KNIGHTS OF THE ROUNDTABLE:
GENESIS OF A KING

BOOK 1

JACK WINNER & MACK DENNIS

A catalogue record for this book is available from the National Library of Australia

*To the people who supported our dreams and celebrated the little things alongside us. We couldn't have done it without you. Thank you.*

## Chapter 1: The Prologue

*"Run, son!"*

*The voice echoed through the woods, drowned out by clashing swords. Through the woods, a young boy ran for his life, terrified of the sound of the swords clanging behind him.*

*A tall, commanding figure stood in a clearing behind the boy, swinging his blade up to defend himself. Black flame surrounded his boots and coated the ground, growing larger every step back from the attack.*

*The swords met again, sliding across one another with a whine. The man looked up at his opponent, daunt seeping through him like ice. Fiery, dilated eyes glared back at him, set in a horned steel mask rigid as his blade and black as midnight. The flaming black shadow stood well over the man, its very existence sapping the light from the sky and the flames that burned among them.*

*The boy hid behind a thick tree not far from where he ran, gaining his breath. He opened his hand, a necklace bound in gold thread glowing in his palm, the blue crystal in the centre glimmering in the small light from the moon peeking through the canopy.*

*Flinching at the sound of a pained yell, the boy peered his head around the tree. The man lay defeated on the ground with a deep gash on his arm, his sword in the scorched dirt beside him. The dark figure stalked over to him, its weapon dangling from its right hand and scraping* the ground as it moved, sparks spitting from the sword as it brushed the stones scattered across the dirt.

The man looked up at the demon-like shadow, his eyes wide as he clutched at his wound. The figure stood over the man in victory, the flames roiling off its shoulders and lapping at the air.

"Just like the legends said, 'the King will fall', and let that be true," it growled, its voice deep like thunder.

"A new King will rise; he will bring peace to Braynor," the man spat, his voice steady as he rose to his feet.

"King Benjamin, how naïve you've become," the figure mocked, a shadowy grin peeking from under the fiery embrace.

"The Born King is destined to rise, and you cannot change that," the King said, defiance entering his voice.

"But you will fall," the figure smirked. "And you cannot stop that."

The King jolted sharply, groaning with pain. He looked down, the sword's tip embedded into him, blood slowly pouring out of the wound. Pain flared through his body, and his knees gave out, sending him back to the ground, his hand holding the blade. A line of blood dripped from his sliced palm, crimson staining the charred grass. Gravity overtook him, and he fell to his side, facing the boy in the woods.

The King's lips moved slowly, the light in his eyes fading as he whispered to him, "Run, Arthur... Run."

The young boy felt tears dripping down his cheeks as he watched him bleed out on the ground, flicking his eyes up to the figure. In a flick of movement, the figure sharply turned its head to the boy. Bright amber eyes glared at him, piercing through the black flames and staring right into Arthur's eyes as if they'd burn him from the inside out-

A fearful cry pierced through the air, and Arthur sprang up in fright, panting heavily. Looking around with wide eyes, he took in the familiar surroundings of his bedroom.

Bedroom.

Reality.

*Right...*

Realising it was all a dream, he calmed himself slowly, his eyes flicking around the room for any sign of the figure he saw, to no avail. He breathed slowly, calming his racing heart.

Rubbing his eyes, Arthur moved himself over to the edge of the bed. That was the first time the figure had looked at him - every other time, it was just his silhouette and voice. The dark, skeletal face with cracks and breaks, and those orange glowing eyes...

Arthur sighed, looking over to his bedside table, the same necklace he held in the nightmare resting atop it. He frowned at it, picking it up warily and hooking it around his neck.

He got up out of his bed, walking over to his wardrobe in the left corner, a mirror seated beside it. He looked at himself, his green eyes irritated at his dirty blonde hair askew from the pillows. He dragged his fingers lightly through it, studying the faint stubble dusted on his jaw. He'd need a shave soon.

He opened his wardrobe, pulling out whatever his hands grabbed first: a black fur coat with regular dark brown trousers. He threw them onto his bed before pulling out a pair of socks and brown leather boots.

Arthur stepped out of his bedroom fully dressed, heading down the long, narrow hallway. The walls were filled with ancient artefacts, mannequins with beaten pieces of armour sitting behind glass panes, broken shards of swords and axes and all other weapons framed beside them with names of famed Knights engraved into small plaques at the bottom.

He made his way down the flight of spiral stairs leading to the lower portion of the castle, torches lighting the way down. The floor glimmered at the foot of the stairs, pearlescent swirls decorating the light marble. A length of red carpet stretched down the hall, reaching to the edge of the tall entryway and splitting around the two turns at the end of the walkway.

He made his way through the twisting castle walls, his feet leading him through narrow hallways, the wooden doors left ajar with servants buzzing through their jobs. A few of the King's Guards passed Arthur, exchanging small respectful nods.

Arthur nodded back, continuing his way forth. Further down the hallway, a larger door sat propped open, warm light pooling out along the floor. Arthur observed the kitchen from the doorway; polished light wood topped the benches, and wood shelves harboured bowls and plates stacked high above one another. Different types of crockery and equipment dangled from the low-hanging ceiling, their shadows sitting over the assorted blocks of utensils.

Pots sat above the woodfire oven, boiling away in the tidy kitchen, a symphony of crackling from multiple pans dotting the sides around the pots. An elderly woman stood at a bench, lining plates and cutlery out for preparation, her apron smeared with grease and splashed up food.

Arthur walked in, surprised to see the woman up this early without any help from the castle Maidens. He peered at the small clock on the other side of the wall; the time displayed five in the morning. Arthur supposed she wouldn't have been up for another hour or so.

She'd been busy after the feast last night that the King organised, the meals becoming a common occurrence lately. Nobody knew what the meetings were for, but rumours did have a hold in Arthur's head.

Arthur strolled quietly toward the bench, a smile falling onto his lips. The woman didn't notice him, gathering another stack of plates off the cupboard, her arms shaking at the weight. Arthur moved to her, gently taking them from her grasp.

The woman looked up at Arthur with a crinkled smile; her warm face was one of the reasons Arthur would come to check on her. Her speckled grey hair and kind, brown eyes gave anyone who met her a sense of comfort that extended to her infinite kindness and patience Arthur had been fortunate enough to have since he was little.

"Thank you, Arthur," she said kindly, her voice not yet cracked with age.

"Up early today, Ms Enid?" he asked, setting the plates in the same order as the others.

"Your uncle had a feast last night, the third one this week," she replied, taking over the job deftly. "He wanted another one for this morning."

Arthur walked over to the sink, grabbed some plates from the night before already stacked on the side and began to wash them in the basin. "He must have something important enough happening to have so many meetings," he shrugged, not quite believing the words himself.

"He is your uncle, after all, he's always busy," Enid muttered. She wasn't wrong; the King of Camelot never had much time to sit down and think, let alone spend time with family.

"Wouldn't surprise me if it was about the uprising near Catarina," Arthur said, rinsing the suds off the bowls and setting them aside to dry. "News has been springing up about that down in the marketplace from the travellers."

"Samqueel mentioned that, I believe," she agreed.

"Seems like a situation for the Knights of the Roundtable to handle," Arthur said, placing the rest of the dishes away and wiping his hands dry on his trousers.

He walked over to a basket on the bench beside small tubs of spices, lifting the lid open only to find it empty. He frowned, closing the lid and straightening it.

"They had the last of the bread. I came here to prepare you and your uncle breakfast, but I found it empty," Enid muttered with irritation, dishing out the food prepared from the pots and pans, boiled eggs and crispy bacon piled up on each serving.

"I'll head down to the Londinium markets and get some more," Arthur said, straightening his jacket.

"No need, son," Enid assured him. "The next delivery should be in by the afternoon."

"A lady like you shouldn't need to wait on bread deliveries," Arthur shook his head. "I was heading down, anyway."

"You're too kind, Arthur," Enid said, a smile stretching across her face. Arthur gave her a slight smile, heading out of the kitchen.

"I'll be back soon."

He dawdled towards the High Gates, flicking his eyes past the same old boring architecture that surrounded him twenty-four-seven. Arthur thought the castle could do with a facelift. Perhaps the bricks needed a clean; moss was indeed growing in that crack further-

Voices echoed down the hallway, coming from the room two doors down. The words grew louder as Arthur neared, too loud for Arthur not to eavesdrop.

Arthur stood beside the two doors, leaning against the wall and peering inside slowly. A large round table sat in the centre, along with twelve seats, three of them empty. Men dressed in fine attire sat around the table, wine goblets and half-empty platters strewn around them.

His uncle sat on the left side of the table, wearing a jewelled crown on his head. The others wore finely crafted jackets, different coloured accents adorning the collars on their formal white and orange coats. The men gathered around the table paid no attention to Arthur, too focused on the conversation.

The Knight in the red-accented coat, a blonde man with sharp silver eyes, spoke up. "If Ariandel overtakes Catarina, what does that mean for us?"

"Our defences are too vulnerable for a frontal assault; we cannot afford to lose more than a few hundred Knights," the blue coat added, his hands neatly folded on the table. His dark hair was pulled back in a hair tie away from his bearded face, blue eyes watching the King.

"And with fewer trainees joining our ranks nowadays, we stand less of a chance leading troops into battle," the gold coat said. His dark skin and hair matched his eyes, intelligence writhing in them. "What are your suggestions, sire?"

The King turned his head to look at him, one leg crossed over the other, his hand folded beneath his chin. His dark brown eyes trailed over each of the Knights, disinterest clear in his gaze. The King picked up his glass of wine slowly, swirling the dark liquid inside.

"The reasonable yet riskier approach to this situation is to confront Ariandel of their transgressions against the Kingdom of Catarina. We cannot allow Camelot to suffer the same fate. We will not allow this Kingdom to fall."

"Reuben is right, sire; our defences are too few to start another war," the red coat reminded him. "The Legion is filled with new men barely a year out of their traineeship, some of them earlier than others, and even then, we have nowhere near enough numbers to take them on. A formal meeting with Ariendal is out of the question; King Solomon made that clear when we tried the first time."

"You're all Knights of the Roundtable, are you not?" the King gritted out, irritation on his face. "You're all the men of many stories. I'm sure you can figure it out."

"That's beyond the point; even with our rank and skill, we cannot take on an entire Kingdom of Barons, and the

Gods know who else they've allied themselves with,"
Reuben answered.

"Precisely," the Knight in gold added. "Even though we
are Knights of the Roundtable, the other Knights of
Camelot don't stand a chance to fend for themselves against
such a dangerous enemy, especially not with the likes of
Dolorous Gard, if the rumours are true."

"Sir Lorsaw," the King started, raising his brows
slightly. "I would've thought you to be above listening to
the common squabble's rumours. Dolorous Gard Drows
meeting in the middle with Ariendal's Barons is simply
ridiculous."

Lorsaw's brows twitched, his face staying immovable.
"Sometimes it is wise to listen to the people of the city you
protect to know if a threat needs to be defended from," he
said, his voice low. "There's no use waiting on words from
other Kingdoms on enemy movements if they come too late
to tell us, let alone local crimes and issues."

"King Ergott," the red coat interjected before he could
retort. "With all due respect to your prioritisation of our
Kingdom's safety, there hasn't been a word against us to
consider them a threat as of yet. If we move now, we could
be accused of inciting a war purely out of spite against
them. That could make our situation worse. I don't think it
wise if we throw a needless war into the mix of our current
issues of trying to gain the city's trust and faith in the
throne since it hasn't proven to get any better in the years
you've ruled. Many people think your rule on the throne is
redundant; I couldn't imagine what people would think of
you if you brought them anarchy instead of the safety you
promised them."

"Watch your words, Samqueel," Ergott sniped,
glowering at the Knight and setting his hand on the armrest.
"I will not have you utter treason inside this castle unless
you want your title revoked."

"I am representing the city's voice," Samqueel replied, vexation sharp in his eyes. "I have my right to express any concerns, whether public or private, and so does everyone else in this room."

"Only one person's opinion matters and that is my own," Ergott snorted, his fingers clutching the chair tightly. Samqueel's jaw flickered, his stare unwavering. The Knights at the table shifted uncomfortably; Arthur could feel the tension in the air as if it were a cat brushing his leg.

"Sire," Reuben cleared his throat, adjusting in his seat. "What if you fall? Who will be King?"

Ergott flicked his eyes to Reuben. "King George will be taking over if I fall."

"Rheged? Why?" the large Knight across from Reuben asked quizzically, his coat decorated with burnt orange. His sizeable brown beard framed his dark blue eyes, and short, clipped hair covered his broad head.

"It's my personal belief that King George is capable of leading in my stead," Ergott said matter-of-factly. "Should the need ever arise."

"And what of the Crown Prince?" Lorsaw protested, nodding outside of the door.

Arthur blinked, backing away from the door slightly. *Does he know I'm here?*

"Isn't he destined to be King? He is the son of Benjamin," the green coat Knight asked, looking around with a raised brow to the other Knights and scratching his short black goatee, brown eyes questioning under spiky black hair.

"You have a point, Arkan. The boy is destined to be King," the Knight in black nodded, leaning back in his chair and fiddling with his fork. Blue eyes widened slightly under preened black hair as he dropped the fork, frowning.

"Arthur is not ready for that type of role, and he never will be," Ergott growled, his back straight and a scowl deep on his face, his hands clenched in a death grip on the armrests.

The room fell silent, the Knights facing Ergott. Arthur's heart sank to the ground bitterly, his eyes scowling at the floor. *Of course, he still believed that.* It wasn't as if Arthur hadn't tried to talk with him about it. Years of tension and disbelief from Ergott had built up Arthur's resentment for his uncle, and it wasn't going to change today.

"You cannot deny the boy his birthright, Ergott," Samqueel warned.

"He is not fit for the role. His father should have known that before his passing," Ergott bit, watching Sam with disdain.

"You cannot speak about King Benjamin in that way, your own brother," the light blue coat Knight protested, anger knitting his brows closer together. Green eyes glared at the King, light brown hair pushed back behind his ears with a dash of stubble coating his jaw.

Ergott glared at him, and Natan glared right back, then blinked in shock. Arthur peered through the doorway as the Knights fell silent again, trying to see what was happening. The Knights were watching Ergott with looks of surprise, their bodies rigid. Reuben's eyes flicked to the door, Arthur pulling back quickly, dread flooding his chest. *What did they see?*

"You must see the potential in Arthur, surely? Benjamin would've wanted him to take over Camelot. I don't understand why you see differently," Samqueel added, his voice quieter than before.

"My brother was naïve," he growled, bracing his hands on the armrests of his seat. "He was too wrapped up in his own beliefs of fantastical worlds and equality. Arthur will not be the King, even if it is his birthright."

"The people believe in the boy. Is he not the King's son?" Lorsaw argued, leaning forwards.

"The city points to its beliefs, as they were taught to. They need their leader," Taryn added.

Ergott frowned. "They already have one; me," he spat.

"The people are looking for guidance and a King who brings them peace and ease of life, not war and hardship," Sam's hands gripped the edge of the table, his knuckles white.

"This conversation is over. Get your troops ready for our departure in two days. Do not keep me waiting," Ergott commanded, standing up from his seat and storming out towards the staircase at the back of the room.

The Knights watched as Ergott dismissed himself. Samqueel snorted angrily and pushed himself away from the table, standing up with a growl.

Arthur felt conflicted, processing everything he'd overheard. *The Born King; that couldn't be me.* All of the prophecies were just myths.

He frowned, moving away from the door and continuing his way to the High Gates, too caught up inside his mind to notice the attention of the guards he'd passed along his way through the castle courtyard.

He opened the side door next to the Gates, stepping outside of the castle boundaries. Below the steep castle steps lay the sparse city of Londinium, a cluster of stone and wooden buildings and marketplaces on scattered small hilltops surrounding the sparse banks of the Castaral River that cut through the Kingdom like a serpent. The sun behind him rose steadily to set the city alight, illuminating the separate districts like lines on a compass. The clocktower in the North began to chime, its mighty bells ringing across the city to reach his ears.

Sighing deeply to himself, Arthur walked down the castle steps. A cool breeze hit him as the wind picked up, the smell of spruce trees, pine needles and woodsmoke as familiar as family. Flags brandishing the Kingdoms of Braynor blew heartily alongside the steps on tall poles, standing strong as soldiers. One in particular caught Arthur's eye: the flag of Camelot, an orange wyvern on a white background, its body bunched and pouncing through the air. Arthur watched it flap around, his brows flicking up as its rings snapped, sending it off into the wild gales. His eyes trailed its journey as it flew towards the city, the sunlight shining on the thin fabric outlining the wyvern perfectly.

He smiled faintly at the flag, burying his hands in his coat pockets and beginning his descent towards the streets of Londinium.

# Chapter 2: Londinium Streets

Arthur scanned the streets as he reached the bottom of the steps, passing by the armoured guards standing at the stone obelisks like statues, the cobblestone streets echoing the voice of a nearby vendor. The ample circular space encompassed the base of the castle steps and split off in three directions, the largest path straight ahead leading into the heart of the city to the central Plaza.

The market locations would shift around the city from time to time, depending on the season or time of year. Typically, the markets were found in the Central District Plaza, but to Arthur's surprise, the stalls were nowhere to be seen. Plenty of citizens moved about still, many crowding the doorways of butchers, bakers, and finery shopfronts. Young children ran around the area with a leather ball, laughing amongst each other as they passed it.

Arthur made his way down the walkway, dodging the carts parked in front of buildings unloading crates and barrels of goods. Nobles walked in groups past him, hosting finery of all colours and extremities, some of them turning to watch him walk by with looks of recognition. He kept his attention forward as he weaved through the city, acknowledging people as they greeted him with a simple nod.

Arthur's mind flicked to the overheard conversation again, Ergott's voice echoing in his head. It was hard to know that even his uncle doubted him; it'd been that way for a long time, but it was still hard for Arthur to take in.

Since his father died, he'd been shoved away from anything to do with the royal throne by Ergott. He may as well have been forbidden from royal duties, his hopes of being King disappearing with his father. So, Arthur took the liberty of becoming a typical citizen of Camelot, blending in with the crowds just about every day. Sure, people still recognised him as the Crown Prince, but that's all he was: a Prince, not a King.

Exiting the alleyway, Arthur came to a busy street packed with people like herded cattle surrounding a few pop-up markets and trade carts. His eyebrows flicked up as he merged in with the crowd, walking with the same slow pace as the citizens, his eyes trailing around to find any sign of a bread market.

Finally, after minutes of searching, he broke through the crowd into a smaller breezeway, the bread stall flush against the wall. He made his way over, wary of the civilians dashing around him with full bags loading their arms. He stopped in place, waiting for them to pass to no avail.

Arthur's patience started to wear thin, annoyance creasing his brow. He had better things to do than wait for this chaos to settle. He should've been returning to Enid by now with bread in hand. He could've been back in his room studying the Knight manuals or watching the Roundtable train in the yards sooner-

Over to his left, Arthur heard a yell from one of the stalls. His eyes flicked over to the disturbance; at one of the stores, a young woman wearing a dark, torn jacket stood in front of the market, her stance startled. A man beside the stall glared at her with his fist raised.

"Put the apple back, thief!" he growled at her. His dreadlocked hair, contrasting his brown and grey jacket, stuck above his brow. His beard framed his deep scowl, cruel brown eyes set in his harsh face.

Arthur ground his teeth; he knew that face. He'd seen him getting around terrorising the people, picking fights with anyone in his way. He stood back and observed, watching through the crowd.

"What apple?" she bluffed, her hands in her pockets.

"The apple that was just in the stash. It was there before you came along!"

"You must be blind 'cause I didn't take anything," she shrugged off and turned to walk away.

Before she knew it, a hand gripped her arm like a vice. Her eyes grew wide in fear, snapping her attention up at the tall man, their eyes locked in a tense battle.

"Londinium doesn't tolerate thieves," he spat, getting in her face.

Her eyes widened further. "I didn't steal the damned apple!"

More men emerged from the crowd and began to circle her, holding planks of wood and small random rubbish, wearing the same jacket as the aggravator. Arthur watched him shove her to the ground, his jaw tightening as she hit the ground with a thud. Her hands flew out in front of her to stop her fall, and a red sphere rolled out from the inside of her coat, one of the men stooping to pick it up.

"Well, well, what's this then?" one of the men said, inspecting the apple for bruises and throwing her a dirty look.

"I… uh," she stuttered, her eyes dancing around to the men surrounding her.

"You know what we do to thieves, boys," the leader growled with a smirk and stalked over to her, the men closing in. Her eyes widened in fear, and Arthur's feet moved, stepping closer.

The man's feet lashed out suddenly and connected with her side, a cry of pain escaping from the girl. She moved her hand to protect herself, her other arm raised over her face, curling in as the men rained harsh blows down on her small frame.

Arthur sped up a bit more, gently shoving people watching the fight out of his way, his voice itching to yell something at them to make them stop.

The man paused for a moment, watching her groan in pain on the cobblestones. He smirked, stepping forward to land another blow. Arthur's hand shot out against his side, shoving him and his men back away from her with enough force to send them stumbling.

"Back away from the girl," Arthur warned, blocking their path to the curled-up woman behind him. The man looked at Arthur, a slight smirk slithering across his rugged face as he drew closer slowly.

"Hello there, Arthur," his slippery voice drawled. "Come to join the affray, have we?"

"Go crawl back in your hole, Leonard," Arthur growled, glaring at him.

"Come *on*, Arthur! She's a thief, and thieves deserve to be punished," Leonard protested, his arms wide as he regarded the audience of people watching them.

"Says the thief himself," he spat at Leonard.

"You nobles don't understand what it means to live on the streets. You never have, and you never will," Leonard accused. "Who are you to call me a thief?"

"Just because you live on the streets, doesn't mean you have the freedom to beat a woman," Arthur scowled, shaking his head. "And don't think these people haven't seen your face before. Your reputation is as spotless as a Dalmatian."

"Still showing off your ego, are you?" Leonard asked, his words turning sharp as a sword.

"Still showing your arrogance?" Arthur retorted, tilting his head back. The people around them began to back up, giving them more space. A larger crowd gathered around, a few standing on boxes to see them.

The scrape of boots on stones sounded beside Arthur, the girl getting slowly to her feet, brushing the dirt off herself.

"You should learn not to get yourself involved in situations that don't include you, Your Highness," he growled, his eyes flicking back to Arthur. Leonard's men crept closer to Arthur, circling like wolves.

Arthur looked to his right, one of the men nearing the girl. Arthur shoved him back with a growl, branding him with a glare as the man stumbled.

"Be careful, Arthur," Leonard warned, his hand hidden behind himself. "This might not go as well as you planned."

Arthur looked back at Leonard, his hand wielding a wickedly serrated knife, the metal glinting sharply. He should've expected something dirty to happen.

The men drew ever closer, their cockiness skyrocketing at Arthur's hesitation. His eyes narrowed at the four men, observing each of them as he let his brain think. He looked to the stall beside him, noting the loose planks that separated the fruits from one another, the piles of sand that sat at the base to hold the table stable.

Leonard smirked, his fingers clenching into a tight fist. The men charged towards Arthur, their makeshift weapons held high. Arthur smirked as he ducked beneath the first attacker, grabbing the nearest separator plank and swinging it around to whack the man in the head with a clack, his boot kicking up the sand pile into the air towards the others in a great arc. They stumbled back, two yelling and rubbing at their faces as sand got in their eyes, the apple dropping to the ground and rolling away.

Within a quick flash, one of the men lunged at Arthur with his plank; Arthur spotted him, lashing his arm out at his chest and kicking his knee backwards. The breath rushed from the man as he hit the ground hard, his plank flying from his grip.

Citizens around them cried out in alarm, a few running from the commotion while others circled to watch. Arthur ignored them, returning to the now recovered men glaring at him. Another charged Arthur with a yell, moving to swing at his legs with a wickedly modified metal bar.

Arthur shoved the girl backwards out of the way, scattering the crowd before her back hit the far wall around a corner with a huff of breath. She stayed on her feet and watched the fight with slightly annoyed eyes. Arthur grabbed the man by the collar of his shirt, thrusting his knee into his chest and discarding him roughly away.

The man groaned in pain, coughing and holding his ribs. Leonard frowned at Arthur, twirling his dagger between his fingers, rooted to the stones. Arthur mirrored his look, watching the knife from the corner of his eye. He wasn't sure how good Leonard could wield a weapon, but he wouldn't put it past him to know at least how to swipe.

Leonard's boots scraped the stones and then stopped, the knife disappearing wherever he kept it. Arthur followed his line of sight; he spotted a band of Knights from the corner of his eye charging through the crowd towards the commotion.

He looked back at Leonard with a faint smirk. At least he knew a little bit better than Arthur initially thought. "Want to continue?" he drawled, relaxing his stance.

Leonard scowled at him. "This isn't over, Arthur," he spat, straightening his jacket.

Spooked by the Knights, Leonard and his men scurried into the crowd, looking back at Arthur with ire before he lost sight of them amongst the flurry of people.

Arthur watched them leave and ducked around the corner where the girl stood, watching the Knights follow after them with a smile. He looked at the girl with satisfaction, her eyes lit in interest.

"Are you alright?" Arthur asked her, turning to her.

"Yeah, I should be fine," she said, her hand still floating on her side. "Thanks for helping."

"No one deserves to be treated like that," Arthur said, bending to pick up the apple.

"He's some gentleman, isn't he?" she muttered, tucking her dirty blonde hair behind her ears.

"Definitely," Arthur lifted a brow, polishing it on his jacket. "He's the kindest man in Londinium."

"I hope we're both being sarcastic here."

"I'd be concerned if we were both serious," Arthur said, smirking at her. "What's your name?"

"Maria," she answered. "And you are?"

"Arthur," he responded, nodding his head slightly.

"Pendragon?" Maria asked, her brows flicking up.

Arthur nodded, handing her the apple. "In the flesh."

"So you're the one everyone talks about," she smiled, taking the apple from his hand.

"Please, no one talks about me," he scoffed, lowering his arm.

Her face turned confused. "What do you mean? Haven't you seen the murals?"

"Murals?" Arthur echoed, looking at her.

"They're all over Londinium," she said, gesturing around the walls. "Paintings of the prophecy - the Sword, more so."

Arthur's brow raised. "You must have confused it for something else. It'd be some sort of guild symbol, for sure."

"Why do you say that?" she asked. "No guild around here has a sword for a sigil. Besides, your prophecy is popular in the city. We believe you're meant to be the real King."

"I'm not, never have been, and never will be," he dismissed. "Even if people believe I can lead this Kingdom, it'll never happen."

Her frown deepened in protest. "Well, why not?"

"It's just not my calling," Arthur shrugged off, annoyance starting to seep into his voice. "Besides, I don't know the first thing about being King. My uncle does, however. Maybe you should turn your eyes to him."

"He's a fake," she spat, to Arthur's shock. "Everyone - even his Knights - disagree with his intentions and acts. He isn't the rightful leader of Camelot. I think you know that, too," she nodded at his solemn expression.

"Who said I thought that?" Arthur gritted out, his face hardening. "My uncle isn't the greatest King, but I'm not fit for that responsibility. It isn't my destiny."

Maria stared at him, puzzled, disbelief in her eyes. He looked away from her, sighing. He'd heard the story a thousand times before, and every time he'd denied it, he'd received the same look as the one she had now.

Her expression changed to Arthur's surprise, hope flickering, and she smiled slightly. "Have you considered Knight training?" she asked, her voice lighter.

"Knight training?" he echoed, his heart almost skipping a beat. The books on his study table back at the castle flashed in his mind. Of course, he'd considered it; he'd wanted to be a Knight since he learned what they were. He'd read and memorised the words of every training manual he'd found in the castle library on the topic and strived to join the yards with the Roundtable at every opportunity he could get away with.

"Why not? It needs more trainees lately," she shrugged. "I've been trying to find more people to help in the kitchens and with a few extra tasks around the hall, but being a Knight would suit you better. I even got Tristan Garrison to join the ranks."

Arthur looked at her curiously. "Tristan Garrison?"

She nodded. "Surprising, I know."

Tristan was known reasonably well around Londinium; his friendly, goofy charm typically was why so many people learned his name. He also happened to be Arthur's best friend he'd met as a young boy down by the Castaral. He wouldn't put much past him in the way of finding a career that was more than what suited him.

But Knight training? Arthur hadn't expected that.

Maybe he could finally put that study to use for something other than to pass the time. If he weren't fit for the role of a King - not that he wanted to be one - then protecting the Kingdom as a Knight would give him some purpose. That's all Arthur had been looking for: a purpose, something to help find out who he was. Something other than everyone else's expectations of him picking up his father's crown.

He looked back at her, his mind made up. "Where does one go to train as a Knight?"

Her eyes brightened, a victorious smile going across her face. "Follow me, King Arthur."

He frowned at her. "Don't call me that."

Maria rolled her eyes playfully, leading the way further into Londinium. Arthur followed behind like a cat being dragged on a leash. The original reason as to why he was here - *the bread stall!* - suddenly flicked in his head. He sighed, debating whether he should go back and get it while she wasn't watching.

As if she'd heard his thoughts, Maria looked back at him from over her shoulder in expectancy, her green eyes glimmering in the sun like a polished gem. He frowned as she took them down the longer path, passing by lesser-known stalls.

Arthur glanced around the stalls half-heartedly as he followed, his frown deepening the further he got from the bread stall. A flicker of a shadow caught his eye as he passed by an alleyway, turning his head to look. A black-cloaked figure stood leaning against a wall, their face hidden under a deep hood. Citizens walked past the figure without a second glance, the figure's head turning to look away, the hood disappearing as two men carried a crate past

Arthur's field of view down the hallway further. Arthur paused in puzzlement, scouring the alleyway. *They just disappeared?*

"Hey, are you coming or what?" Maria called back to him, standing further down the way. He turned to look at her and walked hesitantly away from the alleyway, the phantom feel of eyes still raking over him making the hair on his neck prickle.

## Chapter 3: Night At Camelot

Walking down the alley, Arthur glanced around at the small stalls lining the walls, starting to thin out the closer they got to the Northern District. A few residents stopped to stare at him, faces of hope and wonder surrounding him.

Arthur lagged behind Maria, ignoring them all. He wrapped his jacket tighter around him: the cold weather was becoming unbearable, almost as bad as Amarnia's Northern end or even the Arctic. *No, not quite the Arctic.*

Looking at some stalls, Arthur spotted something on the alley walls, pausing momentarily. He stared at it, taking long enough for Maria to look back at him, stopping her trail.

Paint coated the grey bricks, red and white smeared roughly into the crevasses. A red sword in a rounded stone, the writing beneath catching his attention the most. *The Born King will rise.*

Those words, those exact words, made his heart skip. *Why would this be here, and right now of all times? Is there really a prophecy of the Born King?* The thought turned over in his mind like a whirlwind. Maybe there was such a thing as a Born King, but… it couldn't be him. At least, that's what King Ergott believed.

Maria walked up to him slowly, her eyes flicking between him and the mural, watching his face flicker with emotion. His thoughts turned too wild, and Arthur looked away from the mural, turning to Maria with his face back to neutrality. *No. It's not me. I shouldn't even entertain the thought.*

She looked up at the painting, staring at those words that gave him such conflict. "It points to you," she said.

Arthur looked away from her. "I wouldn't get your hopes up too soon," he muttered.

"My hopes are that you actually see that you're destined to be King," she said, walking up to him. "You can't doubt yourself, Arthur."

"Even if it is my destiny, how would I rule an entire Kingdom alone? You have no idea how much responsibility comes with being the ruler of a whole castle."

"If Ergott falls, who will take over?"

"King George is what I heard my uncle say."

Maria shook her head, a small, exaggerated sigh coming through her nose. "He has no right to decide who should and shouldn't rule over Camelot; it's your birthright-"

"Stop saying it is," Arthur growled, glaring at her. "If it were my birthright, I would be wearing that crown as we speak, but it's clear it isn't."

"You're the son of Benjamin," she reasoned, something like offence sharp in her return glare. "Ergott is using this as an advantage to rule over a Kingdom that wasn't his. The rules are that the firstborn of the King is to take over the throne when he dies, not his brother."

"If a King dies, the eldest in line to overrule the Kingdom takes the throne. Children can't rule a Kingdom. Besides, suppose a new monarch is appointed to a throne. In that case, they rule the Kingdom until they're physically unable, like everyone else," Arthur said, feeling the lie turn to ash on his tongue.

"I don't know what kind of history books they've got in that big brick house, but that ain't it," a male voice echoed from the alleyway to the left of them.

Both Arthur and Maria looked over to the source of the voice in the dark shadows, the street lanterns lighting up an outline of a silhouette leaning against the bricks. The man walked out of the alleyway, the lanterns highlighting him perfectly.

Dark skin stretched over a tall frame, short brown hair falling over light brown eyes lit with mischief that matched his smirk. Arthur shook his head lightly, smiling faintly at the man.

"Couldn't find anywhere else to loiter, Tristan?" Arthur asked.

"It's hard to choose where to stand when walls are everywhere in the city. I just like this particular one," Tristan said, smiling back. "And besides, I live here."

"You've been keeping busy," Maria noted, looking over his shoulder.

Stacked piles of wood at waist height were lined up along the far side of the alleyway, a wood axe resting against one of the carts holding more logs. He looked over his shoulder at it before turning back to the two.

"It's about time we get the fire started," Tristan said, rubbing his hands. "It's too cold for this."

"Perhaps you should wear a coat as well," Arthur suggested, noticing the lack of clothing on Tristan.

"Well, I thought a long shirt would do for chopping wood, but obviously, I was wrong," Tristan frowned, pulling his sleeves down. "What are you two doing down this way, anyway?"

"Wouldn't you know if Marlon's is open?" Maria asked.

"Most likely, considering I'm already late for today's training. Why?"

"Knight trials," Arthur said, folding his arms, trying to hold the warmth in.

Tristan's eyebrows flicked up. "You're signing up?"

"Don't make it a big deal," Arthur frowned.

"If Arthur isn't going to be the King, maybe he can be a Knight of Camelot instead," Maria said, looking at Tristan.

"I mean, yeah, it's close enough. You're still protecting Camelot from danger," Tristan smiled, shrugging.

"You could say that," Arthur replied. "Camelot's in need of new Knights lately."

"Maybe this will finally get in your head about who should be the real King," Tristan smirked.

"That'll never happen. I'd be lucky enough to be a Knight," Arthur snorted.

"You never know, Arthur. This could prove to Ergott that you can be King," Maria looked at him.

Arthur sighed at her. "You and I both know he'd never accept it. Besides, King George is taking his place."

"Pff, please? That looney? He wouldn't be able to handle a *puppy,* let alone a-" Tristan stopped talking suddenly and looked over Arthur's shoulder, his eyes narrowing slightly. Arthur noticed his stare and followed his line of sight.

"Are those new guards?" Tristan asked, nodding in that direction.

Men in black hoods stood at the end of the walkway, swords hanging from their sides and masks covering their faces. Arthur narrowed his eyes, a creeping feeling in his chest. Their voices were harsh, speaking sharply to the people around them.

Maria turned to her side to watch them. "Something's not right," she murmured.

One of the hooded men pushed a civilian out of his way, the young boy hitting the ground hard. The man yelled at him angrily, lifting him by the collar and shoving him to stumble away. A scowl formed on Arthur's face, his teeth grating. *Who are these men in hoods, and what do they think they're doing?*

"They look real friendly," Tristan snorted

"Since when did Ergott get black cloaks?" Maria asked.

"He didn't," Arthur said, pivoting further towards the hoods.

The men stalked further down the alleyway, citizens peeling back to make way. Arthur's feet moved to follow, keeping to the wall. Peeking around the corner, he saw them standing in front of a stall, harassing the older woman behind her wares.

His jaw tightened, and he moved to round the corner. A sudden tug on his bicep glued him in place, and he looked back. Tristan held his arm in a vice-like grip, shaking his head at Arthur. He furrowed his eyebrows at Tristan, and his grip lightened slightly.

"Don't," Tristan warned, looking up at the horde. "Who knows what manner of weapons they're carrying under all that cloak."

"They're on our turf, unwanted and uninvited," Arthur replied, shrugging his arm out of Tristan's grip.

"Tristan's right, Arthur. They don't look like people to mess with," Maria said, peeking around the corner.

"Don't worry," Arthur dismissed. "It'll be a short conversation."

"When you say short, do you mean short as in you'll tell them to leave? Or you'll keep it short by beating them up?" Maria asked with a frown.

"Only time will tell," Arthur smirked mischievously, flexing his hands.

"Arthur," Tristan started, his expression concerned. "They really don't look like people to mess around with. Maybe they're here for a reason?"

"To what, treat the people of Londinium like stacks of rubbish?" Arthur asked.

Footsteps sounded behind them, and the three turned to the noise. Three dark hoods marched down the alleyway, their movements synchronised perfectly. They moved against the wall, watching them pass by; one of the men glanced at Arthur, his hazel eyes raking over him. Up close,

Arthur could see the faint engravings on the ebony masks beneath the hood, swirling and spiking around the eyes.

He kept his eyes trained on the masked hood as they moved around the corner to the others. Maria and Tristan peered beside him, suspicion flooding them all.

The men eyed the civilians that passed them, the townspeople nervous about their presence and attitude. Some children ducked behind the stalls, scattering out of the way. Barked orders echoed from beneath the masks, people flinching around them.

"You think they still have a reason to be here?" Arthur said flatly, glancing above him at Tristan.

"Well, they still look like proper fighting tools, but…" Tristan looked down at Arthur, "Not really."

"I'll keep an eye on them," Maria said. "They're heading down the main way." She shifted around the corner, and Arthur gripped her jacket.

"No," Arthur protested. "Let me handle it." Maria glanced back at him with a scowl.

"Maybe no one should go. I don't particularly want to get my ass *or* your ass kicked and in jail," Tristan frowned, standing beside Maria.

Arthur looked back at Tristan, his scowl deepening. "Do as you wish, but I will stop them." Arthur looked back at the men, clenching his fists and following behind.

Tristan and Maria looked at one another in annoyed defeat and walked behind Arthur warily, moving through the parted crowd.

A distressed voice cried out, metal bins clattering from a further turn. One of the cylinders rolled out onto Arthur's path, followed by yelling. His eyes widened, and he hurried to the corner, Tristan and Maria hurrying after him.

"Arthur!" Maria called out, frustration in her voice.

The three rounded the corner and stopped, eyes widening. The Black Cloaks circled an old woman on the cobblestones against the wall, beating harsh blows to the woman's body. She cried out for help, covering her face with both arms for protection.

Deciding enough was enough, Arthur gritted his teeth and rushed towards them before Tristan could stop him, shoulder barging one of the men into the wall. A crunch sounded as the Black Cloak hit the bricks, grunting and growling at the pain. The others turned their attention to Arthur, facing him with their expressionless masks.

"Get back into your home, civilian," the hood in the middle spat at him.

"Sorry," Arthur growled, straightening up. "I don't take orders from you lot."

"Watch yourself, boy," one of the men growled. "You could get yourself into a lot of trouble."

"No doubt," Arthur agreed, landing a hand on the man's throat and sending him coughing to the ground with an elbow to the temple.

Another hood took a swing at Arthur's jaw, and he grabbed for his wrist. The man's fist connected with his cheekbone instead, Arthur grunting at the force of the hit. The man tried to free himself, but Arthur twisted his arm around his back, launching him into the two other men next to the wall, the frightened woman yelping as they landed beside her.

Tristan snapped to attention, rushing over to Arthur's side. "Maria, stay back. I don't want you caught up in this, too," he said.

"But-" she protested.

"No buts," Tristan barked and swung his fist into the jaw of a nearby mask.

Arthur looked over at Tristan, panting in pain as the men reeled back to size the pair up. Tristan moved to stand beside Arthur, both of them raising their fists.

"I go left, you take right," Tristan growled, shifting his shoulders.

"Done," Arthur agreed.

The two charged forward, Arthur kicking one mask to the bricks and swinging his fist into the next. Tristan set for a larger man, the man lunging at him. His giant fists beat into Tristan's ribs like a sledgehammer, making him grunt at each hit, driving the breath from his lungs, backing into another pair of hands.

Tristan struggled, trying to break out of the mask's grip as the larger man cracked his knuckles, walking up to him slowly. Arthur looked over at Tristan, his eyes widening. A glint of light dragged his attention back to the hood before him.

Arthur ducked, a baton swinging over his head in an arc, and lashed his fist out to hit the mask's ribcage. The man grunted as Arthur smacked the baton out of his hand and slammed his boot into his knee.

Arthur grabbed the baton off the ground and swung it into the hood's mask, sending him sprawling across the stones. Tristan groaned in pain, and Arthur turned back to see him still trapped, the baton weighing heavy in his hand. Maria lashed at the man hitting Tristan with her nails, scratching his arm.

He paused and looked at the thin trail of blood on his forearm, then glanced back at her. She balled her hands into fists and went to swing, the man backhanding her hard. Her feet reeled back, and she tripped over littered debris, grunting heavily as she fell. She held her face and moved towards the woman, holding her ground. He laughed mockingly at her and turned back to Tristan's glare of outrage, flexing his hand.

Without warning, a crack opened up in his mask, the baton shooting sparks through the Cloak's vision as the force knocked him down. The hood held his face, and he glanced dazedly to where Arthur stood. Grunts and the sounds of scuffing boots on the cobblestones turned his attention back to Tristan, seeing his men held under headlock by him.

Arthur looked at the man on the ground, his jaw clenched and eyes narrowed. Steps echoed down the alleyway, and Arthur looked to his left, the other cloaks standing in a line with batons ready.

"Excellent work, Tristan," Arthur said, turning his head to the new arrivals. "Anyone else wish to contribute?"

The men looked at the Cloak with the cracked mask, scowling up at Arthur, a growl of irritation rumbling from his throat. His arm raised in the air, and the hoods lowered their weapons as he stood with a groan.

Arthur raised his brow, lowering his own stolen baton. "Very good."

"You're lucky this time, boy," the man barked. "Next time, we won't surrender this easily."

"We'll see if there's a next time," Arthur scowled. "You don't belong in Camelot."

"The King thinks differently. Who do you think invited us here?"

Arthur's eyes grew in surprise. "He invited you?"

"That's your concern why?" the man scoffed.

"Normally, he invites people who have a shred of decency," Arthur hissed with venom, looking at him up and down. "You're clearly not one of them."

The man snorted at Arthur and walked over to his men, a few of them straightening as he walked past. Arthur watched the men as they walked away down the alley with a scowl. Tristan moved over to Arthur, holding his swollen side.

"Well," he started. "That went *exactly* as I planned it to go."

"Why would Ergott invite those men?" Arthur asked, watching them walk away.

"For some sort of guarding job, though I think the better guess would be for a wedding reception at this rate," Tristan coughed, walking over to Maria and reaching his free hand down to pull her to her feet.

"Is it just me, or did they look like assassins?" she asked, brushing off the dirt from her pants.

"They probably are assassins, but just more asshole-ish than the rest by the looks of things," Tristan frowned, looking at the alley they'd turned down.

"They're not here for anything good; that's all I know," Arthur added, looking at them and throwing the baton down the alley out of sight. "Let's get you two cleaned up, shall we?"

Tristan and Maria nodded, walking back near the first alleyway. Arthur walked over to the woman, helping her up from the ground. She smiled painfully at him, and he smiled back.

"Thank you, Arthur," she grumbled. "There's a King in you, deep down."

"Go find some help, get yourself better," he replied gently, ignoring the comment.

The woman walked off down the alleyway with a hobble, looking back at Arthur one last time, watching him follow Tristan and Maria around the corner.

She smiled to herself. "The Born King."

## *Chapter 4: Jackseye's Fortune*

The three returned to Tristan's alleyway, wary that more guards might be on Arthur's tail from earlier. Arthur peered behind his shoulder, watching for shadows and listening for the telltale clink of armour. Arthur couldn't think of one reason why his uncle would hire those men, especially if all they were to do was oppress the people. *Maybe they never intended to protect the people but followed their own rules.* Arthur frowned, turning back to watch where he was going.

The logs of wood Tristan cut up loomed in a dark pile beside a door, Tristan opening it for Arthur and Maria to step through. He swept his sight down the alleyway before closing them in and locking the door. They stood in the foyer of a small house; wooden shelves and plush seating decorated the open room to Arthur's right, stairs to the left leading up to another level.

The living room appeared surprisingly clean, a lovely leather couch with a maple coffee table in the far corner beside a fireplace stacked with logs.

Tristan walked into the kitchen, heading to a large stone box hidden beneath the floor and lifting the lid. Condensation rolled over the lip, slowly coiling to the floor and wrapping around his arm as he reached inside.

Maria took a seat at the scuffed-up kitchen table, wincing in pain as she touched her face, a red welt swelling on her cheekbone. Arthur approached her, placing a gentle hand on her right shoulder. Her eyes flicked up to him.

"You alright?" Arthur asked.

"Yeah," she winced. "I'll be okay."

"Those guys sure know how to throw a punch," Tristan called out from the kitchen.

"What did you expect?" Arthur said, turning towards him. "They're trained men."

"You were the one who insisted on fighting them; don't forget."

Arthur bit the inside of his cheek.

"Since when did you know how to fight so well, Arthur?" Tristan asked.

"The castle can get boring," Arthur shrugged, sitting beside Maria. In his off days when Arthur was younger, he'd get invited by the Roundtable to practise basic training. Sam would always have a plan for him when he'd join them, stretching out the time for as long as he and the lads could before Ergott could find them and shut it down. It was one of the reasons he wanted to be a Knight in the first place.

"You need to train with Marlon; he'll teach you proper techniques," Maria said.

Arthur looked at her. "You train with him?"

Maria shook her head. "Tristan trains with him," she nodded towards the kitchen.

"Every day for four hours," Tristan added, walking over to them, holding a wooden tray with three wrapped, ice-filled towels.

Arthur and Maria took each of the towels, resting it on their sorest spots. Arthur winced at the cold bite of the ice on his face, watching Maria place hers on her cheekbone, her face grimacing at the sting. Tristan sat across from Maria, his pack on his right rib.

"So what's the plan?" Maria said.

"Plan?" Arthur echoed.

"Are we just going to sit here and keep letting those men terrorise Londinium or what?"

"There's nothing we can do about them," Tristan said, adjusting his posture.

"Unfortunately," Arthur muttered. "We've already made a name for ourselves towards them."

"I don't know about us two, but you certainly have," Tristan frowned at him. "Why would you pick a fight with them, even if we did make them scram?"

"That woman was in danger, Tristan. I couldn't just let them beat up an old woman," Arthur protested, lifting the pack from his face.

"Hey, I understand the part about protecting people from others, but what will Ergott think when he sees you with a welt across your gob?" Tristan asked.

"It doesn't matter what he thinks," Arthur dismissed, turning to face him.

"He must've been drunk to think they'd be good people to hire," Maria rolled her eyes.

"That's my uncle for you," Arthur sighed.

Tristan grunted, leaning back in his chair. "The bastards are going to leave me tender as a babe, the way that big guy was hitting me."

"It's a wonder it's just a rib that hurts," Arthur raised a brow.

"Oh no, it's definitely more than that."

A distant crashing of metal snapped their attention outside, the conversation dropping. They looked towards the window, silhouettes cast on the far wall moving closer; five men passed by the window, dark hooded cloaks blowing in the wind. Arthur stood up from his chair and stalked towards the window, angling his view.

The men stood against the opposite side of the alleyway, two leaning against the bricks. Arthur narrowed his eyes; they were similar to the men they fought, but from what Arthur could tell, they weren't them. The Commander with the cracked mask was nowhere to be seen. *Probably licking his wounds, too.* Arthur smirked.

A sudden knock at the door broke the silence, the wood creaking at the hinges. Tristan and Maria looked at the door, sitting upright in their wooden chairs.

The knocking got louder and louder, rattling the wood dangerously hard. Arthur walked over, placing his ice towel on a side table next to the door, opening it slowly. Three men looked at Arthur, wearing the same black clothing as the others. One of the men wore no helmet or hood; instead, he had a grey beard and long tied-back hair, his left eye replaced with a scar stretching from the top of his forehead to the top of his lip.

"Someone is home, it seems," he said, his voice gruff and deep. "I was beginning to think no one was here since you took so long to answer the door."

"What are you doing here, Jackseye?" Arthur questioned, looking at his two flankers. Rohin Jackseye, the ex-Legion Commander under his father. The man that left on the tenth anniversary of his father's death with no explanation. The man Arthur thought was dead.

"Nice to see you too, Arthur. It's been too long," Jackseye replied.

"Probably for the best," Arthur spat. "Since you betrayed Camelot and its people."

"Men like me have duties. Besides, I'm still a close ally with your uncle," Jackseye smirked, his amber eye glinting maliciously.

Arthur frowned at him. "Answer the question," he growled flatly.

"My Barons and I are here to help defend Camelot, your uncle's special request," Jackseye said. "Wouldn't it be a shame if Camelot fell like its predecessor, Catarina?"

*So that's where he went - Ariendal.* For a man who fought to keep the Barons at bay from Camelot's borders, why would he choose to become one? And why would Ergott bring them here if he's sending a war party to fight them at Catarina? "How can you defend a Kingdom from your own forces? It doesn't make sense," Arthur asked firmly. "And as far as I've seen, you've caused nothing but havoc and street fights."

"Which brings me to why I'm standing here; a patrol of mine was intercepted by three individuals in Londinium's side streets. You three wouldn't know anything about it, would you?" Jackseye asked, eyeing all three of them.

Arthur folded his arms, shaking his head in denial. "Haven't heard a thing, sorry."

"Funny how it sounded precisely like you. You always liked to get yourself into trouble when you had the chance," Jackseye said, smirking faintly.

"Things have changed after eight years," Arthur gritted his teeth.

"That would be true," Jackseye replied, his head tilting up and eyes narrowing slightly. "Now, as described by my men, one of the perpetrators was female, and the other two were males of different ethnicities. Apparently, one of the names was 'Tristan'. Ever heard of the name?"

Arthur fought the urge to look at Tristan, almost feeling his friends' anxiety from the other side of the room. Arthur unfolded his arms, tilting his own head back.

"Never heard of the name," Arthur said casually.

Jackseye scoffed lightly, looking at Arthur in disbelief. "Now, Arthur, lying could get you into trouble, you know," he growled.

"I don't lie," Arthur lied. "You, of all people, would know."

"Well, if you're done with your story, I'll question those two over at the table," Jackseye shrugged, nodding to Tristan and Maria.

"By all means," Arthur said, stepping aside for Jackseye to enter.

Jackseye pushed past Arthur, the two men shadowing behind him. Jackseye's hand rested on the pommel of his curved sword, stopping before the two. Tristan and Maria looked at each other, unsure of what to say or do. Arthur closed the door behind himself, following them into the kitchen with a narrowed gaze.

Jackseye cleared his throat dramatically. "What about you two? Have you heard of the name 'Tristan'?" he asked, looking at Tristan with a slight smirk.

"I'm afraid it doesn't sound overly familiar," Tristan said with a slight waver. "Sorry."

Jackseye looked over to Maria beside him. "Have you?" he questioned, his brow raised.

Maria shook her head, her throat bobbing. Her hand clenched on the ice pack against her face, and she looked down.

"You got your answers, Jackseye," Arthur interrupted, walking over to him. "You can search elsewhere now."

"My investigation isn't done yet, Arthur. Apparently, you were seen around the area of an earlier brawl. One even said you joined in."

Arthur frowned, his brows knitting together. "Who?" Arthur thought the Knights would've been too focused on the street raff to have noticed him.

"Leonard Lionel," Jackseye answered.

"And you believe a thief over someone you've known since they were born?" Arthur growled, angered. *The bastard snitched on a fight he was a part of.* Arthur never would've thought he'd do that, nor did he think anyone would believe *Leonard*, of all people. Then again, this was Jackseye.

"You've never been good at keeping yourself out of trouble, Arthur," Jackseye repeated.

"At least I wasn't the one who started the trouble," Arthur scowled. "I just happened to be at the wrong place at the wrong time."

"I'd say," Jackseye smirked.

Arthur's back heated suddenly as if someone had hugged him. He looked over his shoulder and saw the two

Barons behind him, standing awfully close. The front door swung open, and more black-hooded men poured in to surround the three.

Tristan stood up, scowling at them. "You have no right to storm into my home," he snarled. "Leave right now."

The men stormed to Tristan and grabbed him roughly, Tristan spitting curses at them. Arthur glared at Jackseye, flicking his eyes to the Barons holding Maria and making her drop her pack to the floor. The men behind Arthur gripped his arms tightly, their armoured gloves scraping against his skin sharply.

"I've taught you how to speak but not lie," Jackseye drawled, sauntering to Arthur. "That's why you're terrible at it."

"I wasn't lying!" Arthur yelled, thrashing around in the guards' grip.

"I remember this boy," Jackseye pointed to an angry Tristan. "And I remember his name very clearly. You shouldn't defend others, boy; it never ends well for you."

Arthur bared his teeth at Jackseye, attempting to break loose from the Baron's grip. "You bastard! Let us go!"

"Interfering with the King's Guards is a cruel violation to Camelot, Arthur," Jackseye grinned wickedly. "You, of all people, should know."

"You know I'm a part of the royal family. You cannot arrest me!"

"Are you, though?" Jackseye asked lightly, a brow raised. "'Cause I don't see a crown on your head like you were 'destined' to have. And these two are just regular townspeople who caused a violation. A violation which you interfered with and hence got yourself into trouble."

"Your men hurt an innocent woman!" Maria barked. "That's guard brutality towards the citizens of Camelot!"

"You have no right to arrest Arthur, nor do you have a warrant," Tristan growled, narrowing his eyes at Jackseye.

"Then I guess I have every right to arrest *you*," Jackseye shrugged.

Arthur assessed the situation carefully, tugging in the men's grip. He looked down at their legs, black leather padding on the knees, thighs and shins; that could work to his advantage.

Arthur moved his right leg backwards, hitting the hooded man on his right directly in the shin and making him let his hands go with a yelp. He turned to the other guard, elbowing his jaw and grabbing his sword from the scabbard as the man stumbled. Jackseye spun to face him, unsheathing his khopesh. Arthur swung the blade up at Jackseye, trying to knock his hand away.

Jackseye deflected the blow, kicking Arthur in the abdomen as he shifted. Arthur fell to the ground and landed with a grunt, the air whooshing from him.

"Impressive, Arthur," Jackseye mocked. "Since when did you learn the element of surprise?"

"Ever since you left for the Barons," Arthur spat, trying to sit up on his knees.

"I guess a lot *has* changed after eight years," Jackseye tilted his head.

"You have no idea," Arthur glowered, straightening up toward Jackseye, his arms extended.

Jackseye allowed Arthur to grab his lower body, holding him in place as the two moved backwards. Jackseye slammed into the brick wall with a grunt, Arthur pinning his arms against Jackseye's chest. Before Arthur could lash out at him again, fierce grips tugged him back from the wall, guards holding him in place before he could do more damage.

Arthur thrashed in their grip, watching Jackseye regain his composure, twisting his neck to the right and letting out multiple cracks. Arthur widened his eyes as Jackseye threw punches to his stomach, the armoured gloves hitting hard as bricks. Tristan and Maria watched in shock as Jackseye hit

Arthur over and over again, the guards moving them out the front door, more of the hoods out in the alley.

Arthur looked up at him in pain, his teeth bared and anger flowing through his cells. "You're a bastard, Jackseye," he snarled and coughed painfully.

"March him to the castle; his uncle can deal with him from here," Jackseye ordered offhandedly, walking out of the room.

The guards marched Arthur out of the house, returning to the open alleyway. Jackseye led the three up the main street towards the castle, the passing civilians gaping in shock at the scene. Murmurs and whispers flickered through the crowds, concern and outrage thick in the air. More people stopped to stare at the Barons and the three, eyes widening at Arthur grimacing in pain. The Barons forced them out of Jackseye's road as they moved along to Arthur's demise, shoving a few civilians too slow to move.

At the castle entrance, Camelot guards stand tall at either side of the Gates, peering down at the oncoming party on the stairwell. Torches lit up the Gate with the help of the afternoon sun, lanterns swinging from poles above them.

Arthur looked up at the entrance from the staircase, still within the Baron's tight grip, Tristan and Maria behind him. The Camelot Knights looked at the men approaching them, noticing Arthur being held prisoner. They looked at each other sharply, and one of them stepped forward, Jackseye stopping before them.

"Pleasure to make your acquaintance, Sir Knight," Jackseye nodded. "If you wouldn't mind opening the gates for my men and myself."

"What is your business here?" the Knight asked, suspicion clear on his face.

"King Ergott has requested my arrival, and I delivered on his request," Jackseye answered.

"Who may you lot be?"

"Rohin Jackseye and the Black Guards," Jackseye answered.

"And Ergott is expecting you?" The Knight tilted his head down, resting his hand on his pommel.

"Indeed he is," Jackseye agreed. "And I suppose he'd want his nephew back from getting himself into trouble. He and his friends were interfering with our business, including attacking one of my patrols."

"What is your business here, Jackseye?" the other Knight repeated more firmly.

"My men and I are here to make Camelot a well-protected Kingdom," Jackseye reassured, gesturing to his men to move up.

"We weren't informed of your arrival-"

"Let them pass," a voice ordered from behind them.

Arthur's eyes flicked up at the voice behind the Knights in recognition, Jackseye and the others following his gaze. A figure walked to meet them, his armour built more extravagant than the Knights at the Gate. His blue eyes glimmered in the sunlight, his ears arching from under his long brown hair.

"Ergott is expecting them," he said, stopping beside the Gate Knights. "And so am I."

"Pleasure to make your acquaintance, Wilhelm," Jackseye said.

"Jackseye, it's been a while," Wilhelm replied.

"If we may, my men and I would like to enter the castle and speak with the King," Jackseye said.

"Ergott is waiting for you in the throne room," Wilhelm gestured behind himself. "You may proceed."

The Knights stood aside as Jackseye and his men marched through the castle's entrance, their grip on Arthur's wrist tight.

Arthur snorted. As if he'd run; he was in the castle he *lived in*, for the Gods sake. Arthur knew something wasn't right; the Knights and Wilhelm weren't questioning why they had him bound. Arthur narrowed his eyes at Jackseye as they entered the castle, his hands itching to grab him again.

They turned down the hallway, entering the open Roundtable room. The Knights were still seated at the table, turning their eyes to the incoming group. Samqueel immediately stood up, glaring at the guard holding Arthur.

"Let the Prince go," Samqueel demanded, moving towards him, "right now, or you get your hands permanently removed."

"Now, now, Samqueel, Arthur here interfered with our business," Jackseye said, moving in front of Arthur.

"I don't give a damn about what kind of business you've got your nose all up in, Rohin, I'm ordering your men to stand down," Sam snarled, his teeth bared.

Arthur looked at Samqueel in shock; the Commander of the Roundtable had never been this angry in front of him. Jackseye turned to Arthur, contemplation in his expression.

"Jackseye," Samqueel warned, his voice low and silver eyes burning. "You cannot arrest a royal."

"Perhaps you're right," Jackseye muttered. "Let them go."

The men released Arthur and the other two from their grip, Arthur shrugging semi-roughly out of their grasp. Maria rubbed her left bicep, glowering at the guards. Tristan shrugged out of the guards' grip, flicking his eyes to Sam with gratitude.

"I must say, Arthur, you did hold your ground quite well," Jackseye drawled.

"You knew you had no right to arrest us," Arthur spat. "You don't have that authority."

"Times have changed, Arthur," Jackseye replied. "Perhaps even for the better."

"For the better? You call your men hurting an innocent woman on the streets 'for the better'?" Arthur asked with irritation in his voice.

"She wasn't following instructions. *Muharí* Ryker asked her to return to her home, which she denied," Jackseye said.

"Maybe because she's homeless," Tristan said, stepping to stand beside Arthur. "Her name is Loretta; that alleyway has been her home for a long while."

"You knew her?" Arthur asked.

"I give her food whenever she needs it," Tristan shrugged.

"Her refusal wasn't an attack; she has no home," Maria said softly.

Jackseye looked at the three. "Perhaps my men could've been too harsh to the woman, but she still refused direct orders from the King's men."

"You expected anyone to recognise your men? What in the ether are you even doing here, and bringing Barons into the city? Have you gone mad?" Sam growled.

"Surely the King had let you know of the plans and announced our arrival?" Jackseye huffed, looking at Samqueel and the other Knights still seated at the Roundtable.

"Unfortunately, I didn't have the time to," Ergott said, walking down the far staircase into the large room.

"King Ergott," Jackseye greeted, bowing before him. "Pleasure to make your acquaintance."

"It's been too long, Rohin. Have the Barons been treating you well?" Ergott smiled.

"Not as well as here, I'm afraid," Jackseye said, straightening himself.

Ergott glanced over to Tristan and Maria, his eyebrows furrowing. "Who are these two?" he questioned.

"Ah, you reminded me; Arthur and his friends here interfered with my men's patrol," Jackseye said, smirking at Arthur. "So my men and I arrested them for treason."

"Jackseye, you know you cannot arrest a royal, especially not my nephew," Ergott scowled slightly.

"That's why I brought him to you, sire, so you can decide his punishment," Jackseye replied, beaming.

"Arthur's done more to help out this Kingdom than you've ever done. You should be the one to suffer, traitor," Sam hissed, his jaw clenched.

"Now, now, Samqueel," Ergott started. "No need to lash out at our guests and new colleagues; they've only just arrived. Show some hospitality."

Samqueel frowned at Ergott slightly, nodding shallowly and straightening his back. "Apologies, sire," he muttered, his face returning to neutrality. Arthur could see the shine of ire in his eyes as he glanced back to Jackseye.

Ergott looked over at Tristan and Maria, his face uninterested. "Anything to say in your defence?"

"None, sire," Tristan said, looking down to the floor. "I apologise for my actions against you and yours."

"I do," Maria looked up, stepping forward in front of Ergott.

"That is?" Ergott asked, slightly curious.

"You've robbed Arthur of his destiny," she started, her voice gritted. "He should be the King, not some selfish, arrogant imbecile like you! Saying that King George will take over when you pass on is just downright wrong. It's Arthur's birthright to be the King, yet you're so caught up in your own fantasy that you-"

"Silence!" Ergott barked, stepping towards Maria slowly.

Maria watched him gain closer, defiance and fear in her eyes. Arthur watched her with disbelief, the whole room gaping at her. No one could believe that she just disrespected the King in his own castle, especially not Arthur, especially in Arthur's defence!

"Is that really the proper way to address your King, peasant?" Ergott asked, his voice softer yet mysterious.

Her eyes flashed in protest at the insult, fear still overwhelming her features. "N-no, sire, I was just-"

"Just what? You obviously have your own opinions, and I'd like to hear them," Ergott pushed, his jaw tightening.

"I was just saying that Arthur should be King after you," she repeated, her voice trembling slightly.

Ergott hummed a short laugh, looking at Arthur sideways, then back at her. "March her and the other one back to Londinium. Feel free to lay a few blows if they resist," he dismissed.

Tristan frowned at him flatly. The King knew damn well who he was; *everyone* in the room did. It wasn't uncommon to find him with the Knights around their cabins. Friends in high places was an understatement when it came to describing the lad's friendships.

The Black Guards gripped Tristan and Maria by the arms to their annoyance, tugging them out of the Round Hall doorway and marching them towards the Gates. Arthur's brow creased in worry at the tightness of the guards' hold. Arthur looked at his uncle, his expression turning to anger. Ergott turned to him, a faint smirk on his face, aware of what he'd caused.

"As for you, nephew, don't you have anything to go to?" he asked.

"Since when did that concern you?" Arthur bit sharply.

"I found the Book of Mordred on your desk, a fine read for anything to do with becoming a Knight," Ergott raised a brow.

"Maybe you should consider it as a sign," Arthur scowled, walking out towards the door.

A small figure rounded the corner into the doorway at the same time as Arthur, running into him with a whoosh of air and a startled yelp. Arthur paused in shock, his hands shooting out to catch the tiny woman on reflex.

"You alright there?" Arthur asked in concern.

Brown eyes looked up at him in surprise and delight. "Oh, hello, Arthur," she smiled nervously. "I didn't see you there."

"Aunt Guinevere," Arthur replied, standing her up properly. She brushed her blonde hair back away from her face, fanning herself.

"Pardon me for running into you. I was in a bit of a rush," she admitted. "And you know you can call me Rosaline."

"In a rush for what?" Arthur asked.

"I was called down for an emergency with the Maidens," she explained. "I needed to ask Ergott a few questions, is all."

Arthur frowned. "The Maidens? Is Enid alright?"

"Enid is perfectly fine," Rosaline assured. "One of the younger girls was having trouble with some of the new people getting around the castle and ended up tripping down a flight of stairs."

"What did the new people look like?" Arthur asked, narrowing his eyes.

Rosaline straightened her skirts absently, trying to catch her breath. "They had black cloaks on, from what they described. I've seen a few get around the chambers, and they've caught my attention only recently, so I've come to ask Ergott about them." She peered around his shoulder into the Round Hall. "Is he in here?"

Arthur grabbed her arms gently, taking her around the corner out of the doorway. Queen Rosaline Guinevere was a fragile little thing with a busy streak like that of a bee; Arthur could swear the woman never sat down to rest on a good day.

"They're Barons," Arthur whispered. "Highly trained assassins from Ariendal."

Her eyes widened in startlement at him, shock written across her face. "Assassins in the castle?" she gasped. "What are they doing here?"

"Something isn't right," Arthur said. "Just be wary of them around the castle."

"I will," she whispered. "Thank you, Art." She pulled her arms gently from his hands with a small smile, moving into the Round Hall towards Ergott.

"Evening, everybody," she greeted, watching the Barons at the door with uncertainty. Arthur stood beside her, narrowing his eyes at his uncle.

"Oh, my dear," Ergott said with delightment. Rosaline moved over to Ergott gracefully, and that permanent smile lit across her face. The Knights' eyes glowed in surprise, standing from the table to bow.

"Evening to you, Queen Guinevere," Samqueel greeted, a smile on his face.

"Jackseye, you remember my wife, Rosaline?" Ergott asked.

"Indeed I do," Jackseye nodded, bowing to the Queen. "Nice to see you again, Rosaline."

"Rohin," she greeted politely.

"What can I do for you, my Queen?" Ergott asked, smiling at her.

She walked to him, taking his arm in her gentle hands and smiling up at him. "There's been an incident in the servant's stairwell, with these… um…" She looked at the Barons standing at the doors. "These men that have been in the castle. Why have they come?"

"Rohin and his men are accompanying the castle as our new royal guards," Ergott explained. Arthur watched the Roundtable Knights throw dirty looks at Ergott for the words.

"Oh?" she questioned. "But what about the Knights? *They're* supposed to be patrolling the castle."

"Like I said, *accompanying* the castle," Ergott said, wrapping his arm around her waist.

Her face softened in thought as she glanced back up at him. "Well, the reason I'm here was to seek assistance with the injured Maiden. Her injuries are quite extensive," she murmured.

"An injured Maiden?" Ergott asked, looking at her.

"I was told one of these new guards was involved in an incident with the girl falling down the staircase," she said.

"I don't have time for this," Ergott muttered, rubbing his head. "Samqueel."

Sam's eyes narrowed slightly at the King as he stepped forward. "We're on it," he nodded. "Lead the way, my Queen."

Rosaline let go of Ergott and turned towards the door, the Knights following behind her with Samqueel escorting her out.

"And Arthur," Ergott added. Arthur looked up at him, his eyes narrowed.

"Don't you have studying to get back to?" Ergott asked.

Arthur huffed at the King, walking out of the Round Hall without a word. It irked him how only now Ergott found any interest in his pastimes. *As if he'd care, anyway.*

Ergott watched as Arthur made his way out of the Round Hall, turning away with his usual smirk. Arthur walked past Jackseye, Rohin watching him with a sideways glance.

Walking up to the array of spiral stairs, Arthur heard the slam of the Black Guards shutting the double doors. He furrowed his brows at the figures standing near the doors, continuing his way up the stairs.

Arthur sighed to himself, overwhelmed by the day that occurred, and he didn't even get the loaves of bread. But what did it matter? He wouldn't get any recognition for getting supplies for the castle from anyone but Ms Enid. Hell, it was rare for Ms Enid to even get any praise for her work, and she did just about everything around here.

He made it to the top of the spiral staircase, heading back to his room down the far end, the sun glowing through the open windows across the walls. He opened his room door and looked around; the bed looked made, clean and well-furnished, along with his floor. Some of the clothes that were there before were now gone. On his bed, a note lay sprawled on his pillow. He walked over to it and picked it up.

'To Arthur, thanks for your help and assistance whenever it's needed. Keep your room clean, from Ms Enid.'

Arthur smiled faintly at the note, placing it on his bedside table and lying on the freshly made bed. He stared at the roof, the cold from his blankets seeping through his clothing. He sighed once again, closing his eyes as he listened to the silence.

# Chapter 5: Spectre of the King

*"Run, Arthur!" Benjamin cried. "Run!"*

*Arthur darted through the forest, dirt and grass flicking up behind him, his feet sinking into the land. Benjamin rolled out of the way of a savage blow, the sword from his opponent hitting the ground hard. Benjamin looked up at the figure, orange dilated eyes piercing his soul. Smoke poured from the figure's mouth as it growled, yanking its sword out of the ground, clumps of dirt spraying Benjamin's face. The King groaned, blinking dirt from his eyes.*

*The figure turned to Benjamin, a menacing grin spread on its ghastly face. In the distance, an explosion erupted, tearing the being's attention from the King. A huge fireball erupted from the east past the forest to the base of the coastal mountains, the bang making their ears ring. Benjamin stumbled back onto his feet, his face slackening as he faced the explosion.*

*"No..." Benjamin whispered.*

*"Catarina has fallen, King Benjamin. You have lost," the figure said, its thunder-like voice echoing through the woods.*

*"Why do this? Why hurt thousands of innocent lives?" Benjamin asked, looking at it over his shoulder.*

*"It was never about the people or the throne; it was about getting rid of you," the figure growled.*

*Benjamin turned back to the figure, his eyes narrowing. "The throne never belonged to me. It belongs to the spirit of my ancestors. I just happened to sit in it."*

*"Now the throne will belong to another," it said, sprinting towards Benjamin with its sword raised.*

*Benjamin took Excalibur in both of his hands, his own eyes flaring a bright blue, his sword glowing with runes. He braced himself for the blow, the black flames on the figure's weapon getting hotter the closer they got. Their weapons clashed fiercely, the sound echoing around the trees. Benjamin bared his teeth. "Not if I can help it."*

*Running through the woods out of breath, Arthur looked back towards Benjamin, trying to see him. All Arthur could see were trees and bushes, nothing but thick woodlands. He squinted his eyes, hoping to see something other than leaves.*

*Something caught his attention to his left; a faint silhouette ran through the bushes, their frame too small to be a guard or Knight. He narrowed his eyes at the running shadow; it didn't look like an animal-*

*"Arthur."*

*He jumped in fright and snapped his attention to the voice. His father limped towards him, out of breath and tired... very, very tired.*

*"Arthur," Benjamin said softly, kneeling in front of the boy, his hands on his shoulders. "I need you to be strong for me and run as far away as you can get."*

*"I can't leave you, Father. I won't leave you," Arthur protested.*

*"You must run back to Londinium. Find Jackseye. He'll look after you," Benjamin said, rubbing his son's arms.*

*"I can't do it without you," Arthur whimpered, a tear falling down his face.*

*Benjamin reached his hand to Arthur's face, wiping away the tears. "Yes, you can. You always could. I want you to take this."*

*Benjamin moved his arms towards his neck, unhooking his amulet swiftly, the small blue crystal glimmering in the moonlight. Arthur looked at it, the light making his tears almost burn away from brightness. Benjamin looped the chain around Arthur's neck, letting it settle on his chest.*

*"It's yours now," Benjamin said. "It'll remind you to be brave and to remember me."*

*"Please... don't leave me," Arthur cried.*

*"I'll meet you in the castle, but right now, I need you to find Jackseye-" Benjamin swung his head around quickly with a gasp; black flames surrounded the base of a falling tree, and the world jolted as Benjamin lifted him up and promptly dodged the falling limbs, the tree crashing to the ground right where they just stood. Arthur looked at the flames in horror, looking up to see those glowing eyes in the dark behind the fallen tree. Benjamin placed Arthur back on the ground, standing in front of him like a shield and unsheathing his sword.*

*"Run," Benjamin growled.*

*"I won't leave y-"*

*"Run, Arthur!" Benjamin barked, charging towards the glowing eyes with his weapon ready.*

*Obeying his father's command, Arthur sprinted towards the castle, fear and dread soon overcoming his emotions. Arthur heard the same clashing of metal fly through the canopy. Arthur looked back at his father for a slight moment before a loud screech bellowed in front of him. He flicked his head forward, his eyes widening at the thing before him; a giant black horse reared up onto its hind legs, the same screech emitting from its maw. Glowing red eyes glared at Arthur, smoke pouring out of them in waves, the same black flames as the figure coating its flank.*

*Arthur yelled in fright and stumbled to the ground in fear, scattering back from the creature as it charged at him, its hooves tearing into the earth closer and closer-*

Arthur let out a horrific yell as he jolted awake, sweat dripping from his head onto the bed sheets. His room had turned dark, the moon glowing outside his window shining over his bed. He loosed a breath, resting his head on his pillow, trying to rid the tension in his body.

That dream was way more detailed than what he'd seen before. The flaming horse was new. He touched the amulet at his neck, the crystal cool against his fingers. He saw his father again, and that silhouette that ran past him… Night terrors were an absolute pain.

He sighed deeply, sitting up on the edge of his bed. He wiped the sweat from his forehead with his arm, his sleeve coated in it.

*That horse; what did it mean?* From what he could guess, the horse had some sort of connection to the figure that fought his father. He shook his head, trying to clear his mind as he stood up from his bed. A knock on his door sounded, catching his attention as he stretched his limbs.

Arthur walked over to the door, opening it slowly and peering out.

"Are you alright, Arthur?" Ms Enid asked, her voice laced with concern. "I heard you cry out."

"Just a bad dream, Ms Enid. I'm fine," Arthur reassured her.

"Another one of those dreams?" Her wrinkled brow knitted together.

"Every night, they get worse and worse, it seems," he quirked his mouth.

"Have you told your uncle?"

"Why would I? He wouldn't do anything about it."

"What makes you say that?"

Arthur shook his head, a faint frown on his face. "They're just silly dreams. He'd mock me for being afraid."

"What was your dream about?" she asked.

"It's getting a bit late, Ms Enid. Perhaps you should rest up for the night," Arthur said, purposely dodging the question. He didn't feel like talking about his dreams with anybody, not even with Ms Enid. It felt too personal and silly.

Enid looked up at Arthur, contemplation on her face. "You remind me so much of him. It's… beautiful," she murmured.

"Of who?" Arthur asked, his brows furrowing slightly.

"Your father, Benjamin," she answered with a smile. "You have his heart. It's a shame you weren't of age when he passed."

Arthur frowned. "It's probably for the best. Ergott knows more about ruling a Kingdom than I do."

"He's afraid," she muttered softly.

"Afraid? Afraid of what?" Arthur blinked. *Odd of her to suggest such a thing...*

Enid raised her hand to Arthur's face, her hand cool against his cheek. "Of you, the 'Born King'. He knows your destiny, what you're to become. He wants to remain the King until the day he falls 'cause he knows you'll be the King not only of Camelot but also of Braynor."

*She's been up for so long that she's becoming delusional.* Arthur gave her a slight smile, moving her hand away from his face. "I wish that was true, but my uncle has other intentions."

"That is true, unfortunately," Enid sighed.

"It's getting late, Ms Enid. You need to get some rest," Arthur changed the subject.

Enid smiled softly. "Very well, see you in the morning."

Arthur returned the smile, resting his hand on her left shoulder before she wandered off, heading down the hall to the stairwell. Arthur turned back into his room, allowing the wind to shut the door behind him a bit too swiftly.

Walking over to his desk, Arthur lit a small match from within his drawer, lighting a lantern hanging above his desk. The room turned a hue of orange, the flame illuminating the papers and books stacked in piles.

Sighing to himself, Arthur pulled out the wooden chair tucked underneath the bench, sitting with a thud. Various notes lay scattered on top of their suited books, a larger pile stacked upon a peculiar book of interest. Looking up, Arthur reached up to a shelf above his head, placing more books on his table.

He moved a few pages out of the way and positioned the books in front of him. The books were protected by unique dust jackets, and gold and copper decals decorated the sleeves. Arthur panned over the titles, deciding which of the three he'd like to use his night on studying over.

*The Knights Manual, Knights of Camelot Training, The Darklands*... He placed the Darklands book up to the others above his desk and moved the Knights Manual to the side, opening the training book.

The author's name glittered in black ink on the first page: **Comdrick Mordred**. Arthur flicked the page over, browsing the contents table.

One part in particular caught Arthur's interest: the training of the Knights, lists of all the exercises needed to be deemed fit enough.

His mouth quirked at a few. *Who in their right mind would make a Knight stand on their hands?* As the hours passed long into the night, Arthur's eyes began to grow heavy once more until, eventually, with a slight thud, his head lay to rest against the book on the table.

*Arthur stirred awake from an uncomfortable rest, the side of his head throbbing in pain. He cracked his eyes*

*open, finding himself still sitting at his desk, the book under his face still wide open to the page he left it at. Arthur sighed to himself, sitting up in his chair.*

Good job falling asleep at the desk, Arty. Real intelligent.

*He rubbed his face, groaning at the throbbing in his head. A cool breeze flowed from underneath his door, and Arthur shivered, turning to look. His eyes flashed, flicking towards the gap under the door quickly.*

*He stood up from his chair, trying to get a better look at what he saw. A faint blue light shone beneath the doorway, reminding him of the moonlight glow from outside. He blinked at it, curiosity propelling him forward. He reached his hand out to the door handle, opening it slowly.*

*As if spooked, the light darted across the hallway, heading down the stairwell.*

*Arthur's eyes widened. He'd never seen such a thing before in his life. Arthur followed the light down the stairwell warily, picking up a torch from a sconce on the wall and holding it before him as he walked down the stairs. The further Arthur walked down the stairs, the further away the little blue light went.*

*Perhaps it was leading him somewhere? But where? Arthur already knew the castle inside and out from his, more often than not, bored days of exploration.*

*Hell, he'd even found an extra passageway one time when he was younger, but that didn't go so well for him when the bakers found him stuck and covered in flour in the butler's pantry early the following day...*

*Arthur paused, seeing something standing in the middle of the lobby before the High Castle Gates, his heart skipping a beat. The blue light seemed to materialise before him into a man kneeling in front of a small boy. Arthur turned his eyes to the boy, and his eyes widened.*

*The boy was him, and that man... his face was too blurred out to see who it was.*

*With a slight whoosh, the forms of the boy and the man diminished, the little orb speeding off to leave Arthur gaping to himself in a dark, empty foyer beside the stairwell.*

*He furrowed his brows in confusion and kept chasing after it. He weaved his path down the castle corridors, too focused on the blue light to notice the Knights that passed through him effortlessly, none of them taking any heed to his presence.*

*Heading down a narrow hallway, Arthur stopped as the blue light transformed again, turning into the form of the same man as before, facing away from him.*

*Arthur paused, narrowing his eyes at the spectre in front of him. It stood beside one of the side doors along the hallway walls. Arthur felt the same cool breeze of wind as the one that came from beneath his door, goosebumps dotting his arms as it blew out the torch in his hand. He looked at it with a frown and sat it on the ground.*

*The spectre looked back at him, bright glowing eyes staring at Arthur, the light enveloping the man's entire eye.*

*Arthur's eyes widened, freezing; could it see him? The spectre looked to the door to its left, phasing itself through, the blue light shining beneath the door gap. Arthur frowned and walked to the doorway, inspecting it. Something in Arthur's gut told him to open the door, but another part of him hesitated at the thought.* What if the spectre is dangerous?

*"Open the door, son..." a whisper told him.*

*Arthur turned around in fright, looking down both hallways, but no one was there.*

*"Open the door..."*

*There it was again. Arthur placed his hand on the handle gently, the door swinging open and the cool breeze rushing more intensely to Arthur as it opened, the blue light gone from the hallway.*

*Stepping inside the room, Arthur looked around the dark, looking for anything sticking out of the shadows. Beside the wall on a bracket, a readied torch sat dormant.*

*He grabbed it and swiped the tip along the brick wall beside him, sparking into an intense flame before dying back down to burn slower. Soon, the whole room in front of him lit up, revealing piles of crates and tables dotting the far wall.*

*Arthur looked around curiously. This was one room he hadn't stepped foot into before, simply because he wasn't allowed to. It was one of Ergott's many rules for Arthur to follow. His eyes panned over each side of the room but came to a halt when he spotted a chest at the far end of the room, pressed up against the brick wall.*

*The chest was made of dark wood, rusted metal lining the edges and holding the locks still, the lid completely covered in dust and cobwebs. Arthur felt uneasy but was too invested in the chest in front of him; he had to see what was inside. Arthur walked up slowly to the chest, feeling a strange presence coming from it. Seating the torch in a bracket above the chest, he knelt before it, scrutinising every detail.*

*"Arthur..." the whisper called, sounding closer. Was it coming from the chest?*

*Arthur looked behind himself to see if anyone was in the room, but no one else was there. His bravado wavered slightly, and he thought about leaving the room before Ergott found out somehow.*

*He looked back at the chest warily, slowly placing his two hands on the chest. Arthur pulled the locks undone and opened the chest, a cold breeze escaping and whooshing his hair back from his face. That same blue light glared brightly from beneath the lid. His eyes widened: beneath a white sheet, pristine and glinting in the torchlight, Knight armour edged with copper glinted cleanly, a sword and shield laying down the bottom of the clothing.*

*The metal glinted harshly in Arthur's eyes, a vibrant blue blinding him for a moment. Arthur reached down into the chest, moving the various pieces of armour out of the way, gripping the sword's hilt firmly.*

*He pulled his arm out of the chest, lifting the weapon from within the wooden box. His eyes widened, glued to the sword in his hands. Lifting the blade to the light as he stood, he pulled it from the scabbard a few inches, Arthur's eyes glittering in wonder at the runes etched into the blade.*

*"Arthur..." the voice said.*

*His eyebrows furrowed as he paused in place. The voice was behind him.*

*He slowly turned around to face the voice, a similar blue light shining in the corner of his eye. Behind Arthur, the spectre stood solemnly, staring at him at eye level. It stepped forward, and Arthur stepped back slightly, wary of the spectre's presence. Arthur studied his facial details, clearer than what they were before. A rough-hewn beard coated his jaw, high cheekbones framing the glowing blue eyes, his hair roughed up as if with helmet hair.*

*"You have no idea how long I've waited for you to find that chest," the spectre said in the same gravelly voice as before.*

*"Who are you?" Arthur asked, sheathing the sword. "What are you doing in Camelot?"*

*"Checking on my son," the spectre answered, his voice smooth and soft.*

*Arthur looked at the man, his face slackening. "Father?" Arthur asked.*

*"Yes, my son," Benjamin smiled. "You have grown to look a lot like your father."*

*"Like father, like son, right?" Arthur asked, a small smile forming on his face. His father was here, talking to him, but how?* Is this a dream?

"Exactly," Benjamin said, looking at Arthur up and down. "Something is missing," he noted, looking at Arthur's brow.

"If you're referring to the crown, Ergott is wearing it," Arthur said.

"Why aren't you?" Benjamin asked, his eyes furrowing.

"Ergott's taken over the title of King. He believes I'm not ready to rule, nor will I ever be. People in Camelot and Londinium believe it's my destiny to wear the crown, but I don't know what to think at this point," he said, running his hand through his hair. "I don't want to end up failing this Kingdom, even though people want me to take the lead. All of his negative talk about me not being fit or ready to be King has me thinking he might be right."

"What do you believe, Arthur?" Benjamin asked calmly.

Arthur looked down at the sword gripped in his hands. "I want to believe I'm destined for greatness, that I have a purpose instead of being nothing."

"You, my son, are the Born King. You always have and always will be. It is your destiny to take my place, but you must earn it first."

"Well, how do I earn it?" Arthur asked, looking at Benjamin.

"When the time is right, you must traverse the Darklands and find a man who lives within the deepest, darkest part of the territory," Benjamin said. "He will guide you to finding the key to your destiny. But for now, you must take this sword and this armour and learn the skills necessary to survive."

"This destiny I'm said to have and fulfil; when will it come into place?" Arthur asked softly. If it ever came into place. It sure hadn't in the times he'd wished for it.

"In time, that question will be answered before your very eyes," Benjamin reassured.

"What of my uncle?" Arthur asked curiously.

*"Ergott is withholding dark secrets behind a veil. He cannot be trusted on the throne," Benjamin answered, his eyes narrowing slightly. "Believe me with this, my son; you will take Ergott's place, no matter how long it takes. The throne is your birthright."*

*Arthur looked down at the sword, watching the dreamcatcher-shaped pommel weave the blue spectral light through its strands like a spiderweb. The prophecies - they had to be true. How else would he be in this vision, talking to his father?*

*If nothing else made sense to Arthur regarding the prophecy and his destiny, could he trust that what he was seeing was real? That this wasn't all some sort of twisted dream his brain conjured up like the nightmares?*

*But what about the people who depend on his rule? If the words were valid, he'd save them from great evil in the face of the most significant threat the country had ever known. Who would protect them if it wasn't him?*

*He couldn't leave people to suffer. He'd never been able to.*

*Arthur clenched his jaw and looked up at the spectre. "I'll try my best, Father," he vowed, holding tighter to the scabbard.*

*Benjamin smiled as his spectre began to fade away, the world swirling around Arthur with technicolour waves.*

## Chapter 6: The Roundtable

Arthur jolted awake with a start, his head throbbing just like in the dream he had. He groaned to himself, rubbing his temple as he sat up and lifted his face off the books on his desk. *Well, at least that part of the vision was right.*

That couldn't have been a memory, nor just a random dream like any other person in Londinium; it had to have had a purpose. He looked over to his window, becoming instantly blinded by the sunlight, clamping his eyes shut as the sun harassed his vision.

Arthur stood from his chair, his spine cracking as he stretched his arms up over his head with a groan. Arthur walked over to his windowsill by the far left wall, letting out a tiresome yawn as he shuffled over, his legs not quite fully awake from sleeping in a wooden chair. Yet again, it's not the most ideal sleeping spot of *all* the choices.

Arthur opened the windows to allow the cool breeze to travel through his room. The temperature dipped in and out of all different conditions in this kind of weather; whether it be hot, warm, cold or cool, there was no way of telling what the climate would be doing each day.

Especially in Braynor.

Walking to his cupboard, Arthur opened the double wooden doors, pulling out fresh clothing that Ms Enid had packed away for him. He pulled out an olive green shirt and brown trousers, quickly following a pair of leather boots.

He moved over to his bed, sitting on the edge of it and
placing his clothes beside him.

Arthur took off his long-sleeved shirt, throwing it
towards the clothes basket on the opposite side of the room.
The shirt bounced off the wall and into the basket smoothly.
Arthur grinned faintly, taking the olive shirt next to him
and sliding it over his head.

He stood from the edge of his bed and changed his
trousers. From where he was, Arthur could hear a
conversation coming from the hallway, the voices familiar.
He strained his ears, trying to listen to
them clearly.

"Ergott is the King of Madness," Taryn growled,
leaning against the hallway wall.

"Be careful what you say out loud," Samqueel warned,
his voice stern as he turned to face him.

"Let me ask you, Sam; do you think the Barons are the
right choice for Camelot's new protectors? You know of
their history," Taryn frowned, folding his arms.

"In all honesty, I'd be lying if I said I agreed with
Ergott's choice," Sam muttered.

"You and I both know that he shouldn't be King," Taryn
mumbled quietly, looking around the hallway.

"Speaking about Ergott like that can get yours and my
ass kicked if someone overhears," Samqueel reminded him
with a glower.

"He deserved to be told off by that girl," Taryn said.
"Ground his ego a bit. Satisfying to no end."

"Ergott wants us at the Roundtable in fifteen minutes,"
a third voice joined, Reuben walking to stand beside Sam.
"Another meeting about the assault on Ariandel, I'm
guessing."

"That brings up my next point - he throws us into
stupidly dangerous situations," Taryn added, giving Sam a
sharp look.

"When did Wilhelm estimate our departure?" Samqueel ignored him, turning his attention to Reuben.

"Tomorrow at sunrise, when the men are ready," Reuben replied. "Are we even sure this is a smart idea?"

"I know damn well that it isn't," Samqueel sighed. "Have the boys returned with the others yet?"

Reuben nodded at him. "They arrived early this morning."

"Good. At least we can fall back on that plan if things go the way I'm guessing."

"Surely he's not so stupid to do something like that?" Taryn scoffed. "The city would never forgive him."

"For now, it's just a precaution. They know the plan. As for Ergott's concern with Catarina," Sam shook his head with a sigh, "I don't understand what he's worried about. And why the Hell would Jackseye show up after all these years just to bring Barons back here? Something isn't right."

"Are you three coming? Ergott's waiting for you," Lorsaw's voice sounded from the stairwell.

All three Knights flicked their eyes over to Lorsaw near the staircase, seeing his typical tight-lipped face peering around the corner. Taryn smirked at him from over Samqueel's shoulder, relishing in his irritation.

"A bit tired there, Lorsaw?" Taryn asked, nodding to his knotted hair and messy outlook, his shirt untucked and coat crinkled.

"Since when did you care?" Lorsaw sniped, straightening his shirt.

"Oh, I don't. I just find it funny," Taryn grinned at him. "Normally, you'd never let a single hair on your head be out of place, never mind full-on look as if you got dragged in by the cat."

"In the Round Hall, now," Lorsaw demanded. "We don't want to keep Ergott waiting."

"Last time I checked, Lorsaw, you weren't the ones giving the orders around here," Samqueel frowned at him slightly. Lorsaw sniffed, looking away. "Ergott can wait for another five minutes. For now, go fix your hair, your outfit and your attitude. You look terrible."

"We'll be waiting for you in the Round Hall," Lorsaw growled, walking back down the stairs and threading his fingers through his hair.

From his doorway, Arthur watched the Knights follow Lorsaw down the stairs with grumbles of annoyance, their boots echoing in the hallway. Arthur sighed lightly, reaching over to the back of his neck for the hook on the necklace. Taking it off, Arthur went to gently place it on his bedside table and accidentally dropped it to the floor, hearing it hit the planks with a thud. Arthur shook his head with an annoyed huff, squatting down to the floor to pick it up.

As Arthur turned his head to look up, a shadow caught his eye beneath his bed, his brows knitting together. He placed the necklace up on the bedside table, turning his attention to peer beneath the frame. Arthur reached under the bed, getting a grip on the object.

To his surprise, the object was a lot heavier than he anticipated. He strained his tired limbs as he tugged it out from under the bed, backing up to look at it in confusion.

It was the chest from the dream.

*Had that been there the whole time?* It was a carbon copy of the chest from his dream - the same latches, with the same type of wood and the same rust coating the edges.

There was no way it could have gotten itself into his room; he never went into the door that was forbidden to him… or had he?

Arthur's eyes felt glued to the chest, the whole atmosphere centred on the box. A new question filled his thoughts: *What's in it?*

Arthur hesitated before reaching over to the latches, flicking them lightly as they clicked open. He lifted the chest open, the same cold breeze passing by his fingers, but no glowing blue light.

There it was: the armour, the sword and the shield, perfectly placed within the chest in the same spot as before.

Uncertainty creased Arthur's brow. *Maybe the dream wasn't a dream after all...*

Arthur closed the chest slowly. He knew he couldn't tell Ergott; otherwise, that would mean many consequences. He slid the chest back under his bed, out of sight and out of his mind - for now. Arthur finished readying himself, stepping out of his room to head down the stairwell, looking both ways to see if the Knights were still out there. He sighed in a bit of relief, heading down the stairs.

How in the Ether had it ended up under his bed? It couldn't have just shown up in Arthur's room as a coincidence - maybe someone put it there?

Like Hell they would. His uncle wouldn't - not even his Knights would dare to do it. They'd get into deep trouble if King Ergott found out they'd put it there.

Arthur reached the bottom of the stairs, his mood lifting as he saw Ms Enid in the main room, wiping down the doors with a wet cloth, a wooden water bucket on the ground beside her. Arthur walked over, spotting a spare cloth flopped over the bucket untouched. Without hesitation, Arthur made his way over to the Maiden, eyeing the extra cloth.

Ms Enid turned to look behind her, a broad smile beaming across her wrinkled face. "Good morning, Arthur," she greeted.

"Morning to you too, Ms Enid," Arthur smiled.

"You're up earlier than normal today. Are you heading somewhere?" Ms Enid asked softly.

"Not for a while; I still need to get you your bread," Arthur said, guilt growing across his face.

"Don't worry about the bread, lad; the delivery came on time. I heard about yesterday's incident - those men were too cruel to you, dear," Ms Enid frowned, looking at a spot on his face. "Look at what they did to you."

Arthur turned to look at a mirror seated against the wall towards the door; a purple bruise smudged just under his eye across his cheekbone. It was probably a factor contributing to the pounding in his head.

"It's nothing too major, just a bruise," Arthur shrugged, turning to look at her.

"Do I have to have a word with the men?" Ms Enid asked in a low voice, her eyes narrowing.

"It's nothing, Ms Enid. Trust me, I'm fine," Arthur reassured. An old mistress like her would never be able to fight against the Barons, regardless.

Ms Enid nodded shallowly, turning back to the door she was cleaning. "Did you have another bad dream?"

Arthur dipped the cloth in the water bucket, beginning to clean with the elderly Maiden. "Not a bad one, but an interesting one," he nodded.

"You know me too well to not tell me," Ms Enid said with a slightly expectant tone.

Arthur quirked his mouth. "It was strange. I started in my room, sleeping on the desk. There was this blue light coming from underneath my doorway, so I checked it out, and nothing was there except this blue orb. I walked down the main lobby, and the blue light kept on leading me on a specific path like it was guiding me to a place. I followed it down the Western hallway, and then it became a silhouette, a spectre, I believe." He wiped across the door's surface, dust clinging to the cloth. "It led me into the room Ergott banned me from, and I found a-"

"Chest?" Ms Enid interrupted, giving off a slight grin.

Arthur looked at her sideways. "You knew about it?"

"Of course. I made sure it got moved there," Ms Enid shrugged casually.

"You put it there?" Arthur asked with incredulity, his eyes widening slightly.

"I knew that after our conversation about Ergott not wanting to give up the throne, I had to help you somehow," Ms Enid murmured under her breath, wary of eavesdroppers.

Arthur couldn't believe it. "Ms Enid, that could get you into trouble," Arthur frowned.

"Ergott doesn't control me. The only reason I'm still here is to look after you as best as I can since he won't," Ms Enid dismissed, dipping her cloth in the bucket.

Arthur was stunned. Of all things, he never would have thought Ms Enid would go against the King for him. "Why give me the armour? Why risk getting yourself into trouble for me?"

"Because no one else would have," Ms Enid shrugged, casually polishing away.

"No one should, not even you," Arthur protested. "I'm not worth the risk of you getting your job taken away or even worse. I appreciate the thought, but that was a risky move."

"Ergott needs to understand that you're not just a peasant living in the royal castle under special care, Arthur. Your uncle is a hard man, and I have a gut feeling that something isn't right about him."

"Maybe that's for the better or the worse, but I heard it from his own mouth that he doubts me," Arthur muttered, getting irritated. "I'm going to prove to him I'm more than just his nephew."

Ms Enid looked at him, intrigued. "And how will you prove it to him?" she asked curiously.

"If I can't be a better King than what he believes, then maybe I'll become a better Knight than he could ever think. Other people seem to believe in me, so why can't he?" Arthur declared, frowning deeper.

"Because you're too young and naïve," Ergott's voice snaked towards them.

Arthur and Ms Enid flicked their attention over to his voice, their eyes widening. Ergott, along with two Camelot Knights, stood at the top of the stairs to the High Gates, his expression flat. Arthur scowled, taking a step in front of Ms Enid.

"You two are like Syren's in the castle. I could hear you from a mile away," Ergott grumbled.

"So you got all of that information?" Arthur asked defensively. His heart pounded in his ears. *How much of that had he heard?*

"About you thinking you can become a Knight of Camelot? Yes, I did," Ergott answered, a slight smirk slithering across his face.

Relief flew through Arthur, but he kept his face neutral. "Why does everyone but you believe in me?" Arthur asked, his voice stiff.

"Because everyone else is blind. They're so caught up in their own opinions, imaginations and hopes of you that they've blinded themselves from the truth. You're a weak young boy with a fancy title to your name. They already have a King - a King who can and will do anything for his Kingdom. But they can't see that because all they want is 'The Born King', a myth and a tale," Ergott growled.

"You've blinded yourself, uncle," Arthur glowered. "You keep on telling yourself that you're the only one here who can bear the pressure of being King."

"That's because I am. Being a King has many, many responsibilities, Arthur. People want you dead. I'm doing the right thing by you," Ergott narrowed his eyes back at Arthur.

"You're wrong," Arthur spat, his blood firing up.

"You don't know how well you've got things, boy. I've done so much for you, and you're repaying me by being as selfish as your father," Ergott barked at him.

"You've done nothing for me! You've kept me here and robbed me of knowledge and power, all for your own agenda!" Arthur bit back.

"I'm trying to protect you," Ergott boomed, his fists clenching at his sides.

"You're holding me back!" Arthur barked. "You're pushing me away and telling me no because you couldn't be bothered to face the fact that you're not the rightful King. You're afraid!"

"Afraid of what? My nephew, the street fighter? The saviour of the poor and weak?" Ergott looked him up and down in mockery. "You should consider yourself lucky I was here to clean up the mess your father left behind. Who was going to teach you the ways of the King if you just so happened to pick up the crown?"

"I'd have figured it out. A lot of things would be different around in Londinium, I assure you that," Arthur huffed, his eyes cold.

"And would they have been for the better or the worse?" Ergott asked, his jaw clenched.

"You tell me, your Highness," Arthur glared at him.

"King Ergott," a voice broke the tension from the Round Hall doors.

Ergott pivoted, seeing Samqueel standing with the door halfway open. Sam flicked his eyes to Arthur, his face steeled with tension. Arthur wasn't sure if that was a good thing or not.

"Yes, Samqueel?" Ergott answered, his spine rigid.

"We're ready for the meeting, sire," Samqueel replied, stepping out to the hallway further.

Ergott nodded, making his way over to the Round Hall, glaring sidelong at Arthur. "Disrespect me in such a regard again, boy, and you will find yourself out on the streets as a commoner," he threatened.

"You wouldn't dare," Arthur scoffed, narrowing his eyes in anger.

"Don't test me." Ergott turned his gaze forward, Arthur and Ms Enid watching as Ergott disappeared into the Round Hall.

Arthur glanced at Sam, nodding in thanks. It was one of many times that Sam had broken up a fight between him and Ergott, settling the tension to keep the peace. He'd done it since he was a young lad - came to his defence, fought for his freedom to roam the streets and to train in the castle yards with them, made sure Tristan kept his privilege to hang around the Knight Quarters. All of the Knights had made sure he was kept safe and sane since Jackseye left the castle. He couldn't be more grateful.

Samqueel nodded back to Arthur in acknowledgement, the Round Hall doors shutting with a thud. Arthur turned back to Ms Enid behind him, the old woman fretting with the cloth in her hand.

"Looks like that armour will be coming in handy after all," Arthur smirked, walking back towards the staircase and chucking the rag into the bucket with a sploosh.

"What are you doing, dear?" Ms Enid asked, watching him.

"Becoming a Knight of Camelot," Arthur answered, smiling at her as he walked up the stairs.

Ms Enid smiled proudly as Arthur disappeared up the stairs, dunking her cloth in the bucket. "Well, Benjamin," she murmured, ringing the water out into the bucket. "You might just get your wish after all."

Tension rolled in the air of the Round Hall thick enough that Sam could cut his sword through it. Barons stood on either side of the room along the walls, positioned as if the Knights at the table were the threat. His jaw clenched tightly at Carsen standing on the dais beside a comfortable

Jackseye lounging with his hands behind his head, the quiet Knight's face irritated at the man in his seat. Jackseye didn't notice, his boots up on the lip of the table and a wine glass in his fingers.

*The cocky bastard always did know how to make enemies.* It made Sam want to drag him in the dirt behind his horse tied to a chain.

The Knights watched as the King walked over to his seat, Ergott's anger filling the room like an open tap as he collapsed into the chair with the grace of a giant beast. Samqueel took his seat beside Ergott, Reuben at his usual spot to his right.

"Are you a new Knight of the Roundtable, Rohin?" Samqueel asked Jackseye flatly, keeping his face uninterested.

"Do I look like a Knight to you, Sam?" Jackseye sniped at him.

"The Roundtable seats are reserved for the Knights who serve it, not black hooded strangers," Samqueel hinted, letting an edge enter his tone.

"Maybe I'm allowed to sit at the Roundtable because I have a higher authority than you as of today, Sir Torona," Jackseye replied.

Sam gripped the edge of his armrest. "I believe you lost that privilege when you abandoned your Legions to join a league of assassins," Samqueel added, keeping his voice steady.

"I wouldn't underestimate my status if I were you, Sam," Jackseye growled. "We both know Barons are the proper solution to ending chaos."

"We talk about chaos, but I'm yet to find any other than the stink your forces are kicking up to the east," Sam sniped, turning to look at him sharply. "And to know there wasn't any uproar before your leagues patrolling our streets, I can say for certain that your men have been the root of many headaches caused as of late. Suppose you believe your purpose here is to rule by fear over people who were peaceful before your 'intervention'. In that case, you've got your ideals in the wrong council, Rohin."

"Perhaps my men could bring a new order to this wretched city," Jackseye suggested, leaning closer to Samqueel. "You and your men are too soft on the people. You've let them stew in their belief of a so-called corrupted crown. With our help, this city can go back to believing Camelot is strong under the rule of King Ergott. To make a Kingdom strong, you need to show your people your strength."

"The Barons have swapped your train of thought for one of a weasel, I see," Sam muttered, pinching the bridge of his nose. *What was Ergott thinking, bringing this wreck back to Camelot?*

"They've opened my eyes," Jackseye growled. "And they see better than yours."

"Are you two finished?" Ergott grunted, his patience wearing thin.

Samqueel glanced at Ergott briefly before turning back to Jackseye, frowning deeply. "Apologies, sire," he muttered.

"Dearest apologies, my King," Jackseye smirked, leaning back in his chair, much to Carsen's annoyance, who sat beside him in Joseph's spot. The silent Knight hadn't turned up to the meeting, most likely for the better. Since the Barons showed up, he'd hidden himself out of sight to avoid a fight between himself and his brother.

That's if Voss was even in Camelot. Sam hoped for Joseph's sake that it wasn't the case. He could tell the ink on his body was itching at their very presence.

The room fell silent, the Knights waiting for Ergott to speak. Sam watched the Black Guards closely; it was as if they were statues. He couldn't tell if they were even breathing with how still they were. *Exactly how long do I have to put up with these freaks?*

"I'm only going to say this once," Ergott started. "We are going forward with the attack, and we are bringing Ariandel to its knees."

"Like I have told you many times before, sire - Camelot is not a Kingdom of war," Reuben sighed, irritation edging his words as he glanced at Ergott. "King Benjamin intended to make this a land of salvation, as it was King Uther's and his father before him. We can't just change our values at the flick of a switch."

"Benjamin was a soft King, never doing anything to change Braynor," Jackseye stated, smirking slightly. "Enforcing freedom of speech and the right for a homeless hag to be as equal as the richest person in the Kingdom is just begging for trouble against the crown. What would he have done if someone started questioning his right to lead?"

Lorsaw looked at him flatly from the corner of his eye. "I find it odd when someone can change their opinions as quickly as the weather," he grumbled, his voice dripping with venom.

"Shocking, ain't it?" Jackseye said smugly.

"Samqueel," Ergott turned to him, Sam flicking his attention to the King. "You are the Commander of the Roundtable. You lead these Knights. You've been in worse situations with worse odds and came out better. Convince them to change their minds."

"This isn't what Camelot is known for. We don't just head into battles for the sake of shutting down a threat that's yet to be given. Our job is to protect the Kingdom and our people, sire, not inspire madness," Taryn argued.

"You need to understand that, my King," Reuben added, leaning forward on the table. "Think about the people of Camelot that could die if we did this."

Jackseye looked over at Ergott with his brows high in fake surprise. "They've gone soft on you, Ergott," he drawled. "Look how quick they are to back out of a fight. Mighty men, indeed."

The Knights flicked their eyes over to him sharply, annoyance rippling off their shoulders like fumes.

"You have no say in what the Roundtable does, Baron," Lorsaw growled, scowling at him.

"Please," Jackseye scoffed. "My authority is a lot greater than yours."

"So is your ego," Arkan mumbled. "And that's saying something."

"And your arrogance," Natan muttered. Carsen turned his head, hiding his smirk.

"Why are the Barons even here? Aren't you supposedly sending us to *fight* them?" Brannagh asked, sighing.

"We aren't allied alongside the normal gaggle of Ariendal's Barons," Jackseye corrected sharply. "We're separate, an outlawed force. It's funny what happens when previous connections make your future turn sour. We're here to protect the Kingdom when you leave for the oncoming battle. Myself and Ergott figured that your leftover Knights wouldn't be able to handle the backlash if you failed to bring them down."

Sam's blood roared at that. *And what the Hell was that supposed to mean?*

"And may I add, he is correct," Jackseye continued. "Barons, unlike your sorry lot, actually possess the skill to triumph on the battlefield. Your sorry excuse of a warfront specialises in babysitting. The folks in Londinium know that when their so-called 'mighty' Knights of the Roundtable hold the front line, they're clinging to a small, pitiful thread of hope. But what about the shambles you leave behind yourselves to pick up your scraps, those pitiful, untrained adolescents clutching toothpicks? Barons are warriors, born and bred for battle – we're attackers, not mere protectors. Alone, we're magnificent; together, we're an unstoppable force. Honestly, I can't fathom how you expect to stand a chance against a force like them when you're relying on stable boys and pickpockets to do your dirty work. Your reputation has crumbled to dust since I departed, but then again, I never held high hopes for you, Sam. Ever since you stumbled into the training hall, you've had a knack for wildly overestimating yourself."

The room fell into an ominous, bone-chilling silence, the Knights' collective anger and tension hanging heavily in the air with all eyes now fixed upon Jackseye. Sam, in that unbearable stillness, felt rage surge through his veins like a wildfire in the heart of the Ether Plains. The hairs on his arms stood at attention, bristling as Sam clenched the armrests of his seat. The wooden chair let out a slow, agonised creak, mirroring the strain in his clenched fists. His fingernails dug into the wood like claws, leaving deep, permanent grooves.

How.

*Dare.*

He.

"You're forgetting one significant thing, Rohin," Samqueel growled through his teeth.

"And that is?" Jackseye asked, curiosity laced mockingly in his voice.

"My men did not shed their blood, sweat and tears inside of the training hall and sacrifice their safety to spend three nights in the heart of the Darklands proving their worth just to be called toothpick-wielding teenagers by a man with as much integrity as a wolf in sheep's clothing! You've got some bloody nerve accusing me of hosting weak forces, considering it was you who took Green Thumbs from the hall beneath Commander Mordred's nose to serve the crown untrained and unprepared. You have no idea how much of a mess Wilhelm and I have had to clean up since you left or how much time I've put into fixing all the little mistakes you've conveniently decided to cover up."

Jackseye's face twitched with slight surprise, his easy mask flicking back into place instantly. "In that case, it's no wonder why things have gone downhill since you've made them think using a shield is better than using a sword," he snorted.

Sam sat forward in his seat, pushing his finger into the wooden grooves. "Training a Legion of any sort of fighters based on prioritising attack over defence is foolish! If you meet an attack with defence, you keep your men safe and still on their feet. But if you choose to counter an attack with another attack, your fighters will turn into nothing but bloody debris – and it will happen even faster if a damn volley of arrows is raining down! You attack when there's a clear opening to exploit, or you don't attack at all. Just blindly charging into battle like a bunch of reckless imbeciles, with your stupid methods for training offence with no defence, will leave you and your men torn to ribbons!"

He stood to his feet, bracing his knuckles against the table. "My men once slayed a Darklands dragon in this very Kingdom using the same tactics that I teach to every single lad that comes through the Gates with a title and a badge to their name. I've led my men every step of the way through each battle we've faced and come out victorious *every single time*. I am aware of how to win my battles with defence as our priority. Protection is no laughing matter. The people *need* protection. They will always depend on their Knights to guide them to safety and defend their homes whenever another dragon decides to pay a visit.

"Your men will be the last ones they will ever count on fighting for them. They know of your history of violence and killing. You're proving to them on the streets of your unworthiness as we speak, for the Gods' sake. Poke and prod all you want over my method of battle. In the end, I'm not leaving my home to be defended purely by you. The odds may be stacked against us in that case, but I don't care. I'll continue to know my people's worth, regardless of what you think," Sam spat at Jackseye, standing straight and looking down at him.

The Knights at the table raised their wine glasses high, cheers of support for Sam's words bouncing off the walls as they yelled heartily.

*Let him chew on that.* Sam picked up his goblet, his withering stare burning Jackseye as he raised it with the others. Jackseye glanced at Ergott, a dirty frown coating his face. Ergott's face remained unimpressed, his jaw tight.

Samqueel turned to King Ergott, taking in his scowl. He watched him as he picked up his goblet, waited as the room quietened, and the Knights turned to the King.

"You are all dismissed. Except for Samqueel," Ergott murmured softly, taking a deep drink of his wine.

Sam's heart quickened, watching as the lads around him hesitated a moment before standing from their seats. The Barons by the wall pushed the doors open, moving to let the Knights leave, Jackseye pushing past them with a scowl. Reuben looked back over his shoulder, his mouth quirked in uncertainty as he glanced at Sam. *Good luck.*

Sam felt as if he may need it.

"Disobeying my orders has become your personal goal, has it?" Ergott swirled his wine, taking a sip.

Samqueel sat back in his chair slowly, sitting his glass back down. The room felt remarkably empty without his friends surrounding him. The feel of the Barons' masked faces watching them made his spine rigid. "Using Rohin's Barons to protect Londinium is not a good choice, sire."

"I don't quite understand, Samqueel," Ergott frowned, placing the glass down. "I thought you looked up to Jackseye as a mentor when he was a part of my Legion."

"I wouldn't know where you had gotten that thought from, considering I'd never particularly gotten along with him, sire," he answered, clearing his throat quietly. Sam had hated Jackseye since the day he'd blamed him for tarnishing his reputation for telling Commander Mordred about his ideas of early recruitment. "Besides, he left to fight for Ariendal. Why should I respect him for that?"

"What if he was ordered by me to go to the Barons?"
Ergott looked at him scornfully, the brown in his eyes
warming considerably.

Samqueel observed his face, his jaw clenched. "Then I
would've expected to be informed of his movements
instead of being left in the dark, sire."

"Sometimes, royalty comes first out of all things,
Samqueel. It was the tenth anniversary of Benjamin's death;
I was busy, of course, as we all were. Unfortunately, time is
limited for me to inform you of every little detail of what
happens within the castle walls," Ergott frowned.

Sam's eyes flashed angrily. "I am your Knight
Commander, Ergott," he shot. "I need to know these things
so I can keep a level of order and stability under your
crown. Having the Legion Commander up and leave with
no explanation or foretelling does nothing to help that." He
leaned on the table, lowering his chin to look at Ergott from
beneath his brows. "And if royalty truly came first, then did
you bother to tell Arthur as well?"

"Don't you bring Arthur into this; he has nothing to do
with it," Ergott snapped, thudding the table with his fist.

"Then why not include the boy in any meetings? Why
not involve him in anything he needs to know for when he
becomes King? If royalty was more important than
informing your Knight Commander of key details, then
surely it's within your reasoning to include him," Sam
tested, half raised out of his chair.

"You are stepping on a very, very thin surface here, Sir
Torona," Ergott warned, his eyes heated.

Samqueel resisted the urge to glare at him, his lips
pursed tight. "So we are clear: the movement against
Ariandel is a fool's choice."

"You're the fool. Disobeying the King's direct orders is
a huge mistake to make," Ergott spat.

Sam fixed Ergott with a cold stare. "My orders are to
take care of my men, my colleagues, and my Kingdom.

You're sending us on a death errand, and right now, the honour and safety of my Knights is more important than a King's orders."

Ergott scoffed, picking up his goblet once again for another sip. "Follow me, if you will," he ordered, his voice suddenly calm.

Samqueel observed him, still bristling with fury. Ergott reached the base of the stairs in the far corner before he turned back around, scowling at Sam.

"It would be rude of you to not join me," Ergott hinted, his voice laced with disapproval.

Sam stood straight slowly, straightening his coat before walking off the dais with a barely contained scowl. "Where are we going?"

"To the balcony," Ergott assured. "Fresh air will help us to settle this."

Sam stalked behind him, looking back towards the open doors to watch the Barons walk out of the room, dispersing like shadows to a corner.

King Ergott walked swiftly up the stone stairs, the clack of his boots on the stones bouncing off the curved walls of the stairwell. Sam followed behind quickly, taking an exasperated breath. He was still determining Ergott's intentions, but he knew some sort of power trip was about to happen.

Ergott led Samqueel out to the balcony, the sun glaring down as they stepped out onto the stone platform. Ergott walked to the brick ledge lining the balcony's railing, leaning both hands on the bricks and peering out over the city.

Samqueel stood behind him, keeping his distance. The sun was scorching for this time of year, Sam's coat heating up quickly. He imagined the children in the city to be looking for a good spot on the riverbank to go for a swim as he once did when he was younger.

"Do you see that Kingdom over there?" Ergott pointed, looking at a pale stone castle in the far distance to the west.

He flicked his eyes to look, turning his head. "What about it?"

"They look up to you and your Knights, you know," Ergott reminded him.

Samqueel raised a brow. "Rinecroft? How… weirdly flattering," he mused. Sure, he and his men were no secret to the rest of the world, but to be an object of idolisation in a Kingdom known for farming? Odd indeed.

"Jackseye and I believe that Rinecroft will be Ariandel's next target," Ergott muttered, looking back at him from over his shoulder. "Wouldn't it be a shame if they fell?"

Sam chewed his tongue. *Why would Ariendal want to take a young Kingdom that has little benefit to them?* "You're certain of their movements? This isn't just Rohin leading by emotion?" he asked.

"I'm afraid it isn't," Ergott answered, turning around to face him. "If the Knights of the Roundtable aren't out to protect them, who will?"

"We have allies, or *had*," he tilted his head slightly at Ergott accusingly. "Sending a Legion of our Knights will cover their territory just fine if the need ever arose."

"Ariandel will go through them like a knife to paper," Ergott frowned slightly. "The Knights of Camelot aren't properly as trained as your Knights."

Samqueel looked at him sharply. "You underestimate your Knight's capabilities, sire," he protested. "Marlon trains the lads to the highest quality. You're aware of the extensive boundaries pushed before they're deemed acceptable."

Ergott chuckled deeply, shaking his head. "You really don't know about this situation, do you?"

"I'd know more if you would inform me of any reports from the front lines of our allies," he gritted out. "Sending my men to find out from halfway across the country is redundant. We have couriers. Pigeons, even."

"I'm going to tell you this one last time," Ergott growled, walking closer to him. Sam straightened, meeting his stare equally. "Your men will be leading the front line on the raid at Catarina. You have absolutely no say in it, and you will follow through with my lead. Am I understood?" Ergott growled deeply.

Samqueel narrowed his eyes, ire burning deep in them. "I'll be researching the defence of Ariendal for myself this evening. If I do not find a crack for us to slip through, consider your task forgotten."

Ergott's smirk was one of wickedness, his eyes malicious. "In that case, you can consider your titles revoked," he threatened.

Sam's heart skipped a beat, his stare wavering. "You're not serious," Sam spat, his teeth baring a little.

"You don't want to let go of that position now, do you?" Ergott asked menacingly. "All that hard work you've put in to get to where you are now, wasted with a single sentence. It would be a shame to put all your years of service down because of a refusal."

*You twisted bastard.*

"I would rather let my men live another day to fight a real war and forsake my title than lead them to their deaths over a war no one wanted to fight," he muttered, his jaw clenched. He turned on his heel and walked towards the door, leaving it open as he stormed through.

Ergott smirked as Samqueel left the balcony, his eyes glinting with irritation. "I suppose we'll have to wait and see what you come up with," he muttered quietly to himself.

Ergott turned back around to the balcony's ledge, scouring his eyes over the outskirts of Camelot. Silently, Black Guards moved to stand behind him on the terrace, shifting into position from their various spots. Ergott

looked at them over his shoulder, their mask revealing
nothing.

## Chapter 7: Knight's Training

Arthur opened his door, stepping into it as the sunlight lit up the space through the window. He pushed his hair out of his face and let a breath loose, his heart still thundering in his ears.

That had been the first time he had ever stood up for himself in front of his uncle; it felt unnatural to him, foreign as a drug. He was never normally allowed to speak for himself in those situations, but it must've been a rare day.

Arthur walked over to his window, leaning on the lip of the skirting and looking down at the people below him. He could pick out a few Knights and the shadowy forms of the Barons within the crowd. Arthur watched the Barons closely, noting the way they moved.

The largest man led at the front, his men trailing behind in a cluster. It was like a wolf pack. An alpha who led his hunters to stalk their prey.

Only a fool would believe that the Barons would be a good choice for protecting an already well-guarded Kingdom such as Camelot. Just as well, Ergott had to be the fool to hire them. It was only time before he realised his mistake.

Arthur frowned at them, watching the patrol push and shove any civilians that stepped within their proximity. His eyes glued to the Barons, he moved away from the window ledge-

"Arty! Oi!"

Arthur paused, turning back to look down at the castle courtyard.

"Arty! Arthur! I see you up there!" Tristan called out from below. His arms waved above his head in a wide arc, his beaming grin visible even from the tower window. "Remember me? Your best friend?! Can you see me? Hey!"

"How could I forget the most annoying person in the Kingdom?" he muttered, rolling his eyes. "I'll be down in fifteen minutes," he called down to Tristan, who whooped in celebration.

Muttering to himself, he moved over to his wooden cupboard, opening the double doors with ease and digging through the clothes folded high on the overhead platform. Arthur eventually found what he was searching for; a brown satchel, the leather faded with frayed strips ripping off the surface. He coughed as the dust swirled in the air around him.

Arthur walked over to his desk with the satchel in hand, opening the latches as he shuffled over to the desk. He grabbed a water bottle from the corner of his desk, opening the satchel wide before placing the water bottle gently inside, stashing a few of the training books inside as well. Arthur flung the strap over his shoulder and stepped out into the hallway, the door shutting loudly behind him as he continued along his path.

Walking down the stairs, Arthur began to feel different, a mix of nerves and excitement stewing in his chest. After all, he was heading to train to become a Knight of Camelot, and that was a big thing. Refining his skills instead of relying on his street fighting skills could help him find his way or stop some sort of fight between him and the Barons when it came down to it, especially against someone like Jackseye.

Coming to the bottom of the stairs, Arthur walked into the castle lobby, seeing a few familiar faces standing around the pillars to the left, their attention turning to him.

"Going somewhere, are we, Arthur?" Sir Natan asked, his shoulder pushing off the pillar he leaned against.

"Possibly," Arthur answered, walking over to them.

"Is that a purse?" Arkan asked, raising an eyebrow at Arthur's satchel.

"No," Arthur replied slowly, confused. "I'll be back in the next two hours."

"Don't go getting yourself into any strife now," Sam said from behind him on the stairs, walking over to them.

"Since when did I get into trouble?" Arthur asked with feigned hurt, looking back at Sam.

Samqueel gave him a look, raising his brow. "From what I recall, getting shoved around in the streets with scuffed and muddy trousers at the age of ten was when your fighting career happened to become a reality," he chuckled.

"At least I know how to defend myself from an attacker. I don't see anyone trying to tell me any different," Arthur frowned. "Nor have I got anyone to teach me anything."

Sam straightened his back, his mouth quirked to the left. "I suppose all you had to do was ask, but it seems you've taken the initiative to learn the right way. I'm proud of you for doing so."

Arthur flinched; he hadn't heard those words in forever. "You're proud? Of what exactly?"

"For becoming the man you want to be."

"For standing up to your uncle," Reuben chimed in. "That was a huge thing to overhear."

"For getting yourself involved for the sake of your people," Natan nodded, moving to clap his shoulders.

"For following in your father's footsteps," Brannagh said, giving him a soft smile. "He'd be proud of you to no end."

"For taking the time to learn to fight for your Kingdom," Lorsaw said and muttered quietly, "Even if it goes against everything Ergott asks of you."

Karsol heard him and slapped the back of his head, Lorsaw grunting and glaring up at him.

"For always, *always*, protecting the people of Londinium. Even though it isn't your duty yet," Taryn said with a smirk.

"For being yourself," Carsen piped up, his voice strained. Joseph nodded in agreement, thumping his chest with a fist.

"For being our Crown Prince. We're honoured to serve alongside you, Art," Derak said, placing a hand on his back.

Samqueel smiled down at him, approval in his eyes. "We all believe in you, Arthur. What will it take to make you believe it, too?"

Arthur looked at each of the Knights around him, taking a deep breath in. "Myself," he murmured. "Proving to myself that the prophecies have a hold in more than just stone and story. For me to find my place in the world, where I belong."

"You belong here, lad. Camelot is your home. Who is it you want to be?" Forlorn questioned, folding his arms.

"What I'm destined to become. I just need to figure out what that is," Arthur answered, furrowing his eyebrows lightly.

"Whoever you decide to be, we'll be here," Samqueel promised. The Knights nodded to Arthur, adding their agreements.

Arthur nodded back at all of them, standing up tall with a slight grin on his face. "It's time to prove to Ergott that I've got a place in this Kingdom."

Arkan grinned. "Go show the world you're more than just a pretty face," he joked. "Show us what you're *really* made of."

"I'll do my best," Arthur replied. "That's if I'm not killed in the process."

Lorsaw snorted. "Please, the whole thing wraps you up in armour with the squish factor of a marshmallow. Training's easier than fieldwork, I can tell you."

Taryn groaned. "Lorsaw with the ever-so-inspiring cheer factor. You should start a cheerleading squad since you're so fantastic with your motivations," he drawled.

Arthur frowned slightly at Lorsaw, raising his eyebrow at him. "Thanks for the encouragement."

"I'm only giving educated information-"

"Oh shoosh, Lorsaw," Arkan interrupted with a sigh.

"Sit down, Lorsaw," Reuben said.

"Take a few calming breaths, Lorsaw," Taryn grinned slyly.

"Don't be a cranky Knight today, Lorsaw," Derak rolled his eyes.

"Have you had your morning snack yet, Lorsaw? Is that why you're so moody?" Brannagh raised a brow, smirking.

Lorsaw scowled. "No..."

"Damn it, Lorsaw!" Taryn scorned, lifting his hands in the air. "No wonder you're grumpy."

"You ought to go feed your face, then, Lorsaw," Brannagh looked over at him with raised brows.

"Ms Enid can cook you some eggs. We all know that's your favourite dish," Reuben suggested with a grin.

"I'm allergic to eggs!" Lorsaw growled in protest.

"No wonder why you're always refusing to eat rations," Sam muttered.

"I'm just going to go now…" Arthur muttered awkwardly, slowly stepping back to exit the gates.

Arkan looked over at him. "Hey Arthur, a word of advice?"

"Sure," Arthur said cautiously.

"Take out his left knee; you'll know who." They all rolled their eyes and groaned. It seemed a shared joke sat with them that puzzled Arthur.

*What the hell could that mean?*

"Who?" Arthur asked in confusion.

"You'll know when you know, trust us," Forlorn chuckled.

"Trust anyone but Arkan," Reuben reassured.

Arkan frowned. "I have ears that work just fine, and they can hear the liquid crap pouring from your mouth," he said flatly.

"You have ears and hearing; you just use them whenever you think it's necessary. Which is *never*," Brannagh added, staring pointedly at Arkan.

"At least my diet doesn't consist of just plants."

"Don't you judge my food," Brannagh growled.

"What are you gonna do, nibble on me? You rabbit," Arkan maliciously grinned, backing up quickly with a laugh as Brannagh chased after him.

Deciding to leave them to it before he got caught up in a wrestling match he'd never escape from, Arthur slipped out of the castle quickly, chuckling under his breath.

The Knights were either a laugh, a fight or a terrifying thing to behold. There wasn't much in between to label them. Considering the men were capable of both taking down a dragon and beating the entire Kingdom in a drinking contest, it wasn't hard to get along with the protectors of Camelot.

Arthur stepped onto the stairs leading down to Londinium's streets, looking around the area to spot Tristan anywhere in the vicinity.

"Ah, there you are! I was starting to think you got lost in that massive boulder," Tristan grinned, popping beside him quickly from the Gates' wall.

"How long have you been waiting for me?" Arthur asked, walking down the steps.

"About half an hour probably, according to the sun," he said, holding his hand up to the bright star. "I don't know exactly how people tell the time like that, but from what I'm guessing, you tell the time by rating on a scale of one to twelve how much it hurts your eyes to look at." He squinted at the sun.

"Are you finished with your time theory yet, or would you like a script about everything you just said?" Arthur said to him. "I mean, you could make serious gold with those kinds of philosophies."

Tristan looked at him, blinking harshly. "Is that not how that works?"

Arthur shrugged. "Your choice of if it does."

Tristan smiled slightly, looking at the satchel tucked beneath Arthur's arm. "Is it a trend to wear purses in the royal family now?" he observed.

"It's called a satchel, not a purse," Arthur frowned at him. "It was my father's before he died, and of course, he left it for me."

Tristan hummed. "What's in it?" His eyes lit up. "Do you have food?"

"A bottle and some books," Arthur answered. "And what makes you think I'd give you my food if I had any?"

Tristan raised his hands in a shrug, waving them slightly. "No one said you'd *give* it to me," he reasoned.

Arthur frowned at him, a ghost of a smile pulling at the corner of his mouth. "Because it's you, and you're always looking for food," he shook his head.

"Ask your uncle to lower the taxes. Then, I could afford to buy more food than a lump of bread and some cheese."

Arthur scoffed at that suggestion. "Like he'd listen to someone else's opinion."

Tristan shrugged again. "Who knows? Anyway, let's go before Maria gets cornered with the normal tools in the training hall," he said joyfully, walking down the stairs.

Arthur followed behind him, keeping close as they snaked through the crowds bundled in the alleyways. The Northern District path led past homes decorated with frilly flowers and well-maintained gardens, the noble citizens buzzing around their district cheerily. Tall terracotta-coloured walls met the multi-coloured shingles topping their roofs, birds of all colours flying through the sky with cheery chirps. Knights in training moved around the small square plaza beneath the clock tower, some seated at the benches near the wall of the stone training hall.

"Hopefully, somebody decided to leave the door unlocked this time," Tristan muttered to himself.

"Who trains you?" Arthur asked, looking at him sideways.

Tristan stood in front of a wooden door, steel reinforcing the edges. He gripped the handle and looked through the small window in the centre of the wood. "An old guy known as Marlon," he answered and twisted the doorknob, swinging it open. "A-ha, finally."

"Since when did you want to train as a Knight? You always said you wanted to be a blacksmith when we were young," Arthur said.

"Well… there aren't many blacksmiths that are willing to take me in," he shrugged, his voice a little strained. "They all think I'd try and melt the tools or something."

Arthur looked at him, his head tilted. "Who told you that one?"

He grimaced slightly. "All of them."

Arthur frowned. "Right."

Tristan walked inside, leading Arthur inside. A small foyer peeled off in three directions, the sound of sparring lads coming from the long, straight hallway in front of him. Glass lined the sides of the walls, and chunks of old beaten-up pieces of armour were stashed in alcoves behind the panes similar to the hallways in the castle. Iron plaques engraved with the names of Knights widely varied throughout history adorned the spaces between, some of them shinier and more recent than others.

Arthur looked around curiously, peering closer at the cleaner plaques. The names of the Roundtable stared back at him, their rankings engraved beside each of their names with their assigned colours polished into the inlays. Arthur smiled and turned to keep heading down the hall. A light flared in front of Tristan, his silhouette breaking through the end of the hallway into a massive room, Arthur blinking the light from his eyes rapidly.

"Well, this isn't what I expected," Arthur muttered to himself, looking around the building.

Lads stood below him on the lowered flooring at the base of the stairs leading down to the stone arena pit, a few of them training in drawn chalk squares on the ground, hitting each other with savage blows. Each corner of the large room was coloured with faded paint, viewing platforms with wooden rails lining the space behind the bleachers on the far wall stretching around towards the entrance where Arthur stood. A door could be seen in the gap near the stairs between the red and blue bleachers, large windows shining light inside from a sizable fenced-off grass area outside. To his left, an arched doorway sat behind a stone table holding empty, crumbed platters, the smell of cooking food wafting to his nose quickly. The roof reached high above him, rafters supported by the pillars standing at attention beside the bleachers glowing with sunlight that streamed through the circular window.

Tristan looked back at him. "I mean, it's not a whole place of pain and torture, but it's not a tea party either," he shrugged.

"Tristan!" A voice called out from the red corner.

Tristan perked up, turning to the voice with a grin. "Oi, Peter," he greeted.

"Training started two hours ago," Peter said while walking up the stairs to him. "Marlon was missing you." The trainee looked at Arthur with calculating blue eyes, his brown hair stuck to his forehead with sweat. A nick in his eyebrow was slashed on a slant through the middle of his left eye, a small scar stretching along the length.

"Apologies, I was waiting for this one to come out of the big fancy brick house," he nodded to Arthur.

"My liege," Peter bowed his head to Arthur.

"First time I heard that one," Arthur's eyebrows flicked up unenthusiastically.

"Yeah, but you haven't heard 'your absolute outstanding, praise-the-Gods, golden-hearted majesty' before," Tristan huffed.

"Thank you for that overview, Tristan," Arthur frowned lightly. Tristan held his grin in.

"He isn't exactly wrong, you know," Peter chimed in. "I mean, you are the King's son, aren't you?"

Tristan looked at Arthur funny, his brows low. "You're Ergott's son now?"

"He is my uncle," he corrected. "My father was the King before Ergott took his place."

"But he just said the King, as in the current King…" Tristan frowned, thinking to himself. "Which means… there's a Queen, too?"

"Tristan, you're thinking too hard," Peter said, furrowing his eyebrows.

"Who's the Queen?" Tristan asked confusedly, ignoring Peter.

"You mean my mother or my aunt?" Arthur asked.

His eyes widened. "You have a mother?"

The pit in front of them fell silent, their eyes trailing a man walking towards the three. Arthur flicked his eyes to the man, and Tristan turned to look. "Oh, look, it's Marlon," he said in a high voice, watching him tower over him as he climbed the stairs to stand in front of him.

"Tristan, you're late. Again," Marlon growled, his voice deep and mysterious. His brown skin reflected that of Tristan's, dark eyes set in a scowl of disapproval. Long dark hair sat atop his head in a tight bun, leading across his jaw in a thick bundle.

Marlon looked over at Arthur, his eyes narrowing slightly. "A guest?" he pondered.

"Arthur," he introduced himself.

"I know who you are. I knew your father as well," Marlon answered.

"You knew my father?" Arthur asked, looking at Marlon curiously.

"Of course I knew Benjamin," he frowned. "Being a Knight doesn't come without affiliation to the royal family."

"Interesting," Arthur said quietly. *I suppose that's correct...*

Marlon looked him over, studying the satchel at his side. "Why have you come along today?"

"Observation mostly," he said. "I'm looking to join the Knights. I thought I'd come along and bless you all with my presence while I watch how this place works before deciding if I'd like to join."

Marlon tilted his head to the side. "I'm sure the helpers in the kitchen feel honoured," he said flatly. "As for your plans - you don't learn from just observations."

"I won't be joining in the fighting today, I'm afraid. I've already had a run-in with the Barons the night before," Arthur reassured.

"Nonsense," Marlon dismissed and pivoted to look to the far corner.

Arthur furrowed his eyebrows. "I don't mean to disappoint, but I'm only observing today. If there's a next time, maybe. I don't have any skills-"

"Kyan!" Marlon boomed across the hall. A lad looked over to them and stood up from the floor. "Over here, now."

Tristan blinked in surprise. "You're going to verse him against Kyan?" he questioned incredulously.

Arthur looked at Marlon, narrowing his eyes. "I'm not fighting anyone-"

Marlon turned his stare on Arthur, his eyes intense. "You're here to either train or help clean up afterwards, not sit in the corner to watch. So yes," he growled. "You will be fighting."

"I appreciate your encouragement," Arthur drawled sarcastically. "But I have no intention of landing any blows to anyone today."

"Well, that's just too bad, isn't it?" Marlon said back with equal fire.

Arthur looked at Tristan. "Did you know this was going to happen?"

Tristan's smile waivered with nerves. "I didn't think he'd verse you against *Kyan*-"

Arthur narrowed his eyes at him. "So you *did* know," he accused.

He chuckled nervously, touching the back of his neck.

"Who am I fighting now, Marlon? Is it Tristan again?" Kyan asked, standing beside Marlon. The trainee stood up to Marlon's shoulder, his black hair falling about his shoulders in a fluffed-up mess. His green eyes flicked to Arthur with curiosity.

Tristan's eyes widened. "I'm just going to…" he quickly dashed down the stairs, heading towards the corner with the faded green paint.

Arthur looked at Tristan with a deep frown. "Well, thanks for your help, Tristan," he called to him sarcastically. Peter sighed through his nose and followed after Tristan.

Marlon glanced at Kyan, shifting his weight to one foot. "I'm setting you a starter," he nodded towards Arthur.

"I told you, I'm only observing-"

"Hush!" Marlon snapped, his voice echoing through the rafters. Arthur blinked at him. *Is everyone here as rude as this Marlon? Because I'm starting to have second thoughts.*

"Shouldn't be too hard. He doesn't look like a fighter to me," Kyan shrugged with a faint smirk.

"I can fight," Arthur growled. *Who do they think they are, talking to a royal like that?*

"Show us then, *Your Highness,*" Kyan mocked.

Marlon moved back down the stairs towards a chalk outline, Kyan following him loyally. The other trainees looked over and gathered to watch, many recognising Arthur at the top of the stairs. Arthur narrowed his eyes, reluctantly following the two over to the outlined square.

"In the square, feet at nine and four, begin on my word," Marlon ordered, standing at the edge. Kyan shifted his feet to the proper position, his arms loose at his sides.

"I don't want to fight you," Arthur said softly, setting his satchel down and moving inside the square. He shifted his feet to copy Kyan, his muscles bunching.

"It's not a fight, Arthur," Kyan smirked, curling his fists. "It's a test."

Marlon nodded. "Begin!"

Arthur flicked his eyes to Marlon. "You just want to see me get hurt-"

His sentence was clipped short as a sharp pain lanced through his chest, making him stagger back. Arthur held his chest as the pain dashed across where Kyan struck him.

Kyan danced back, shifting his shoulders. "Now that I've got your attention," he grinned. "Maybe you'll learn to watch your opponent."

Arthur narrowed his eyes at him, getting himself ready for Kyan's next blow. *The bastard doesn't know who he's messing with.*

Kyan's feet shifted, and his fist rocketed towards Arthur's shoulder, his other hand shooting towards his jaw. Arthur grabbed his outstretched arms, folding them back into his chest before pushing him back fiercely.

Kyan gained his footing quickly, grinning at him. "There you go, a small glimmer of fight," he observed. "What else you got?"

Arthur narrowed his eyes at him. "You want to try me?"

Kyan shrugged casually. "If you insist," he said lightly.

Arthur glared at him, shifting his feet. "I'd prefer to observe," he growled.

Kyan smirked at Arthur, pacing to circle him like a vulture, watching Arthur with calculated eyes. His fists bunched, ready to strike. Arthur looked over at the benches, spotting Maria moving amongst the crowd towards Tristan, carrying a tray of food.

"What's Arthur doing?" she asked, looking at Tristan on the bench.

"Getting beaten by Kyan," he said simply, eyeing the sandwiches.

"I thought he was observing?" Maria commented, unconsciously moving the platter towards Tristan. Tristan's eyes widened, his hand snaking up slowly towards the sandwiches.

"You don't learn anything from observations, Maria," Peter remarked, folding his arms. "This'll teach him better than the sidelines ever will."

"By hurting him even more?" Maria looked at him flatly, turning to face him. Tristan looked at her with a frown, dropping his hand from the air. "The Barons already landed a few hits on him. Didn't you see his eye?"

"The Barons aren't ones to mess with," Peter murmured, looking at her sideways. "I thought he would've known that."

Maria frowned at Peter, turning back to Arthur and Kyan in front of them. Kyan stepped over to Arthur, swinging at him wildly from all different angles, landing a shot on his ribcage and shoving Arthur back. Arthur stumbled to the ground, landing with a loud grunt, his shoulder barking in pain.

Kyan looked around at a few of the onlookers, giving them smirks as they cheered for him. Arthur slowly pushed himself up off the ground, his ribs sore. Kyan looked back over at Arthur, his eyebrows raised cockily.

"Still want some more, do you?" Kyan asked, watching Arthur getting up from the ground.

"You'd be surprised," Arthur returned, wincing as he stood to his feet.

"You've had your fun; now you can return to your other activities," Kyan jived, sneering.

"The fight will not stop until one of you yields," Marlon said. "Continue, now."

"With all due respect, you're all trained fighters. The only experience I've had was street fighting and a few sword basics, not whatever multitude of training you do here," Arthur protested, looking around the room. "I'm sure you all don't want to see your 'Future King' be beaten senseless."

Marlon looked at him with disinterest. "Status doesn't matter in the training hall. Just so long as you're here to become a Knight, you're equal to the person next to you," he growled. "Now stop finding excuses to sit out and raise your arms."

Arthur turned back to face Kyan with a scowl and grunted, Kyan's fist connecting with his jaw. Arthur collapsed to the ground, his face merging with the stone flooring with a thud. He coughed, groaning as he slowly rose back up.

"Had enough yet?" Kyan teased, standing over him.

Arthur narrowed his eyes, quickly wrapping his leg around Kyan's ankles and sending him to the ground. Kyan grunted and lashed his boot towards him, flailing around. Arthur stood up from the floor, taking off his coat before chucking it to the side. Arthur rubbed his jaw, wincing at the pain as a welt formed where Kyan hit him. Arthur glowered at Kyan, looking down at him on the floor. *How does that feel?*

Kyan growled, standing up. Arthur returned a slight smirk and began circling Kyan, their roles switching almost simultaneously. Marlon grinned faintly, watching Arthur with interest.

Arthur pounced on Kyan and landed a hit on his chest, the impact making his breath whoosh out of his mouth with a grunt. Kyan stumbled back, his footing unsteady. Seeing an opening, Arthur punched the side of his head, rocketing him to the floor.

"'He doesn't look like the fighting type'," Arthur mocked him with a smirk, curling his finger in a come hither.

Kyan launched at Arthur from the ground, swinging towards his ribs. Arthur's eyes flashed, deflecting the blow with his forearm.

*Again, too easy.* He launched his hand to grab Kyan's arm and twisted it behind his back, pinning him. Kyan yelled in pain, struggling.

"What was that about this being a test, Kyan?" Arthur drawled. Kyan seethed, trying to pull his wrist from his grip.

"Little known thing about me; I know how to pass my challenges," Arthur grinned cockily, gripping him tighter.

Pain rocketed through Arthur's foot, Kyan yanking his arm free from his loosened grip and shoving him back with his shoulders. Arthur hopped on one foot with a hiss for a moment, the pain subsiding slowly.

Kyan spun around to face him, his fist shooting towards Arthur's temple. He ducked in time to avoid a headache but was too slow to dodge the second swing to his right shoulder. Pain shot up his neck, Arthur grunting and putting his hand against his shoulder.

Tristan looked at Marlon with a concerned expression, seeing his slight grin growing wider with amusement.

Kyan used his hesitation to kick Arthur in the thigh, a loud thud echoing across the hall. Arthur yelled in pain, gripping his thigh with his hand - it felt as if he'd hit him with a sledgehammer. Kyan watched as Arthur knelt on the ground, smirking at him from over Arthur's head.

"You should've studied harder for this test, I'm afraid," he growled, a venomous grin on his face. Before Arthur knew it, he was launched across the floor just outside of the chalk line, the cheers of the trainees drowning out as his head smacked into the stone floor.

Arthur groaned as he stirred awake from a dreamless sleep, his entire body barking in pain. His eyes squinted open, and he found himself in a bed surrounded by stone walls, more beds aligned against the wall to his right through the long room. Tall wooden cupboards sat against the walls, their handles knotted with locked chains. Drapes of grey sheets were tied back with thin ropes on hooks along the walls, their ringlets holding onto wood rods nailed to the ceiling.

*The infirmary, then.* Arthur sighed, sitting himself up hesitantly on the bed, his body aching with every move.

"To say the least, I am impressed with your skillset," Marlon said, sitting on a chair beside him. "For a so-called street fighter."

"Why did you make me fight a Knight in training?" Arthur groaned, rubbing his head.

"So I could decide if I should let you join or not," Marlon said simply. "Watching you watching others wouldn't have been any help in the decision."

*Asshole.* "Observation would've allowed me to learn my targets better," Arthur hinted, looking over at him. "Who was that man I was fighting anyway?"

"Kyan Bors, he's one of our newest trainees," Marlon answered, ignoring the snipe. "You're lucky I didn't put you up against Dagonet."

"Dagonet?" Arthur asked, an eyebrow raised. "An odd name for a man, don't you think?"

Marlon frowned at Arthur. "Peter Dagonet," he corrected.

The memory of the blue-eyed boy from earlier flicked into his head at the name. "Seems like everyone has unusual names these days," Arthur muttered, groaning as he shifted against the pillow.

"I'd say," Marlon looked at Arthur sideways. "What brought you here to train?"

Arthur glanced at him. "Ergott has been holding me back for as long as I can remember. It was time I proved him wrong."

"Why come here with no clue of our process?" Marlon asked. "Your father had at least some knowledge of what to do."

"I'm nothing like my father," Arthur replied with a slight frown. *And I'm sick of everyone saying so.*

"I'm sure you've seen the murals around Londinium," Marlon said as flat as his stare. "Question is, do you believe in what the murals foretell?"

Arthur mirrored Marlon. "You mean the murals of the 'Born King'? Yes, I have seen them. And even if they were true, I couldn't hold that responsibility."

"Well, how would you know if you've never tried?"

That stumped Arthur. "I've never been given the choice," he replied, almost as a question.

Marlon shook his head. "Choices aren't given," he growled. "They're taken."

"What would be the point, anyway? My uncle wouldn't allow me to try and learn to take on that responsibility," Arthur said bitterly. "I'm lucky I'm even in this building."

Marlon stood up, looking towards the door. "Then you damn well better make the use of your time while you've got it," he dismissed, walking towards the doorway.

*As short as it would be.* Sometimes, Arthur liked to wonder how different things would've been if Ergott never came into power. If his father and mother were still alive.

Sometimes, it was more than occasionally.

"What was he like?" Arthur asked, watching him leave.

Marlon paused, pivoting halfway and looking down. "Brave. Selfless. A true leader and King to his people," he muttered.

"People tell me I'm like him, that I'm selfless like him. But I'm nothing like him."

Marlon looked at him, distant memories flicking emotions across his face in a blur. "Then you insult your father by saying so."

"How can I be the man my father was? When I'm not even given the chance to do anything for this Kingdom?"

Marlon's stare became solid, his back straightening. "You make your chance," he sniped. "You get up off your ass, go out there into the big scary world, and you prove yourself to your people. Benjamin gained the favour of his people by paving his path to lead Camelot along; go pick up the shovel and start digging your trail."

Arthur looked at him, his eyes wide with shock and defence. He had never been talked to like that before, and maybe Marlon was right, but could he have been a little less snappy about it? It wasn't as if Arthur wasn't trying to do anything for this Kingdom like his uncle.

Hell, he'd fought a Baron troop for an elderly lady. Couldn't Marlon see that he was trying?

*No. Marlon can shove his words right up his-*

"Marlon!" Peter called from down the hallway.

Marlon turned to the hallway, dragging his eyes away from Arthur. "What is it?" he demanded.

"Some visitors are outside. Are you expecting anyone?" Peter asked.

Marlon sighed through his nose. "Not particularly."

"They said it's urgent," Peter said, walking around the corner. "Safety inspection; the guy doesn't look too pleased."

"Didn't know Camelot had safety inspections now," Kyan scoffed, standing beside Peter.

Marlon's eyes narrowed. "They don't," he rumbled, moving past the lads down the hallway.

Arthur stood from the bed and limped after Marlon, the two others following closely behind. Something was wrong, and it surely had something to do with the Barons. It was the only explanation Arthur could think of.

Arthur followed them down the hallway back to the small foyer at the front door, the long hall to the training pit to his left. Marlon peered through the small window on the door, his hand pressing against the handle. "Who's there?" he commanded.

"Open on up," a man said. "Just doing an inspection."

"Identify yourself," Marlon growled.

"Rohin Jackseye," he answered. "Go on now, open it up. The inspection will take five or so minutes; better save us both the hassle."

"Shit," Arthur whispered, backing away from the door.

Marlon's eyes flashed. "Rohin?" he said with astonishment, reaching to open the door.

"You know him?" Arthur asked Marlon, raising an eyebrow.

"Old friend turned sour," he muttered.

"Open the door now," Jackseye insisted, knocking on the door.

"Peter," Marlon growled.

Peter nodded, looking over at Arthur and Kyan. "Follow me, you two," he walked past them, heading down the long hallway.

"Where are you taking us now?" Arthur asked.

"To play hide and seek from the Barons," Peter answered, leading them down the hallway.

"Can I get some context here?" Kyan piped up.

"No," Arthur and Peter said, frowning slightly.

"Tristan! Maria!" Peter yelled, looking around for them.

"Knowing Tristan, he's probably harbouring all the food he lays his eyes on," Arthur said, smirking to himself.

Tristan turned around from the kitchen food table with a mouthful of food, chocolate covering his mouth. "What?" he said through muffled chewing.

"What did I tell you? Harbouring the food," Arthur smirked.

"Get your ass out of the kitchen and follow me," Peter commanded.

Tristan swallowed, wiping his mouth on his sleeve and following after him. "Where are we going?" he questioned.

"Jackseye and the Barons found us," Arthur said, his expression and voice changing to a more serious tone. "Where's Maria?"

Tristan shrugged. "Got caught up with the tools, like I said," he said.

"Where can I find her?" Arthur asked, looking at him sternly.

"Probably in the stay room."

"Kyan, go and look for her," Peter looked at him.

"On it," Kyan nodded and ran down the hallway towards a far door.

"You two, this way," Peter ordered, nodding towards a far hallway across the pit.

Arthur followed, feeling the pressure on his leg strain his bruise. Tristan scampered behind, looking longingly at the kitchen.

Marlon opened the door, looking Jackseye up and down, his lip curling. "You've got a lot of nerve showing up back in Camelot," he sniffed.

"Good to see you too, Jonathan," Jackseye said, stepping into the building. "Looks like you haven't changed much, at all."

"You got yourself a new decoration, it seems," he noted flatly, looking at his eye.

"That's what happens when you gain more power; you change," Jackseye shrugged, scouring around the interior, the Barons following behind him.

Marlon blocked off the Baron's path, looking down at them with a frown.

"Don't be rude to your guests. Let them pass," Jackseye scowled.

"*Uninvited* guests," he sniped.

Jackseye turned to him, his hands folded behind his back. "You, too, had no idea of our arrival, didn't you?"

"If I had known, I would've prepared the kettle," he said with sarcasm.

"It goes to show how much attention you give to important circumstances."

"You mustn't have been important enough to be given my full attention."

"Weren't you told?" Jackseye asked, walking up to him slowly. "The Barons are now here to protect Camelot, perhaps as a replacement for your Knights. Maybe a new business wouldn't be a bad idea," he smirked faintly, standing right in front of him at eye level.

Marlon glowered at him in disgust. "You truly believe your guild will overtake Camelot without some sort of resistance?"

"Ask the King yourself," Jackseye shrugged.

As he followed Peter down the hallway, Arthur overheard the echoes of the conversation, stopping in place to listen carefully. Tristan bumped into his back, shoving him forward slightly. Arthur gave him a stern look.

"Whoops," Tristan murmured, smiling apologetically.

"Luckily for you, I've had enough fighting for one day; otherwise, I would beat you senseless right here," Arthur frowned at him.

"No, you wouldn't," Tristan waved his hand dismissively in the air, watching him with a bit of nervousness.

Arthur stared at him flatly with an eyebrow raised.

"...You wouldn't, right?"

"Shove me again, and we'll find out," Arthur said, smirking lightly at him.

"You're smiling, which means no," Tristan grinned and stepped around him.

Arthur fake lunged, growling at him. Tristan yelped in fright, darting after Peter. Arthur shook his head amusedly at Tristan, returning to listen to the ongoing conversation between Jackseye and Marlon with interest.

"I'm not asking for the 'King's' opinion," Marlon bit.

"You should," Jackseye said. "He could put you into order."

"Order? Last time I witnessed a Baron in Camelot, the order went right out the window," he spat. "What in your right mind thinks this time will be any different?"

"You best believe that something is going to happen sooner or later, my dear friend," Jackseye muttered softly. "You won't just be a Knight trainer."

"If you're so inclined to take over the Kingdom, why inform your enemies of your plans? I would have thought you'd know better, considering you were one of us once."

*One of us?* Arthur's eyes widened, the conversation getting more interesting by the second, placing new thoughts and questions in Arthur's mind. *Who exactly is Marlon? And how does he know Jackseye so well?*

"Oh, that isn't what I'm *planning*; it's what's *going* to happen, whether you like it or not," he chuckled, his grin audible in his voice.

"What exactly are you here to inspect?" Marlon ground out.

"Where is he?" Jackseye asked simply.

"Where is who?" Marlon said flatly. "There are many 'he's' here."

"Don't play dumb now," Jackseye growled with annoyance. "Arthur, I overheard him and the Knights of the Roundtable discussing that he will attempt to become a Knight of Camelot."

"Benjamin's son hasn't shown up today," he lied. "Perhaps he chickened out."

"Are you seriously going to lie to the King's men?" Jackseye asked with a frown.

Arthur could feel the heat of Marlon's glare from across the hall. "You call yourself that out of the pain and suffering of others," he growled. "You do not wear that title around me. I am *well* aware of your wavering loyalty."

"I'm impressed, *Marlon*. Has your English improved?" Jackseye asked with a grin.

A thud echoed down the hallway, an angered snarl following it. "Either learn to shut your trap right now and get the job done you were sent to do by your King, or keep talking, and I throw you and your Black Cloaks out to the stones," he snarled. "Your choice."

The sound of drawn blades whined, Jackseye's amused chuckle bouncing off the walls.

"I wouldn't go any further, Jonathan," Jackseye smirked.

Tristan turned back around the corner, staring at Arthur with raised brows. "Are you coming?" he asked.

Arthur looked forward at Tristan, nodding at him before limping after him hesitantly, straining his ears to hear the rest of the conversation.

"I can go as far as I like while on *my* ground," Marlon hissed.

The rustling of cotton and leather filled the hall, the Barons moving away from Marlon and sheathing their swords promptly. "You people in Londinium better watch yourselves, aye?"

"This is our Kingdom. You cannot change that no matter what you think."

"I beg to differ," Jackseye scowled, the sound of boots leaving the hall trailing after him reaching Arthur's ears.

The door squeaked as it moved to shut slowly. "Don't expect such a warm welcome the next time you show up here again," Marlon said sharply, closing the door and sliding the lock into place.

## Chapter 8: Destiny Awakens

Arthur's mind turned over the conversation he overheard with Marlon and Jackseye. None of what Jackseye said had to be true, especially since his army was nothing but cold-blooded murderers from the darkest part of Braynor: Ariendal. The Barons were infamous for how they preyed on the weak, as Arthur had seen in the alleyway. They had no sympathy for other lives that weren't of Baron blood, and the way that people became Barons was no simple or exciting task.

Arthur had read about the training they had to undergo before they were deemed acceptable; they would have to sacrifice a bit of their blood to pledge themselves to the allegiance, train for hours upon hours, night by night, day by day until their feet were bleeding beneath them. Their skin was marked with purple tattoos of all designs, their meanings known only by the Barons. He'd seen Joseph's tattoos on occasion peeking out from beneath his long sleeves - the purple thorns that wrapped around his throat and the savage tiger stripes that covered his brow and temples.

Arthur couldn't imagine what it would be like to go through that training - hell, the Knight training was rough enough. Although he could stand his ground for as long as needed, he would have to learn more than what Sam had taught him.

Peter led them down the hallway, spotting a door at the end with a small window covered with a little curtain, the

chill breeze creeping inside beneath the crack in the door.
Arthur shivered as they gained closer to the door, watching
Peter open it with a creak.

"Are you seriously taking us back outdoors?" Arthur
asked.

"Do you *want* the Barons to find you?" Peter scowled.
"What's your deal with them, anyway? I heard a lot of them
talk about you."

"That's a story to tell later on," Arthur said, starting to
walk out of the door.

Peter stopped him in his path, frowning at him. "You're
on our turf, and those Barons want to know where you are.
Answer my question."

Arthur scowled back at him. "What makes you think it's
any of your business?"

"I just told you, it's our turf, *my* turf," Peter said stiffly.
"Barons don't just look for people for the sake of it. They're
a pack of wolves, and they only hunt the prey they want to
take down."

"We interfered with one of their patrols by accident,"
Tristan said, stepping beside Arthur.

Arthur turned to Tristan with a scowl. "Thank you,
Tristan, that was really needed."

Tristan looked at Arthur, frowning. "Well, *you* weren't
going to say anything."

"I don't know what part of Londinium you grew up in,
but the rest of us know that performing that kind of act
could get you into strife," Peter said, folding his arms.

"Trust me, I already found that out the hard way,"
Arthur said.

Footsteps sounded behind them, and Tristan pivoted to
look. Kyan and Maria caught up, their breath short. Maria
held Arthur's satchel tightly, passing it to him.

"What's happening?" Maria panted, looking at Arthur.

"Jackseye found us," Arthur said, looking at her as he
slung the strap over his head.

Her eyes widened. "How?" she said with shock.

"That's not important," Peter interrupted. "What's more important is that we need to get you three safe."

"By throwing us back into the frost land where the Barons will be patrolling? Great safe spot," Arthur scowled.

"Trust us."

Arthur sighed, nodding at them faintly. "Alright then, Maria, you go first."

Maria squeezed past them, poking her head through the doorway and wedging her way out.

"Tristan," Peter said, nodding towards the door.

"Where, exactly, do I go?" he questioned, walking towards the door.

"You'll see Maria outside the door," Arthur said, exaggerating his words.

Tristan popped his head out the door, looking around. "Oh, there you are," he said, opening the door and walking out.

Arthur looked back at the two trainees before he exited. "Send Marlon my regards."

"I'm sure he'd be happy to have Jackseye off his land, don't worry," Peter frowned.

Arthur nodded at him, making his way out of the building. The three found themselves on the streets of Londinium, the air cold with snowflakes spread across the ground. Arthur looked back at the door, seeing Peter lock it behind them.

Tristan shivered, wrapping his jacket around himself tightly. "So," he said, his breath fogging. "Where to?"

"Did you not warn them that the Barons were on our trail before?" Arthur asked.

Tristan frowned. "Well, no," he said slowly. "They either ignore my words, or they ain't understanding my English well."

"You're telling me *they* don't speak English well?" Arthur raised an eyebrow.

Tristan scrunched his face, shrugging. "I mean, they don't take notice of nothing I say when it's important, so I don't think so."

"They know it better than you, that's for sure," Arthur muttered. Tristan stuck his tongue out at him.

Arthur groaned as he moved, his thigh throbbing in pain from Kyan's blow. "That bloody bastard," he muttered, rubbing it gingerly.

Maria looked at him with concern. "Come on, we can go back to Tristan's and get ice on it," she suggested.

"What's the point? That just proves my point to the both of you," Arthur said.

"What point?" Tristan asked, looking at him.

Arthur looked back at him, his mouth quirked slightly. "I can't be a Knight, let alone a King."

Maria glowered at him. "Just because you got hurt doesn't mean you're useless," she said impatiently.

"I'd beg to differ."

The three pivoted to their left, Leonard leaning against the brick wall down the alleyway with a smirk stretched over his face. "Arthur was always going to be trash at fighting; I should know."

"You again," Maria growled.

"I didn't know this was the scoundrel's part of Londinium," Arthur started, straightening his back. "Where's your hideout with your other pals?"

Leonard pushed off the wall, stalking close to them slowly. "Somewhere close by," he said casually. "They'll come when they hear you."

"And that will be when?" Arthur growled, limping up to him. Tristan watched carefully, a frown starting to form.

"Is now really the best time to fight, Arty?" he asked. "I mean, you literally just got-"

Leonard's fist lashed out into Arthur's stomach. Arthur groaned at the hit, tackling Leonard into the wall behind him.

"Gods be loving," Tristan cursed, stepping forwards.

Leonard elbowed the side of Arthur's head, the thud sending a ringing noise through Arthur's ear. Maria and Tristan felt hands grip them tightly from behind, tugging them backwards.

Leonard's men circled them, blocking their exits. Tristan snarled and pulled one arm out from their grip, swinging it back into one's chest and whipping his head back into the other's nose. The two men behind Tristan collapsed to the ground, groaning in pain.

Leonard slapped over Arthur's ears, making him stumble back, his hearing hollowed out. Arthur tensed his jaw, glaring at Leonard and landing a punch to Leonard's ribcage, followed by a knee to his chest. Leonard grunted, ricocheting back into the wall, his knees giving out beneath him.

Two thuds sounded behind Arthur, and he turned around, the two men who held Tristan lying spread-eagled on the stones. Tristan struggled with three more gripping his arms, Maria straining against the iron grips holding her in place, grunting and cursing. Arthur watched in shock, limping over to them as fast as he could move.

The world shifted out from beneath him, and he fell to the pavement, grunting in pain. Arthur looked back at Leonard's hand wrapped around his ankle, his smug look painted on his face. Arthur kicked at him from the ground, trying to break his grasp.

Leonard yelled in pain and let go of Arthur's ankle, a crack echoing down the alley as he covered his face. Arthur kicked Leonard's wrist hard, feeling a snap as it connected. He cried out again, blood leaking through his fingers down his chin as he held his wrist. Arthur gave him a smirk, slowly standing up from the pavement.

"Arthur, look out!" Maria cried out.

Suddenly, the back of his head exploded in pain, his vision following him falling to the cobblestones hard. Arthur groaned in pain, the back of his head pulsing. Leonard's biggest man towered over him and kicked him away from the wall roughly, pain shooting sparks through Arthur's side as he rolled.

Arthur looked up at him in agony, gritting his teeth with a growl.

"You bastards!" Tristan snapped, writhing in the men's grips. One of them punched his jaw, Tristan yelping in pain. Arthur looked at Tristan and Maria from the ground, his heart sinking. How was he going to get them out of this?

"Not to be rude, but I reckon those three have had enough, don't you think?" a voice said from the end of the alleyway, his accent foreign. The men pivoted to the voice, Tristan raising his head to look, blood dripping down his chin. Maria gasped, her eyes widening. The man stepped forward, a black hooded cloak covering his face; Arthur blinked in shock. *It's the hood from the alleyway!*

"By the looks of things, that one on the ground is as good as gone, and the other two don't stand a chance," the man observed, looking down at Arthur. "So, I believe it's fair to say that you've claimed victory."

"Who the hell are you?" Leonard barked from the ground.

"Just a good Samaritan," the man assured, looking at him on the ground. "Like all of us, except for Arthur, of course, since he's a royal. And I believe it's illegal to attack a royal."

Arthur looked at Leonard from the ground, blood dripping from his mouth. Whoever this man was, he was on Arthur's side.

Leonard curled his lip at the man, getting up with a groan and clutching his wrist. "It's none of your business what happens on these streets," he sniped. "What are you going to do about it anyway, Kandor?"

The man looked into his eyes, removing the black hood from over his head. "I'd be careful of who you threaten," the man narrowed his eyes at him. Dark brown hair was slicked back from his forehead, sapphire eyes glinting with challenge framed by a thick, short beard.

Maria's eyes widened further, her breath catching. "Sir Jameson Galahad," she breathed.

Arthur looked over at her, then back at the man, his eyes wide. *This man is a Knight?*

Galahad looked at Maria with a pleased smile. "Ah, at least someone remembers," he said.

"Sir Galahad," Arthur whispered to himself. Arthur's mind spun. What in the Ether was going on? The Barons show up to watch over Camelot while the Roundtable are gone, Jackseye speaks to Marlon as if he were his brother, and then an old Knight appears? This couldn't be a coincidence, especially because the old Knights were *dead*!

Leonard backed towards his men, looking at the four carefully.

"I'm going to give you two choices; first," Galahad listed, holding up a finger towards Leonard. "You walk away somewhat unharmed and untouched, or two," he lifted the other finger, "you and your boys will be walking away with a few more broken bones than what you've already gotten, your choice."

Leonard glared at Galahad and spat blood on the ground. "Damned Knights," he cursed. "Let's go," he barked at his men. The ones holding Tristan and Maria let go, shoving them away before turning back the other way.

Galahad twiddled his fingers at Leonard mockingly, a slight smirk on his face. "Toodle-loo, sweetheart. Don't run into anyone else that bruises your ego," he cooed after him.

Leonard and his men growled and peeled away down the alley. Galahad looked down at Arthur on the ground, shaking his head. "Just like your father, always lounging on the job," he joked, bending down and grabbing Arthur gently by the bicep. "Come on now, upsie daisies."

Arthur allowed Galahad to help him up, groaning slightly as his thigh barked under pressure. He stood beside Galahad and looked him in the eye, giving him a nod of thanks.

Tristan stared at Galahad, rubbing his jaw and wiping the blood away. "A Knight of old?" he questioned quietly.

Galahad looked at all three of them, pondering over their bruises on different parts of their body. "You three must *love* street fighting," he said quizzically. "You've got a knack for attracting it, that's for sure."

"Not entirely our fault, might I add; they seem to be at the wrong place at the right time," Arthur said, folding his arms. "We don't find trouble; it finds us."

"All the damn time," Tristan shook his head, throwing a look at Arthur.

"Every time," Maria frowned at Arthur.

"Most of the time," Arthur admitted, looking at the both of them. "But we manage, most of the time."

"Barely," Tristan muttered to himself.

"We manage to get things done, even when it involves us getting our shit kicked in," Arthur muttered, his eagerness slowly deviating.

"So you prefer to battle the streets?" Galahad asked, his eyebrow raised.

"Potentially, yes," Arthur nodded.

"That's an odd way to oversee your Kingdom."

"Tell me about it," Maria rolled her eyes. "I've known Arthur personally for two days, and both days, I've been involved in some sort of *'interaction'*."

Arthur shrugged. "And that's just two days," he huffed in amusement. "Tristan has seen it since we were ten, isn't that right?"

Tristan puffed his chest out proudly. "Friends for years with many shared tears," he grinned. "And a few dozen boots launched up the-"

"Tristan," Maria scolded.

Tristan laughed, his grin returning from the scowl he'd worn.

"Never let him finish that one," Arthur shook his head.

"I was going to say launched up the alleyway," Tristan said disappointedly.

"We still get the meaning, Tristan," Arthur said, looking back at him.

Galahad grinned at Tristan. "Always good to have a sense of humour," he nodded. Tristan beamed proudly.

"Can't argue with that," Arthur shrugged. "Anyway, I'm heading back to the castle. You might see me back here tomorrow," he said, limping down the alleyway.

"Are you sure you want to walk that far?" Maria questioned.

"You sound like you don't know me," Arthur called back. Maria frowned, opening her mouth to say something but stalled.

"Bye, Arthur," Tristan farewelled cheerily. "Don't fall down the stairs on the way up like I did!"

"It'd be funny to see you do it again!" Arthur called back, rounding a corner.

Galahad rumbled in laughter. "The castle steps, eh?" he said to Tristan.

He nodded. "It took me ten minutes to reach the bottom."

Their voices gradually faded from earshot, Arthur pushing through the crowds to the castle. His teeth gritted against one another at the pain in his leg, his head worse. *Damn you, Leonard.*

Returning to the castle steps, Arthur limped up to the Castle Gates, his bruised thigh straining with every ounce of pressure. Maybe it was more than a bruise, he realised glumly.

The wind stung his cheek, his hand reaching to touch it gently with a wince. He looked at his fingers, blood caking his fingertips. *Leonard knew how to fight, but he only knew how to fight dirty.*

Finally, he'd made it to the Gates, the great iron grates not yet shut. The castle courtyard was unusually empty, with no marching guards or Wilhelm at the top of the wall. He stepped inside, heading straight to the kitchen for an ice pack, his eyes roving around the castle.

The castle seemed more hollow than usual; there were no Knights in the foyer or the Round Hall. There weren't even Knights guarding the Gates. *Where did they go?*

His memory switched back to the argument he overheard with Ergott and the Roundtable. *Is the attack on Ariendal tomorrow?*

He looked down all the hallways in view, no telltale shine of armour or clank of metal on metal to be heard. It must be; it would explain the lack of security. It was common for Knights to return home to their families the night before a war to say their possible final goodbyes. Tonight would be no exception.

Arthur narrowed his eyes, heading towards the kitchen. He limped down one of the hallways, looking around at each room and corridor he came across.

*Empty, empty, empty.* It was spooky enough as to how open the castle was with the Knights still patrolling, never mind having absolutely no one in any place in the palace.

He walked into the kitchen, looking around for anyone in the room. *Again, empty.* Arthur walked to the cooler, taking out a bundle of ice for himself. He grabbed a towel on the kitchen bench, placed the ice he held in it, formed it into a ball and rested it against his cheekbone.

*Why would Ergott send us to fight a war party we're not threatened by? Who's going to stay behind to protect Camelot if push comes to shove?*

Arthur frowned. *Unless it's those wretched Barons that he's using.* They wouldn't protect much of the Kingdom if they could help it. *What a stupid idea: using the enemy to protect from the enemy.*

Light footsteps echoed down the hallway, moving quickly towards the kitchen. Arthur turned to look at the doorway and saw Rosaline walking in, tying her hair back into a ponytail. She wasn't in her usual garb: a soft grey long-sleeve shirt with a white coat wrapped around her waist by the sleeves, long black trousers and leather boots. Arthur blinked in shock; *the Queen hardly ever wears anything other than gowns in the castle.*

She spotted him and placed a hand over her heart in fright. "Arthur!" she exclaimed. "You frightened me half to death. Look at you!"

"You should see the other guy," Arthur sighed, holding the ice up to his cheekbone.

She gave him a worried look and moved over to him. "What happened to you? Was it those Barons?" she asked.

"No, it wasn't the Barons," Arthur said with a frown.

"Who was it?" she asked, moving her hand over his face to inspect the cut.

"It was one of the street fighters," Arthur said, watching her hand. "Leonard Lionel."

Rosaline frowned and turned to the kitchen bench, picking up a dry cloth and rinsing it in the sink. "What are you doing down there with the fighters? I would've thought you'd know better," she said.

Arthur sat down on a bench stool, looking at her eye level. "I don't go searching for them. They always seem to find me," he frowned.

"Even if they do find you, you shouldn't choose to fight them," she pressed the towel onto his cut, the wound stinging. "It only gets you coming out looking like this."

"Leonard gets every beating he deserves," Arthur muttered, frowning at his name bitterly. "He's a good-for-nothing thief."

"Maybe you shouldn't be going down there if you can't avoid them," she scolded. She wiped away the blood on his face and sat the towel on the bench, opening a cupboard door.

"What else am I meant to do? Stay in the castle and do servant jobs?" he scowled.

"I didn't say you were to be locked in the castle. I just think it wise to avoid them. Or at least take an escort with you." She pulled out a small wooden box and placed it on the bench, opening the lid and taking out a needle and thread. "How often is this happening?"

"It doesn't matter," Arthur dismissed. "I can handle it on my own. I don't need an escort."

"You shouldn't have to need one, but if this keeps happening, I'm not sure if Ergott would let you go without one," she said, pulling the thread through the eyelet of the needle. "Where else are you hurt?"

"My thigh," he said. "A trainee landed a good hit on it."

She looked at him in interest, turning to him with the needle in hand. "Trainee?" she asked. "You were at Marlon's?"

"For a little bit," he admitted. "Though I didn't get far."

"Are you going to become a Knight?" she asked, lifting the needle towards his cut.

"I was thinking about it," he said, wary of the incoming needle.

Her hand grabbed the top of his head, holding him still. Her brown eyes stuck him in place. "If you keep moving, it'll hurt more than it will when you're still."

"I'm not a fan of needles," Arthur frowned at the point of the needle inches away from his eye.

"You should think about that before you get yourself all scraped up," she frowned. It looked odd for her to frown.

"It wasn't entirely my fault," Arthur told her.

"I'm sure it wasn't," she said gently and pricked the needle through his skin.

Arthur winced, clenching his eyes and jaw shut as the needle connected.

"If you don't open your eyes, I can't stitch it properly," she said, pausing.

"What are you, a nurse?" Arthur asked, opening one eye slowly.

Rosaline continued to stitch the wound, pulling it through gently.  "I may as well be. I'm everything else in the castle except the Queen," she sighed. "I may as well be your mother, too."

Arthur frowned, his mouth quirked. "Whatever happened to my parents?"

She threaded the needle through again, a sharp pain shooting through his face for a moment. "Well, your father passed away the night Catarina fell, as you know, and your mother… Well, no one really knows what happened to Emilie."

Arthur narrowed his eyes slightly. "Why do I keep having dreams about my father? As if I watched him die?"

She pulled the thread tight, tying it off. "Some dreams aren't real," she said gently. She snipped the thread and cleaned the needle. "Your mind might just be trying to make sense of it. Many people with trauma go through the same thing."

"Each dream feels real like it actually happened. He even calls my name," Arthur said.

She smiled at him softly. "That's why I said 'some'." She placed a small cover over his stitches, packed the box up and waddled back to the cupboard.

Arthur rubbed his face, wincing at the pull of the stitches. "That feels a lot better, at least."

"Maybe you should channel that fight into your training," she pointed out, sliding the box back into the cupboard.

Arthur looked up at her. "I attempted to train today and ended up with a bruised thigh."

"Well, no one can be the best at something the first time. Your uncle should know," she chuckled.

"I don't know," Arthur sighed. "I don't know if it's worth going back there and giving it another go."

"Well, why not?" she asked, a confused look on her kind face.

"I just don't think I have what it takes," he said to her, fiddling with his hands.

"Well," she said, picking up the bloodied rag and placing it in the sink. "If you want it bad enough, you'll work for it. You can be the greatest Knight *or* King," she looked at him pointedly, "in the land if you tried. Everybody faces hardships and downfalls on their journey. If there weren't any steps to take, then how would you learn? Everyone would be able to do it if it was easy. That's why there's only a special few who can." She rinsed the blood from the towel. "But that's the difference between being given something and working for it. You overcome your hardships, and you become the things you want to be."

Arthur took in her words, nodding at her silently. "You're right. I wouldn't give up over one fault."

"For every fault, there is a lesson learned," she nodded, looking at him. "You're a smart one, Arthur. I'm confident you can learn to overcome your downfalls."

"Learning some courage would be the best start," Arthur chuckled softly.

Rosaline laughed gently, wringing the towel dry. "Confidence, even if it's faked, can persuade you to be brave enough to face the challenges. Take Samqueel, for example."

Arthur nodded at her. "He's the best Commander I know."

"Did you know he never wanted to be a Knight?" she asked.

"No," Arthur answered, his eyebrows raised. "Sam didn't want to be a Knight?"

She shook her head, spreading out the towel over the faucet. "When he was a young boy, he hated the Knights. A rumour I've heard was that they supposedly murdered his father."

"That doesn't sound like the Knights of Camelot," Arthur frowned. "They're not murderers, they're protectors."

"The story was they showed up to his doorstep the night Catarina fell with his father's chain covered in blood. The report noted that Dawson Torona was murdered in a drunken brawl hours before the war broke out, but Sam didn't believe the story. Unfortunately, Dawson wasn't unfamiliar with the watches of the Knights and prison walls."

Arthur's mouth quirked, looking at her. "I wonder if he still holds that grudge."

Rosaline shrugged, polishing the bench with a clean cloth from the drawer. "Who knows," she pondered. "He told me the story years ago when he was young and drunk and stranded in the stairwell."

Arthur couldn't even begin to picture that sentence. Arthur had known Sam and his mother, Erin, personally for years but had never thought to question where his father had gone. He'd figured that he passed away the night Catarina fell - many people were caught in the crossfire that night. It was one of the worst attacks on the Kingdom in centuries since his great-great-grandfather overtook the land from the elves that were here beforehand. He wasn't aware of how close he was to the truth.

"Why is he so protective of me?" Arthur asked.

"Perhaps he's taken you on as a little brother of sorts," she suggested. "He is one to stand up for people who need it. Especially you."

Arthur nodded, standing up from the wooden chair and stretching his limbs, yawning widely.

"Perhaps some rest will do you good," she smiled at him, wiping her hands dry on the cloth.

Arthur smiled back at her. "Thank you for your help, Rose," he said gratefully.

"Now, no more fighting with the alleyway men," she told him with a pretend frown, wagging her finger at him. "If I hear about it one more time, you won't get any pie for dessert."

"No promises," he held a laugh in, his lips twitching upwards.

"I'm being serious," she joked, a pretend look of scorn on her face.

"I'm sure you are," Arthur said, smiling lightly at her.

The Queen chuckled softly and turned back to the kitchen bench. "Off you go, son, before your leg gives out," she dismissed.

Arthur smiled at her, turning back to face the stairs before making his way up to the upper level of the castle. The torches lit his path up the stairs, the shadow of his silhouette stark against the grey stone wall, following behind him loyally as always.

He reached his room after walking from the stairs past the corner, eager to see the armour he had uncovered earlier that morning. He shut his door as he stepped into the room, immediately moving to reach beneath his bed and pulling the chest out of hiding. He opened the lid with a bit of struggle, the armour, sword, and shield still lying in the wooden box. His heartbeat quickened, and with a slight hesitation, Arthur gripped the sword's hilt with one hand, pulling it out gently. The gleaming metal shone silver in the afternoon sun, illuminating the ripples in the blade like ocean waves. He trailed his finger along the groove carved through the middle, following it up to the guard, his fingers bumping against hidden engraved runes towards the bottom.

Arthur blinked and raised the sword higher to his face, squinting at the engravings. Whorls of metal scarred the blade, each overlapping the next in a rhythmic pattern, trailing out over the sword until it faded towards the centre. Three in particular stood out, their carvings deeper than the rest.

Arthur traced his thumb over them; they were old English symbols, each embossed with black. One was a scale, its arms stretched wide and holding to two plates. The next beneath it had a cross with two zig-zags meeting each of its corners, and the last symbol was a circle with a pupil slitted like a lion's eye. *Justice, mercy, command.*

Scraping his finger across the edge carefully, the razor-sharpness of the blade bit his skin, a faint trickle of blood leaching out.

Arthur wiped the blood on his pants dismissively. He felt the leather wrapped around the handle, following the stitching from the gold-dipped guard down to the round dreamcatcher-like pommel, the black hide unbroken and sturdy.

*A fine sword fit for a King, alright.* Arthur set it down in the crate gently, flicking his eyes over the armour, dusty and in need of a polish. Maybe he could learn how to be that man after all. He had the things he needed; all that was left was for him to do as he said he'd do.

If he could figure out how to do so without dying along the way.

Sliding the chest back under his bed, Arthur laid down on the mattress with a pained groan, glad to finally be off his leg. Now, to rest.

The sun peeked above the land and set the frost alight, glittering on the grass and dewy rooftops. Small clumps of half-melted snow lay scattered around the castle courtyard, horses' breaths fogging in the air as they snorted.

Shouted commands fly through the air, Knights in full-clad armour readying up, packing saddlebags full of various items, sharpening their swords and some on their knees with their heads bowed. For many of them, this would be their first battle outside of Camelot, fresh faces mixed with excitement and daunt.

That was another thing Sam didn't like about this army; too many of them needed to be more experienced, and some of them had only just been appointed Knights. Ergott gave him no choice but to take the men. Desperation was never a good thing to give in to at a time like this, especially in a fight no one asked for. *And against an enemy we're leaving to defend our Kingdom, no less.*

The Knights of the Roundtable stood beside their horses, each looking around the courtyard with uncertain looks. Samqueel mounted his horse, holding the reins steady, his crimson-edged armour gleaming in the morning sun.

"Alright, men, listen up," Sam called, facing his horse to the gathered Knights.

The Knights looked up at Samqueel, their attention focused on him. The nearby Knights turned to face him, calls of attention going up across the yard.

"I understand the situation you've been asked to participate in," he said, looking at the younger lieutenants behind the Roundtable. "Trust me, if I had more sway in the matter, I wouldn't be leading you out to a battle we know nothing of."

Reuben leaned on a wooden hitching post beside Arkan, his arms folded. "What does the situation look like from outside our view?" he asked, shifting slightly.

"Sources from Northumbria have reported that Ariendal has moved its forces to their Northern boundary. It's left us an opening to tear through and infiltrate the South. I'm not sure what that means for us or if it's a trap, but I'll be able to tell more details when I see it first-hand," he said, looking at Reuben.

"Does no one else see that this could be a set-up?" Taryn asked, standing beside his horse. "I mean, who sends their forces directly to raid an army that we sure as hell know could kick our ass even if we fought with a literal dragon on our side? We're leaving a league of them to defend the Kingdom, for the Gods' sake," Taryn frowned, looking at the others around him.

"I'm aware of the dangers, Taryn. That's why I never wanted to lead this Legion to this war," Sam sighed and looked at the other Knights. "Ergott has given us barely anything to work off. I'm flat out getting a straight answer anymore out of him. But I need all of you here," he turned to the Legion and raised his voice, "the experienced, the new kids, the people who've been here long before me; I need you to put your faith on your sleeves and take that sword, or that axe, or that bow at your side, and raise it ready to help your Kingdom.

"I'm asking you all to rise to the challenge of this fight, to be brave in the face of death - to go down swinging if you have to. I trust every single one of you to lead yourselves with an iron will into the enemy's territory," he boomed. "I trust that you *will not back down* from this fight, that you *will not give up*. You all have the power to rally against Ariendal, no matter what they say. I know you all have the strength to do so, no matter what they say. You survived the depths of the Darklands, for the Gods' sake! We are the only force in Braynor able to say that about our Knights; that is why we are the strongest in the East! Do you believe it? Do you understand what I say?"

The Legion cheered in the winter air, fists raising and horses spooking. Inspired faces shone up at Sam, conversations rallying through the crowd.

Sam smiled at them. "All of you are Knights of Camelot; all of you were born to do this. You will all become your own legend once we get through this. Right here, right now, is the start of your storybook, the first chapter of your greatness. If you're with me, you better damn well start listening for the war songs that will be written about you." He looked around at the hope in their eyes, heads held high and spirits lifted. "Get ready to make history."

Reuben stood up off the hitching post, walking up to stand in front of him. "You've been there since the very beginning, and you've led me to victory countless times," he stuck his hand out for an honourable shake. "I'm not about to turn my back on you now."

Sam smiled at him and took his hand, both their grips iron strong. "Good, because I was kind of counting on it," he chuckled.

"What would you do without your right hand Knight, huh?" Reuben asked with a laugh.

A smirk spread across his face. "Find a left-hand one," he jousted.

"A typical Samqueel Torona response," he smirked.

"Expect no less, good sir." Sam straightened in his saddle, patting his horse's neck gently. "Everyone saddle up, it's time to move."

"You heard the man, saddle up," Reuben said, walking over to his horse beside Sam's. "Arkan, try not to fall off before you've got onto the horse."

Arkan gave him a look of pretend hurt. "You really think I'd get my shiny new armour covered in mud the moment I get on the saddle?"

"Definitely," Brannagh smirked, saddling up on his horse.

"Most likely," Taryn added, straightening himself on the horse's back.

"Certainly," Lorsaw nodded, pulling the reins tight.

"There's a one hundred per cent chance," Derak said with a smirk.

Arkan snorted and looped his boot into the stirrup. "You all have such little faith in me-" his sentence cut short with a yelp as he pushed himself up into the saddle and slid over the horse onto the ground with a metallic clash.

"*Nice*," Reuben drawled slowly. "Well done, Arkan," he clapped sarcastically.

Sam snorted in laughter, shaking his head. "We really wonder why, Arkansas."

"Arkansas?" Arkan frowned, looking up at Samqueel, mud coating his face and splattered over his chestplate. "You actually remembered my full name?"

"Oh, we remembered it alright," Forlorn said. "We just didn't bother to say it completely."

"His name is Arkansas?" Natan asked, an eyebrow raised.

Dominic looked at Natan with a shrug. "You wouldn't get it."

"We just removed the "Sas" because that's what he lacks in his personality," Brannagh chuckled.

"Ex*cuse me*," Arkan protested.

"Brannagh isn't wrong, you know," Derak said with a shrug, a grin spread over his ginger bearded face.

Arkan stood up, scooping a wad of mud off himself with a disgusted look. "I am *filled* with sass, thank you very much," he said dramatically.

"It doesn't get you anywhere, I'm sure of that," Reuben said, adjusting his posture.

"It gets me more women than Brannagh," he smirked and chucked the mud at Brannagh.

"I wasn't wrong when I depicted you all as children," Lorsaw sighed, shaking his head.

"Shut up, Lorsaw," Arkan grinned.

"It's got nothing to do with you, Lorsaw," Taryn said.

"Don't be a control freak, Lorsaw," Brannagh drawled, wiping the mud from his side.

"You're too observant, Lorsaw," Reuben scoffed.

Karsol reached into his saddlebag, pulled out an oat bar and handed it to Lorsaw. "Here, since you seem to be stiff as a board," he said in his thick voice.

Lorsaw glowered and turned his horse away from Karsol, clopping towards the Legion.

Sam watched him ride out and looked up towards the castle balcony. Ergott watched from above, his golden crown glimmering in the sun, scouring over the Legion. Three Barons stood behind him, their dark hoods stark against the stone wall.

Samqueel shifted his jaw and nodded to Ergott. Of all the things he'd asked of him, never had Sam wanted to refuse more. But he knew if he didn't do as he was told, that Jackseye would win.

He couldn't let Camelot fall under the reign of this tool and his cronies. So he'd do this final task. Sam knew he'd have to fight his way back inside the castle. If this war was going to happen in the way everyone was predicting, at least the backup plan would keep Arthur out of Ergott's reach. Until he could get the bastard off the throne. He just hoped Rosaline had made it on time.

Turning his horse toward the gates, he rode forward, leading the Legion of Knights behind him. Banners bearing Camelot's wyvern coat of arms rose into the air, the clack of hooves on stone clattering behind him like war drums, shifting armour singing a familiar symphony.

If any luck was on his side, Sam could bring them back home again. He just wasn't so sure if he really could.

# Chapter 9: March to Catarina

The sharp Winter wind seeped through the castle walls, the torches in sconces giving both light and a glow of faint warmth as King Ergott passed by. Ergott walked along the hallway corridors, standing up tall with two Black Guards following behind him.

As much as he wanted the Barons to rule Camelot's citizens, it often bothered him to have these two, in particular, follow him like dogs everywhere he went in the castle - on Jackseye's command, no less. Ergott supposed he needed an entourage, anyway. But not here.

Ergott turned to them with a deep frown. "You are dismissed, Guards. Your presence won't be needed for the time being," he said flatly. The Barons looked at each other, their masked faces unreadable. It infuriated him how their identities were hidden from him, *the King.*

"Leave," Ergott barked, and the two Barons bowed to him, moving off silently back towards the stairwell.

*Right, now that that's dealt with...*

Ergott continued his way downwards, approaching another set of stairs leading further down into the castle floor. The torches lit the way down poorly, like they were dying to the cold winter's presence. The humidity made his handheld torch sputter, the flame dimming and twisting.

The stairwell ended with a doorway, a large iron knocker centred on the wooden door. Seating the torch in its sconce, he lifted the knocker and banged it to the wood three times and two more times after a short pause.

"Open up, woman," Ergott growled to himself.

He banged the knocker another three times, getting more impatient by the minute. The woman did nothing but sleep and read down here. What was keeping her from answering? He glowered darkly at the door and went to bang the knocker another three times.

The door swung open ominously with a creak, wind whooshing out through the doorway. Ergott stepped into the room slowly, looking around the dimly lit chamber from the top of an altar stairwell. A table set with unlit candles sat in the centre of the room, a white cloth seated beneath them.

"You can come out, Vivien," he called out, hearing the echo fading into the abyss while he walked down to the dusty carpet.

"Why, hello, my King," a feminine voice purred from behind him.

Ergott looked back over his shoulder. "You need to learn to answer the door," he looked towards the empty space, scouring the wall beside the stairs.

"Oh, but I still did," Vivien chuckled softly, her voice to his left. "Excuse a girl for resting peacefully."

"The Knights have left Camelot," he said, looking around the room to spot her.

"I've heard the news - the speech said before their departure was extraordinary, don't you think?" Vivien said lightly.

"What speech?" Ergott asked.

A female figure emerged from the shadows, long slender legs poking through her black and white, extravagant short-cut dress, her brown hair pulled back and tied over a shoulder, complimenting her pale skin and freakishly yellow eyes. "Sir Samqueel Torona is quite the motivator," she purred, fiddling with her hair. "Half of Braynor has already heard of his words, and the plan to attack Catarina is no secret."

"What did you call me for that was so urgent, Vivien?" Ergott scowled. "I have royal issues to attend to."

Vivien walked to the table, the candles flickering to life with a wave of her hand. The room lit up in orange hues, the corners fading into the shadows, a pile of hay and dirty blankets heaped against the far wall beneath a vent. The flames made her eyes glow pale; their citrine depths turned to him with a mad glint. "I know of the boy's destiny," she said.

"Arthur?" Ergott asked with an eyebrow raised.

"Indeed so."

"Arthur has no destiny to fulfil," Ergott sniped. "We discussed this numerous times."

Vivien smirked like a cat, her voice velvety smooth. "And each time, the same visions come to me: a King with hair of spun gold and a sword of legends with the strength of his ancestors fueling his will."

"Enough," he dismissed. "This sword of legends, where can it be found?" Ergott asked with a slight frown.

"The Blade of the Blood Ties is already in the hands of its protector," she prowled closer.

"Arthur has the Sword?" Ergott frowned deeply, disbelief spreading over his chest.

Her red lips parted to reveal too-sharp teeth. "Destiny has left its mark on the wounds already dealt; only the healer can fix them now."

"How did *he* get it?" Ergott lashed out. "*Where* did he find it?"

"The spirits of those once living have strong wills," she whispered.

"Spirits? What spirits?" Ergott asked furiously.

"The souls of His ancestors; the connections to the castle run deep even in death," she laughed.

"Benjamin," he growled. *The stubborn bastard still manages to rule over me without me knowing. Typical.*

"Indeed so," she said delightfully, clasping her hands together and pacing closer to Ergott.

Ergott turned to her, his eyes narrowed. "How do you know this? You know our deal."

Vivien trailed her fingers across a piece of his cape along his shoulder, her eyes trained on the fabric. "The visions," she said simply. "Our deal outlined that I report what I see, even if it did not satisfy you."

"Our deal was that you could remain here underneath *my* castle to help me with my achievements; you could not leave this chamber," Ergott reminded her.

She flicked her eyes to his, her head tilting slowly. "You think I've left the chamber? You believe the visions to sprout from opinion and not fate," she chuckled.

"I would certainly hope not," Ergott scowled. "You're lucky I even agreed to this deal. Sometimes, I wonder why I keep you here - for years, you've given me nothing but the same words."

"Tell me, Ergott," she moved closer to him, her hand inching up along his shoulder towards his neck. "Even if I did leave the chamber, would you live in fear of not knowing your future? Or would you continue to follow your path of ignorance?"

"I will do what's right for me and for the people of Camelot," Ergott said, watching her closely.

She hummed a laugh, tracing her nail over his jaw. "Whatever you wish to believe, my Lord."

Ergott flinched away from her touch, narrowing his eyes at her with a frown.

"Surely I'm not that repulsive?" Vivien drawled.

"I'd prefer if you didn't touch me, Vivien," Ergott said firmly.

Her eyes turned mischievous, her smirk sharp. "Who would've guessed you would be so squeamish," she purred and moved her hand back to his cape.

Ergott moved away from her, heading back towards the door. "I will be back once the war is finished," he said, one foot on the step.

"A woman gets lonely all alone in a hidden chamber in a castle, you know," Vivien said with her brow raised. "A little company would be appreciated more than once in every while when you require input."

Ergott looked back at her from over his shoulder. "Once our deal's requirements have been met, you can have a room in the castle for yourself and all the company you want," he said, continuing up to the door.

She hissed behind him and stopped at the bottom of the altar staircase, an invisible barrier blocking her path. "Send food for once," she barked. "It's been weeks!"

Ergott opened the door to the chamber, shutting it forcefully behind him with a loud bang and scrape of rusted metal hinges. He looked up the stairwell and began to make his ascent, his head pounding mercilessly all of a sudden.

A scrape of boots on stone echoed in the stairwell, coming towards him. Ergott looked up as he walked, hearing the sound. Had someone followed him down here?

The shadow of a female figure rounded the stairwell, a blonde woman peering down towards him with wide brown eyes. "Ergott? What are you doing down here?" she asked softly, her voice cautious.

"Rosaline," he smiled, walking up to her. "Nothing, I was just… we had a stray mole rat issue, nothing I couldn't handle."

Rosaline Guinevere was a dashing young thing, the loyal wife to Ergott for many years before he was King. Her curiosity wasn't unheard of in the castle, often seeking answers to things she shouldn't be, to Ergott's disdain. Still, he kept a smile on his face as he took her arm to lead her upstairs gently.

"A mole rat?" Rosaline asked.

"Nasty critters they are," Ergott muttered. "They got into the walls and into the basement."

"Who was the woman that shouted after you?" she questioned, touching his arm.

"The woman?" Ergott asked. "There was no woman, Rosaline."

She looked at him bemusedly. As curious as she was, she wasn't stupid, either. Ergott's heart raced beneath his calm exterior, his mind racing over different excuses.

"It could've been a Maiden or Enid," he said, keeping his smile. "I never heard a voice."

Her mouth tilted slightly. "Maybe you're right," she murmured, walking alongside him. "But I was sure I heard someone-"

"Rosaline," Ergott cut her off. "You're hearing things."

She frowned at him slightly, suspicion hinting in her eyes. "Why have you never come down this stairwell before? And where are the Knights?" she pushed.

"The Knights are marching to Catarina as we speak, and like I just told you, we had a mole rat problem," his voice turned stern. "You have your answers, Rosaline. Now, no more questions."

She sighed through her nose silently and bowed her head to him. "Yes, my King," she muttered.

The rain pummelled down in drenching sheets, the ground soaked in water from the dark clouds above. Mud stuck to the horses' hooves like glue as they travelled in rows of two along the dirt path. The trees overhead dripped water down the backs of their cold armour, the creak of wet metal echoing through the pines with the frosty wind.

Sam gritted his teeth against the breeze that froze his bones under his armour. Looking around, his Legion were shivering atop their steeds, a few barely clinging to their reins. The Roundtable kept up, too used to the conditions to keep the chill from slowing them.

"It's so Gods damn *windy*," Arkan called out from his right, his sodden black hair blowing around his face.

"Shut up, Arkan," Natan called from behind him, his back straight and hair flicking around his head. "You should be used to this shitty weather."

"Just because you grew up in the North doesn't mean you get to brag," Arkan protested.

"Actually," Natan smirked, "it does. Maybe you should've trained in the tougher conditions," he said, a cold breath blowing from his mouth as he talked.

Arkan huffed loudly, pulling his reins tighter. "I prefer the warm sands of Hanalei to this."

"So the desert, then?" Derak chimed in with a question.

Arkan raised a brow at him. "Do you know nothing about geography, Derak?" he questioned him.

"Hanalei is in North Armania, a subcontinent if you will," Brannagh said, taking a sip from his waterskin.

"Actually, it's in the territory of North Armania," Lorsaw corrected. "An island along the tropical line of the realm, known for their great coconuts."

"Hey, Lorsaw," Taryn called over to him.

Lorsaw frowned and looked at Taryn, his hair sticking to his dark skin.

"No one cares," Taryn said, smirking at him lightly.

"Shut it, casual," he spat.

"Oooh, fighting words," Taryn teased.

Samqueel flicked his eyes between them, watching with annoyance. *Not again.* Every single time they travelled in a war party, there was at least one fight between the two, naturally started by Taryn. Sam's breath fogged through his nose as he sighed.

"I can use a lot more than just my words," Lorsaw growled in annoyance.

"Sure, you can," Taryn drawled.

"Why don't you come over here, and I'll show you how to dismount your horse like Arkan?" he threatened.

"Oi!" Arkan protested with a frown.

"Sam!" Taryn yelled at him.

"Don't go crying to me, Dawn," Samqueel warned. "You started it."

"I didn't threaten him," Taryn protested.

"Riding with those two is a pain in my neck," Reuben said with a deadpan look. Samqueel grunted in agreement.

"I fell off *once*," Arkan argued. His horse snickered in the rain, shaking its mane out.

"Once is good enough to set an example," Brannagh teased, looking around through the rain.

"How far off are we from this stupid Kingdom anyway?" Karsol growled.

"Too far," Samqueel muttered, pulling his horse to a stop, facing the Legion. "Hold your horses, men. We'll stop here until the rain subsides."

"Couldn't have told us that earlier?" Taryn frowned, ringing out his soaked cloak. The Legion behind him groaned in relief and protest, dismounting their horses and moving beneath the cover of the trees.

Sam threw him a look. "Would you prefer to rest in the mud tonight, Taryn? Cause you're heading down that path pretty quickly," he asked sharply.

"You wouldn't leave a man behind," Taryn dismissed while dismounting his horse. "You'd feel bad straight away."

"I wouldn't test the Commander," Reuben warned, calming his horse.

"When will we reach Catarina?" Brannagh asked.

"When we damn well get there," Samqueel growled sharply, dismounting his horse and leading it further under the trees. All this bickering and questioning was setting his nerves on a thin edge. It didn't help that he didn't want to be out here in the first place, either. He had bigger things to deal with on his plate than answering the same repeated questions over and over, like figuring out a way to get these lads home.

"Most likely within a day's travel," Reuben answered Brannagh, dismounting his horse next to Samqueel.

"Commander!" A Knight called out from the crowd.

Sam pivoted towards the voice, pushing his hair away from his eyes with a sigh. Tying his horse to the nearest tree, he walked back out to the rain, his armour heavy with water. "What is it?"

The Knight made his way over to Samqueel, his helmet bundled under his arm, his long brown hair resting at the shoulders soaked in sweat and rain.

"The Legion requests we devise a clearer plan before we continue further along," his voice sounded worried.

Reuben's eyes flicked over to Sam. Sam's brow, already creased in frustration, turned to a glower, his quicksilver eyes burning through the lieutenant. "The battle right now is the least of my worries," he growled. "A clearer plan will be made once more information is given to me. I need to be informed before I make our next decision. For now, organise a few of you to begin setting up camp under the higher trees a few paces off the path."

"It might be the least of *your* worries, but consider the others you're leading into this mess," he narrowed his eyes at Samqueel.

"Boy, I suggest you choose your next words very carefully if you wish to keep your sword at your side," Sam snapped, his voice flying through the rain. "You will address me as Knight Commander, and I will not hear another word against my orders again, understood?"

He'd never seen this lad before in the ranks, and he already had a line on his shoulder pad. *Are they giving out ranks like sweets, too, now?*

"You're starting to sound like Ergott, Torona," a voice said from his right side. Sam snapped his attention to the voice.

A man with short brown hair and grey eyes much like Sam's own strode over to him, his armour decorated in maroon patterns with three silver chains on the left-hand side of his chest plate. Three marks dashed his shoulder pad, carved through the metal - not filled with gold, however, like Sam's own. Sam's shoulder pad had three lines underneath the right lower side of the Braynor Cross, three stars in the remaining gaps, all inlaid with gold, and three strands of golden chains hanging from his shoulder to the neckline of his chest plate.

"Obviously, these men are sodden; perhaps you should ensure their safety rather than lash out at their necks," the man said.

Sam burned with anger, his jaw tight. "I would prefer if I could let my Legion be dry and prepared before any intervention on my part. Nobody wants to stand out in the rain all night and wait for answers," he said sternly. "Keep to your job, Cole, and I'll keep to mine."

"You're speaking to a Legion Commander, Torona. I speak for these men when no one else will. Everyone has their own opinions; you're just too egotistical to listen to anyone else, like the King's Pet you are," he frowned at him, standing close to him.

The Knights turned to face the two, overhearing the words, tension thick in the air. Samqueel's eyes turned cold, his body relaxing. He'd hated Cole since the day he'd met him in the Hall all those years ago, and he hadn't done anything to lessen the feeling within that time.

"Cole, I recommend you-"

"Shut your mouth, Solas," Cole scowled at Reuben, turning his eyes back to Sam. "Go on, reassure these men that you, their *Commander*, will lead these poor souls into a battle unknown."

Arkan looked around the forest, his eyes wide, running his hand through his hair. "The audacity of this man," he said to Taryn.

"Cole has always been an asshole," Taryn whispered to Arkan.

"I'm going to give you a moment to think about your choices before you end up with your backside in the mud beside that tree over there," Samqueel pointed to a fallen tree calmly, his voice steady. "Would you like two moments or just the one?"

Cole scoffed, meeting him at eye level. "You don't intimidate me, Torona."

Sam raised a brow. "Really?"

"That one over there scares me more than you," Cole pointed to Arkan. Arkan looked at him with wide eyes, signalling to cut it out.

"Oh, that's hilarious," Samqueel laughed, looking around at the Knights gathered. They laughed nervously, unsure where it was going.

"It sure is," Cole laughed, his expression blunt.

Sam chuckled, shaking his head. "You know what else is funny?" he asked, grinning at him.

"What?" Cole asked.

Sam's fist smashed into Cole's neck, his left hand following through with a punch to his unprotected side gap. Cole gasped for breath, coughing as he reeled to the side, touching his throat. Samqueel kicked him in the stomach, sending him rocketing through the air over to the exact tree he'd pointed to, grunting and landing with a squelch in the mud.

Cole coughed, spitting mud from his mouth with a groan. Samqueel dropped the grin, his eyes cold once more. "It's hilarious how you forget your manners to a Knight Commander who'd fought more battles than you," he spat, his voice dripping heavily with venom. "Next time you want to make fun of my leadership style, take it up with my

Knights. They might pay it back a little more kindly than I did."

"He had it coming," Derak smirked, leaning against a tree.

"Who's the egotistical one, now?" Taryn called out to Cole, his arms folded.

"I tried to warn you, buddy," Reuben shook his head at Cole.

Cole growled, sitting back against the log and glaring at Samqueel.

"Oh, and another thing," Sam said mockingly to him. "Ergott is *not* my King. I am nobody's pet, and I am *not* taking orders from a man who inflates his sense of self-worth by telling others how to do their job. So again, keep to yours, and I'll keep to mine." Samqueel walked away from them, heading to his horse.

Before he'd even made it ten paces, another Knight sought his attention. "Commander Torona!"

Unimpressed, he turned to the Knight. "Yes?"

"You might want to see this," he said cautiously, noting the annoyance on his face.

Samqueel sighed. "What does a man have to do to get a change of clothing and a cup of tea around these forests?" he muttered.

"A lot more than what you're displaying," Reuben smirked at him.

Sam looked at him flatly, his mouth twitching in a ghost of a smile. "Then I expect a boiled billy and a pitched tent waiting for me when I get back, Commander," he joked.

"Second Rank Commander," Reuben corrected him.

He waved dismissively. "Specifics," he rolled his eyes playfully and turned to the Knight. "Lead the way, son."

The Knight, along with two other men, led Samqueel into the forest clearing, the vines from the trees dangling to the ground in swinging ropes. The foliage around them thickened gradually as they prowled deeper, the ground becoming uneven with roots and boulders as they entered the denser parts of the forest. Sam scouted out his surroundings with creased brows, looking up into the trees to spy large shadows of birds moving around.

The young Knight crouched down in a small pathway, the grass fading into a mottled ashen grey. He trailed his finger along the edge of the dead grass, tracing the outline in thought.

"Have a look at this," he said after a minute of analysing.

Samqueel knelt beside him, looking at the patch on the ground, his brow creased in interest.

"I don't think this is a safe territory to camp in," the Knight said. "That looks like the footprint of some animal."

Indeed, the grass formed a sizable oblong shape, five smaller circles the size of Samqueel's fist dotted above it. His jaw feathered. The forests never were a safe zone to stay in, no matter where you were. But this was new, and, looking further down the trail, there were more prints than just this one patch.

He stood back up, looking to where the prints led. "We've camped in forests like this before and have come out the other end fine," he said, turning to the men standing around the footprint. "We will have to keep vigilant of our surroundings and stay away from this area in particular."

The crouching Knight looked up at his Commander, a drop of water sliding down his face from the pouring rain above. "What animal does the footprint belong to?"

Sam looked at the Knight grimly. "Unless a new animal is getting about with human-shaped feet, I'd narrow this down to a Giant," he said.

"Guessing those other footprints belong to it?" the Knight asked, pointing down the path. Sam nodded and turned back towards the direction they came from.

"It's heading away from the area," he said, watching them stand to join him. "It shouldn't bother us as long as we're careful. Now come on, we'll get this camp set up so I can get out of this suit."

"What of the other creatures?" another Knight asked.

"The general rule of thumb is if we don't disturb them, they won't disturb us," Sam looked at him. "If you're overly concerned, set up a few outposts." *Or send Cole after them since that's about all he's suitable for.* Samqueel smiled to himself faintly. "Make sure you're out of the rain. I don't want you to get sick."

"Right, you are, Commander." The Knights trailed past him, disappearing through the scrub towards the camp.

Sam hung back a moment. He could tell they were nervous; their voices were thick with it. The pressures of uncharted territory and the battlefield were always too much for new Knights. And with a whole Legion of mainly fresh faces, Sam couldn't help but sigh in annoyance at yet again another setback from Ergott's spontaneity.

*Surely, a Knight of my rank could set up something as simple as a tent.*

It had been a while since he had been out on a battlefield, or even camping, for that matter.

Probably too long for his liking.

Reuben had learned about surviving in the wilderness when he was training alongside Sam all those years ago; the two were like brothers, and they always had each other's backs, side by side at swordpoint and willing to do anything for the other.

Even if it meant doing things at a low level, like tent prep.

*Gods*, did Reuben hate tent prep.

"Struggling there, Reuben?" Brannagh asked, walking up to him from the right.

Reuben paused and looked up at Brannagh. "How does it look from your perspective?"

Brannagh peered over Reuben's shoulder, spotting the tent pegs strewn across the mud. "Looks like you could use a hand," he hinted.

"I know how to set up a tent," Reuben scowled. "I just haven't done it in a while."

"Well, for starters," Brannagh started. "You have the pegs in the wrong order, and secondly, how are you going to stick them in the ground?"

Reuben looked to his side, the mallet missing. He frowned back at Brannagh. "Smart ass," he muttered.

"Gods, you both are so loud," Taryn complained, walking up to the two with an annoyed expression.

"Says the loudest one of us all," Reuben shot back, raising his eyebrow at Taryn.

"Arkan's the loudest, actually. Aww, are you learning how to set up a tent?" Taryn asked, peering at Reuben's efforts.

"I know how to set up a tent," Reuben glowered at him. "Why does everybody have to have a go at me?"

"I offered to help," Brannagh said, raising his hands in protest.

"What? Who's loud?" Arkan called from his tent, poking his head out into the rain.

"*You!*" the three called back at him in sync.

"Am not," he replied quieter.

"Are you sure you can handle the tent by yourself, Reuben?" Brannagh asked.

"Yes, I'll be *fine*," he rolled his eyes, picking up another tent peg and looping it through the rope.

"You heard the man, Taryn; time to leave him alone," Brannagh said cheerily, leading Taryn away from Reuben and his tent.

Reuben looked at them with a quirked mouth, then back at the mess of rope and pegs. He sighed through his nose. "Surely," he muttered to himself.

"Surely what?" Samqueel questioned, walking out from the treeline behind the tent.

Reuben scowled at him from over his shoulder. "Surely I can be left alone to set up this wretched thing," he growled.

Sam chuckled. "You've forgotten again," he laughed.

"Helpful, Sam, thank you," Reuben replied, sarcasm thick in his voice.

"You know I was joking when I said I expected it done, right?" Samqueel knelt beside him, picking up the pegs.

Reuben frowned at him, stopping his work. "I have been working on this for thirty minutes, and you just tell me now that you didn't want me to do it?" he said flatly.

"Getting the fire going would be impossible in this weather, and I'm familiar with your struggles with tent pitching," he grinned, picking up the mallet from beneath the tarp.

"Have I ever told you how much I hate you?" Reuben asked with a laugh.

"Oh, plenty of times," Samqueel said lightly, pulling the ropes taut and tapping the pegs through the dirt. "Like that one time you insisted on going to town for a drink, and you ended up face-first in the gutter in front of that girl you liked," he grinned mischievously.

"That never happened," Reuben dismissed. "I didn't face plant; I tripped over an uneven surface."

"Yeah, my left boot heel."

Reuben frowned at him, slowly changing into a smile. "Whatever,"

"'Whatever', he says, as if he didn't gain a scrape to the noggin," Sam smirked at him and pulled the last of the ropes down, pitching the poles up to stand.

A groan sounded behind the two. "I hate camping," Derak said, stretching his arms over his head.

"And here I thought you loved it, old man," Natan said.

"No," Derak sighed. "But he does." he pointed over to Carsen sitting in his tent under an overstretched tarp between two trees, his eyes bright with a smile.

"Can't judge a man for having a hobby," Reuben said, turning back to the tent.

"A hobby for nature?" Derak asked.

"It's what he likes."

"And it's something you're not good at," Sam prodded, standing up and opening the tent flap, escaping the rain.

Reuben sighed, flinging his long black hair away from his face. "That's all set up then?" he asked.

"Sure is," he said from inside.

"Just as well," Reuben muttered while standing from the ground with a grunt. "I was about to give up, mind you."

"We're fairly sure you gave up halfway through," Dominic called to him from two tents down.

"You could've helped, you know, Dom," Reuben called back.

"I mean, Henry asked," Dominic shrugged.

"I was willing to lend you a hand," Brannagh said from a tent next to Forlorn. "But it looks like you handled it semi-well," he chuckled.

"No thanks to you lot," Sam smirked, coming out of his tent to his horse.

"I'm glad Arkan didn't offer a hand," Reuben said, looking over at his tent.

Carsen took one look at Arkan's tent, a mess of rope, textile, and tarp pulled over a low-hanging branch, and stood up, walking through the rain to the makeshift hut.

"Looks like a Kobold's hut," Taryn said, looking at Arkan's creation in question.

"More of a bird's nest," Natan muttered, scratching his chin.

"In Arkan's words, it's called *Art,*" Karsol gestured, standing next to Taryn with his arms folded.

"Damn right, it is!" Arkan called from inside it. Carsen shook his head at the tangle of junk.

"It's called an abomination!" Derak yelled at him, his Northern accent thick.

"It's fine, it's doing its job- *Hey*!" Arkan poked his head out into the rain to glare at Carsen, who was rearranging the ropes to pull tighter. "Mind your own tent!"

"He's adding the final touches," Reuben chuckled.

Carsen stuck his finger up at Arkan and kept fixing the tent, Joseph joining in on the other side. "Fussy bastards," Arkan growled.

"Who knew that the silent duo could create such an effective team," Brannagh said while scratching his goatee. "Fascinating."

The two stood back, admiring their work. The tent actually represented a tent, the fabric straightened out, and ropes pulled neatly together, with a decoration of a grumpy Arkan at its foot. They high-fived each other and grinned at Arkan, moving back to their tents.

"They've always been that way, Brannagh," Samqueel nodded to them, pulling his sleeping bag from his horse and carrying it towards his tent.

"The two are almost inseparable," Reuben said, helping Sam with his gear.

Natan shrugged to himself, walking over to his tent. "Meh, I don't know about *inseparable*," he mused.

"The two are like brothers almost," Dominic said to him. Carsen gave him a thumbs up. Dom returned the kind gesture, giving him a nod.

"How much stuff did you pack, Sam?" Reuben asked, looking at the gear on his horse.

Samqueel gave him a look. "It's just my battle armour," he shrugged. "And a change of clothes and the sleeping bag."

"Did you think this was a holiday of sorts?" Reuben asked. "Don't forget you brought the tea set, the tent, and a backpack to put your toiletries in, except the utensils you bring to polish your armour off before a fight-"

"Okay, okay," Sam interrupted, his eyes slightly wide. "Let's just rattle off everything I pack for every battle right in front of everybody, Reuben."

Reuben gave him a mischievous smirk. "Oh? You're embarrassed?"

Samqueel looked away, a faint bit of colour staining his cheeks. "Shut up," he dismissed, carrying the bag in the tent.

"What if I told the *entire* Legion?" Reuben asked teasingly.

"Then you're sleeping in the mud with Arkan."

Reuben scoffed. "As if you'd do that."

"Wouldn't I?" A thud sounded from inside the tent, followed by zips being undone and fabric wrinkling.

"Nope," Reuben dismissed. "You care about me too much."

"Well, if you want to keep talking about my polishing tools," Sam poked his head out through the flap to give him a flat look, "then make yourself comfortable right where you're standing, boy."

"Take a joke, will you, Sam?" Reuben said, giving him a smirk.

Samqueel narrowed his eyes playfully at him and ducked back into the tent.

"What polishing tools?" Dom laughed. "I always thought he got new armour."

"He's not rich, Dom," Reuben said to him.

"I'd beg to differ," Lorsaw protested.

"You're not rich either, Lorsaw," Derak prodded.

"You might be broke, Lorsaw," Taryn grinned, catching the bandwagon.

"I'm richer than *you*. I don't blow my money on cheese crackers and women every Saturday night," Lorsaw sniped.

The Knights around Taryn burst into laughter, Karsol nudging him on the shoulder. Taryn frowned at Lorsaw, moving away from the nudges.

"Lorsaw got Taryn good!" Natan laughed.

"The better part is he doesn't bring any of them back with him to the castle," Lorsaw grinned.

"Which ones, the crackers or the women?" Arkan laughed. They all laughed again, hunching over on their knees.

"I do!" Taryn protested. "It's just rare!"

"Okay, buddy, we believe you," Brannagh said with a smirk.

"I'll believe it when I see it," Dominic shook his head, a grin on his face.

"You guys are assholes," Taryn frowned.

"Did you pack any cheese crackers with you, Taryn?" Arkan asked. "Or did they run away after getting a whiff of your socks, too?"

"Wouldn't you like to know, Arkansas?" Taryn frowned at him.

"Damn, poor Taryn," Reuben said, watching the exchange happening in front of him with a smirk.

Rustling echoed from Taryn's tent, and Joseph poked his head out, holding a box of crackers in the air with a fiendish grin.

"Put them back!" Taryn yelled in frustration, the others laughing again. Joseph narrowed his eyes at him, opened the box, put a cracker in his mouth, and slowly backed into the tent.

"Should we be worried about the assassin?" Brannagh asked, watching Joseph in question.

"Possibly," Natan said. "I'd be more worried about the ones in the castle. At least Joe's tame… ish."

Carsen chuckled hoarsely from his tent, his hand on his chest. Joseph appeared beside him suddenly, sitting with the cracker box cross-legged on the ground. Taryn looked at him, flabbergasted. "Wh-what? How?!" he protested, his hands in the air.

Joseph pointed towards the back of Taryn's tent with a cracker in between his fingers, the ropes strung up just high enough to slip beneath.

"You sneaky little sausage," Brannagh said with high brows.

Joseph grinned and shrugged, turning to Carsen and signing to him, his fingers moving sharply in the air.

"There's a second box," Carsen translated, his voice gravelly.

"Did you really need two boxes of cheese crackers for this journey?" Natan asked Taryn.

"I was going to eat some on the way," Taryn growled, heading into his tent and zipping it up angrily. The side flap snapped shut with a crack, and the rope pulled taut.

Reuben laughed along with the rest of them as they moved out of the rain, Reuben moving his gear from his horse into his and Sam's tent.

Nightfall laid across the campground like a thick blanket, the rain clouds long gone. The shifting of metal echoed through the trees, the sentries at their outposts shifting on their feet nervously.

The Roundtable Knights kept to their tents, snores sounding from inside a few. The mud outside the tents slid under Sam's boots, puddles squelching with his weight.

The wind rustled the leaves above his head, following him on his patrol towards the Camelot Knights. He figured he may as well make himself visible to his men; sometimes, it was better to mingle with the young ones to gain their trust and respect rather than demand it. After all, Samqueel could settle down for a drink or two.

A campfire lit up the muddy patch of forest, the Knights huddling around it shivering. Samqueel huffed in amusement at them. "Not used to the wintry conditions, are we men?" he asked.

They pivoted to turn to him with respectful nods, some holding mugs of ale while others polished and sharpened their weapons. "First time on the battlefield, Commander," the closest one to him said, his teeth chattering.

"You'll learn to toughen up," Sam shrugged, sitting on one of the logs in front of the fire. "The cold only gets worse when it's snowing."

"Have you ever fought in the snow, Sir?"

"Gods, no," Samqueel scoffed. "I'd rather keep my toes and fingers than fight in an ice chamber."

The men chuckled softly, their shoulders starting to relax slowly. "How long has it been since your last fight, Commander?" one of the men sitting on the log across from him asked.

"When we were little lads, weren't we, Sam?" Reuben said, walking up behind the group with Brannagh and Dominic by his side.

Sam looked at him, his brow raised. "Little lads? My last fight was when I was twenty-three."

"So, two days ago?" Brannagh smirked.

"Flattering, Henry," Sam replied.

"Well, how old are you now, Sam?" Dominic asked, sitting himself beside the fire.

"Last time I checked, I was thirty-two."

Reuben took a seat next to Samqueel on one of the logs, nodding to the younger Knights seated around. "Keeping a lookout, are we lads?" he asked the Knights.

"Sure are, Sir," one said.

"Don't worry about the battle for the moment, yeah? Just enjoy the peace while you have it," Reuben said with a smile.

"The battle won't be the hard part about this whole thing," Dominic muttered.

Reuben looked at Dom. "What are you talking about?"

"I'd imagine carting everyone home would be harder," he mused, a hand against his cheek.

"Especially with rookies and the likes of your lazy bones," Sam smirked, nudging Reuben.

"Says you," Reuben narrowed his eyes at Sam playfully. "You always ask me to do your hard work."

"A cup of tea every now and then is hard work?"

"Shut up."

Samqueel grinned. "You volunteer half the time; I don't even need to tell you."

"What else am I supposed to do when Ergott or you aren't barking orders at me?" Reuben asked.

"Pick up knitting," Samqueel smirked widely, his eyes lit with mischief as the Knights around them chuckled quietly.

"Or pick up eating a nice salad with me," Brannagh suggested.

"No one in any of the Kingdoms would do that," Reuben said to Brannagh.

"Well, why not?" Brannagh asked. "Just because you're not into salad doesn't mean others aren't-"

A shriek split through the air, the voice pained and hoarse. Sam looked up sharply, scanning the forest. The Knights of Camelot looked around in surprise, their eyes wide. "What on Earth was that?" one asked to the open air.

"Weapons ready," Reuben ordered, unsheathing his sword. The Camelot Knights picked up their discarded weapons from around them and on the weapon stands near the tents. The howls sounded closer, the snapping of teeth echoing through the trees. The lads at the outposts dotted around the camp moved around the shadows quickly, trying to find the source with nervous calls to one another.

"Werewolves," Reuben growled.

Dom stayed on the ground, looking at the fire in realisation. "They don't like light," he muttered.

Reuben looked over at Samqueel. "Your thoughts?"

"Stay quiet and mind your shadows," Samqueel commanded, his hand hovering over his pommel.

Reuben nodded, looking at the Knights beside him, their young faces stricken with fear of the unknown. Brannagh reached for his longbow, watching the forest carefully.

"Don't go crashing through the forest or lifting bows just yet," Sam warned.

"Didn't you hear the howl?" Brannagh asked, looking at Samqueel in confusion.

"Of course, I heard the howl, but if we leave them to pass, they won't disturb us."

"Sam's right," Reuben said, looking at him sideways. "Don't engage."

The forest around them crackled with leaves, foreign growls and yips sneaking through the trees. The Camelot Knights at an outpost closest to the treeline spooked, snapping their attention towards the noises with their weapons raised.

"Commander Torona! There's something in the woodlands!" a Knight from the outpost yelled.

"Steady yourselves," Reuben barked.

Sam looked at them with his hand raised to his mouth, glaring sharply. *Gods, did they* want *to attract them?*

The growls grew closer, surrounding the outpost, the bushes and leaves crackling as they neared. The lads kept shouting at one another, their weapons swishing around them in panic.

*Gods help me.* Sam set his jaw, moving over towards the outpost quickly, his boots muffled on the mud. It was as if they'd never been in the damn forest before, which was impossible. *The Darklands must have scared them silly.*

Reuben scowled at them with frustration, he and Dominic trailing Sam silently. No one liked how nervous the new kids became. It was always a bad sign when dealing with conflict; nervous mannerisms always lead to critical mistakes.

They watched the Knights closely, their boots causing heavy irritation amongst the leaves. Samqueel reached the outpost, listening to the growls around him as he stood beside the fire. "Right," he growled to the Knights, irritated. "When I say so, get up into either the closest tree or *quietly* go to your tent; you've made way too much noise."

"But Commander," the Knight from earlier with the shoulder marks - Vincent, Sam had learned - protested. "We'd have more of a chance if we all defended the camp-"

"I'm not sending you into an unnecessary fight with a pack of *werewolves*," he interjected, his teeth clamped.

Right on cue, a howl to their right split the air, and three heads tore through the shrub, the werewolves' bulky form snarling at the Knights. Their terrifyingly gruesome snouts barked at them with rotted, protruding fangs. The muscles along their muzzle were torn back away from their gums, the rot following up to their eight, flamelike eyes that glared at them from inside a huge furry skull. The bones of their haunches stabbed the air with razor-sharp edges, their six huge, clawed paws dug into the ground, and their skeletal tails slashed the air.

"Oh, Gods!" Dom cursed quietly, his face paling.

Sam faced the werewolves, his anger at the Knights forgotten. The Knights behind him froze with their weapons at the ready.

"Lower your Gods damned weapons, you tools," he spat at them.

The werewolves gained closer to them, their bristling fur dark in the shadows. The muscles bunched over their abnormal forms rippled in the light of the campfire behind Sam, heatwaves rippling into the air from their heated breath.

Reuben turned to Samqueel, his eyes wide with uncertainty, noting Remedy was not in his hands. "Sam?" he whispered.

Samqueel crouched slightly at the knees and raised his palm flat toward them, extending it to the closest wolf. He could feel his heart pounding inside his ears and felt the lump of uncertainty he swallowed down his throat sink to his stomach. He trusted this to work; she wouldn't lie to him about it.

Werewolves were elves once before their transformations; Drow Elves, specifically, although it wasn't uncommon for other races to get the wild shape gene. The legend was that when the Drow Elves had crossed from the Etherrealm to the Overrealm and into the Darklands, like the other Etherspawn, they'd come into contact with wolves that had attacked their groups. When the victims healed, the bacteria from the wolves had bonded with the genes of the Drows, and because their ever-evolving immune systems couldn't handle foreign entities, the genes evolved to incorporate the bacteria into its system. As a result, it had turned them into Werewolves and spread the shifter gene to other races as they'd mingled and come across them in their territories.

*They are only aggressive to the things they perceive as threats.* Sam just prayed to the Gods that they didn't think him to be one.

"What are you doing?" Vincent asked incredulously, his sword in both of his hands.

"Lower your weapon," Sam growled at him. "They won't think you're a threat if you don't give them a reason to."

"Are you *crazy*?"

The Werewolves snarled at them, snapping their teeth at their blades. Sam sheathed his sword slowly, keeping his eyes forward.

Vincent jolted at the snap, backing up and sheathing his sword with daunt. Reuben followed Sam's word, sheathing his sword slowly and keeping an eye on the Werewolves. The rest followed suit, all of them backing away slowly, watching Sam warily.

The closer wolf sniffed at Sam's hand, all eight eyes glaring at him. He watched it cautiously, trying to steady his breathing. *Friend, not enemy.*

The glint in the wolf's eyes changed, pulling away sharply and turning to dart back to the scrub, its brothers following quickly behind, the crashing of leaves underfoot drowned out by barks and yips. More footfalls joined in - a *lot* more, Samqueel realised - and he sighed in relief, the noise fading gradually.

"How many do you reckon were actually surrounding us?" Reuben walked up beside him, looking out into the shrub.

"Too many," Dom shuddered, a howl sending goosebumps down his arms.

"Thanks for the specifics, Forlorn," Taryn frowned, walking over along the trail with his sword in hand.

"Look who decided to wake up after all the action was over," Dom frowned at him.

"The hell was all that howling?" Taryn asked, rubbing his left eye.

"What do you think, genius?" Reuben asked, brushing past him to return to his tent.

"It was your mother wailing over the lost opportunities for a grandchild, naturally," Brannagh teased, pulling his bowstring absentmindedly. "All hopes are on Elaine, now."

Taryn flipped him the bird, not making eye contact with him. "So who's going to tell me, or do I need to figure it out?"

"Werewolves, dumbass," Sam sniped at him, turning to the Knights behind him with a scowl. "If they come back, drown the fire and let them roam, do not engage. Do not leave your tents. Understood? Good. Go."

The Knights scurried off, placing their weapons back on the racks and in sheaths before making their way over to their places. Taryn frowned, following Samqueel's demand with a sigh; Reuben and Dominic moved off to sort out the rest of the camp.

*That was too close.* Trust the Darklands to give them a lick of the Ether on the first night. He sent a silent word to the Otherworld, looking at the stars before turning around to face the Knights walking away.

"Taryn," Sam called.

"Yes?" Taryn answered, looking over his shoulder.

"Apologies."

"For?"

"Attitude," Sam answered, walking towards the Roundtable tents.

Taryn rolled his eyes, turning back to him with a makeshift smile. "Sorry, Sam, it won't happen again."

Samqueel raised a brow. "I was apologising to *you*," he said slowly, walking past him.

"Oh?" Taryn straightened. "Wait, what for?"

He frowned, pausing to look back at him fully. "Well, it was for calling you a dumbass, but I'm starting to think it's true."

"Keep dreaming, Samuel," Taryn smirked, jogging past him to his tent.

Sam scowled at him, his back straightening. "Did you just call me Samuel?" he called to him.

"Guess we'll find out in the morning!" Taryn called back.

Sam narrowed his eyes, walking to Taryn's tent and kicking one of the pegs out of the ground. The rope flew up into the air, and the tent poles collapsed, sending the material crashing down.

"You asshat!" Taryn cursed, frisking around underneath the collapsed tent.

Brannagh laughed from his spot near his horse, shaking his head. "Ah, the consequences of your own actions," he chuckled.

"I take back the apology," Samqueel sniped, walking to his tent. "You're one hundred per cent a dumbass."

"I'll get you back! Ow!" Taryn struggled, poking his head out of the tent.

*Sure you will.* Samqueel smiled to himself, zipping up his tent.

The night was dead silent, the eeriness of nothing swamping Sam's ears as he lay awake staring up at the tent's roof. Reuben's quiet breathing across from him kept his guard down; at least something sounded alive. He longed for the feel of a warm bundle of brown fur at his side, for the companionship he'd been missing for years now. It was always times like these that he missed his best mate.

Gods, he missed her, too. Both of them. All of them. It'd been forever since he'd seen the flash of white appear at his window, felt her touch or heard her voice. Since he'd seen the marshlands in the North. He'd need to take a trip soon to see them if he could get away from Ergott.

He sighed through his nose, his hand fiddling with the chain resting on his chest absently, the overlapping triangles on the pendant poking his fingers gently. Sometimes, he wondered if he should've stayed with them there. Other days, he wondered what would've happened if he'd never met her, if only because the stress of knowing he'd never have time for them would weigh on his mind.

But he would never regret meeting her, never regret belonging to her, and her to him. If things were different, he'd have them both in the castle with him, safe and close by. If only she wanted that. If only she was allowed to be.

Sam shook his head clear, sitting up and leaning on his elbows against his knees. He rubbed his face, his calluses scratching at his short beard. Remedy sat in its scabbard at his right beside his bedroll, the dark metal of the hilt almost invisible in the dark. He looked at the rounded pommel, tracing down the blade to the matte silver cross guard that hugged the entrance of the leather scabbard.

He had a job to do. He had men to protect and a Kingdom to serve. An oath to uphold. Mates to fight for. He would never dare to leave his friends behind for his own gain; they were everything. Always had been since he'd met them in the hall.

Even if a select few got on his nerves often.

"WHERE'S MY CRACKERS, DAMN IT!?"

Sam's eyes widened in amusement, clamping down on his lip to keep from laughing. The crackers box in question sat behind him, emptied of all but crumbs and cheese dust. He'd snuck into the tent while Taryn had gone to scout the trees for a bathroom break, sharing the treats with Reuben and keeping their laughter quiet when they'd listened for Taryn's return. Sam was surprised he hadn't found it earlier.

*At least I can get the select few back for their pestering on occasion.*

# Chapter 10: Seasoned Oak

The streets were more relaxed than Arthur would've guessed them to be on a Sunday morning. Usually, they'd be flooded by people looking to go to the stalls for a feast at the midday mark. You'd be flat out seeing the produce over someone's shoulder; many people would dig elbows in to get a glimpse of the sweets and meals on offer. Even the poorest citizens get fed on Sundays.

Except there was no one. Not a single soul.

Arthur trailed down the alleys, looking around at the empty streets. In his left hand, he held a heavy bag that burned his arm from the weight, the objects inside sticking their corners into the material.

*Maybe taking the armour wasn't the best idea.*

Arthur turned the corner down the left alleyway, finally arriving at his destination: Marlon's Knight Training Camp. Arthur scoffed to himself, looking at the new large wooden sign stuck to the bricks above the door. "Interesting name," he snorted. *As if everyone didn't know where this place was.*

Stepping up to the door, Arthur knocked with his free hand, taking a step back to wait patiently. Small thuds sounded faintly through the door, slaps of skin on concrete echoing. Arthur frowned at the noise. *What the hell is that?*

The sound got louder, travelling towards the door, heavy breathing accompanying it. The sound stopped, heavy panting whooshing behind the door.

Then a knock.

Arthur knocked once again, his eyebrow raised in confusion. The knock sounded again, a giggle behind the door. Arthur rolled his eyes, a small smile slipping on his face.

"You've given away your identity, Tristan. Open the door," Arthur said, looking around the alleyway with a small smile.

"I have?" Tristan asked. "I mean, uh," his voice deepened, "this isn't Tristan, this is… Peter?"

"I can tell it's you," Arthur reassured.

"No. It's Peter, who are you?" Tristan coughed, clearing his throat and muttering.

"Kyan, now open the door," Arthur played along.

"Kyan!" Tristan said in his normal voice, opening the door excitedly. His grin dropped, then picked back up. "Arthur!"

"You're so gullible," Arthur scoffed, looking at Tristan and noticing the amount of sweat dripping from his forehead. "Did you just run a marathon?"

"It's a long way between here and the training hall," he panted. "Plus, I wanted to answer the door before Peter did."

"Marlon around?" Arthur asked, stepping inside.

"He's training the new lot."

"Well, he's got a new trainee," Arthur said, walking down the hallway with his bag.

Tristan closed the door, following after him. "Who?"

"Who do you think?" Arthur asked, looking back at him.

Tristan pursed his lips in thought, his eyes glazing over. *Oh gods, he's actually thinking.*

"Me, you chip idiot," Arthur told him.

"Oh. Well," Tristan looked him over, "you look better than when Kyan beat you up a few weeks back, so that's a good plus."

"I had stitches pulled out of my face, hence the bruise," Arthur said, turning a corner.

He walked over to the green corner benches, setting his bag down on the wooden bench with a metallic thud.

"What have you got in there, bricks?" Maria asked, coming over from a group.

Arthur looked over at her, his face passive. "Armour," he said simply. "My father used to wear it when he was a Knight."

Maria blinked at the bruise on his brows. "I bet that hurt," she nodded to it.

"You have no idea," Arthur scoffed.

She frowned slightly, looking back to the group she was watching. "So you decided to come back?" she said, her voice light.

"That's surprising to you?" Arthur asked, opening his armour bag.

"I would've thought-"

"You'd give up by now," a voice interrupted from beside them.

Arthur looked up towards the voice, frowning slightly. Kyan grinned at Arthur from the higher benches in the orange corner, leaning his forearms on his knees. "Good to see I haven't broken you yet," he prodded.

"Good to see you too, Kyan," Arthur snided. "Were you looking for a round of applause? I can give you one if that boosts your ego."

"Clever words for someone who can't use a sword," Kyan teased, standing up and jumping down the benches.

"I've trained with a sword before; I know the basics," Arthur said, watching him.

Kyan landed beside Maria, leaning an arm on her shoulder. "I'm sure you have," he dismissed. "Playing with sticks in the courtyard of the royal gardens classifies as formal training nowadays, it seems." Maria looked at Kyan's arm uncomfortably.

Arthur reached into the bag and pulled out his father's sword. "Does this look like a stick to you?"

Kyan's eyes glittered in amusement. "So you have a real sword," he said, surprised. "That's a start."

"You don't say," Arthur said, narrowing his eyes at him. Tristan frowned at Kyan slightly, looking at his arm on Maria's shoulder.

"I'm sure using your endless amounts of wealth and education will help you wield that chunk of iron, especially all those books you read," Kyan snorted.

"How wealthy do I look to you?" Arthur asked.

"You're the son of a *King*," he said slowly.

"I'm just as wealthy as a person in Londinium," Arthur admitted. "I have nothing in that castle. All I have is that title of a royal, nothing else. I might as well be living down here in Londinium 'cause that would make me wealthier."

"Yeah, yeah, sad rants, big deal. We all know how *hard* it is for the famous," Kyan waved his hands in the air dramatically. "Just admit, you've got more than the majority of people down here. Everyone knows it."

"Everyone *thinks* it," Arthur corrected him, frowning. "King Ergott has taken it all for himself."

"Now *that* I can believe," Kyan raised a brow.

"Kyan, can you quit being a jerk for five minutes?" Maria sniped at him, moving his arm off of her shoulder.

"Do as she says," Arthur said, narrowing his eyes at Kyan.

"Ooh, the future King is giving me commands," he mocked, his eyes wide.

"Watch it, Kyan," Tristan said in a low voice.

Kyan looked at Tristan, amused. "The hell are you going to do about it, Garrison? Stress eat?"

"Don't test me, Kyan, I'm warning you," Arthur warned.

"The street fighter with a stitch in the eye challenges a Knight trainee," Kyan sighed dramatically, clenching his hands together beside his face.  "Oh, the romance here is so… dead," he smirked.

"Let's take the romance over to a date in a chalk box," Arthur challenged, nodding over to the empty box.

"Oh? You want to spark the relationship back up, I see?" Kyan grinned darkly.

"I never got to say my goodbyes after your carriage left," Arthur shrugged, playing along with his little word game.

"A pity it went the way it did," Kyan pulled a sad face. "It could've led to a fantastic marriage of my foot to your face if we'd held on longer."

Arthur handed Tristan the sword in his hand, narrowing his eyes at Kyan and clenching his jaw.

Tristan looked at the sword in his hands. "Arthur, I don't think this is a good idea-"

"Hold the sword, Tristan," Arthur said firmly.

"At least wait for Marlon-"

"Marlon doesn't matter," Arthur dismissed. "Kyan wants a challenge, and I will deliver."

"Let's build this love back up," Kyan grinned, walking to a box.

Arthur followed him, staring him down with a stern glare.

"The hell is going on?" Peter asked, walking up to Maria and Tristan, who was unsheathing the sword.

"Kyan is being a domineering prick," Maria scoffed, folding her arms.

"And Arthur gave me this," Tristan said, turning to him with the sword.

Peter jumped back, the blade swishing a few inches away from his chest. "Gods above, Tristan!" he said, taking the sword off him.

"Hey, that's mine," he protested, going to grab it back.

"You need to watch where you point swords," Peter scowled, putting the sword back in the scabbard he swiped off Tristan's other hand and setting it down on the seats.

"I know how to point swords," Tristan scowled back.

"At the things you *shouldn't* point them at," Peter frowned, looking up at Arthur and Kyan. "Gods, what on Earth are those boys doing?"

"Bickering," Maria scowled. "One wanted to fight, and the other was in a bad mood, it seems."

"And which order is that?" Peter asked, folding his arms with a frown.

"Kyan is the former," she said, sitting down on the bench beside Arthur's bag.

Peter rolled his eyes. "Not surprising, to say the least."

Tristan edged around Peter, sitting beside the bag and eyeing the sword.

"Take the sword, and you won't be training for a month," Peter warned, spotting Tristan at the corner of his eye.

Tristan frowned at Peter. "Arthur told me to hold it."

"Before you almost stabbed me," Peter reminded him, giving him a look. Tristan slouched sulkily and watched Arthur.

Arthur stood opposite Kyan inside the sparring box, removing his fur coat and throwing it on the floor outside the line.

"Oh, look out, things are getting serious, the coats coming off," Kyan jested, grinning at him.

Arthur glared at Kyan. "Make your move, sweetheart," he taunted.

"Let me just decide how I want to hand your ass to you this time," Kyan pondered, scratching his chin dramatically with an over-thoughtful look on his face.

"You haven't seen me at my prime," Arthur said.

"Was that last move close to it? Or are you all words?"

"Well, if you stopped moving your jaw, you'd see this coming," Arthur said, launching his leg into Kyan's thigh. Kyan stepped back a little too late, Arthur's boot grazing him sharply. He hissed and touched his leg.

"Going to retaliate? Or sulk about a small graze?" Arthur asked, standing over him.

Kyan growled and barged his shoulder into him, digging his elbow into his rib and spinning to launch a foot into his chest. Arthur grunted, landing on the concrete with a loud thud inches away from the line.

"Going to get up? Or just sulk about a sore shoulder?" Kyan mocked.

Arthur moved his leg underneath Kyan, swiping at his ankles with his boots. Kyan jumped over his feet, moving back. Arthur growled, getting up from the ground in frustration.

"Come on then," Kyan beckoned to him with his fingers. "Since you haven't shown me your 'full power' yet."

Arthur glared at him, walking up to Kyan with a clenched fist.

"What is going on here?" A commanding voice boomed through the hall, trainees turning to look. Kyan looked over to the voice, taking his eyes off Arthur.

Arthur threw a punch at Kyan, stepping forward with a growl. Kyan saw it from the corner of his eye too late, copping the punch to his cheekbone. He touched his face, looking at Arthur.

"You just felt my full power, you bastard," Arthur glared at him.

Kyan's eyes went dark, and he bunched his fists hard. He swung one into Arthur's side, the punch hitting him like a sledgehammer. A blinding pain shot through his nose with a crack as Kyan headbutted him and made Arthur stumble, collapsing onto the floor with a groan after a hit to the temple.

"That didn't sound pleasant," Peter said, quirking his mouth. Maria's eyes lit in worry, her face still a mask of annoyance.

"Headache," Tristan winced.

Arthur rolled over in pain and held his nose, blood pouring down his face onto the ground beside him. Arthur glared up at Kyan standing over him, his teeth bared. Blood flowed over his teeth, the metallic taste strong in his mouth.

Kyan frowned down at him. "And *that* was my full power," Kyan spat. His cheek was blooming a deep red, and his eye started to swell.

"Cocky bastard," Arthur growled.

"Somebody tell me why Arthur Pendragon is back in my training hall," Marlon growled, standing outside the box.

"I couldn't tell you," Peter sighed, looking at him. "I came out here just as they started throwing hands."

"He's training, obviously," Tristan chimed in.

Marlon ignored Tristan, standing over Arthur with a glower. "I get pulled out of training the younger boys just to find the old King's son getting beaten yet again?" he growled. "When will you learn, boy, that you can't fight?"

Kyan chuckled, walking out of the box in victory and spitting at Arthur's feet as he walked to the far wall with the other trainees.

"You send your trainees to teach me instead of showing me yourself; how about you show me how to fight then? Since you're the trainer, after all, or was that just a lie you told me?" Arthur growled, standing up from the floor and spitting blood.

"You can't expect to be thrown into a pride of lions and come out of it best off," Marlon frowned. "Patience with little steps is what you need."

"Maybe if you taught me how to fight, then you wouldn't have to babysit me," Arthur sniffed, looking up at him with a clenched jaw.

"You will be taught what you need to learn when you are ready to do so."

"Why not give me the chance now?" Arthur asked, pressing him.

Marlon frowned down at him. "Because you're too busy with your head in the clouds to see what you're missing," he growled.

"A crown? A magical sword?" Arthur asked sarcastically, narrowing his eyes at him. "Thanks for the obvious information. If you know where to find either, a hint would be great. Or were you talking about the level of sarcasm and attitude you and the rest of your trainees have, 'cause I'm almost certain you've pulled that one right out of your-"

Marlon's hand slapped him across his head sharply, the impact stinging. Arthur flinched in surprise, touching his temple and blinking rapidly. *Um, oww!*

"What was that for?" Arthur asked with disbelief, turning back to him with widened eyes.

"To smack the arrogance out of you that you're throwing at the world like it's rice at a wedding ceremony," he snapped.

"Like father, like son, right?" Arthur growled, his shoulders squaring.

"Your father was the polar opposite of what I see before me. The man I knew had common sense with what challenges he could face without major consequences; he had *respect*. I wouldn't have expected his son to become this worm of a boy."

"You have my uncle to thank for that part," Arthur said.

"Your uncle doesn't influence your choices to resort to this attitude. You *chose* to be like this," Marlon glared at him.

Arthur scowled at him bitterly, rubbing his head. *You don't know what I've had to live through, so don't tell me he didn't do anything to me.* He looked over at Tristan and

Maria - Tristan sat pale on the seat, his hand resting on the bag of armour. Maria stared at the ground, her face impassive. How she'd reacted earlier - she'd looked away then, too. Was he really that much of a tool?

"Sure," Arthur said quietly.

"So pull your head in, boy. You've got a long way to go before you make your mark, but Gods help me, if this attitude keeps up, then Londinium's doomed," Marlon sighed, squeezing the bridge of his nose.

Arthur glowered at Marlon. "I don't understand how I'm destined to be someone I know I'm not."

Marlon lowered his hand from his face. "How do you know you're not that man if you haven't lived to see the day it comes to light?"

"Are you always this good with speeches? Cause you're kind of cheesy with the inspiration," Arthur said, his mouth turning up in a sly smirk.

Marlon's lips twitched. "I was a motivational speaker once," he said. "And now I'm a trainer. It's what I'm meant to do."

Arthur smiled faintly. He supposed it was only a matter of time before someone cuffed him one around the ear and told him what for. Not that he appreciated being hit in the melon.

Maybe it was because he knew Marlon knew his father, maybe because of the brash new way he's being treated by the trainer, but either way…

This time, he'll put his head in the game. He had to, for his father's sake. And his own.

"Have you fought in a while, Marlon?" Arthur asked curiously.

Marlon's face darkened slightly. "On the battlefield, no," he muttered.

"I meant in general," Arthur corrected.

"Almost every day," he said, looking at him. "Training involves fighting, as you can see."

"I've got a sword," Arthur said, nodding over to his bag.
Marlon frowned. "What sword?"

"This one!" Tristan said, holding the scabbard in the air.
Arthur looked over at Tristan, beckoning him to come over.

"Found it a few weeks ago," Arthur said, watching
Tristan. He handed it to Arthur with a dramatic bow,
humming trumpet noises as he held it up to him. "My
liege," he said with a thick accent.

"Thank you, Sir Tristan," Arthur said, taking the sword
from his hands. Tristan grinned, sitting cross-legged on the
floor. Arthur unsheathed the blade from the scabbard,
holding it in front of him for Marlon to see.

Marlon froze on the spot. "You… you found the crate,"
he whispered.

Arthur looked at him, slightly confused. "Is everything
okay?" he asked. *He knew about the crate?*

Marlon's breath shuddered, his eyes trailing the sword's
runes, the blood draining from his face. "Benjamin, you old
tool," he muttered softly.

"It doesn't look all that *magical* if you ask me," Peter
said, watching the exchange from behind Tristan.

Tristan frowned at him over his shoulder.  "You're such
a buzz kill," he protested.

"What's so important about this sword?" Arthur asked,
inspecting the runes.

"That sword," Marlon said softly, "is the carbon copy of
Excalibur."

"Excalibur?" Arthur echoed.

"The magical sword Peter rolls his eyes about," Maria
said, walking over to them.

"What magical enchantments does it have?" Arthur
asked, looking up at Marlon.

"This one here?" he asked.

Arthur nodded. "This one in particular."

Marlon looked around the hall at the trainees standing
around, their attention stuck on the conversation. "Leave,"

he boomed. "The break rooms are open; get your own food from the kitchen if you have to."

The trainees peeled off towards the doors and down the hallway quickly, mutters of curiosity flicking between them. Marlon looked back at the sword once they'd cleared out and said simply, "None."

"Oh," Arthur frowned. "Well, that's… exciting." *Underwhelming, even.*

"The sword doesn't have magic?" Maria questioned, eyes lit in confusion.

"This one doesn't," Marlon repeated. "It was created to be a stand-in more than a magical weapon, but it will still do the same damage as a normal sword."

"What about the *real* sword?" Arthur asked, looking at the sword in his hands.

"The real one has magic, yes."

"Specifics?" Arthur asked.

"Well-"

"It makes the ground tremble beneath the feet of its enemies," Maria interrupted, her eyes glittering. "It's said to make the wielder of the sword, specifically of the Pendragon bloodline, more powerful in battle, the magic in the blade sending pulse waves through the air with each impact, weapons breaking under its might, the runes glowing as bright a blue as the sky. Its magic is a mighty force that takes a long time to master once unlocked and will be the first and last defence in battle," she finished.

"Can anyone lift it?" Arthur asked, looking at Maria curiously.

"Once it's been pulled from the stone it's stuck in, I'm sure it'll be the same weight as a normal sword," she shrugged. "It's just that other people won't be able to use the magic."

"So you're telling me I'm the only one who can pull the sword from the stone?" Arthur asked, his curiosity spiking.

"Unless you have another older sibling or something, then yes," she nodded.

Arthur looked down at the sword, inspecting the runes again. Could it possibly be his destiny to pull the blade from the stone? Where *was* this stone? And did it exist, or was it more of a legend?

*No*. Arthur wouldn't let his mind doubt this one. He couldn't possibly doubt this, especially since the exact duplicate is in his very hands. And Marlon's reaction was too real to be anything else. *Was this the prophecy? The prophecy of the Born King?*

"So let me get this straight," Tristan said from the floor, turning all eyes onto him. "There are two swords."

"Correct," Maria said.

"One of them is magic."

"Yes," Arthur nodded.

"This one," he pointed to the sword, "is *not* magic."

"That's right," Marlon said.

"So… where's the magic one?" he asked, looking up at them.

"Have you been paying attention?" Peter asked, looking down at Tristan in surprise.

"For once," Maria smiled.

"Good on you, buddy, you finally paid attention to something important," Arthur said, smiling at him.

Tristan beamed, grinning. "I do listen, just subjectively," he said. "Or at least that's what Henry said before he left for his vacation."

"Tristan," Arthur said, looking at him with a flat expression. "They aren't going on a *vacation.*"

Tristan looked at him with a frown. "Yes, they are," he protested. "I dared him to so I could have the salads he was leaving. They had the horses ready and everything the next day."

"The horses?" Marlon frowned. "They don't use horses for nothing."

Arthur looked at Marlon, his mouth a thin line. "Ergott's sent the Knights to attack Ariendal at Catarina," he said.

"He's *what?*" Maria, Marlon and Peter asked in combined surprise.

"The Barons are now guarding Camelot," Arthur said.

"There's no Knights?!" Marlon asked in outrage.

"I couldn't see any in the castle," Arthur shrugged. "Ergott's using the Barons as the protectors of Camelot. I caught them negotiating about the attack on Ariendal a few weeks back, and they were sent two days later. They were as enthusiastic about going as you'd expect," Arthur explained, his eyes flicking between the group.

"Ergott left his castle unprotected by proper men and gave it to Jackseye of all people," Marlon frowned, shaking his head in disgust. "All for what? There's been no word of harm against the Kingdom."

"Surprising, I know," Arthur sighed. "Bit of a poor decision by the so-called Great King Ergott."

"No wonder he's disliked by the people of Londinium," Peter chimed in. "All they ever talk about is his ambitions for his own personal reasons."

"And he's proven that theory by sending our protectors and leaving us with madmen," Arthur said, crossing his arms over each other.

"Surely he's not *that* foolish," he growled.

Arthur turned to Peter, shrugging. "He seems to think himself intelligent," he rolled his eyes.

"He's up to something," Maria muttered.

"Without a doubt," Arthur agreed.

Voices surged from outside, blaring like trumpets in the air. Arthur turned to the door, the others following his line of sight. Suddenly, loud knocking echoed from the front entrance, thundering within the hallway.

"Open up, private inspection now," the voice barked.

Arthur looked over at Marlon. "Friends?"

"Them again?" Peter asked, looking at Marlon.

"What do they want this time?" Marlon sighed. Tristan stood up from the floor, moving out of the way of his hulking form before he got trampled.

"We need to get you out of here now," Peter said to Arthur.

Without warning, the door burst open with a thunderous bang, splinters of wood scattering all through the hallway. Arthur jumped, snapping his head over to the door. Barons flooded through the hallway into the training hall, spreading around in search. A slim figure strode out of the hallway, his black hood adorned with purple embroidery of a higher quality than the other Barons.

"Sorry about that mess," he said, stepping over shards of wood. "We promise to clean up once we're done with the inspection." The black mask covering his face was different from the others, the whorls filled in with gold and purple pigments, tiny jewels adorning the under eyes.

"I told Jackseye your kind were not to come back here," Marlon barked.

"Calm yourself, tool," the Baron said, flicking his violet eyes over to Arthur. "He's the one we're after."

"Yeah?" Maria challenged. "And what for? He hasn't done anything wrong!"

"My King demands he returns to the castle this instant," he shrugged, striding over to Arthur.

"Don't you lay a hand on me," Arthur sniped.

"Or you'll regret it," Tristan growled, moving next to Arthur, his shoulders square.

The Baron scoffed, looking at Tristan up and down. "What are you going to do, boy?"

"Want to test it and find out?" Tristan scowled.

"I don't want anything to do with you, peasant. Arthur is to return to the castle this instant," he spat.

"He's not going anywhere, Voss," Marlon glared at him, stepping in front of him. "Not while he's in my hall."

Arthur looked at Marlon, questioning how he knew the Baron by name.

"Have you taken it upon yourself to care for the boy?" Voss asked. Arthur looked at Marlon.

"Anyone who enters my training hall to become a Knight is under my protection," he gritted his teeth. "And many others will agree that I'm not the only one who would protect them."

"You really think he could be a Knight?" Voss asked, a smirk laced through his voice.

"Wanna find out?" Arthur challenged. *Another one of these damn higher Barons.* What was this one's agenda? And where was Jackseye skulking if he wasn't here?

"What makes you think he can't be one?" Maria growled.

"Take the King's word," Voss said, looking down at her. "You should start believing in your King more often."

"Everyone in Londinium knows that his words are false," Arthur glared at him. "You Barons have no right to be here."

"Especially when all you do is hurt people," Tristan growled. "That's not cool."

"That's called discipline, you idiot," Voss hissed at him.

"Disciplining the poor Londinium citizens, is that your way of bringing order to an already falling apart city?" Arthur protested. "Because all it's doing is tearing it up more, and none of you see it."

"What's your King's plan?" Marlon spat. "Take away the strong to maim the weak?"

"None of your concern," Voss growled.

"It's *all* my concern! I train men to serve the Kingdom; I *deserve* to have an answer for these foolish notions! I deserve to know why the new Knights with no experience were shipped off to fight a battle no one can win!"

"Then why aren't you there with them?" Voss asked, smirking at Marlon.

Marlon's eyes flashed with hate. "You know why," he growled.

"Do *they* know?" Voss asked, pointing at the rest of the group.

Arthur looked at Marlon, his mind turning over the conversation he'd overheard. "What's he talking about?"

"Know what?" Peter spat.

"So they don't know," Voss drawled. The Barons forced their way through into the locked doorways, startled yelps of protest sounding around them. Marlon looked around at them, eyes lit in worry.

"Marlon?" Arthur asked, looking at him in concern.

"It's not important," he said stiffly. "You're just trying to make it seem like it."

"Tell them," Voss pushed. "If it's not so important, it won't matter, will it?"

Arthur stared at Marlon, his suspicions confirmed. Something was amiss, and from what he'd heard when Jackseye was here, Arthur was sure it wasn't a coincidence.

Marlon gritted his teeth, his jaw tight. Peter looked at him in confusion, a scowl creasing his brow. "What is he on about, Marlon?" he demanded. "You're just a trainer, aren't you?"

The trainees growled and yelled at the Barons as they forced them all out to the hall, some being dragged. Arthur watched in horror, his eyebrows furrowing in anger.

Kyan shoved one off of him as they pulled him out of the doorway, more of them grabbing him as he struggled, protesting against them.

"Go on," Voss insisted. "You've got your trainees here to hear who you really are," he smirked.

Marlon growled and looked at Arthur. "I knew your father a lot better than you think," he said, turning to face them all.

"How?" Arthur asked. Tristan and Maria looked at each other in confusion. It seemed no one had any clue as to what he meant.

Marlon sighed in frustration and looked at his trainees surrounded by the Barons. "All of you have known me long enough to believe the stories I've told of the Roundtable, yes?" he asked them.

They nodded, a few murmurs flitting through them.

"They weren't made-up stories," he shook his head. "They weren't tales of sacrifice, or bravery, or righteousness." He looked back at Arthur, his face dead serious. "They were memories."

Surprised gasps popped up from the trainees, eyes wide as saucers stared at him. Peter looked at Arthur with a confused frown, then back at Marlon, disbelief glinting in his eyes.

"Did you fight by my father's side?" Arthur asked, looking at him in curiosity.

"I did," he admitted. "And more than once."

Arthur baulked, looking at Marlon carefully. "When did you?" he asked.

Marlon looked at the sword in Arthur's hands, his eyes glazed. "The last battle was eighteen years ago," he muttered. "In the forest just outside the Darklands."

Arthur's heart skipped a beat, the blood draining from his face. *Eighteen years ago...*

"But that would mean you were there when..." Maria's eyes widened as Marlon looked at her solemnly. Arthur's world stopped, the hall slowing down around him as it processed through his mind.

*He was there when my father was killed.*

Arthur looked down to the floor. "You were there when he... died."

"You lied to your trainees, *Marlon*," Voss drawled, circling the group. "I wonder what they must be thinking now... let's ask one." He turned to one of the Barons, gesturing to him to bring an onlooker over. The Baron dragged the girl over roughly, gripping her by the arm. She cursed at him, trying to fight him off of her before another Baron grabbed her other arm, making her kneel in front of Voss.

Voss crouched down in front of the girl, removing his face mask to reveal a rugged face, his teeth stained yellow and purple ink smeared across his cheekbones up to the piercings in his brow. His black hair was cut short on the sides, with a long strip of hair left along the middle of his head brushed back, fussed by the hood. "What's your name, sweetheart?" he asked, his voice poisoned with honey. She squirmed away from him, her face wrinkled at his sour breath.

"Get back away from her," Marlon commanded, grabbing his shoulder roughly.

Voss smirked up at Marlon, a dagger appearing in his hand that slashed across his arm. Arthur's eyes widened as Marlon barked curses, a few Barons grabbing him and pulling him away. Marlon fought against them, shoving them back.

"Wouldn't it be a shame if this girl's blood was painted on your walls?" Voss asked, smirking at Marlon before turning back to the girl.

Tristan's eyes lit in worry, and he moved towards the girl. "Don't hurt her," he said sternly. She looked at him, her eyes wide and fearful.

The two Barons behind Tristan grabbed him tightly, pulling him back away from the girl. He snarled at them, reefing at their grip viciously. Arthur narrowed his eyes, the sword gripped in his hands firmly.

"You spill her blood, and I'll kill you," Tristan roared. "She doesn't deserve this!"

"So, what is your name, girl?" Voss asked, twirling the dagger in his hand, Marlon's blood flicking off it.

She watched the blade dance in the air, her breathing ragged. "Lucy," she breathed.

"Lucy," Voss repeated, tasting the name slowly. He reached down to grip her hair roughly, scuffing the chestnut locks and making her wince. "Tell me, Lucy, why did you want to become a Knight? Especially under the care of Xavier Marlon," Voss turned to him with raised brows. "Or at least that's who he says he is."

"She's not training," Tristan barked, pulling an arm free and launching his elbow into a Baron holding him. The Baron punched him in return, Tristan doubling over in pain with a groan.

Voss looked at Tristan with a raised brow. "So you say?"

Arthur looked at the Barons around him, one of them grabbing the sword from his grip with a fight. He glared at the Baron, the black mask revealing no emotion, more hands catching his elbows and holding him in place.

Arthur narrowed his eyes with a growl. How were they going to get out of this wretched mess of a situation? *These pesky Barons and their black masks.* He gritted his teeth in anger. "Watch it," he growled deeply. The Baron snorted at him.

"She's a helper," Tristan hissed, half crouched over. "She works here in the kitchens."

"Let her go!" Peter yelled, thrashing in the Baron's grip.

"You all care so much about a *peasant*?" Voss mocked. "No wonder why you all belong in brothels."

Kyan snarled in outrage at him, barking obscenities at the Barons. Maria stood quietly in the Black Guards' grip, her head bowed and her lips moving quietly. Arthur watched her in interest, blinking at her.

"Maria," Arthur whispered. She didn't look up, her lips not pausing. *Is she praying?* Arthur's eyebrows creased.

"Don't forget you were once a commoner, Urhen," Marlon sniped, stilling in his struggles.

"I learnt etiquette and took a better path in life. *You* can't seem to move on from Knights or the royal influence," Voss said, standing up from the ground.

"Is that what your brother did, too?" Marlon snorted.

"We don't speak of him," Voss growled, standing close to Marlon, his eyes glinting dangerously.

"Is that because he chose to be who he wanted? Or because you can't accept the fact he knows what's best?"

Voss reeled his arm back, clenching his hand into a fist, and threw it into Marlon's ribcage. Marlon buckled slightly, leaning into his hand with a huff of breath.

"We. Don't. Speak. Of. Him," Voss repeated, his voice stronger than venom.

Maria tilted her head up, her eyes still closed, and her lips slightly parted. Arthur watched her carefully with concern and curiosity.

Marlon looked at Voss from beneath lowered brows, his body relaxing slowly. "You still don't know how to punch properly," he commented.

"Possibly," Voss agreed. "But I know how to break your spirit. Stand her up."

Tristan thrashed in the Baron's hold, snarling at them. They pulled Lucy to her feet, her brown eyes wide and her breathing too fast. Voss walked over to her, the dagger gripped firmly in his hand.

"One slice to the throat can leave a person bleeding for several seconds," Voss said, springing the dagger up against her throat, holding the back of her head with his free hand. "I wonder how long your throat will bleed?"

Maria's eyes flew open, and Arthur took a double look; evergreen eyes were replaced by full amber, her pupils swollen into a large circle. He blinked in surprise, confused as to how her eyes looked like an-

"Eagle!" one of the Barons called out, a scuffle moving behind him. Arthur turned around to face the far window, the glass pane smashed to pieces as the giant bird ploughed into the hall. It flew towards the Baron that called out, hooking its talons viciously into his mask, shredding it from his face with a shriek. The Baron screamed, trying to bat it away as it soared around the room.

"Kill the bird!" Voss commanded. The Barons let the trainees fall from their minds, chasing after the bird with their weapons raised, the eagle swooping down to gouge their arms deeply, blood spraying across the hall. The trainees scattered, barging down Barons as they ran towards the doors, fighting their way out.

While the Barons were distracted by the eagle, Arthur launched his head into the Baron behind him with a sickening crack, landing an elbow into the other, spinning to knee his crotch and watching him drop to the ground. Free of their holds, Arthur turned to the one he headbutted, his sword on the ground beside him. Arthur bent down, picking up the blade from the floor, looking at the Baron wryly.

"Thanks for holding it, lad," Arthur smirked, twirling it in his hand.

Tristan stomped his heel down on his Baron's foot, swinging his arm up into their mask, the Guard's head whipping back and falling to the ground. The other Baron gripped his shoulder, and Tristan pivoted, pummeling him in the stomach with unmatched force. The Baron dropped like a stone beside the other.

"You got a crush, Tristan?" Arthur asked, looking at him from a few feet away. Tristan looked at him with a frown for a moment before launching himself at the guards holding Lucy.

*One hundred per cent he does.* Arthur grinned, then caught something in the corner of his eye, swinging the sword up in defence. A Baron lashed at Arthur violently with a thin-edged sword, pushing Arthur back away from the sparring boxes. Arthur swung the sword in front of him, barely blocking a savage upper blow aimed at his chest.

The Baron kept shoving him back, the clash of swords getting too fast to parry-

The Baron paused his attack, his head jerking to the side before collapsing to the floor. Peter stood in the empty space behind the Baron, his pommel raised in his grip, looking at Arthur. "We need to get you out of here *again*," he growled.

"Tristan! Maria! With me!" Arthur commanded, nodding at Peter for his help.

Tristan kicked away the last Baron and grabbed Lucy's arm gently, pulling her along with him towards Arthur. Arthur and Peter rushed to the hallway, awaiting their arrival at the entrance.

"Where's Maria?" Tristan asked, panting as he stopped beside them.

"For the Gods sake, wait here," Arthur growled, rushing back out to the rivalry.

The hall was a bundle of chaos, Barons and trainees locked in an intense battle, more than a few bodies littering the floor. Arthur searched the cluster for any sign of Maria, nothing standing out.

"Maria!" he yelled, defending himself from a few incoming blows from Barons, slicing them down with some struggle.

Golden hair caught his attention, and he turned to see Maria running towards him, her eyes still eagle-like.

"You got a death wish, do you?" he asked, panting heavily.

She blinked, and the familiar green eyes came back, realisation glinting in them as she looked around. "Holy cow," she cursed.

"Since when could you control eagles?" he questioned, giving her a look.

"Doesn't matter, let's get out of here," she said, looking towards the hallway.

"Follow me, and stay close," Arthur said, running in front of her with the sword at the ready. She ran after him, dodging a few wild swings from the fight surrounding them. Kyan looked over at them running and pummelled a Baron once more, standing up and joining them, his arm bleeding.

Arthur led them over to the others, standing aside for them to go in first. They squeezed past him, looking at one another with startled looks.

"Where's Marlon?" Peter asked, looking around the hall for his familiar figure.

"He's fighting Voss," Kyan panted through his teeth, gripping his injured arm.

"I'm not leaving without him," Peter said, panting.

"He can find his own way out; there's no way we can pull him out of that," Kyan protested.

"You guys go, I'll wait for him," Peter insisted.

"Peter, get your ass moving down the hallway," Arthur commanded.

"I'm not leaving him!" Peter scowled at Arthur.

"We don't have time to argue! Move!" Arthur barked back.

Tristan moved down the hallway quickly, seemingly determined. "I know of a way out," he said.

"You, of all people, know a way out?" Kyan asked incredulously, following him.

"Yeah, it's called *the front door*," Tristan said with his hands raised, his fingers twiddling.

Peter shook his head and went to shove past Arthur, who stood in his way with his hand on his chest.

"Peter, we don't have time," Arthur growled. "I'd go back for him too if I could-"

Shouts boomed from behind them, Barons running towards them with their weapons drawn. Maria's eyes widened, and she shoved Arthur and Peter forward. "Go, just go!" she cried.

Peter's eyes widened and he spun around, pelting after Tristan quickly, Arthur hot on his tail with Maria. Arthur looked back, seeing an array of Black Cloaks following their path, gaining closer.

On one of the walls, sconces with lit torches sat dormant within reach, buckets of burnt coals hanging beneath glowing red. Immediately, Arthur had an idea. He stopped dead in the tracks behind the group, gripping the sword tightly in his hands. He waited for the Barons to gain closer, narrowing his eyes at them as they rushed to him.

Maria turned around to see him stopped, pausing her run. "Arthur!" she called him. He ignored her, watching the Barons as he adjusted his grip on the sword.

"Get closer," he murmured to himself.

"Move it, you tool!" she yelled at him.

The Barons came a few feet away from Arthur, their yells echoing through the hallway. Arthur raised the sword above his head, hitting his blade against the two torch buckets in the hallway, sending a massive spray of hot coals straight towards them. Arthur turned away and covered his eyes, glaring at the hot air in front of him. The Barons hissed in pain, the burning coals scattering over them, searing through their cloaks into their under armour.

Arthur grinned and lowered his sword, spinning around and sprinting after the others. Maria looked at him incredulously, running alongside him. "You're crazy," she scolded.

"I know," Arthur agreed. "But it paid off."

Tristan flung the door open the wrong way, the hinges creaking and snapping off the door frame. His eyebrows flicked up at the door cascading down the stairs. "Whoopsies," he murmured, laughing nervously.

"What did you do?" Arthur asked, stopping beside him, panting heavily.

"He… broke the door," Lucy said with wide eyes.

"Really? Now of all times you decide to break our only exit?" Arthur scowled at him.

"At least it's open," Tristan shrugged and moved out of the building.

"That's not your doing," Peter said, looking at the splinters across the ground. "You just happened to break off the rest of the door from the Baron's entrance."

"Don't steal my thunder," Tristan frowned at him from outside.

Arthur followed behind him, stepping out into the street grounds and looking back at the others. Arthur held his hand out gently to Lucy, his face soft.

"Down you get," he said with a small smile. She looked at him nervously and took his hand, her skin smooth, and walked down the stairs.

Arthur turned to Maria and gestured his hand out to her. "You too."

"You don't get to steal *all* of the girls from this area, Arthur," Kyan smirked, swooping in to take Maria's arm and lead her down.

Arthur straightened, scowling at Kyan. "What a tool," he muttered to himself.

Peter shoved the remainder of the door back in place, wedging it in an awkward spot. "That should hopefully stop them for a moment," he nodded to the door and jumped down the stairs.

Arthur jumped off the steps, twirling the sword in his hand as he landed. "What were they talking about with Marlon?"

Lucy blinked at Arthur, observing the sword, a glint of - *wait, is that admiration?* - in her eyes.

"Marlon never said anything about those stories being memories," Kyan said, looking back at Arthur.

"It's odd, but at the same time," Tristan shrugged, moving closer to Lucy, "it explains why he went into so much detail."

"Jonathan," Arthur pondered. "Jackseye called him by that name the last time I was here," Arthur's eyes furrowed.

Peter snapped his head to Arthur, his eyes locked on him. "What did you just say?" he said intensely.

Arthur looked up at him, his eyebrows creasing. "The leader of the Barons called Marlon by that name weeks ago."

"Jonathan Gawain," Kyan breathed, looking at Peter with wide eyes. Tristan and Maria shared the same expression, Lucy covering her mouth in shock.

Arthur looked at them in puzzlement, unsure of their shared look. "The name is significant because?"

"Marlon would tell stories of Sir Gawain all the time," Peter breathed, his jaw slack. "He always had a tale about him. I thought he was just a relative of his or something and figured that's how he knew, but now…"

"It all makes sense," Kyan touched his forehead with a hand, his eyes wide.

"A few weeks back, another man saved us from Leonard and his street gang, too," Arthur recalled. "His name was Jameson Galahad."

"*Sir* Jameson Galahad," Maria corrected, running her hand through her hair.

"*The* Sir Jameson Galahad?!" Peter asked.

Arthur looked at Peter, raising an eyebrow. "And *he's* relevant because?"

"Do you know nothing of Knight history? Sir Jameson Galahad and Sir Jonathan Gawain were members of your father's Roundtable," Peter said, starstruck.

Arthur's face dropped, his heart skipping a beat. "They were Knights of the Roundtable?"

"This whole time, we were being trained by an ex-Roundtable Knight?!" Kyan laughed incredulously, looking around the alleyway. "No *wonder* they were pumping out Knights like a production line!"

The blockade behind them shifted, the sound of bashing wood splitting the air. They turned and looked at the door fragment, the wood dislodging dangerously.

"Time to go," Tristan said quickly, turning to Lucy and leading her down the alleyway at a run.

"Go! Now!" Arthur commanded, leading them further down the alleyway. They all ran further down the alleys of Londinium, the streets still void of any citizens. The wood splintered and scattered from the last of the door, Barons filing over it carelessly as they gave chase.

Tristan darted around the corner, pausing for a second with Lucy. "Run home, don't stop until you get in the door," he said gently to her.

"What about you?" she stammered, looking up at him with wide eyes.

Arthur looked back at Tristan, pausing in his tracks. "Tristan!"

Tristan looked at Arthur, then back at her. "I'll be okay, just go."

Lucy nodded and glanced down the alleyway, running as fast as she could. Tristan watched her go, then sprinted after Arthur. Arthur raced beside Tristan, looking back at the Barons for a split second.

The Barons gained closer, their black capes flapping in the wind behind them. They split up down multiple alleyways, commands being thrown across to different men. Three of them shimmied up onto the roofs of the buildings, and Arthur looked up at them, watching them run along the gutters like cats.

Tristan cursed, and Arthur felt a sharp tug on his arm. He spun back around in alarm to see a wall in front of him, his body jerking awkwardly from Tristan's tug. His footing stumbled for a moment, and Arthur collided against the wall, his head hitting it hard.

Arthur's vision swam, and he shook his head, stumbling after Tristan.

"Thanks for that!" Arthur growled, rubbing his head.

"It's better than running full pelt into it!" Tristan called back.

"I basically did!" Arthur said, running back up to him at full pace.

"Stop looking at the pigeons and run straight, then, you tool!"

"Head down the left turn two blocks from here!" Arthur commanded.

Tristan looked at him with a grin. "Ah, the old manoeuvre, eh?"

"Let's test the tools out," Arthur grinned back.

"Alrighty, here we go," Tristan whooped, running after Maria and the others. Arthur sprinted at an equal pace a few feet beside him, the both of them overtaking the group. Peter looked at them in astonishment, slowing back in shock.

"Maria, lead them back to my place; take the long way," Tristan shouted to her.

"You got it," she called back and skidded to a slower pace, doubling back down an alleyway to her left, Kyan and Peter following after her hesitantly.

Arthur gripped the sword tighter, adrenaline surging through his body. Tristan huffed as he ran and looked at him with a nod to the left. Arthur nodded back, and as the Barons split off to chase after Maria and the others, Tristan and Arthur split apart, darting down opposite alleyways.

The Barons paused for a moment, looking at them separately before darting after Arthur, their voices echoing across the brick homes.

Arthur looked back at them, scowling. "Of course you follow me, you big bastards," he bit, running faster.

The alleyway flew under his feet, eating up the cobblestones with ease, his boots clacking harshly. Shutters on windows flew open, curious eyes peering out at the disturbance down the way.

Arthur darted to the right, gripping a pole to swing around faster. The Barons reeled back, taking time to turn back to the alleyway. Arthur grinned and spotted a carriage filled with barrels and crates beside a building.

"Brilliant," he muttered, darting over to the carriage. The Barons watched him as he sprung up onto the back of it, vaulting onto higher crates and jumping up to grip the ledge of a roof, pulling himself up and over the shingles.

Arthur looked down at them with a grin. "Bet you can't climb up here without a carriage at your disposal," he teased. The Barons jumped up onto the carriage, and Arthur moved to the far end of the roof. He picked up a stick inside the gutter connected to a rope hidden down the drainpipe and pulled it.

A snap sounded from the alley below, and the Barons yelped as the cart jolted beneath them. The wooden pegs at the front of the carriage pulled loose from the rope, the wheels rolling down the hill and sending the carriage toppling down the alleyway, Barons scattering out of the way of the boxes.

"And that is called *Seasoned Oak,*" Arthur grinned and bowed to them, turning and making his way towards the centre of the roof, a ladder leading down inside an old chimney. Arthur squeezed down it, black soot covering him from head to toe as he pushed out of the hearth.

He looked at the soot in disgust, brushing it off his jacket half-heartedly. "I always forget about this part," he muttered to himself.

He made his way through the house down a set of stairs, lifting a trapdoor down into a secret tunnel. Jumping down, he felt around in the dark for the table with the torches, his hand fumbling the handle before he grabbed it, scraping it across the bricks to light it on fire. He jogged his way down the tunnels, burrowed-out stone edges prodding his boot soles sharply.

Arthur and Tristan had accidentally found these tunnels the same way Arthur came in. They were exploring the abandoned house as children no older than twelve, not knowing what to expect, and ended up finding the trapdoor. Ever since, they'd mapped out the tunnel's directions by memory, leaving torches like the one in Arthur's hand at convenient spots throughout.

Arthur figured they were old spy tunnels from years and years ago or some sort of servant system. Either way, he knew where to go.

A familiar gait echoed down the tunnel, a light in the distance illuminating Tristan's figure. Arthur smirked and made his way to him, dodging the muddy puddles littering the ground.

"That was easy to do," Arthur said with a smile.

"Fools them every single time, no doubt," Tristan grinned.

"I'd say we've got a high chance we've lost them in the confusion," Arthur said, walking with Tristan down the tunnel.

"They shouldn't be able to tell where we've gone," Tristan said, walking up a small set of stairs. "Hell, the other guards haven't every other time. They wouldn't know about the tunnels. And besides, if anyone comes down, we'll hear the trap go off."

The trap consisted of a mismatched-sized pile of wooden oak planks; if any of the openings they used to access the tunnels were opened too wide, the trap would set off, dropping a load of wood into the tunnel and making a big enough ruckus to warn them from anywhere in the tunnels. Hence the name "Seasoned Oak".

Arthur followed Tristan up the set of stairs, winding round and round in circles until they'd reached the top. A bucket of water sat at the table with the spare torches, Arthur dunking his torch into it with a loud hiss, Tristan doing the same.

The trapdoor above their heads was outlined in daylight, and no voices came from above. Well, since the Knights were gone, of course there wouldn't be anyone patrolling the High Gates closest to the staircase.

Tristan and Arthur braced their legs on the steps and pushed up in unison, the trapdoor heaving open with a clunk against the wall beside the Castle Gates. Arthur peered his head out, looking around cautiously.

"Anyone out there?" Tristan asked him, slowly peeking his own head up.

The castle courtyard was awfully silent, too eerily deserted. Everyone really was feeling the Knights' absence; the castle wasn't the same.

"All clear," Arthur confirmed, climbing out of the trapdoor and holding it open for Tristan to roll out, the both of them laughing to themselves.

Arthur stood up, closed the trapdoor, and hooked the trap back up promptly. *Better safe than sorry.*

"Alright," Tristan sighed, looking at Arthur. "Where now?"

"To prison," a voice growled to their left. Arthur and Tristan snapped their heads to look at the Baron, more of the Black Guards peeling out from behind him, the few on the closeby roofs pointing crossbow bolts at them. Arthur raised his hands with Tristan, backing up towards the Gates, their eyes wide.

The sun glared in Arthur's eyes, squinting at the Barons on the roof. He was done for now; he had no way out of this one. Somehow, they'd known about the tunnels and exactly where they'd come out, but how? He'd been sure to keep it a secret; even Tristan knew not to tell anyone about them…

Where was Maria? Did she make it back to Tristan's house with Peter and Kyan? Arthur frowned slightly. He wouldn't mind if Kyan got lost along the way, but if they'd gotten ahold of her, then they were in deeper trouble than what he and Tristan already were in.

"Taking us back to my uncle, are you? You know he'll do nothing about it like he always does," Arthur bluffed, looking back at the Barons.

"You're at the top step of the castle. It'll be an easier trip than the last time," the Baron replied with a laugh that echoed through the rest of them.

"Go on, drag me inside if it'll fulfil your ego," Arthur smirked to himself. Something blocked the sun faintly, and he sighed inwardly, blinking the light out of his eyes, looking at the smoke crossing the sky-

*Hold on a minute.* Arthur looked more closely, trailing the smoke in the distance to its source.

"The hell is that?" he asked, squinting his eyes at the horizon.

The Barons followed Arthur's eyes, their yellow eyes dilating. The smoke became thicker from a distance, and a massive ball of flame erupted into the air, a loud explosion reaching his ears.

Arthur's eyes widened in realisation.

*That was Catarina.*

# *Chapter 11: Chaos & Flames*

Everything was pitch black, the world spinning around him in circles like he was falling through the sky, a low ringing noise piercing his eardrums. His body was numb, the world cold and distant. *Where am I?*

Samqueel's eyes cracked open, blinking at the harsh light glaring at him from above, shooting pain lancing through his skull. His hearing slowly returned to him, the world muffled like his head was underwater. Sam groaned, moving his head slightly and squeezing his eyes shut. Something was wet under his face, rough and sharp against his skin. Opening his eyes again, he looked at the fuzzy world, seeing it in double vision.

*Mud.* It was mud under his face. And his hands, he realised, moving his fingers along the ground. He moved around slowly, the numbness giving way to pain. *Pain, pain, pain,* his body seemed to throb, his side screaming with it. He lifted his head, blinking the mud from his eye, shifting to look at the blood pouring through the tear in his chainmail. "Shit," he cursed, his breathing bated.

His vision cleared, and he dragged his eyes across the battlefield; fire sprung up in patches alongside the-

*Bodies.* Sam's heart skipped a beat, looking around in horror at the piles of young Knights strewn across the ground, their armour glinting dully in the sun, coated in ash and mud.

His breath shook. *What happened?* The battle was going their way; they were pushing forward at a better pace than he would've expected…

His stomach sank, and he looked up at the destroyed castle ruins to his right. *The towers.*

A soft, pained groan whispered beside him; his ears started to clear further, and he shook his head, looking towards the noise. His heart stopped.

His armour was coated in black soot, half of the leather wholly burned off. Blue metal peeked through the mud staining his body, blood running thickly from the wooden splinter wedged through his abdomen. Skin peeled from his arms and face, crimson glistening in the sun. The man coughed, blood dripping from his mouth in rivers.

"Reuben," Sam coughed, his voice cracked and hoarse. Smoke blurred his vision once more, but he ignored it, digging his fingers deep into the mud. Pain barked at him from his side as he pulled himself across the gap between them, his heart racing too fast. *No, no, no, no, no, please, no, not Ben!*

Reuben shivered in pain with gasping breaths, his head turning to face him.

"Ben," Samqueel cried out, trying to move his numb legs. *Damn it,* move, *you tool!*

"S...Sam," his weak voice called back, shuttering with every breath.

He reached his side, his ribcage screaming in agony as he sat up on his legs, willing himself to stay upright as he kneeled beside Reuben, his eyes wide. Reuben looked up at Samqueel, his mudstained face pained and tired.

Sam's hands trembled, staring at the plank pierced through his friend. His blood was spilled in a puddle around him, Sam's legs seated in it.

"That bastard…" Reuben struggled. "That bastard lied to us…"

It was true. The Barons led them into a death trap. And Sam knew it the whole goddamn time! He should've known this would happen; he *did* know this would happen. And he'd still dragged them into it.

"I'm sorry, Ben," he choked out, his voice thick with emotion. "I'm so sorry."

"Promise me... Sam," Reuben said quietly.

"Promise what?" he asked, looking at his torn face. It killed him to see his friend like this, lying broken like a child's toy in the dirt. His jaw tightened hard enough that it ached.

"You kill that son-of-a-bitch... no matter what," Reuben said sharply, gripping Sam's forearm tightly as he coughed.

Samqueel's breath staggered, looking at Reuben's hand on his arm. He still had enough strength to get his point across. *Typical Reuben,* he thought, swallowing the lump lodged in his throat.

"She's waiting for you, brother," Sam whispered to him. "It's time to go home."

"I'll give her a hug for you," Reuben's eyes lit faintly in reassurance, and his heart cracked. Never has he had a more loyal friend by his side. Reuben had been there for everything ever since the day he'd saved him in the alleyway. But this time, Sam knew he couldn't save him. "Damn you and your magnetism for wooden planks."

Reuben huffed with a slight smile on his lips. "Something about them, isn't there?" he breathed, blood leaching from his face. Sam's lips turned up in a ghost of a smile, tears springing to his eyes.

He could see Reuben was trying to hold on for him, but Sam could feel his grip getting more and more loose on his arm, his fingers trembling. There was just too much blood on this Gods damned land.

"Brothers, until... the end," Reuben wheezed, his breath getting shallow.

Sam's eyes creased in pain for his friend, and he touched his other hand laid across his chest, gripping it softly. "Brothers," he croaked. "Until the end."

Reuben's face slackened, his head falling back down onto the hardened ground, his eyes unseeing. His chest fell still beneath Sam's hand, the steady beat of his heart fading to nothing. The grip on Sam's arm slipped, his hand falling into the bloodied mud.

Reuben was gone.

*No.* Samqueel's eyes flooded, his grip tightening on Reuben's hand. No, *not Reuben.* His teeth gritted together painfully, his breathing becoming unsteady. His friend lay dead before him, and it was Sam's fault. All of this, every single body laying on the field-

A glint of purple metal struck his eye, and he looked at it sharply, his heart shattering. Joseph lay sprawled not ten feet away from him, his body mutilated and twisted. And beside him laid Brannagh, his bow nothing but fire fuel.

Samqueel swivelled his head around him desperately, trying to find his brothers - Carsen, Natan and Derak behind him, their swords stuck in the ground in front of them; Arkan, the bright green armour everyone picked on him for, speared through the chest into the ground by a metal rod; Karsol, his shield blown to bits around him; Taryn - Sam looked away from him. His black armour was lit in flames, a sight no one would wish to see.

Beside him laid Dominic. *Oh, Dom...* Sam's jaw started to quiver. Ten Black Cloaks lay beside Forlorn, his spear lanced through his chest. Lorsaw's hair shone from beneath a pile of Knights, his sword buried beneath them. Sam's eyes stung with tears, realising what they'd done - their last stand, the protective circle.

They laid down their lives to protect him. Samqueel didn't know if he hated them or loved them for it.

He looked down at Reuben's Commander badge on his shoulder pad, the golden chains broken off and shattered in the mud. *Brothers until the end.* Hot tears flowed onto the mud-stained metal, his body shaking with sobs. "Damn it, you tools," he barked at them. "*I* was meant to keep *you* alive!"

*And now look at what I've done.* Sam's head drooped onto Reuben's chest, the metal cold against his skin as he let his heart break. *Gods be damned.*

His teeth bared in an anguished wail, the cry echoing across the field, sending birds scattering from the untouched trees. He'd cry; for them, he'd mourn. The world be damned, he didn't care if they saw him cry. These boys meant more to him than anything else, and he'd just let them die on his watch.

*"Sam. What are you doing here?"*

His tears flowed hot down his nose, his hand digging into Reuben's chest piece as the memory flashed in his mind.

*"Hey, don't cry," Reuben said to him, kneeling down beside him, the barrel blocking them off from the corner view. "Don't get yourself all red and splotchy."*

*Sam looked up at him, his hand gripping his shattered arm. "It hurts, Ben," he gritted out through his teeth. "I don't know if I can take it anymore."*

Sobs racked through his body, his side becoming unbearable.

*"Can't take any more of what?" Reuben asked, looking down at him.*

"I was never fit to be a Knight," Samqueel whispered against Reuben's chest.

*"Get off your ass, and give them what they have coming to them!" Reuben commanded.*

*Samqueel looked at him, blinking.* "But they're stronger," he whispered painfully. Blood kept leaching through his armour. "I can't fight… when I'm broken."

*"Someone has to finish the fight; is it going to be you? Or them?" Reuben asked.*

Sam's eyes flickered, the words cutting through him just like the first time.

*"You got what it takes, and even if you fall down, only you can pick yourself up off the ground. And even if I'm not there to babysit your ass, I will always have your back 'cause you're my brother."*

Sam's breath shook. *"Brothers until the end,"* he *smirked up at him.*

*"Brothers until the end,"* Reuben grinned.

His bloodstained hand shifted to the ground beneath him, his knees finally moving to slide under him.

*Get off your ass, and give them what they have coming to them.* His feet pushed up, a pained growl escaping through his teeth.

*Only you can pick yourself up off the ground.* His side killed him with pain, but he ignored it as he stumbled to his feet, his balance off.

*Is it going to be you or them?*

Samqueel looked at his men scattered around him, lifting his hand to wipe away the tears on his face, mud smearing across his cheekbone. "It was never until the end," he said to them.

*Samqueel grinned smartly at Reuben, standing up and holding his arm. "It's more like brothers always," he jested.*

"It's always been more than that," he whispered, swallowing the lump in his throat.

The familiar glint of black and silver sat in the mud, Remedy glaring in the sun. He bent to pick it up with a bark of pain, wiping the muck off the hilt and shaking the rest of the blade in the air. The runes on the blade caught the sunlight: the wolf, the tower and the eyes. *Lead, protect, oversee.*

Footsteps sounded around him; Sam turned his head to look toward the noise, straightening his back. Their voices were muffled, covered up by masks. The men marched closer to Samqueel, blood splashing from the ground in puddles as they walked.

"Last of your kind, are you?" one of the men asked.

*Barons.* Sam looked away from them, looking at his brothers in sorrow, his breath steadying. *So this is what it's come down to.*

"Pretty impressive, Commander," he said. "Unfortunately, your survival wasn't a part of the plan."

"I suppose that's too bad," Sam said calmly, turning his eyes to the leader. "Because it's part of mine."

"Surrender now, Commander," The Baron barked. "Ergott would be surprised to see you."

"I agree," he nodded, turning to face them, his sword loose in his hand. "Ergott will be surprised."

The Baron looked at the sword in his hand, looking back up at him and shaking his head. "I wouldn't do that if I was you."

Sam shrugged, his eyes turning dark. "If I'm going to go out, I may as well go out with a bang," he growled and lifted Remedy, twirling it ready to meet them.

The Barons readied themselves, watching Samqueel carefully. Ignoring the pain in his side, he lunged forward, swinging the sword backhanded at the leader of the group, slashing down across his thigh. The Baron groaned loudly, collapsing down onto one knee hard. The other Barons lunged at Sam with their weapons high, slashing wildly at him.

His focus snapped into place, and he ducked beneath the blade of one, swinging his leg around the back of one's knees and thrusting his sword tip into another's stomach. They both dropped to the ground, blood gushing down the sword's blade as he met the other's swing. The leader growled at Samqueel from the ground, a dagger in his hand, standing up slowly.

Sam's rage flared high, his eyes glaring daggers at the Baron he parried. The Baron stumbled back, and one from the ground slashed at his feet. Sam jumped over the blade, landing beside the injured Baron and stabbing him through the heart, stomping on their wrist with a crack.

The leader threw his dagger at Sam, pulling out two more from his back sheaths. A Baron lunged for Sam, and he lanced him through the chest, spinning him around to face the leader, the dagger embedding itself into the Baron's back. He kicked the Baron off his blade and rocketed around to slash the other Black Guard from hip to shoulder, blood spraying across his armour. The Baron dropped to the ground on top of his colleagues, their blood adding to the puddles. The leader charged at Sam, his shoulder barging into his chest roughly, his side barking in protest sharply.

Sam reeled back with a hiss, gripping Remedy tight. The leader slashed Samqueel's shoulder gap with his dagger, followed by a slash to the thigh pad, shoving him to the muddied ground with a grunt.

Sam glared up at him, his shoulder stinging.

"You should've died along with your Legion," the leader snarled.

Metal flashed up at the Baron's arm, a sharp pain ripping through him as the dagger fell to the ground. The leader yelled in pain, reeling back as blood poured out of his forearm, his hand falling to the mud with a thud.

Samqueel rocked back onto his spine and launched both feet into the Baron, making him stumble around uncontrollably. His boots caught on the hand of a fallen Baron, and he tripped to the ground, the mud squelching beneath him.

Samqueel stood back up, wiping away the blood from his shoulder as it beaded through his chain mail, his sword pointed towards the Baron. "It's just your luck that you'll be meeting them at the Gateways," he spat.

"You'll suffer from this! You failed your Knights; you let them die!" The Baron snapped at him.

Sam's nose flared in anger, and he moved the sword aside, launching his iron boot into the Baron's face. The Baron's mask cracked into splinters, his head rocketing back with the force. Purple skin gleamed with blood under the fragments of the mask, and the black hood pulled off to reveal horns like that of a ram on each side of the Baron's head.

Samqueel paused for a moment, staring at the horns. *What's a tiefling doing with the Black Cloaks?*

"A shame, isn't it?" the Baron asked, coughing up blood. "You won't get to see Camelot crumble."

Samqueel scowled coldly at the Baron. "Neither will you," he growled.

The Baron smirked at him, letting out a deep chuckle with a mixture of coughing as he laid his head back in the mud. Samqueel lifted his blade with both hands and stabbed the sword through the tiefling's teeth, blood spraying with its startled cry. The Baron gurgled on his own blood for a moment before his eyes glazed over, his chest falling still.

Reefing the sword out of his head, he shook the black blood off the blade. "Let's see how you deal with the dead down there, shadow dancer," he spat at him.

*Kick his ass back to the Ether for me, Ben.* Sam smiled slightly at the thought and pivoted towards Camelot. The castle sat dormant in the distance, too far away to make anything out.

But Sam felt his stare on him. He glared back hot enough to make sure he felt his, too.

Scouring over the plains on the balcony, King Ergott watched silently, spotting the fires in the distance. He knew the work was done; he could feel that the work had been done, but something troubled him. His headache grew thicker and thicker, his skull pounding painfully with each heartbeat. He tensed, moving his hand over to his pained temple.

Ergott could feel that one of the Knights had survived, and he knew exactly which one.

He opened his eyes, turning around to walk down the hallway, the Black Guards standing on either side of the doorway. Ergott made his way down the hallway to his right, coming back to the staircase leading down deep into the castle below.

His steps echoed loudly as he trotted down the stairs, coming to the platform separate from the quarter. He reached for the door handle, and it suddenly opened by itself. He pulled his hand back from the door with a frown. *Has Vivien somehow escaped?*

The door swung open, and a woman's gasp echoed from behind it, blonde hair glinting in the torchlight. "Ergott," her voice said in shock, her brown eyes wide.

"Rosaline," Ergott froze. "What on Earth are you doing down here?"

Her face flickered in guilt, and she opened the door completely, stepping outside of the chambers. "I-I went exploring, I wanted to know-"

"You know you aren't meant to come down here!" Ergott snapped at her.

Rosaline flinched away from him, her eyes lit in fright. "What's down here that's so important?" she asked, her voice small.

Ergott slammed the door shut, glaring at her. "All Kings have their secrets, Rosaline, and some aren't meant to be seen by others," he snarled.

"I'm your *wife*, Ergott," she protested, moving against the far wall. "If you can't trust me with what's in this chamber, then how can I trust that what you're doing is the right thing?"

"Don't use this against me, woman," Ergott growled deeply, his eyes burning like a flickering light.

Her face paled in fear. "And your eyes," she said. "They've been changing ever since Benjamin passed away."

"Find yourself somewhere safe to hide," Ergott ordered. "The castle won't be safe for a while."

"Why won't it?" she questioned.

"Samqueel has gone rogue," he said, walking back up the stairs.

"Sam? He'd never!" She chased after him up the stairs, hoisting her skirts high enough to not trip over.

"He led his Knights into a battle I told him not to fight, and everyone but him died," Ergott explained.

Rosaline struggled to keep up, her breath fast. "But you ordered him to go and fight Ariendal," she protested.

Ergott stopped, turning his head back to her slowly. "Who told you?"

"I overheard Arthur talking with Enid," she said, pausing her pursuit.

"Arthur…" Ergott growled, narrowing his eyes.

Rosaline stepped close to him, touching his arm. "Is there something going on in the castle? Are we under threat from a neighbouring Kingdom?" she questioned.

Ergott looked down at her, stern and frustrated. "Gather the Maidens into a safe area and meet me back in our room," he commanded.

"Only if you promise me you'll tell me what's going on," she growled frustratedly. "You've been keeping too many things to yourself, and it's got me worried."

"I'll explain when you've returned from gathering the Maidens," Ergott said, walking back up the stairs.

Rosaline followed him up the stairs with a sigh, splitting away from him at the hallway door, looking back at him with a worried glance before disappearing around a corner.

*The woman was too wise for her own good.*

"Commander Jackseye!" Ergott yelled as he trailed around the corner.

Jackseye walked out of a room, adjusting his hood quickly. "You called?"

"Gather your Barons, lockdown the castle and Londinium," Ergott ordered.

Jackseye's brow furrowed. "Why?" he asked.

"Samqueel survived," Ergott said. "And he's coming back."

Jackseye blinked in shock. "Surely not? No one could survive that blast," he said incredulously.

"He did; I can feel that he did. Now do as I commanded," Ergott said, making his way up to his room.

Jackseye muttered to himself and headed down the staircase, his boots clacking out of earshot. Ergott frowned at the sound. *At least Samqueel did what he was told when commanded without a second word.*

Ergott trailed up the stairwell, passing by two patrolling Barons in the hallway. "You two!"

They snapped their attention to Ergott immediately. "Sire."

"Head down to the High Gates and shut them," Ergott commanded.

The Barons look at each other quickly. "Is there an issue, sire?" one asked.

"Yes, there is," Ergott glared at them. "Now get down there!"

They both moved quickly towards the stairwell-

"One of you get back here!" Ergott commanded. One of them paused and pointed at their chest.

"I don't care, get here," Ergott growled. The Baron moved back to Ergott, uncertain.

"Give me a dagger," Ergott demanded.

The Baron hesitated. "What?"

Ergott glared at him, his eyes glowing brighter. "*Give me a dagger,*" he growled.

Horse's hooves pounded the grass through the forest, clumps of earth spraying up behind it as it ran. The castle's shadow hovered above, blocking the sunset from blinding Sam's eyes as he scoured the sides for any movement as he rode, torches lit in sconces illuminating the windows.

The horse snorted beneath him in exhaustion, its heartbeat banging against Sam's thighs. The poor beast had been pushed to run a two-day ride in less than an afternoon, and it began tiring two hours ago. Samqueel finally let the reigns go slack, coming down to a trot and letting it stop for breath.

Sam hadn't stopped in his tracks once before now, afraid if he did, he'd crumble. His mind kept replaying over and over the vision of the explosion, of his men scattered around in the mud, damaged and broken, and the sound of Reuben's last breath. His mind became numb along with his body after the first hour of the ride, propelled by pure rage alone.

He would not stop until he saw Ergott's blood splattered across Remedy. And he didn't care how he'd do it.

*Someone has to finish the fight.*

Patting the horse on the neck, he urged it on gently, the loyal beast pushing on to walk out of the treeline towards the gates. The stone wall passed by him as he trained his eyes on the castle steps, his chin raised high despite the agony in his body. Lanterns strung up on the buildings swayed in the cool evening wind, the silent chatter of families in buildings muffled behind closed doors.

The few civilians of Londinium watched out and about as he rode through the city's central alley, looks of surprise and joy flitting throughout their faces at his return.

"But where are the others?" "Why is he back alone?" "Has something gone wrong?" He could hear them murmuring between themselves. Amongst the crowd of onlookers, a few Barons shoved past them. They immediately drew their weapons, yelling viciously at the civilians to move out of their way. The civilians scattered by their commands, screaming in fear and worry.

Sam looked sideways at the Barons, his eyes cold. His horse buckled beneath him, stepping away from the Barons with a nervous snicker. *These assassins didn't know when to step aside.*

"Warn Ergott!" one of the Barons yelled at another, and the Black Guard darted off towards the castle.

Samqueel snorted at the Baron. *Like he doesn't already know.*

The Barons surrounded him in a circle, a few of them holding shields they took from the Knight's armoury, barricading his way up to King Ergott. Sam wouldn't have guessed they'd known where their weaponry was stored; he shouldn't be so surprised. But what *did* surprise him was the fact they were using *Knight* shields.

Sam's head tilted to the side, looking at each of them around him. "Evening," he said flatly.

"Stand down, intruder!" a Baron commanded.

"Intruder?" he raised a brow, turning his eyes to the Baron. "You've got it wrong, I'm afraid. I've come home." *The real intruder is in the castle, and you're blocking my way.*

"Stand down! King Ergott's men forbid you to enter Camelot!" The Baron interrupted.

*Oh, you've taken the title of the King's men? Hilarious.* Samqueel sighed and let go of the reins, swinging his leg off the horse and dismounting the saddle, raising his arms in the air. His face was a flat expression of calm, and he let boredom seep through. *Unoriginal commands. I wouldn't expect anything less from Rohin.*

"Cuff him," the Baron said, gesturing to him.

One of the Barons pulled out a pair of iron cuffs from his back pouch, prowling over to Samqueel with caution, aware of his reputation.

Sam smirked at him and held his arms out willingly. The Baron stepped forward in front of him, looping the metal cuff around his wrist.

*Dumbass.* Samqueel's arm snapped down, the cuffs falling to the ground as his other arm flew back up into the Baron's jaw, the mask dislodging from the force. His leg lifted up and kicked the Baron in the stomach, sending him back into the other Barons standing behind him. The other Barons acted, drawing their weapons simultaneously, Sam drawing his own sword.

"Let's get this over and done with," Sam growled.

Three Barons advanced from his right, and he pivoted to them, raising Remedy to meet their blades, shoving them back and punching one in the head. His reinforced gauntlet knocked the Baron out cold to the ground, the others gathering their balance. More pressed on his left, and he slashed in a wide arc, hitting one's knee deeply and shoving him back into his mate's blade, the dagger in the Baron's hand slicing through the side of the held man's neck, blood pouring to the ground as Sam dropped him. He spun around and slapped the horse's flank with the flat of his blade, the tired stallion rearing with a loud neigh, his hooves flying through the air and kicking at the surrounding Barons, forcing them back to avoid the impact.

Samqueel ducked in front of the horse, guiding it towards them with loud shouts to startle it further, Barons dropping to the ground beneath the kicks. A dagger flew into the horse's flank, and it screamed in pain. Sam let the reins go for it to run away from the area, Barons scattering out of the way of the wild horse.

A flash of steel sliced open two of the Barons' chests, Remedy flying through the air at stunning speed, Sam's hands braced on the handle as steel broke through bone in splinters, whirling back around to meet the Barons' oncoming blades, duelling fiercely with the assassins.

*Slash, thrust, swing, duck, kick, grab, punch, slash again, parry-*

Pain sliced across his already injured side, a Baron's dagger piercing through his chainmail further, burning like a hot flame on his skin. He roared in pain and blindly slashed at the source, a jut against the sword coming clean. A masked head rolled across the cobblestones, crimson rivers seeping through the cracks from the bloody stump of the corpse's severed neck.

The remaining Barons hesitated, watching the head roll towards the leader's feet, the mask tinged red at the chin, the trail of blood welling behind it as it came to a stop. Samqueel panted with his teeth bared, blood sprayed across his face, holding his side and panting, his sword at the ready. "Anyone else?" he snarled.

The leader snarled back, his eyes filled with anger. "The King will have your head, Torona," he growled.

"Extraordinary how your mate just lost his first," he prodded, twirling Remedy in his hand.

The leader narrowed his eyes, standing aside for Sam to make his way to the castle. "King Ergott awaits," he said, gesturing his arm to the palace.

Sam glowered at the leader, eyeing the dagger in his hand as he passed by, his sword angled and ready if need be. Barons parted the way forward, watching him walk up to the castle, civilians in their homes gaping from windows and doorways.

Sam kept his sight forward, his eyes glimmering in pain at the blood leaching from his wound, the air stinging it greatly through his armour. *Just keep going. You're almost there.*

Footsteps rushed up the grand staircase to Camelot, the Baron out of breath and tired, wheezy from the amount of running. Approaching the High Gates, the Baron demanded they let him in, screaming at the top of his lungs. The side door opened, and three men stepped out, looking at the deranged Baron standing at the Gates.

"Is he here?" Wilhelm asked.

"Torona has arrived in Londinium," the Baron panted, his voice shaken.

Wilhelm turned to the Barons behind him. "Warn the King," he ordered. They peeled off back through the side door, their cloaks disappearing quickly into the castle.

Wilhelm turned to the Baron, his face serious. "Where was he last?"

"Mid-town, arrived on a steed," the Baron described.

"The damage?"

"I left before they apprehended him," he said.

Wilhelm huffed, shaking his head. "If you believe Torona would willingly be cuffed without a fight, then you Barons have another thing coming."

"Is he dangerous, sir?" the Baron asked.

"He's the Knight Commander of the Roundtable," Wilhelm sighed. "Of course he's dangerous, you tool."

"King Ergott needs protection," the Baron said, heading through the Gates to get inside the castle.

Wilhelm put his hand on the Baron's chest, stopping him. "You are of no use in this state of exhaustion to protect the castle," he sniped. "Go back to wherever you shadow dancers dwell."

"Yes, sir," the Baron nodded, heading down to the castle's side.

*And take your friends with you.* Wilhelm frowned, turning back to look towards the plaza in the middle of Londinium.

The Baron walked around the side of the castle, panting while taking his mask off, sweat gleaming across his brow. He took a breath, pausing in place for a brief moment, sighing to himself.

His chest jutted forward, making his feet stumble. He frowned and looked down at the glint of blood-stained steel protruding from his chest. Pain spread across him like wildfire, the breath whooshing from him as blood leached through his robes, dripping down his legs to the stones. A sharp tug left his chest feeling void, and his legs collapsed beneath him, his body dropping to the ground in the puddle of his own blood.

A shadow stood over him, the figure tall and broad. "Voss stole the lives of my trainees from me," the voice growled. "So I'll take my share of lives back."

"W-who.. are you?" the Baron wheezed, turning his head to look up at the man.

Dark brown eyes glared at him, rich, deep skin gleaming with blood and bruises in the light seeping through the shadows. "I'm your worst nightmare," Gawain growled deeply.

"Gawain…" the Baron's eyes slowly shut, his blood leaching from his mouth. The Baron's chest fell, his neck falling limp.

Gawain wiped his blade on the Baron's leg, standing back up straight and walking back around the corner, crushing the mask underfoot as he picked up his burden of a bag. *Damn young lads and their forgetfulness.*

# Chapter 12: The King Who Cried Wolf

"Rosaline!" Ergott's voice echoed throughout the castle like a blaring siren, marching down the hallway.

Shuffling feet sounded down the hall, the small woman coming to the call. "Ergott, is everything okay?" she worried.

"Samqueel has arrived. We need to get you to safety," he said, grabbing both her biceps.

Her eyes widened, looking at him in shock. "Where do we go? The Maidens are in the Knights' quarters," she stammered.

Ergott looked around, spotting their room across the other side of the walkway. "Our room, quickly," he demanded.

She pulled away from his hands, turning and running to the room, Ergott following behind her. A few Barons ran past them along their way, their weapons at the ready with shields strapped to their other forearm. Rosaline gasped, moving out of their way, keeping towards the wall as one brushed her shoulder roughly.

"Move it, wench," the Baron spat at her.

"Watch who you're talking to!" Ergott barked at them. Rosaline and the Barons looked at him, Rosaline holding her shoulder. "Your Queen deserves more respect than what you'll ever receive in your lives."

Beneath the mask, the accused Baron's eyes widened, looking at Rosaline. Queen Rosaline Guinevere wasn't very popular in the Kingdom; it was no surprise the Barons hadn't recognised her. "A-Apologies, Your Highness," he stuttered. She looked away from the Baron, shifting her shoulder.

"Now get down there and defend this castle, and you may just earn an ounce of respect!" Ergott snarled, ushering Rosaline to continue on. The Barons continued down the stairwell with their swords at their side, Rosaline slipping through the doorway to their chamber.

Ergott shut the door behind them, panting heavily while keeping both of his hands on the wooden handle. Rosaline moved to the window across from the four-post bed, standing to look out at the city. "How do you know of his return?" she questioned, looking at him. "The Barons are already in the plaza and at the Gates. If he was coming back, he'd still be a day's ride-"

Ergott turned to her, reaching out for her to stop talking. "That's enough, Rosaline," he said, moving away from the door. "I don't want to worry you any more than what I have done," he said softly.

Worry spread across her face, facing him completely. "You've been distant since Jackseye arrived," she said. "I've felt as if I'm invisible to you."

"And I deeply apologise for my absence, my dear, but I'm here to give you my full attention," Ergott said gently, walking over to her.

She looked up at him, the light from the city illuminating her face. "The chamber beneath the servant's quarters," she murmured. "What's there?"

"My thinking space," he brushed off. "I've been thinking I haven't been the husband I should be, and I'm deeply sorry," Ergott said, a small tear forming in his eye.

Rosaline reached her hand up to his face, brushing his cheek comfortingly. "The stresses of being King are getting to you, aren't they? The power you have is hard to control, the responsibilities too much," she said softly.

"Yes, it's all converting around me, and I feel...
trapped," he admitted, looking down at her.

Her face softened, a gentle smile forming on her lips.
"You're strong enough to work your way through this," she
assured. "Have you found your way to become free?"

Ergott shook his head. "I'm trying to."

"Tell me what I can do to help," she said. "I can
shoulder your burdens if you need me to. You're not alone
in leading this Kingdom."

"I need you to forgive me," he whispered to her.

"Oh, Ergott," she breathed. "I never held anything
against you. I knew what I was getting into when we got
married. I may not understand your predicament, but if
you'll let me help you, let Arthur help you-"

"Arthur doesn't want anything to do with me," Ergott
interrupted. "He believes I stole his birthright from him,
which isn't all a lie."

"You didn't have a choice," she cooed. "If you hadn't
taken the throne, Camelot would be in ruins. Arthur was
too young to take on the responsibilities. You did the right
thing by the Kingdom. But maybe if you talk to Arthur, let
him into what it's like to rule, he can learn from you. You
could teach him to be the next King."

"Thank you, my love. I will always love you and your
words of wisdom," Ergott smiled, hugging her gently.

Rosaline wrapped her arms around his neck, resting her
head on his shoulder. "And I will always love you too, my
King," she smiled.

Ergott flicked his eyes up to the window, the glow of
amber eyes reflecting in the glass back at him. The stars
forming outside glimmered at him as if in accusation,
judging him silently. "I'm sorry..." he said softly.

"It's okay," she looked up at him, her eyes crinkled in
Ergott's favourite smile.

Suddenly, something sharp jolted into her abdomen,
searing pain dashing across her side as it ripped upwards

towards her throat. She cried out, her eyes widening in pain as Ergott shoved her down.

Ergott looked stricken at his wife, tears streaming down his rugged face as he clenched his fist around the dagger in his hand, dripping with her blood. "I'm sorry, my love…"

Tears of pain welled in Rosaline's eyes, disbelief and shock written across her face. A strangled cry escaped her throat, her hands shaking violently over the bleeding slash across her body.

The glow from Ergott's eyes faded away, his body slumping like he was released from a spell. Ergott dropped the bloodied dagger to the carpet, kneeling beside Rosaline with a shocked gasp, picking her up and cradling her in his arms.

"No… no, no, no," he half whispered, his voice strained. Her blood stained his dark pants and ran out in rivers from her mouth, her eyes staring up at him unseeingly. Breath wheezed past her mouth in short bursts, fading to nothing. Ergott moved his hand up to her soft face, sobbing as the loyal, gentle Queen faded away.

His breathing was ragged, the thing roiling beneath his skin growing harder to resist. He rested Rosaline down gently on the floor, brushing her hair back off her face. *This better be worth the pain.* He picked up the dagger from the floor, his eyes burning like lava inside his skull turning to face the empty doorway.

The wooden door burst open, hitting the wall with a loud bang, torchlight flooding the dark chamber. "Vivien!" Ergott barked, walking down the steps, dust scattering underfoot.

"My King," her velvety voice purred from the far wall, her figure spread across the piles of hay and blankets.

"I've done what you asked, Witch! What else do I need
to do to please you?!" Ergott snarled at her, tears falling
down his face.

Soft laughter echoed around the room, her slender
figure standing up gracefully, yellow eyes aglow. "You
could feel it, yes?" she drawled, coming closer to him. "The
power that crawls in your veins is begging to come out, is it
not?"

"What are you talking about?" Ergott asked, narrowing
his eyes at her.

"Don't play dumb with me, Ergott. I am fully aware of
your capabilities," she grinned. He could feel his eyes
turning hot, an orange light glowing off the bridge of his
nose.

"Your tasks are almost complete enough for it to form
completely," she tilted her head, her hand coming up to rest
on her cheek. "I wonder, if I tell you what the last one
would be, would you let me go?"

"Depends on what the task is and what you would do
when released," he said, observing her.

Vivien smirked slowly at him, prowling closer still.
"The path to glory is still divided before you. Destiny
cannot rewire its roads at the snap of a finger or a whisper
of a chant," she said.

"What is the last task, Vivien?" Ergott asked, frowning
at her.

"Prophecies are grand things made by the Mage, aren't
they?" she pondered, looking up at him.

"What Mage?" he asked, looking down at her.

Her eyes lit in surprise, the golden glow flaring
brighter. "You do not know of the legends?" she smiled.

"All I'm interested in, Vivien, is knowing what the last
task is and killing the man who's coming for me," Ergott
scowled at her, moving her hand off his face.

Her voice lilted in laughter, and she brushed her hand
across his shoulder, her nails dragging. "Powerful, yet

ignorant," she said slyly. "You're nowhere near as smart as you believe to be."

"I take my chances with intelligence to be higher than most commoners," Ergott sniped. "I won't ask again, Vivien. What is the last task you'll have me do?"

"The only way to solidify your future on the Throne of the World is to change the future," she growled. "The Born King has a strong future ahead of him, whilst you do not."

"You want me to kill Arthur?" Ergott asked.

"If you remove the problem from the situation, the rest resolves itself," she murmured, her long fingernail tracing down his jacket.

"Killing Arthur will be a hard one; the boy has a group of trained Knights with him," Ergott said, looking away from her.

"And it'll get even more difficult before you even know it," she agreed, moving her finger up to his jaw.

Ergott hesitated, sighing before turning back to her. "How much do you want your freedom, Vivien?"

Her face turned feral, a glint of madness in her eye. "More than you want to keep the throne," she said calmly.

"I have a proposition for you," Ergott said.

"I'm listening," she drawled.

"If I let you out of this chamber, right here, right now," Ergott turned to face her. "You will give me more abilities every full moon, and you must remain my sorceress until the day I die," he proposed.

She hissed, and her nail scratched his jawline, pain stinging from the cut. "You bastards and your desperation for power," she spat.

Ergott held his bloodied jaw, scowling at her. "I guess you don't want your freedom then," he growled.

"I'll take your offer, King," she tilted her head back. "But I wish to have the freedom I desire, not be locked in this stone Hell."

"That can be arranged," he said softly.

"Then we have a deal." She rubbed her fingers together, feeling his blood dry on them.

Ergott made his way towards the chamber door, walking up the steps to the small altar, shadows swarming around him like tendrils of smoke. He walked towards the doorway, the shadows engulfing him and moving through the door, the handle left untouched.

The Round Hall sat quiet, nothing but a few gushes of wind howling through the cracked open windows. At one of the corners, a Baron slouched against the wall, not moving a muscle. Boredom was written across his short bearded face, his hazel eyes unamused.

*Why would they put me in the one room that nobody used in the castle anymore?* He sighed through his nose, looking at the mask in his hands. He looked up, his eyes searching around the empty room, nothing but the large round table in the middle, the dust visible from where he stood. *What a waste of time.*

Commands shouted from outside the door, more boots running past in groups. More of them were going out there to fight a singular man. *Surely we don't need to use* all *of the Barons?* It was ridiculous.

The light blew out from the lantern in the hallway, and the sound of scraping metal and jangling chain mail sounded past again, then a muffled grunt, a thud of flesh on stone emitting from the hallway. The Baron squinted his eyes, walking towards the door curiously, his right hand hovering over his scabbard. He opened the door, looking around to locate the source of the sound. Three Barons lie flat on their faces in the hallway, a shadow standing off to the side.

The Baron's eyes widened, and he drew his sword quickly. The shadow pivoted and looked at him, red metal gleaming in the further torchlight down the hallway, a blade gleaming in its hand.

"They said you'd come," the Baron scowled.

"Here I am," Sam said calmly.

"Did it hurt?" the Baron asked, lowering his sword. "Seeing your entire Legion dead in front of you?"

"More than you'll ever come to know."

"They deserved everything they got," the Baron shrugged. "Disobedience doesn't come without its consequences."

Samqueel shook his head slowly. "These ones," he gestured to the Barons on the ground with his sword, "they got nowhere near enough of what they deserved. Your King killed his men."

"Is that right?" the Baron asked. *Your* King, not *our*. *Interesting how he phrased it.*

Samqueel's side glistened in the dark as he turned to face the Baron fully. "A leader doesn't bring down others to keep on top," he said. "The leader lifts them, pushing them in front to grow and thrive. Ergott is not a leader, and he never will be."

"We'll see about that," the Baron challenged, darting towards Sam quicker than a blink of an eye. Sam's sword flashed in the air, meeting the Baron's blade equally. His eyes were intense, almost wild with anger. The Baron growled viciously at Samqueel, gritting his teeth. Sam shoved his sword further down the Baron's blade, moving to the side to miss the Baron's sword as his guard smashed into his fingers. The Baron barked in pain, shoving Sam's sword back off his broken fingers. The Baron glared up at him, snarling in anger before charging at him.

Samqueel let him, reeling his feet back to match his speed. The Baron jutted into him, Sam's head racking back against the wall, his sword flat against his side. He smiled faintly, his eyes watching the Baron closely, tilting his head.

"Any last words, Commander Torona?" the Baron asked, smirking at him as his other hand reached behind himself for his dagger.

"Say hi to Amelia for me when you go home," Sam said simply and swung the sword pommel-first into the Baron's head.

The Baron reeled back with a grunt of pain, his head throbbing. He looked back at Sam, gritting his teeth in anger. Steel flashed in his vision, and pain seared through the Baron's face, a hot line of it dashing over his nose to his left brow. The Baron cried out in pain as blood flowed in rivers through his fingers, his sword flying across the hall.

The Baron snarled at Samqueel, unsheathing his dagger. "Vermin!"

A heavy hit to his stomach made him fly backwards, making him roll across the floor through blood puddles to the wall beside the Round Hall doors. He grunted as his head smacked into the bricks, his hand fumbling the dagger.

"Now, unless you can see past the blood in your eyes, I suggest you put that back in your pocket, boy," Sam growled at him. "You don't want to lose both an eye and a hand, even if the latter is already broken."

"I hope hell treats you well, Samqueel," the Baron spat, putting the dagger back in his pouch.

"That's a lad," he said, turning to walk inside the Round Hall. "Looks like Rohin didn't fail to teach you something, at least."

"The Jackseye family is smarter than you think," the Baron sniped. "Unlike your father's."

Sam stopped.

"Rohin did a fair job disposing of Dawson good enough to make it look like the brawl they said it was," he smirked, rolling with the hesitation. "He's quite easy to tempt with a bottle of ale. It always has been, by the looks of things. His prison reputation wasn't a secret to us, you know."

"What do you know of my father's death," Sam asked quietly, still facing the other way.

"Only that my father did a number on him," the Baron shrugged. "And that apparently, his screams of anguish were music to his ears."

Sam's shoulders rose and fell slowly, the sword in his hands quivering under a white-knuckled grip. The Baron's eyes lit in mischief, realising he'd hit a nerve.

His head turned slowly to look at the Baron from over his shoulder, his stare sharper than razor blades. "Rohin is lucky I'm not the revenge type," he hissed.

"Then why are you back here wanting to kill King Ergott?" the Baron asked, sitting up slowly.

"This isn't revenge. This is justice; it's vengeance for the fallen. It's about the people in the city who can't fight, whose voices have been silenced to the void. It's about the people who deserve better than what they've got." Samqueel turned his head to face the far wall, stalking towards the staircase.

The Baron chuckled darkly while watching Sam leave, laying back down on the ground. Faint footsteps caught his ears, and he looked around with his good eye, seeing a shadow of a girl disappearing around the corner quickly. Pain throbbed across his eye as he narrowed them in suspicion.

His heart was beating too fast, the blood roaring in his ears and sticking his undershirt to his wounded side. Rage flowed through him like a river, refreshed by Edward Jackseye's words.

*Rohin killed my father.* He should've known that backstabbing *liar* was involved. He should've known the day he'd met him with that smug look on his face in the training hall, the sabotage he'd committed against the crown and Commander Mordred…

The staircase opened to the room levels, the doors sealed shut, and lanterns glowing softly on the stones. Sam's feet carried him onwards, watching as three Barons rounded the corner in front of him. His hand tightened on Remedy as they shouted and ran towards him, their weapons raised and shields at the ready.

Remedy flew through the air, blood spraying onto the walls of the castle, the crack of skulls on stone echoing as their heads ricocheted back into the walls, the clatter of weapons dropping to the ground a symphony to the thump of bodies falling one by one.

Sam never missed a breath as he prowled towards the door he knew Ergott was behind. The proud bastard was always perched up on that balcony like a cat on a stool.

Boots stomped down the hallway to his left, and he ducked behind an open doorway, tucking in Remedy to his side as the door inched shut. Holding his wound, he looked back down the way he came, a blood trail following his path. If anyone wanted to trail him, it wouldn't be too hard to do so. He scowled to himself.

A patrol of Barons stormed past the door, the swish of their cloaks and leather armour subtler than their footsteps, the noise fading down the stairwell he had just come up. They'd find Edward there and start raising the alarm. He should've just knocked the boy out and thrown him out the door.

It was too late to do anything about it. He had to get to Ergott *now*.

He opened the door, peering out to check they'd gone completely, and slipped through the hallway. He walked to the arch above the balcony door, listening for any hint of a sound as his hand twisted the door handle.

"I was beginning to wonder if you'd show up," a voice said from the balcony ledge.

Sam opened the door completely, walking out onto the platform, his eyes shifting to the King. "Surprised to see me?" he asked, standing in front of the open door.

"I could see everything, you know?" Ergott said. "The fires sprouted along the ground, the deaths of everyone on that field." He turned around to face Samqueel. "How was it from your perspective?"

His grip on Remedy tightened, his teeth grinding together. "About as wonderful as you could imagine," he growled.

"Charming," Ergott grinned, his amber eyes glowing brighter.

*That orange glow*... he'd only seen it a handful of times before now, thinking it a trick of the light from the lanterns in the Round Hall. Now Sam knew for sure that he wasn't seeing things. Ergott was harbouring magic. "Does it hurt when your eyes glow?"

Ergott frowned at him. "Every time," he said coldly.

"A pity," Sam shrugged. "The fires of the Etherplains could warm them further for you if you need. Just let me escort you there. I'm sure you'd fit in just fine with the rest of the corrupted souls."

"I see your ego wasn't killed," Ergott chuckled, amused. "Unlike your Legion."

Sam's teeth ground together. "You sent us into a fight we told you we couldn't win. Why?"

"Times have changed, my old friend. I knew if I went through with my plans while you were still living, you'd attempt to stop me."

"Because your plans are horse shit!" Sam snapped. "Using the Barons against us, abusing the power of whatever magic you've got stowed under your skin? You are the most selfish bastard in Braynor."

"No," Ergott disagreed. "They're selfish plans, yes, but they were for the greater outcome."

"Greater outcome of what?" Sam raised his arms in disbelief. "Your people? Your Kingdom? If that's what you believe, take a look at the citizens hiding away from your 'plans' in their houses, locked behind closed doors, fearing for their lives because of these black-cloaked heathens patrolling the city! That's not the greater good."

Tears like fire trails fled from Ergott's ethereal eyes, a taint of madness hiding inside them. "I had no choice, Sam. You'll never understand why I did what I did, but you need to understand that this was nothing personal," Ergott said.

Sam scoffed in disbelief. "Then why use *my* men to do your dirty work? You sent your entire defence to be slaughtered at the hands of Ariendal," he snarled.

"It was the Witches' exchange," Ergott admitted.

"What *witch*?" he spat.

"The Witch of the Darklands," Ergott said. "She promised to strengthen my abilities if I completed her said tasks. Killing you was one of them. The rest of them wouldn't have let me get you where you are now without them lying dead on a battlefield, wouldn't they?"

Disgust coursed through Samqueel. The selfish bastard valued power over his own men's lives. *How did I not call him out on this before?* "What does Rosaline think of all this? Or have you kept it from the Queen as well?"

Ergott's expression flickered, his stone-cold mask dropping a fraction. "Rosaline…"

Sam caught the look, his heart skipping a beat as he roved his eyes over Ergott. There was blood on Ergott's hands, his pants stained dark at the knees. "You didn't," he growled, his voice poisonous with scorn.

"I had to, and it caused me great pain to do so," Ergott admitted, a tear streaming down his face.

"You *didn't* have to! You *didn't* have to kill her! You *chose* to kill her, *chose* to murder Rosaline like an *animal*!" Sam roared in anger. "The woman was nothing but loyal to you. She was too sweet to be around your corrupt, selfish ways. She deserved a better life than this. You ought to be ashamed of yourself."

"Enough!" Ergott snapped, his eyes glowing fiercely. "She was my everything, but you wouldn't understand."

Anger stabbed through him like a hot knife, his teeth baring. "I wouldn't understand? *I wouldn't understand?!* I know *exactly* how it feels to lose *everything! You* were the cause! *You* were the reason I had to leave them! I had to abandon my *family* for *you*! And what happens in return? You stab me in the back!"

Ergott reached to the scabbard on his right hip, pulling out a sword with deep engravings along the blade that caught the sun like mirrors. He brought the sword up near his face and rubbed his hand along the edge, his eyes glowing brighter and brighter. Soon, the blade was engulfed in black flames, the heat glaring off his weapon.

"A poor choice, wasn't it?" Ergott asked, his voice rasping deeply with a demonic echo.

Sam's feet shifted into position, his sword raised before him in both hands, anger overtaking every sense and thought he had. The pain in his body ebbed to nothing, razor-sharp focus centring on Ergott.

*He's taken everything away from me.*

*Someone has to finish the fight.*

"I feel sorry for you, Samqueel," Ergott said, his voice deepening. "But unfortunately, you won't be joining Dolorous Gard."

"I wasn't planning on it," Sam said. His legs bunched, and he sprang at Ergott, Remedy slashing through the air.

Ergott swiped his sword along the platform, black flames covering the entire surface around them. Sam's eyes flashed, the fire catching him off guard as he dashed to the side to dodge them. *Was this his magic?*

Ergott turned to him, swiping his sword close to Sam's chest. Sam leapt back, the blade glancing off his breastplate, sparks shooting from the metal. Ergott lashed the sword up from the ground, fire dashing to Samqueel in a wave of heat.

Eyes wide, he tucked and rolled across the balcony, landing on a knee behind Ergott. Ergott turned around, swiping the sword with his momentum, glaring at his former Commander. Remedy met the blade in time, and Sam's boot lashed at his knee, landing with a jolt. Ergott collapsed down onto one knee with a grunt, his gaze burning at Sam. Sam sprang to his feet quickly and slashed towards Ergott's shoulder, the blade sinking deep into his flesh.

Ergott growled at the sharp metal within his arm, turning back to Samqueel.

Sam gave him a feral grin, his teeth bared. "Sorry," he mocked.

"Your pride still stands strong," Ergott said, bashing the sword out of his shoulder. "That's a good thing to keep before dying."

Sam yanked the sword away, the blood dripping to the stones. "Glad to know I'm still worthy of praise from the likes of you," he sniffed.

"A privilege if you ask me," Ergott growled, rising from the ground slowly.

"Too bad your opinion isn't valid on Sundays," he snorted. "The Gods forbid heathens from their rights on their day."

"Says a murderer," Ergott scoffed.

"Murderer?" he raised a brow. "Enlighten me with how you've come to that conclusion."

"You've killed Barons, and you led your Legion into a battle they couldn't win."

"Protecting my Kingdom from invaders does not amass to murder. Secondly, that was *your* doing, and I'm sure Rosaline could back me up for my next point when I say you can't say a damn thing about me being the murderer."

Ergott snarled at Samqueel furiously, darting with his sword pointed at him. Samqueel parried him, ducking beneath the arch of fire that waved towards him, his back hitting the wall with a grunt.

*This is going to be a long fight.*

"The brick house looks a lot bigger from the inside than the outside," Tristan said nervously.

"It's a castle, Tristan," Arthur said. "What else did you expect?"

The Barons holding them remained silent as they pulled them through the winding staircases and hallways of the castle. Tristan looked as though he'd be sick. From what Arthur could tell, he'd never been past the Knights courtyard before, other than the Round Hall.

"Well, I didn't expect to see thirty bedrooms, five levels of stairs, a dining hall and a room filled with different-sized mirrors-" Tristan muttered.

"Yeah, I get it," Arthur interrupted.

"Why do you need so many mirrors, Arthur? Are you summoning a spirit from the Otherworld?" Tristan gasped.

"Why do you ask so many questions?" Arthur asked, slightly irritated.

"Because I know Face-less here won't say anything," he nodded to the Baron.

Arthur looked back at the Barons from over his shoulder. "Where are you taking us?"

The Baron remained silent.

"See? It's like they're on mute," Tristan sniffed. He looked at the Baron, pulling a face. "Hullo? Anybody in there? Or are you hollow with robotic legs?"

Arthur knew that their focus wasn't on them; their masks were trained at something in the castle. He looked down at the cuffs wrapped around his wrist, the iron biting his skin, and glanced at one of them. The one behind him had a metal key dangling from his belt. With no prior warning, Arthur went down on one knee, fiddling with the straps on his boot.

The Baron holding him paused, looking down at him and tugging his arm. "Get up," he commanded. Tristan looked at Arthur, brows raised.

Arthur didn't respond to his command, ignoring him completely.

"I said get up!" The Baron bent to grip his arm-

Arthur smacked his head back into the Baron's face, elbowing him in the ribs quickly after. A hiss of pain echoed behind the mask, the Baron's grip loose. Arthur grabbed the back of the Baron's collar with his cuffed hands and threw him over his shoulder, the assassin landing on his back with a thump.

The Baron holding Tristan stopped, drawing his weapon and moving towards Arthur. Tristan's hands shot out, wrapping the chain of the cuffs around the Baron's neck, tugging him back against his chest tightly. The Baron beat at the chain mercilessly, choking for breath.

Arthur snatched the keys from the Baron's belt, standing up quickly as the Baron turned to reach for him.

"Nuh-uh," Arthur smirked, shaking the keys. His foot lashed out to the Baron's face, rocketing his head back into the ground with a crack, the thump of another body following as Tristan dropped the passed-out Baron.

Arthur reached for the key slot, hearing the key click into place as the cuffs loosened, collapsing onto the ground

in front of him. Arthur turned to Tristan, gesturing for him to give him his hands.

He held them out to him. "That was easier than I thought it would be," he said.

"The old shoelace trick always gets them," Arthur smirked, throwing the cuffs to the side. "Grab his sword," he pointed to the passed-out Baron.

"I think the best part was that you don't even have shoelaces," Tristan laughed, pulling the sword from the Baron's scabbard.

Arthur walked over to the other Baron, pulling the sword from his scabbard. "It still fools them even if they're intelligent," he said.

"Hell, it fooled me the first time, too," he shrugged.

Arthur held his tongue on that one. "We've got to find Peter and the others," Arthur said, turning back to the way they came from.

The crash of boots sounded from their right, and Arthur pivoted to look, a group of Barons charging towards them, barking orders.

"Great, we have company," Arthur frowned.

Tristan looked and spooked, darting off down the hallway.

Arthur looked back at Tristan, raising his arms. "Thanks for the backup, Tristan!"

"I don't know where I'm going!" he shouted back, turning a corner.

Arthur shook his head, turning back to the Baron's gaining closer. "Oh shit," he muttered with widened eyes, darting after Tristan.

The friendly tool darted down a servant's hall, Arthur catching up behind him. "Why, of all places to turn, did you take this way?" Arthur called after him.

"It looked exit-able!" Tristan said.

"That isn't a goddamn word!"

"It is now!" Tristan took a right, a stairwell in front of him.

Arthur followed Tristan up the stairwell, which was the last thing he'd expected to ever do. He looked back, hearing the Barons coming for them with yells and boots trotting in unison.

"Where do I go?" Tristan paused, two hallways splitting off in front of him.

Arthur paused beside him, looking around their area. "One of the towers," he panted. "They should lead down to the throne room."

"You lead, I don't know this castle from a bar of soap," Tristan pushed his hair from his eyes.

"Follow me," Arthur said, darting to the left. Tristan watched him for a moment before dashing after him, his eyes wide.

Arthur made his way around the farther end of the left-side hallway, winding down the spiral staircase with practised speed. Tristan caught up with him at the bottom, sweat coating his forehead and gasping for breath as he bent forward. "How do you live in this place?" he breathed incredulously. "It's *huge*."

"I only live in one section of this castle," Arthur said.

"You'd need a map to find it," he panted.

Finally, after racing down levels of spiral staircases, they reached the throne room, empty and hollow from the lack of noise. Tristan flopped to the floor, breathless. "Let's not do this again," he huffed.

"Agreed," Arthur panted, looking around the throne room. "It's all clear," he said, sitting up against the brick wall.

Tristan whooped in a weak celebration, the noise carrying up towards the viewing balconies above them.

"If you give away our position with your noises, I'll kill you myself," Arthur scowled at him, breathless.

Groans echoed from down the hallway to the left of the throne room, echoing into the large space. Arthur looked toward the faint noises, squinting his eyes while standing up slowly.

Tristan raised his head from the floor, looking over at the noise. "Did you hear that?"

"Wait here," Arthur ordered, making his way over to the noises.

"Gladly," Tristan put his face back on the cool marble floor, breathing fast.

Arthur walked over to the source of the noise, listening out for it as he drew closer. Blood pooled across the marble floor, the trail leading to a Baron laying against the wall. Three more lay piled beside him, their bodies dead still.

Arthur narrowed his eyes. *This is an absolute blood bath.* Arthur walked around the bodies, assessing their wounds, weary of the blood pools around each body.

The Baron against the wall moved his head to look at Arthur, making him jump. A thick trail of pierced skin slashed across his face, stretching from his right cheekbone over his left eye, blood leaching in rivers. He'd only been there for a moment by the look of it.

Arthur bent down in front of him, resting the sword's blade near his neck. "What happened here?"

The Baron angled his head away from the blade, his eye swollen red and half shut in pain. "Torona," he choked out.

"Sam?" Arthur asked in disbelief, his eyes widening. *He's home?*

"You shouldn't be here…" the Baron groaned.

"And why's that?" Arthur asked coldly.

Shouts echoed from inside the Round Hall, the familiar sound of yet another pile of Barons coming toward him. *They just never sit down, do they?*

"What's happened?" Tristan said suddenly behind Arthur's shoulder.

Arthur looked back at the Baron, pressing the sword closer to his neck. "How many of you are in the castle?"

"Enough," he grinned with a deep laugh, blood coating his teeth.

"Arthur, we've got to hide," Tristan said quickly and grabbed his arm, tugging him away from the Baron.

Arthur scowled at the Baron, standing up before walking quickly with Tristan into the Round Hall. They darted behind the wall of the staircase, the stomp of boots trailing down past them out to the hallway, the door shutting closed.

Red glints caught Arthur's eye; looking at the wooden floor of the staircase, fresh blood glinted in the torchlight leading up the stairs. Arthur followed the trail of blood, narrowing his eyes. *Since when was Camelot such a warzone?*

"Your house is full of pests," Tristan remarked, following him and eyeing the bodies littering the staircase.

"I knew they were no good the first time I saw them step foot into Londinium," Arthur growled, looking at Tristan.

The creak of a door sounded from the top of the stairs, silent footfalls padding farther away from them. Arthur frowned in confusion and continued up to the top, peering around the edge of the wall.

"That sounded like metal armour," Tristan mused, peering out beneath Arthur.

"Stay silent," Arthur told Tristan, slowly moving against the wall.

Samqueel snarled, the pain in his ribs getting worse as he slashed at Ergott ruthlessly, their swords clashing and echoing off the castle wall. Ergott parried Sam's blow, shoving him to the balcony ledge.

He spied the ledge beside him, darting to the right and swinging his sword towards the back of Ergott's legs, jumping over the flames lapping at his boots. The heat from the black flames made the fight all that much harder for a parched Samqueel, his head spinning.

Ergott groaned in pain, staggering to the hardened balcony flooring. Ergott turned to him with a snarl, the black flames surrounding him on the platform.

Sam panted, backing away from the flames, his arm raised to shield his face. Ergott looked at the sword in his hand, eyeing the flame around him with a slight grin. He raised the sword high above his head and slammed it into the platform, a massive gust of black fire sprouting out from the impact.

Sam ducked, his armour searing his skin with the heat of the flame as it hit him. He groaned in pain, falling to the stones.

His breath couldn't seem to catch up to him, the air too hot to breathe. Sweat drenched his body, his head spinning round and round in circles. He needed a drink.

"Given up?" Ergott growled.

Sam's eyes glared at him from lowered brows. "You underestimate your Knight's capabilities, sire," he mocked.

"Do I?" Ergott asked, his head tilted back. Sam could tell he thought he'd already won; that glint in his eye told him everything.

*Perfect.*

"You know what happens when you corner a wolf?" Samqueel growled, getting to his feet, the leather across his armour crumbling.

Ergott lifted a brow, holding his sword steady. "It cowers in fear?" he suggested and swung his sword down atop Samqueel, waiting for the crunch of bone-

Remedy stopped the blade in its tracks, hitting it with great force back away from him. Ergott's eyes flashed in surprise, the orange burn flicking to Sam's face.

Quicksilver glared sharper than steel. "It fights its way out," he snarled and launched his fist into Ergott's throat.

Ergott's eyes flew wide open, grabbing his throat and choking violently, reeling back away from him-

An elbow connected with Ergott's temple, his knees buckling beneath him. Remedy flew, and Ergott roared in pain, a trail of blood splashing against the castle wall and running down his side deeply, flowing to the balcony in waterfalls.

Sam launched his boot into Ergott's back, forcing him down to the cobblestones face first. He pointed his sword to Ergott's neck, rage growling through his teeth as he panted. "You made a bad move cornering this wolf," he snarled.

"Finish it," Ergott growled at him. "Kill your King!"

"With pleasure," he huffed and braced his hand on the pommel. His hand shoved down on the pommel-

His feet gave out from underneath him, his body rocketing back through the air. Shock flitted through Samqueel at the sudden force, Remedy flying from his grip as he smacked into the balcony railing, his head cracking against the stone painfully. He slid onto the stones weakly, his head pounding with pain, warmth seeping down the back of his neck. His vision blacked out for a moment, coming back to double vision, his ears ringing.

Ergott chuckled deeply, grabbing his sword from the ground beside him. "Despite your greatest efforts, you still couldn't find yourself to do it," he growled.

Pain seared through him as he lifted his head, grunting. "You'd be bleeding from the neck if you didn't do whatever that was," he wheezed.

Ergott prowled over to Samqueel, the sword scraping the ground beside him. He placed his foot on Sam's chest, pressing down hard. Sam's ribs screamed in agony, a groan of pain escaping his lips before he could stop it.

"But despite your failure," Ergott said, "I respect your efforts."

Sam struggled to breathe under the weight of Ergott's foot, his face crinkling in pain and anger. He grasped his hands around Ergott's leg, trying to push him off to no avail. "I never failed to do what I set out to do," Sam huffed.

"What did you succeed in doing?" Ergott asked.

Sam glanced up at him, blood trailing out of his nose. "I gave them time," he seethed.

"Given who time?" Ergott asked curiously.

Sam smirked despite the pain. "Wouldn't you like to know?" he coughed.

Ergott pressed down harder, glaring down at him. "*Who?*"

A loud crack sounded from his chest, and Samqueel roared, pain dancing across his face. He could feel his lungs getting heavy with blood, desperation the only thing keeping him alive.

He looked to the door, his eyes adjusting to the distance, seeing him there through the gap. His face turned surprised. *Why was he not gone? Where was Jon-*

"Tell me!" Ergott roared.

"Ergott!" A voice yelled from the door. Ergott snapped his head to the voice, his eyes widening.

"You've gone far enough," the voice said, walking closer to him.

"Arthur," Ergott growled. "You're not supposed to be here."

"You're not supposed to be killing your Knight Commander, but here we are," Arthur said, pointing the sword at him.

Ergott sneered at him, his teeth bared. "You *wouldn't* understand," he snarled.

"Oh, I understand it very clearly," Arthur sneered back.

Sam wheezed from beneath Ergott painfully. *Why aren't you halfway across the territory by now?*

"Get out of here before you get hurt," Ergott snapped.

"You'd kill your nephew?" Arthur asked, narrowing his eyes at him.

*I wouldn't put it past him.* "Run, Arthur," Samqueel strained. "He won't hesitate…"

"Is that true?" Arthur asked Ergott, his sword pointed at his uncle.

"Go, Arthur," Ergott growled deeply, his eyes flaring brighter.

Arthur blinked at his eyes, his face paling with realisation. The boy knew something; Sam could see it click in his expression.

"Those… eyes…" Arthur said, his voice shaking. Ergott watched Arthur, his foot lifting ever so slightly on Sam's chest.

Samqueel looked up at Ergott, baring his teeth. *Distractions are always welcome.* "Long live the Born King," he snarled and reached down into his boot, pulling one of the Baron daggers out into the sun, slashing it up into his leg deeply, blood spraying wildly from the wound.

Ergott roared and turned back to Sam, lifting his sword into the air with both hands.

Sam glared at Arthur, gathering the last of the air in his lungs. "Get out of here, boy! Go!" he yelled.

Arthur's eyes widened, hesitance freezing him. "Sam!"

Ergott's sword slammed through Sam's chest, bones splintering apart beneath the steel, crimson rivers leaching through the armour to the cobblestone balcony. Pain flared through Sam, and he cried out, his voice carrying through the doorway into the castle, echoing through the building.

Arthur glared up at Ergott, gripping the sword tighter in his hands. "You bastard!"

Ergott's hand flew out towards Arthur, making him ricochet back into the castle wall with a thump. Samqueel turned his head to face Arthur, his vision blurring as his hearing disappeared. The pain in his body went quiet, a stillness creeping over him like a blanket. The weight finally lifted from his chest, Ergott's figure stalking towards Arthur's prone form on the ground.

Sam's sight left him, the warmth of his blood turning cold as sensation disappeared, his lungs shuttering. *Go, boy. Get away from this mess.*

# Chapter 13: Escaping in Style

The ground was hard underneath Arthur, the cold seeping through his clothes. His body ached every time he breathed, his pulse throbbing through him like a drum beat. He stirred, groaning quietly to himself. Faint light cracked through the sky above him, the scent of dust and rotted wood stuffing up his nose.

*This isn't the castle. Where am I?*

His mind spun as he gained his bearings. The last thing he remembered was facing King Ergott on the balcony. Those Gods damned orange eyes were Ergott's this whole time; his uncle was the one in his nightmares. It gave him a headache to even think about it. *Is that blood on my neck?*

*And seeing Sam die…*

He opened his eyes with effort, adjusting to the low light. *It must be dawn.* How long had he been here?

He slowly got to his knees, his body creaking with aches. Arthur looked around the area, realising where he was. The sword was nowhere to be seen, he realised with a scowl. *That's just great. First the armour, now the sword. What next?*

The Londinium alleyway was cold, a cool breeze whistling through like a mournful cry, wooden planks and old garbage surrounding him. *This had to be the poor Southern District.*

Arthur leaned against the alley walls, sighing deeply to himself. *This whole destiny thing is a mess. How could a bunch of words and a blood tie possibly dictate one's* future? Especially when it leads to things like waking up in an alleyway after finding your corrupt uncle murdering his Commander. Who made this stuff up?

Rattling sounded from beneath a pile of wood, the planks bouncing around sharply, falling from the stack with a clatter. Arthur looked over at the rattling with high brows, moving his legs away from it.

A loud thud echoed from beneath it. "Ow," a muffled voice complained from beneath it.

"Who's there?" Arthur asked, his voice stern.

A metallic clunk slid across the stones and the woodpile scattered across the alleyway, one sliding to a stop at Arthur's foot. Arthur frowned at the wood in front of him, looking back up with a scowl.

The ground seemed to lift up from underneath the remaining planks, a curious head popping out to scout around with wide, familiar brown eyes. They looked at Arthur and lit up in delight. "Arty!" Tristan smiled.

"Tristan? Since when did you create another tunnel to the Southern District?" Arthur asked, narrowing his eyes at him.

Tristan pushed the trap door up completely to rest against the wall, a grin on his cheeky face. "It's always been here," he said. "You just don't have enough time to explore anymore."

"You don't have to remind me," Arthur grunted, getting up from the ground.

"I also found some cool stuff while I was leaving the block," he added, pulling himself up to sit on the lip of the entrance.

"Is it a dog?" Arthur asked with a huff of sarcasm.

"Quite the opposite, in fact," he nodded and reached into a bag on his hip, muttering to it softly. He pulled out a small bundle of golden fluff the size of his palm, pitiful mewls squeaking from the tiny beast. Bright green eyes looked at Arthur wildly, its little body shaking.

Arthur raised a brow, looking at the golden kitten in Tristan's hands. "A kitten?"

"Indeed," he beamed. "I found it in one of the tunnels just outside the castle walls."

"That's… cool?" Arthur questioned.

"I think it's cute." He sat the kitten down gently onto the cobblestones, the little ball of fluff laying flat on its stomach with its ears pressed back.

"Tristan," Arthur said, his voice suddenly turning serious.

"Before you say anything else," he slid back down into the tunnel, his head popping down for a moment. "I've got something cool for you too."

"Tristan, I need to tell you som-"

"Voila!" Tristan's voice echoed, his hand lifting a long leather object into the alleyway, his head raising through the hole with raised brows.

*That's my father's sword.*

"My sword? You got it back?" Arthur asked with delight.

He sat it on the stones beside the jumpy kitten, leaning his arms on the edge. "Eh, it wasn't too hard," he shrugged.

"How? Where did you get it?" Arthur questioned.

"Ergott likes to talk too much," Tristan grinned. "While you were knocked out, he went on some rant about random rubbish and talking to himself. Your uncle's a right madman in more ways than one."

"Tristan-"

"I'm not finished yet," Tristan complained. "After he dragged you out of the balcony, he left the sword on the floor-"

"This is important, Tristan," Arthur scowled at him.

Tristan looked at him flatly. "I grabbed the sword and ran."

"Tristan! Let me talk," Arthur snapped in frustration.

"Okay, I'm done," he said quietly, shrinking back with wide eyes.

"Samqueel is dead," Arthur said, his throat tightening. "*All* of the Knights are dead. Ergott sent them into a death trap."

The kitten looked at Arthur as if in shock, its small eyes wide. Tristan shared Arthur's expression, his hands clenching and unclenching. "I know, Arty," he said solemnly. "I saw him die. The news about the explosion is already flying around the Kingdom. What in the Ether do we do now?" His face was haunted, his eyes bordering on tears.

"I'm sorry, Tristan," Arthur said, kneeling to place a hand on his shoulder. Mournful mewls sound from the kitten, and Arthur looked at it; curiously, tears flooded the cat's eyes, distress stiffening its little frame. *Did it understand him?*

Arthur turned back to Tristan. "We need to find the others and leave Camelot," he said softly. "It's not safe here anymore."

Tristan looked at him sadly, tears welling. "I feel bad for stealing Henry's salads now," he whimpered.

"I'm sure he's forgiven you by now. He'd want you to have them," Arthur tried to cheer him up. The poor lad would be distraught. Tristan was known to be close to the Knights beyond all reason. He was just the kind of soul who connected with anyone. Arthur couldn't blame him for being distressed over it. Tristan sniffled and petted the kitten, who looked at him with fright.

Footsteps barged around the corner behind him, coming to a stop. "There he is," a familiar voice called.

Arthur turned to the voice, a sigh of relief escaping from his mouth. "Maria," he smiled.

"We've been looking all over for you since Tristan came back through the tunnels," Maria said, moving over towards Arthur.

"We've?" Arthur asked, standing up from the ground.

Three shadows turned the corner, Kyan, Peter and Marlon coming to stand behind Maria. Arthur's eyes flicked to Marlon's face: bruises peppered his dark skin, a cut on his jaw scabbing over.

"We need to get you out of Londinium," Marlon growled, his voice hoarse.

"The Roundtable-"

"Dead, we know," Kyan interrupted. "There's a whole story flying around the city."

Arthur scowled at him. "Nice to see you too, pest."

Kyan grinned at him, facing his palms to Arthur with his arms spread slightly. "At least I'm here ready to escort your royal ass out of this city," he drawled.

"Did you really have to bring him?" Arthur asked, frowning at Marlon.

"More is better than less," Peter grumbled. "The people need you more than you need us. That's what's more important."

Tristan pulled himself out of the tunnel, standing up with the kitten in hand. It wriggled around and hissed at him, its tiny claws scratching his skin like daggers. He frowned at it and put it gently back on the ground. "That's not very nice of you," he scorned. The kitten sniffed at him and flicked its tail, darting off down the alleyway. Tristan frowned sadly after it.

"Better to let it go than to carry it around all day," Maria said to him. "It could've been a bigger burden than what we need." Tristan pouted at Maria, his brows lowered.

"So what now, then?" Arthur asked, looking at Marlon. "We can't stay here, and they'll search the training hall."

"We find the next alley out and walk down it," Peter said, unfolding his arms.

Arthur frowned at him. "Anyone have a better, unboring plan?"

"You sure don't," Peter snorted. "If you think of a better idea, sound it out."

"We could… go on a proper vacation," Tristan said from behind Arthur.

"Good idea," Arthur added, pointing to Tristan. "But where do we go? The Barons are practically everywhere."

Maria looked down at the tunnel door. "We could always use those, right?" she asked.

"No," Arthur and Tristan said at the same time.

She frowned at them in confusion, Kyan reflecting on her look.

"The tunnels are off limits," Arthur said firmly.

"They'd be a better way out," Kyan suggested, shrugging.

"We're not using the tunnels," Arthur repeated firmly.

"They're too complicated and full of rats," Tristan frowned. Kyan's eyes flickered at the word. Arthur caught the hesitance, wicked delight making his smirk stretch.

"Have you got an issue with rats, Kyan?" Arthur grinned, turning back to Tristan. "Maybe we *should* go through them."

Kyan's back straightened. "No," he protested. "I'm not afraid of stupid little rodents."

"So, if we send you down there, you wouldn't be scared of a rat if it comes near you?" Arthur asked, raising an eyebrow at him.

He huffed, lifting his brow at Arthur. "If I sent you into a room full of women, would you know what to do with them? Don't be daft."

*As arrogant as ever, Kyan.*

"Any other suggestions?" Arthur asked, ignoring Kyan.

"Surrendering," a voice said from further down the alleyway.

All of them snapped towards the voice, Arthur tightening his grip on the sword. Arthur narrowed his eyes, moving forward in front of the group. Maria's eyes widened as she backed up, running into Arthur with a thud. She looked back at him for a moment apologetically, moving away from him to let him pass.

More Barons rounded the corner behind the speaker, their hoods making them wraiths in the morning shadow.

"Let me guess, the King sent you?" Arthur asked uninterestedly.

"By the order of King Ergott, you will be taken to the castle to face your trial," he boomed.

"My trial?" Arthur asked, raising an eyebrow in confusion.

"For partaking in the murder of the Knights of the Roundtable," he said.

Arthur blinked, his heart stopping for a moment. "What are you talking about?"

Tristan's brow crinkled in confusion. "Arthur didn't kill them; Ergott did," he defended. "We were at the castle-"

"The order given was to retrieve you in order to judge your actions. Now come along quietly, or we will be forced to reprimand you," the Baron interrupted, their voice firm.

"You've got the wrong man," Arthur scowled. "Ergott murdered them, not me."

The Barons advanced towards them, hands on their weapons. "We will see whether you're guilty or not under the judgement of the Law," the Baron growled. "Arrest them."

Marlon stepped forward, a deep scowl on his face. "If I may, I'd like to suggest a-"

The closest Baron to him smacked him in the jaw with a baton, his head reeling to the side. Blood spurted across the ground from his mouth; Marlon spat it out and turned back to face them with a glare.

"I'm telling you lot right now! I didn't kill the Roundtable!" Arthur snarled at him.

The Barons inched closer to them with shackles in their hands, ready to spring.

"Gentlemen," a voice from behind the group of Barons said. The Black Cloaks turned their heads to the voice, Marlon's attention turning to the shadow standing behind the Baron group.

"Might I suggest refraining from using your weapons on the future King," the man stepped closer to them.

The Barons closest to him turned around, batons at the ready. "Stay back away, citizen. You don't have any involvement in this situation."

"Oh, but he does," Marlon muttered, his jaw set and aching.

The man removed his hood from his face, looking up at them. "Allow me to introduce myself," the man drew a sword from his side, swiping at the Baron's feet.

They quickly jumped out of the way, scattering around him. The man turned to one of the Barons, snatching away his baton before pinning him against the wall and smacking his face with the weapon.

The Baron in front of Marlon lurched to the suddenly, Marlon's fist outstretched in the air. The cloaked man turned to face Arthur and the others with a beaming grin, nodding in greeting.

"What are you guys waiting for? Jump in," he said, swinging back around to the next Baron.

Arthur smiled widely at Galahad, buckling the sword around his waist. "I was wondering where you went," he said half-heartedly.

"You weren't bullshitting us after all." Peter raised his fists, battling the Barons as they launched at him, Kyan fighting by his side.

Galahad moved over to one of the Barons, kicking the back of his knee. Tristan moved in front of Maria, his teeth bared as he defended her from the baton-wielding assassins, keeping them back.

More Barons started to charge towards them from further down the street, Marlon throwing the one he held captive towards them like a bowling ball.

"We need to move now!" Marlon yelled at the group.

Arthur spotted an opening between the affray, darting towards the alleyway's exit. Tristan saw him and followed with Maria behind him, kicking the planks back over the tunnel door as he went. Kyan and Peter trailed after them, shoving off more Barons as they went.

Marlon moved to Galahad's side, the two moving backwards to block off the alley Arthur ran down. Marlon rubbed at his sore jaw, Galahad looking at him with a friendly smirk.

"You're still old," Galahad greeted.

"You're still hiding."

"What the hell is this Marlon business?" Galahad asked.

"An alias so people don't come and ask questions," Marlon looked at him.

"Have you told the boy the truth?"

"That wretched Voss squeezed it from me," Marlon growled and watched a Baron come closer, launching him across the alley with a kick.

Galahad looked at him in surprise. "Voss is here?"

"Rohin, too. Ever since these pests showed up, we've had nothing but Baron after Baron," he panted.

"I see. Were you the one to draw the attention?"

"Try the boy instead." Marlon dodged a swing, gripping the Baron's arm and tossing him over his shoulder.

Galahad connected his blade with that of a Baron's, shoving him back into the others behind him. "We'll take him to the caves; I've got an escort awaiting us at the edge of the forest," he said with a grunt, kicking another Baron away.

"Don't tell me it's who I think it is," Marlon sighed.

"Ryan will be happy to see you again," Galahad assured, darting after Arthur and the others.

Marlon chased after him, flicking a sword up to his hands with his boot. "The question is, am *I* happy to see him again," Marlon muttered.

Arthur panted as he ran down the street, hearing Galahad and Marlon trailing behind him. He looked forward to the others, Tristan right beside him.

"If you don't keep your face forward, it'll smack into a wall," Tristan panted.

Arthur scowled at him, looking back again; Barons chased behind the older Knights, coming in floods and joining from the side alleys. "We've got company," he sighed.

"Look out!" Tristan gasped and grabbed Arthur's jacket, pulling him back behind him to a sharp stop. Arthur spread his arms wide as he stumbled slightly, watching Tristan smack into the wall Arthur was about to hit with a hard grunt, the lad flopping to the ground in a heap.

Arthur's eyes widened, and he moved to his friend, crouching beside him. Maria caught up to them, her knees skidding against the concrete as she slid beside him. "Gods, are you alright? That looked like it hurt," she asked, her voice laced with worry.

Tristan looked at Arthur groggily, holding his head. "I told you you were going to run into the wall," he groaned.

Arthur reached down, Maria helping to pull him to his feet. "We've gotta get to the city entrance," he said, continuing to run down the streets. "Come on."

Tristan held the wall beside him, shaking his head clear. Arthur looked back, slowing back with a frown. He looked back at the Barons darting to them, uncertainty rooting him.

"Come on, Tristan, let's go," he repeated, urging him on.

Tristan shook his head, his vision swimming. "Just go, Art," he slurred. "I'll catch up."

"I'm not leaving you here; can you walk?" Arthur asked, slight worry in his expression.

"My head…" Tristan winced as he pressed his temple. "Everything is spinning."

Maria brushed the dust off of his back, rubble falling off his clothes back to the ground. "He's gonna need help to get going," she said, gently wiping away the blood trail that moved down his face with her sleeve.

"What's the hold-up?" Peter called from behind them, he and Kyan catching up.

"Kyan, you need to help Tristan," Arthur ordered, looking over at him.

Kyan sighed at Tristan, shaking his head. "You tool, what have you done this time?"

"I flew into the wall," Tristan grumbled, blood beginning to patch on his brow.

Kyan rolled his eyes. "Go, I'll deal with this," Kyan waved off Arthur and Peter.

Arthur and Peter bolted, Maria following after them with a slight hesitation. They dodged and weaved through the crowd of citizens, running through the main street past wagons and carriages full of hay.

Kyan sighed and grabbed Tristan's arm. "Come on, we've got to catch up," he groaned.

Tristan shook his head. "I'll find my own way out, trust me," he said.

"Don't be a tool. Get moving, now."

Barons exploded around the corner, Galahad and Marlon running straight for the pair.

"The Hell are you two doing? Run!" Marlon commanded, turning around to scatter a row of boxes stacked against the wall across the alleyway.

Tristan shoved Kyan off his arm. "Go already. I'll just drag you guys down."

"If you end up dead, Arthur will kill me," Kyan growled and ran off after the rest of them.

Marlon and Gawain ran behind him, Marlon looking back at Tristan with a scowl. "Garrison!"

Tristan blinked his eyes hard and turned down the other alley, waving towards the Barons. "Hey you, you big-robed bastards!" he shouted. "Come and get me if you know what's good for you!"

The Barons turned to him and immediately ran after him, Tristan's eyes widening as he staggered down the alleyway, cursing to himself.

"Stop!" a Baron yelled at him.

"You stop!" he shouted, running around a corner.

Tristan found himself in a crowded marketway, wagons and carriages riding past him down the alleyway. He grinned mischievously and ran down the alleyway, dodging around the carriages with a stumble. His shoulder clipped one as it passed, making him groan in pain and clutch his arm.

The Barons made their way out of the alleyway, scouring over the market area. Tristan looked behind him in alarm and quickly ducked around a cart, sliding in underneath it and balancing himself on the axles.

"Search the area!" the Baron commanded, people scattering from their presence. Tristan watched them walk past the cart he hid beneath with a sigh, resting his head on the wooden bar beneath him. The cart suddenly jolted and began moving, Tristan gasping and holding on tightly with his legs. *Uh oh.*

"Where did he go?" the Baron called, looking around behind the dormant carts and behind crates. The Barons around the marketway peered through the windows of the shops sprouting along the walls, people moving out of their way in fright.

Suddenly, the tailgate of the cart that passed them fell open, apples spilling over the heads of the Barons. The

Black Cloaks shouted in surprise and pain, the commotion turning the heads of the other Barons down the way. Four men stood on the back of the cart, feigning looks of surprise. All were dressed in farmer's clothes, their skin covered in dust and specks of charcoal.

"Oh, sorry there, boys," one of the men said, leaning off the side of the cart. "They're a bit heavy, you see." His grin shone against his deep brown skin, his black hair scrambled above his grey-brown eyes gleaming with mischief.

One of the men on the cart chucked the crate onto the nearest Baron, the assassin exclaiming in protest as he fell to the ground onto the apples. He laughed at the two Barons jumping onto the carriage, their weapons at the ready. He offered his arms up towards them, his skin light in the sun beneath the dirt coating him. His moustache crinkled with a grin, his brown hair smoothed back by the wind hovering over blue eyes set in a strong face.

"If you need more apples, give us a yell," he said to them and kicked more crates at them powerfully. One of the Barons shot off the cart as the crate barrelled into his chest, landing on the ground with a grunt.

The man on the side pulled back onto the small platform at the front of the cart and slapped the horse's rear, saluting the fallen Barons as the cart rocketed through the alleyway. Citizens and Barons scrambled out of the way of the wild cart, the man grabbing the reins and steering it down a clear alley, seating himself on the front bench and bracing his legs on the pole with a laugh.

The Baron remaining on the cart stumbled at the sudden shift of gravity, falling to his rear end into the boxes bouncing against the barriers. Three of the men picked the Baron up by the limbs roughly and swung him overboard, the Black Cloak rolling down the alleyway uncontrollably.

The moustached man laughed hysterically, holding the side of the cart and raising his hand up in the air as they left the Barons in their dust. A faint knocking noise sounded from underfoot, getting faster the rockier the road became.

The man looked down in confusion. "Stop the carriage," he called to the front.

The driver pulled the carriage into a secluded alleyway, their carriage hidden from view behind another cart holding barrels of wine. The man jumped onto the ground off the edge of the carriage, kneeling down to examine the underside.

A wide-eyed Tristan clung to the axles for dear life, shaking in his boots and staring at the man. "Where in the Ether is this carriage going in such a hurry?!" he asked, his voice high-pitched in anxiety.

"Looks like we got a stowaway," the man huffed in amusement.

Adrenaline rushed through Arthur as he led the group down the streets, looking back at his group and counting heads, seeing Marlon and Galahad catching up to them. *Gods, they're fast.* They were almost at the Southern Gates now; it wasn't too far…

Maria ran beside him, her breath rushed. "Where's Tristan and Kyan?" she breathes.

"They're back there somewhere. Maybe they took another route?" Arthur answered, looking at her.

"From your left!" Peter shouted, barreling towards Arthur.

Arthur flicked his eyes over to his left, his eyes widening. An apple cart came speeding towards him from the intersection, the horse running rampant.

"Shit!" Arthur yelled, trying to slow down. Maria gasped and slowed back, grabbing for a gutter pipe and pulling back behind the wall.

"Jump, now!" Galahad yelled from behind Peter.

Arthur's breath rushed from him as Peter jump-tackled him across the alley, the cart speeding past Arthur with a hand's breadth to spare, his heart skipping a beat at the closeness. He and Peter rolled across the cobblestones, the small rocks on the path scratching Arthur's arm as he rolled. They both looked up to watch the cart speed past, getting back on their feet quickly.

Marlon panted as he watched the cart go by, looking at Galahad. "Typical apple carriage," he snorted.

"And guess who's on it?" Galahad said with a smirk.

Marlon rolled his eyes and turned to Arthur. "That's our ticket out of here, so start running after those apples," he commanded.

"The apple cart?!" Arthur exclaimed, looking back at him with widened eyes.

"It nearly killed us!" Maria cried. "And *that's* our escape route?"

"Oliver never was a subtle planner," Marlon muttered.

"I am, too!" the man on the carriage yelled at him, grinning widely.

"Well, he's not stopping anytime soon," Peter observed, unsure whether to run.

"We're busting through the Southern Gates; make sure you lot are behind us!" Oliver explained, turning back to the front.

"Come on!" Arthur said. The group ran after the carriage quickly, dodging the debris flying out from behind the carriage.

Behind them, an entire array of Barons followed, a few of them wielding bows. A handful of Barons stopped in place, loading their bows with three arrows each.

Maria looked back behind them, exclaiming in alarm. The Barons fired their arrows straight at them, all grabbing another three arrows from their quivers.

The arrows flew past Arthur, zooming over his head and embedding into the wood of the carriage crates. A few arrows speared into one of the men on the carriage, his cry of pain echoing the thud of his body landing on the deck of the cart.

"Get down!" Oliver yelled at the others on the carriage.

Peter yelled in pain, and Arthur looked over to him; an arrow shot through his arm, the head sticking out through his bicep. Maria slowed back slightly, her eyes tilted up to the sky.

The archers lined up their shots, aiming the second round of arrows straight towards them. Maria snapped her attention around to them, her eyes glaring as they changed colour to a rustic gold that enveloped her whole eye.

Barking echoed from around the Barons, packs of wild stray dogs leaping onto them with snarls, ripping at their limbs. Their bows scattered across the alleyway as they yelled and fought the dogs, whines of pain filling the air.

Arthur paused and ran back to her, grabbing her arm and spotting her eyes. "And you talk to dogs too?" Arthur asked.

She turned to him impassively, her gaze unseeing with the dog-like eyes pinned on him. "I can summon any animal, Arthur," she said, her voice hollow.

"Talk sounds better," Arthur muttered.

Shadows clouded over the top of them from the roofs, Barons darting across the shingles. Oliver looked up at the sudden shadows casting over him, his eyes widening. "Look out from above!" Oliver warned the others.

Marlon looked up at the rooftops and darted towards the walls. "Stay under the gutters!" he barked.

The group shifted under the overhanging gutters out of view from the rooftops, dodging the shingles being thrown at them. Slate shattered on the ground in front of Arthur, shards flicking around them dangerously.

The cart barrelled down a new alleyway, slowing back as it crawled underneath a small footbridge. "Quickly," Oliver waved, opening the tailgate of the carriage. "Jump in!"

Arthur boosted Maria up first into the back, her eyes blinking clear as she took Oliver's hand. Arthur looked back at Peter, the trainee's face scrunched in pain as his hand pressed against the arrow wound.

"This is going to hurt like a bitch," Peter growled and gripped the side of the carriage with both hands, pulling himself up with a painful roar.

A few of the Rebels inside helped him up, holding their hand out for the others. Arthur looked back at Galahad and Marlon, the two men catching up and pulling themselves onto the carriage expertly.

A familiar figure darted from around a corner, Kyan's chest heaving heavily as he sprinted towards the cart, Barons trailing behind him closely.

"Kyan! Where's Tristan?" Arthur demanded. *Don't tell me he's left him!*

Kyan ran to the base of the cart, holding his hand up to one of the men to pull him up, collapsing to the wood breathlessly. Sweat coated his clothes and face as he panted, looking at Arthur.

"Where is he?" Arthur yelled at him.

Kyan shook his head, lifting his hands to gesture back where he ran.

Arthur scowled at Kyan, gripping the rail on the side of the cart and putting his feet up on a small platform to the side of the wheel. "Unbelievable," he growled. *I left this tool to defend Tristan, and he ended up saving himself.* Hatred blossomed in Arthur's chest.

Oliver pulled the tailgate shut, sliding the bolt into the lock and finding a seat. Galahad looked around the carriage, his brow crinkled. "Where's Arthur?"

Marlon reached down to grip Arthur's arm, heaving him on board the carriage like a ragdoll. "Right here," he said.

Arthur immediately moved over to Kyan and landed a punch to his jaw. "You left Tristan!" he yelled at him.

Kyan's eyes widened in alarm and he raised his arms up in defence. "He said he'd catch up-"

"I told you to help him! No matter what he said!" Arthur yelled furiously.

"Arthur, stop!" Maria said, trying to grab his arm.

"You never leave your men behind, you coward!" Arthur snarled at him.

"Leave who behind?" a voice said from behind a barrel.

Arthur looked over to the voice, panting heavily in anger. Wide eyes peered over the barrel, as familiar as breathing air to him.

"What are you doing on the apple cart?" Tristan asked, a half-bitten apple in hand.

Arthur scowled over at Kyan. "You're lucky," he said.

Kyan spat blood at Arthur's feet. "Royal prick. I ought to kick your ass," he snorted, turning away from him and moving over to Peter.

"How did you get on this cart, Tristan?" Arthur asked, calming down.

"Well, the Barons were chasing me down the market alley that was packed full of people buying-"

"The short version, please, Tristan," Maria said.

He frowned. "You guys never let me explain a full story," he grumbled. "I hid under the cart from the Black Cloaks and ended up finding Sir Geraint by accident."

"I'm sorry, who?" Arthur asked, his eyes widening slightly.

"Sir Oliver Geraint, at your service, my liege," Oliver smiled, bowing at Arthur.

Peter's eyes widened, amazement on his face. "What is the meaning of all this? The old Roundtable was thought dead, and now three of them are before me."

"Well, we're not dead," Geraint said simply. "Not yet, at least," he added.

"Though for a good while, I thought *he* was dead," Galahad nodded to Marlon. "With all this fake name business."

"Fake name?" Geraint asked, looking at him with a raised brow. "Don't you take pride in your name, Jonathan?"

Marlon sat against the side of the carriage, scowling at them. Kyan looked at him, his eyes suspicious. "So it *is* true," he said.

"Your name truly *isn't* Marlon," Arthur muttered, looking at him.

Marlon looked at them flatly, taking in their curious eyes and bated breath. "No," he grumbled.

"So, what is it then?" Arthur asked, folding his arms.

"This old bag is Sir Jonathan Gawain," Galahad nodded to him. "The good old Red Knight of the Roundtable, King Benjamin's Legion."

"Second in Command of the Roundtable and a close friend to all of us, who he loves very much," Geraint said, smirking at Gawain, who snorted at him.

"Where are the rest of you? Where have you been hiding all this time?" Maria asked, her face curious.

Geraint looked at Maria, smiling at her faintly. "That will be explained shortly, my darling. Firstly, we've gotta get out of Londinium."

A crash sounded from outside, the cart jutting sharply upwards. Arthur's hand gripped the side of the cart tightly, keeping him in place as the others shifted about, the crates knocking against each other. Maria cried out in shock as she was flung back, landing onto Arthur's lap as Tristan flew over the barrels, yelping as he landed on his back on top of Kyan. Kyan growled at him, shoving him off, Peter cursing as his arm bumped the wall.

"Well, we're out of Londinium," Gawain murmured.

Arthur's eyes widened, looking at Maria, her arms pushing awfully close to parts he valued. "Comfortable?" he asked.

She looked up at him, her flushed face making her green eyes stand out. "Apologies, Arthur," she said faintly, peeling herself off of him.

"Where are you taking us?" Arthur asked, looking at Geraint.

"To a safe haven of sorts," Geraint answered.

The cart stopped after a while, a few voices sounding around them, horses hooves trotting around them. Arthur's eyes flashed in alarm, getting to his feet; *more Barons?*

The tailgate flung open, people dressed in tunics - *not Black Cloaks, thank the Gods* - ushering them off of the cart.

Peter held his arm, blood staining the sleeve of his grey shirt as he moved towards the edge, jumping down to the ground. The others followed suit, Tristan almost tripping over the lip but, thankfully, catching himself.

Arthur exited the cart, looking around the area; they were at the edge of the forest, quite a bit away from Camelot on a small crest to the right of the river. The castle sat to his left, the sun glancing off the windows of the façade glaring at him as if accusingly...

Arthur stared at the castle while walking down the small hill, sighing deeply to himself. *Things will never be the same now.* But wasn't that what he wished for? Change was all he wanted for himself. But this was a whole other level he wasn't expecting.

Maria looked over at him, her face softening as she followed his gaze. "It feels huge, right? To be outside of Camelot?" she asked.

"This isn't what I was expecting," Arthur admitted. "Being a wanted man in my own home and having to flee the Kingdom wasn't on my card of things I predicted."

Her mouth quirked, eyes flicking to him. "It could be worse," she suggested.

Arthur looked back at her. "How?"

"You could be alone."

Arthur nodded at her, a small smile stretching on his face. "It's just lucky that I'm not." He wouldn't know what in the Ether he'd do if the others weren't here. He probably wouldn't have even made it out of Londinium without them.

Her lips spread in a bright smile, her eyes glittering in the sun. Something about them made Arthur feel safe, something stirring in him he couldn't quite name.

He pushed it to the side, thinking it was irrelevant. "I probably could do without Kyan, if I'm honest," Arthur said with a smirk, clearing his throat.

"I think everyone can do without Kyan," she sighed, looking at the troublemaker. "He doesn't know when to use his head right."

Arthur chuckled, walking up to the group on top of the hill. "And probably never will."

She chuckled softly, following behind him closely. "He can't use it for attracting women, despite his beliefs," she muttered.

The two walked up to the others, a Rebel assessing Peter's wound with a grim look while the others recovered from the chase, spread out amongst the piles of hay and parked carriages.

Galahad walked up to one of the Rebels, panting faintly. "Connor," he greeted.

The Rebel turned to look at Galahad, sharp features lifting chestnut brows at him. "Jameson? It's been, what, three hours? That was a quick run," he mused.

"Where's your leader?" he asked, looking around.

"I wouldn't know," Connor shrugged, lifting his tankard. "You'll hear him before you see him, though."

"Now *there's* a statement I can get behind," a voice sounded from beside a carriage.

Galahad turned to the carriage, raising his eyebrow at him. "Were you standing there the whole time?"

"You're awfully unobservant, Galahad," he purred. A man with long black hair leaned against a cartwheel with his arms crossed, smirking at Galahad.

"Hey, Gawain, I found your buddy," Galahad called to him.

Gawain looked over at Galahad, his eyebrows lowered as he walked over. "What makes you think anyone is my favourite Knight here in particular?" he sighed.

The man's eyes lit in surprise, his smirk turning to a grin. "Jonathan Gawain," he said incredulously. "I thought you were-"

"Dead, so did I," Geraint interrupted, fixing the saddle on the horse next to him. "He had a fake name."

"Fake name? Who wouldn't recognise that mug?" the man gestured to Gawain. "The man is a walking legend."

"One, I'm not *dead*," Gawain sniped. "Two, how did you think Camelot kept getting Knights? Someone had to train them after Mordred retired. Three, you'd be surprised how gullible some of them are," he growled, looking over at Tristan.

"You've got a point," Galahad nodded, folding his arms.

Arthur walked over to them, spotting the man leaning against the carriage. "Who's he?" he asked, looking at Gawain.

"This tool is-"

"Sir Ryan Bedivere," the man bowed dramatically, smirking at Arthur. His soil eyes seemed to be living with mischief; Arthur couldn't decide if the glint in his eyes was the sun or madness. "Now, who are you?"

"Arthur Pendragon."

Bedivere frowned, his brows knitting together. "Who?" he turned to Galahad. Arthur blinked. He had to be the only person in Braynor that didn't know who he was.

"Benjamin's son, you idiot," Galahad sniped.

"Benjamin had a son?" Bedivere questioned, looking over Arthur. "He sure doesn't *look* like him."

Arthur frowned, a huff of disbelief escaping his nose. He thought he looked at least a *little* like his father, from what he could remember. He wouldn't know what his mother looked like, so it was hard to judge.

"Yes," Galahad sighed. "Ergott has overruled Camelot and killed the Knights of the Roundtable, and he's framed Arthur for their murder," he explained.

Bedivere snorted, laughter riddling across the camp. "He tried to frame the Crown Prince?" he chuckled. "What an absolute tool."

"We barely escaped the Barons; they're Ergott's new protectors," Arthur said, looking at Bedivere with narrowed eyes.

"Well, at least you got out of that hellhole," Bedivere shrugged. "The Black Cloaks are daft and difficult to deal with."

"So what happens now?" Arthur asked, looking at the four men.

"Well, the plan was to get you to the party on time, but I think we're past the deadline," Bedivere mused, a sly look on his face. "Even Cinderella had better timing than you."

Galahad frowned at Bedivere, looking back at Arthur. "We need to get you somewhere safe," he said.

Tristan walked over to the group, holding a wrap in his hand, a mouthful already bitten off. "Where are we going? What party?" he asked through the mouthful.

Geraint looked at Gawain. "Where to?"

"Is that my wrap?" Connor frowned, his brown eyes squinting at him in suspicion. Tristan looked at him with wide eyes.

"We go to the hideout," Gawain nodded. "It's the only place we *can* go."

"Well," Geraint said, mounting the horse beside him. "What are we waiting for?"

"Peter to get the arrow from his arm," Gawain said, looking down the camp.

"The arrow isn't out?" Geraint asked.

A pained yell echoed from one of the carriages, a stream of curse words following it.

"It is now," Bedivere laughed.

"How long will the trip take?" Arthur asked.

"A few hours, it's only just south of here," Galahad shrugged and moved towards the carriage.

"It's a wonder nobody's found you tools yet," Gawain snorted. "You make yourselves present everywhere else."

"You say that like it's a problem, Gawain," Geraint looked at him.

"It's a problem if we get caught."

"Don't be so glum, old boy," Galahad grinned, stepping up into the carriage. "We've been hidden for this long. We can hide for another two or so decades."

"If anyone can get us caught, it's that one," Geraint pointed to Bedivere.

Bedivere lifted his arms up in protest. "Since when do I bring any attention to myself?" he sniped.

"Remember the trip to Sarrum?" Galahad lifted a brow.

"Where you stole multiple pairs of socks to keep your hands warm," Gawain rolled his eyes.

Bedivere shrugged nonchalantly. "It was cold, and I didn't want *your* germy foot mittens," he said.

Arthur climbed inside of the carriage. "You lot are an interesting bunch," he said.

"Welcome to the life of a bunch of old Knights, sire," Geraint grinned, turning his horse around.

The group gathered themselves and jumped on board the carriages as the Rebels began to depart from the hill, heading into the forest in front of them on carriages and horseback. Arthur settled himself beside the door, waiting for the others to join him. *Gods help me.*

# Chapter 14: On The Beaten Track

The carriage rattled along the dirt road quietly, rocks jutting the wheels occasionally to the side. Camelot was well behind them, the castle far off in the distance through the window of the carriage door. Arthur watched it as it shrunk, leaning his head back against the wall with a sigh through his nose. *How long would it be before I get to go back again? If I ever go back.*

He flicked his eyes over to the left wall. Maria laid down in a tight ball against it, her blonde hair a strewn mess around her head. He'd never met someone who could summon animals before. Evergreen eyes flicked to him in curiosity, Maria lifting her head to look at him.

"You're staring, Arthur," she noted.

"Does it hurt your eyes?" Arthur asked.

Her brow crinkled. "What hurts my eyes?"

"When you… talk to animals?" he asked, unsure.

"No," she said, resting her head back down on her arm. "It makes me sleepy, though."

"So, you're a Mage?" Arthur asked, shifting up to a comfortable position.

"I suppose so," she shrugged. "I'm not sure where I got my powers. My best guess is my mother."

"I never really knew my mother," Arthur said, a bit saddened. "She died when I was young."

Her face softened in sympathy, her warm gaze settling on him. "I lost my mother when I was young, too. I was raised by a nanny instead," she said.

"In Camelot?" Arthur asked.

She nodded. "My father would visit from time to time when I was young, but he went away, too. At least, I think he was my father."

"Everyone is expecting me to be like mine," Arthur said, looking at Galahad at the front of the carriage. "Especially them."

She sat up onto her knees, rubbing her eye with a balled hand. "I don't expect you to be like Benjamin," she said. "No one can be like another person. You've got to find your own way, you know?"

Arthur nodded at her. "Yeah, I suppose you're right," he said.

"Don't suppose it, know it," she grinned.

"Okay, Enid," Arthur joked, chuckling lightly.

Her brow raised in question. "Enid?"

"One of the Maidens in the castle. She was the only one besides Aunt Rosaline who believed in me in that wretched place," Arthur explained. *And the Knights...*

"So, you're calling me a Maiden?" she asked slowly, angling her head downwards to look at him beneath lowered brows.

He blinked, confusion flooding him. "What? No," he shook his head. "I was just trying to make a-" he stopped then, seeing the mischief in her eyes and the smirk across her face. *What a little trickster you are, Miss Maria.*

"I'm not calling you a Maiden," he reassured.

"I know," she smiled, sitting up and crossing her legs. "I'm just messing with you."

Arthur hummed a laugh, watching her as she inspected her nails for dirt. The same feeling as before stirred in his chest at the sun lighting up her golden hair through the window, her eyes glowing lime green as they lit in surprise at the dirt coating her nail-

Arthur mentally slapped himself. *Stop it. Focus.*

"Why join me?" Arthur asked, looking towards the far wall.

She glanced at him, lowering her hands. "Because I believe you can be King of Camelot," she said. "And I wanted to be a part of that. I don't think it was a coincidence that you saved me from that tool with the apples that day."

Arthur nodded. "Leonard will probably miss us," he joked.

"I won't miss him," she huffed. "I've still got a mark where he kicked me in the ribs."

"Me neither. That prick can stay in the gutters," Arthur scowled, his mind looking back over that day.

She smiled faintly, a slight glow settling across her cheekbones, looking away from him. Arthur took a double look, interest lighting him up.

"Are you blushing?" he asked her, raising a brow at her. *Is it because of me? Since when did she find me attractive?*

Her brows raised, and she looked back at him, her blush deepening. "Huh?" she stammered.

Arthur chuckled at her. *Gods, I'm not that good-looking, surely.* "You're blushing," he pointed out, smirking slyly.

"Oh," she breathed, huffing a laugh and covering her face with a hand. "I'm just thinking, is all."

"About what?" Arthur asked, lifting a brow.

"About how I got my ass handed to me," she admitted.

"Huh?" Arthur's smirk faltered, his brow dropping. "You got your ass handed to you?"

She looked at him quizzically. "When Leonard beat me up," she said slowly.

"First time?" Arthur frowned. *So it wasn't that after all.* Disappointment deepened his frown, bitterness coating his tongue and settling in his chest. You *idiot, Art.*

She looked away from him, turning her head to look out the window. "Yeah, actually," she muttered.

"It seems to be his own personal goal to ruin my life. He always picked on me when I was young," Arthur muttered. "Now, all we do is fight."

She nodded in acknowledgement, pulling her legs up to her chest and resting her arms on them. Arthur looked at her for a moment, turning to watch where the carriage was heading, a faint view of dense foliage surrounding them.

"What are we talking about over here?" Kyan asked, walking over between the two, Maria ignoring him.

Arthur looked over at him flatly. "Personal business," he said irritably.

Kyan's eyes lit in mischief, a smirk stretching over his lips. *The bastard saw everything.* "Well, pardon me for interrupting your deep background information sharing," he replied.

"You're not forgiven," Arthur narrowed his eyes at him.

Kyan shrugged. "I guess that's too bad," he said and sat down beside Maria, blocking off Arthur's view of her. Kyan wrapped an arm around Maria's shoulders, pulling her closer to him. "How are we doing over here? Not bored of this poor sod's voice, are we?" Kyan asked her.

"I'm not sure if you've gotten the hint already, but she doesn't like you," Arthur scowled at him.

Maria glanced up at Kyan, her eyes annoyed. "Please remove your arm from around me," she said flatly.

"Naw, you like it," Kyan jested, shaking her gently. "You don't protest against it when we're alone."

*Who does this tool think he is?* Arthur stood up and held the side of the cart, walking over to him. "Kyan."

Kyan glanced up at him flatly. "What?"

"She asked you to remove your arm from her," Arthur scowled. "I suggest you do it."

Kyan gave him a mockingly sulky look, his lip wavering. "I'm sure if she really wanted me to stop, she'd do something about it," he drawled, looking at her. "Ain't that right, darling?"

Anger fired up in him a lot faster than he would have thought, his jaw clenching. "Listen, jackass," Arthur growled through his teeth. "You've got three seconds to get off her before I remove you myself."

Maria pulled Kyan's arm off of her shoulders, shifting away from them. "If you both don't mind, I'd rather be left on my own for however long we've got left on the carriage ride," she muttered.

"That means get off her and piss off, Kyan," Arthur said, frowning at him.

"Gods, you're such a royal buzz kill," Kyan rolled his eyes at the both of them, standing up. "All I was doing was giving her something more comfortable to lean on, you know?"

Arthur huffed at him, sitting back down on the carriage floor, turning over to lay on his back and closing his eyes. Kyan walked past him back to his spot, looking down at him with a frown.

"I know you're staring at me, Kyan," Arthur said, his eyes remaining shut. "You're not subtle whatsoever."

"Oh, you don't want the attention anymore?" Kyan snorted. "Now that you can't get it from a woman."

"I'd rather not worry about anything for the next few hours," Arthur snorted. "Go sit back down and feel rejected."

"At least I made a move," Kyan smirked, walking away from him.

Another set of footsteps echoed beside Arthur, along with a flop of weight. The crunch of an apple split the air, chewing noises loud in his ears.

Arthur cracked open an irritated eye, looking at Tristan. "Do you ever stop eating?" he frowned.

"When I'm full," Tristan said, swallowing the mouthful.

"Which is never," Arthur muttered, closing his eye.

"Are you calling me fat?" Tristan looked at Arthur.

"Maybe." Arthur smirked slightly.

"That's hurtful."

"Truthful."

Tristan scoffed in disbelief at him, flicking his elbow. "You don't have any manners today, sour puss," Tristan frowned.

Arthur opened his eyes, looking up at him. "It's been a tough couple of days, buddy; it's nothing personal."

Tristan narrowed his eyes at him and poked his ribs playfully. Arthur squirmed, trying not to laugh. "Cranky butt," Tristan teased.

"That's a bit mean, don't you think?" Arthur said, grinning at him.

"You've said worse," Tristan lifted a brow.

"Yeah? Like what?" Arthur asked, sitting up from the hardened wooden floor.

"Chip idiot."

"That one was a good one."

"You're a chip idiot."

"No," Arthur said. "Kyan is."

Tristan giggled to himself. "Yeah."

Arthur chuckled, looking over at Kyan. "Definitely."

Kyan stared flatly at the pair. "I'm not deaf," he muttered.

"No, but you're a chip idiot," Tristan grinned.

"And *you* are a dumb tool."

"Don't say that to Tristan; he's sensitive," Arthur scowled at Kyan. Kyan snorted, looking away.

Tristan looked at Arthur, his face flat. "Am I?"

Arthur shrugged. "I mean, you can be."

Tristan looked down slightly, taking another bite of his apple. Arthur glanced at Maria in the corner, her face hidden in the shadow. Arthur frowned, Kyan's words mixing around in his head. *What a jerk. As if he'd know how to get girls, anyway.*

The cold breeze blew rapidly through the castle of Camelot, the Barons inside patrolling every corridor and every hallway. Maidens scattered out of the way of them in fright whenever they passed, steering clear of the stairwells.

In one of the rooms, a Baron sat on the edge of a ward bed, a Maiden standing in front of him with a medic box beside her. His face was tilted up and his eyes closed in pain as the stitch pulled through his eyelid, hissing at it. The Maiden kept calm as she threaded the needle through and tied off the suture, clearing up the cut delicately with a cloth.

"I suppose your Barons weren't the best defence when it came to a rogue Knight," a voice from the doorway said.

The Maiden picked up a patch of gauze and pressed it over his eye gently, pain shooting through his head like an arrow tip. He growled through his teeth.

"And now Arthur has escaped Camelot," the voice purred.

"I assure you, sire, we are doing our best to track him down," his father's voice followed.

King Ergott stepped into the room, his crown jewels set alight from the lanterns, pale bruises adorning his skin. "We need to find where he's heading," he said.

The Baron looked at the King, holding back a grunt at the pressure on his eye. *How was he so quickly healed?* His fight with Samqueel had left him with more of his blood over his clothes than Torona's. It was impossible how fast he was recovering.

"My men are tracking his movements as we speak," Jackseye said, following behind him.

"And Voss?"

"We're not certain of his location," Jackseye admitted.

"No matter," Ergott dismisses. "He was never the best of Masters."

Edward frowned at the pair, holding the gauze in place as the Maiden wrapped a bandage around his head. "Voss is gone?"

Ergott looked at him. "We're uncertain at this point. Perhaps you know where he could be?"

Edward shrugged. "Last I heard, he was on a mission to capture Arthur from Marlon's Training Hall."

"Marlon… and who is he in relevance to Arthur?" Ergott asked.

Jackseye looked at the King with raised brows. "Sire, are you seriously unaware of who your Knight Trainer is?" he asked incredulously.

"Of course I know him," Ergott sniped. "What I don't know is why he would go against his King's orders to have him returned?" he muttered bitterly, turning away from him.

"Then you knew Xavier Marlon was really Jonathan Gawain?" Jackseye asked, his voice expectant.

Ergott paused, turning back to him slowly. "What did you just say?"

Edward's eyes widened, looking at his father. "Sir Gawain was the Knight Trainer?"

"In the flesh," he nodded to his son.

Ergott turned back around. "No wonder why we were getting so many Knights so quickly," he muttered. "Now he's gone with Arthur and will train him."

"Reports of more Knights were told to me this afternoon again," Jackseye turned to him.

"Which ones?" Ergott asked, looking at him from over his shoulder.

"Jameson Galahad and Oliver Geraint, heading out of Londinium on the back of an apple cart."

Ergott narrowed his eyes with a frown, clenching his jaw. "So they aren't dead."

"I'm afraid not," Jackseye muttered.

Edward's heart thundered, looking at the two men with his stomach sinking in realisation. *If they're alive, then how many more of them are out there?*

"Rohin, send a patrol to search over the outskirts of Londinium, find out where they went off to," Ergott said.

"Already on it," Jackseye frowned. "Patrols were dispatched this morning."

Ergott looked over at Edward. "And you, be prepared for another departure in the next coming days."

Jackseye looked at Ergott in protest. "The boy is injured, at least let his wounds heal before he's sent-"

"I can handle it," Edward said firmly. "A scratch on the face won't slow me down."

Ergott smiled faintly, looking at Jackseye with a grin. "You have a strong boy, Rohin."

Jackseye frowned at Edward, scorn sharpening his scowl. "Perhaps a little too strong," he mumbled.

"I can still fight with one eye," Edward challenged, standing up and spooking the Maiden, who darted back away. "This won't make any difference. I've fought with worse."

"Ms Ruth," Ergott said deeply. The Maiden looked at the King, bowing.

"You are dismissed," Ergott nodded. She gathered her box and tied it up, walking quickly from the room.

Edward's good eye trailed after her, watching her leave. "A pity," he shrugged. "She was such a lovely little thing."

"And new to the job," Ergott said, watching her leave. "Ruth is only in her mid-twenties."

Edward's appreciation for the Maiden rippled further, a slight smirk on his lips. Ergott looked over at Edward with a frown.

"The Maidens are off limits," he growled.

"Yes, my liege," Edward nodded to him. *But what would you know if I did?* He smirked at the thought.

"That's your first and final warning," Ergott added firmly, frowning at Edward.

"I'm sure he can handle the rule," Jackseye dismissed. "Boy's never been with a woman in his life."

Edward raised a brow at Jackseye. *That's where you're wrong, father.*

"My castle isn't the place to find love," Ergott said, turning to Rohin.

"Barons are sworn to chastity when they sign up," Jackseye recalled. "Too many loose ends otherwise."

"A fair rule," Ergott agreed.

*And full of bullshit, wouldn't you think?* "If you'll excuse me, I have duties to go back to," Edward bowed to Ergott.

Ergott looked back at Edward, nodding slightly at the boy. He walked out of the room, looking back over his shoulder to make sure they didn't watch him turn down the servant stairwell after the pretty Maiden.

Ergott turned to Jackseye. "And what of Ariendal's condition?"

"Strong and ready to go," Jackseye said. "The fight against the Knights was considered a warm-up amongst them."

Ergott walked over to the windowsill, watching Barons order the city. "Excellent," he said coldly. "Now, all we need is to find the boy."

The night sky darkened the carriage to almost pitch black, the stars aflame outside the window. The moon lit the horse's path forwards, the driver yawning widely.

Tristan lay on top of a few stacked crates, groaning. "I thought you said only a few hours, not a full *day*."

"If you keep complaining, it'll go for longer," Geraint said through the open window, his horse walking beside the carriage.

"I'm hungry."

"Not surprising," Arthur grumbled, rubbing his eyes from a rough sleep.

"Where are we even going?" Tristan drew out.

"A safe place," Kyan mocked with his hands twinkling in the air.

"Somewhere with food if you shut your gob," Peter muttered, his bandaged arm deepening his scowl.

Arthur opened an eye, peering over to the group. "You know of this place, Peter?"

"No," he said, looking at Arthur. "I was saying it to make him stop complaining."

"He's not wrong," Galahad added. "We've got plenty of food there."

"Great," Arthur said. "Cause I'm actually starving."

"Do you have apple buns?" Tristan asked, eyes wide in hope as he looked at Galahad.

Galahad looked back at him, frowning. "What kind of question is that?"

"Do we look like scavengers?" Geraint frowned at him through the window.

Tristan looked at them with a flat expression, waiting for an answer.

"Of course we have them!" Geraint laughed.

"Ah, good," Tristan smiled. "They're the best thing ever. Sam's mum, Erin, makes *the* best apple buns."

Kyan looked over at Tristan with a brow raised in disbelief. "Commander Sam? Like the one that led the Knights?"

Tristan looked at him blankly. "Do you know another Sam?"

Kyan snorted. "There's no way you used to hang out with the Roundtable," he huffed.

"Why? Just because he's Tristan?" Arthur frowned at him.

"Exactly why," Kyan agreed.

Arthur scowled at him. "You like to make yourself seem better than everyone, don't you?"

"Well, if he really did hang out with them," Kyan sneered, "then let's ask him a few questions about things no one in the city knew about the Knights. Shall we?"

Everyone looked at Kyan, shrugging at one another.

Arthur scoffed. "Sure," he said.

"I mean, I'm down," Tristan shrugged, sitting up. "Who wants to know what?"

"Smartass can go first," Arthur smirked at Kyan.

Kyan mocked his smirk and looked at Tristan. "Where did they stay in the castle?"

"Oh easy, they've got cabins outside the Knights Quarters, about fifteen of them," Tristan said. "Though I don't know why if there's only twelve of them."

"Who was the heaviest drinker?" Arthur asked.

Tristan chuckled to himself. "You'd think it would be Karsol, but no. It was actually Joseph."

"The quiet ones are always the most chaotic," Arthur smirked.

"Favourite snacks for each of them?" Kyan shot.

"Uh, well, Sam loved apple buns," Tristan counted on his fingers. "Taryn always had a box of cheese crackers on him. Carsen loved marshmallows, like *loved* loved marshmallows. It was crazy. Henry had salads that I always stole when I could, Lorsaw liked peanut bars, Karsol always craved some sort of sugar cereal no one ate, Reuben loved bacon, Joseph kept beef jerky in his pockets all the time, Arkan practically *inhaled* cheese puffs and pickles, Dominic liked milk biscuits, Natan would always eat cashews and Derak just constantly drank sweet tea. If that counts as a food." He looked around at them.

Arthur smirked at Kyan. "How about that?"

Kyan huffed, a mildly surprised look on his face. "Yeah, right," he mused.

The carriage began to slow down, the road becoming rougher. Maria stirred from her sleep on the other side of the carriage, opening her eyes to look at them. "What was that?" she mumbled.

Arthur stood up and faced out the window, the moonlight illuminating the stone path brightly. His eyes trailed along to a large cave opening dug into the side of a rocky hill, more Rebels standing with torches around the entrance. The carts in front of them pulled to a stop off the road, more of them peeling out of the doors towards the cavern.

Geraint dismounted his horse, petting it on the neck gently before handing the reins to a Rebel, walking around the back of the carriage and opening the door. "Alright, up we get lads," he grinned and looked down at Maria. "And lass."

They all stood up, making their way out of the carriage, Tristan actually falling out of it this time with an "Oof!". Peter stooped to pick him up with his free arm, pulling him to his feet.

"Here we are," Galahad said, facing the camp with his hands on his hips. "The Reigate Caves."

Arthur stepped out of the carriage, looking around the area with wide eyes. Vines hung over the edge of the entrance, swishing as people moved in and out of them. Sandstone peppered the outside, the rocks forming a circuit for the carriages to go, leading around the other side. Many of the rocks were explicitly carved as seats, divots burrowed into the stone like dimples.

A man walked out of the tunnel, his short gray hair bleached white in the moonlight. His jacket was well maintained, the buttons done up against the cool night. He walked towards the apple carriage, two other Rebels following after him.

Galahad smiled at one of the younger Rebels, dismounting from the carriage with a grunt. Arthur watched Galahad walk towards the Rebel; the lad had to be no older than sixteen, his blonde hair stuck up in a cowlick at the top of his forehead.

Joyful blue eyes glimmered at Galahad, and the lad ran towards him, his arms outstretched. "Dad, you're back!" he grinned.

Galahad stretched his arms out wide. "Hey, buddy!"

The boy barrelled into Galahad, wrapping his arms around him tightly. Galahad laughed as he tried to keep his balance. "Did you do it? Did you get him?" the lad asked, looking up at him.

"Why don't you ask him yourself?" Galahad asked, nodding over to Arthur.

Arthur looked at the lad, a small smile on his face. He looked at Arthur, his eyes widening. "Are you really the Born King?" he asked with awe.

Arthur glanced at Galahad, looking back at the lad with an open mouth.

"I knew it!" the boy grinned, joy lighting his eyes up. "I knew we could find you and bring you back!"

Tristan looked over towards Arthur with his eyebrows raised. "A little ball of energy he is," he said.

Arthur looked at Tristan. "Did you know he had a son?"

"Not at all," Tristan shook his head.

Maria walked up to Arthur's side, her eyes droopy as she looked at the lad. "He's got more energy than me, that's for sure," she murmured.

"You just woke up," Arthur said. "I'm sure you both would have the same amount of energy," he grinned lightly.

She narrowed her eyes at him. "You try sleeping in a carriage full of loud men," she grunted.

"I did," Arthur looked at her.

"You must be an awful deep sleeper, then."

Arthur frowned at her. "I didn't get any sleep," he growled, looking over at Tristan.

"Exactly my point," she muttered, irritated.

"Who are these people?" The lad asked Galahad, looking at Tristan and Maria.

"This one," Galahad pointed to Arthur. "Is your King. This is Tristan, and what was your name darl?" Galahad asked Maria.

"Maria," she said.

"Maria, and you remember the stories about Uncle G, don't you?" Galahad nodded to Gawain.

"Oh, yeah, I do," the boy said, smiling at Gawain. Gawain nodded to the boy, a small smile on his face.

Galahad looked over at the three. "This here is my son, Baeydn," he smiled.

Tristan peered at the boy curiously. "Why, you don't look like Jameson," he observed. "You've got a blonde mop."

"I look more like my mother," Baeydn said to him. "I've got Dad's courage, though!"

"Which one of you is Arthur Pendragon?" the elder man asked, looking around at the new arrivals.

Arthur flicked his eyes over to the man, walking over to him. "That's me," he said.

"Good to hear it," the man smiled. "We've been waiting to get you for a long time."

"What exactly is this place?" Arthur asked, looking at the cave's entrance.

"This is Reigate Caves, son," he said. "We've hidden here for the past eighteen years after your father died. We've made an awful good residence out of it."

Arthur nodded, looking back at him. "Looks comfortable," he noted.

"It's more comforting on the inside, trust me," he said with a warm smile. *For a man who looks no older than sixty, he's awfully grandfatherly.*

"And your name?" Arthur asked with a soft smile.

"Rodney Lancelot," he said, extending his arm to him.

Arthur blinked, a warm grin on his face. "Another one of you?" He shook his hand, his calloused skin rough on Arthur's palm.

"There's more where I came from," Lancelot smiled. "They're all eager to meet their new recruit and future King."

"Do you believe it's all true?" Arthur asked, frowning slightly. "The Born King?"

"The Mage was never wrong before," Lancelot shrugged, letting his hand go.

"What Mage?" Arthur asked.

"*The* Mage, boy," Lancelot answered.

Arthur looked at him, raising a brow. "There's a whole Kingdom of them, specifics would help," he said.

"Not a civilian Mage, Arthur," Gawain chimed in. "He means the real deal."

Arthur looks over at Gawain. "Merlin?"

Gawain nodded at him. "Merlin," he confirmed.

"Where is he?" Arthur asked.

Gawain's eyes lit in puzzlement, taken aback by the question. "Why would you try to find him?" he questioned.

Arthur raised a brow at him, frowning slightly. "Isn't that a part of the journey? To find him?"

Maria looked at him, uncertainty on her face. "Not unless you want to travel through the Darklands. I know *I* sure don't," she said.

The Darklands was a mysterious land in the deepest part of the forest, with mountains filled with treacherous monsters and wild animals alike. Anyone who entered unprepared wasn't known to come back out alive, and those that did come back came out in pieces, or as Knights, the stories say. At least that's what Arthur read in a book, anyway. But it never mentioned Merlin.

"Aren't we in the forest?" Arthur asked.

"Not the Darklands," Lancelot shook his head. "It's a fair way from here. This is a part of the temperate forests south of the Darklands. It's pretty rare to see any Etherspawn in the area."

"Well, that's a good thing then," Arthur said.

Lancelot took in their tired faces, his face softening. "Come on, I'll take you guys through the caves. It looks like one of you needs help anyway," he said, looking at Peter in the background.

Arthur nodded, looking over at Peter. "Escaping Camelot wasn't easy."

"It never is; the place is a rabbit warren," Geraint shrugged, moving towards the cave.

Arthur looked over at Maria, seeing her tired expression. "Come on," he said, walking over to her. "Let's get you inside."

She looked at him with a faint smile and followed after Geraint, pushing her hair from her face. Arthur smiled back at her, following Geraint into the cave's entrance. The Rebels took the carriages into the opening, the rest of the group following behind them in the moonlight.

## *Chapter 15: The Reigate Caves*

Torches lit up the cave in sconces along the sandstone and slate walls, the crunch of gravel underfoot making Arthur wonder if where they were going really was as fancy as he initially thought. *Living in a cave is a significant difference from living in a castle.*

Around them, a few Rebels stared at Arthur, murmuring amongst themselves as he passed by. Arthur looked forward and saw a large clearing within the cave, a lobby filled with oak wood laid out across the floor in even panels, fur rugs dotted around decoratively. The walls were smoothed back, and alcoves were carved into the stone, serving as shelves and beds. Stone-carved and plush furniture sat around the space in equal proportions, much of it to his taste.

Arthur looked around the lobby in awe, smiling faintly at the cave's interior. *How did they do this all on their own?*

A few men walked up to the group, wearing rugged clothing with different coloured jackets. Arthur blinked at them; *they must be more old Roundtable Knights.*

"So you're the Born King?" one asked, his blue eyes glimmering in the moonlight seeping through the hollowed roof that turned his mousy hair silver.

"That's what people have been calling me," Arthur frowned. "But just call me Arthur."

"Aaron Percival, but you can call me Percy if you forget the last name," the man said, his arm outstretched.

"No one's gonna call you Percy!" one of the Rebels yelled from afar.

"We're flat out calling you Aaron!" another voice called.

"Believe it or not, Aaron, you're not hard to forget," Bedivere added behind Arthur.

Arthur shook Percival's hand, looking back at Bedivere. "Neither are you, by the sounds of things."

Bedivere lifted a brow at him with a delighted smile. "That's the whole point of this pretty face," he drawled.

"That wasn't a compliment," Arthur frowned at him.

"It is now." Bedivere walked around him, heading towards a walled-off area, tempting smells wafting from the carved windows.

Tristan smelt it, and his mouth dropped, his feet shifting to follow after Bedivere like a zombie. "Food," he muttered to himself.

"Feel free to make yourselves at home and get a bite to eat," Lancelot said to the group. "We've got plenty left over."

"Food and a good mug of ale sound great right about now, if I don't say," Kyan smirked, moving off after Tristan. Gawain stood with Peter, muttering to him as he led him to another area of the cave, no doubt to get his arm fixed.

Arthur sighed to himself, looking around his supposed new home. He couldn't have imagined this would ever have happened to him, that this was how his apparent destiny would start. *Well… at least they have a floor.*

"Hey, Simon," Geraint called to the far wall, walking down a carved-out walkway. "Come check out the new lads and lass that we picked up in Camelot."

Across the cave, a man stretched across a fur rug laid along a wooden bench chair, a book pinned underneath his hand. His blue eyes flicked up from beneath light hair to look at Geraint, then to Arthur. Curiosity entered his gaze, and he closed his book, standing up and shuffling over to them, a lopsided smile wrapped on his face.

"Pleased to meet you," the man greeted with a sharp accent. "Name's Simon Ector."

Arthur nodded at him. "Arthur Pendragon," he greeted.

Simon blinked in surprise, grinning widely. "Pleasure to finally meet you, my liege."

"Just call him Arthur; it's all he'll respond to," Maria said tiredly, leaning against the wall and rubbing her eye.

Simon looked over at Maria, smiling at her more widely than he did with Arthur. Simon's eyes lit in interest, and Arthur grit his teeth as his gaze drifted over her. "And your name?"

She looked at him, her eyes foggy with fatigue. "Tired is what it is," she muttered.

Arthur looked at Simon with his arms folded. "That's Maria. The journey up here was a bit rough, to say the least."

"Would you like me to walk you to your room?" Simon asked her.

Something shot through Arthur at his words, an emotion he couldn't quite name, especially when she said, "That would be great, thank you."

"Come with me then," Simon said, grabbing her arm gently. "Are you joining us, my liege?"

Arthur frowned lightly, his chest feeling heavy with annoyance. *Why am I so annoyed?* "I'll find my own way there," he muttered.

Maria moved closer to Simon, letting him lead her down another part of the cave. Simon linked his arm with hers, watching her with an acute interest that set the hair on the back of Arthur's neck bristling.

Arthur scowled at him, turning away before he became too angry. He looked around, trying to think about something else. *What was that emotion?*

Then it hit him. It was *jealousy. Of* what*? Simon Ector?* He huffed at himself. *Come on, Art. There was nothing to be jealous of... except for the way she moved closer to him when he touched her arm...*

*Why am I even thinking about this? Maria is just a girl.*

Arthur looked towards a new corner, shrugging off his thoughts as he walked up the stairs to the small platform. He took a stool out from underneath a low bar table, sitting down with a sigh. He looked down the bench, noticing he was the only one there until a larger man sat down three stools to his left. His white jacket was spotless, the seams intact, and the material practically glowing underneath the torchlight. Arthur looked at him from the corner of his eye, trailing his gaze up and down. Dirty blonde hair was smoothed back across his head, stretching down into a trimmed beard dusting his jaw. Blue-gray eyes stared flatly at the bottles on the stone shelves beneath low brows.

"Do you have any drink service here, or is it just for show?" Arthur asked, trying to locate the bartender.

The man lifted a brow at him and knocked a rhythmic beat onto the bar. "You got to know how to work the show to get the goods, boy," he said. A Rebel woman rounded the corner from behind the stone wall, saw the white jacket, and instantly grabbed a bottle of whiskey.

Arthur scoffed. "Already knew."

"If you had known, you'd have a drink halfway down your throat," the man growled and took the drink from the woman.

Arthur knocked on the bench, getting the rhythm spot on.

The bartender looked at him up and down. "Are you sure you can handle whiskey?" she questioned.

Arthur looked at her, unsure. "I guess we'll find out."

The man smirked at his drink, shaking his head. The bartender poured another knuckle, adding a chunk of ice into the glass before sliding it in front of him.

Arthur caught the glass, watching the ice swish around the amber liquid. "Thanks," he said.

"You've got no idea about the knocks, do you?" the man grumbled.

Arthur looked at him with sly challenge. "Bet."

He looked at Arthur sideways, taking a sip from his drink. "Go on," he prompted. "After you down that, do the rhythm for vodka."

*Rhythm for vodka?* Arthur took a sip, allowing the drink to settle in his system. Nothing happened but the bitter taste of the sour honey infused in it. "That wasn't so bad-" Arthur coughed at the aftertaste, placing the empty glass back on the bench. *Gods, it burns like fire!*

"Kay!" a deep voice called out from behind him.

Kay chuckled at Arthur and turned around to face the voice. "What do you want? I'm busy."

"Care for a round?" the man asked. Arthur turned around to look at the voice; a man, possibly even bigger than Kay, was strolling over to them.

Kay waved him over, a challenging smirk on his face. "Get on over here, Chris," he said, his eyes narrowing slightly with interest. "Let's show the lightweights how it's done."

The larger man wore one of the colour-coded jackets, dark orange lining the base of the fur collar and at the end of his sleeves. The man had a massive brown beard that came down to the top of his chest, his long hair tied up at the back. "Come on then! Let's see what you got this time!"

"The same thing as last time, where I beat your ass," Kay lifted a brow, shifting to face the man. Soon enough, a large gathering of Rebels focused on the corner, Percival and Bedivere coming over quickly to stand near Arthur.

Arthur watched the two curiously, shifting to sit side-on to the bar. "How regularly does this occur?"

"Every damn night," Percival said, folding his arms. "It's always them two."

"They wonder why they wake up with hangovers in the morning, and it's no wonder why Kay is always such a sore-headed bear when he does," Bedivere added, leaning against the bar.

"They still do this?" Galahad asked with a sigh, folding his arms and standing behind Arthur.

"Oh, all the time," the bartender rolled her eyes. "And neither of them bother to *pay* afterwards either."

"Gawain!" Percival yelled.

The dark man walked out from behind the wall, appearing beside Percival to look at the two big men. "I'm not at all surprised," he muttered, watching the two line up their shots. "They're going to drink themselves to death one evening."

"If only," Bedivere rolled his eyes.

"Come on, Gaheris!" Percival shouted.

Arthur looked at the Knights, smiling faintly. The way they were acting made Arthur feel as if Sam and the lads were here with him. *It must be a Knight thing.*

"Okay, Sir Henry Kay," Gaheris smirked. "How many shots?"

"I can sweep you twenty shots," Kay challenged.

Gaheris scoffed. "Do I look like a man-child?"

"In less than a minute," Kay finished with a smirk.

"Thirty shots," Gaheris said, raising an eyebrow.

Geraint looked over to the crowd of people from his spot near the entrance, sighing to himself. "Lancelot!"

"Thirty-five, with three knuckles of brandy on top," Kay growled. The crowd exclaimed in surprise, looking at each other, gold being tossed around in bets of who would win this round.

"You have yourself a challenge," Gaheris smirked, reaching his hand out.

"Thirty-five shots each with three knuckles of brandy to top it off?" Bedivere's brows raised. "Gaheris would die."

"Gaheris is going to win, for sure," Galahad said.

"I'm voting Gaheris; Kay will pussy out," Percival smirked.

"My gold is on Kay," Gawain nodded, pulling ten gold pieces out to lay on the bar. "Toss it in."

Percival tossed in ten gold pieces, followed by Galahad. Bedivere slid his stack into the pile, the gold glimmering in the torch light.

Arthur stood up from the bar, nodding to all of the Knights around him. "I'm going to find my room; the way you lot drive is torture to my back," he said, walking away from the scene.

"Goodnight then, lad," Percival grinned, quickly snatching Arthur's spot.

"You'll miss all the action," Gawain said, watching Arthur. "It's actually very humorous to watch these two get more and more stupid."

"I've seen enough action for a day," Arthur dismissed.

"Very well, you'll probably hear the cheering regardless," Gawain nodded and turned back to the men.

Arthur nodded. "Probably," he said, walking down the steps leading to the bar.

The crowd began to grow louder as he rounded the walkway corner he remembered Simon and Maria walking down, the voices echoing on the stone walls as he climbed the carved staircase up higher. Arthur looked around each corner of the cave walls. The stone was cut decoratively, with displays of animals and Knights alike painstakingly etched from the rock.

He found an empty room down a left corner, seeing a nicely made bed against the right side wall, a candle lighting the space from the stone bedside table. A large cupboard sat against the wall opposite the bed, standing on top of a plush fur rug that matched his blankets. The room was surprisingly warm, an updraft of hot air blowing through his boots at ground level.

*I wonder where everyone else is bunked in.* Tristan was most definitely making himself known in the kitchen. Peter would be getting stitched up and probably asleep in his own room. He didn't particularly mind if Kyan lost his way in the tunnels. Maria was wherever that accented tool took her, most likely fast asleep.

Arthur sat on his bed, sighing deeply to himself. "What a mess," he muttered, looking at the rug on the floor.

A shadow crossed over the floor at the doorway, Arthur lifting his eyes to look at Lancelot. The man smiled warmly at him, his white moustache wrinkling like a caterpillar. "How are we settling in?" he asked softly.

"Getting there," Arthur said. "Still hard to believe it all happened the way it did. It's overwhelming to know how many people actually want me to be King here; I wonder how quick it'll take them to realise I'm not that person."

The old Knight moved into the room further, his face gentle. "Nobody here is expecting you to be perfect on your first day," he reassured. "You haven't even begun training yet."

"I did at Marlon's- I mean, Gawain's training hall, but even then, I couldn't impress him," Arthur said, frowning at the memory.

Lancelot chuckled softly. "It takes an awful lot to impress Jonathan Gawain," he assured. "But I'm sure you've got the goods to come through. You just need a bit of proper practice, is all."

Arthur glanced at him. "So I'm guessing you all will train me?"

"The majority of the time, Gawain will train you," Lancelot nodded. "But if he needs help with other things he's not so great at, the other Knights will step in to assist. It's all a team effort."

"And they all believe in The Born King?" Arthur asked.

"Well, not only is it a prophecy created by Merlin," he started, clasping Arthur's shoulder gently with a squeeze.

"The proof is sitting right here in front of me. The son of the late King Benjamin foretold to rule the land of Braynor. If your presence isn't enough for them, I don't know what is."

"All of Braynor?" Arthur frowned lightly. "Surely that's not possible. No man can rule an entire continent."

Lancelot smiled down at him. "If the legend is true, and you do become the King of Camelot, pretty soon you'll be the man to rule it all. People have heard your name far and wide, not just in Londinium. War-ravaged Kingdoms have turned to your name with hope, their faith given to you to help reunite the country once again. It's a great responsibility but a great honour at the same time."

Arthur looked down, taking in what Lancelot had told him. *It's my destiny to bring peace back to Braynor and lead these people?* He'd often tried to imagine what that would look like - if the prophecy existed - he couldn't have pictured it more differently.

How was he going to lead a handful of Rebels and forgotten Knights to victory against his uncle, who has some sort of magic? *And when the Hell did he get magic, anyway?* If his dreams were anything to go off of, Ergott must have had it under his skin for years. His arms flared with goosebumps at the realisation, the amber eyes flicking back inside his mind again.

"Your father was a great, inspiring man, capable of anything he set his mind to. You are his son," Lancelot said. "We don't expect you to be the carbon copy of Benjamin. But we are excited to see what kind of man you become throughout all this. No matter what you think or what you've been told, you were born to lead. Don't let your potential go to waste, son."

Arthur looked up at Lancelot."What of the Sword? How do I get that?" he asked.

"I'm afraid I'm as knowledgeable about Excalibur as the next man," Lancelot admitted. "It disappeared the night

Benjamin passed away. Books mention it to be in the Darklands, but beyond that, you'll have to ask around or find some information on it."

Arthur looked at Lancelot with a smile. "After all this time of being told I'll never be King, I've found a bundle of people telling me otherwise. Who knew the believers were here all along?"

"Everyone's always believed, boy," he smiled. "You just didn't see it."

"There's one thing I don't understand, though. Why were you all hiding this whole time?" Arthur asked. "Why not come back to Camelot?"

Lancelot let his shoulder go with a soft pat. "Things became very… hectic in the castle when Benjamin passed away," he said.

"With my uncle?"

"Exactly," he nodded. "He didn't want us to stick around. He wanted to wipe the castle of anything under Benjamin's influence. So he sent us out on a mission to try and trap us, and we led him through it to make him believe us dead before we left to discover this cave."

"He tried to kill you all?" Arthur frowned.

"He did with a few of us," Lancelot admitted solemnly. "Close friends and brothers were killed in his plan. But those of us who escaped are still here today."

Arthur scowled, looking down. *History does repeat itself, huh.* "He did the same thing to the Roundtable yesterday, and now he's framed me for killing them and Aunt Rosaline," he growled.

Lancelot went still, his kind face turning to one of shock. "Pardon?" he asked.

"He framed me for killing the Roundtable," Arthur repeated, looking up at him. "He murdered Rosaline to keep his power."

Lancelot's face saddened considerably, and his brow crinkled. "Rosaline is dead?" he echoed, his voice pained.

Arthur watched him carefully, hesitance halting his words. Lancelot's hand passed through his gray hair and rubbed his face absently, a mournful noise sounding from his throat. "Not Rose," he shook his head. "Rosaline was a very important woman to us."

"How was she?" Arthur asked curiously. He couldn't possibly see how the old Knights would've known Rosaline; they were gone before Ergott and Rosaline had married. Rosaline had come to Camelot as a young princess for an intermarriage alliance, bonding Nemeth and Camelot fifteen years ago. Arthur could still remember the wedding: purple and orange banners flying through the city, hundreds of esteemed houses and royals showing up for the celebrations in the castle, the grand feast and ball where he'd danced with the young princesses that had come to the wedding with their parents. He'd hated the look of the frilly shirt he'd been made to wear by Ms Enid; her argument was she thought he'd looked 'rather dapper' in it, and asked if he'd want to go in clothes covered in charcoal from his adventures in the city instead.

"She would report back to us on the movements of the castle," Lancelot said, his face laced with sorrow. "She was the reason why we were there to get you. The Knights were aware of the situation, as well. And now that the lot of them are gone... Oh, Rosaline," he sighed.

Arthur watched Lancelot, sympathy looming on his face. "I miss her too," he murmured.

Lancelot smiled faintly at him, tears springing to his brown eyes. "If things were different, and she wasn't married to that tool of a King, she'd be here in the cave," he said. "She was a beautiful woman. Her heart was too big for the role she played. I wish I could've just made her stay all those weeks ago."

Arthur nodded at him in agreement, then paused. *How could he have seen her?* "All those weeks ago? You visited Camelot?" Arthur asked.

"She would ride here on her good old mare every once in a while," he answered. "She risked a lot to keep it under wraps, but she claimed no one ever noticed her absence in the castle."

"That's why she's never around," Arthur murmured to himself. "She was reporting to you." Arthur would barely see the Queen around the castle. If he was honest, he often forgot she was around half the time. She never was frequent with any appearances at any gatherings or amongst the citizens. When she was, she would stay out for hours and talk with anyone she could, helping them with anything they needed. It made him feel a little guilty. "What information were you told?"

"She informed us of any movements within the castle. We knew the day the Roundtable was Knighted and ranked, when Jackseye was sent to Ariendal, the decisions of Ergott to join with the Barons, and any major milestones that were celebrated in the castle. She would find anything of interest and ride out the next morning." Lancelot nodded to himself, sighing quietly. "That's why she didn't come back with you."

"I wish she did," Arthur quirked his mouth. "The people loved her."

Lancelot huffed softly. "It wasn't just the people."

Arthur looked at him. "Did you?"

"With all my heart," he admitted. "She was too blindsided by Ergott to see it though. She loved the man despite his actions, and I just had to accept it."

"What was he like when my father was around?" Arthur asked, looking at him with a slight frown.

Lancelot sat down and took a deep breath, bracing his hands on his knees. "Ergott was quiet, to say the least," he said. "Always sneaking around the city and castle like someone painted a target on his back. He'd push his opinions of battle often with anyone who arched against us. Benjamin would always put him in line with any far-out suggestions and would trump him tenfold. It almost often ended up in a fight with those two after that. It seems his influence won this time around."

"I wish I knew my father," Arthur sighed. "I only know him partially through the nightmares I have and when I found the crate. But now I've lost the armour and the shield, so that was smart of me," he rolled his eyes. "It's just lucky Tristan got the sword back for me. I know he would want me to be the King, but I don't know if I have the strength to continue his legacy. I'm sure he's *incredibly* proud of that."

Lancelot looked at him curiously. "I'm sure time will tell for you," he nodded. "Nobody becomes a King in a day. And Benjamin's armour?"

"Yeah," Arthur nodded. "I lost it when the Barons stormed through the training hall."

"Well, you're lucky Gawain isn't very forgetful," he smiled.

Arthur raised a brow. "What do you mean by that?"

"I suppose you'll find that out tomorrow morning," he answered and stood up, grunting inwardly.

"Leaving me in suspense, are you?" Arthur asked with a smirk.

"I don't want to spoil the surprise," he smiled, turning towards the door.

"The surprise would be that he hands my ass to me," Arthur huffed.

Lancelot laughed softly. "Everybody believes that, but people don't seem to see how big of a softie he really is," he chuckled. "Get some rest, boy. You've got a big morning ahead of you."

"Thank you, Lancelot," Arthur nodded with a smile.

"Call me Lance," he smiled warmly and closed the door gently behind him.

Arthur smiled at Lancelot, laughing softly to himself. *Gawain a softie? I'd like to see how.*

Arthur removed his boots, placing them next to his bed. He laid back on the mattress, grunting lightly to himself. The furs beneath him were soft and warm and more comfortable than the goose-feather down blankets back at the castle. He could get used to this, he supposed. *At least I don't have to sleep in the mud.*

He turned his head to the candle and blew it out, the room plunging into darkness, light seeping through the crack beneath his door from the hallway. The cheering of Rebels echoed down the tunnel from a distance. *The drinking competition must be still going.* The men were more outgoing and kind towards him than he would've anticipated. And they actually believed him to be the next King, along with the rest of the Kingdom. And he didn't even know who they were, aside from his father's old Knights. *Maybe this prophecy isn't just a myth after all.*

"Wake up! Come on, Born King, time for your first training session!"

Arthur's eyes flew open, looking around the room still plunged in darkness, the doorway wide open with a man's silhouette shadowing over him. "Is it even day?" he mumbled, sitting up on his forearms and blinking the sleep from his eyes.

Percival stood at the doorway, leaning against the door. "Last time I checked, the sun was up outside," he said. "Now get up and put these on." Percival threw him new clothes, landing across Arthur's legs. "And put those ones you're wearing in the water fountain," he said, walking away from the door.

*Water fountain? What water fountain?* Arthur didn't recall seeing a fountain on his way in. Then again, it was dark when he arrived.

Arthur rubbed his eyes, sitting up on the side of the bed with a groan, picking the clothes up as they fell to the floor. He looked at the clothes: a new tan long-sleeved shirt with a dark pair of trousers. He got to his feet, walking over to the door tiredly before shutting it closed, a cold draft of wind blowing across his feet. *Thanks for leaving it open, Percival.*

He dressed quickly, picking up his old clothes in a heap and bundling them beneath his arm as he slid his boots onto his feet. He walked out of the room, looking around the hallways with a yawn. Inspiration lifted his chin; he felt proud and motivated to keep going on this unorthodox journey, strange as it was.

A door opened up from further down the hallway, and a bedraggled Maria stepped out of the room. Her hair was a mess of tangles around her head, fluffed up like a lion's mane. The dark circles from under her eyes were gone at least, her green eyes looking at Arthur with clarity. Her clothes were loose and untucked; she must've just passed out in them because it looked like she'd been dragged through the door by a cat.

"Get a good sleep, did we?" Arthur chuckled.

"The beds here are *way* more comfortable than Camelot," she yawned, her hand brushing over her hair. Her eyes widened slightly in surprise. "Gods almighty, that's a bad sign."

"There's a water fountain somewhere in this place," Arthur said, looking at her hair with a humoured face.

"I think I just need a bath in general," she muttered, looking down at herself. "And a change. Gods, I'm a right mess."

"Might need to get changed, especially since you're talking to your future King," Arthur smiled, laughing at her.

Her eyebrows flicked up at him, her face jokingly stricken. "Pardon me, sire, for the disorganisation of my presentation," she fawned, her hand on her chest.

"That's quite alright, Lady Maria," he chuckled.

"I must organise the Maidens straight away to run me a bath in my gold-plated chambers," she held in laughter, holding herself regally, her nose in the air.

"Sounds like a spectacular idea. Tell them to run their King a bath while you're at it, won't you?" he asked jokingly, his own hands raised in mock etiquette.

"Oh, right away, my liege," she nodded enthusiastically, raising her hand to flick her tangled hair back behind her shoulder. "Wouldn't want you stinking up the courtyard, would we?"

Arthur lifted up his own arm and sniffed, his face turning into a fake shock. "Good Gods! I smell like a werewolf!"

"Been playing amongst the common rabble, have we?" she snivelled, turning accusing eyes to him, laughter glinting in the emerald depths.

"Now, let's not perform accusations, Lady Maria," he said with a chuckle. "I already called myself out on it."

"Guilty pleasures have no place for a man as high up as thee," she gasped, pretend shock on her face.

Arthur scoffed at her, putting his hand on his chest. "Thou shall not have guilty pleasures!"

The both of them looked at each other with their lips pursed, then burst into laughter, their howls echoing down the tunnel. Maria doubled over in laughter, holding her arms against her stomach, her eyes glowing. Arthur chuckled to himself, his grin spread wide, shaking his head.

"Coming down the training circle?" he asked.

"I'll come down later," she said. "First, I need to find the bathing chambers to get rid of this scary sight."

"Percival said there was a water fountain somewhere," Arthur raised a brow. "But I didn't see one last night."

"I'm not bathing in a water fountain," she huffed.

"No, to wash these," Arthur raised the clothes he held in his arms.

"See, now that's more reasonable," she said, turning to walk down the hallway with her arms raised again. "Now, I shall return to attend to Your Majesty, but I shall take care of this whirlwind of a do before I even think about going outside."

"Excuses, my fair lady," Arthur shook his head. "You're missing out on a real exciting exercise that could result in me getting hurt or worse… dying," he said with a grin.

"Bollocks," she called back, rounding the corner. "If someone killed you here, we'd never hear the end of it."

Arthur shook his head with a chuckle, making his way down to the lobby. His mind ran the scene over in his head, his mood keeping up as he walked through the hallways, a smile sitting easy on his lips.

The hallway opened up into the main cavern, Rebels sitting around in the furniture socialising with one another, a couple groups banded together and jogging down the tunnel to head outside. Arthur looked around from the top of the staircase, letting out a sigh of relief and making his way down to the floor.

A few of the Knights sat around at a table against the far wall, mugs sitting on the table with small plates littered around them. The white jacket Knight - Kay, as Arthur recalled - sat slumped in his chair, his brow creased in fatigue with his eyes squinting at his plate, an arm resting on the table holding his head up.

"There he is! The Born King!" Geraint called from the table, leaning back in his chair to grin at him.

"Just call me Arthur, would you?" he chuckled lightly.

The rest of the Knights, minus Kay, turned their heads to look at Arthur, their faces changing to expressions of welcome delight. Bedivere raised his arm to Arthur, waving him over. "Get on over here, boy," he greeted. "Sit down and scavenge a plate."

"I wouldn't touch Kay's bacon, though," Lancelot advised. "He's grumpier than usual."

Kay glowered at the older man from beneath lowered brows.

Arthur made his way over to them, looking around for the fountain. "Umm, where do I put these, exactly?" he asked, raising his clothes.

Galahad lowered his fork to the table, turning behind him to a group of younger Rebels. "Baeydn," he called, the boy looking up and coming over to him. "Take Arthur's clothes to the fountain for us, buddy. That can be your first task for him."

Baeydn looked at Arthur with eager eyes. "Sure, no problem," he said, reaching his arms for the ball of clothes.

Arthur looked down at him. "Are you a fan of the Born King?" he asked.

"I've loved the stories since I've heard them," Baeydn said, a smile on his face. "The man that'll be the ruler of Braynor through blood ties, who'll save the land from evil! Somebody's gotta do it, right? And you're the one who will; Merlin said so. You'll be the coolest ever King."

"Cooler than your dad?" Arthur asked, whispering to him.

Baeydn looked at Galahad quickly, his face scrunched in thought. "Hmm," he thought.

"He'll give you all the chocolate in the castle," Arthur said.

Baeydn's eyes widened, and he nodded eagerly. "Oh yeah, definitely," he said quickly.

"Good choice," Arthur smirked, handing him the clothes."Thanks, lad."

Baeydn took the clothes and passed by his father with a grin, disappearing down the tunnel. Galahad chuckled at him, watching him go. "What's he so happy about?" he asked Arthur.

Arthur sat down next to Lancelot and Bedivere, looking at Galahad. "What do you mean?" he asked innocently.

"Ah, never mind," he said, turning back to the group. "Anyway, back to the conversation. No, you cannot fit an entire omelette inside your gob, Christopher."

"Watch me, Jameson," Gaheris grinned, picking up his fork. The omelette in question was the size of the plate, filled with all sorts of vegetables and thick as Arthur's thumb.

Arthur raised a brow at Gaheris. "You're eating that whole thing?"

"That's if he doesn't have a heart attack first," Percival rolled his eyes, eating a piece of bacon.

"He may be able to do it if he rolls it up," Bedivere muttered. "But that's beyond his mental capacity to think up."

"Aren't you hung over from last night?" Arthur asked Gaheris.

"Oh, very," Gaheris nodded. "And so is he."

Kay scowled at Gaheris, shovelling a piece of egg into his mouth.

"Don't mind Henry Kay, he's just sulky that he lost," Percival smirked. Something bumped the table from beneath, and Percival grunted in pain, holding his leg.

"Okay…" Arthur said, dragging his eyes away from Kay to Galahad. "Where's Gawain?"

"Probably out running," Geraint said through a mouthful, covering his mouth. "He took a couple of the Rebels out with him - cold bones, I'm guessing."

"Eager to train, are you?" Percival asked Arthur, leaning down to rub his shin.

"Well, thanks to Lancelot, I'm excited to start," Arthur nodded, turning his eyes to the Knight.

Lancelot smiled at him. "I'm sure it wasn't just me that helped," he said humbly.

"And, of course, everyone who believed in me," Arthur added promptly.

"Hey, who invited this guy to the party?" a familiar voice said from behind Arthur, hands clasping his shoulders.

Arthur looked at Tristan behind him, a warm smile on his face. "This lot did," he nodded to the Knights.

"They certainly know how to chow down," Tristan grinned, looking at the plates strewn across the table.

"I bet you could beat Gaheris in an eating challenge," Arthur added, looking over at Gaheris.

"Who? Me? No one can beat me in my own challenges," Gaheris boasted.

Tristan looked at him, eyebrows raised. "I mean, I'd give it a shot," he shrugged. "They kicked me out of the kitchen before I could grab anything. Ooh, nice omelette."

"Thank you," Gaheris beamed. "I cooked it myself."

"No wonder why it's burnt then," Percival observed, raising an eyebrow at the burnt surface.

"Should we do it then? I'm starving," Tristan challenged, smiling at him.

"Of course you are," Arthur sighed. "It's up to Gaheris if he wants another challenge."

"I assure you, this young man here won't last a minute," Gaheris laughed. "Surely he isn't serious about it."

"I wouldn't be so certain, Chris," Galahad warned. "He ate half a crate of apples on the way here. And *still* ate a whole meal when he got here."

Gaheris looked over at Tristan, surprise in his eye. "No lie?"

"No lie," Arthur nodded.

"My mother always said I could eat a horse and chase the rider," Tristan laughed and pulled up a seat. "I don't think I'd like horse meat, though. Or rider meat."

"Alright, well," Bedivere clasped his hands together. "Let's get this man a plate."

Arthur stood up and walked over to Tristan, placing his hands on his shoulders. "Now remember, your whole reputation with your fellow colleagues is on the line here. We will probably make fun of you if you lose, okay? No pressure," Arthur said in his ear.

Tristan looked at him bewildered, his eyebrows raised. "You doubt my capabilities of consuming omelette?" he asked, his voice confused.

"Absolutely not," Arthur assured. "*They* do, and I'm sure if you won, Gaheris would probably rip your head off."

Tristan swallowed nervously, looking at Gaheris. "He is a big guy," he stammered.

"Like I said, no pressure," he patted his shoulder, a mischievous smirk on his face.

A rebel brought Tristan a plate, sitting it in front of him; an omelette of equal size was piled on it, a jug of water following after it. Tristan's eyes settled on the food in front of him, any fear instantly wiped from his face.

"Alright, the first one to down the egg omelette wins," Bedivere announced. "If you both tie, there will be a continuous train of food until one of you gives up, throws up, or goes ass up. Any questions?"

"What happens if Tristan wins?" Arthur asked.

"We never came up with a reward," Percival admitted. "No one's beat Chris in an eating match since we met him."

"Do you have a question?" Gaheris asked Tristan, unsure of his name. "Your name?"

"Tristan Garrison," he squeaked. "And will you kill me?"

Gaheris burst into laughter, looking at the other Knights around him. The others laughed with him, and Arthur joined with uncertainty. Tristan shook in his seat, watching him nervously.

Gaheris looked back at Tristan with a flat expression. "Possibly," he said coldly.

Tristan's eyes widened, sweat coating his forehead. He looked at the plate in front of him. "I don't think this is a good idea, Arty," he whispered.

"You'll be fine as long as you lose," Arthur whispered into his ear.

"Alright, no more questions," Bedivere slammed the table with a fist. "Go!"

Immediately, Gaheris dug into the omelette, eating an entire chunk of the side in one single bite. Tristan jumped at the thunk and grabbed his fork nervously, digging into the omelette. Arthur looked at his friend in pity and turned to watch Gaheris. Gaheris shovelled ounces of the omelette in his mouth, half of it already gone. The Knights around him cheered him on, the large man confident as he stuffed his face. He looked up at Tristan; his fork dropped to the table, his eyes wide and jaw dropped.

Tristan's plate sat empty, the lad swallowing the last mouthful with a glass of water. He sat the glass down, a relieved smile on his face, wiping his mouth with the back of his hand. "Ooh, that was good," he burped. "Pardon me."

Arthur looked at Gaheris warily, looking at his plate, the omelette sitting half done. Gaheris swallowed what was in his mouth and stared at Tristan, dumbfounded.

Tristan smiled at the Knights, sitting up in his chair. "Anyone for seconds?" he asked.

Percival looked at Tristan in shock, turning to Bedivere. "He beat Gaheris," he said breathlessly.

Geraint's jaw dropped, speechless as he stared at Tristan. Bedivere's brows were almost reaching his hairline, his raised arm stuck in the air in shock. Galahad sat still as a stunned mullet, glancing between the two.

Kay dug into a piece of bacon, chewing on it thoughtfully. "Looks like you've got competition," he said simply.

Gaheris stood from his chair and made his way over to Tristan. Arthur backed up, looking at Tristan in concern.

Gaheris stood in front of Tristan, looking down at him. The lad shrunk in his seat, staring up at Gaheris anxiously.

"Stand," his deep voice ordered. Tristan flicked his eyes to Arthur, alarm on his face.

"I won't ask again," Gaheris growled.

Tristan slowly stood from his seat, his knees crouched as he held the seat in front of him.

"Never before have I had a man beat me in a challenge, and for that, I shake your hand and give you my deepest amount of respect," the Knight smiled at him, reaching his hand to him.

Tristan yelped and ran away in fright, disappearing around a random corner. The chair fell to the ground in his stead.

"Tristan!" Arthur called his name. The Knights watched Tristan with confusion, the Rebels in the cavern pausing to watch him run.

"I'll find him," Arthur sighed, following his tracks.

"By the Gods, Chris, you've scared him off," Galahad said, sitting straight.

"Meh, it was bound to happen at some point," Percival shrugged, turning back around to eat his meal.

"The lad was jumpier than a mouse in a room full of cats," Bedivere joked, straightening his green jacket.

"They always get frightened," Gaheris chuckled, sitting back down.

Arthur walked out of earshot of the Knights, jogging after Tristan. "Tristan!" he called, rounding the corner. Tunnels met Arthur like a brick to the face, carriages rolling past him out of the entrance, his friend nowhere in sight. He sighed, looking at the tunnels and trying to guess which way he would've gone.

*Think like Tristan.* Arthur looked down each tunnel; one led into stables, another crate stashes, the next what looked like more rooms, and the last a lighter room with the sound of running water coming from inside it. *Knowing Tristan, he'd be attracted to the lighter tunnel.*

He walked down the tunnel, strange patterns of light reflecting on the wall. As he moved closer, a water body came into view, a small white fountain bubbling away in the centre of the small pool of water.

"Well, there's the fountain," he muttered to himself. Sunlight streaked through a hole in the top of the cave, glancing off the water brightly as it moved, the water lapping away at the edge of the bowl carved into the floor. Crystals hung around the cave and caught the light, bouncing it around onto the walls.

A few of the Rebels knelt beside the water, Baeydn being one of them with his clothes in hand, rinsing them in the water against a washboard. He smiled at the boy and swept his eyes further, spotting Tristan sitting beside the water, curled up in a ball.

"Tristan," Arthur called out, walking over to his friend's side.

He looked up at Arthur, his eyes glittering in mesmerisation. "It's so pretty," he said, a smile on his face. "Water in a cave."

"It is, isn't it?" Arthur nodded, looking across the water.

"Gaheris scares me," Tristan murmured, resting his head on his arms. "You were right, Arthur. I am sensitive."

"He is intimidating, I'll give him that," Arthur agreed. "But he respects you now."

Tristan looked up at Arthur, uncertainty on his face. "He said he would probably kill me if I won."

"I'm pretty sure he was joking," Arthur reassured.

"That omelette was really good, though," he smiled.

"Want another one?" Arthur asked, raising a brow.

"Can I have gravy this time?"

"Ask the chef."

"Then yes."

"Gravy on an omelette."

"What's wrong with that?" Tristan raised a brow, sitting cross-legged.

"Tristan, gravy doesn't belong on an egg omelette," Arthur said. "We've discussed this."

"Yeah, and every time, at least one other person agreed that gravy belongs on an omelette," Tristan recalled.

"You asked a blind man," Arthur frowned at him.

"Just because he's blind doesn't mean he can't taste," Tristan protested.

"He doesn't know what gravy looks like," Arthur argued.

"It's not about the look," he shook his head, standing up. "It's about the *taste*."

Arthur looked up at him from an angle, chuckling lightly at him. The floor must have been slanted, Arthur standing closer to the water than Tristan. "You finally grew some height to be taller than me," he grinned.

Tristan huffed lightly. "I've always been tall. What do you mean?" he asked, slowly inching up higher on his toes.

"I've always been about a hand taller than you," Arthur grinned at him.

Tristan raised his hand to his head, hovering it above Arthur's, narrowing his eyes at the gap. "Well, now I'm the taller one," he gloated.

"You're standing on your toes, Tristan," Arthur raised a brow, pointing to his feet.

He promptly flattened his feet back down, his palm lightly smacking Arthur in the forehead.

"You right there?" Arthur frowned at him.

Tristan grinned and did it again, the slap making him laugh.

"Ow!" Arthur barked, rubbing his forehead. "That one was harder," he frowned at him.

"I can do it again," he laughed, raising his hand again.

Arthur stared flatly at him. "Do it again, I dare you."

Tristan dropped the smile, his hand lowering an inch.

"Good," Arthur said, keeping a straight face. "Now, let's go back to-"

"Boop!" Tristan laughed, his finger pressing Arthur's nose.

"Oh, for the Gods' sake!" Arthur growled at him.

Tristan laughed maniacally and ran away back down the tunnel. "I got you with the boop!" he yelled. "Maria! I got him!"

Arthur grunted deeply at Tristan, soon dropping the anger and grinning wickedly, laughing at his friend before chasing after him. Tristan laughed, looked over his shoulder and exclaimed in fright, bolting faster around the corner. Arthur darted around the corner, almost bumping into a few Rebel helpers along the way.

"Sorry!" Arthur called back to them. They muttered amongst themselves as they watched him go.

"He's gonna kill me!" Tristan cried out, sprinting towards the cavern tunnel, his boots skidding on the gravel.

At the table, the Knights talked amongst one another, stacking the plates up neatly.

"I'd figure if he's Ben's son, he'd have some resemblance to him at least," Bedivere argued. "The blonde hair is throwing me off."

"His mother had blonde hair, Ryan," Galahad said, picking up some empty mugs.

"When will he begin his training?" Percival asked, picking up his empty plate.

"When Gawain returns, I'm guessing," Geraint shrugged. "The courtyard is ready to go."

"Lancelot?" Percival looked at him.

The Knight raised his hand to answer, then paused as Tristan's voice echoed from the tunnel, the source quickly following after it. The Knights watched as the lad streaked across the floor, Arthur following swiftly after him.

Galahad's brows raised up. "What on Earth?"

"I'm going to beat your ass!" Arthur yelled at Tristan.

"Not if I can help it!" Tristan called back, darting up the stairs. Rebels jumped out of the way of the dark-skinned lad, watching him run with startled looks.

Arthur passed the Knights, stopping immediately as he noticed them watching him, panting heavily. "He's a bastard, that one," he laughed, out of breath.

"What in the name of the Gods is going on?" Gawain frowned, walking up to the table and watching Tristan disappear from view.

"Oh, good," Arthur smiled. "We can begin training then?"

Gawain looked at him, his frown deepening. "I'd say you were in need of a warm-up, but it appears you've done it already," he observed.

"I don't have my gear, only my sword in the room," Arthur panted.

"That's where you're wrong," he sniffed and turned away from him, walking back down the tunnel.

"Wrong?" Arthur asked in confusion. "They're back at yours, remember?"

"Enjoy the ass-kicking," Gaheris called to him, lifting a stack of plates up and walking to the kitchen. The rest of the Knights followed his lead, picking up their mess.

Lancelot looked at him encouragingly. "You'll be fine," he assured, picking up the glasses. Arthur frowned slightly, following Gawain down the tunnel.

## *Chapter 16: Other Kind of Training*

Walking down the tunnel behind Gawain, Arthur began to feel anxious, uncertainty flickering through his stomach. The entrance to the cave loomed before him, the sun bearing down on the courtyard in the mid-morning glow. Rebels were already outside stretching and exercising amongst themselves, soaking up the sun-

*Where is he going?* Arthur frowned as Gawain turned left sharply down another tunnel away from the entrance. Hesitantly, he followed after him, not entirely certain if the old Knight knew what he was doing.

"Why are we going down here?" Arthur's voice bounced around the tunnel.

"Well, since you couldn't be bothered to keep your things in order, I did it for you," Gawain answered, facing forwards.

"What do you mean?" Arthur asked.

The Knight stopped before a door, twisting the handle to open it up. Inside was dark and cold, a slight wind whooshing past Arthur as he paused behind Gawain to look in.

"Disorganisation is a bad habit to have," Gawain said, picking up a candlestick from an obscured table. "This will be one reason for you to keep your things in sight."

"I kept the sword, so I'm not all that disorganised," he protested.

Gawain reached his arm around outside the door, lighting the candle on a torch and bringing it back into the

room. "But you didn't remember to grab that, did you?" he questioned, holding the candle up to him.

"Of course I did," Arthur lied. "I wouldn't lie to you, Gawain."

"Good thing I know better." He moved the candle over to a looming shadow in the room, the light bouncing off shining metal. A mannequin stood solitary against the wall, armour adorned on it decoratively. It was more polished and kept than Arthur remembered, the copper finishes gleaming brightly in the small flame.

"You got my father's armour?" Arthur asked, looking at the polished suit of metal in surprise.

"You're lucky I managed to grab it before Voss did," he growled, looking at him. "Next time, you shouldn't be so forgetful."

"Whatever happened to Voss, anyway?" Arthur asked curiously.

Gawain walked to the walls, lighting more candles as he went. "He got taken care of," he said dismissively. "He shouldn't be a bother anymore."

Arthur frowned at him slightly, turning to the armour, the shining metal glimmering in his eyes. *How did he remember to grab it through all that chaos?*

"Put it on then," Gawain said.

Arthur looked at him. "What?"

"The armour. Put it on."

Arthur blinked at him confusedly, and Gawain sighed impatiently. "Have you never worn a piece of armour before, boy?"

"I'd be lying if I said yes," Arthur admitted.

"Right," he gritted out, setting the candle on the table and walking to the mannequin. "This will be a process."

Arthur walked up to the mannequin, taking in all the pieces of armour he'd need to wear. *This shouldn't be too hard, surely.*

Gawain pulled the chest plate off the mannequin easily, holding it by the leather straps. "Arms up."

Arthur raised his arms above his head. "How heavy will this be-?"

Gawain slid the armour over his head quickly, the piece dropping onto Arthur's shoulders with astounding weight, making his knees buckle. *Gods! It weighs a tonne!*

"Heavier than what you can handle," Gawain answered, tightening the straps.

Arthur tried not to sway with the weight, resisting the urge to grab Gawain's shoulders. "And you wear this on a battlefield?"

"I wore more than a chest plate," he grunted, securing the buckles and turning to grab the gauntlets. "You should try wearing the rest of the set beneath it. You'd die in the heat before you get crushed by the weight."

"Guess my father wasn't as fancy as his Knights," Arthur scoffed.

"The outside iron is the lightest you can go without wearing underarmour for proper protection," he turned to Arthur. "Anything below that makes it more of a decoration rather than any protection. Hands up."

"Noted," Arthur nodded, raising his hands to him.

Gawain slipped the padded gloves onto his hands, settling the metal plate along his forearm and buckling the straps. Arthur flexed his fingers, the plates along his knuckles folding and shifting with the movement.

Gawain fixed the leg armour to the chest plate's side, the weight pulling him down further. It got worse as the shoulder pads were added one after another, Arthur almost toppling over on his side. The boots weren't helping either; he couldn't lift his leg without scraping the metal on the ground. Gawain looked him over, checking the straps.

"Please tell me that's the last part?" Arthur hoped, trying to move properly.

"Unfortunately for you," Gawain stepped back to observe him. "This is only the outside layer."

"You're kidding, right?" Arthur frowned.

Gawain's face remained impassive, but something lit up in his eyes, a spark of light Arthur hadn't seen in him before. "Not at all," he said softly, his lips turning up in a ghost of a smile.

"You good? You've got a smile on your face," Arthur inspected, looking at him in confusion.

Gawain huffed faintly. "It just reminds me of Benjamin's first time trying the armour," he said. "He hated the weight too, don't worry."

"Like father, like son?" Arthur grinned.

"Spot on," Gawain nodded. "Although he didn't forget to keep his belongings together."

"Are you going to hold that against me?" Arthur asked with a frown.

"Until you learn how to keep your things on you while lost in a city full of thieves."

"The only thieves I know of in Londinium are Leonard and his gang," Arthur said, walking around the room in his armour, getting the feel of the new weight.

"Nothing new," he snorted. "Now come on, we're going for a walk."

"Do I go and get my sword, then?" Arthur asked, following Gawain.

"You won't be handling a sword for a while," he answered, the candles flicking out with a whoosh of air as the door opened.

Arthur frowned at him from behind. "You're boring," he muttered.

"And you're unfit."

"I'm not unfit!"

"You will be using a sword once you can run ten kilometres non-stop in that suit," Gawain growled. "And not until then."

"Alright," Arthur sighed, his brows low.

Gawain walked back the way they came, this time taking the right turn outside to the courtyard. Arthur followed him, the armour slowing him down. It squeaked and clashed as he walked, making him frown.

"Stand up straight," Gawain called back. "You sound like a tin can being dragged on a leash."

Arthur stood up straight, the annoying sound clearing from his ears. "So, are we doing hand-to-hand combat then?"

Gawain walked onto the grass behind the wall of sandstone chunks, the clearing of the courtyard buzzing with training Rebels. He turned to watch Arthur walk across the grass to stand in front of him, panting with exertion. "No," he said simply.

"What kind of training, then?" Arthur frowned at him.

"The other kind," Gawain answered and lashed his hand out against Arthur's shoulders, shoving him back.

Arthur hit the ground hard with a gasp, the metal armour pinning him to the grass. Arthur blinked in shock, looking at Gawain stunned.

"Get up," Gawain commanded.

"Have you forgotten what kind of clothing I have-"

"Stop your whining and get up!"

Arthur shifted onto his stomach with a groan, trying to raise himself off the ground. A foot hooked beneath his leg and swept him back down with a huff of air, Arthur glaring up at Gawain.

"Have you gone mad?" Arthur accused him.

"On your feet before the worms get you," Gawain said, standing back.

"That's what I was doing!" Arthur protested, trying to get up once again.

"You're slower than a slug," Gawain bit.

Arthur scowled, pushing himself up from the ground and getting onto his knees.

Gawain's leg shot out to sweep him down once again, Arthur landing back on the ground in a heap. "Come on, Arthur! Get to your feet."

"How am I supposed to when every time I get closer, you kick me back down?!" Arthur barked at him, gritting his teeth.

"Good, get angry," Gawain smirked, prodding his side with his boot.

"Don't touch me!" Arthur snapped, pushing himself back onto his knees quicker than before.

"What will you do to stop me, boy? Roll back on your face again?"

Arthur went back onto one knee, pushing himself to stand up, his knee raising from the ground with effort. *What kind of training* is *this?!*

"Is it all too much to handle yet?" Gawain barked, shoving at his shoulder roughly.

Arthur staggered back, barely keeping himself from toppling over once more, baring his teeth at Gawain. "Would you cut that out?!"

"Do something about it, Arthur," Gawain jested, raising his arms up at his sides.

"Like what? I don't have a weapon," Arthur panted.

"Come and get me," Gawain challenged, glaring at him.

Arthur ambled towards him, feeling slow as a turtle. Gawain darted to his left, slapping the back of his chest plate as he passed him. "Too slow."

Arthur swung his arm at Gawain, baring his teeth in anger. "No thanks to this armour!"

"Go on," Gawain shouted. "Shove me down!"

Arthur narrowed his eyes at him, his muscles straining as he raised his arms towards Gawain. Gawain dodged to the side yet again, and Arthur looked back over his shoulder to see his foot lash out to push him further. His eyes widened as he stumbled forward, the weight of the armour overcoming him as he fell back to the ground once more.

Arthur punched the grass in frustration, snarling in anger. *This isn't training! This is mockery!*

"Your balance is terrible," Gawain criticised, standing behind him. "It's a wonder you can stand up without falling. Oh, wait, you can't even do *that*."

Red-hot anger seared through Arthur, and he rolled back onto his stomach, pushing up against the weight back onto his feet angrily, spinning around to face Gawain with a snarl.

"Well, look, you've found a bearing," Gawain snided sarcastically. "I wonder if you can use it to run towards me without flopping like a tool once again."

Arthur glared at him, his anger overcoming his senses as he sprinted towards Gawain. Gawain's feet moved, the Knight running backwards as he watched Arthur, goading him on with a beckoning hand.

"Come on, you sloth," he barked.

"This isn't training!" Arthur snapped. "This isn't what I was told would happen! How am I supposed to take on my uncle when you won't let me train properly?!" he protested, slowing down to a stop. "I'm done."

"You're even more lopsided than how you run!" Gawain called to him, pausing at the edge of the grass.

"Whatever, Gawain," Arthur scoffed, turning to walk back into the caves.

"So just like that, you'll give up?"

"You're not teaching me anything! You're pushing me around like my uncle did!" Arthur turned back to him, a growl in his voice.

Gawain stalked over to him, his hulking figure staring down at Arthur tensely. "I'm pushing you around," he growled. "I'm shoving you down. I'm making you angry and getting all those feelings into you to make you move. That armour is making you move; your anger is making you move with your armour. You are *learning* to carry that armour, one way or another. You feel the sweat drip down your back, boy? Are your muscles screaming at you to take off the burden? Is the sun warming you up like a furnace? Guess what? It's meant to. This may not be what you expected, but it's what you're getting, got it?"

Arthur looked at him, his teeth gritting together. He was right, though; indeed, sweat did coat him, his body was aching in every spot, and the sun felt like a brand.

"It's all little steps, boy," Gawain growled. "You've got to start at the start, and *this* is the start."

Determination flowed through him, and his breath caught anew. "Teach me."

"Run and keep up."

"Run? Run where?"

Without warning, Gawain sprinted off across the grass, a lot faster than what Arthur would've expected from the old Knight. Arthur's eyes widened, and he moved after Gawain, going a lot slower than he did.

"Faster, boy!" he called back to Arthur, turning around to face him. "Get those legs pumping!"

Arthur's face went dead flat as he pushed himself, going as fast as he could in the armour. The armour held him back as if he were dragging an anchor behind him, his lungs burning with every gasp of air.

"Control your breath! Take it steady!" Gawain ordered, his feet slowing back to watch Arthur.

Arthur calmed his breath - *in, out, in, out* - and ran towards Gawain, his legs picking up speed. He went almost as fast as Gawain did, gaining closer and closer to the Knight.

"Good," Gawain barked. "Now slow it back."

Arthur straightened himself and slowed down as he approached Gawain. The weight of the armour disagreed with him, shoving him forward as his legs tried to slow, his heart jumping in fright.

"Stop! You'll barrel through the forest!" Gawain said, his eyes wide.

"I'm trying!" Arthur leaned back, trying to stop gravity from pulling him on, his legs slowing faster as his steps got wider, the trees getting frighteningly closer.

He squeezed his eyes shut and held his arms out in front of him, waiting for the force of the armour to drive him into the tree. Something pulled him to a sudden stop, his chest plate jutting into him and pushing his breath out of his lungs.

Opening an eye, the bark of the tree seated right in front of his face, he turned his head to see Gawain gripping the back of his chest plate, his breath coming to him in bouts of relief.

"I could've handled the impact," Arthur laughed nervously.

"I was more concerned about the welfare of the tree," Gawain said, standing him upright.

"Oh, thanks," Arthur frowned at him. "That makes me feel appreciated and loved."

"You're not here to be loved; you're here to train. Tired yet?"

"Do you take yes for an answer?" Arthur asked, panting heavily.

"All the better," he smiled, thumping his back. "It means you're still alive and ready to do some core work."

"Oh great," Arthur panted. "I can't wait."

"Keep up the sarcasm, and it goes from fifty push-ups to one hundred."

"Fine."

"On the ground, don't stop until it feels like your arms are about to fall off," Gawain commanded.

"Can I take the armour off?" Arthur asked.

"No."

"Saw *that* one coming," Arthur sighed, lowering himself onto the ground with high brows.

The courtyard at the front of the castle was fraught with Black Cloaks, Barons standing in uniform lines across the grass, and shouts of command echoed up to the Kingdom windows from the city below. In his room, King Ergott stared at a frame within his hands, a river of tears streaming down his face.

Rosaline's portrait stared up at him with her comforting smile, her sweet face as beautiful as he remembered. The painting captured her likeness down to the kind glint in her eyes; they seemed to burn a hole right through him at that gentle gaze. His heart ached with longing and guilt.

"Oh, my dear Rosaline… I'm so sorry," he mourned, tracing her face with his finger. He could almost feel her soft skin beneath it, the warmth of her body a haunting memory, her phantom blood coating his arms. The stain on the carpet beside his bed was long gone; the Maidens had cleaned it upon finding the Queen's frail body.

He sensed her before she made it near the door, anger burning his eyes to glow again. "What do you want, Vivien?" he growled.

The door creaked open slowly, the yellow-eyed woman walking into the room with a contemplative look, taking in his tears and the portrait in his hand. "Just to check up on my King," she said. "I could hear you from the hallway."

"I'm fine," he dismissed, wiping away his tears. "You don't need to check in on me."

"I felt you need somebody," the witch shrugged, shutting the door and leaning back on it. "So, here I am."

"I don't need you. You're lucky I even let you out of the chamber," Ergott sniped, looking at her from under low brows over his shoulder.

"Lies," Vivirn purred. "You *do* need me, and you know it."

"For one thing: to give me my magic, that's it."

"What if it became more than just the one thing?" she mused, pushing off the door.

"What are you implying?" Ergott asked, his eyes narrowing.

"It is indeed a sad thing for a man to lose his other half," she said sadly. "It breaks them apart and makes them hurt for the rest of their lives."

"You made me kill her," Ergott snarled, his body pivoting towards her. "That's why I feel this way."

"Oh, but I didn't," she shrugged. "I merely informed you of your options to gain your power. You decided to take the hard way."

Ergott looked down, sighing to himself deeply. She was right, in a way. Ergott yearned for his power and chose to get more of it over the life of his most prized possession.

"And a King can't rule a castle without a Queen," Vivien purred, walking closer to him.

Ergott looked up at her, watching her closely. "I suppose you're right," he murmured.

Vivien's eyes set alight, the golden glow washing something over Ergott, his grief and anger ebbing away into nothing. "If you take me as your next Queen, I can give you more power than you've dreamt of," her voice echoed inside his head, whispers winding around the room. "We could lead the Kingdom as an impenetrable force."

His mind seemed to hollow out, his vision tunnelling on Vivien's figure, her voice pinging in his mind. "Camelot would be unstoppable," Ergott smirked, his voice distant in his ears. His mind was reeling over the possibilities, visions of him and Vivien ruling over the Kingdom flashing past his eyes, thousands kneeling before him at the castle steps.

Vivien smirked at him, the pulse around Ergott's mind growing stronger, the whispers becoming more intense.

"With both of our powers leading the throne, we could take over Braynor and bring the whole country to its knees," she growled.

"Arthur would never become the King with us in the way," Ergott said, standing up from the bed. Rosaline's portrait dropped forgotten to the ground from his hands, the world around him becoming sharper and clearer with every pulse of his slowed heart.

*Yes, I can see it so easily now.* Ergott pushed aside his grief, replacing it with cool contemplation. The temptation of the vision took him over, drowning him in sour envy.

Vivien strolled closer to him, her hand coming up to trace his jawline gently. "The Born King will be no more in the eyes of legend," she whispered.

"Braynor could be ours if I had a Queen to rule the castle with me," Ergott whispered, looking at her with hunger in his eyes.

"It's only a matter of words away, my liege," she smirked, moving herself closer to him still.

With her, he'd get all the power he ever wished for. She was the key to his success. *How did I not see this before?* "Will you be my Queen, Vivien?" Ergott asked.

Her golden eyes flared, a wash of magic seeping through his bones. "I accept your proposal, my King," she smiled. The thing beneath his skin writhed, the power growing within him. Red-hot fire burned inside of him, sending pain and pleasure shooting down his spine, the strength in him so very satisfactory. He could feel the magic expanding in him, revelling in the feeling.

Ergott smiled back, his eyes glowing hot, the pain gone and replaced with vision sharper than a sword edge, the amber glow mingling with Vivien's own golden eyes. He slipped an arm around her waist, all thoughts of Rosaline gone from his mind. *My Queen,* something inside of him growled. "Very good," he whispered, leaning his head down to her.

Arthur's breath was still trying to catch up with him as he pushed open his bedroom door, walking in and letting the door swing into the wall. The armour was long off him, and thank the Gods for that; the suit was a burden. *And I wasn't even in full armour, apparently! How ridiculous.*

He loosed a breath in an exhausted huff, his body going limp as he moved to his bed, flopping onto the furs in a heap. Sweat still drenched his clothes, sticking them to him uncomfortably. *I need a bath.*

He slid his boots off with his toes, the smack of leather on wood echoing in the small room. He stuffed his face into the furs, the fine hairs stuffing up his nose and wicking away the sweat on his forehead. *Gawain's method of training is* brutal. *Do people do this every day? Will I have to do this tomorrow or the next few weeks?!*

He grumbled in the fur, shifting his face to the side to breathe easier. "This Knight business is ridiculous," he muttered to himself.

"You look like you got thrown in a river," a familiar voice said from the doorway, laughter in their voice.

"I feel like I *did* get thrown in the said river," Arthur groaned.

The scent of warm bread and meat wafted under his nose, his stomach growling. *How long has it been since I last ate?*

Arthur shifted up with a groan, sat up on the edge of the bed, and looked towards the door. Maria stood with two plates of food in hand, humour in her eyes. She looked less ruffled, at least, her hair smooth once more. She was dressed in a long sleeve gray shirt, dark pants rolled up to her knees, and white socks covering her feet up to her ankles. "A bit sore, are we?" she goaded.

"Oh ha-ha," Arthur laughed sarcastically. "Gawain's training is torture."

"And that's just his way of warming you up," she said, walking into the room and kicking the door shut behind her. "Thank the Gods that was open when I got here; I wouldn't know how I'd have opened it."

"Luckily I didn't have the energy to shut it," he added, looking at the plates. "What's on the menu?"

She handed him one, reaching into her jacket for a set of cutlery to sit beside him. "Chicken cooked in gravy with a bread roll," she said, seating herself on the end of his bed cross-legged, placing her own plate on her lap.

"Thanks." He took a huge whiff of the wafting steam, the scent making his mouth water in anticipation. "Smells nice."

"You can thank Simon for it," she said, grabbing her own fork from her pocket.

"I don't particularly like that Simon guy," Arthur admitted, taking a mouth full of chicken. *Oh, it's absolute heaven!* The gravy was spiced with rosemary and lemon, the taste fresh in Arthur's mouth. He hated himself for liking it.

Maria piled the chicken shreds onto her bread roll, tilting her head at him. "Why? He's a nice lad," she asked, taking a bite. "His cooking is great, too."

"The way he was eyeing you wasn't exactly *gentlemen-like*," Arthur frowned, taking another mouthful of chicken.

She raised a brow at him, her green eyes considering him. "Eyeing me?" she huffed.

"Someone has a crush on you, Maria," Arthur said, looking at her.

"And if he does?" she questioned, lowering her roll.

"Does what?" Arthur asked.

She rolled her eyes. "If Simon was crushing on me, why would you be so concerned about it?"

"Because we only just got here, and none of us know him."

"What does it matter? We're getting to know them. You'll meet him more formally eventually anyway," she frowned. "I could go and get him now if you wanted."

Arthur nodded at her, looking away awkwardly. "You have a point, I'm sorry." *What the hell was that, Art?*

"Anybody would think the way you've gone about the lads being around me that you were protective," she said pointedly, spearing the chicken with her fork.

"Well, you're like my little sister in a way," Arthur shrugged, his stomach flipping a little with nerves.

She snorted, eating the chicken. "Imagine me going rampant in the castle," she joked.

"I can imagine it alright," Arthur chuckled, eating the piece of bread.

"You, good sir," Maria pointed to Arthur's discarded boot in pretend command. "Fetch me my robe. I desire to be pampered with a side of cranberry juice and a violinist playing Christmas music."

"The hell are you going on about?" Arthur asked, an eyebrow raised.

Maria looked at him with raised brows, looking down her nose at him. "Why, my good fellow," she said in a thick, mocking accent. "I'm ordering my servants at my command. They should know to follow the princess's orders without question, though it seems they're a bit soulless. Or even sole-less," she laughed, looking at the boot.

Arthur laughed with her, shaking his head. *She's absolutely bonkers.* "Good luck ordering them lot to do anything productive," he snorted.

She waved in dismissal at the boots. "Oh, bother," she sighed. "They're probably too exhausted carrying the weight of your behind around all day. No matter."

"Exhausted of me?" Arthur gasped, pretend shock on his face.

"You are very high maintenance to keep protected from any sharp rocks in your path, sire," she shook her head, looking at him from beneath her lashes. "Wouldn't want you to stub a toe."

"As your King, I demand an apology at once," Arthur demanded, pretend anger on his face.

She tutted with a big grin on her face and her hands raised in the air. "Alas! The truth demands no apology!" she declared. "For the soles of your leathery disciples lay on the floor at the expense of their own pitiful lives of travel."

Arthur chuckled softly at her, finishing off his plate of chicken.

She laughed at herself, settling back down to finish her plate off. "You've changed your attitude," she observed. "Normally, you'd be all frowny at jokes like that."

"Lancelot is quite the motivator," Arthur looked at her, smiling.

She smiled back at him, her eyes crinkling. "It looks good on you," she noted.

"What does?"

"Confidence," she answered. "And that smile you've got on your mug."

"Well, get used to seeing it," Arthur said, grinning at her.

Her own lips parted in a grin, mirroring him. "I'm sure it won't be too hard," she shrugged. Her skin seemed to glow with her smile, the light catching her eyes like the moon did before. Warmth spread through Arthur's chest, his heart beating just a little quicker than before. He felt heat starting to crawl up his neck, something stirring in his stomach at her look.

Arthur cleared his throat, looking down to her neck, noticing a strap under her shirt as he sat his plate down on the bed. "What's that?" he asked.

She blinked and touched her throat, pulling the strap out from beneath her shirt. "My necklace?" she asked, holding the pendant. The purple stone glimmered in the candlelight, silver swirls holding it at three points to the leather band.

Arthur nodded. "It's pretty," he said, looking at the gem in her hand. He clenched his thumb in one hand at his side, trying to stop the blood rushing through his system as quickly as it was.

"I've had it since I was little," she said, letting it rest on her chest. "I was told it used to be my mother's."

"What's the gem?" Arthur asked, inspecting the purple stone.

"Amethyst," she answered. The gem seemed to glow faintly, a slight glint of purple light shining on her shirt.

"I like it," Arthur smiled. "It suits you."

She tucked it back beneath her shirt with a glow on her cheeks. "Thank you," she said.

Arthur couldn't help but think it seemed a little familiar. Just like how she was, in a way. Arthur wasn't sure exactly why, but she stirred something in him every time he looked at her.

He averted his eyes away as she moved her shirt, thankful the room was dark enough for Maria not to see the furious heat reddening his face. Arthur leaned back onto his bed with a groan, his head thumping into the pillow. "Gawain has officially broken me," he declared.

She laughed, picking up his plate from the bed and stacking it under hers, sitting it on the floor. "It's only been a day," she teased. "Imagine the next month."

"That's the concerning part," Arthur sighed.

"You'll be fine," she dismissed. "He's just pushing you to get fitter, then he'll give you something to train with. He does it with everybody."

Arthur looked over to the corner of his room, the sword's pommel glinting in the candlelight. "I've already got something to train with," he frowned.

"Not *literally*," she huffed. "Figuratively, as in he'll train you the way you thought and read about."

"I know how to fight," Arthur sighed. "And he's holding me back."

She uncrossed her legs and shifted to sit on her knees, facing him. "Everybody has to go through fitness training before they pick up a sword. No good giving a lad a weapon if they can't hold the weight of their protection first," she said, resting her elbows on her knees and leaning on her hands.

Arthur looked up at her, nodding lightly. "I suppose you're right."

"I know I'm right," she wrinkled her nose at him, her smile lopsided. "I'm a professional." She shifted herself to lay on her stomach beside him, her legs swinging in the air. "You just gotta trust the system."

"Have you seen Tristan anywhere? He was supposed to be out watching," Arthur said, looking at her with slight surprise as he shifted back to give her more room, laying on his side. He felt his heart skitter, his mind throwing itself into a panic. *Stop it, for the Gods' sake, Arty! Calm yourself.* It felt like more of a workout than training to stop his body from embarrassing him.

"Last time I saw him, he was running down the tunnel," Maria said.

"Because he hit my nose," Arthur frowned.

Her eyes widened in mischief. "He got you, did he?" she smirked.

"Yes," Arthur narrowed his eyes. "He got me."

"It was about time," she chuckled, shifting to get more comfortable, to Arthur's mental dismay. "He was waiting for the day when he could finally do it. He's gotten everyone in the training hall with it."

"Speaking of the training hall, I haven't seen Kyan or Peter since we arrived here," Arthur said. "I hope Kyan's gotten lost, but it's odd for Peter to be absent."

"Peter is making a recovery," she said, picking her teeth clean with a fingernail. "He can't draw back a bow without a proper arm."

"And the other less important one?" Arthur asked.

"Who knows, out of sight, out of mind."

"Amen," Arthur nodded.

She rested her head against the mattress, her hair spilling onto the furs. "He's such a bother, Kyan Bors."

Arthur sighed, raising his hand to lean his head against. "You can say that again."

"Rugged, a little cute, but a bother."

"A little cute?" Arthur's eyebrow flicked up.

"Black hair and green eyes aren't a bad combination," she shrugged, fiddling with the fur blanket.

"What do you like in a guy?" Arthur asked curiously.

Maria shifted her head to look at the bed head, her face contemplative. "Calm, strong, protective, thoughtful," she listed. "It's not hard to fit the 'taller' bracket."

Arthur's mouth quirked lightly. "Do you know anyone with those qualities?"

A small smile rested on her lips, her eyes looking down slightly at her hand. "A few," she admitted.

"Would I know them?" Arthur asked, keeping his voice easy.

Maria huffed a laugh, looking up at him. "Curious to know if you meet the standards?" she teased.

"A Magician never tells," Arthur smirked at her, watching her mischief grow.

"It makes it funnier how *I'm* the magical one here," she laughed, turning onto her side to look at him.

"I'll be getting Excalibur, remember?" Arthur reminded.

"That doesn't mean *you're* magic," she pointed out. "It means you have an *item* of magic."

"That I'll wield, so therefore, I'll be magic."

She tilted her head with a sarcastic look, a smirk on her face. "It's *still* not how that works. It's like saying you bought a watermelon, and therefore you're a watermelon farmer."

"Different concept, but alas," Arthur grinned at her.

Maria scoffed jokingly at him, rolling her eyes. "Nobles and their supposed education," she said. "You think too hard."

Arthur scoffed at her. "I think you mean the opposite," he corrected.

"You're right. You think too little."

"Not as little as Tristan."

"He tries his best."

Arthur nodded. "We all do."

She hummed a small laugh and pushed herself back up onto her knees, twisting to put her legs over the edge of the bed. "I suppose I should go and find where he ran off to," she muttered.

"I need to get some rest, anyway," Arthur said, sighing quietly to himself in relief as his stomach stopped fluttering like a fish. "Gawain's pushed every last drop of energy out." He shifted up on his bed with a groan, pulling his knees up slightly.

"You should look into getting a bath, too," she smirked, wrinkling her nose. "You smell of stale sweat."

"Thanks," Arthur scoffed at her.

She grinned at him fiendishly and stood up from the bed in a flourish, her hand accidentally brushing his leg. Arthur flinched, looking at her hand leaving his skin, his eyes widened slightly. The touch sent lightning coursing through his veins, his breath leaving him as flat as he was at training. His heart pounded in his chest like a galloping horse, everything centred on that touch. He didn't know if it hurt or tickled.

She hadn't seemed to notice his change as she picked up the plates and strutted to the door, pulling it open. "I'll send word if I find Tristan somewhere other than the kitchen," she joked. "It'll shock me if he's elsewhere."

"He won't be," Arthur said, his voice raised a few octaves higher than usual. He cleared his throat, watching as she pulled the door closed behind herself.

He shook his head clear, his heart still thundering in his ears. *What the hell was all that?* He couldn't figure out a single reason why her hand simply brushing his leg could do… *that. Did it have to do with her magic?* And Gods, the heat on his face was worse than the Summer sun! Let alone the fight he'd fought with himself just then. *What in the Ether is wrong with me today?*

He brushed the hair back from his forehead and laid back down on the pillows, his skin still tingling where she touched him like it was on fire. Arthur sighed to himself and stared up at the roof, a ghost of a smile forming on his lips. He moved his hands behind his head, the bristles of his hair poking through the gaps of his fingers.

He just couldn't seem to get the picture of those green eyes out of his head or that stunning smile, no matter what he tried. Not even the thought of Ergott could calm the fire Maria caused in him.

## *Chapter 17: Ash & Cinders*

The sky opened up above the people clustered in the alleyways surrounding the main road in Londinium, rain falling on the roofs with gentle fingers. It seeped through the cracks in the streets underneath the hooves of the horses riding past the prone citizens, snorting the rain from their noses. The Barons riding the horses were wrapped in soaked black cloaks, their masks as expressionless as ever.

Thunder rolled overhead as the band of horses behind Edward pulled along the small carts, their wheels squeaking inaudibly against the roar of water on stone. Twelve wooden carts pulled along twelve wooden caskets in rows of two, the spray of lightning flashing off the water coating them. Coloured cloths were draped over each side of the carts alongside the orange and white flag of Camelot, red and blue leading the way at the front.

Amongst the crowded townsfolk, an array of Barons lined up in front of the onlookers, holding up spears by their side, shields held up on their left arm. Above the people, a flock of crows harassed their ears, their cries echoing from the rooftops. Tears mixed with the rain on people's faces, their eyes trained on the caskets as they travelled past them.

A sudden loud sound came from the lined-up Barons, their spears rising from the ground to slam into the ground with a loud thud. Edward looked at the people surrounding him, the rain running into his eyes and stinging his stitches.

Movement in the crowd caught his eye, and he turned his head to look; people shifted out of the way of one particular woman shoving her way through, the Barons in the line turning their heads to her. Her eyes were wide, face locked in disbelief at the rows of carts with their colours and flags. She seemed to scan them, looking for something in desperation.

She must've found what she was looking for as she locked eyes with the carriage at the front of the line: the red-flagged casket. Her wail pierced the air, echoing across the buildings with her anguish.

Edward watched with interest as she fought the Barons trying to hold her back, her grief and fury fueling her strength.

"Stay back!" one of the Barons commanded her, trying to grab her arms.

"No! Let me through!" she screamed at them, pulling out of their grip.

"Get back in line!"

To Edward's surprise, the woman snapped, shoving her way past the Baron with a great deal of force, sending the Black Cloak sprawling onto the road. She sprinted towards the carriage, her dark brown hair strewn in the wind behind her.

The commotion gained the attention of the leading party as the crowd murmured and cried out at the woman, the Barons pulling the horses to a stop long enough for the woman to reach the cart with the red flag, anguish written across her face. Barons moved to warn her off, and Edward rode up to her, blocking the Barons off.

"Let her be," he commanded. "I want to see where this goes."

"Yes, *Hari*," the Barons stepped back.

The woman hadn't noticed his actions, clamouring onto the cart deftly and kneeling beside the casket with shaky hands. Edward turned to watch her mourn over the dead

Knight, looking her over. Sharp gray eyes were red with tears and outrage, her mouth open as she sobbed uncontrollably. "My boys! My Sam is gone!" she wailed.

An onlooker growled in outrage and looked up towards the castle balcony in the distance. "This is all *his* fault!" he protested. "He killed our Knights!"

"Damned Ergott! Murderer!" Another yelled.

"False King!"

The crowd around them began to join the man, shoving against the Barons lined up in front of them. The Barons tried to hold them back, the lines caving in on the road and spooking the horses.

Edward frowned and pulled his reins tight, moving away from the crowd. "Move it on! Keep going!" he barked at the leading party. The carriages led on through the chaos, forcing people to move.

"He's no King! He's a fraud leader!" a man yelled, followed by the yelling of others.

"Death to the King!" a woman snarled, shoving a Baron.

"Death to the King!" others yelled, the crowd taking up the chant and pushing against the Baron's line.

The Barons fought them back, spears swinging against the citizens and pushing them down the alleyways, more than one of them falling to the ground as the thunder boomed overhead.

A frightened woman's scream pierced through the crowd as a Baron stabbed a man with a spear straight through his abdomen. The cries of protest turned to cries of fear, the citizens that weren't still fighting running for their homes.

The woman on the cart watched it unfold in horror, her eyes wide in dread, hair stuck to her face with the rain. A flash of white crashed down onto the cart, a bird landing on the floor of the carriage beside the woman. She jumped in fright, looking at the white crow. She leaned her arm down to let the crow jump onto it, holding it up to the casket. Its feathers fluffed out, unusually bright green - not red, Edward puzzled - eyes taking in the box with what seemed to be shock. Its beak opened with a mournful cry, jumping onto the lid to lay down, its wings seemingly feeling the wood.

The woman, Edward supposed to be Samqueel's mother, copied the bird, lying against it with a mournful cry. There was something very odd going on between these two, and Edward had a feeling it had a more significant meaning than what he saw.

From the castle balcony, King Ergott scoured over the streets, watching the parade of carriages wheeling the caskets in. His crown was drenched with rain water, along with the rest of his attire. A smirk sat on his face, delight coursing through him at the people's outrage. *Let them fight. Make them think they can.*

Beside him, a woman's laugh trilled, Vivien's own yellow eyes lit in amusement at the crowd. "Oh, the joy in the air," she smiled. "The grief hits me in waves even from up here."

"I want everything to do with them erased from the castle," Ergott said, watching the flagged caskets with a frown. "Including the Roundtable."

"Why, of course, my dear," she purred, looking at him sideways. "Their memory must be quelled."

"And have Rohin sent to speak with me, dear," Ergott added. "There's important things we need to discuss."

"The woeful cries of a mother have certainly done their part in triggering the turnaround of the people's perspectives," Vivien smirked.

"They don't matter; their opinions are invalid to us," Ergott scoffed. "They will soon see a greater change to Camelot, and they will learn to respect and love their King."

"And that they will," she purred. "But not in the way you think." She turned around and walked towards the balcony door, her newly acquired black cloak billowing behind her.

"I hope you're ready, Arthur," Ergott murmured to himself. "I hope you're ready to see the fall of your home." He turned away from the fighting crowd on the street below, following behind Vivien.

The weight at his side slapped against his leg annoyingly; the scabbard was too small to harbour the infamous blade. The burden was enough to drive Ergott insane and lean him over, the guard digging into his hip like a persistent child. Winding down the staircase, he gripped the handle, trying to relieve the weight of the bastard sword to no avail, irritating him further. Today would see the end of its reign, anyway.

The Round Hall was empty, the table scattered with unwashed crockery and discarded weapons. Jackseye stood behind one of the chairs, standing to attention as he walked into the room.

"Fascinating, isn't it?" Ergott asked, moving his hand along the surface of the Round Table. "How one simple thing can cause tragedy throughout the Kingdom. The bigger picture has been painted for them to see why I have made this decision, but they'll never understand why it's so necessary."

"Their simple lives and ways of thinking are beyond understanding our reasoning, sire," Jackseye agreed. "They will always see evil in the face of your plans."

"And yet the Devil has to show them the true path to his reasoning," Ergott said, looking up at him. "But then again, they refuse to believe anything other than what my brother had taught them. Frustrating, to no end."

"The Roundtable had a large influence in the Kingdom," Jackseye stated. "Wiping them out caused a reaction that was bigger than we anticipated. We've broken their hopes but ignited their fury."

Ergott looked at the Round Table, taking his hand off the surface, dust smeared on the tips of his fingers. "They looked up to the Roundtable and saw them as guardians and protectors. And now that the Knights are gone, they have no true protection, no one to look up to. They will change their minds to follow us soon enough."

Jackseye chuckled darkly to himself. "So much for Torona's big speech," he shook his head. "A waste of breath."

"The fool saw himself as an icon to the people," Ergott looked up at Jackseye. "A symbol of *hope*, as some would say."

"He was right in that aspect," Jackseye nodded. "All the better for us, now that the people have seen their hope die in front of them."

"But they still have one last piece of hope," Ergott frowned.

Jackseye scowled, turning to look out the window. "The boy."

"Arthur must be found," Ergott said firmly. "The Born King prophecy must die."

"The search party will be led out tomorrow morning to look for him," Jackseye informed. "Only the best of the best will be in the team. We will drag him and his traitors home."

"The others with him don't matter to me; dead or alive, I don't care. But I want Arthur alive. I will deal with him once he's brought back to Camelot. Understand?" Ergott explained, looking Jackseye dead in the eye.

He met Ergott's gaze steadily, nodding slowly. "It will be done, sire," he said.

Ergott nodded at him. "Very good."

Jackseye glanced at the weapon at Ergott's side, a cool calculation on his face. "If I may ask, sire," he added, "why is Remedy at your side? I would've thought it would be discarded by now."

"It won't be here for long," Ergott dismissed.

"I see," Jackseye grumbled and straightened up. "I will go and tend to the carts on the way and finish this whole funeral ordeal before someone decides to torch a building. I'll be back by the afternoon."

"I'd be careful going down there with those rats," Ergott scowled. "They're known to be a fierce society, especially toward us."

"I'm sure Edward has it under control," he assured. "The boy is smarter than the common rabble. He knows what he's doing." Jackseye turned and strode out of the Round Hall, two Barons on the other side of the door peeling off to follow him.

"Let us hope so, Rohin," Ergott muttered to himself. "Let us hope."

The carts reached the bottom of the stairs to the castle, the horses pulling to a stop, making the woman lift her head from the casket. Edward watched her as she tilted her head up to look at the castle, fear and hatred on her face. The bird on the box shook out its feathers, cawing at the castle softly.

Edward pulled his horse up beside the cart, watching them with interest. They mourned for a killer Knight, the one who slaughtered his men, no less, and gave him the slash across his face. He should hate them. He knew better than to hate the innocent.

"*Harí*," a Baron said to his right.

Edward looked down at the Baron. "Yes?"

"The caskets, where do we place them?"

"Take them to the cabins," he said finally. "Put them wherever *Muharí* Rohin commands. I'm sure he knows where."

"Yes, *Harí*," the Baron nodded, turning to the others and shouting the order down the line.

The woman's face filled with possessiveness as the Barons closed around her son's casket, the white crow hissing. Edward turned to them, pulling his horse in close and watching one of the Cloaks near the woman.

"Out of the way, miss, mourning time is over," he said, gripping her arm.

She cried out, pulling against his grip in protest, holding onto the side of the carriage. Edward's eyes flashed, and he rode closer, bearing down at the Baron. "Let her be," he ordered.

"I said move it!" the Baron commanded, tugging her roughly. She yelped as her grip loosened, the Baron pulling her to her knees at the foot of the cart.

Edward dismounted his horse and grabbed a fistful of the Baron's cloak, tugging him back as rough as he had to the woman. "I said leave her be, *Almúr*," he hissed.

The Baron turned to look at him, their eyes protesting beneath the mask. "She disobeyed orders, *Harí*!"

"And you disobeyed mine," Edward barked. "Now let the woman go. She will leave willingly, or you will leave in a coffin yourself!"

The Baron looked down at the woman, her clothing now covered in mud. A flash of white feathers smacked into the Baron's mask, feral cawing loud in his ears. Edward jumped back away from the bird, the Baron swatting his arms at the crow as it sank its talons into his cloak. *Gods, the bird has a mind of its own.*

"Get off me, feral bird!" the Baron barked, waving his arms in the air. His hand smacked the bird, sending it with a puff of feathers down to the ground, its tiny frame rolling across the cobblestones. It stood up with a hiss and jumped over to the woman, its feathers fluffed out and wings shifting.

"Take that feral thing with you, peasant," the Baron scowled, storming away from the casket.

Edward watched him go with gritted teeth. He'd find out the name of the *Almúr* soon enough. He sniffed at him and turned back to the woman, extending a hand. "I apologise for the-"

"Stay away from us," she snarled, picking up the bird carefully and shrinking away from him. "You Barons are nothing but trouble!"

Edward raised a brow, lowering his hand. "I'm going to give you five minutes to find a place for you and your people to run to," he said quietly. "It starts now. Run."

The woman got to her feet, her quicksilver eyes filled with grief and hate as she looked at the casket her son lay inside one last time before she darted off towards the crowd. Edward watched her go, sighing through his nose quietly. *Even courtesy is overlooked for purple ink.*

"There he is!" a man pointed up to the balcony. Edward followed the man's direction, turning his eyes upwards.

King Ergott looked down at the people below, scouring once again over the corrupted Kingdom. *Gloating over his people's reactions as if he needed the ego boost.*

The King pivoted to glance behind himself, a womanly figure approaching the balcony railing. Edward squinted up at the woman, recognition stilling him. The people around Edward who saw the strange woman had daunted, confused looks on their faces.

"That's not Queen Guinevere," he heard one say.

"In here, quickly!" a man said, holding open a stone door for Erin to walk through. A few others followed through with her, eager to get inside.

"Inside, now!" the man ordered them. Erin cradled the white bird in her arms closely, keeping her from being hurt further. *Who knows what that brute did to her?*

A young lass led her with a gentle hand on her back through the stone house, though it seemed a lot larger than a house. The hallways were dark and filled with rubble, shattered glass from the alcoves in the wall scattered on the floor beneath her boots.

Shouting from the outside bounced through the walls and the open door, a mixture of commanded orders and protests beating Erin's ears. The man ushered in the last few citizens inside before slamming the door shut, bolting the locks into place and turning around to them, counting heads; eleven, Erin could see.

"Is anyone hurt?" the man asked, walking into the crowded hallway.

"None over here," a voice said.

"We're okay," a woman chimed in.

Erin looked down at the crow in her hands, inspecting the frail body of the alert little beast. "Are you okay?" she asked.

The crow turned its head up to look at her, reassurance in its green eyes as it croaked. Erin smiled slightly and stroked the bird's feathers.

The man peeked through the blinds, shaking at his head at what was happening outside. Erin looked up and peered over his shoulder; smoke started billowing through the alleyway from a source she couldn't see, people running with children away from the armed Black Cloaks. Horses ran madly down the way, scattering people out of the way in their wild rampage.

"It's pandemonium out there," the young lass said, standing beside the man.

"I knew this would happen the day they showed up," the man scowled.

To think this was all because of the Knights' deaths saddened Erin, her grief for her son still fresh in her heart. *Sam died protecting the people from things like this. He'd hate to see this.* She turned away from the window. *All because of these black-cloaked heathens.*

"He's not coming back for us," the man growled. "Like the coward he is."

Erin blinked in shock. "Who do you mean?" she asked.

"The Born King," the man turned to her, his brown eyes filled with bitterness. "He left us here to fend for ourselves. Now look at Camelot; it's falling into pieces."

"What makes you think he isn't coming back with something better, Owen?" the young lass questioned.

"He isn't coming back, Lucy," Owen growled. "He never will."

"I can tell you right now, he and the other lads will return," she protested. "I saw with my own eyes who was with him. Tristan even swore to come back."

"What other lads?" Owen interrupted her.

"Haven't you heard? The old Knights are returning," she replied. Erin gasped, looking at Lucy, the bird in her arms flicking its head to her. *Benjamin's Knights?*

"They're all dead, Lucy," Owen sighed, putting his hands on his hips and shaking his head. Rugged dark hair fell over his face, and he flicked his head back to move it from his eyes.

"Bollocks!" Lucy spat. "I was there when one of them saved us from the fight."

"Which one?" Owen asked, frowning at her.

"Sir Galahad."

"Impossible," Owen denied. "Galahad died in the forest to the North along with the rest of them," he said.

"If you don't believe me, then explain to me who you believe the Knight Trainer is," Lucy frowned. "'Cause I can tell you, it's not who you think."

"It's Xavier Marlon," Owen frowned.

"Wrong," she said.

"Then who is it?"

"Tell me the story of how the bodies of the Knights were found," Lucy started, folding her arms.

"They weren't found; they were crushed into dust," Owen explained. "After they went to fight the invaders, fire erupted beside the castle, they went to see what it was, they lost and were covered in ash and cinders."

"And how many lumps were under the ash and cinders?" Lucy questioned.

"Twelve," he answered.

"Wrong again," she tutted. "There were eight lumps under the soot. How many Knights were there in the Roundtable?"

"This discussion is over, Lucy," Owen scowled, walking away from her.

"I'm getting there, hang on," Lucy protested, grabbing his arm to make him stop.

Owen released himself from her grip. "Save it, Lucy," he growled.

"There were twenty," she continued. "And the other twelve weren't found, including the man who took the name Xavier Marlon instead of-."

"Name the last eight, then," Owen interrupted.

Lucy scowled and let him go, putting her hands on her hips. "Gallehault, Hoel, Lanval, Morholt, Safir, Pelleas, Dinaden and Erec," she listed.

"So you know your old Knights?" Owen asked, folding his arms with a raised brow.

"And I know for certain at least two that survived," she scowled. "And his name isn't Xavier Marlon."

"You really think they're going to come back with the supposed Born King and take back Camelot?" Owen asked.

"I *know* they will," she corrected. "Tristan's never lied to me, and I don't think he's planning to."

"Your boyfriend?" Owen smirked. She slapped his arm, glowering at him.

Erin tried to process the information thrown at her: *the old Knights are alive? Arthur was coming back with them, but when? And will it be too late by then?* Unease settled in her chest.

"Look, little sister," Owen belittled, "you may think you know these things will happen, but I know for a fact that they aren't."

Lucy's face turned red with annoyance, stomping her foot at him. "You never believe me even when I turn out right," she growled.

"You know why?" Owen asked.

"'Cause you're a chip idiot," she barked.

"'Cause I'm older, and I'm smarter than you," he smirked, poking her nose roughly.

She slapped his hand away with a growl and stormed off down the hallway, glass crunching underfoot. "You're so unbearable, Owen!" she stormed.

Owen chuckled at her, shaking his head. "Still likes to chuck tantrums."

Erin watched the scene unfold, frowning slightly. For everything the girl said, the boy had a witty comment to pile on. She wasn't sure if she was glad she hadn't had another child with Dawson so as to avoid this level of bickering. Not that she didn't get her fair share from all of Sam's friends when they'd come to the house, their banter and laughter flooding her memory. They all may as well have been her children.

Grief pinged through her at the thought. *Now I have no children to listen to complain.*

Erin moved to the least glassy part of the hallway, brushing it aside with her foot to sit down and placing the bird onto the floor. It hopped around the strewn debris, inspecting the people surrounding it. Its wing hung limp on one side; *her arm is broken.* Erin frowned in worry at the bird. "That will hurt later," she mumbled to herself.

Suddenly, a scuffle sounded right outside the door. A loud, knocking thud echoed through the hallway. Erin turned her head to look at the window, an ominous black mask staring straight at her.

"Open the door!" the Baron ordered.

The crow grumbled lowly, hopping to Erin's feet. She picked her back up carefully and stood up once more, the people in the hallway gasping and moving back from the door. Owen narrowed his eyes at the door, gesturing to the people to move.

Erin looked down the hallway after Lucy, the young girl's eyes wide as saucepans. "Quickly," she half whispered to the citizens. "Follow me."

"Everyone, to the sleeping chambers, now," Owen whispered to them, rushing them to Lucy. Erin followed after the girl, her shadowy frame flitting in and out of the light of the shattered windows of the rooms they passed.

The stone door echoed ruthlessly with the thud of the Baron's fists. Lucy propped open a door with a shard of wood, moving to the side to let people in. "Find somewhere to duck," she said.

"Go inside, now," Owen ordered them all, standing on the opposite side of the door. They all filed through into the room, scattering across and over to the beds, some ducking behind the frames. The window on the far wall was still intact, block-out blinds covering it thickly.

"Lucy, go in with them. I'm going to distract them," Owen ordered.

The girl looked at Owen with a frown. "I knew you were stupid, but I didn't think you were *this* stupid," she scolded.

"Lucy, we don't have time to argue-"

A loud thud echoed through the hallway, and the sound of marching men erupted from the hallway.

Lucy's eyes widened, and she grabbed Owen's arm. "Just get in here," she whispered.

Owen frowned and followed after his sister, kicking the wood out and shutting the door behind them. Erin watched from behind a cupboard, the bird hopping from her arms onto a bed frame. *These Barons are relentless.*

Owen crouched down in between the people scattered around, looking at them all with his finger hovering over his lip. They fell silent, only the muffled sound of the bird's talons scraping the blankets audible.

The Barons searched the training hall eagerly, their voices muffled behind the closed door. Lucy looked at Owen in uncertainty, her brown eyes worried. Owen looked at her, raising his finger back up to his lip at her. Lucy's hands raised, her fingers flowing through the air rhythmically around her face. Erin blinked in realisation: *sign language.*

Owen copied her, doing different rhythmic movements near his face. Erin thought back in her memories to her younger years when her parents taught her the artistic language, translating the hand movements.

{Stay silent, Lucy.}

[You're not planning on going out there, are you?]

{We don't have a choice.}

[Yes, you do!] Lucy signed furiously.

Owen raised his head slowly, trying to see any Barons nearby.

{Five Black Cloaks, maybe.}

Lucy peered her head around the door, looking out.

{They look armed.} Owen signed.

Lucy gave him a flat look. [Oh, really? I never would've guessed.]

{Now isn't the time for that.} Owen frowned at her.

[You're telling *me* that?]

{If we wait here *quietly*, they won't find this room}

Lucy rolled her eyes and shifted her feet beneath herself slowly, sitting down on the planks. [They know we came here. The door was locked.]

{They don't know about this room.}

Everything went silent. Lucy frowned and looked at Owen. [Weird.]

Owen raised himself once again to peer through the window; everything was almost pitch black.

{I don't see-}

A sudden black mask appeared in front of the window, the Baron's eyes boring down onto Owen's face. Owen jumped back onto the ground, his heart racing out of his chest.

"Everyone hide!" he yelled, moving in front of the door.

Lucy's eyes widened, and she tried to grab her brother, but his arm was too quick to catch. The Baron burst through the door, the wooden door slamming into Owen with a good deal of force, shoving him back and making him roll across the ground with a grunt.

The people hid under their spots of choice, covering their mouths to stay silent. Erin ducked back behind the cupboard, her eyes wide. *How did they know?*

"Owen!" Lucy gasped, moving out from her spot to him.

"In here!" the Baron yelled down the hallway, drawing his weapon and advancing towards the pair.

Owen groaned, lying on the floor stunned. Lucy's eyes were wide as dinner plates, her face pale as the Baron moved closer. Erin peered out to watch; they were doomed!

A sudden flare of white light erupted from the bed frame, and a nimble figure sprang toward the Baron, a woman's voice roaring in pain and challenge. The Baron turned his attention to her, stepping back in surprise. The woman tackled him to the ground, yelling in pain at her broken arm. Hair whiter than snow practically glowed in the dark, those brilliant green eyes luminescent against her pale skin. She pinned him down beneath her knees, her good arm morphing into a lion's paw.

The Baron's eyes widened, raising his shield in front of his face. She swiped her arm down onto his shield, the wicked claws slashing straight through the leather like paper. The Baron grunted, dropping the torn shield to the side, looking up at her in terror.

She grabbed his mask with the paw and ripped it off, chucking it to the side and pressing her claws against his exposed throat, a feral snarl on her face. Her muscles were bunched beneath her loose black clothes, and power writhed through her lean form.

"You took everything away from me," she snarled, her accent foreign and angry.

"What would that be? Your land?" the Baron snarled back.

She dug the claws in further, blood pricking the man's skin. "Your bastard King took away my mate's life," she bared her teeth, long fangs glinting sharper than razors.

The Baron struggled to breathe, his tan face turning bluer by the second.

"I will hunt down every single last one of you parasites and your families until the rage your men have put in me no longer burns," she vowed and slashed her long claws across his throat. Blood sprayed across the room, splattering against the wall colourfully.

The Baron's eyes widened, his gashed throat bleeding heavily and bubbling with air. She stood up when the Baron stopped moving, shaking the blood off her furry hand. The claws shifted back into long feminine fingers, blood dripping off of them onto the floor.

Lucy stared up at the woman, her eyes locked on the delicately arched ears beneath the snow-white hair. The woman turned to the people staring in shock and fright, her eyes losing their glow. "I am a friend to the people. I mean you no harm," she said, her teeth shrinking back to normal size. "My name is Laruen Ramondo. Yes, I am an elf. I will protect you as long as it takes for you all to get to safety."

Erin looked at Laruen's right arm, the bone hanging limp in her forearm. *She must be in agony, surely.*

Owen stirred on the ground, his head throbbing wildly. Lucy looked back at him, her hand hovering over a lump forming on his head. "Got a headache now?" she asked.

"Don't make it worse," he growled, sitting up from the ground.

Laruen's eyes snapped to the doorway, hearing something Erin couldn't. "Go, now," she said. "Whichever way is faster out of here."

Lucy stood up, lending her brother a hand. "Come on," she said. "There's a back way out."

"Who is she?" Owen asked, looking at Laruen.

"The bird," Laruen muttered and stalked towards the door.

"Since when did elves live in Camelot?" he asked, standing up from the ground.

"I don't," her voice trailed back into the room.

Erin stood up and walked over to the siblings, the people behind her following closely. "It's a long story," she assured them.

"Everyone move," Owen ordered the people. "Stay together, and watch your surroundings."

"If you keep yelling, you'll alert *more* of them," Lucy scowled.

"I'm not yelling," Owen scowled back at her.

"Nah, you're just speaking at a higher volume." Lucy walked to the door, gesturing for the others to follow. Erin followed after her, the shuffle of feet following closely behind.

An animalistic roar echoed from down the hallway, men's yells of pain following after. They moved faster, spurred on by the noises as they winded through the hallways, Lucy opening the door to peer out quickly.

"Okay, no one's there," she said. "Let's just stay here until the elf lady comes back."

Owen sat in the hallway, his head spinning ferociously. He leaned his back against the wall, turning pale in the face. Erin furrowed her brow in worry, going to the boy. "How are we doing?" she asked him softly.

"Not too good," he said, lifting his head to lean against the wall.

"You hit your melon pretty hard," she noted, looking at the bump forming under his hair. "We'll have to find you some ice later."

"I'll be fine," Owen growled, trying to get himself onto his knees. Erin held her hand out to him, and he looked at her. "What?" he asked.

"Well, are you going to stand back up?"

"We have to keep moving," Owen said. "So yes."

Lucy tutted at him, turning around to face him. "I think that head knock has made you lose the last brain cell you had," she sighed. "The woman is trying to help you, you gnat."

Owen looked at Erin with slight disgust, moving onto his right knee. Erin lowered her hand awkwardly and stepped back from him.

"Who even are you, anyway?" Owen asked her.

"Erin," she said. "Erin Torona."

Owen looked at her differently than before, sympathy and realisation changing his scowl. "I'm sorry about what happened to Sam. He was a good leader."

The people murmured around her, offering condolences and surprised whispers. Her heart ached, the picture of her boy still fresh in her mind. She could still see his face lit with joy the day he'd come home from his graduation, the lads following him inside to celebrate with her; she could see his young self bringing in that stray little pup he'd found in the rubbish, determined to fight Dawson to keep her. She could almost feel the heat from his head resting against her shoulder as he hugged her for the last time before he'd ridden off to fight in Catarina. *If only I'd held him for longer.*

A shadow stalked from out of the hallway, Laruen walking back to them covered in crimson, her white hair stained with it. "Okay," she said. "Let's go."

Owen looked at the blood covering her in shock, standing up slowly. "How do you know where to go?"

"Friends in high places," she smirked, opening the door beside Lucy.

Owen looked back at the people, nodding at them. "Stay together."

"You could start an inspiration novel," Lucy muttered, following after Laruen. "'Stay together, be a team, keep it up.'"

"Whatever," Owen grumbled. He stood to the side, allowing the others to go out first. Erin walked out after them, the rain drenching her instantly, cracks in the cobblestone paths running red with the bloodied water like sanguine rivers. *Gods rid the Kingdom of this chaos, and soon.*

Horse hooves beat the mud on the track like muffled drums, bouncing over the river that rolled on at King Ergott's side, the stars glimmering off the surface brightly. The sword at his side threatened to leave the sheath, but he held it in with one hand beneath his cloak that billowed in the wind. *It won't be gone just yet.*

The riverside opened up into a wide valley, foliage scattered around the border of the water on top of large boulders and slate planes. Ergott remained emotionless as the horse trotted across the rough surface, the river bank a few feet away from the trail. The horse snorted beneath him, hesitant to go near the lake. Ergott protested against the horse's discomfort and pushed down to the river bank. The horse buckled, backing up against its master's orders.

"Wait here," Ergott frowned, dismounting the horse near a tree. He grabbed the horse's reins and looped it over a low-hanging branch, turning back down to the river below.

Mud and clay stuck to his boots the closer he got to the water, slowing him down to a careful stepping game. He held Remedy at his side, almost in comfort. It was a pity to discard a fine blade, but it had to be done. He had to get rid of Samqueel's mark.

A melodic voice sounded from somewhere further on the lake, piercing through the eerie silence. Ergott looked around for the voice, but no one was in sight; only a thick fog, overgrown foliage, and the lake that sat in the middle. He frowned, walking further down along the slippery slate, aware that he wasn't alone.

The water lapped at the bank gently, a calming contrast to the voice piercing the air. Bats flew up into the sky, their wing beats flitting through the air. Ergott scoured over the water, the fog lying over it like a blanket.

Something pierced the surface, a ripple spreading out to his right. Ergott snapped his eyes to it. *What was that?*

The water eventually settled back down, but Ergott remained on edge, his grip on the sword's handle tightening. He stopped at the water's edge, scouring over the surface, his eyes narrowed.

The thing broke through again - a tentacle, it seemed. A very, very long tentacle, with spines like a fish sticking up along the top. The moon shone off its skin, slowly dying as it dipped back beneath the surface. Ergott narrowed his eyes, unsheathing the sword slowly, his eyes glued to the water.

Everything was calm around him; not a sound was coming from the trees. Even his horse was quiet. It seemed as if the whole world held its breath to listen to the song lilting through the air. And so Ergott listened, as well.

The water in front of him exploded, waves flying through the air with an inhumane screech, spraying Ergott with water and something a bit thicker that stuck to his face. Ergott turned his head away from the water, the sword gripped firmly in his hand. He looked back with a scowl, his teeth gritted. He wiped his hand over his face in disgust, slime coating his fingers.

Feminine laughter echoed across the water, the singing stopping to echo its sister's amusement. The thing poked its gruesome head out of the water, sharp fangs and white eyes glowing in the moonlight. Ergott scowled at the thing. Its tail was the tentacle he saw, the same spines stretching up along her spine to the back of her neck.

"Leave me be. This business doesn't concern you," Ergott snarled at her.

"You are at the edge of my home," she drawled, her voice surprisingly woman-like. "Anything that touches my territory is my business."

"I'm discarding a memory," he said. "It will take no time."

"But this place is not for you to disregard your rubbish," another head poked out of the water next to its sister, a grim snarl on its face. "The waters here are sacred."

"I am your King," Ergott told them. "I decide what gets thrown into this lake."

They tilted their heads at him with their teeth bared, one of them snarling animalistically. "The King, you are not," she spat. "An imposter to the throne."

"Then who is the King to you beasts?" Ergott asked snappily.

"The one true King of legend," she answered, swimming closer to his feet. "The one who will reveal the Sword and claim back his Kingdom."

"*You* are not Him," the other snapped.

"He is dead," Ergott snarled. "I will wield the sword and reign over the throne!"

"Not with those chicken arms, you're not," a head further in the water called, her voice younger than the others. She rose in the water, her arms crossed and teeth bared in a wicked grin. "Especially when you don't have the right blood to begin with. Do you plan on getting fitter any time soon? How will you get the sword to pull to your command? Explosives? Please, tell us of your plans, False King."

"Once I throw this sword in, I hope it decapitates one of you ferals," he growled at them, stepping an inch closer to the water's edge. His boot tip touched the water, and the one closest to him lunged, swiping for his leg with outstretched claws.

Ergott swung the sword down at her, the blade cutting her arms off below the elbows. She let out an ungodly screech, reeling back towards the water uncontrollably. Black blood spilled over the mud into the water, the severed limbs fading into dust. Her sisters snapped to him, their fangs bared and tails coiled.

"Get back! All of you!" he warned, pointing the sword at them.

They hissed like demonic cats at him, watching the sword as their sister disappeared under the water. The Syren taunting Ergott straightened, turning her head towards the centre of the lake as if listening.

"Back!" he warned again.

"She watches, Sisters," she said softly. The Syrens froze and turned towards the lake, their lithe bodies swishing through the water. Ergott watched them curiously, a slight smirk forming on his face.

The youngest Syren turned to Ergott, swimming closer to replace her injured sister's spot. "You have something worthy of the Lake," she said, her milky gaze raking him.

Ergott glanced at the sword in his hands, looking back at her. "This belongs in the waters."

"You harbour the blade of many battles, the cure to end all problems and plagues wherever it is taken. Why discard the Remedy?" she tilted her head.

"It has become ineffective against its injustice. It is time the sword joins the fallen," Ergott said.

She held out her clawed webbed fingers, looking at him with her head lowered. "I will take it into the depths for Her Majesty to have."

Ergott looked at her warily, reaching down and handing the sword to her. She wrapped her fingers around the blade, pulling it back to the water with her. Her eyes were distant, her face twitching sharply. A hard mask fell onto her expression, accusing eyes fixing him with a glare.

"You are a disgrace," she hissed. "A failure to your land, a murderer."

"The King must make hard choices to grow his future, and those beneath the royal line are subject to sacrifices," Ergott growled, looking down at her coldly.

She bared her teeth in a hiss and ducked under the water, her slippery form lashing through the water. The other Syrens followed after her, the last one flicking her tail sharply out of the water to splash the King again.

Ergott darted back away from the water's edge, the splash landing where he was just moments ago. He turned around to where he came from, making his way back up to his horse.

*I'm no murderer. All of these actions are to make a better Kingdom. They're all too blind to see it.*

He grabbed his horse's reins and mounted the saddle, his face set in a glower as he kicked the beast's side. *They'll all see one day. I'll* make *them see.*

## Chapter 18: Midnight Duel

"Come on, Arthur, get those arms swinging," Gawain growled.

Arthur panted in heavy breaths, running down the hillside with the armour on, feeling like a cart was pulling him. Gawain jogged steadily beside him, the old Knight wearing a bit of armoured plate himself. Albeit, it looked lighter than the armour Arthur was wearing.

His feet chewed up the distance between the courtyard and the hill, but he still had yet to get past the worst bit: the upward slope. He'd run this track a thousand times by now for the past month, but every single time, he'd hated this damn hill.

And what annoyed him further was that the trainees in front of him were running up it efficiently. He frowned at them, going as fast as he could to catch up with them. At least there was always one person who lagged behind him.

"By the Gods, my side feels like it's being stabbed," Tristan puffed behind him.

"If you keep complaining, you'll fail the training," Peter said from ahead of them.

Tristan staggered a bit as he ran, his breath uneven as he watched Peter run easily. "Showoff! Pull me along like a sled dog, yeah?"

"Ask the bottom of my boot," Peter called back.

"Thanks, Peter!" Arthur scowled at him.

"I can't bloody well breathe," Tristan squeaked, slowing back down.

"Tristan," Arthur breathed, scowling at him, "I will trip you over if you keep complaining, and Gawain will help."

"You should be grateful," Gawain snorted at Tristan. "You're only wearing chainmail."

"It's still heavy!" Tristan complained, trying to keep up, the chains rattling as he jogged. "Why is all this heavy crap necessary?"

Arthur rolled his eyes. "Let's swap armour, then."

"Noooo," Tristan protested, his voice getting hoarse. "I'm flat out in this stuff. You can keep your fancy plate."

They followed the trainees around a corner, heading into the dense forest, a creek splitting across the marsh. *Away* from the cave. *How long does this track go for again?*

"Kyan, stop going off the track," Gawain barked at him from further up.

"It's a faster route!" Kyan protested, moving back onto the track.

"The point of the route is to go for as long as you can," Gawain sniped at him. "Stay on the path."

"I'd let him go on his own route, Gawain," Arthur chimed in. "No one would be concerned if he got lost."

"Despite what you believe, Kyan is a valuable asset to your team," Gawain said to Arthur. "You might not get along, but he's been in this longer than you have."

"A team member who *left* Tristan," Arthur scowled at him.

"I told him to go," Tristan puffed. "I had a plan."

"Right," Arthur mumbled, his chest burning from the weight.

The trail led them through a cluster of close-knit trees, vines hanging down to brush Arthur's hair. A small clearing opened up, the dirt stretching out like an old dry riverbed, cracks breaking up the dry mud. Trainees crouched around the area, some sitting down to catch their breath.

Arthur slowed himself down, the weight of the armour helping him this time to stop. The breath whooshed from him in great gasping breaths, his body straining to stay standing. Tristan saw the clearing and whooped weakly, falling to his knees.

"Finally, the torture is over," he smiled, flopping to the ground.

"I wouldn't get your hopes up just yet," Arthur panted, his heart racing.

Peter walked over and nudged Tristan's side with his boot; he looked as if he'd never broken into a sweat. "I think he died," he raised a brow. Tristan's shoulders jumped as he giggled.

Arthur turned to him. "You'd need to do a lot more than that to kill him."

"I'm invincible," Tristan joked with his face in the dirt.

"Get out of the dirt, you grot," Peter frowned. Tristan grunted in protest.

"Give him an hour," Arthur said. "He'll eventually get out of it."

"Make it two," he groaned, rolling onto his back.

Arthur looked around the area; nothing but dense forest and trainees were in sight. Galahad's young boy, Baeydn, approached Arthur with a straw crate. Arthur looked down at the lad, looking at the crate in his hands. Waterskins were stacked in a row inside the crate, a few missing and in the hands of various trainees. Arthur smiled at him, grabbing a waterskin from the crate.

Tristan's head lifted from the ground, his brows lowered in focus. "Do you hear that?" he asked no one in particular.

Arthur looked down at him. "Hear what?"

"Splash noises."

Arthur furrowed his eyebrows, listening out for what he was talking about. He couldn't hear any splashing. "No?"

"I swear I can hear water," he frowned, getting up onto his feet.

"Baedyn has a crate of waterskins," Arthur pointed out, taking a sip of the drink.

"No, not like *contained* water," he said, looking around.

"Has the isolation gotten to that thick skull of yours?" Kyan smirked, walking over to stand beside Peter with a hand in his pocket.

"You've got bugs in your ears," Peter snorted.

Tristan ignored them, frowning towards a bush. "It's just..." he walked towards the scrub, his words trailing off. Kyan and Peter looked at one another confusedly.

Arthur looked at Tristan. "Tristan?"

"I can hear water. I'm not joking," he frowned, looking at Arthur.

Arthur looked at him in curiosity, following behind him. Gawain watched them, frowning as they parted through the trees.

Tristan walked through the small bushes in his path, dodging the tree roots sticking out of the ground. Arthur trailed behind him, navigating over logs and large foliage.

"It's getting louder," Tristan noted. "Can you hear it?"

Arthur listened out again, this time hearing the familiar gurgle of water. "Yeah," he said, his eyes lighting in realisation. "It sounds like a waterfall."

"That's exactly what I was thinking," Tristan agreed and pushed through the trees onto a big rock. "Ooh."

Arthur walked over to his left. "What?"

Tristan's hand grabbed the top of his head and spun it forward slowly, Arthur's eyes settling on the body of water in front of them. Arthur's eyes widened in delight, and he smiled at the body of water, walking out from the tree's edge.

A rock jutting from the small creek on a higher ledge spilled water in cascading flows into the small pool surrounded by mossy rocks, the bubble and gurgle of water stronger here. The water was surprisingly deep in the smallish rock pool, the bottom seen clear as day. At the left end, a small ledge layered with rocks in a natural slope spilled water further down into the forest, the creek continuing away from the dry riverbed. Waterlilies floated in the water, purple and yellow hues stark on the green lily pads beneath them. Tiny fish swam in the water lazily, one jumping through the surface to catch a low-flying bug.

"It's so pretty," Tristan whispered.

Arthur walked over to the water's edge, crouching down with a grunt. He removed his gauntlet from his right hand and lowered it into the water, splashing up on his sweat-covered face. The water was deathly cold, hitting his face with a sharp, ice-like sensation that numbed his fingers almost instantly.

"Pretty cold, too," Arthur said, the water dripping from his face.

Tristan stood beside him and looked at the fish in awe. His eyes were lit like stars, watching them swim, bending down to see them closer.

"Reckon Gawain noticed?" Arthur asked, looking out across the water's surface.

"I noticed, alright," Gawain said, standing behind them. Tristan yelped in fright, spinning to face him and just catching himself before he slipped into the pool. Arthur stood up from crouching, his eyes wide.

"You're not hard to miss in all that armour," Gawain said, looking at the copper details flatly.

"Like the waterfall we found?" Arthur asked, ignoring his anger.

"It's been here for a long while," Gawain snorted. "Where do you think we get the water from?"

Arthur shrugged. "Thought you had it delivered."

"What are we, a monastery? The Rebels find their things out here; it's better to stay hidden that way."

"Can't argue there," Arthur muttered.

"What about the ale and bread?" Tristan asked, seating himself cross-legged.

"Get off the ground," Arthur frowned at him. Tristan poked his tongue out at him.

"The Rebels bring them back from markets in Londinium and other nearby Kingdoms," Gawain answered. "You saw the apple cart."

"And haven't been caught?" Arthur asked curiously.

Gawain shook his head. "They're pretty clever for a bunch of strewn-together randoms.".

"I'll admit," Arthur started, "they did hold their ground when escaping Londinium, especially Geraint."

"He may have held his ground, but he's never really secretive about it," Gawain muttered. "He never has been, the sod."

"Neither are we," Arthur huffed, pointing to Tristan.

Tristan looked up at him. "We've been secretive about the tunnels," he frowned.

"Until the Barons found out about them," Arthur frowns. Tristan scowled, looking back down to pick moss off a rock.

"We knew of them," Gawain said. "Never used them, but knew they were there."

"How?" Arthur asked, looking back at Gawain.

"They're old spy tunnels," Gawain explained. "They were used as a last resort to escort the royal family from the castle if things ever came to it. All the Knights of the Roundtable knew. I'm not overly sure how the Barons would've found out, but it wouldn't surprise me if Jackseye told them."

"We uhhh…" Arthur muttered. Tristan held his tongue, picking moss faster. "Found them by accident."

"In an old shack," Tristan added. "I squeezed through the chimney one day out of curiosity because someone didn't want his clothes covered in soot," he looked at Arthur.

"And I had a valid reason," Arthur added. "Imagine walking through the castle covered in head-to-toe soot, then have your uncle force you to jump in the pool only to then walk back to your room with no towel with a bunch of elderly Maidens watching and laughing."

Tristan paused. "You have a pool?"

"No, you idiot," Arthur frowned. "I didn't want to get dirty."

"Gnat," he grinned.

"Anyway," Arthur smirked at him, looking back to Gawain. "It was an accident that they found the tunnels. It was sincerely Tristan's fault."

"Oi!" Tristan frowned.

"However," Arthur went on, "they don't know what parts of the Kingdom the tunnels connect to. So they shouldn't bother to search them."

"That's a pretty thin 'shouldn't'," Gawain muttered, straightening himself up, his armour shifting.

"But it's a shouldn't, nonetheless," Arthur grinned.

"Like how you shouldn't be here," Gawain raised a brow.

Arthur frowned at him. "What's wrong with exploring?"

"Didn't anybody ever teach you not to go wandering through the trees?" Gawain growled. "You can find things nastier than a pond."

"Like what?" Arthur frowned.

"There have been rumours of wild animals getting around the trails," he said. "Bears, wolves, cats, whatever tickles your fancy. I don't want to have anybody off the path or out of my sight because if anyone gets hurt, it's on me. Now let's go; the others are still on the riverbed." He turned back around to stalk through the trees, waiting with an eye over his shoulder for them to join.

Tristan stood up and tossed the moss ball he'd been rolling up at Arthur, darting towards Gawain with a grin. It flew right past him and plopped into the water.

Arthur sighed. *Not more torture!*

Back at the clearing, the trainees sat around and socialised, Baeydn sitting alone at the edge of the trees against a rock with his crate. Arthur walked back onto the riverbed, his legs starting to burn again. He sat himself down to lean against an old stump, the armour thudding against the wood. It poked and prodded him uncomfortably in places, and he shifted to move it. *You'd think they would design this stuff to be more comfortable.*

Across from Arthur, Baeydn grinned at him. He couldn't believe that his King was right in front of him and that he was real. *The Born King. I knew he was real.* He reached into his pocket and pulled out a wooden Knight about the size of his thumb. It had a sword and a shield made of small metal pieces and armour painted with gray clay. He smiled at it, observing the small wooden figurine in his palm. *I want to be one, one day, like my father.*

The underbrush beside him rustled, leaves crunching softly. He looked over beside him, hearing the rustling clearly. A leaf blew out toward him, the red hues turning brown from the cold. Baeydn watched the leaf blow towards him, laying his palm flat for the leaf to fall onto.

A sudden ball of fluff sprang out of the scrub, catching the leaf beneath its little white paws. Baeydn yelped in fright, moving back away from the fluffy object. It snapped its attention to him, its big green eyes wide. Its fur was like spun gold, the kitten's tail curled up in fright.

Upon realisation, Baeydn relaxed and smiled at the kitten, shuffling back to his spot. The kitten flattened itself to the dirt, its ears pinned back against its head.

"Hello there," Baeydn said softly. "What are you doing out here?"

It blinked at him, its eyes searching over him with a shred of intelligence. Baeydn tilted his head at the kitten, looking at it curiously. It tilted its head, copying him.

He tilted his head to the other side, observing the kitten as it copied him again.

"Do you want some water?" Baeydn asked curiously, reaching into his crate and grabbing out a waterskin. The kitten mewled, its squeaks high.

Baeydn opened the lid to the waterskin and poured some of the water into the lid, holding it out to the kitten in his flattened palm.

It watched him warily, moving to his hand and sniffing at it. It sprang its front paws onto his fingers, the pads soft, and lapped at the water. Baeydn smiled at the kitten, watching it drink from the lid. It flicked its eyes up to watch him, a small purr forming in its throat.

"Why are you out here?" he asked softly, looking at the kitten curiously. It meowed at him as if in answer. Baeydn tilted his head again, looking at it with interest. The kitten looked over to Arthur, its ears pricked up.

Baeydn followed its gaze, then looked back at it with a smile. "That's the Born King," he said.

The kitten seemed to nod in agreement. Baeydn smiled at her, a warm feeling in his chest spiking. He reached down to the tiny kitten and picked her up gently, sitting her down in his lap. It looked at him with a high wrinkled brow, claws poking through his pants as it balanced.

"Don't play with my pants," he frowned at her. It purred, shaking the material free from her snagged claw and finding a loose thread. Its eyes dilated, and it swatted at it, fiddling with the small string. Baeydn smiled at the kitten, chuckling at it as it played with the string.

It meowed and looked up at him, its eyes narrowing. *What are you laughing at?* It seemed to say.

"You can play with the thread," Baeydn smiled.

Her tail flicked his hand.

"You're so soft," he noted.

It purred in agreement and moved beneath his hand, the golden fur like cotton. He patted the kitten gently, smiling down at the feline.

"Were you all alone out here?" he asked her. She blinked up at him, its head nodding again. He blinked. *Did it just nod again?*

"Do you understand me?" he asked her. It meowed, nodding again. Baeydn grinned and patted it softly. *This is so weird.*

She flopped onto her side on his leg and scrambled for a hold, falling onto the dirt with a rumpled hiss. Baeydn picked her up gently, standing her up on his lap once again. She shook out her fur, grumbling.

"Baeydn," Tristan called to him.

"Yeah?" Baeydn answered, looking up at him.

The tall, dark lad walked over to him, the chain mail on him rattling like a maraca. He looked down at him and opened his mouth, then paused, looking at the kitten. "Oh, hello," he said to the cat. "I remember you."

The kitten's eyes widened, and it shrank back into Baeydn's hand. Tristan frowned slightly at it. "How did it get all the way out here?" he mused.

"I don't know," Baeydn shrugged. "It just came to me."

"Strange," he hummed and bent down to pick up the crate. "It ditched us back in Londinium after I let it go. Anyway, we're heading back to the cave," he said and looked around the clearing to see if anyone noticed. "Bring the kitten," he whispered.

Baeydn looked down at the kitten and smiled. "You're coming with me."

It curled under his hand in a ball, its ears poking through his fingers.

"Where will I put her?" Baeydn asked Tristan.

He shrugged. "I don't know, ask your dad," he said and followed after the group.

"Come on, kid," Arthur called to him, following the group back to the caves. Baeydn stood with the kitten in his hand, carefully tucking it into his arm as he walked after the trainees. *Dad's going to be so excited.*

The armour was becoming more unbearable by the minute. But, at least, it was getting easier to manage. Sort of. Arthur was still yet to wear the whole thing, but he could probably deal with it now.

Maybe. He hoped.

Arthur walked over to a wooden chair, his legs aching fiercely. He sat down with a grunt and began to unbuckle his leg guards. *Gods, it feels nice to sit down.*

"Hey, stranger," Maria said, walking over to his seat.

Arthur looked up at her, a wet strand of blond hair covering his forehead. She wore a short-sleeved blue shirt today, matched with black trousers and leather boots. It suited her. "Why weren't you out there?" he asked with a grin.

"I'm not a Knight, remember?" she pointed out, looking at his armour.

"Lucky for you then," he said, placing the leg guard on the floor beside him, going to the right leg.

"Need a hand?" Maria offered, gesturing to the buckles.

Arthur looked up at her, a smile forming on his face. "Sure," he said.

She moved over to him, going to his side and reaching for his shoulder pad, holding it still as she loosened the buckle with deft hands. Her scent washed over him, strawberries and sugar sweet over his sweat. "Have you been baking?" Arthur asked.

"I have, actually," she nodded, sitting the shoulder pad on the floor. "Some tarts are loaded up in the pantries, ready for later."

"Any left for us?" Peter asked as he walked past, stretching in front of them.

She looked at him as she unfastened his other shoulder pad. "There's three or so in the oven, but," she fixed him with a look as he moved towards the kitchen, "they're for *later.* If I see one missing, I'll bite your fingers."

"Noted," Peter nodded, walking away from the kitchen with his hands raised.

"Are you a kitchen hand now?" Arthur asked, moving to his knee guards.

"I'm more of an all-rounder," she shrugged and put the other pad down. "I get any job thrown at me just about. But I do love making food."

"Can you cook?" he asked, placing the thigh plate down on the floor.

"Can a blind man hear?" she huffed.

"I'll take that as a maybe," Arthur chuckled, unbuckling his second thigh plate. Her hands moved to his sides and pulled the chest plate free, that same shock flitting through him at her touch again. His breath hitched slightly, and he felt his heart kicking back up to speed. *Damn it, not again.*

She lifted the chest plate by the shoulder straps up over his head. Arthur raised his arms high, groaning slightly at the slight strain in his underarms.

Maria let out a disgusted groan, staring at his back. "Did you go swimming, or is that all the proof of your *manliness*?" she curled a lip, setting the chest plate down and wiping her hands on her pants. "It's disgusting."

A large patch of sweat stuck his white shirt to his back, more of it beading on his neck and in his hair. It stuck the front to his chest, too, the cool breeze hitting him and making him groan in satisfaction. "You try wearing it all day," he said to her. "It's like wearing a furnace."

She laughed softly and knelt beside him. "I can tell you're not joking," she grinned. "You look like a tomato."

"I feel like one," he chuckled, taking off his right gauntlet.

Her hands flipped the clasps holding his boots together, the metal falling to the ground with a minor clash, the other quickly following. She stretched over to pick them both up and sat them beside the rest of the armour. "Right," she said, sitting on her knees beside him. "That's the easy part done."

"Of what?" Arthur asked with a raised brow, unbuckling the second gauntlet and sliding it off.

"Getting all that armour off you," she looked up at him. "Now we've got to put it back and find someone to clean it."

"I might be able to help with that," a familiar voice offered, walking up to them.

Maria looked at the voice with a smile, standing back up and turning to him. "I thought you were busy helping the younger ones?" she smiled.

Arthur looked at him with a flat expression. "I forgot your name. What was it again?" he said with a voice just as dull.

"Simon, my liege," Simon smiled. "Simon Ector."

"Right, Simon," Arthur said. "Where can we clean the armour?"

"I'll take it to the fountain and scrub away the dirt."

"Are you sure?" Maria asked him. "What about the others?"

"Session is done for the day," Simon shrugged.

"What exactly do you do? Besides smiling?" Arthur asked, standing up from the chair.

"I mainly teach the young kids the skills to use a sword, and I also help in the kitchen," Simon said.

"I knew about the cooking," Arthur nodded.

"And it's always nice to have a beautiful helping hand in the kitchen," Simon smiled at Maria. She rolled her eyes playfully, a glow on her cheeks.

Arthur frowned lightly at him, hatred seeping through his chest cold as ice. Even his accent was annoying him. "Are you a Knight?"

"An old trainee, my liege," Simon smiled. "I was training as a young lad in the hall twenty-two years ago."

"Arthur is fine," Arthur scowled at him.

"A-apologies, sire," Simon replied, noticing his annoyed look with slightly creased brows.

Maria looked at Arthur questioningly, her brows furrowed. *What is wrong with you?* she seemed to say.

"Right," Arthur grumbled firmly, turning to Maria with a more friendly face. "Should we take the armour to the fountain?"

"Sure," she clipped, picking up the chest plate and looping it over her arm. "Are you still willing to help, Simon?"

"I can help if needed," Simon repeated, watching Arthur warily.

Arthur picked up a few pieces of armour from the ground and walked off to the fountain. "We should be fine. Thank you for offering," he dismissed.

Maria threw Simon an apologetic look and picked up the rest of the armour, following after Arthur. "I'll see you later?" she asked.

"Sounds good to me," Simon nodded, smiling at her. She smiled at him and nudged him with an elbow jokingly before she stormed after Arthur.

Arthur walked to the fountain with a slight frown, carrying the heavy pieces with all the energy he had left. The light was brighter in the afternoon inside the cave, the water reflecting more harshly onto the walls.

Maria stormed past him and dropped the pieces onto the stone next to the water, the clang of metal echoing around the chamber.

"What's wrong with you?" Arthur asked her, sitting down the pieces of armour gently.

"The better question is, what's wrong with *you*?" she sniped, looking at him with a scowl.

"What do you mean?" Arthur asked. "I'm fine."

"Every time Simon shows up, you get all puffed-up and flat-faced," she pointed out.

"I'm not the King yet," Arthur shrugged. "He shouldn't call me those silly names."

She spread her hands out slightly with a sceptical look. "You're a *royal*," she scoffed. "Would you rather be called Your Highness? Or Prince? Or something even worse? Take it as a compliment that he still likes you after the way you've thrown him dagger-eyed looks."

"Maria, just calm down-"

"This is calm, Arthur," she growled, her voice flat. "If I weren't calm, I'd be yelling."

Arthur looked at her, his frown gone. "I just think he's too much, and he's really up in my space," he said.

"You rarely even interact with him," she protested. "You know he's actually charming to be around? He's better than the gutter crawlers back at Londinium; I'll tell you that."

"Anything is better than the gutters in Londinium," Arthur muttered.

She sighed, pinching the bridge of her nose lightly. "Tell me, Arthur, and be honest; why don't you like him? It's the same reaction with Kyan, though I don't blame you for that one, but *Simon*?"

Arthur looked at her, taking a deep breath. His heart pounded a little too hard, his blood rushing in his ears. *What do I tell her?*

"I just think you could do better," Arthur offered, looking at her.

Maria was taken aback, her head flinching backwards with a disbelieving stare. "Excuse me?"

"The way he looks at you is *more* than just friends, Maria," Arthur added, walking up to her. "And I have a feeling that he just isn't the one to make you happy."

She stared up at him, her brows furrowed in irritation. "What would you know, Arthur?" she growled. "Where is all this conspiracy stuff coming from? You *watch* him as he's talking to me? Do you know how weird that sounds? Do you know how it makes me feel when you say you think you know what's *best*?"

Arthur looked down at her, guilt squeezing his chest. "I'm just trying to protect-"

"You don't need to protect me! I did just fine before I met you, and I'm doing fine now!" she barked. Her voice echoed around the cave, and she covered her mouth, looking at the others staring at them around the fountain.

"This isn't exactly the best place to yell," Arthur said, furrowing his brows at her.

She gritted her teeth, holding in a growl. "For a man who is fated to be a generous and loving King, you're awfully controlling," she muttered.

"Now you know what I've grown up with," Arthur scowled at her.

"Don't you try and tell me it was hard to grow up," she hissed. "You think you're the only one who had a rough start?"

"I'm not saying I'm the only one who did," Arthur growled. "I'm saying I grew up in a wretched castle with a man who disrespected everyone. I won't be like that man. I won't allow it."

"Then why do you act like a bodyguard any time any guy approaches me? You don't help me in any way with it," she growled.

"Because I like you, Maria!" Arthur blurted angrily. "Alright? I like you. I like the way the light hits your eyes and makes them glow like gems, and the way your smile makes me feel like I'm home, and… well, it doesn't matter. I shouldn't have gotten jealous, and I'm sorry, I'm sorry. I just, I didn't want to lose you as a friend."

Her glare disappeared to a stunned look, her green eyes wide. Her mouth gaped with unspoken words, her face flickering with emotions. Arthur felt his face light on fire, his hand reaching up to brush his hair back nervously.

"I've lost too many people who were my loved ones," Arthur added. "And if you don't want to go any further than friends, that's okay. I just don't want to lose you all together." *Gods be damned.*

She ran a hand through her hair, looking towards the water with a whoosh of breath. *Gods, she looks like I slapped her.* A bright glow of red stained her cheeks, rising from her neck. "Of all things you could've said, I didn't expect *that*," she whispered.

"Look, it's fine if you don't feel the same way, but I needed to tell you why I acted that way," he breathed, his heart pounding in his chest like a drum. He fought to keep his breath even, embarrassment squeezing his throat.

Maria sat down to the ground, loosing a breath and putting her hands on her face. Arthur frowned in worry, his hands fidgeting. He walked over to crouch beside her, trying to look at her face.

"Maria?" he asked her softly.

"Mm?" she replied, turning her face to him.

"Are you alright?"

She chuckled softly into her hands, lowering them. "It's quite funny, actually."

Arthur frowned lightly. "Why?"

"Because for a good while…" she started and trailed off, a small smile on her lips. "For a good while, I liked you too, yeah?"

Arthur chuckled, shaking his head. "So you kept it a secret, too?" his voice wavered, the tightness in his throat abating.

She laughed softly, looking at him. "I suppose I did."

"You did well."

She grinned slightly, shaking her head. "I didn't think so," she shrugged.

"I'm happy to just stay as friends," Arthur reassured her.

She smiles slightly, looking down. Arthur tilts his head at her, looking at her curiously.

"Is that what you want?" she asked quietly.

"I'm not sure," he admitted. "Simon likes you, so you can go with him if you want." Bitter sparks flew through his blood at the words, but he had to say it for her sake.

She chuckled softly. "You know he and I are just friends, right?" she asked, looking at him.

"I reckon he's had some thoughts come into his head."

She scoffed playfully, slapping his foot. "You're gross," she scorned.

"It's truthful," Arthur shrugged.

"The only way to get those thoughts in your head from someone else is to think them yourself, and we both know that happened," she grinned mischievously.

*Oh, clever witch.* "Touché," Arthur grinned at her.

Her eyes lit up in amusement, leaning on her knuckle to face him. "So you admit it?" she asked lightly.

"Admit?" Arthur asked, watching her closely.

"You, good sir, have been thinking about me."

"I, as the King, do think tremendously."

"Indeed, sire, your brain capacity is that of an elephant," she jested.

"I do not have big ears, my dear lady. Therefore, it is eccentric for you to say that," he frowned playfully.

She grinned and shot her hand out to flick his ear. "What's this then?" she asked.

"Ow!" Arthur frowned, flinching back. "That hurt."

She grinned amusedly, scrunching her nose in mockery. "Aww," she drawled. "A flick to the ear causing immense pain to His Highness? Shame."

"I'll flick your nose," Arthur grinned mischievously.

"Oh?" her brows raised, her hand moving to hover over his face. "Like this?"

"Don't you even think-"

Her hand flicked the tip of his nose lightly, a smug look crossing over her face. "Boop."

Arthur frowned at her, sighing deeply. "About it," he scowled.

She laughed at his reaction, lowering her hand slowly. Arthur looked at her with a playful frown, shaking his head.

The pad of her finger just touched his nose again, and she grinned. His arm shot out to grip her wrist, moving it away from his face. "Don't," he warned. Her eyes widened slightly, a flash of alarm on her face.

"Don't touch my nose," he repeated softly.

She pulled her wrist from his grip slowly, lowering her hand back down to her side. Arthur tilts his head at her, confusion flicking through him at the wariness in her eyes. *Did I scare her?*

"I uh," she stammered, turning to the armour. "I suppose I should get this cleaned."

"It'll get dirty again tomorrow, I bet you," he chuckled, trying to lighten the mood back up again.

"We know, but Gawain is picky," she said quietly, picking up a piece of the iron plate and sluicing water over it.

Arthur stood up from the ground, groaning lightly to himself. "You alright?" he asked her.

"Yeah, I'm okay," she said softly, focusing on the armour.

"I'll see you later?"

"Count on it."

Arthur nodded and walked out of the fountain room, looking back at her a few times, watching her hunched form getting lower each time. He mentally kicked himself, cursing under his breath. *Idiot.*

Night fell over the cave's exterior, the Rebels and Knights inside all in their comfortable beds with layers of covers. Soft voices echoed down the tunnel outside of Arthur's door, and he listened as they faded off further.

He still wore his boots and an extra jacket he found, his sword tucked up under his shirt along his back. The training wasn't enough for him; he needed more than what Gawain was doing. And tonight, he planned on doing just that.

He cracked open the door and peered out to the torch-lit hallway, seeing no one in either direction. Arthur walked out of his room quietly, closing the door gently behind him, making sure it made no sound.

He made his way down the tunnel quietly, pausing by an open door to check no one watched. A small figure lay bundled up in the furs on the bed against the wall, the familiar blond hair glinting in the faint torchlight. He smiled slightly and continued, leaving Maria to sleep. Arthur walked down the small staircase leading to the foyer, finding it empty with no one in sight. The torches lit the area wonderfully, the wood shrivelling down to its final stump in each sconce.

*This is a lot easier than I expected.*

He crept towards the cave's entrance, making sure he wasn't followed. Only his boots crunched on the gravel the closer he got to the entrance and made his way out, grinning to himself as he jogged towards the track.

The moon shone brightly from above, lighting up the crushed sandstone like chunks of stars littering the ground he jogged on. Shadows stretched across the track he ran through, the rustle of leaves in the wind filling his ears. Nightingales tweeted overhead as he ran, owls joining the symphony surrounding him.

*Let's put this sword to good use.* He grinned to himself; adrenaline surged through his veins the closer he got to the training grounds. He finally broke through the treeline, the familiar dry riverbed flooded with cracked gray light. Arthur looked around the forest; he hadn't seen this area at night before - it looked odd, the broken moonlight deepening the mud cracks like scars and sending shadows to tower over him.

The slight splashing of the distant waterfall touched his hearing to the right of the clearing, the sound more defined in the quiet of the night. Arthur smiled at the sound, walking along the track beside the low-running creek.

The moon lit up the water like liquid silver, leading him to the pool of water in the rocks. Being out of the armour felt even better; the weight and the orders of Gawain didn't constrain him. He could do what he wanted, and he liked the absence of the other trainees. It was more peaceful that way.

The night air wasn't as cold as he would've expected, the breeze brushing his face gently. He pulled the scabbard out from beneath his jacket and gripped the sword tight in his palm, wandering over to where the Rebels trained with swords. Chipped trees stood at the edge, battered from endless hits from blunted blades. The stumps surrounding them were six feet in height and made of oak trees, common around their area. The wood was strong enough to withstand the training blades, but… Arthur looked down at his sword. *What about this one?*

He looked forward to the array of training stumps and placed the sword on the ground beside him a moment, shrugging the jacket off his shoulders and throwing it over the top of a stump. He bent down and picked up the sword, sitting aside the scabbard before walking over to the nearest stump.

*It's time to see what it can do.* Arthur tightened his grip on the handle and swung, the blade etching through the air and embedding itself into the side of the stump with a loud crack.

He blinked. *Is it stuck?* He tugged it, and it stuck into the stump further, his grip tightening around the handle. He pulled it harder, and it came free with a jut, the pommel smacking into his gut.

"Ow! Bastardly thing," he growled, holding his stomach. *Okay, lesson one, don't get it stuck.*

He looked at the blade's edge; it was hardly dented, still smooth and sharp. He straightened and moved over to a more crowded area, four stumps surrounding him. He flicked his eyes to note each of them as he stood in the middle. *This won't be so hard, right?*

He gripped the sword tight with both hands and spun closely to the one on his right, using the momentum to slash at the first one he saw. The wood splintered its bark across the clearing, his sword whooshing close to his leg as his hand slipped.

He jumped out of the way of it, his heart skipping at how close it came. He blinked and stumbled forward, realising he was only holding it with his dominant hand. *Okay, lesson two, don't use one hand on the sword.*

*Or let go.*

*Definitely don't let go.*

Arthur frowned slightly at the sword and regained his footing. *This is harder than I thought.* Doing it alone was terrible compared to when he'd train with the Roundtable. His heart pinged with longing at the memories, wishing Sam was here with a shield and Remedy in his hands.

He sighed and took the sword in both hands, looking at the stump in front of him. *This whole sneaking-out thing was a ridiculous idea.*

"Use your strength, Arthur…" a familiar voice said to him, faint and soothing.

Arthur turned around to find the voice, but no one was there. He blinked in confusion, trying to see through the dark.

"Use my strength?" Arthur muttered, lifting the sword.

"The sword… is yours," the voice whispered. "Cherish it, nurture it."

Arthur took a deep breath, letting his arms go loose. The sword gripped in his hands tightly, Arthur lifted it into the air and swung it towards the centre of the stump with all his might, grunting with effort. The forest split with an almighty crack, the sword cutting clean through the wood and coming to a stop. Arthur looked at the split wood, the sword sitting right in the middle of the two halves. He smiled to himself slightly and lifted the sword out, the wood from the top of the stump clattering to the ground with a thud.

"Well, that was unexpected," Arthur said, rolling the log away with his foot.

He inspected the blade for any marks but, to his surprise, found nothing. *What is this thing made of? And if this is only the false one, then how strong is the* real *Excalibur?*

He grinned at the sword and took it up again, slashing behind him in a flurry of twirls, the sword sending chips of wood flying through the air as it struck the stumps. The thud of the sword reverberated up through his arms and stung his already sore muscles, but Arthur relished it. It made him feel like he had power for once. The sword made him *feel* powerful.

He turned to another stump beside him and slashed it fiercely on an angle, the top half of the stump sliding off onto the ground. He grinned and laughed, looking at the sword in his hand and nodding his head at the weapon.

"What a little legend you are," he said to it, spinning it in his hand. The sword glinted in the moonlight, the runes engraved on the blade flooded with silver. The blade was so shiny he could've sworn it was a mirror reflecting the forest around him. The lion's eye stood out the most, its detail seemingly more lifelike, it was as if it was actually watching him.

He blinked. It blinked. He frowned and moved the blade, the eye going back to the normal etching. *What?*

Arthur turned around, lowering the sword to his side. His breath caught, his eyes widening; the sword *was* reflecting the forest, alright. A huge golden lioness stood behind him, its green eyes watching him closely.

"You from around here?" Arthur asked it nervously. Everything in him told him to run to the cave, but what if it was faster? Surely, if he ran, it'd catch him.

The big cat blinked at him calmly, sitting back on its haunches. Its tail flicked in the air on its own accord, the lion shaking its short mane out, sending dust flying through the air.

Arthur locked eyes with the lioness and slowly walked backwards away from the beast. He wasn't planning to take his eyes off it, not even for a second. The beast growled at him, the sound like thunder. Its face seemed to be scowling at him, weirdly enough.

"Didn't you know it's rude to look the King in the eye?" Arthur frowned, taking a few steps backwards.

The cat averted its eyes away from him. Arthur blinked at it. *Did it just understand me?*

The great cat shifted its paws to lay down on its stomach, grumbling like a bickering child. Arthur looked at it curiously and walked towards it slowly, placing the sword on the ground gently. It watched him closely, fixing him with its green-eyed stare.

The eyes seemed familiar to Arthur. Where had he seen them before? Arthur tilted his head at the big cat, watching it with interest. It grumbled at him, its paw patting the ground. *Sit.*

Arthur glanced at it uncertainly, trying to work out what it meant. It - it *rolled* its eyes - and growled at him, patting the ground again.

Arthur nodded at the lioness and lowered herself to the ground calmly. The lioness wasn't any average lion, Arthur knew. It was too bright, the light in its eye too sharp to be just an animal.

It huffed a great breath of air and rested its head on its paws, the moonlight washing its fur white. *No, that's not the moonlight.* The lion was *glowing.* Arthur watched it with wide eyes as the light got brighter, the form of the lion becoming a silhouette, shrinking down to a smaller size.

*What is going on?*

The light flared, and he covered his eyes, looking away.

"What in the Hell?" he muttered. As the black faded from his eyes, he could see a small figure sitting on the ground, her hair white in the moonlight. Ragged, dirty clothes clung to her small body, and the same bright green eyes stared at him, though more nervously than when the lion did.

*A child?*

"I'm guessing you're a cat lover?" Arthur asked, chuckling lightly.

She stared at him, her face coated in dirt. Pain and sorrow glittered deep in her eyes, the girl almost frail enough to fall apart.

Arthur tilted his head at her and smiled gently. "You're lost?"

She shook her head. *Not lost.*

Arthur looked at her curiously. "How could you change into a lion?"

She shrugged nonchalantly. *I don't know why.*

Arthur looked down at his waterskin on his belt, grabbing it from his belt. Her face floods with longing, watching the flask keenly.

"Come get some," he said. "I won't hurt you."

She stood up and moved to him gracefully, reaching for the flask hesitantly. He handed her the flask gently, noticing a chain around her neck. She looked at the flap on the flask and flipped it open, drinking from the bottle messily. Arthur smiled at her warmly, wrapping his arms around his knees. "What's the necklace you've got?" he asked her.

She blinked at him, pausing her drinking. Arthur blinked at her, noticing her reaction to the question. Tears began to well in her eyes, her breath quickening. Her small hand reached underneath her shirt and pulled out the chain, the length of it reaching almost to her stomach. The chain was a simple silver link, the pendant in her hand the shape of two metal triangles overlapping one another.

Arthur sighed in realisation and looked down at her. "I miss him, too," he said softly.

Tears spilled over her face. "He was my father," she whispered, her young voice cracked with disuse.

Arthur looked at her sadly and sighed. "And he was my mentor." *Sam had a daughter?* He'd never once spoken about a family other than his mother, Erin. *Maybe to protect her?* He noted the delicate arches of the girl's ears, confirmation settling his mind.

*How had she gotten Samqueel's chain? The Commander never took the thing off.* Then it came to him. Tristan found her in the tunnels underneath the castle. She was the cat. The tunnels had holes everywhere leading through the castle walls; Arthur never thought anything of them. She must have been there when… *oh, Gods. She watched her father die.*

"I wish I were there earlier to save him," Arthur murmured. "I'm… I'm sorry."

She looked up at him, her small hand gripping the necklace. Her body was shaking with grief, her breath ragged. "The King is a bad man," she said. "Mama hates him."

He tilted his head. "Do you believe in the Born King?"

She tilted her head with him. "The boy talked about that," she murmured.

"That man who killed your father won't be the King for much longer."

Her posture began to relax, her shoulders slowly winding down. She trusted him, Arthur realised. He'd gained the trust of this small girl, the daughter of Samqueel no less, and as insignificant as it seemed, it made his heart swell in happiness. *Is this what it feels like to be a King?*

Arthur looked at the dirt all over her cheeks. "Let's get that dirt off your face," he said calmly.

She nodded and averted her eyes once she realised she was staring.

"Hey," Arthur mumbled. "You can look me in the eyes, okay? I don't mind."

She flicked her attention back to him hesitantly. He reached back down to his belt and grabbed a second waterskin, pouring some onto his hands. She watched him with big eyes, staying still.

"Come a bit closer," he beckoned. She shuffled forward to stand near his knee, a hesitant hand touching it.

He moved his hands to her cheeks slowly and calmly, rubbing off the dirt with his wet fingers and palms. Her eyes squeezed shut, and she huffed air from her nose, peeking at him through one eye. He wiped his thumb along the creases of her face, occasionally tipping more water into his palm.

She watched him calmly, letting him do it. Arthur looked at her, smiling warmly at her. He didn't get all the dirt, but at least it looked better than before. She smiled faintly at him, her hand feeling his knee with interest; the texture must be different to her.

"What's your name?" Arthur asked softly.

"Sariel."

"I'm Arthur," he said. "Nice to meet you."

"Meeting strange children in the middle of a forest is not a good hobby to have, Arthur."

Sariel snapped her attention to the voice, crouching away from him. Arthur stood up and turned his head to the voice, frowning slightly at the man. Gawain stood at the edge of the trees on the path, a sword in hand, his dark hair ruffled from sleep. He scowled at Arthur and glanced down at Sariel, narrowing his eyes. "What are you doing out here at night?"

"I was training," Arthur answered. "Then this girl came from the bushes; she's a shifter."

Gawain's face flashed with hostility. "A Wildshape? In the forest around our cave?" he growled.

"She's harmless, Gawain," Arthur growled back. The child ducked behind Arthur's legs, her eyes wide as she stared at Gawain.

"And she is Samqueel's daughter," Arthur added, reaching one hand back behind himself to touch her hair gently.

"Samqueel never had a wife, nevermind a daughter," he snapped and turned to the girl.

"She has his necklace," Arthur scowled.

"Anyone can have a necklace, Arthur. Be gone, pest!" Gawain snapped at her. Sariel flinched and pulled away from Arthur, sprinting towards the trees. A bright flash of white illuminated the forest for a moment, and the crash of leaves underfoot went silent.

Arthur watched her leave, then huffed towards Gawain. "Aren't you a gentle soul," he scorned. "Lancelot was right; you do have anger issues."

"Any shifter is dangerous," Gawain spat. "I don't care if it's a child. Now get your stuff and get back to the cave."

"No," Arthur argued.

Gawain glared at him, moving closer to him with a tighter grip on his sword. "Get back to the cave, Arthur," he growled with venom.

"Why don't you make me?" Arthur challenged, shrugging to him.

"You asked for it." Gawain's sword cut through the air towards him, the flat of the blade tapping Arthur's thigh with a thud. Arthur stepped back, hissing at the slash, grabbing the sword from the ground beside him.

"Do you think you are above the word of your mentors?" Gawain spat, slashing for him again.

Arthur deflected the sword with his blade. "I'll take my chances."

"You ought to learn how to do as you're told." He swung the sword backhanded, coming at Arthur's left side.

Arthur's eyes widened, and he skipped out of the way, looking back at Gawain in shock. "Are you trying to kill me or something?"

"You think you're good enough to pick that sword up," he barked. "So show me, boy. What have you got up your sleeve that I can't see?"

Arthur narrowed his eyes and gripped the sword with both his hands, positioning his feet.

"Look at that. All that reading taught you to place your feet correctly, at least," Gawain smirked.

"You start to remember a few things after a couple of reading sessions," Arthur grumbled, watching Gawain closely.

Gawain's hands shifted on his blade's handle, gripping one over the other and one hand beneath the guard. Arthur narrowed his eyes, his grip tightening. He seemed to be waiting, just standing casually. *What does he want?*

"So, who attacks first?" Arthur asked, tension halting him.

"You're the big shot here. You came out here breaking my word; you back yourself up."

"Just for the record, your word isn't very clear-"

Gawain's feet propelled forward, and his sword clashed against Arthur's, the sound reverberating around the trees. Arthur's wrists burned with the impact, and he swiped to keep it in contact with Gawain's blade, the two locked together.

"You talk too much," Gawain said simply.

"Did my father used to as well?" Arthur asked, trying to keep the lock steady.

"Most definitely." He shoved the blade to the side and shouldered Arthur back, the breath driving from him as his back hit the ground. Arthur groaned on the ground, coughing a few times before slowly getting back up.

Gawain watched him with boredom written across his face, his sword dangling from a hand. "Come on, then, don't dawdle."

Arthur looked to the ground and grabbed a pile of dirt in his left hand, standing back up and facing him. Gawain twirled the blade in his hand and stepped towards him, Arthur following his movements, narrowing his eyes at his mentor.

"Did you know everybody used to do this when they were younger?" Gawain asked.

"Fight you?"

"Go out into the forest to spar or sword fight or some other stupid thing," Gawain said. "Some brought back terribly bleeding wounds."

"Let me guess," Arthur added, "you told them the same thing as you've told me?"

"None of them listened, naturally," Gawain huffed. "It's like herding cats."

*I bet they never did this before!*

While Gawain was distracted, Arthur pegged the pile of dirt at Gawain's eyes, rushing up to him with the sword raised. Gawain growled, his eyes clamped shut as he raised a hand to wipe them, his arm coming up to meet his sword blindly. Gawain's form buckled, his legs shuffling back almost with a limp.

Arthur's memory hit him with a quiet gasp. *You'll know who.* Arthur kicked his left knee, shoving him back with the sword, the old Knight roaring and falling to the ground.

"Did they do that before?" Arthur asked, looking down at Gawain.

Gawain's teeth were gritted in pain, looking up at Arthur with interest, his hand gripping his leg. "How did you know about that?" he asked, his voice calm.

"A good old friend, Arkansas," Arthur smirked, twirling his sword.

Gawain laughed, rubbing the dirt from his eyes. "That little bastard," he shook his head. "The whole lot of them. Absolute smartasses. Good to see they didn't keep that under wraps."

Arthur looked down his nose at Gawain, mocking his stoic nature. "Come on then, don't dawdle," he teased.

Gawain chuckled and stayed where he was, lowering his knee. "No matter how much you think you know-" his sword swiped towards Arthur's ankles, the flat slapping the bones beneath his boot painfully.

Arthur yelped and fell onto the ground with a thud, gritting his teeth at the impact. Gawain's figure stood above him, the sword pointing down at his chest. "There's always something you haven't learned," he finished. "Keep your eyes open."

Arthur looked up at him, scowling. "That was cheating," he said.

Gawain raised his eyebrows at him in mock surprise. "And throwing dirt wasn't?"

"There's no section in the rule book that says I *couldn't* do it," Arthur protested.

"The rulebook isn't the Bible on how to fight, son," Gawain said, moving the sword away from him. "Textbook fighting is useless on the battlefield or anywhere else. You just need to learn with experience and use the book as a guide."

Arthur rolled his eyes, getting up slowly. Gawain offered him a hand, and he took it, pulling him up to his feet.

"So, how about you let me do more sword training?" Arthur said, looking at him.

Gawain thumped him on the back with a hand, smiling at him in a way that made Arthur unsure what it was about. "You know what? Tomorrow morning, in the courtyard, except not with that thing," he nodded at his sword.

"Isn't that what I need in the style of 'Sword Training'?" Arthur asked, raising a brow at him.

"If I let all my trainees have sharpened swords to train with, how many do you think would still be alive?"

"Depends on how good they are," Arthur shrugged. "I'd expect Kyan to, you know, *not* live."

"You'd be surprised how often the more experienced trainees fall on their asses to a new kid," Gawain huffed. "But Kyan with a sharpened sword against someone like Simon? I wouldn't like to clean that up. On either side."

Arthur chuckled lightly. He couldn't imagine Simon fighting someone like Kyan and coming out on top. Even he couldn't beat Kyan - not that he wanted to admit so. He looked up at Gawain. "Why are you hard on me?"

Gawain looked at him thoughtfully. "I'm hard on all my trainees," he said. "I need to be because, by the time they're out in the real world with a real sword at their side and a real threat in front of their faces, they'll have the brain to remember not to wet themselves. I push them to their limits to show them they can go further. I push you specifically that extra mile to show you that you can go further than what you thought. Tell me, how far do you think you've gone?"

Arthur looked down to the ground. "I wouldn't know at this point."

"Have you looked at yourself in a reflection? Have you seen how different you look from the scrawny rat of a kid that came in an apple cart to the caves all those months back?" he asked.

"I wouldn't call me a scrawny rat," Arthur frowned at him. "And no, I haven't looked at a reflection."

"Next time you come across a mirror, do so," Gawain smirked mischievously. "And rats live in tunnels, boy."

"Are you saying I live in a tunnel?" Arthur asked.

"I'm saying you were tunnel-visioned," he corrected. "You had your mind set on being a failure like your uncle led you to believe. You were told you were nothing, and you believed it without a doubt. To say you were oblivious is an understatement."

"You know something, Gawain," Arthur narrowed his eyes at him. "You're an asshole."

"Look at you now, though," he continued, smirking. "You think you're a hot shot, you don't look like a chicken with fleas anymore, and you've got a Legion of Knights at your back. Don't give me that look; you know you were thinner than my wrist," he frowned.

"I guess I was," Arthur chuckled. "It's still hard to believe that I've gotten to this point. I'm still framed for the murder, and my uncle wants me dead. I'm only hoping that this Born King prophecy is real, 'cause if it isn't, all this has been for nothing, and it's extraordinary how-"

The world tipped out from underneath him, and he gasped as his rear end met the ground with a sharp thud. His hands shot out behind himself, softening his fall backwards. Gawain laughed beside him, his leg extended out in front of Arthur's feet. "You still talk too much," he chuckled.

Arthur frowned at him. "And you're still a cranky old prune," he said.

"Prune? I'm not *that* withered," he chuckled, extending a hand down.

Arthur rolled his eyes and took his hand. "You're more withered than the Maidens at Camelot."

Gawain's other hand swooped down and tapped his forehead lightly as he pulled him up to his feet. "I think you're referring more to your void inside there," he joked.

"Don't touch my forehead," Arthur scowled at him.

"Never kick my knee again, and I'll call it even."

"At least I know your weak spot."

"You'll keep it to yourself, or Gods help me," Gawain snorted and sheathed his sword.

"No promises," Arthur said, picking up his jacket and sword from the ground.

"Come on, boy. Let's get the last wink of sleep before Percival demands coffee again."

## Chapter 19: Hunting Season

*Row after row after row. Same old positions in front of the castle as per usual. How dull.* At least Edward wasn't going to be here for much longer. A pity and a blessing; the only thing he'd miss on this mission was the Maidens. The same stone and mortar walls that surrounded him constantly he wouldn't miss. If he ever saw the inside of another castle again in his life, it'd be too soon.

Edward stood straight-backed at the front of the Baron *Shueba*, his face overwhelmingly bored. He'd been standing for what felt like an eternity. He'd be grateful when the time came to leave. At least he could get off his feet.

Footsteps sounded faintly from behind him in the Castle Gates, harmonised by Ergott and Jackseye's rugged voices. He turned his attention to them, keeping his gaze forward.

"Remember, Rohin," Ergott said. "Arthur returns here alive; injured is an exception, but he's of no use dead." He stopped in front of the gates, two Barons standing on either side of the King.

"Crystal clear, sire," Jackseye sighed. Edward could tell his father had been told the same words too many times before, the look of annoyance he tried to hide lacing his voice.

"When should I expect your return?" Ergott asked.

"When we find him, is what I'm supposing," Jackseye said. "We're still unclear of his location just yet."

Ergott nodded slightly. "Head south first. The forests are an easy hiding spot for any fleeing fugitive."

*And if he'd been pounced on by a pack of wolves and eaten alive?* Edward tried not to roll his eyes, clenching his fist at his side.

"Yes, sire," Jackseye nodded.

"Good luck," Ergott nodded at him, walking back into the castle with two Barons following closely behind him.

Edward turned his head to watch the King walk away, a frown deep on his face. The man was insane. His idea to recruit the Barons came out of thin air with no reasoning other than to replace the Knights he murdered. Something didn't sit right with him, not now that he knew Vivien was working with him. *Is no one else picking up on any suspicion?* Every single *Almúr* behind him was more oblivious than a deaf man to a scream as if they were dogs stuck to their master's command.

He looked back at his father. The old man hadn't seemed to see it, either. His and Ergott's history together must've blindsided Rohin too much to see the flags flying in front of him. And his hatred against the Knights wasn't helpful, either; his plan succeeding had closed his eyes to all the damage that'd happened. And Edward was the one who got his face scarred by the Commander himself. Edward ground his teeth in contemplation.

Jackseye mounted his horse that sat at the front of the search group, grabbing the reins in his right hand. He turned to the *Shueba* and whistled sharply, the Barons standing to attention in unison, their boots thudding the ground. Edward didn't move.

"If you can't keep up, then head back in the direction we came from," Jackseye said, flicking his eyes over to Edward. "I cannot afford to have an army of children for a task made for men."

"They will keep up, *Muharí*," Edward said. *It's more a question of if they are motivated enough to follow.*

Jackseye frowned. "I will be leading the search. You will follow my orders with no questioning. Understood?"

Protest flashed through Edward, and he opened his mouth to snap back, a retort itching to bark from his throat.

"Understood?" Jackseye repeated, giving him a sharp look.

Bitterness coated Edward's tongue, and he shut his jaw tight. His *Shueba - his -* was just as easily taken away as it was given. *What was the point of all my purple ink and rituals if I'm discarded to the side regardless?*

*I'll remember this, Father. I won't forget the day you pushed your rule onto me.*

Jackseye nodded at the Barons and flicked his reins to trot away from the castle. Edward stalked over to his horse and mounted it swiftly, kicking it sharply to chase after his father, the Barons behind him following. The glare he threw at his father's back made his scar sting, but at least his eye was getting clearer every day.

Jackseye slowed back down to ride next to his son, looking at him flatly. Edward fought a snort. The man never showed any emotion besides anger, jealousy or the face he pulled when he was plotting something. It'd been the same since the day he'd pulled him from the house in Southron and dragged him to the East Coast with one less eye and the other burning amber. *Today must be no exception.*

"You must learn to respect my choices, son," Jackseye said.

"I'll respect your choices when you respect my rank," Edward sniped, holding the reins in one hand.

"I respect your rank, but I don't trust your acts."

Edward curled his lip. "What acts are you referring to? One of actual human decency or the ones Voss taught me?"

"Voss was never a good teacher. He's made you change more than you realise. You never used to be an entitled, snarky pup. You've only learned your attitude from him, not his skills," Jackseye huffed.

*He did a better job than you.* "At least I didn't go missing after my first mission in the Kingdom."

"You made a worse decision," Jackseye said. "You tried to fight a Knight of the Roundtable."

"Oh, really? You were there to see what happened when he came in the door now, were you?" Edward sniped sharply. "You were there to see him split my face open with his bastard sword and leave me be instead of-"

"Instead of finishing the kill, like I once did to his father," Jackseye finished.

"I don't know what plans we are a part of, Father, but the Commander was more intent on stopping them than we are on fulfilling them. Is this even worth it?"

"King Ergott intends to take Braynor for himself, and he's agreed to allow the Barons to be his army," Jackseye told him. "And it's something that we will participate in for the sake of our status."

Alarm hit Edward like a brick to the face. "Are you implying that my hands are bound under Ergott's madness because of an ultimatum you agreed to?"

"He is your King, and you will respect him," Jackseye growled. "You may not like him, but he is your ruler."

"Answer the question, Rohin," Edward demanded.

"Don't call me by my first name, Edward," Jackseye warned. "I am your father."

"Fathers don't lie and cheat their way into hierarchies at the expense of their children."

"You should be thankful for the life I've given you and your siblings," Jackseye huffed. "To answer your question, the deal we have made with Ergott is to protect his rule from the prophecy of the Born King in exchange for immunity when he expands his rule across Braynor."

*Good to confirm that we're dead if we don't find this prince.* "The life where three out of six of us are dead? Thankful doesn't cover it."

"Your brothers fought for the Barons and they were leaders of their own *Shueba*."

"And what happened to them? How exactly did they die?" Edward sniped. His grip on his reins got tighter and tighter.

"I will not discuss their fate with you, boy," Jackseye scowled.

He snorted angrily. "Just like with everyone else, you refuse to speak. Why won't you tell anybody how they really died? The whole secret business is more hurtful than you think, and not just to mother."

Jackseye looked down slightly. "It hurts me, too."

"Marley, Jase and Arlo do not deserve to be hidden away from us. Keeping secrets and following orders blindly isn't helping your family love you." Rohin never heard the strangled sobs from Lana's room every night; he didn't understand the grief it caused his little sister to lose her three bigger brothers. *Does he even have a soul anymore?*

"Your brothers died in a fight I knew they couldn't win, and I warned them not to, but they never listened. This is why I never wanted you to become a Baron," Jackseye murmured.

*Liar.* "You dragged yourself into this mess yourself and brought me with you. Tell everybody all you want about how righteous and sensible your actions were," Edward growled, facing forwards to hide the silver in his eyes. "But I'll never believe you." He flicked his heels against the horse's flank, the beast trotting forward faster.

"That's why I can't tell you the truth."

"You don't even know it yourself," Edward muttered quietly and spurred the horse forward faster, outrunning his father length by length. *Damn Rohin and his lies. Damn him to the Ether's Black Pit.*

"Arms up, Arthur!" Galahad shouted at him.

Arthur took a savage blow across the jaw from Gawain's knuckles, staggering back with a groan. The pain shot through him like an arrow and throbbed as it swelled, Arthur hissing as he touched it. The courtyard was filled with trainees sparring and watching the fights, the old Knights in particular seated on the stones around Arthur.

"Don't just rely on that sword to help you," Gawain growled, pushing his sword blade away. The blunted training sword was heavier than Arthur would've expected; it was like lifting a small child with one hand.

"Were you trying to break my jaw?" Arthur asked, holding his jaw and shifting it around.

"Intentionally, no."

"Well, if you were meaning to, you succeeded."

"You're still yapping on like a hyper dog; you'll be fine." His sword cut up and blocked Gawain's swipe, dodging back away from his charged shoulder.

"That pep talk makes me feel so much better, Gawain. Thank you," Arthur frowned sarcastically.

"You should hear when he *really* gets into it," Bedivere called to Arthur from the sidelines.

"It's like a war horn," Percival chimed in, taking a spoonful of his soup bowl.

"Worse, an angry wife," Geraint grinned, stirring his drink.

"And even worse than when Kay disciplines us," Galahad said, giving Kay a smirk.

"I don't know why I try," Kay growled, his hair ruffled and messy. He'd been drinking again, Arthur could tell. "None of you tools listen."

"You all seem to be enjoying this. Want to actually give me tips?" Arthur asked them, panting heavily.

"Tip one," Percival started. "Give up on trying to beat Gawain. Not happening."

"Helpful, thank you."

"Tip two," Bedivere added. "Don't look away."

"Don't look away?" Arthur asked, turning back to Gawain. He wasn't there. Arthur blinked in confusion, looking around for the tall Knight, his grip on the sword tightening. A tap on his shoulder turned him around, Gawain standing behind him an inch away. Arthur yelled in fright, falling to the ground in surprise.

Laughter burst from the Knights on the rocks, a few trainees turning their heads to look. Arthur scowled at him, standing back up from the ground.

"Was that a part of your plan?" he asked, brushing the dirt off his clothes. He was out of the armour for once; Gawain let him wear just normal clothes instead of roasting in the iron death trap for this training session. And thank the Gods, because it was hot as the Ether.

"Always," Gawain said. "There's not one person that doesn't look away. Ryan learned that."

"No surprises," Percival nudged him, chuckling to himself.

"The bastard was watching a two-year-old waddle to a stream," Bedivere protested. "How was I supposed to see him coming after me for stealing a tart?"

"Because you stole a tart," Galahad raised an eyebrow. "And we all know that you're the only one who would steal a tart."

Bedivere looked pointedly at Gaheris. "And that tart wouldn't?" he drawled.

Gaheris looked up at the Knights, a caramel tart in hand. He gave them a smile, his teeth filled with pieces of shortcrust and caramel.

"My, I wouldn't mind some of that, actually," Bedivere murmured, his face turning thoughtful.

"You're not getting any," Percival said. "You already stole a piece." He grabbed another spoonful of soup.

"Bollocks," Bedivere dismissed and plopped himself down beside Gaheris. He looked up at the big man, watching the tart with subtle side eyes. "Care to share, Chris?"

"Go eat my sweat-crusted pillow," Gaheris said with a mouthful of tart.

"That doesn't sound very appetising," Bedivere frowned.

While the Knights chatted amongst themselves, Arthur observed Gawain, his sword glued to his palms. Gawain stood calmly in front of him, sword raised in defence. "Perhaps it's time to fair you against someone else," he muttered.

Arthur stood up straight and twirled the sword in his hand. "Like who?"

Gawain pondered a moment and looked around the courtyard, his gaze settling on Tristan. The lad was seated underneath a large oak tree, a bored look on his face as he drew in the dirt with a stick.

"You want me to fight Tristan?" Arthur asked, raising an eyebrow with a small smirk.

"He hasn't trained with a partner before, so why not? Tristan," Gawain barked, the lad looking over to him with raised brows. "Over here."

He threw the stick into the shrub and stood up, coming over to them with interest. "Do I need to fetch water or something?" he asked.

"Take this," Gawain said, reversing his sword to give him the handle. "You're getting a session."

Tristan's eyes flicked between the sword and Arthur, a grin flashing onto his face. "It's about time," he said, taking the sword.

"No pressure on us?" Arthur nodded to Gawain.

Gawain shook his head. "Practice rounds only," he said. "Don't go chopping each other's heads off."

"That's good enough for me," Arthur said, positioning his feet correctly.

Tristan beamed and inspected the dull blade, twirling it around to watch the metal gleam. "It's been forever," he said.

"Like Gawain confirmed, no pressure," Arthur reminded him with a grin.

Tristan looked around at the trainees, his face worried. "Where's Peter?" he asked. "I don't want him coming in and stealing this one, too."

"Peter's in the main room," Percival confirmed.

"Good." Tristan raised the sword, shifting his feet into place. "I'd like to train for once."

Bedivere turned away from the tart to look at Tristan with the sword. "Gods, this won't go well," he muttered, settling back to watch.

Arthur watched Tristan carefully, gripping the sword tightly in his hands. Tristan caught his hesitance, a small frown on his face. "What?"

"Are you sure about this?" Arthur asked.

Tristan lowered the sword with a sigh. "I know how to fight with a sword," he said. "Why is everyone doubting me?"

"I'm not doubting you," Arthur assured. "Maybe you can teach me a few skills."

"I doubt it," a voice muttered from a fair way.

Arthur glanced behind Tristan's shoulder, narrowing his eyes slightly. "And you would know, Kyan?"

"Yes, actually, I would," the trainee nodded, crossing his arms and leaning against a tree. "He's more likely to throw the sword halfway across the courtyard than parry."

Tristan looked away from Arthur down to the ground, his shoulders slumping. Arthur ground his teeth, setting his sword into the dirt gently. "Your input isn't needed, Kyan," Arthur scowled. "Go and hit on the helpers. That seems to be the only thing you're great at."

"Funny how you say that after everyone heard what went on between you and Maria in the fountain room," Kyan smirked. "Get rejected already, did you? No surprises there."

Arthur dropped the sword to the ground completely, walking up to him. "Even if I did, it's none of your business," he scowled.

"And yet you two carried on like a pair of strangled geese at one another for everyone to hear. If you didn't want anyone to know, then why shout it out?" Kyan stared flatly at him, sizing Arthur up.

"I'm not afraid to punch you in your perfect teeth," Arthur growled.

"Go ahead, I'll make you go crying back to your bedchamber like the last time, remember that?" he grinned.

Arthur grinned back, laughing in front of his face. He looked back at the other Knights. "He's funny, isn't he?"

Tristan glanced at Arthur briefly, offering the handle back to Gawain with a disappointed sigh. Gawain took the sword back and patted his shoulder, watching Arthur with interest.

Arthur turned back to Kyan, smiling widely at him. Kyan looked at him with boredom.

"Go back to your jousting. You won't win," Kyan shrugged, pivoting to turn around.

Suddenly, a heavy pain shot through Kyan's neck. His hand flew to his neck, his eyes wide as he choked, coughing violently. Arthur grabbed his shoulder and brought his knee up into his chest, making the breath rush from his lungs with an audible whoosh. The trainee dropped to the ground on his knees, gasping for breath around his swelling throat.

"Let's get one thing cleared up," Arthur said, kicking him onto his back. "I will be your King in the future to come, and Tristan will be my right-hand Knight, and unless you want to live in the Darklands with killer beasts," Arthur crouched down to him, "you will show me the respect your King deserves. Am I understood?"

Kyan glared up at him, a glint of fear and hatred in his eyes. His hand was still on his throat, his breath wheezy.

Arthur hit the side of his neck, and Kyan's breathing cleared up with a cough. "Do you understand, Kyan?"

The trainee stayed on his back and glared up at Arthur, his face conflicted. Finally, submission cemented his jaw, and he averted his eyes. "Whatever," he muttered.

Arthur placed a foot on his chest, pressing down. "Wrong answer," he scowled.

Kyan looked up at him with wide eyes, fear on his face as his breath left him again. "Stop! Gods, I said I understood!" he groaned, trying to shove Arthur's leg off.

Percival walked over to Gawain, slightly worried. "Are you sure this is a good idea?"

Gawain frowned. "This is going further than I thought," he muttered.

"Do we stop it?"

"Arthur," a quiet voice said behind Gawain. Arthur looked over to the voice.

"This isn't like you," Tristan said worriedly. His face was unusually scared - of him. Arthur blinked in realisation and looked down at Kyan, took his foot off him, and offered Kyan a hand. "I'm sorry," he said quietly.

Kyan just stared up at him, panting breathlessly. Gawain breathed out with a whoosh, looking at Percival. "Count on Tristan to do so," he muttered. "He's always the peacemaker."

Arthur looked at the rest of the Knights, their expressions of uncertainty matching one another. Anxiety shot through Arthur like an arrow, freezing his blood. *What did I do?*

Kyan sat up and moved away from him, his throat turning a deep shade of red and swelling quickly. Trainees around him were stopped in place and staring at him, murmurs flitting among them. Shame burned him up from the inside as Arthur sprinted away, his mind driving him to follow the jogging path.

"Arthur!" Tristan called to him, but he didn't stop. His head raced with anxious thoughts, every emotion mixing and coursing through his body with adrenaline that drove him forward.

Lancelot stepped out of the cave's entrance with a mug in hand, watching Arthur sprint away with wide eyes. "What's happened?"

Geraint moved over to Kyan, kneeling beside him to check his neck out. "A bit of a scuffle in the courtyard, Lance," he said.

Lancelot walked over to Gawain quickly with concern. "What happened, Gawain?"

"Arthur drove his point home a little too hard," he said, sticking the training sword into the grass point first.

"And where's he off to?" Lancelot asked.

"Who knows?" Bedivere said, miraculously holding a piece of Gaheris' tart. "Off to sulk about failing as a King, probably."

Percival smacked Bedivere on the back of the head, the force making him drop the slice of tart. "Watch it," he warned.

Bedivere spun around to face Percival with a glare. "Do you have any idea how long it took me to get that?!"

"Oh boo hoo, you can get another one in the kitchen!" Percival barked back.

Bedivere growled at him and smacked him back, the soup bowl falling from his hands to the grass.

Percival glared at him. "I hadn't finished that."

"I didn't finish the tart either, but here we are," he sniped.

"Can he sleep outside tonight?" Percival asked Gawain.

"You'll both be outside in a moment," Gawain snorted.

Percival flicked Bedivere's earlobe, quickly running away from him. Bedivere barked curses at him and chased after him, the food quickly forgotten.

"Idiots," Galahad shook his head. "Are we going after Arthur?"

"Let him be for a while," Lancelot said. "He might need some time to himself." He petted Gawain on the shoulder and walked back inside the caves. Gawain followed after him, the rustling of the two fighting Knights wrestling on the ground to his right bothering him. Galahad stood up from his stone, following after them.

Peter walked out past them, his arm free of bandages and stitches, and spotted the Knights on the ground, pausing.

"That was my favourite soup!" Percival growled.

"That was my favourite tart!" Bedivere snapped, pinning him.

"Your tart was the only love you'll ever get!" Percival struggled under him.

"I've bedded more women than your sorry ass," Bedivere growled, digging his knees in deeper.

"I've bedded five, and one of them was the best. Wanna know who she was?"

"Your mother?" Bedivere snarked.

"No," Percival smirked. "It was your sister!"

"Um," Peter frowned, watching the two.

Bedivere's face dropped, violence entering his face. "You *what*?" he snarled.

"She was a psycho in bed," Percival added, grinning fiendishly. "She had fun; I made sure of it. I even convinced her to-"

His words cut off as Bedivere punched him right in the mouth, blood pouring from his lip to the ground as Percival spat. "Ow, you bloody turd!"

"That better be a joke, Aaron!" Bedivere gripped his collar tightly, his finger pointed beneath Percival's chin. "I will skin you from fingernails to ass hair if you're telling the truth."

"Of course, it was a joke, for the Gods' sake! Get off me," Percival bit, gripping beneath Bedivere's arms and throwing him sideways. Bedivere rolled across the stones and got back onto his feet, dusting himself off and watching Percival sit up, rubbing his jaw.

"I hope that stops your fat mouth from eating for a while," Bedivere snorted. "You might just shed some pounds."

"Says the one who stole a tart," Percival retorted, wiping the blood from his mouth. "I think you should opt for fruit instead, considering you nearly flattened my ribs."

Bedivere huffed slightly and offered a hand down to him. "Touch my sister, and you'll lose your hands."

Percival took his hand and got up on his feet. "I'm *so* scared," he smirked at him.

"You should be. I ate the last of your soup and left that bowl for you to find on purpose."

"You bastard," Percival muttered at him, frowning. Bedivere grinned and smacked his back.

Peter cleared his throat. "Speaking of food," he started. "I was sent to tell you lot that the kitchen needs a hunt done today. Apparently, we're getting low on meat and berries."

"The berries don't surprise me," Bedivere shrugged. "That wench you lot brought in has been baking tarts nonstop. Not that I'm complaining."

"I'm not hunting," Percival chimed in. "I did it last week, and I almost got bitten by a wild pig."

Peter looked at him in bewilderment. "A pig?" he asked in disbelief.

"Yes," Percival nodded. "It was a wild pig, and it was a violent critter. Like this one next to me," he pointed to Bedivere.

"I doubt you were anywhere deep enough inside the forest to be telling those sorts of porkies," Bedivere snorted.

"You weren't there to see it, Bedivere," Percival growled. "Geraint was."

"He was probably the one who shot it, too."

Percival shook his head impatiently and made his way into the caves.

"Sore loser!" Bedivere called after him. He turned to Peter with a chuckle. "Alright boy, looks like he's out of the question. So let's go find some more people to drag along."

Peter nodded and followed him to the courtyard, Percival muttering as he walked past Lancelot, straightening his collar. Gawain watched him absently and leaned against the wall facing Galahad, his arms crossed.

"Arthur is learning quickly?" Lancelot asked, standing in front of Gawain.

"Quick enough," he said. "Though if he would use that brain of his for listening other than this stubborn will he's gotten. It'll help him quicker."

"Independence is a good thing to have, Gawain," Lancelot said. "The human mind is incomplete without it."

"Though he does need to learn how to control his anger," Galahad chimed in.

"In all honesty, I wasn't expecting him to crush Kyan beneath him like glass," Gawain nodded. "He's getting aggravated, and it's showing in the way he deals with people."

"Then we need to help him," Lancelot said. "Teach him how to be the second Benjamin."

"You can't force that upon him," Galahad shook his head with a frown.

"No one can be the same as another," Gawain agreed. "Not even Benjamin's son."

"Do you still believe he is to be King?" Lancelot asked.

"Why wouldn't I?" Gawain frowned, turning to him.

Lancelot turned to Galahad. "You too?"

"He's our King," Galahad nodded.

"State your point, Rodney," Gawain said.

"We need to help him become who he is meant to be, and that means that you mustn't be hard on him. We need to teach him more gently, like how Benjamin wanted."

Gawain frowned. "Are you doubting my method of training?"

"You're making Arthur less and less motivated to fulfil his destiny."

"What I am doing," Gawain stood up from the wall, "is getting him mentally ready and physically fit. The brutality of my training is necessary for development to take hold. It's worked for all the times I've trained my trainees. I don't see why I should treat him any differently."

"What would Ben want?" Lancelot asked, staring at him eye to eye.

"If Ben was here and getting what he wanted, we wouldn't be in a cave three hours away from the castle we were meant to be living in," Gawain sniped.

"Be thankful I provided us with these caves," Lancelot scowled back.

"I'm sure you weren't the only person who chipped in to build it up," he sniffed and looked at Galahad.

"I'm not a part of this, sorry," Galahad said, raising his hands slightly.

"Then why are you here?"

"To listen to this," Galahad said. "And to make sure you two don't rip each other's heads off."

*Sticky beak.* "Give an input or go hunting," Gawain said, turning to Lancelot.

"Arthur needs to work on his issues *and* balance his emotions," Galahad said, looking at the both of them. "Neither of you are wrong. I think you should find a way to combine the two methods."

"He can work on his issues before or after his training," Gawain dismissed. "He doesn't mingle with anyone else other than his friends, and the people he does talk to make him think they're trying to dominate him; we saw that just then. I don't know about the anger issues."

"He will learn," Lancelot nodded. "And he will learn properly, under the guidance of us."

"You can teach him how to deal with his life problems or whatever you want to call it. I'm here to make sure he can fight. Now, is there anything else you want to tell me other than what I'm doing wrong?"

"So you don't care for the boy?" Lancelot asked, crossing his arms.

"Of course I care for the boy," Gawain growled. "But his issues aren't my concern. He can sort them out himself."

"Let him know that you care, Jonathan," Lancelot said. "At the moment, he feels like you only want to shove him around for your benefit."

"He's an adult; he can handle it," Gawain muttered. "I caught him going out last night to train himself. He should know by now what I think."

"And what *do* you think?"

"What I think is that he's a stubborn mule with a god complex. He doesn't need to be reassured and coddled like a child; he needs to grow a backbone and get out of this 'little poor me' mindset."

"It's our responsibility to take care of the lad and guide him to his true destiny. He needs to be taught to control himself and advance in his training."

"I'm sure you're more than capable of making him pull his head in," Gawain frowned, meeting him at eye level. "You're the behavioural wizard; that's your job. I'm the trainer, you're the teacher, and Jameson is the sticky beak in the corner."

"Not entirely true," Galahad frowned. "I was almost certain you were going to break Lancelot's nose, and I'd have to calm you both down again."

"I have changed in the eighteen years you haven't seen me, you know," Gawain snorted.

"I'll believe that when I see it," Galahad smirked, walking off into the main room. Gawain trailed his eyes after him as he left and looked back at Lancelot. "Anything else?"

Lancelot smiled warmly at him and patted him on the shoulder. "Keep training the lads well. I do advise you to take on a less aggressive approach. However, if you feel like your methods are working just fine, I'll be more than happy to counsel."

"I'll try to keep an open mind, but I can't guarantee it," Gawain sighed. He looked outside to the Rebels in the courtyard, a slight smile touching his lips. "It's good to see many of the runts back here, and better still, that they've survived living out here." Many of Gawain's past trainees were rejected from a full Knighthood, either by becoming a target of the Crown or because they needed somewhere to go. Some were injured in their traineeships and couldn't continue their training, while others weren't strong enough to complete the trial from red to blue. But each one of them was sent here to Reigate under sworn secrecy to live with the Knights and train amongst them to help in the future under the Rebel banner. "They've flourished well in the caves."

"They're learning from the best and learned from the best in the past," Lancelot smiled.

Gawain's lips turned up in a ghost of a smile. "How many made it last round?"

"Twenty-one."

Gawain nodded. "Good numbers," he muttered. He'd sent out  twenty-four; he never expected all of them to survive the trip.

"Now, go and find Arthur before he ends up dead," Lancelot shook his head.

"He'll be fine," Gawain snorted. "He's got an eye in the forest." The girl still hung on his mind like an old picture, the flash of white in the forest burning his memory. *The daughter of Samqueel. I'll believe that when I confirm it.*

Lancelot nodded at him, patting him on the shoulder before walking off to the main room. Gawain watched after him, sighing through his nose. The white-haired Knight wasn't one for much of a violent pathway when it came to dealing with, well, anything.

Not that Gawain thought his training was particularly violent. It could be worse; Arthur could've been trained by twenty-five-year-old Jonathan Gawain, who couldn't keep his cool at the mention of his accent or skin colour. Nowadays, he was a tad more thick-skinned, and it helped that everyone thought him dead in the Kingdom. The weight of the Sir title was heavier than most thought.

What did it matter? They were going to find out eventually once more. He may as well get used to it. Gawain turned back around, his boots crunching on the gravel as he walked back out of the cave.

Arthur rested his head back against a thick tree base, frustration at himself still burning inside him. The waterfall was the only place he could think of to go; no one else came here. The water seemed to be higher, the creek flowing more than usual.

He sighed, watching the water cascade down the rocks. *What in the Ether was I thinking?* He'd pinned Kyan down after he'd submitted. That wasn't what a King was supposed to do. It was hard for Arthur to believe he had even gotten so angry at one person, and he knew he shouldn't have, even though Kyan wasn't the best person.

And he'd done it on purpose, too. He did it to see the fear in his eyes, saw it on his face, but… it was on Tristan's, too. He'd scared his friend. He'd scared himself.

"What am I doing?" he sighed to himself, shaking his head frustratedly. This was all wrong. This isn't what people want from him. This isn't what his father would want.

He reached to the ground beside him and picked up a rock from the  ground, feeling it in his hands. The pebble was smooth, flattened by years of corrosion. Arthur looked down at it and frowned, turning back to the waterfall a few feet away from him and tossing the rock across the body of water out of anger, the stone skimming across the surface before sinking through to startle the fish beneath. He rested his head in his hands, rubbing the back of his head with a sigh.

A faint flapping noise came from his left, and he turned his head to look; a small fowl looked around at the water, its round feathered body fluffed up. The rustle of its wings sounded again as it shook and walked over to the water with a cluck.

Arthur creased his brow. *A chicken? In the woods?* He looked it over; it wasn't golden, so it wasn't Sariel. Its feathers were a light brown like any normal kind of chicken. *But in the forest?*

"Did you run away from your farm?" Arthur asked, raising a brow at the animal.

It looked at him, its round eyes inspecting him dumbly. It wasn't another shifter; there wasn't any intelligence to be seen in the bird. *Just a normal chicken.* It clucked and dipped its head to the water.

Arthur sighed, looking away from the bird and focusing on the scenery around him-

A deep throng sounded from far behind him, and the chicken exploded in a ball of feathers, the poor bird screeching. Arthur looked back, and his eyes widened; *where did the chicken go?* Across the other side of the waterfall, the chicken was pinned against a tree by an arrow in its side, hanging limp.

"That's… great?" Arthur said aloud, looking at the lifeless bird.

"Ha! You got him!" Tristan whooped from further in the trees, his voice echoing.

"Shut your gob before you scare the rest of the game away," Kay's voice growled.

Arthur's eyes widened, standing up from the tree. "Tristan?"

"Go and get the bird, Tristan. I think it shot across the water," Peter's voice quietly chimed in.

"For a lad with a bad arm, you're a good shot," Percival said.

The crash of leaves and sticks sounded closer to Arthur, Tristan running straight past him and looking to his left. "Alright, chicken, where did you go?" he muttered to himself.

"Try that tree over there," Arthur smirked at him, pointing to the other side of the waterfall.

Tristan yelped in fright, spinning around too fast to face Arthur, his face pale as he tumbled backwards. Arthur clenched his lips shut in amusement, looking at Tristan on the ground.

Tristan blew a leaf from his face and looked up at Arthur, blinking. "Arty? When in the name of the Gods did you show up?" he said breathlessly.

"I've been here for a while now," Arthur said, offering a hand to him.

Tristan held a hand up, the other one resting on his chest. "One moment," he panted, putting his head back on the ground. "I need to find where my heart went in the leaves."

"Come on," Arthur rolled his eyes. "Don't be dramatic."

"Do you know how scary you actually are when you appear out of thin air?"

"No. But by the looks of it, pretty scary," he smirked at him.

"I think I saw the Otherworld for a moment," Tristan brushed his hair back from his face.

"By the Gods, you're so dramatic," Arthur said to him, grabbing his arm and pulling him up from the ground.

"Great job, Tristan. Now you've scared all the food for the next mile radius," Peter sighed, breaking through the treeline.

Arthur looked over at Peter, his eyebrows flicking up as he saw his arm healed. "Good to see you on your feet again," he smiled.

"The Baron did a number on it," Peter muttered. "It's not as good as it was."

"What are you lot doing out here?" Arthur asked him.

"Hunting for more food for the kitchen," Peter shrugged.

"It's hunting season," Percival chimed in, breaking through the leaves.

"It's always hunting season," Kay said. "You just think Winter is better for it."

"Technically speaking, it is," Percival frowned at Kay. "It's way easier to hunt in Winter than it is in Summer. There's less of a chance of heat stroke."

Kay snorted. "Heat stroke? In Braynor? Only you could pull that off."

"Hurtful," Percival huffed, folding his arms.

"When have you ever gotten heat stroke, Aaron?" he grumbled crabbily.

"Like two months ago," Percival scowled. "And don't call me Aaron."

"It's the name your mother gave you, ain't it? And I don't believe you."

"Of course you don't," Percival snorted.

Tristan walked over the stream of water and yanked the chicken free from the arrow sticking it to the tree, the bird flopping to the ground with a thud. Arthur grimaced at the sound of its bones cracking on impact, looking away from it.

"Poor chook," Tristan mumbled and picked it up, holding the arrow in one hand.

"Since when were you good at archery?" Arthur asked, looking at Peter.

"I've always done archery," Peter said, watching Tristan. "Swords are just a second thing I don't use often. I prefer ranged combat."

"Following in Brannagh's footsteps?" Arthur asked.

He smiled slightly, looking at him sideways. "Maybe."

Arthur smiled back and nodded. "He'd be proud."

"He'd be more so if I had shot its eye instead. Tristan, be careful with the arrow. It's sharper than you think," Peter called to him. The lad held the arrow close to the tip, the chicken in both hands.

Arthur looked over at Tristan, frowning at him slightly. "Keep it away from yourself."

"Well, if you could've got the chicken instead, it would've made things easier," Tristan argued with a waver in his voice.

"And attitude won't get you anywhere," Arthur rolled his eyes, grinning at the lad. Tristan looked up from the bird at Arthur, not reflecting his amusement.

Peter sighed and walked over to where Tristan stood, crossing the creek effortlessly. "Here, pass the bird," he said, holding his hands out. Tristan gave the bird to him and put the arrow back in his quiver, walking back across the creek with his hands in his pockets.

Arthur looked up to the sky and frowned, seeing dark clouds forming overhead. "We better get moving before the storm comes."

"It looks like it'll be a nasty one," Peter agreed, looking up at the sky.

"I'll get the rest of them out of the woods before they get drenched," Kay sighed, turning around.

"Who?" Arthur asked him.

"The rest of the trainees and Knights and everybody else that joined the hunt to feed you," he sniped and walked through the trees with a sharp whistle.

Arthur frowned at him and turned back to Tristan. "Did Maria come out?"

Tristan shrugged slightly, still looking down. Arthur tilted his head at him, walking over to him. "What's the matter?"

He shook his head. "It's stupid, don't worry about it," he grumbled.

"Hey," Arthur said warmly. "We've been friends forever; you can tell me."

Tristan sniffed and looked up at him slightly, silver lining his eyes. "Stupid bird," he muttered, wiping his face with his sleeve. "You were right, Arty. I am sensitive."

"You're not sensitive. You have a heart and a good one at that," Arthur smiled warmly. "I don't know anyone else who has a heart like yours, but people need it."

Tristan huffed. "But it's just a bird," he shrugged. "Or it's just a dog or a lizard or something. Insignificant little things that don't matter. Things that won't always be there. And I still care, even though people tell me it's dumb."

"Tristan," Arthur said, placing a hand on his shoulder. "Don't beat yourself up about being a caring person. Those people don't have a good heart like you do. Hell, your heart is better than mine. If this weren't my destiny, this would be yours 'cause you'd be a better King than me."

Tristan chuckled lightly, mischief entering his eyes a little. "Imagine me on the throne. The Kingdom would be chaotic."

"Oh, no doubt," Arthur chuckled. "There would be a whole new tradition in Camelot."

"'Go Feed Your Neighbor Day' or something," he huffed, a small grin on his face as he looked at Arthur.

"There always has to be something about food with you," Arthur shook his head in amusement.

"Because I'm always hungry. No matter what I eat, there's still room for more in the void," he grinned. "I should try my hand at a King's feast, see how much of the table I can eat before I pass out."

Arthur rolled his eyes playfully at him, nodding over to the others. "Let's get back to the caves."

"As soon as we're back, I'm raiding the kitchen for Maria's tarts," he declared and tapped Arthur's back, running off. "She'll kill me, but it'll be worth it!"

"Silly tool definitely will lose some fingers to Simon's knives if he doesn't lose them to a stray arrow first," Peter muttered, looping the chicken's neck through a rope on his belt. "It'd be just my luck that it'd be one of my arrows to do it."

"You wouldn't be able to hit him," Arthur said. "He can run quicker than you'd expect."

"Sometimes that's his downfall," Peter smirked. "I've cornered him a couple of times in the training hall, holding one of my bows captive. He didn't run anywhere with them after the last time."

"How's Princess going?" Arthur asked, looking at Peter.

"He's breathing and living as usual, just a tad more spooked than before. I wouldn't expect much from Kyan for the next month or so."

"Who said I wanted to talk to him anyway?" Arthur frowned.

Peter snorted and slung his bow back across his chest with a small wince. "He's better to talk to when he's drunk. He's less of a tool that way," he smirked, flexing his arm.

Arthur nodded at him. "How's the arm?"

"A few more weeks, and it'll be back to normal. Hopefully, then I can shoot chickens through the head and not the chest."

"You'll make Tristan cry that way," Arthur huffed, walking over to the tree line.

"Pah, he'll still eat it anyway." Peter followed after him through the trees, the two leaving the waterfall behind as thunder rolled overhead.

"While crying," Arthur said.

"That's when you give him a sweet or whatever Maria harbours in the kitchen," Peter laughed. "He'll shut up real quick then."

"That's the way he works," Arthur shrugged, walking into the forest, Percival following after them. It's how Arthur first bonded with Tristan, sharing a piece of cake with the lad by the Castaral River. He didn't realise how much of an influence it could be on him until he kept coming back and hanging out with him. Eventually, it stopped being about food, and the friendship kicked off.

"Motivation by food never fails. I wonder what his limits are?" Peter hummed.

"No limits," Arthur shook his head.

"I wonder if we can convince him to clean the main cavern for a free tart," Percival smirked, finding the trail.

"Who even makes the tarts anyway?" Arthur asked.

"Simon, Freya, sometimes Gaheris," Percival chimed in.

"What would be fun to have is a baking showdown between the lot of them," Bedivere walked from out of the trees, holding a turkey in his hand by the neck.

Arthur flinched slightly, looking at him slightly startled. "How long have you been there for?"

"Not long," Bedivere shrugged. "I heard you lot trumpeting around and found the path back. The rain is about to hit."

"That means we need to go," Galahad said from beside Bedivere. "Finish up your hunt, and let's get going."

A spit of rain smacked into Arthur's forehead, and he wiped it away, the group collectively speeding up to get to the courtyard. They followed the dirt track with autonomous feet, the rain turning it muddy with each drop that hit the dirt.

Arthur jogged along with them steadily, surprising himself as he kept up easily. All that training with the armour must be paying off. *There was a method to Gawain's madness, after all.* He felt stronger as he ran, his breathing calm and collected, his body falling into that familiar rhythm alongside the others.

*Easy does it.* He smiled to himself at his progress.

Thunder cracked overhead, another low thrum echoing after it that sent shivers over Arthur's arms. Arthur frowned and looked around at the others, Peter frowning and looking at him.

"You heard it, too?" Peter asked, slowing to run beside him.

"Yeah," Arthur said, listening out again for it. Leaves rustled around them in the bustling wind, blowing Arthur's hair every which way around his head.

*There!* The howl split through the air closer now, off to the right just inside the treeline. They all stopped, pausing and glancing around, alert with the howl so close.

"Wolves," Bedivere growled, pulling his sword from his sheath and looping the turkey through his belt.

"You don't happen to have a spare sword on you?" Percival asked Bedivere.

"Trust you not to bring a weapon out hunting,"
Bedivere snorted and looked at him, scowling. "What are
you on about, you silly tool? You've got one at your side!"

"I knew I had one," Percival drew his sword. "I'm
talking about Arthur."

Arthur looked at them, flicking between Percival and
Bedivere. Uncertainty dashed through him - *why did I leave
the sword back in the courtyard, damn it?* - and he looked
back at the trees to see a dark shadow flit through the gaps.
*It's too late now.*

# Chapter 20: Against Pack Law

Arthur widened his eyes at the silhouettes in the trees; wolves were common around the forest and sparse plains, and they were a terror for most small villages scattered around, especially villages with rabbitfolk. He hadn't expected to come across them anytime soon.

The shadows quickly materialised, the wild dogs leaping out of the trees and landing in front of them, their snarls and barks matching the thunder rolling overhead. Arthur backed away from the wolf in front of him, watching its glittering amber eyes glare at him.

The wolves circled the Knights, snapping at their ankles as they sprang back away, darting back from swords slashing at them. Bedivere cursed as one grabbed hold of the turkey at his side, pulling it free of his belt and sneaking off with it. "Little shit!" he spat at it.

Percival slashed at one near his ankles, kicking it in the snout. It yelped and snapped at his foot as it backed up. Percival moved away and pointed his sword at it, blinking the rain from his eyes.

"Where did these stupid mutts come from?" Kay growled, slashing at one and splitting it up the side, the wolf yelping as its blood sprayed across the mud.

"Deeper within the forest," Galahad said, kicking one away from him to land in a puddle.

"Exactly how deep? They mustn't have been far enough away to smell the game we've got on us," Peter asked, holding his bow in front of him, dripping with water.

Arthur watched the wolf in front of him as it snarled with its teeth bared, its haunches bristling. A bigger shadow appeared in the trees behind it, and Arthur looked up; glowing golden eyes glared through the brush, towering above the bushes as tall as a horse.

"I've got eyes on the alpha," Arthur said, glaring at the larger wolf.

Bedivere spun around and stared right at the wolf, his eyes wide and his long black hair stuck to his face with the rain. "By the grace of the Gods!" he cursed. "That's a huge wolf!"

"Give me a sword," Arthur muttered to him.

"Are you mad?"

"No," Arthur said. "Well, maybe, we'll see."

Bedivere's head flicked in front of Arthur, and he raised his sword, slashing towards Arthur and jumping in front of him as the smaller wolf lunged, his sword streaking straight across the wolf's eyes. It yelped,  scattering backwards with a whine.

"You can't even keep your eyes on the smaller targets, let alone the large one," Bedivere scoffed, his eyes back behind him to the wolf he was focused on.

Arthur glanced at Bedivere's side and saw a short sword in a leather sheath, his hand grabbing for it quickly without a second thought. He spun back around and sprinted toward the beast of a wolf, his heart racing.

Its eyes danced with the challenge, and it sprung out of the tree line towards Arthur, its paws darting sideways out of Arthur's beeline. Peter cursed at the sight of the wolf, swinging his bow into the side of a gray wolf.

*This will either be the stupidest thing I've ever done or the best thing.* Arthur paused in front of the enormous wolf, his sword arm braced beside him. It regarded him with a snap of its teeth as it bunched in front of him, its black-red claws digging into the earth.

"Come on, then!" Arthur challenged, baring his teeth at the beast as thunder split the sky, running towards it. The large dog barreled towards him with an explosive kick of its hind legs and leapt into the air, its front claws outstretched.

Arthur quickly slid underneath the wolf, swinging his sword at its leg. Blood rained down on him as the blade pierced through its hide, a loud bark echoing through the trees. It landed on the earth lopsidedly, rolling onto its side. Arthur got up from the muddy ground, wiping away the blood from his face with a grimace.

"Well, look at that, you *are* mad!" Bedivere barked at him and hacked at another dog.

The rain made the blood and mud run off Arthur in rivers, the gold-eyed wolf's pelt sticky with it. It stood back up and looked at him, and hostility turned to interest, its ears pricked up. Arthur stared at the beast and shook his head at it. *What was this wolf doing?*

Its head snapped to look over his shoulder, sniffing the air. Not a moment later, a blood-curdling scream sounded from further in the trees behind him. Arthur flinched at the scream and followed its eyes, the smaller wolves following his gaze.

Peter gasped and paused, looking towards the scream. "Arthur," he said with daunt.

Arthur looked back at him, his eyes wide. "We need to move, now!" he barked, sprinting towards the scream. The wolf watched him with a grin, the other wolves gathering around it as the Knights battled them back away.

The forest was dark, leaves surrounded him, and he couldn't find the path. But, at least Tristan had optimism on his side. Birds were flying around in the air, and a deer was over there in the trees. *It's a wonder Peter hasn't shot it yet.*

The lad hummed as he walked along, keeping an eye out for any sign of anything familiar that would take him to the path. *Leaves, sticks, rocks, plants, leaves, trees, ugh.*

*Hmm. Come to think of it, it's awfully quiet.* He sighed through his nose and turned around in a circle on the spot. No one followed him? *Weird. Usually, someone's always on my tail.* It annoyed him greatly, sometimes. He might act stupid, but he wasn't actually as dumb as people thought.

"Hullo?" Tristan called to the trees, looking through them lazily. "Did anyone follow after me, and they're just hiding to make me feel independent?"

No one answered him but the thunder overhead and the drops of rain that got heavier by the second. Tristan frowned slightly and kept moving through the trees. "Uh… Peter? Are you there anywhere?" he asked loudly, a slight edge of nervousness in his voice.

Tristan pushed the rain out of his hair with a swipe of his palm. *Where am I?* All the trees looked the same around here. *Tree, tree, tree.* Forests were dull compared to a Kingdom. At least Kingdoms had people. Oh, how he missed people and talking to someone who wanted his company. Unlike a cranky Peter or Kyan.

Or a nutter Arthur.

Arthur was turning scary now; it was starting to worry Tristan. He'd never seen his friend like that before. It was unnatural. *Maybe introducing him to Marl- Gawain wasn't a very good idea.* Then again, it brought them here, and Arthur wanted to be King now. But the anger? It was new. Tristan didn't think it was even possible for him to be so-

A stick snapped to his left. Tristan turned his head with a grin, expecting Peter to jump out of the bushes at him. "Is that you there?" he asked the noise.

Nothing replied back to him.

Tristan frowned and laughed nervously. "Peter, if that's you, I'd like it if you'd come out instead of trying to scare me because it's working too well."

A low growl rumbled amongst the bushes, sending shivers up Tristan's spine. Uncertainty flooded him, and his brow creased, moving back away from the shrub. "Arthur? I know you can growl, so stop, please," he said with fear.

A thunderous snap sounded behind him, followed by a deep snarl. Tristan gasped and spun around, feeling for a sword that wasn't there. *Damn it!*

The wolf stalked around Tristan, its teeth bared and razor sharp. Fear spiked through him, seizing his throat as he tried to breathe.

"Okay, okay, calm down. They can probably smell the chicken all over you. They're probably harmless," Tristan reasoned with himself, his eyes wide as dinner plates.

Another snarl sounded from behind him, and two more wolves breached the shrub, barking at him. The wolves stalked closer to him, their eyes glued on Tristan.

Tristan's heart raced at a million miles an hour, spinning around to look at the wolves. "You guys can't smell fear, right?" he asked them with a shaky voice.

The bigger wolf barked at him, its eyes lit with hunger. Tristan swallowed the lump in his throat and took a deep breath, his eyes racing between the dogs. *If I keep running east, I'll find the cave eventually.* He braced his legs and sprinted through a gap between the wolves, running with every ounce of desperation he had.

He heard the wolves run after him, their large paws thudding the ground hard as their barks. Tristan ducked beneath low branches ahead of him, keeping his head forward and his eyes wide. He couldn't see any sign of the path through the rain, the muddy ground too mixed around by the water and shadows to pick through. Thorns snagged at him as he leapt over bushes in his way, his boots slipping in the puddle on the other side and sending him to the forest floor. He rolled down the slight incline with a yelp, rocks and mud clinging to his clothes like a second skin. He groaned at a pain in his arm as he stopped rolling, a sharp piece of slate sticking out of the ground cutting him as he moved.

The snap of teeth sounded above him, and Tristan looked up in fright, claws lunging for his chest, pushing him back to the ground, driving the air from his chest with a whoosh. Alarm spiked through Tristan, his hands grabbing instinctively at the wolf's muzzle as he rolled again down the slope. The dog snarled and ripped its face out of his hands, biting at his fingers as it rolled down the hill with him. Tristan barked in pain and pulled his hands away, stopping at the bottom of the slope.

His eyes were coated in sludge, his bloodied hands wiping it away. He blinked quickly, turning his head to watch the wolf get back onto its feet, raising its hackles as it faced him. The other wolves emerged through the rain from down the slope, their feral fangs bared at him in threat. Tristan scattered backwards through the mud in panic, his back meeting a fallen tree with a jolt of his heart. He didn't even recognise this part of the forest at all.

The wolves lunged at him with savage barks, agony shooting through Tristan as they ripped at his body, claws and teeth shredding his clothes and through his skin. Tristan yelled in pain as one tore through the sensitive skin of his abdomen, the sound echoing across the forest. One of the wolves gripped his ankle and yanked him to lay flat on his back, and another wolf dug its claws into his chest, tearing his shirt to shreds as it ravaged his arms. He punched at it wildly, the wolf yelping as his fist connected with its nose. His legs screamed with pain as the dogs bit through the fabric savagely, the sound of ripping flesh and cloth filling his ears. He kicked and writhed against the wolves, yelling in pain and fear as his blood soaked the ground with the rain and his bones broke beneath their bite.

Mud choked him as their paws kicked it up, his body stuck in the sodden dirt as if it held him still.

"Tristan!" a voice called from the forest beside him. "Tristan, where are you?!"

His eyes widened further as he tried to see past the bundle of wet, muddy fur on his face. "HELP!" he screamed.

Tristan dug his fingers into the pelt of the wolf on his chest and threw it off of him to the side, his boot lashing towards the ones at his legs. Pain swamped him from all over like a suffocating blanket, his voice breaking as he yelled.

"We're coming!" a second voice called to him, two sets of footsteps catching Tristan's ears over the snarl of the wolves.

From the forest edge, two Rebels breached the tree line drenched in rainwater, their weapons in hand. Tristan kicked one of the wolves in the face, the dog yelping and snapping back at his ankle with a crunch. He cried out in pain as he felt the bone snap. Rain flooded his vision, mud splattering up on his face as the dog he threw off himself lunged back towards him.

One of the wolves yelped as a Rebel launched himself at it, tackling it to the ground and piercing its throat with his short sword. The other - Connor, Tristan realised as he spotted him - whistled at the other two, his hands waving in the air. The one at Tristan's chest looked at Connor with a ferocious snarl, blood coating its muzzle. The other paused its tearing on Tristan's leg, its ears pinned back against its head.

"Come over here! Come on!" Connor yelled at it, picking up a stone from the ground and throwing it at the wolf at Tristan's chest. It flinched away from the stone and barked at Connor, barreling towards him.

The tackled wolf struggled savagely beneath the Rebel, scratching and biting at his arms and stomach. The Rebel pinning it down twisted his sword sharply, moving away from the beast's mouth and struggling to stay balanced on its flank. The wolf yelped and went limp, blood gushing out of the stab wound into the mud, washed away quickly by the heavy rain.

Tristan looked at the other wolf at his feet, the dog bunching its muscles to spring at the Rebel. His eyes flared wide. "Look out!" he warned, his voice fractured with overuse.

The Rebel looked back at Tristan, his eyes soon widening in realisation. The wolf sprang onto him with a snap of its jaws, the dog biting at the air savagely. The Rebel fell beneath the weight of the wolf into the mud, his yell of fright cutting off as the wolf snapped its jaws around his throat.

"Gods!" Tristan cursed with fear, trying to get up and failing, his legs failing to shift beneath him.

Connor yelled in pain, the wolf latching onto his thigh with razor-sharp teeth. He slashed at it and pierced it through its skull, the wolf dropping to the mud dead.

"Jack!" Connor called to the dead Rebel, anguish in his voice. The wolf let go of Jack's neck and spun around, barreling to Connor and lunging up at his chest. Connor exclaimed in fright, falling backwards into the mud, the wolf yelping as Connor's blade sank through its belly.

"Connor!" Tristan yelled, dread filling him up. *By the Gods, the wolves are killers!*

Connor shoved the wolf off him into the mud, looking at Tristan in shock as he rolled onto his side. His hand reached up to the slash at the base of his throat pulsing out crimson with every heartbeat, his face paling at the realisation. The lad choked, blood rivers spitting out of his mouth. Tristan's eyes filled with tears of fright and pain as Connor's chest went still, his eyes glossing over and the rain washing his blood away.

The lads just died to save him. It was the first time he'd seen anyone die. The scent of blood made his stomach turn, his breath quickening.

"Tristan!" a familiar voice called to him.

He looked around, agony making him stay still as the rain drenched him. "Arty?" he yelled, looking around.

Arthur bolted over to him, kneeling beside him. Tristan looked up at his blurred form, rain smearing his vision and lack of blood making him see double. "Woah," he murmured. "There's… a lot of you."

"He's losing blood, Peter!" Arthur called, applying pressure on his chest wounds.

Tristan yelled in pain at his touch, squirming in agony. "Ow! You're hurting me!"

"You're losing blood, Tristan. Stay still!" Arthur commanded.

"Arthur, look," Peter said, standing over where Connor lay with the wolf.

"Connor…" Arthur breathed, looking at his body in shock.

Behind Arthur through the shrubs, Galahad and the Knights burst through the tree line, their eyes taking in the bloodshed around them. Galahad spotted Tristan and immediately knelt beside Arthur, warm hands piercing through the cold numbness chilling Tristan's skin.

Blissful warmth overtook Tristan, and he blinked slowly up at the Knight, his head swimming. "Hello…" he said weakly, his chest breathing easier.

A distant feel of pressure on his wrist registered somewhere in his mind. "We need to get him back to Reigate," Galahad's muffled voice said. *Am I underwater?*

"How far is it?" Arthur asked.

"Just through the trees, around half a mile."

*Half a mile?* His hearing faded out to almost nothing, the roll of thunder overhead rumbling through his mind and blocking out any conversation.

Pairs of hands helped Tristan to his feet, holding him up gently. He yelped as pain lanced up his ankle, gripping onto Arthur's shirt.

Galahad's familiar foreign voice rumbled somewhere nearby, and he felt someone touch his forehead, heat like summer honey seeping through his blood. He sighed in relief as the pain started to drain away, his body relaxing against Arthur's.

He sank into the feeling of weightlessness. The cold and wet of the outside world traded for a place safe and cosy, like a mother's womb or a patch of sunlight in a grassy field, far away from the threat of wolves and death.

"Wolves in the forest? It's rare for them to be anywhere near here," Gawain frowned, a cup in his hands that didn't smell of coffee.

Arthur sat across from Gawain, holding his own cup and leaning on a wooden table in the main cavern, the Rebels murmurs and whispers echoing off the walls. "It was an entire pack," he said. "Three attacked Tristan while the rest surrounded us."

Gawain squeezed the bridge of his nose between his fingers with a sigh, resting his arm on the table. "And we lost two Rebels," he muttered.

"We didn't get there on time," Arthur said shamefully. "We were lucky we got to Tristan when we did." The lad was halfway to death, Arthur could've sworn. He was out of it more than usual when they'd found him, and the amount of blood that pooled in the mud scared Arthur half to death himself.

"We'll skin the pelts off the wolves for later use and start organising a burial for Connor and Jack. There were more than a few people here who knew the two. They will be missed," Gawain sighed, resting his arm on the table.

"The alpha was different to the others," Arthur muttered, his mind flicking back to its unnatural behaviour.

"How different?"

"It challenged me like it wanted me to fight it. Then when I did, it grinned, and it didn't go any further," he explained, his brows creasing.

Gawain chewed his tongue in thought. "Interesting," he grumbled.

"I'm thinking they were sent to find me by someone, and that wolf isn't truly a wolf," Arthur added. "It was too smart."

"Wolves are smart creatures, smarter than we know. They're capable of using their families to an advantage, something we can learn from them. I'll make sure the rest of the wild dogs are out of the boundary as soon as this rain is done," Gawain said to no one in particular. "We can't afford to lose more Rebels to petty things like wolves."

Arthur looked down with a different matter on his mind. *What was my uncle doing? What has become of Camelot?* He had a funny feeling the wolf attack had his name written in it somehow. Arthur wasn't sure how, but something didn't sit right in him with the way that wolf looked at him.

"Are you open to wild suggestions?" Arthur looked back at Gawain.

Gawain raised a brow. "As long as they're not stupid."

"Sneaking into Camelot to find out what Ergott is up to."

Gawain frowned. "I said as long as they're not stupid," he repeated.

"It's the only way we'd be able to see what we're up against," Arthur protested. "And we need to know exactly what's happening in Camelot."

"Not by sending you to go and find out. We can still send Rebels to mingle with the citizens in the marketplace like they've done for years," Gawain muttered, fiddling with his cup.

"When are they heading out next?" Arthur asked, his eyes lighting up in interest.

"You're not going," Gawain growled, taking a sip of the brandy.

"Will Lance tell me if I asked him?"

"Who's asking me for what now?" Lancelot's gruff voice said, walking up behind Arthur.

Arthur stood up and smiled warmly at him, Gawain throwing him an impatient glower. "When are the Rebels going back to Camelot?" he asked.

"The next carriage leaves tomorrow morning," Lancelot said bemusedly. "They just need to restock up on a couple of fruits and do the rounds first."

"Excellent," Arthur smiled. "Tell them I'm going with them."

Lancelot blinked at him astoundedly. "Why?"

"The lad went nutters and wants to see what's happening," Gawain growled. "And he is *not* going."

"It's the only way we can see what we're up against," Arthur repeated. "We have to give it a shot, at least. It's the only viable chance we have to see what's happening."

Lancelot scratched his chin in thought. "It's a plausible idea, but what if you get caught?" he asked him. "What would you do then?"

"Trust me, I won't."

Lancelot and Gawain shared a look; Arthur noted the tension weaving through the air like a strand, Gawain's death stare meeting Lancelot's look of scorn.

"I mean," Lancelot looked at Gawain, who scowled deeply, "he can fend for himself now. He's got your training under his belt, now, and the Rebels will-"

"No, I refuse to let it happen."

"Jonathan," Lancelot sighed, "he'll be fine. He'll stick with the Rebels, and we'll give him a disguise so no one recognises him that he'll wear. Won't he?" Lancelot looked at Arthur.

Arthur nodded, folding his arms proudly. "It won't be too hard."

Gawain growled curses under his breath. "I'm not letting you get yourself captured as easily as fish in a barrel. If you get your ass caught, I'd have to be the one to come and get you, and I'm telling you now, the Kingdom will not survive."

"Then all three of us are in agreement," Arthur clapped his hands together. "I'll go with the Rebels, and Gawain will set me free if I get caught."

"That is not what I meant," Gawain sniped, standing up. "You are too inexperienced. I can tell you right now what we're up against - *assassins*, lots of them, under the influence of your uncle. There's no doubt they've taken over the Kingdom by now."

"Surely, the Barons aren't that observant," Arthur scoffed at him, picking up his cup. "They were terrible fighters when I met them in the alleyway."

"Do you see what I mean about god complex, Rodney?" Gawain turned his gaze on Lancelot. "You can't seriously think this is okay?"

"If anything, it'll give him a chance to prove himself," Lancelot argued. "Arthur is capable of staying within reason. I see no harm in letting him learn more about what the Rebels do on their expeditions."

Gawain shook his head sharply with a scornful sigh. "This is too far. He cannot afford to be imprisoned, and he cannot make any risky moves right now," he bit. "This isn't how you prove yourself to me."

"Then how do I? Because it feels like you're not impressed by any Gods damned thing I try to do," Arthur barked, scowling at Gawain.

"You keep your common sense and your head straight," Gawain snapped at him. "I knew you weren't the brightest when it came to making plans, but I didn't think you were this stupid."

"Jonathan, that's enough-"

"And I didn't think you'd be the kind of man to advocate this kind of behaviour," Gawain turned his anger to Lancelot. "If you want to pretend like everything he wants to do is the Gods-given word, you can. When the cart comes home without him, don't blame it on me." Gawain stormed out of the room, slamming his cup on the bench before he rounded the corner out to the courtyard.

Arthur glared after him, his hands clenching on his cup. *Why can't he just trust me?* Every time Arthur had voiced his ideas, Gawain had been the first to shut him down. *Just like Ergott. It's a wonder they weren't best friends.*

Lancelot sighed quietly, taking a seat at the table. "Headstrong as always," he muttered, rubbing his face.

"Why is he like that?" Arthur muttered bitterly.

"He's been like that forever. Benjamin picked him for his mental strength, although it is a little too old-fashioned nowadays," Lancelot said. "I've tried to get him to see differently, but I don't know if he will anytime soon."

Arthur shook his head, sighing. "I need to go check on Tristan," he said, setting his cup on the table. "I'll see you later, Lance."

Lancelot bid him a quiet farewell, watching Arthur walk down the tunnel towards the medical ward further within the caves. Arthur was more worried about Tristan than what Gawain thought of him. He was going to go on that trip regardless of what the bitter old Knight wanted. He could afford to lose Gawain's respect. He couldn't afford to lose his best friend.

He passed by the rest chambers, Rebels walking in and out of the doors and dodging past him, more than a few looking distressed. Connor and Jack's loss really was leaving an impact - he couldn't blame them. Bedivere would be distraught about Connor's death. The brown-haired lad had been his ward for a long time, Arthur had been told. He glanced back at the Rebels with a shred of pity and continued walking.

The medical ward door sat half open, light glowing out of the doorway. Arthur peered in cautiously; the room was lit up by the sun shining in through wooden shutters pinned back against the stone wall. Beds sat along the length of the walls with injured Rebels laying around on them, a window carved out every so often with the shutters open like the first. A stone desk sat beside the door, and recessed shelves burrowed into the walls held all kinds of concoctions and different aid kits.

Arthur wandered in slowly, trying not to make any disturbances for the resting patients. Galahad sat at the far end of the ward on a stool beside a bed with his back to Arthur. A strange sensation flew up Arthur's spine as he gained closer, peering at the bed he sat by.

Tristan lay dormant on the bed, his eyes closed, and his body relaxed. His arms and legs were bandaged in bloodied wraps, bruises dark on his brown skin. Mud still caked his clothes, most of it washed off of his face. Arthur walked up beside Galahad, peering down at Tristan with worried brows. "How's he doing?"

Galahad jumped in fright, his eyes flying open to look at Arthur as he rose halfway out of his stool. His eyes were a starkly bright yellow, glaring at Arthur for a moment before realisation kicked in. Arthur stepped back away from him, his eyes wide in fright. "It's just me," he reassured him.

"Gods, Arthur, you frightened me," Galahad breathed, his eyes fading back to their normal blue shade. "You've got the feet of a cat."

Arthur looked at his eyes curiously, his brows creasing in interest. "Your eyes changed," he muttered.

"A lot more changes, too, don't worry," Galahad huffed in amusement, lifting his hands. An orange-yellow light glowed around his fingertips, his eyes illuminating back to the yellow once more. "I'm sure the legends would hold some sort of facts about me?"

Arthur looked at him in amazement. "You're a healer," he said.

"That's correct," he nodded, the light in his hands fading away. "It takes a lot of energy out of me to use it, but there's plenty of it. Plenty of tools to use it on, too."

"How is he doing?" Arthur repeated, turning back to Tristan.

"His wounds were not great to start with," Galahad admitted, placing his hands back on the lad's arm. "He was practically standing outside the Gates of the Otherworld. But his skin is starting to knit back together, and I've healed some smaller fractures. His ankle will take a little while longer. I don't know what he's going to do when he wakes up."

"Will he be alright?"

"He should be. I've healed the deepest wounds first, so the only thing he should feel is the bruises and broken bones, but they'll deal with themselves."

"And personality-wise?"

Galahad quirked his mouth. "That's up to him, I'm afraid," he said, his hands hovering over Tristan's side.

Arthur nodded lightly, turning back to Tristan. Footsteps echoed down the hallway towards the doorway, and a bedraggled Maria hurdled through the door, panting hard. Her eyes were wide as she searched through the ward and saw Arthur standing at the far end with Galahad, moving over to them quickly.

"I just heard what happened," she panted, her face pale. "Is he okay?"

Arthur turned to face her. "He's resting."

"Well, can I at least see him?" she asked, worry on her face.

Arthur nodded. "He'd want you to know he's okay," he said, moving to the side closer to Galahad.

She moved over to the bed, her eyes taking in the lad's wrappings and the patches of mud blotting his skin. She sighed in relief and sorrow at the rise of his chest, and her eyebrows creased together. "Gods, Tristan, how did this happen?" she whispered to him.

"He'll be okay. Tristan is strong. Probably stronger than me," Arthur murmured, putting an arm around her in offer.

She leaned into him, looking at her friend in grief. "Connor and Jack are gone," she muttered. "They apparently found them near him."

"We were too late to save them," Arthur sighed. "Tristan is lucky we got to him when we did."

"Silly lad," she mumbled, touching his arm gently. She reeled back her hand sharply, gasping in shock. "Ow!"

"Sorry," Galahad said. "I should have warned you. My magic makes a barrier around the patient to protect them from outside forces trying to hurt them further."

Maria rubbed her finger gingerly. "That's one hell of a zap," she grumbled.

"I didn't do it," Arthur smirked.

"Oh shoosh, you." Maria touched Arthur's arm, a zap of electricity flicking him sharply.

"Ow!" Arthur reeled back from her, shaking his arm around.

"It transmits like normal, too," Galahad chuckled.

Maria chuckled quietly and smiled at Arthur, her hair floating up around her head slightly. Arthur smiled at the sight, and she frowned slightly, smoothing her hair back down with her palm.

Galahad opened his eyes, his hands moving away from Tristan's body, his magic dimming. "He's coming back," he said quietly.

Arthur looked over at Tristan and knelt beside his bed. Maria stood beside him, watching the lad with wide eyes. Tristan's face twitched, scrunching up with a groan. His hand moved up to his face, and he winced, flexing his fingers.

"Ow, what the Hell?" Tristan murmured, blinking minimally.

"Hey, buddy," Arthur said quietly.

Tristan turned his head to Arthur, his eyes squinting against the light. "Arty?" he croaked.

"How are we feeling?"

"Like I got attacked by a pack of wolves," he groaned and opened his eyes completely, blinking a couple of times.

Maria gasped in disbelief. Arthur looked at him in shock, confusion moulding his brows together. Tristan frowned at the both of them, looking between them. "What?" he asked.

"Tristan, your eyes!" Maria said breathlessly.

Tristan's eyes widened, his eyebrows flicking up. "My eyes?" he asked cautiously.

"They weren't blue before," Arthur huffed, looking at him astoundingly. Tristan's soil-brown eyes had turned icy blue, like the point where the ocean met the sky.

Tristan frowned. "Are you two toying with me?" he asked. "My eyes aren't blue."

Arthur looked over at the table beside Tristan and grabbed a small handheld mirror to pass to Tristan, who took it gingerly in his wrapped hands. He stared at it for a moment, his face flicking with emotions Arthur couldn't place. "What in the name of the Holy Gods of the Otherworld?" he cursed, clenching the mirror. "Why are my eyes *blue*?"

Galahad smiled faintly. "Sometimes there's a couple of side effects of healing magic," he shrugged. "Eye colour changes can be one of them. The effect is harmless, but once it's changed, it won't go back to how it was before."

"This is so bloody weird," Tristan breathed, his brows creased in confusion.

"The blue suits you," Arthur said, trying to lighten his mood.

"I don't understand how I'm not dead," Tristan said, trying to sit up with a grunt.

Arthur gently laid him back down, positioning the pillow better for his head. "You need to stay," he said.

"Everything hurts," he groaned, holding his side.

"We can get you tarts," Arthur offered.

"Tarts are not what I'm thinking of at the moment."

"It's either tarts or some sort of sandwich," Maria said with a slight chuckle, her own brows creasing inwards.

Tristan glanced at her with a hint of offence, Arthur clearing his throat awkwardly. Tristan's hands began to shake, his eyes drifting off into oblivious thought. No doubt remembering the attack since his breath began to pick up, his anxiety warping his frown.

Arthur swept his eyes over his many bandages, the sound of Tristan's screams coming back to mind. *Gods, it's a miracle he's even here.* "Are you alright, buddy?" he asked softly.

Tristan flicked his eyes to Arthur. Fear sat in the newly blue depths, his jaw quivering. "Where did everyone go?" he asked shakily.

"We got caught between a pack on the way to the Caves," he said. "Most of us were certain you made it back here long before we did."

"Y-you were right behind me, and then when I turned around to see if Peter was there, no one was around," he stammered, looking at his hands. "I thought you guys were tricking me."

Maria glanced at Arthur, uncertainty on her face. He looked at her in shame, unable to meet his friend's stare.

"I was frightened," Tristan shivered. "I didn't have my sword, and there were things in the shrubs, and then the wolves sprang out..." He shook even more violently, tears springing to his eyes.

Arthur moved closer to him, placing a hand on an untouched part of his arm. Tristan flinched at his touch, snapping his eyes up at him in fright. "Hey, hey, you're safe now. You're with us," Arthur reassured him.

"Why weren't you there? You're always there," he whimpered.

Arthur looked at him guiltily and sighed. "I'm sorry."

"No one was there," Tristan repeated, his breaths of panic turning angry. "The one time I needed someone to watch my back, and no one was there! Connor and Jack *died* for me! I watched them both die!" Tristan gripped his hair with his hurt fingers, hissing in pain. "I watched the wolf spring on Jack and heard his neck break, a-and Connor's life fading away as he looked at me," his voice broke. "I watched him bleed to death in the mud, for crying out loud!"

Arthur tried to calm him down, moving his hands gently away from his hair. "Tristan. Tristan," he breathed, nervousness in his voice. "Calm down."

"Don't *touch* me!" Tristan barked at him, pulling his arms out of Arthur's grip. His eyes glared accusingly at Arthur, his teeth bared.

Arthur moved back, standing next to Maria in shock. This wasn't like Tristan at all. This wasn't the careless lad he'd grown up with. A tinge of hurt stabbed through Arthur, and he glanced at Maria, looking at her with a silver tint in his eye.

Tristan panted through his teeth, putting his face in his hands with a pained growl. "I'm just the tool that keeps on screwing up, right?" he hissed. "I'm not smart enough to know how to find a stupid path in a forest that I ran into myself."

"No, that's not true," Arthur croaked, feeling the words turn to ash on his tongue.

"Everyone was right about me when they said my stupidity was going to get me killed," he growled. "And it almost did."

"You're not stupid, Tristan."

Tristan peered at Arthur through his fingers with a glower. "What am I then, huh? Other than the one who makes everyone laugh at his own expense. The one everyone makes fun of and calls stupid, or takes weapons off of because they think I can't handle it or rejects me from jobs like blacksmithing because they think I'm not smart enough to know how to use a hammer without breaking something."

"You're my friend," Arthur whispered, his words stunted with remorse. He hadn't realised until now just how bad he'd really been treating his friend all this time. His mind reeled back over all the times he'd ignored Tristan's looks of hurt and confusion, all the insults he'd thrown his way without a second thought. Arthur's stomach churned.

Tristan shuddered and laid back against the pillow, his breath shaky with tears. The anger seemed to drain out of him like a wrung towel, his shoulders slumping and his head turning away from them. "I'm sorry, Arty," he choked out, lowering one hand to his side. "I'm very overwhelmed."

Maria looked away from him, her face burning in shame as she folded her arms around herself. She would've seen the numerous times he'd been pushed away from training and, by the looks of it, didn't do much about it. *What did he say back at the courtyard? I don't want anyone coming in to steal this one, too?*

"Rest well, buddy," Arthur said quietly to him, turning to Maria and walking her out of the ward. He flicked his eyes to Galahad, who offered him a look of sympathy, the warm glow of his magic humming back to life around Tristan once more.

Arthur and Maria walked silently out of the ward, all kinds of emotions flowing through both of them, especially Arthur. Tristan watched after them, regret and sorrow in his eyes. Arthur knew he wouldn't have meant to snap; it was something he hadn't expected to ever come from Tristan.

Arthur exited the ward entrance and leaned against the wall, resting his head back on the sandstone. Maria stood in the walkway, a hand over her mouth. She was just as shocked as Arthur was. Guilt was written across her as clearly as if it was inked on her skin.

"I should've been there," Arthur muttered, shaking his head. He'd been so caught up with Peter and Percival that he'd forgotten somewhat about Tristan. Guilt hit him with the thought. He thought Tristan would've been fine on his own. *Stupid wolves.*

"I didn't know it hurt him that much," Maria whispered, both of her hands on her face.

"I've never seen him like that," Arthur admitted. "And I don't like it, not one bit."

"Me either," she said, moving to lean back against the wall beside him. She slid down to the ground slowly, her hair falling across her face.

Arthur sat down slowly next to her, sighing deeply to himself. "It's my fault."

"It's mine, too," she said muffled. "I didn't say anything against the trainees for all those months. I saw him get pushed around and sat in the corner and did nothing about it."

"I haven't been the kindest to him either," he admitted, looking at her sideways. "I've been pretty negative towards him for a while now."

She moved her hands down slightly, her green eyes stained red with tears. She stared down at the floor, sniffling. "If I had known he wasn't taking it as well as I thought he was, I would've told Kyan to shove off months back. I thought he was just playing along with it like he normally seems to, but," she shuddered, "I don't know what to think anymore."

"That's why Kyan got the beating he deserved," Arthur frowned. "He's nothing but a self-centred asshole with no respect."

"It wasn't just Kyan," she said quietly. "It was just about everyone in there. Everyone knew him somehow, and everyone treated him either like he wasn't there or like a kid." She sighed, dropping her head down and curling into a ball, resting her forehead on her arms. "I feel terrible."

Arthur looked at her and moved his arm slowly around her, pulling her closer to him. "It's not your fault."

She sniffled and shifted closer to him, leaning against him. "I could've said something," she muttered sadly.

"We all could've," Arthur sighed, rubbing her shoulder gently. She leaned her head into his shoulder.

"Is Tristan alright?" A familiar accented voice asked from down the hallway, jogging up to them. Maria flicked her eyes to the voice, a small smile on her grieved face. Simon jogged up to them, his face distressed.

"I heard what happened," Simon panted heavily, stopping in front of them. "I wish I was there to help you."

"He's okay, but he's not himself," Maria said quietly, looking down to the floor.

Simon glanced over at Arthur. "Are you alright, my liege?"

Arthur held his tongue at the word and collected himself. "I'm unscathed, thank you for asking," he said.

Maria sniffled against Arthur and wiped at her face, sitting up. "How much did they end up bringing in?" she asked Simon.

"Enough to last us two months. We're heading back into Camelot tomorrow morning for fruit rations," Simon said.

"And I'll be joining you," Arthur chimed in.

Maria turned her gaze on Arthur. "You're going back into Camelot?" she raised a brow.

"Isn't that too dangerous for you?" Simon asked carefully. "You're basically a wanted man in that Kingdom, and if you get caught, you'll surely be killed."

"They won't find me," Arthur reassured. "Even if I get caught, I can use the tunnels underneath the kingdom to flee, or I do a swift manoeuvre."

"A swift manoeuvre?" Simon raised his brows curiously.

"It's called Seasoned Oak," Arthur grinned.

"How'd you come up with it?"

"It was improvised," Arthur shrugged. "We realised gravity was an effective tool." *And it still is.* "It's not fun to haul the carriages back up, though."

"Clever," Simon nodded, intrigued by the manoeuvre. "It would act as a good escape plan."

"That's its whole purpose," Arthur said, standing up from the ground with a groan. "It's how we evaded the Barons. Maria was there."

"I didn't get to see it because I was halfway to Tristan's with Peter and Kyan, though," she admitted.

"Missed opportunity," Arthur smirked at her. She smiled faintly back up at him, looking away. *She still feels guilty.*

"Maria, would you be interested in organising the new kitchenware?" Simon asked politely, trying to turn her mood around.

"Kitchenware?" Maria echoed, looking at him.

"We got new equipment from Camelot as well," Simon said. "And they're in wonderful conditions for elegant cooking."

She laughed faintly at his wording and looked at him with a small smile, unfolding herself from the ball. "I'd be delighted to," she said.

"Splendid," Simon smiled, turning over to Arthur. "Would you care to join us, sire?"

"I'm not much of a chef," Arthur dismissed. "I've got other things to attend to."

"I'm no chef either," Maria shrugged, standing up and brushing the dirt from herself. "I just know how to make tarts and sandwiches."

"I appreciate the offer, but I'll pass," Arthur said.

"Not a problem," Simon shrugged, turning to face Maria. "I've got all the help I need here."

Arthur frowned slightly at his words and glanced over to Maria. She smiled warmly at Simon, the guilt and grief gone, it seemed. *He made her happy.* It didn't sit well with Arthur, but… didn't they establish they didn't want it to go further?

"I suppose you do," Arthur sighed, looking back at Simon. "You look after her."

Maria looked at him with a blink, a small glimmer of surprise there. Simon smiled and nodded to him, placing a hand on Maria's back gently. "I'll make sure she's okay."

Arthur nodded at him. "I'll see you both around," he said, walking down to the main room. He listened as their footsteps went down the other way further, their conversation getting further away.

*Even if it did go further, it wouldn't work.* The law required noble blood to marry noble blood. And if Arthur was going to be the King, he couldn't have Maria at his side. She was an orphaned peasant raised by a nanny on the streets. The Kingdom would laugh and spit in her face. He couldn't subject her to that.

He sighed in defeat. He'd lost his Kingdom, his love interest, and now possibly his best friend. *Is this what being a King is? When everything is so bloody complicated that it drives a man to want to throw in the towel and lose everything?*

Arthur shook his head in frustration, walking down the hallway towards the main cavern. He needed a drink, and a strong one.

# Chapter 21: The Unwanted Visitor

The sun sat on the edge of the world, the bright orange
ball of light glaring at the entrance of Reigate. Three
carriages were set up on the gravel track, horses snorting in
the chill air as the Rebels hooked them up to the front.

Arthur walked out from the cave's entrance, wearing
similar clothes to that of the Rebels; he'd found the bundle
of clothes waiting for him at the edge of his bed. A dark
cloak sat around his shoulders, the fur on the shoulders
tickling Arthur's neck. Underneath, he wore an old
overused gray tunic riddled with holes and dirt stains, his
trousers patched and scraped at the heel of his boots. It had
Lancelot written all over it.

He walked up to the middle carriage, peering inside it
curiously. Empty boxes sat haphazardly around the seats, a
couple of the Rebels seated on them and waiting. They
turned to look at him with a nod, Arthur nodding back and
sliding into the carriage.

"Mind if I join you?" Arthur asked, sitting down beside
a Rebel.

"Go ahead, plenty of room," he said, crossing his legs.

Arthur did a double take of the Rebel - he was the same
lad that was on the apple carriage when they'd left Camelot.
Arthur recognised his mischievous gray-brown eyes and
dark complexion, the lad's black hair ruffled up as before.

"You lot would be used to sitting in this uncomfortable
piece of transport, wouldn't you?" Arthur asked, frowning
at the wood digging into his back.

"We mostly make do with anything we find," the same Rebel said, reaching inside one of the boxes. "If we're lucky, we get one of these." He pulled out a thick rug, unfurling it open on his lap.

"Go on then, roll it out for us," another Rebel said, standing up with the others. The Rebel rolled onto their knees and flicked out the rug to settle on the wooden floor. He looked at Arthur and gestured to it. "Grab a piece of land before they go," he hinted, moving to sit on it.

Arthur nodded, moving down to sit on the rug. "I'm guessing every carriage has one?"

"Nope," he replied, crossing his legs again. "We're lucky. Like I said, the others don't know this is in here."

"You always consider yourself the lucky one, Eylan," a Rebel frowned at him.

"That's because I am," Eylan looked at him. "I know how to *get* lucky, too, don't you worry."

"How long will we be in Camelot?" Arthur asked, wrapping his arms around his knees.

"Well, it'll take us about three or four hours to get there, so roughly a couple hours before we turn back," Eylan shrugged. "Or just whenever we get full crates."

"Perfect," Arthur grinned, nodding at him. The carriage driver shut the door, the nearest Rebels sliding the bolts into place. The floor beneath Arthur rumbled as the horses started off, the road bumpy.

"Don't get any ideas about running off, though, please," Eylan said. "We'll get our shit kicked in by Gawain if you don't come back."

"You let me handle that part," Arthur assured. "I need to see what's going on from the inside."

"Inside of what? The castle?" one of the Rebels against the other wall questioned. "Are you nutters?"

"Possibly," Arthur smirked lightly. "You just do your end of the plan, and I'll do mine."

"Our end was to make sure you stay in sight," he said with a frown. "Theoretically, you're not supposed to leave the carriage."

"Make it a lesser priority," Arthur shrugged. "It's crucial I see what's going on."

The Rebels looked at one another with pursed lips, doubt flickering among them. The carriage fell quiet as it pulled along the track, the horses' hooves clattering from gravel to dirt.

Arthur grunted at the uneven ground, rocking side to side as the carriage moved along the track.

"Get as comfortable as you can, Sire," Eylan grumbled. "It's going to be a long ride."

"Comfortable doesn't exist in carriages," Arthur muttered, shifting himself on the rug.

"It exists, just not for the small-minded," a woman's voice said from the front of the carriage.

Arthur looked towards the front, smiling faintly. "I didn't know they had women driving the carriages," he mused.

"Drive? More like steer now and then," she scoffed. "The poor beasties have been down the track so many times they already know where to go." She sat stretched out along the front seat, the overhang pinned up above her shading her from the sun. A guard rail wedged her in comfortably with stashed furs, a filled hay sack underneath her back propping her up. The reins hung limply from a hook on the rail as the horses walked.

"Horses are smart animals," Arthur smiled.

"They've certainly got both sides of the brawn and brains," she agreed, twiddling with the strap of leather that tightened the front of her white shirt. She peered back at him with dark eyes that contrasted her blonde hair and fair skin bright in the morning light.

"And what do they call you?" Arthur asked curiously, interest glimmering in his eyes.

"Other than the driver? Hannah," she answered, smiling lopsidedly.

Arthur smiled back and nodded. "Arthur."

"I know. Everyone knows who you are around these parts," Hannah propped her head on her hand, leaning against the makeshift pillow.

"Sometimes I wish they didn't," Arthur huffed. "It gets hard to introduce yourself when everyone knows who you are."

"Well, at least you can save your breath," she chuckled. "The famous, or infamous, don't need an introduction."

"At least that's a positive aspect," Arthur huffed in amusement. He glanced back over to the Rebels seated around him and frowned slightly. *Is he hanging out of the window?*

The Rebel was communicating to the carriage beside them, muffled cheers erupting from the other carriage. The Rebel tutted, sighing as the lads around him picked up on chanting.

Hannah looked over to the two carriages with a laugh. "The games begin," she announced.

Eylan looked out the window and to the Rebel standing at it and made a delighted noise. "We have a game of Roshambo," he grinned, standing up to peer out of a closer window. The Rebels turned their attention to the lad at the window, shouting encouragement.

The lad shook his arm in the air, his balled fist hitting his other palm three times before turning flat. He cheered, and the whole carriage filled with celebratory yelling.

"Are they playing rock paper scissors?" Arthur asked with a raised brow.

"Roshambo," Eylan corrected, looking away from the window for a moment. "The same thing, but it's just less Armanian, you know?"

"You Rebels are a strange collective of individuals," Arthur said with amusement. Cheering went up from the other carriage, and the lad groaned with the others.

"You should see them when they get *really* bored," Hannah laughed, settling back into the hay sack. "It gets worse than this."

"No kidding?" Arthur huffed, watching the two with a smile.

"Sometimes they like to race beside each other."

"Sounds like something Tristan and I would do."

Hannah laughed and looked back towards the front. "You two have already done it through Reigate. Everyone either saw or heard it."

"He did something he shouldn't have," Arthur frowned.

"By the way he was yelling out that you were gonna kill him, I gathered as much," she grinned.

Loud yells of protest sparked up in the carriage. "Oh, come on, you delayed your hand flat!" the playing Rebel yelled out of the window.

"Sore loser!" the faint reply came back.

Arthur flicked his eyes back over to the two. "Rematch then!"

"Rematch!" he called over to the carriage, and all three erupted in cheering.

"Oh, I've done it now," Arthur grinned, shaking his head lightly.

"They'll never stop with that kind of encouragement," Eylan laughed.

Arthur grinned and looked towards the front of the carriage. He got up with a grunt and made his way over to the driver's area, seating a crate behind Hannah.

"Mind if I join you?" Arthur asked, sitting down with a groan.

"Sure, why not?" she said, looking at him.

"Consider it a privilege you get to sit with the future King," Arthur grinned at her.

"Ah, but you see, the future King sat with *me*," she said, placing a hand on her chest. "So consider it a privilege yourself to be in the company of such a delightfully sensible being compared to those tools back there."

"Anything is better than dealing with them for a few hours," he said jokingly.

"Try doing it every day," she smirked. "Or just about, anyway."

"I'd prefer not to," Arthur frowned lightly.

Hannah shrugged and looked down at her fingernails, clearing the dirt from them. "You get used to it," she murmured.

"So, what made you want to join the Rebels?" Arthur asked curiously.

Hannah glanced at him. "I'm a rejected Knight."

Arthur looked at her in interest. "You trained with Gawain?"

She nodded. "I was under General Mordred and Gawain's training. I almost made it through, but not quite." She glanced down toward her legs, her right crossed over her left-

Arthur blinked as he looked. Half of her left leg was gone, the leg of her trousers folded up beneath her thigh. "Oh Gods," he gasped.

"That's what I said, too," she smirked.

"If you don't mind me asking, what happened?" Arthur asked, looking back up at her.

"The end Knight trial, they send you into the Darklands for a few nights," she explained. "I was one of the unlucky ones that got mixed up with the beasts that roamed around in there. A stray Shadow Mastiff found me a few hours into the trial, bit my leg and tore me all up. I didn't get out of the Darklands until a few days later with a bad infection at the bite wound, so when they found me, they threw me to the medics and cut my leg off. I got all stitched up and recovered eventually, but I could never be a Knight with just one leg, so my Knighthood stopped, and Gawain sent me to Reigate."

Arthur looked at her in pity. *To come that close to getting an achievement, then have it all crumble over one thing, would be heartbreaking.* "I'm sorry that happened," he said.

She smiled and shrugged casually as if it were just a tiny inconvenience. "Whatever happens, happens," she dismissed. "It just wasn't meant to be, I suppose. History would've been made for me to be the first woman Knight, but I guess the Gods didn't want that. So here I am now," she said, waving a hand to the carriage. "I'm travelling places with a bunch of other rejects that live in a cave with Knights of old. It's not what I would've thought would happen, but I'm happy with life the way it is. Who knows, maybe the dog did me a favour?"

Arthur smiled at her and nodded. "Things happen for a reason, to all of us. Both for the better or worse, but you never know until they happen which outcome it'll be."

"Exactly," she agreed. "Just rolling with the punches instead of letting them hurt you is a better way to keep fighting for life."

Arthur nodded with a grin and looked out towards the road. It was good to see that someone who could go through something terrible could come out of it happier than what most people would. It gave Arthur hope to know there's still good in someone after the bad happens. Tristan flashed in his mind briefly, and he chewed his tongue. *He'll come out of it. He always does.*

"Camelot up ahead," Hannah called back in the carriage. The sun sat higher overhead the carriage, the warmth welcome in the still chill air that flowed through the holes in the carriage.

Arthur looked ahead and felt his heart rattle slightly. *It's been so long...*

The Gates stood open as always, the dark walls glinting in the light reflecting off the Castaral. The castle towered over the expanse of Londinium, the familiar sight of the gray brick spires and the orange-white flag of Camelot flying from the poles on top stirring something in him.

"Back home," Arthur sighed.

Hannah sat up suddenly, leaning forward and grabbing the reins, squinting towards the Gates. "What's all this, then?" she murmured and reached back to thud the wall. The Rebels straightened from their seats, peering out the windows.

Arthur followed her gaze; Barons stood surrounding the entrance to the South end of Londinium, carriages stopped between the hoards of the Black Cloaks.

"Hoods up," she called quietly to them, pulling her hood over her hair. The rustle of leather and furs echoed through the carriage as they pulled their hoods on, the order travelling across to the other two carriages.

"I haven't missed them," Arthur scowled at the Barons.

"Come here a moment, Arthur," Eylan said, beckoning him.

Arthur looked back at Eylan and moved over to him. "What is it?"

In Eylan's hand was a tub of charcoal powder, the burnt wood ground fine enough it was practically black dust. "We're giving you a new style," he smirked.

Arthur glanced at the tub, looking up at him beneath low brows. "I'm not wearing that."

"You can wash it out of your hair later," Eylan assured and tugged his hood down, and before Arthur could object, he grabbed a fistful of the black dust and smeared it through his golden locks.

Arthur flinched back from him and glared. "I said I'm not wearing that in my hair," he growled.

Another puff of dust wafted over his head. Eylan smeared his thumb across his eyebrows, dusting away the excess charcoal from his face. "Too late," he grinned and shut the lid.

Arthur frowned at him, sighing deeply. "Why did you do that?"

"In case the Barons got extra perceptive about who they're stopping and decide to reef the hood off your head," he said simply. "Now your hair looks dark as the night instead of a blonde mop. You'll be a tad harder to recognise now."

"Thanks, Eylan," Arthur said flatly. "I appreciate it."

"You'll appreciate it more when they don't realise who you are," he grinned and flicked a handful of charcoal at him.

Arthur coughed at the dust particles, waving his hand in front of his face. He blinked it out of his eyes and wiped his face, smearing it over his skin further.

"Well, now you look the part at least," Eylan said, closing the tub and sealing it back in the crate.

"I'll look like part of the common rabble now, thanks to your artistic skills," Arthur scowled at him and pulled his hood back over his head.

"Better than standing out in your current predicament."

"Is that supposed to make me feel better?"

"It should have," he shrugged.

The carriage pulled to a gradual stop, the low barks of the Barons' voices muffled from the outside. Hannah looped the reins back on the hook and moved to the edge of the carriage, smiling down at the Barons. "Morning lads," she said, a friendly tone to her voice.

"We need to do a carriage search," the Baron ordered. "What is your purpose in entering Londinium?"

"Picking up some stock and dropping off some apples for the markets," she said, gesturing in the back.

"What stock?" the Baron asked, two others moving to the back of the carriage.

"You see, my colleagues and I in the next two carriages, we trade rather than buy," she replied, leaning against the rail. "We've come here for years, swapping out our produce for anything of interest. Our little village towards the ocean doesn't have the best ground for crops-"

"Enough," the Baron interrupted her. "Have your helpers and yourself step out while we search."

"Not a problem, just give me a moment," she said, reaching beneath the seat for her cane. She tapped the floor three times before she grabbed it, and the Rebels switched their acting on, filing out of the carriage with curious glances and murmurs.

"Keep your head down," Eylan whispered into Arthur's ear and jumped down from the back of the carriage.

Arthur followed behind Eylan, keeping his hood over his eyes and his head down. The Barons stood aside as each of the Rebels exited the carriages, keeping a close eye on each of them.

"Say, this whole searching thing has been new for the past month," Hannah mused, sliding to the edge of the carriage. "Any reason why you're being so thorough?"

"We have a fugitive on the loose," the Baron said flatly.

"A fugitive?" Hannah said with shock, bracing herself to jump down. "My, what happened?"

"The prince killed the Knights of the Roundtable."

*Liars, the lot of them.* Arthur frowned underneath his hood and flicked his eyes over towards Hannah and the leader, watching the exchange.

"Oh? That's a very drastic thing to do," she murmured, jumping down off the carriage and stumbling a bit. "Any reason why he would've done that?"

"We're here to search your carriages, peasant, not answer your questions. Now form a line," the Baron barked at her.

"Certainly, good Samaritan," she grinned and hobbled over to the rest of the Rebels. They lined up against the carriage, leaning back against the wood. They kept their curious looks going, scratching their heads and murmuring to each other.

"You," the leader pointed to another Baron. "Go around and identify each one."

The Baron saluted and moved to the nearest Rebel, tugging off his hood roughly. The Rebel blinked at the sudden bright light, feigning fright. "Name," the Baron barked from beneath their hard mask.

"Quincy Morholt," he replied, shifting away from the Baron. Arthur glanced down the line, his mind reeling. *Come up with a name; think of a name…*

The Baron moved to the next Rebel and tugged down their hood, the young woman flinching away. "Hailey Gallahault."

*Think of a name, damn it!*

"Daniel Hoel," the Rebel next to the woman said.

*Why is it so hard to think of a-* then it clicked.

"Thomas Safir," the next Rebel said, looking away from the Baron.

"Jace Lanval," Eylan said beside Arthur.

The Baron turned to Arthur, tugging down his hood. "Name," he asked flatly.

"Name?" Arthur echoed, staring at him flatly.

"The words your mother called you," the Baron sniped. "What is your name?"

"Benjamin," Arthur said.

The Baron glanced back at the leading Baron, the two sharing annoyed looks. "Last name?" he spat.

"It isn't exactly legal for you to search carriages, plus you're distracting yourself from bigger issues," Arthur glared at him. "It's Benjamin Pelleas."

"The opinions of commoners do not control our tasks," the Baron sniffed at him.

"We have more common sense than you."

Eylan nudged him sharply, throwing him a look that appeared scared on the outside and frustrated in his eyes. Arthur looked at him, giving him a slight grin. Eylan shook his head at him.

"Smart mouth for a lad with plenty of teeth," the Baron growled and moved on, tugging down the hood of the Rebel beside him.

"James Dinaden," he said, looking at Arthur with a frown.

The Baron looked at Hannah. "Freya Erec," she smiled, nodding once.

"*Hari,*" one of the Barons inside the carriage called out.

The leading Baron looked at the back of the carriage. "What?"

The Baron walked out of the carriage, holding something fluffy in his hand roughly. "They're lovers of stray animals," the Baron chuckled. The kitten clawed at his gloves, mewing desperately. Arthur's eyes widened; he recognised that golden fur.

The Baron held it tighter in his hand, hurting the tiny kitten. "Do we throw it in the Castaral?"

"Do as you wish with it," he dismissed. "It's not our problem."

"Let it go," Arthur said with a growl.

The Baron turned to Arthur. "What's the cat's life to you?" he sniffed. "It's just a street pest."

"More than you know," Arthur narrowed his eyes.

"A sympathiser for the less fortunate," the Baron mused, looking back at the kitten in the Black Cloak's hand.

"I won't tell you again," Arthur sniped, walking up to him. "Let it go!"

Several weapons drew and pointed to Arthur, the Baron holding the kitten watching him with a chuckle. The Rebels' eyes widened and they raised their hands, Eylan throwing Arthur a filthy look.

"Woah, boys, let's not be touchy," Hannah said, raising her arms.

"Let the kitten go!" Arthur demanded.

"Fine, have your pitiful moggy," the Baron mocked and tossed the cat back inside the carriage. The kitten squeaked from inside the carriage with a thud. The Baron jumped down from the back and laughed, dusting his gloves.

Arthur scowled at him and felt two Barons tugging him back in line. Arthur moved around in their grip and growled at the Barons. "Get your hands off me!"

"Benjamin! This isn't the way to act around authorities," Hannah said with a bite, then laughed. "Apologies about him; it's his first time out on the run, and he's a moody one."

Arthur looked over at her and reluctantly cooperated. "Sorry," he muttered.

"There's no sign of him in the carriages, *Hari*," a Baron called from the other carriage down the end.

The leading Baron nodded at him. "You're right to enter, but keep an eye on that one, yeah?" He nodded over to Arthur. Arthur frowned at him and walked back into the carriage.

"Will do. You've got nothing to worry about," Hannah nodded and clapped. "Alright, lads and lass, back in the carriages all."

The rest of the Rebels followed after Arthur, and in no time, the doors were shut and the carriages were rolling through the Gates towards the plaza of Londinium.

Arthur sat back down in his spot, glowering out of the window. The kitten limped over to him from the shadow of a crate, dodging around the feet of the Rebels to rub against Arthur's leg with a purr. "You alright?" he asked softly.

It meowed at him, lifting her hind leg behind her. A scratch stretched over her ankle; a loose nail must have got her. Arthur reached down and petted her softly, smiling faintly at the furry animal.

"What in the name of the Gods was *that*?" Eylan growled at him, standing beside him.

Arthur glanced at him defensively for a moment, looking back down at Sariel. "They deserved a beating."

"I told you to keep your head down! You're lucky the charcoal worked. Otherwise, they would've recognised your royal ass."

Arthur stood up from his seat and looked at him. "Look, they have no respect for us, so why should I show any respect to them?"

"It wasn't about *you*. It was about getting the rest of us through for *your* sake," he snapped. "You could've kept your trap shut, and we'd be halfway in the marketplace by now, but you stood up for a stupid little kitten! You really are nutters."

"That kitten is actually a shifter," he corrected. "And yeah, maybe I am crazy, but we all need crazy in this world, don't we? And you know, I am sorry, truly, but *they* don't have a right to treat us like dirt now. Do you think that's fair?"

"We *let* them treat us like that," he growled. "We *let* them see that they can push us around."

"Well, maybe you shouldn't," Arthur scowled.

"Are you truly daft? Do you not see the point of what we do? We are *actors*, Arthur. We pretend to be lesser than what we are so we avoid suspicion. If they so much as catch a whiff of what we're doing, they'll trace us back to the Cave. It's all a façade that we've used for years, and we're not going to let you screw it up over a Gods damned cat!"

"That *cat* is actually a sweet little girl and is Samqueel's daughter. So have an open mind, will you?"

Eylan looked down at Sariel, the kitten shrinking back towards Arthur's feet. "Samqueel had a child?"

"My reaction exactly," Arthur nodded. "I've sworn to protect this child, no matter what, 'cause that's what a King does for his people."

Eylan sighed, sitting down on a box. "A King may want to protect his people, but what about the people protecting him? If you had kept going, I don't think they would have taken that as lightly as they did. I'd apologise to you," he said to the kitten, "but I'm afraid I don't believe you're anything more than a stowaway."

Arthur grunted, sitting down next to him. "I should be the one saying the apology."

Sariel looked up at Arthur and put a paw on his foot, watching the two of them. Arthur looked at Eylan sideways and nudged him lightly. "And to you, too."

Eylan sighed and shrugged. "At least we got through the Gates," he muttered.

"Where do I meet you after I finish scouting?" Arthur asked, looking forward and seeing the streets through the open curtains.

"We should be in the North District, near the training hall."

Arthur looked back at the other Rebels, some throwing him frowns. "Anyone care to join?"

"On that suicide mission? No thanks," the Rebel named Quincy said, leaning against the wall.

"It's not a suicide mission," Arthur corrected him. "Just a very dangerous one."

Quincy raised a brow in question and looked away. Arthur looked back towards the front and sighed, nervous to return to the place he once called home.

Something sharp gripped his leg and he looked down, Sariel clawing her way up. Arthur frowned and picked her up, setting her on his knee gently. She purred and looked up at him, glancing between him and Eylan.

"Happy now?" Arthur frowned at her playfully. She purred loudly at him, her tail swishing. Arthur smiled at her and looked back towards the front.

Eylan reached a tentative hand down towards her, and she looked at him with big eyes, shifting backwards on Arthur's leg.

"Guess I'm the favourite," Arthur smirked at him.

"Pah, animals never favour me," Eylan mumbled bitterly, moving his hand away. She meowed at him, her brow creased in a frown. "She's got an attitude."

"Maybe because you just called her an animal," Hannah suggested from the front seat, looking back for a moment with the reins in hand. "Arthur did just say she is a shifter."

"I'll believe it when I see it," Eylan dismissed.

Arthur looked down at the kitten and nodded at her. "Wanna show him?"

She looked down and massaged his leg with her paws. Arthur patted her softly, smiling at her. *Too shy.*

*Who would her mother be?* It wasn't anybody from the castle, that's for sure; her ears were arched when she shifted back. *An elf?* Arthur wouldn't have guessed Samqueel was one for elves. *It makes this all the more interesting.*

The carriage slowed steadily as they passed by rubble on the cobblestone alleyways, homes and shopfronts wrecked from the outside in. Doors lay strewn across the road, glass smashed from windows and smoke pluming the sky from burnt-out flames inside the houses.

Arthur watched it all with dread through the front of the carriage. This is what has become of his Kingdom. Ergott and his Barons had wrecked the city. *How many people would've died from this?* Horror sank into his stomach.

The marketways were almost like a ghost town, markets dotted across the alleyway with only a few people at each one. Hannah looked around with a frown, pulling to a stop. "This is worse than last week," she said, looping the reins tight on the hook.

Arthur frowned at the state of his Kingdom and put Sariel down gently, walking up to Hannah. "Ergott is responsible for all this," he scowled.

"How can one man destroy everything his people have done for his own gain? What is his motive?" she said, looking at him with saddened eyes.

"Change," Arthur growled.

"This change was never a good idea," she murmured, watching a Baron walk by. The Rebels behind Arthur flicked down the latch holding the door, sliding the crates, both empty and not, towards the end and hauling them off.

"I won't be long," Arthur said to her, making his way out the back entrance. "If I'm not in the Northern District in time, just go. It's better if only one of us gets caught."

"We're not planning on you being that one," she said. "We'll be waiting. Now go."

Arthur nodded at her, flipping up his hood and exiting the carriage, wandering down through the marketplace. Vendors watched him with little interest, the usual bustle of people pushing through the crowd a phantom memory as the wind brushed him instead. *Where is everyone?*

The slight patter of feet followed him, Sariel keeping up with his long strides. Arthur looked back at her, his eyes widened.

"Sariel," he said, looking at her. "What are you doing?"

She looked at him with bright eyes and limped down an alleyway, looking back at him expectantly. Arthur sighed and followed her, keeping up with her steps.

*For a cat with a hurt leg, she's fast.* The kitten zipped around the corner, waiting for him to follow before she ran off again. Arthur looked around for her and frowned. "Where did you go?"

A meow sounded from a box beside him, and she sat on it, purring. Arthur turned to her. "Don't run off."

She jumped down from the box and sprinted down the alleyway, her tail high in the air.

"The hell did I just say?" Arthur frowned at the kitten, following her down the alleyway with a sigh.

She wound down the alleyways for a while before she stopped, the castle looming over Arthur like a frowning marble giant. Arthur looked up at the castle and narrowed his eyes at it. *Damn you, uncle, inciting revenge on the people.* It made Arthur ashamed to be related to him, embarrassed that they shared their last names.

The kitten walked down a bend that goes beside the castle steps, following the curve downwards. Arthur followed the kitten, keeping both his eyes on her.

She turned a corner and paused, sniffing the air with her ears pricked. Her fur stood up on end for a moment, and she darted back towards Arthur. Arthur looked at her questioningly and looked up to where she backed away from.

A grate sat in the wall, the vent echoing with noises from within the castle. Multiple holes were burrowed through the stone, some filled and some not. Arthur looked at the grate curiously and stepped towards it. Sariel followed him, staying near his feet.

The vent whooshed cool air over Arthur as he got closer, the voices becoming clearer. Sariel squeezed into the hole near the bottom, her meow echoing.

"I understand your concern, Wilhelm, but I can assure you that these are steps to a greater kingdom," a familiar voice echoed down the vent. "Even if the people aren't happy with the state of their home, they will be grateful when we've begun the expansion."

"Nobody asked to do this expansion, Ergott," Wilhelm's rough accent grated down the vent. "You've taken it upon yourself to ally with these Black Cloaks, and they're raining the Ether down on the city. This isn't something we need."

"And an excellent job they're doing," Ergott said. "Camelot was always meant to fall. But we will take refuge in another, better Kingdom."

"You're destroying Camelot to live elsewhere? Why don't you just leave instead of causing so much suffering to the people?"

"Because then *he* would return," Ergott growled. "He would take his throne."

"What would it have mattered if you were gone? You're not making any sense of your actions," Wilhelm growled. "Especially with this new woman who has done nothing but lounge around demanding tasks of unnecessary burden."

"I've opened my eyes, General," Ergott said coldly. "Vivien helped me to see more clearly what needed to be done."

"How? What has she done for this Kingdom other than help destroy it with the likes of you?" he spat.

"Are you doubting my leadership, Wilhelm?"

"All that out there, that's not leadership. That's destruction. You're destroying this Kingdom so that Arthur can't have it. That is incredibly selfish of you. Sam was right for coming back to stop you. I should've followed him to the balcony." The sound of receding footsteps echoed over Arthur's head.

"You're right," Ergott said. "And you won't be there to see it fall completely."

The sound of tearing flesh ripped through the vent with a pained yell. The drip of blood on marble echoed a heavy thud of a falling body. Sariel's eyes widened, and she looked up at Arthur. Arthur's eyes widened in shock as blood slithered through the vent down the wall in rivers.

Wilhelm was dead.

The kitchen was hot, as always; the ovens were on full blast from the coals of the fire in the hearth. Simon stood at the kitchen bench, a wooden chopping board placed in front of him, a sharpened knife in his left hand. Sliced chicken pieces sat in a bowl beside him, his knife adding more pieces quickly into the mix.

On the other side of the kitchen, Maria held a large bowl in her left arm, whisking a thick combination at record speed. Flour dusted her clothes and across her face, even more of it on the bench in front of her.

Simon glanced at her for a moment and took a double take, chuckling with amusement. Maria huffed and looked at him. "What are you laughing at?" she asked.

"Do you have much experience in a kitchen?" he asked.

"Not really, but I'm working on it," she puffed, resting her arm and sitting the bowl on the bench. "I'm uh, self-taught from when I was in Gawain's hall. I don't think I'm *that* bad, though, am I?"

"You're actually pretty good," he said, smiling at her.

"Ah, finally, appreciation," she laughed, wiping her face with a spare cloth.

"So, what's your relationship with Arthur now?" Simon asked curiously.

Maria looked at him with a smile, rolling her eyes playfully. "We're going down this path?"

"Why not? A chat between good friends is one in confidentiality," Simon assured, tossing more chicken pieces into his bowl.

"We're just friends," she said, tucking the towel in her belt. "We had a bit of a moment, but we both agreed it could never happen. You know, all the common sense around a royal marrying a noble or another royal. It wouldn't work."

"You like anyone currently?" he asked, grabbing an onion from the top of the bench.

Maria picked the whisk back up and stirred the bowl a little more gently this time. "I mean, no one is really at the front of my mind," she mused. "I guess I'm just kind of living for the moment."

Simon nodded at her. "I'm kinda the same. Plus, after the last relationship, I need to gain trust back."

"Last relationship?" Maria asked, reaching for a cake pan. *Getting some spicy details over here.* Maria smirked to herself. "Do tell, my good consort."

"They left Reigate a few years ago," Simon said. "Went to live in another Kingdom far away. Rebel life wasn't for them. You ever had a lover?"

"No, not really," she shrugged. Her mind flickered over the faces of the ones she wasn't proud of, her jaw clenching a moment.

"That is a face of regret," Simon said, looking at her with a smirk.

Maria shook it off and smiled slightly. "It was a long time ago, and I'd never call them lovers." *Not even close.*

Simon chuckled and sliced the onion up into pieces. Maria's smile dropped slowly as she poured the batter into the tin, scraping the sides of the bowl. Simon glanced at her, looking at her curiously. "Why the long face?"

"Ah, just memories," she dismissed, her smile coming back slightly.

Simon hummed in thought, turning to face her and wiping his hands on his apron. "Did you know I'm not from Braynor?" he asked suddenly.

Maria looked at him, raising a brow. "I kind of figured with your Joran accent," she shrugged.

"Well, as you can tell, I am from Jorandi," Simon nodded. "I came to Braynor when I was a boy with my mother. I had several brothers and sisters back home with my father and cousins. You are aware of the wars happening over there?"

"Can't say I've heard of them," Maria shook her head.

"The Remon Empire from Itreni wanted to expand their territory further, and Jorandi was next in line. Their warriors came into the land and started taking over and building fortresses, slaying people standing against them and bringing war to my home. All of my older brothers and my father were fighting against them in rebellion. I remember when they reached my village, some of the Remon warriors who would use two swords to fight were there. They were called the Dimachaeri. They are where I picked up my inspiration for dual wielding in training."

He cleaned off his cutting board and rinsed his knife in a water bucket. "They did not spare many people from their wrath. My family were forced to leave their homes and find a safe place elsewhere. My cousins and sisters went to Armania on a large ship, and my mother took me to Braynor. My brothers and Father… I do not know of their fates. But in my mind, I like to think they are still well and fighting bravely. They would have made great Knights." His hand scooped up a bundle of wrapped herbs, his knife swiftly mincing them.

Maria watched him with interest, leaning against the bench. "Wow," she said quietly. "I had no idea, Simon. I'm sorry that happened to your family."

"It is okay. It is my story, and it made me who I am. Now, it's your turn to share," Simon replied, sprinkling herbs into his chicken bowl.

Her heart flickered a little. "Share what?"

"Life story," Simon said simply. "I shared mine. Now you share."

She sat the empty bowl down gently, thinking. "A question before I say anything. What's your opinion on courtesans?"

"I feel bad for them," Simon sighed, placing his knife down. "They have so much potential in life, but then they're made by cruel men to do unspeakable things. It is unacceptable."

Nerves got the better of her voice. "And the children raised in them?" she wavered.

"I wish I could give them a better life and have them come here. To our sanctuary, to Reigate. To train to fight instead."

She turned to look at him, a nervous smile on her flour-coated face. "If I had known this place existed, I would've come here a long time ago," she said quietly.

Simon looked at her with high brows, pausing his cooking. "You were raised in a brothel?"

Maria nodded, swallowing the lump in her throat. "I'm not proud of it at all. I lost my parents when I was a baby. I was found in a box near the Castaral bridge, I was told. The only thing I have of my parents is my necklace." She sighed quietly. "I've told everyone I was raised in an orphanage because I'm ashamed of what I've been taught to do. I didn't want anyone getting any ideas, you know. I didn't want to be taken advantage of again."

Simon placed a gentle hand on her shoulder. Maria looked up at him, feeling her nerves leave at the warm smile on his face.

"You are safe here," Simon assured her. "We will protect you. No one will know."

Maria felt her heart warm, a faint glow forming on her cheekbones. "Well, that's good," she said with a shrug and reached to his nose, dabbing flour on it. "Because I'm counting on it."

"Well, you can count on the Knights," Simon groaned, taking off his apron and wiping his nose.

"Are you planning to be one or just being a kitchen man?" she asked, laughing at the dot on his nose.

"I would love to become a Knight," Simon said, hooking his apron on the wall. "I would wield my two swords with grace and strength better than the Dimachaeri."

"Two sounds a bit extreme, doesn't it?" she grinned.

"*Nein*," Simon shook his head. "It would work well in battle, don't you think?"

"What if you need to block? You won't have a shield to protect you."

"I can parry," he shrugged, moving closer.

"That's a pretty difficult manoeuvre," she mused.

"But it'll do the trick."

"Can you count on that?" she asked softly, her head tilted almost all the way back to look up at him. *Gods, he's tall.*

"I can count on me," he said.

She laughed. "You've got a lot of faith in yourself."

"If you have faith in yourself, then you can achieve anything. Arthur needs more faith in himself," Simon chuckled. "And you can use more faith yourself, too. Maybe you'd get a chance with someone here," he smirked.

Mischief stirred in Maria. "Oh?" she asked lightly. "Faith in oneself can lead to chances now?"

Simon nodded with a grin. "That's the Reigate people's charm."

She laughed a bit and smirked at him with her scrunched nose. "Your charm is pretty flattering," she drawled.

"Is it now?" he asked, folding his arms with a raised brow.

"More flattering than Kyan," she huffed and pulled her cloth from her belt, hitting him with it gently as she turned back around.

"That was unnecessary," he laughed.

She looked back over her shoulder at him with a wide grin. "Oh, it was one hundred per cent necessary," she joked, laughing. "I would've gotten the flour from your nose but you're too tall for even the towel to reach."

Simon chuckled, shaking his head at her and grabbing his bowl again. "You're a troublemaker, Maria."

"That's me," she grinned and picked up the cake tin. "I am the ultimate problem creator." *And you, my friend, are becoming quite the catalyst.*

"I'm certain I could verse you for that title and win," a male voice said from the kitchen doorway. Maria turned and looked at the man, freezing with a gasp.

An unmasked Baron leaned against the skirting, blood coating his leather armour. He inspected his hands like he'd been waiting a while for them to notice him. "A great little show you had going on there. A pity neither of you were bold enough to kiss," he smirked, his scar pulling at his lip where it crossed from his eye over his nose.

Simon looked at him with a deep frown, standing in front of Maria. "Who are you, and what are you doing in Reigate?"

"I'm the one who came here to say 'surprise'," he said, waving his hands in the air mockingly. "We found you."

"Leave now," Simon scowled at him. "Barons aren't welcome here."

"Good luck with getting us all out since we've already swamped the place," he said, standing with a shrug. "I'd like to see you try and fail to defend yourself from the others that took your mates down. It'd be fun to watch."

"What?" Simon asked in disbelief. Maria looked at the Baron with wide eyes from behind Simon. *He looks familiar.*

"Edward!" a voice called from down the hallway.

The Baron turned to look behind himself, lowering his hand. "Yes, Father? What is it?"

From the shadows, Rohin Jackseye stepped into the kitchen with two other Barons by his side, his scar stark in the light from the oven. Maria froze. *Jackseye is here.* Cold fear seeped through her veins, and she sat the cake pan back down on the bench before she dropped it, her hands shaking.

"Help the men gather the peasants outside," Jackseye ordered his son.

Edward frowned at Jackseye bitterly, standing his ground. "Look what I found in my explorations," he said casually, gesturing to Maria and Simon.

Jackseye glanced over to the two, his amber eye lighting in recognition. "I remember you," he said coldly. "Where is he?"

"She does not answer to you," Simon interrupted, standing tall.

"Perhaps *you* will," Jackseye glared at him. "Where is he?"

"Whom?" Simon asked.

"Don't play dumb, boy. Where is Arthur Pendragon?"

"Not here," Maria said quietly. "He's not here." *How did they find this place? Were the Rebels caught?*

"Well, if you and Tristan are here along with the other runaways, where is Arthur?" Jackseye asked, stepping closer to them.

Simon angled himself between him and Maria, his jaw clenched in a glare. "Do not touch her; do not near her," he warned.

Jackseye lashed his fist into his stomach and shoved Simon to the ground. "Don't stand in my way," he growled.

Maria gasped and bent down to Simon, touching his shoulder. He groaned and clutched his stomach, glaring up at Jackseye. *Gods almighty.*

"Get her up," Jackseye said to the Barons.

The Barons nodded, marching over to Maria and standing her up roughly, holding her by the biceps. Maria struggled against them, her breath turning panicked. Jackseye walked up to her, stepping over Simon on the floor.

Simon growled and launched his leg up towards Jackseye's thigh, Rohin's hand lashing to grab his ankle without looking away from Maria. Simon's eyes widened and he swept his other leg towards him, twisting to try and get his leg out of Jackseye's grip.

Jackseye tossed him against the kitchen bench by the leg, slamming his boot onto his knee. A crack sounded from beneath his boot, and Simon roared in pain, curling his leg towards his chest.

"Simon!" Maria gasped, fighting against the Baron's iron grip.

Jackseye let go of Simon's ankle and walked over to her, gripping her jaw tightly. "I'm going to ask you one last time. *Where is Arthur?*"

## Chapter 22: Baron Land

It felt like forever since Arthur had walked the Londinium alleyways. Remembering the tunnels took over remembering his Kingdom, and he wasn't sure if he was comfortable with that. What he wasn't pleased with was the hidden vent he followed Sariel to that he had no idea about before that moment. How many people would've listened in like he did? *And to overhear a murder that way was just...*

Arthur shook his head clear, the charcoal dust from his hair flying around him in puffs. Arthur scowled at the charcoal ashes, wiping away a few pieces that landed on his nose, huffing in annoyance. *Damn you, Eylan.*

Turning a corner, he came to a sudden stop, staring down the alleyway; a pair of Barons marched the opposite way, their boots thumping in unison on the cobblestones. He quickly ducked back behind the wall, looking down either end of the alley. The bastards were everywhere, and everywhere they were came the same destruction of broken glass and battered doors. The further to the West, the worse it got it seemed. *Was there an uprising?*

The sound of laughing children erupted from the same direction as the patrol, then as soon as it began, it stopped. Arthur frowned and peered back around the corner.

"To your homes, now," a Baron ordered.

The two red-haired boys stood facing the Baron who spoke, putting on a brave face. "You can't control us, Black Cloaks," one said.

"You're not the Knights. You can't tell us what to do!" the other said, sticking his tongue out at them.

The Baron slammed his spear into the ground, the children flinching back. "I said, now!" he shouted.

Arthur felt a spark of frustration flowing through him; he couldn't do anything, otherwise he'd be caught red-handed, and he couldn't afford to be seen, not now.

A woman with hair as red as wine ran out of a doorway towards the children, grabbing their arms and pulling them to her protectively. "Harley, Bretton, what are you doing outside?" she asked them with panicked eyes, watching the Barons.

"Control your pests," the Baron scowled at her. "They should know the rules, and so should you."

The woman frowned at the Barons as the boys moved to her in fright. "They would be easier to control if you didn't kill their mother," she accused them.

"Aren't you the mother?" the Baron asked.

"I'm their sister," she spat. "You murdered my mother at the funeral uprising. How is that being a protector of the people?"

"It's not, that's not our duty," the Baron said, his mask emotionless.

"Then why did Ergott say so?" she growled, standing up with the boys holding her hands. "Come on, lads, back inside."

"Your King has told many lies to you," the second Baron said, standing up straight.

"Yeah, no kidding," she scoffed, walking to the door and watching the boys walk in. "This whole Kingdom has become a joke. The King is the castle clown, and we're nothing but pawns, right?" she sniped at them, shutting the door behind the boys.

"How dare you!" the Baron shouted, grabbing her by the shoulder. She gasped and spun around, shoving his hand off her shoulder. The Baron threw her down the steps

of her house, the girl crying out in pain as she hit the
cobblestones hard.

"You do not speak of the King in that matter, peasant,"
the Baron scowled, walking down the steps.

She looked up at the Baron in fright, scrambling
backwards and bumping into the other Baron. They
grabbed her by the arms roughly, dragging her towards the
alleyway, kicking and screaming.

"Let me go! Help!" she yelled, struggling against the
Barons in panic.

Arthur scowled and hid behind the wall quietly. He
waited patiently for the Barons to round the corner,
listening for their footsteps.

"You never talk about the King with disrespect," the
Baron growled at her.

"You lot are mental! Let me go!"

The Barons tossed her to the wall roughly next to
piled-up rubbish, scowling down at her beneath their
masks. She scrambled up the wall, her back pressing into it.
She trembled as she watched them gain closer, her eyes
wide and filled with tears. The leading Baron connected his
foot with her ribcage, chuckling at her as she cried out in
pain and fell back down to the ground.

*Gods be damned.* Arthur peered around the corner and
walked up to them slowly. The girl covered her chest with
an arm, hissing in pain as she pressed her ribcage. She
looked up at the Barons and flicked her blue eyes behind
them, pained tears falling.

"Do you really think someone will come and help
you?" The Baron chuckled deeply.

She watched Arthur get closer for a moment before she
looked back at the Barons, curling in on herself.

"I thought not," the Baron laughed.

Behind the Baron, his comrade pulled back sharply
with a gasp, the thud of meat on stone echoing. He turned

around with hesitation; his partner lay defeated on the ground, their sword missing from their hands.

Arthur twirled the sword in his hand, looking at the Baron with a grin. The Baron frowned at him and unsheathed his own sword, tossing the spear to the side.

"Get back into your home," the Baron growled. The girl blinked at Arthur in surprise, uncurling slightly. *The charcoal's working better than I would've thought.*

"How can I go back home if it's filled with black-adorned pests?" Arthur drawled, frowning at the Baron.

"Arthur," the Baron growled, looking at him up and down. "It was about time you returned."

"A lot of changes have been made, but you lot haven't changed one bit," Arthur mused.

"You don't fit the 'skinny lad' description we were told, and your hair is black."

"Charcoal. And you haven't seen all the changes yet," Arthur smirked lightly. "I can show them to you if you'd like, or you can bother someone else. It's up to you."

The Baron growled and swung towards Arthur at lightning speed, Arthur's sword knocking the blade away, staggering the Baron. The Baron stumbled back and looked at Arthur in surprise.

Arthur frowned at him, positioning his feet as Gawain taught him. The Baron growled and swung at him again, cutting upwards. Arthur blocked his sword from the right side and shoved the Baron away with the force of the blow.

The girl scrambled out of the way as the Baron tumbled back towards the wall, his head colliding against the bricks with a sickening crack. Arthur cringed at the thud, watching the Baron collapse to the ground. *That was easy...*

The girl looked up at Arthur with hopeful eyes, standing back up with a stumble. Arthur glanced over to her and moved to her aide, helping her stand.

"You alright?" Arthur asked.

"A bit sore in the ribs but otherwise fine," she breathed, staring at him, her eyes trailing over his appearance. "Are you really him?"

"Really who?" Arthur asked.

"Arthur," she said. "The 'Born King' one."

Arthur smiled at her, scruffing the charcoal out of his blonde hair. "Yeah, that's who I am."

Her face lit up with a smile. "Good to see you've come back," she grinned. "We were all starting to lose hope."

"I won't be here for long, I'm afraid," Arthur said. "But myself and my Knights will be back, and we'll take back what's ours."

"Excellent to hear," she said, bowing her head to him. "I'll keep your appearance under wraps from my end. Don't want that pest in the castle knowing just yet, do we?"

"Not until I return with my father's Knights of the Roundtable," Arthur mused.

"The Knights? They're dead," she frowned.

"Not all of them," Arthur shook his head. "They've been hiding in the Reigate Caves. That's where I've been training all this time."

"It's a good thing that. You're going to need that strength with those lads to get rid of these blowflies," she muttered.

"I could do it *without* Sir Bedivere," Arthur shrugged. "But everyone else is a good pack of men."

She laughed softly, holding her rib with a slight hiss. "Pardon my pain here," she winced. "The bastard got me good."

"You should go home and get some rest," Arthur suggested. "Put some ice on it for about half an hour, then warm it with a hot cloth."

"You don't know much about first aid, do you?" she grinned. "No rest for me anyway. I've got a handful of rats to look after by the names of Harley and Bretton. They never do as they're told."

"You tell them that King Arthur will put them in line," Arthur grinned at her.

"You can tell them yourself when they're older. They're gonna be Knights the first chance they get, just like their papa."

"They can be my Knights of Camelot if they pass the training," Arthur said.

"A Knight of Camelot? Awesome!" a small voice said from around the corner.

The woman looked at the boy with a sigh. "Bretton, why do you *always* have to be a sticky beak whenever you're told to stay?"

"I got curious and heard you screaming. I wanted to help. Who's your friend?"

"Have a guess, you looney," she said, walking over to her little brother. "It's King Arthur."

Bretton's eyes widened, and he turned to Arthur with a slack jaw. Arthur turned to the boy and smiled at him. "I heard you want to be a Knight?"

"Yeah," he said, a voice echoing behind him. Harley stared at Arthur from behind the door, peeking around the corner. The woman rolled her eyes and gestured for him to come forward.

"You both can be my Knights when you're old enough," Arthur said warmly. "Just give it a few years. You have to be twelve to join."

"Really?" Bretton asked, his eyes filled with excitement. "I'd be one of your Knights?"

"Me, too!" Harley said, nudging his brother.

"I'll need Knights to guard the Kingdom and castle, won't I?" Arthur asked them. They both nodded their heads quickly, their eyes wide.

"Keep yourselves safe for the time being, okay?" Arthur patted them on the shoulder. "Listen to your sister, and keep off the streets. Follow those instructions until I return and take back the Kingdom, understand?"

Bretton turned to Harley with a joyful look. "We're gonna be Knights of Camelot!" he grinned from ear to ear.

"We're going to be the best Knights in Braynor ever!" Harley beamed.

"What do you boys say to your King?" Arthur asked, looking at the both of them. "Did you boys listen to what I told you?"

"Yeah, uh, listen to Jacey, and stay off the street… um, sire," Harley said.

"Good man," Arthur smiled. Harley beamed in joy. Bretton whooped and waved his arms in the air, Harley laughing along with him as they ran towards the house.

"Look at that, you got them to listen," Jacey said, chuckling softly.

"And now they'll listen to you, 'cause their King told them to," Arthur grinned.

"We'll see just how long that part lasts."

"Just say that if they don't do as they're asked, they won't be Knights."

"That might work, actually," she mused. "I'll give it a shot."

"That rule goes for you, too," Arthur said, his voice turning serious. "The streets are too dangerous, and you need to stay inside and look after those boys."

"That's what I was doing before the Barons came along," she said. "Long before they ever showed up. Both parents weren't super into staying home to watch those two."

"At least they have a good sister like you," Arthur smiled at her.

She smiled back with a faint blush and looked down. "Thank you for helping me. I'm Jacinta, by the way," she said. "Jacinta Pelleas. Just Jacey is fine, too."

Surprise flitting through him. *Pelleas?*

"Suppose I should go and get the lads' lunch ready," Jacey said, walking towards the door. "Guess I'll see you on the throne sooner or later, yeah?"

"Only time will tell," Arthur nodded at her.

"Here's to hoping," she smiled, turning back and walking up the steps to the door, opening it up and closing it behind herself.

Arthur watched her walk back home, smiling widely to himself. *How coincidental was that? I should've said I was Benjamin Pelleas.* Arthur shrugged his hood back over his head and continued down the alleyway.

"Oi! Stop right there!" a voice yelled from down the alleyway.

Arthur froze and turned back around slowly. A group of three Barons ran towards him, their cloaks trailing behind them in the wind.

"Damn it," Arthur growled, running off down the alleyway.

"Stop in the name of King Ergott!" the Baron barked at him.

Arthur darted down the alleyway, turning the corner down to a marketway, surprisingly lively with a few civilians. They gasped and dodged out of the way of the hooded Arthur, pivoting to look as the Barons trailed after him. Arthur shoved a few of the civilians out of his way gently, dodging the older ones carrying heavier bags. They cursed towards him as he barreled through and made it to the other side, pausing to look around.

The Barons lagged behind him in the crowd, but more came from another alleyway to his right. *They must have heard the commotion.*

"You've got to be kidding," Arthur scowled, rushing down the opposite alleyway.

The carriages blocking the alleyway bore fruits of all kinds; Arthur looked around each of them, but the Rebel carts weren't there. *Damn it.* He kept pelting down and around the corners, squeezing through a particularly tight gap he would've fit in three months ago with ease. Arthur groaned as he squeezed through the brick walls, popping out the other end and pulling his leg free.

He didn't stop to check for Barons before he kept going; he could hear their boots stomping after him and the delay as they filed one by one through the gap. It gave him enough time to run towards the markets closest to him. He jumped behind the nearest crate, panting to catch his breath.

He looked around where he was, a rack of jackets and hat stands surrounding him, two women behind the stall bench blinking at him blankly. He smiled at them and had an idea.

"Had any customers buy anything today?" he asked, out of breath. They were too stunned to answer.

The Barons ran into the market, searching around the stalls for any sign of Arthur. The stall owners watched the Barons nervously, the few customers backing away from their paths. Their eyes flicked over to the clothing stall, seeing three women sitting around on the crates in floppy hats and elaborate robes, inspecting their nails and fiddling with tags. They moved on, calling amongst each other for any information.

Arthur smirked beneath his big floppy brown hat, watching them go as he lowered his hand. *Gullible, the lot of them.*

Arthur glanced at the women with a grin. "Thank you," he nodded at them, pulling the robe off his shoulders.

"Good luck," the eldest lady smiled at him and watched the Barons. The younger woman watched him, curiosity in her brown-eyed gaze.

Arthur looked down the alleyway for a moment before he walked out of the stall, making his way delicately towards the furthest alleyway from the Barons. *At least some of Tristan's acting ideas help sometimes.*

He kept his head lowered while making his way over to the alleyway, glancing his eyes around the marketway. He rounded the corner and pulled off the hat, flicking his hood back around as he sat the hat on a box. Arthur cautiously walked down the alleyway, gathering his breath after running for a while. *It wouldn't be long before they-*

"Down here!" a Baron called, his boots thudding after Arthur.

Arthur sighed to himself, glaring back at him. "You lot don't leave anyone alone, don't you?" he said, sprinting away from the oncoming Black Cloak.

He ran towards a cross in the alleyway, two more Barons cutting in from both sides. Arthur gasped and ducked beneath their arms, his feet still keeping him going as they stood dumbly for a moment before they chased after him with their mate.

*Alright, Seasoned Oak it is, then.* Arthur doubled back on himself and turned a sharp corner down a narrow alleyway, the Barons slowing back to dart after him. Arthur kept his footing steady as he ran uphill, the carriage in front of him ready to go. He jumped up on the back of it and sprang up to the gutter, quickly pulling himself to the roof with the momentum.

A crate fell from the back of the carriage, toppling over to spill watermelons as it burst open. The Barons jumped over the melons with ease, dodging the flying pieces of the crate.

Arthur looked around from the rooftop for a moment; he was in the Eastern District. *This works, too.* He reached into the gutter for the rope, kneeling down on the shingles and waiting for the first Baron to jump onto the cart before yanking it with a mighty tug.

The wheel stump pulled free, the Baron on the carriage falling to their knees as the cart gave way beneath him. The Barons on the street paused and jumped out of the way of the frantic cart, the Baron on board clinging to the sides as it rolled down the hill.

Arthur laughed and got to his feet, disappearing back behind the gutter. *Never fails.* The hole in the roof was big enough to squeeze through without struggle, and the inside lit up with the sun beaming directly down onto the tunnel entrance.

He jumped through the hole onto the rafters and landed on the hay strewn around the flooring, put there for the purpose of a softer landing. Arthur pulled open the tunnel trapdoor and slid down into the dark void.

*Back here again.* He sighed in relief, taking his hood off to let his dirty blonde hair breathe. He scuffed his hair roughly to get rid of the extra charcoal still stuck to the strands, seeing the dust splinter through the air in the sunlight beam.

He grabbed the torch from the familiar table by the water bucket and lit it up across the tunnel sides, the light flaring alive brighter as he shut the trap door. His footsteps echoed down the muted tunnels with the occasional wet plop of a puddle underfoot. The tunnel walls were getting more and more covered in moss and creeping vines, and the cracks filled with green plants. It made sense, considering the Castaral was right over them. Although the tunnels only flooded in Autumn, and it's been a while since they've had good enough rain to do so. *Odd for the floor to be so wet this time of year.*

A quieter set of footsteps came from in front of him, the source lighting up in his torchlight; Sariel's green eyes reflected the light, and her golden fur turned orange in the little light. Her purr echoed around the chamber, a meow of greeting following it.

Arthur smiled faintly at her. "Did you find what you were looking for?"

She shook her head, shaking her back foot free of water. Arthur nodded and crouched down to her, laying his hand flat in front of her. She put her paws onto his hand and squished his palm, purring.

"Let's go," he smiled, picking her up gently with his hand, then tucking her into his arm. He kept going down the tunnel way, a place in mind he and Tristan scouted out; there was a newly abandoned house in the Eastern District. The inside was connected to the tunnels and more maintained than the rest of their hideouts. It was a better place to stay for the moment, especially since the house wasn't damaged, and as far as Arthur knew, no one had the key to get into the stone door.

It puzzled both of them as to why it was connected to the tunnels in the first place, but it didn't matter; there were a lot more houses with lower basements connected to the tunnels the owners never knew about that people still live in today. Tristan accidentally found out about that one day when he located one beneath the house of an older man with a not-so-welcoming attitude when he found him scouting out around his canned food.

Arthur continued his way down the tunnel, keeping his torchlight up high to see further; he was lucky he even had a torch to use, considering that the stormwater must've gotten down into the tunnels. Still, he didn't know how it could've. *Were there grates around here somewhere?*

The trap door rope hung in front of him, the torch sconce on the wall waiting. That was another thing about this place: there was a torch sconce as if someone constantly used this spot to seek shelter. He slotted the torch into the sconce and tugged the rope, the trapdoor springing open on a mechanism and folding up into the building with a quiet thud.

Voices echoed above in hushed tones, going quiet at the sound of the thud. Arthur paused, listening quietly. *People are here? More Barons? How did they find this place?*

Arthur placed his foot into the carved slot in the tunnel wall, pulling himself up with the kitten still in hand. A light like the soft glow of a hearth fire lit up the room behind the doorway to his right. Someone was definitely here.

Sariel wriggled in his hands, struggling around and batting at him. Arthur placed her down on the wooden floor and pulled himself up out of the tunnel. The kitten darted through the doorway excitedly, her tail held high and meowing. Arthur frowned slightly at the kitten and followed her, walking down the hallway curiously.

The polished stone walls bounced with light from the fire further down the hallway to the left. Sariel darted around the corner, a few gasps of surprise echoing from around it.

"What the Hell?" a male voice said, the floor thudding with the shifting of boots.

"Sariel!" a female voice said in surprise, light footsteps rushing towards the corner Arthur stood at. "Where have you been? You've had me worried sick!"

Arthur's eyes widened, and he turned the corner. A group of eight refugees sat around the stone hearth on the beaten-up fur rug, turning to look at Arthur with wide, alarmed eyes. The voice in front of him belonged to a white-haired woman, her green eyes piercing through him like a knife.

Arthur raised his hands up, looking at her with widened eyes. "I don't mean any harm," he said. He looked her over; her arm seemed jutted as if it had been broken for some time. Her ears were arched and delicately pointed at the tip. She was an elf. Arthur's eyes widened. *Sariel's mother?*

"Arthur!" a familiar voice said, a girl standing up and running over to him. "You came back! I knew you would!"

Arthur looked at the girl and smiled. "It's good to see you again, Lucy."

She barreled into him and threw her arms around his waist tightly, Arthur staggering to keep upright. Almost as soon as the hug began, she let go, turning back to look at the brown haired man she sat beside. "See? I told you he would come back, didn't I?" she sneered at him. "You should trust me more often, Owen, especially when I'm right."

Owen scowled at her and walked over to Arthur, looking at him up and down. "Where have you been all this time?"

"I've been in hiding," Arthur said, observing Owen.

"That's charming," Owen growled. "Cause while you've been gone, the Kingdom has gone to shit, and you should've been here to stop it, *my liege*."

Arthur narrowed his eyes at him. "Watch it," he warned. "Your sharp tongue can get you in trouble."

"Owen, why do you have to be so argumentative?" Lucy barked at him. "He came back to fight. Is that not good enough?"

"Look around you, Lucy," Owen said. "Camelot and Londinium have fallen, and we were supposed to be saved by the one Born King who has been *hiding* for over six months!"

"I've been training with the old Knights of the Roundtable, douchebag," Arthur scowled at him. "If I were you, I'd think about the next thing you're about to spit at me 'cause it won't go well for you."

Owen opened his mouth to bite back, but a quiet voice interrupted him from the corner. "You trained with the Knights?"

Arthur looked over at the corner and nodded at the voice. "All of them," he said. "Well, almost. And they're ready to take back this Kingdom for the sake of our people."

Lucy looked at Owen smugly, and he glowered at her. The voice from the corner stood up into the light and came a little closer, her quicksilver eyes looking up at Arthur with hope. "You've taken the title upon yourself?"

*Those eyes…* Arthur smiled at her. "I most certainly have, Erin," he said. "And when we come back here and throw away Ergott from the throne, I'll be ready to lead you all after the guidance of King George. I'll lead you as your King."

Her eyes crumbled slightly, pain sharp in their gray depths. "He tried to stop him, they said. The Barons say he went wild with madness, but I know my son better than that. I know he was doing something to help. And he's gone."

"I know," Arthur said sadly. "I was there when it happened, and I'm sorry I was too late to help him."

"You were there?" the elf said from in front of him, her accent dwindling.

Arthur turned to her. "I tried to save Samqueel, but Ergott was too strong. I think Sam was trying to help me in a way, but I wanted to help him. After Ergott… was done, he knocked me out, and I woke up in an alley. Myself and my friends were chased out with a bounty on my head. If I had stayed, I would've been killed," he explained.

A bright flash of white blinked from beneath the elf's hands, and Sariel appeared before her, leaning into her mother and holding her arm tightly. The chain around her neck dangled down her chest, the slate triangle glinting in the firelight. She looked at Arthur from the corner of her eye as the elf's face flickered with pain and anger.

"Samqueel was my mentor. I'm sorry I couldn't save him," Arthur said quietly. "I did all I could."

"The best is never good enough," she said quietly, looking down at her daughter and the chain that hung around her neck in shock. "Where did you get that?"

Sariel looked up at her, pulling it off from around her neck and offering it to her shyly. "He was on the balcony," she said quietly. "He wanted me to have it."

"Child, you know better than to go near that devil house," she hissed at her, and Sariel flinched, looking down. Erin looked at the chain with a pale face.

"That devil house was my home, and I lost that," Arthur frowned. "I lost *everything*. Your daughter has been with me at the caves for a while. She did the right thing by getting that chain."

"You act as if you're the only one who has lost everything," she said to him with a tight throat.

"I didn't say I was the only one," Arthur said. "Look around you. Everyone has. I'm here to take back what we've lost."

"I know everyone has! I've been here fending for them for the past month, waiting for you!" she snapped.

"Laruen," Erin said quietly to her in warning.

"I'm here for Sam," Laruen snarled. "He would've wanted me to help these people. I stayed because of him. I didn't stay for you."

"I have no doubt that you loved him, and what you've done for these people is heroic and brave," Arthur said to her. "But you need to listen when I tell you that people are coming to save you all, and I'm a part of that. I'm not asking for forgiveness, I'm not asking for your support, but I am asking for your trust."

Laruen stared up at him for a while longer before Sariel nudged her leg, the two sharing a look for a moment. Erin sighed, looking at Arthur with a set jaw. "We've stayed in this spot for almost a month," she said. "If you can get us out to a better place, we will appreciate it, no matter our differences. We will follow you."

Arthur nodded at her. "I can get you to a better place, but we need to go to the training hall first," he said.

"Is that where Tristan is?" Lucy asked, her eyes bright.

"Tristan is at Reigate, but the carriages that will meet us at the training hall will take you back there," Arthur told them. The refugees gathered around looked up at Arthur with renewed hope, some of them hesitant.

"Yeah, great," Owen snorted. "Let's follow the great leader back to wherever he's dug a ditch for us to die in, where the Barons will never locate our corpses."

"If none of you believe me, I don't blame you," Arthur said, looking at Owen in particular. "But if you all want to get out of this mess, you need to follow my lead and do exactly as I say."

"These people can follow the lead of that deadbeat," Erin nodded to Owen, who protested against her with raised arms. "They can follow the man they believe in. Lead the way, son."

Arthur smiled as the refugees stood and gathered their small belongings, turning to him expectantly. "Follow me," he said and led the way down to the tunnels.

"Sit them down in a line!" The Baron's voice echoed through the opening of the cave, other Barons forcing the Rebels onto the ground. Maria struggled in the grip of the two Barons that held her, landing on the ground roughly. Her tailbone barked in pain at the tough floor, and she winced as she shifted upright. They threw Simon beside her, the lad growling in pain at his injured leg.

"Simon," she breathed, moving closer to him. He'd tried to defend her from Jackseye, of all people. The least she could do was make sure he was okay.

He looked at her, his eyes lit in pain and worry, holding his arm out to her. "Are you okay?" he asked her. She nodded and moved closer to him, wary of his leg.

"Is that everyone?" Jackseye asked the Barons.

"As far as we know, there may be a few still coming from the infirmary, *Muharí*," a Baron said.

"You all know what we're here for, don't you?" Jackseye looked around at all of the captives. The majority of them stared daggers back at him, some keeping their head down. Maria watched him with daunt.

"Get off me!" Percival growled, struggling in the grip of three Barons that shoved him to the ground with a grunt.

Maria flicked her eyes over to where the Knights were held captive, noting a few missing. *Did they go out with the carriages?* Lancelot was held between two Barons, Gaheris beside him pinned on the ground by larger men. Geraint sat on the concrete floor with a sword at his throat. *Who's missing? Wait, Gawain...*

The sound of boots thudding echoed from behind her, a few men struggling behind them. A group of seven Barons held the remaining four Knights, Bedivere struggling in their grip, needing two of the Barons to hold him steady. Kay's snarl echoed around the tunnel like a fire alarm, the white Knight managing to pull an arm free and smack an elbow into the side of a Baron's head, the Black Cloak dropping like a stone.

Three guarding Barons sprinted over to him, grabbing ahold of him firmly as he thrashed and shoved against them. One of the Barons kicked the back of his knee roughly, pushing him down to the cobblestone ground and gripping his hair.

"Who can tell me why we're here?" Jackseye said. "I'm open for volunteers."

"Shove a stick in your ass, Rohin," Bedivere spat.

"It's been a while, Ryan," Jackseye smirked faintly. "It's nice to see some faces stay the same."

"Yours got uglier," he sniffed. "Was it the wife who got sick of you finally who gave you that ornament? Or did someone finally give you a taste of your own medicine?"

"You finally grew a pair of balls," Jackseye mused. "I remember when you were in training, you were nothing but a sulky, stubborn bastard of a trainee."

"Some things never change," Bedivere smirked. "I'm still a bastard."

"And a stubborn one by the looks of things," Jackseye raised a brow, glancing over to the Barons holding him. "Feel free to throw him to the ground harder than the others."

They held his arms wide as another Baron shoved him to the ground with a foot, the breath whooshing out of Bedivere like a popped balloon. He huffed and glared at Jackseye with gritted teeth.

"Tell us how, exactly, you came to find this place," Gawain growled, keeping still in his captor's grip.

"We all know how much you love the sound of your own voice," Galahad said, swivelling his head around in search.

"Friends in high places, Jonathan," Jackseye smirked at him. "Very, very high places."

"Is that all? I expected a speech," Gawain shrugged. "Your flamboyance is wearing off."

"You don't have the right to know how we found your humble abode," Jackseye said softly, walking up closer to Gawain. "Maybe you should've kept track of the wolves in the shadows after all."

Gawain growled, set his jaw, and smacked his forehead into Jackseye. Jackseye groaned and reached his hand up to his nose, blood dripping through his fingers to the ground.

Maria watched with wide eyes as Jackseye turned hostile eyes on him. "That's not a good way to greet old friends," Jackseye said calmly, wiping the blood onto his shirt.

"No one ever called your mongrel ass a friend," Kay spat, baring his teeth.

"They called me a mentor," Jackseye said, sniffing at the feeling of blood in his nose.

Pained protests sound from down the tunnel to the right, and Maria snapped her head to the voice. Two Barons held Tristan between them by the arms, his face twisted in pain at the tight grips on his bandages. Tristan cursed at the

Barons and tried to pull their hands off, his legs almost tripping over one another.

"Is there something you'd like to say, Tristan?" Jackseye asked.

"This hurts, you bastards!" Tristan snapped and looked at Jackseye. "When did you get here?"

"When we arrived at the cave's entrance," Jackseye glanced at him.

The Barons shoved Tristan down to the floor with a yell of agony, his hands shooting to his legs and gripping them. Maria almost got up but remembered the guards standing by. *His wounds must be killing him.*

"Now that we're all here," Jackseye growled, looking around the cave, "who would like to answer my question? Where is Arthur Pendragon?"

The cave stayed silent, the Knights growling angrily. Lancelot looked over at Gawain, his face daunted. Maria watched as Gawain turned his gaze to Lancelot with clenched teeth. *Looks like he managed to leave, after all.*

"Anyone?" Jackseye asked. "Any hints or clues?"

Not one voice spoke up. Jackseye chuckled under his breath, shaking his head. "Alright, then." Jackseye looked back over the group of Rebels and spotted a young boy within the mix, raising his eyebrow. "Bring the boy to me," he ordered.

Maria's heart jumped. *Not Baeydn!*

Galahad thrashed around in the Barons' grip, growling in anger. "Don't you touch him! That's my son!"

The familiar Baron from before - Edward, if Maria remembered right - picked up Baeydn by the back of his shirt, gripping his arm as he dragged him to his father. Baeydn struggled uselessly against him, his eyes wide with tears.

"Since no one wants to answer," Jackseye pondered aloud. "We'll do a little bargain instead."

"You leave him out of this!" Galahad snarled.

Edward threw the lad to Jackseye, Baeydn landing roughly at his feet with a yelp, the sharp gravel cutting his arms. He scrambled to his knees and froze as he stared up at Jackseye in fright.

Jackseye crouched down to Baeydn on the ground and looked up at Galahad for a moment. "What's your name, lad?"

Baeydn stayed silent, shaking as tears flooded over his cheeks. Galahad's heart raced within his chest, still fighting the Barons. "Don't you touch my son!"

"Is he mute, Jameson?" Jackseye laughed, facing Galahad with a sly smirk. "Or does he have the same brain space as his father?"

"You touch him, Rohin, and I will kill you!" Galahad snarled at him.

A glint of metal flashed as Jackseye flicked open a hidden dagger, gripped Baeydn by the back of the neck, spun him around to face Galahad, tugged him up to chest level and pressed the blade against the lad's throat. Baeydn's eyes widened, and he whimpered, freezing against the prickle of the knife on his skin.

Galahad's eyes widened and struggled harder, yelling in protest towards Jackseye. Maria's breath was bated in panic; *they wouldn't kill a child?!*

"Leave Baeydn alone!" Tristan barked, straining against the Barons that held his arms.

"You all have two options," Jackseye said aloud. "You either tell us where Arthur is hiding, or I will take this lad's life in front of his father."

"Jackseye," Gawain growled. "You wouldn't stoop so low as to murder a child for information."

"Why don't you test me, Jonathan?" Jackseye growled deeply, pressing the knife harder to Baeydn's neck. The boy winced as a thin line of blood trickled down his throat.

"You bastard!" Galahad yelled at him. "Let my son go!"

"Kill the boy, and you will not get out of here alive,"
Kay growled through clenched teeth, the Baron holding his
hair pulling tighter.

"I will give you five seconds to tell me where Arthur
Pendragon is hiding," Jackseye warned. "Five…"

Galahad thrashed desperately, Maria's stomach sinking.
"He's not serious?" she said in shock.

"Four…" Jackseye counted, the knife pressing on
Baeydn's neck.

"I don't think he's horsing around," Simon breathed, his
skin turning pale. The Barons were more cruel than Maria
realised.

"Three…"

"Leave him be!" Bedivere snapped. "He's just a child!"

"Two…"

Maria flicked her eyes to Edward, the Baron's eyes
alarmed as if he didn't anticipate this.

Jackseye grinned maliciously at Galahad and raised his
wrist higher. "One," he purred, angling his arm.

"Alright! Alright!" Galahad shouted, his voice echoing
around the tunnel. "I'll tell you where he is, just let the boy
go…. please," he pleaded, a tear streaming down his face.

Jackseye's arm paused, a brow raised in interest.
Baeydn sobbed quietly beneath the knife, watching his
father with frightened eyes. Maria watched shakily. *No,
Galahad!*

"Arthur went with a group of Rebels to Camelot in
carriages," Galahad admitted, looking down in shame.
"They left at first light. They should be back by the
afternoon."

Jackseye grinned, his hand still not shifting from
Baeydn's throat. "Anything else?" he asked lightly.

Galahad shook his head. "That's all, I swear," he said
with a strained voice. "Please, just give Baeydn back."

Jackseye looked at him contemplatively, his eyes cruel. "And if I don't?" he pondered, his finger shifting on the blade.

"You have to kill me as well," Galahad growled, glaring at Jackseye.

"Rohin," Edward said quietly, his voice somewhat defiant. "Let the boy go."

Jackseye flicked his eyes to Edward, his glare sharp. Edward's face remained impassive, his stare unwavering. His hand hovered over a dagger on his thigh, Maria watching the Baron's muscles bunch in anticipation. Tension hovered in the air, thicker than glue.

Jackseye clenched his jaw, narrowed his eyes at his son, and leaned down to Baeydn's ear, turning his burning eye to Galahad. "Give your father a hug," he purred into his ear, lowering the knife and shoving the lad towards Galahad.

Baeydn yelped as he stumbled, landing in front of Galahad with a thud. The Barons holding Galahad let him go, and he grabbed his son off the ground, holding him tightly to his chest, tears falling down his face. Baeydn shook violently in his arms with frightened sobs, burying his face into his shoulder. Maria breathed a small sigh of relief.

"Oh, my son, my boy," Galahad cried, his heart pounding. "You're okay, you're okay."

Jackseye stood from the ground and sheathed his knife back into its mechanism, smirking at the Rebels' shell-shocked expressions. "Right, then," he clapped his hands together. "Now that *that's* settled, how about a game of who can run the furthest?"

"Don't you play your tricks on them," Gawain snapped fiercely, fighting the Barons holding him. "Do you want to end up like Voss?"

*Voss? What happened to Voss?* Maria glanced between the two men.

"Voss was weak," Jackseye growled. "And his death was… uneventful."

"Considering he knew how to fight to the death better than you, I'd rank him higher than you," Gawain barked.

"After years of training with the Barons, I don't think you'd stand a chance," Jackseye smirked.

"Have you found his carcass yet? I made sure it was decorated especially for your eyes," Gawain growled.

"No," Jackseye said flatly. "And nor do I care." Jackseye walked over to the cave's entrance and looked at Edward sharply. "Enjoy your pitiful cavern. It won't be here for long."

Edward followed after him with a purposeful delay, looking at Galahad and Baeydn on the ground with a clenched jaw. There was something odd about that Baron, Maria knew. *The son of a Muharí doesn't act like that.*

"I hope you like sleeping with worms, Rohin," Kay spat at his feet as he walked past. "Because that's where you're going." The Barons holding him smacked him across the face hard enough to topple him to the ground. Jackseye just smirked as he and his son left the cave, the Barons shifting around the cave on a silent command as they started to let people go. Maria shared a worried look with Simon. *This isn't going to end well.*

<h1 style="text-align:center">*Chapter 23: Allies & Enemies*</h1>

The tunnel North was more rank than Arthur remembered. *Something had most definitely died down here.* The harsh smell of rotted meat and the scent of unwashed body odour from the people following behind him made him wish there were air vents, but to his disappointment, there was none to be found. Arthur glanced over his shoulder at the following group, their worried faces catching the light of the torch. Distressed about what was going to happen once they exited the tunnels, no doubt.

A cat followed behind his trail alongside Laruen, Sariel's fluffy exterior damp in the humidity and puddles of the tunnel floor. She hadn't gotten her shifting ability from her father, so there was only one option left to ponder over. Laruen stared flatly at him with eyes green as spring leaves.

"Do you even know where you're going?" Owen questioned, continuing to doubt Arthur.

Arthur sighed and glared at him. "I can remember these tunnels inside-out, backwards and upside down."

"If you think you can do a better job, Owen," Lucy said, "Then please lead the way."

"We've been walking for over two hours," Owen scowled.

"One, that's an over-exaggeration," Arthur scowled back. "And two, if you feel you can navigate yourself through these tunnels, then go ahead, be my guest."

"Smartass," Owen muttered to himself. Lucy looked at him and signed something particularly vulgar at him. Owen frowned, shaking his head at her.

The trapdoors overhead became more frequent, some older than others and muffling the sound of footsteps and street chatter. Light peered through from above and led the way around a bend, the tunnel falling dark.

Arthur held his torch higher to watch the roof, looking for anything shiny. The rock of the tunnel made the torchlight seep into it like a dampened blanket, almost muting the torch entirely.

The rocks were different under the training hall, and Arthur didn't really know why. The reasons he narrowed it down to were structural or mute magic. Either way, it didn't help his vision.

*There.* The glint of the metal latch for the trapdoor shone dimly. Arthur reached his hand up and flicked it over, shoving the trapdoor slightly upwards to fly back into the wall with a clatter. Arthur peeked his head out of the trapdoor and scanned his surroundings, looking in every direction. Scattered glass littered the floor from the cabinetry along the walls, the windows cracked and broken. The furniture was strewn about the room haphazardly, bits of splintered wood stirring in the whoosh of the door.

"Anything up there?" Lucy asked.

"Nothing," Arthur said. He looked back down and scanned the wall for a sconce, slotting the half-dead torch in it to sputter out. "Be careful, though; there's stuff everywhere on the floor."

"I wouldn't doubt it," Erin said, moving towards the front of the group beside Arthur. "Barons were tearing up the place when we were here before."

It would make sense for them to come here at first, Arthur supposed. "Alright, the weakest up first, the strongest help them from below with me, someone go up top to pull them through," he said.

Owen sighed and shoved his way through the crowd of refugees, climbing the inlaid ladder. The scattering sound of moving glass echoed overhead as Owen brushed it away from the entrance with his boot. Owen looked around the hallway, making sure they were clear before giving them a thumbs up.

"We're clear," he said, looking down the hole. "Start sending them up."

Arthur nodded at him, turning back to the refugees. "Any volunteers?"

"I'm staying down here to help," Laruen said, standing opposite Arthur.

Arthur turned to Lucy and tilted his head towards the inlaid ladder. "You're first."

"Easy," she said, slotting her foot into the inlay and pushing herself up through the trap door. An older man followed after her lead, just managing to pull himself up on his own.

"Come on, Erin," Laruen said to the woman. "You're up."

Erin nodded and moved to the trap door, slotting her foot into the wall. Laruen grabbed her other foot and pushed her up, straining against the pain in her arm as the older woman went inside the room.

Arthur looked towards the group and spotted a younger girl. "Your turn," he smiled warmly. She walked up warily and looked at the trapdoor entrance, frowning.

"Just push with your legs. Owen will pull you up," Arthur said to her. She glanced at him for a moment before she started to climb, Owen leaning over and grabbing her outstretched hand to pull her up inside the room. Arthur looked at Laruen and nodded at her.

"You go," he said. "I've got the others."

Laruen nodded shallowly and picked up Sariel, placing her inside the room gently before jumping up into the room in one swift movement.

Arthur glanced at the remaining refugees and nodded towards a girl in her late teens. "You're up."

She smiled slightly and moved towards the ladder, pulling herself up onto the edge, gasping a bit as her fingers slipped. Owen grabbed her wrists and pulled her up with a groan. Arthur turned to the next refugee and nodded for them to go up.

The lad hesitated, uncertainty on his face as he peered up at the hole. "Is that really the best thing to, I don't know, try and climb through?" he asked nervously. "What if I slip?"

"I'm right beneath you to catch you," Arthur reassured warmly.

The lad quirked his mouth and moved beneath the hatch hesitantly, looking at the holes in the wall. "That's probably not safe," he muttered.

"What's your name, kid?" Arthur asked, crouching down to him.

He looked at Arthur with a raised brow. "Kid? I'm nineteen," he said.

Arthur blinked, looking at him. His face was chubby at the edges still, his long brown hair curly and tufted up around his head impish-like. And he only stood to Arthur's torso. *Is this kid really nineteen?*

"Right, my apologies," Arthur cleared his throat. "What's your name?"

"Tyler," he said quietly, averting his eyes.

"Tyler," Arthur nodded. "Everyone else got up there alright, you'll be just fine. I'm sure you're strong enough to make it up. Even if you do fall, you'll find a way to lift yourself back up."

Tyler flicked his eyes to Arthur with a small smile, looking back at the wall and sliding his foot into the first divot. Owen looked flatly down at them in boredom.

"Do you have any patience, Owen?" Arthur asked with a frown.

"What's taking so long?" Owen sighed, reaching an arm down to the boy.

"Tyler needed encouragement," Arthur said, making sure everyone was out of the tunnel.

Tyler got halfway up and then stopped to look down, his eyes wide at the distance. Owen sighed and reached down beneath his armpits and yanked him up, Tyler yelping in fright. Arthur looked up and began to climb, making his way out of the tunnels without an issue.

Arthur grabbed hold of the trapdoor handles and shut it with a slide of the lock, placing a few crates and trash on top to hide it. Sariel sat beside the tunnel entrance, looking up at him with a purr.

Arthur turned back to the refugees gathered in the room. "Stay close," he said. "And dodge the debris."

"Gods, there's more glass than the last time," Tyler muttered to himself, moving away from the piles on the floors.

"Where to now?" Owen asked, frowning at Arthur.

"Now we get you all onto the carriage and take you to the safe place," Arthur answered, looking back at him.

"Carriages? So, like horse-drawn carriages? Full of crates and things?" Tyler asked him.

Arthur nodded. "That's right."

The boy looked down a bit. "I don't like horses," he said quietly. "They're weird and big."

"We'll leave you here with the Barons then," Owen rolled his eyes.

"What is the Barons' deal, anyway? They just sprung onto the crowd for no reason," Tyler said with a confused face. "I thought this was a market Kingdom, not a war zone?"

"The Barons are heartless assassins filled with nothing but torture and agony," Arthur frowned. "They've turned Camelot into their playground and the people their toys."

"Huh," Tyler muttered. "Sounds similar to what happened beforehand." He closed his mouth then, and Laruen threw him a sharp look.

Lucy blinked at Tyler. "Beforehand?" she asked.

"Nothing, don't worry," Tyler said quickly, withering under Laruen's glare.

"Lucy, come with me," Arthur said. "The rest of you just relax."

Lucy stepped over to Arthur, following him as he led the way through the training hall. Arthur walked down the hallway, heading straight through the main entrance.

"Gods almighty," Lucy murmured to herself at the destruction around her. Blood trails dragged around the floors through the glass, and crimson was splattered on the walls like flicked paint. But no bodies were around to be seen.

Arthur opened the main door and pushed it to get it open. The hinges creaked, and the door rattled, the bottom dragging across the floor to a stop. He wandered outside and looked around for the carriages.

The world went suddenly dark as something covered his eyes, and he spooked, spinning around and grabbing an arm tightly. Lucy gasped and squeaked, and Arthur pulled back his hood slightly, looking at the spooked girl.

"Sorry," she said, flushing red. "Your hood was down, and I just thought to grab it for you."

Arthur let go of her arm, and she took it back, rubbing it tenderly. "Sorry," he said. "Next time, just give us a heads up."

She smiled back nervously and peered behind him, moving to walk further down the alleyway. "I can hear a market," she said, stopping at the corner and looking around.

"They should be here by now," Arthur scowled, looking around for the carriages.

"There's carriages down there," she said, looking back at him and pointing down towards the alleyway. Arthur flicked his eyes to her and walked over to the young girl.

Down the alleyway, a carriage sat with its doors open, a few of the Rebels pulling crates down and stacking more up inside. They were throughout the small crowd, mingling with the vendors and the citizens.

"Gather everyone up," Arthur said to Lucy. "The cart to the right is the one you want."

"Okay," she nodded, turning and heading back inside the hall quickly.

Arthur jogged over to the carriages cautiously, keeping an eye out for a flicker of a black hood. No Barons were around to be seen.

*That's a first. They're probably* still *trying to find me in the East.*

The Rebels standing around looked dismissively at Arthur, acting as if he were a stranger. All a part of their act, still throwing off any onlookers. Arthur walked around the back of the carriage, squeezing between the wall and the cart before popping up onto the front. "Hannah."

The woman nearly jumped out of her skin, yelping in fright as her food went flying through the air. She turned to Arthur with a frightened look, putting a hand on her head. "By the Gods," she cursed. "Don't *do* that!"

"Not the welcome I was after, but alas," Arthur said with a smirk. "I hope you have enough room in these carriages for more travellers."

"More? Who have you found?" she asked him, brushing the food off her clothes with a disgusted face.

"Refugees from one of the safe houses," Arthur looked back at her. "They've been in hiding for over a month, and they're important people, too."

"I dunno, Gawain is particular about who gets sent to Reigate," she hummed.

"One of the refugees is Samqueel's mother," Arthur told her, moving stuff around for them to sit down.

"Be careful you don't stack things too far apart. They can topple pretty easily," she said, pulling herself over the seat and turning around to enter the inside of the carriage, hopping over to the nearest box. "Watermelons are heavier than people believe."

"They'll be fine," Arthur shrugged off, looking out towards Lucy. "Lucy, start bringing them out."

"They're already coming," she said, climbing up into the carriage. "Laruen is watching for Barons."

Arthur nodded at her. "Make sure they all get aboard," he said, jumping back off the carriage.

"Don't go too far, Benjamin," Hannah called to him.

Arthur looked at her, his brow raised. "You think I'm going to wander off?"

"Better to be close by," she shrugged. "Might need you to help out with stock in a moment."

Lucy looked between the two in confusion, her face starkly blank. Arthur shook his head amusedly, jogging back inside the training hall. He nearly barreled into Tyler around the corner, the young boy moving around at the last moment with a "Woah! Sorry."

"Everyone else following?" Arthur asked, holding him by the shoulders.

Tyler watched his hands with wide eyes, shrinking down a bit. "Yeah, slowly," he squeaked.

Arthur nodded and patted his shoulder. "Head to the middle carriage," he said. "Lucy is waiting for you inside."

"Okay," he said quickly and shuffled around the corner to the carriage.

Arthur watched as Tyler made his way to the carriage, giving him a slight smirk. *Good kid.* More of the refugees passed by him after Tyler, boarding the carriage. Erin smiled faintly at him as she passed by, Arthur smiling back with a gentle nod.

"Right," Owen said from around the corner. "They're all in the wooden death box, now where?" He folded his arms and scowled at Arthur. "And don't just say 'a safe place'."

"You seem like you have an issue with me," Arthur assumed, looking at him in question.

"I have an issue with anyone who decides to leave behind people in need," he spat. "I don't care if you were caught up in some framing job."

"You really think I wanted to or chose to flee?" Arthur interrupted, frowning at him.

"You did choose to flee because you *left*," Owen growled.

"Owen, I've known you for a month, and I think it's safe to say," Laruen spoke from behind him, "that you're an opinionated little prick that doesn't sympathise with people with problems bigger than your own. Put yourself in his shoes. Pretend your sister shoved you out to the streets to die. How would that feel?"

"She wouldn't survive three minutes without me," Owen spat at her.

"Sit your ego aside for once," Laruen snapped. "Your sister is stronger than you. You rule with arrogance, not smarts. If you want to see what your sister can really do within three minutes, have a look at the carriage."

Owen raised a brow at her, then peeked around the corner towards the carriages. The refugees were loaded neatly inside the carriage, the stacks of crates arranged in files for them to sit both on and beside.

"She's a people person, and people like her. People do not like you," Laruen sniffed and glanced at Arthur. Her eyes seemed to say, "I've had enough of this kid's crap."

Arthur nodded at her in respect, giving her a slight grin. Owen scowled at her and walked out towards the carriage.

"Look, he shut up," Laruen huffed, a look of mock surprise on her face.

"Thank you," Arthur said.

"He's been a misogynistic trash pile for a while," she dismissed.

"I mean for helping me. I couldn't have done this without you and Lucy."

Laruen nodded and picked up Sariel from the cobblestones, the kitten squeaking. "I will see the carriage out of here, then we will leave Camelot."

"There's a place for you at Reigate," Arthur offered. "You don't have to search all your life for a haven. You shouldn't have to."

Laruen's mouth quirked slightly. "It's pretty obvious that my kind does not belong here," she said. "It was a miracle I stayed hidden for as long as I have. Your King-Ergott," she corrected, "is not fond of us, nor has any of your bloodline been. Maybe one day, when the racial divide is settled, but not now. I no longer have a reason to stay."

Arthur nodded at her reasoning. "Come back here when I'm the King. All races will be welcome, and I won't allow you both to live without a roof over your heads."

Sariel looked wide-eyed between them, wriggling in her mother's hold. Laruen hushed her quietly, petting her fur. "Silence, child," she said quietly. "I know you don't."

"I can give you both a place in the castle," Arthur said.

"I do not belong in a castle," Laruen shook her head. "That was Sam's dream. I do not wish to be surrounded by stone walls." She hissed slightly as the kitten bit her fingers.

"Will you return to Camelot once Ergott has fled?" Arthur asked hopefully.

"We shall see," Laruen said and held Sariel up to her face. "What? What do you want?" The kitten meowed loudly at her mother, clawing her fingers hard enough to draw blood. Laruen's hand moulded over into the shape of a lion's paw. "Stop it," she glared at the kitten.

Sariel hissed and wriggled free, falling towards the ground with a flash of white light. The girl hit the stones roughly and rolled onto her knees, glaring at her mother. "I don't want to go to the Marshlands," she cried, "The others scare me."

"You cannot stay here alone," Laruen frowned. "You are but a child in a land of dangerous games."

"I want to go with him," Sariel pointed to Arthur. Laruen flicked her eyes to Arthur. Arthur glanced down at Sariel, then looked over to Laruen. *What?*

"He knew Father," Sariel said, holding her shoulder. "He understood. Some people like me back at the cave. People hate me in the forest for who I am."

"They can deal with the fact you're a half-caste," Laruen spat. "There's more of them than just you that live there."

"They hate them, too," she protested. "I want to be with the humans. Please," she begged, looking up at her mother desperately.

Laruen's hand shifted back to its slim normality, her eyes like jade fire. Arthur watched the emotions flicker over her face: anger, grief, longing, frustration and finally, acceptance. She turned her gaze to him, fixing him in place at the intensity of her stare. "It is true that the elves back in the woods are cruel to humans and half-castes," she admitted. "The world is a different place around them. They prefer tradition over modernity. I hate to think of a world that includes both her living there with me and a world where she isn't there."

"You're not the first elf I've interacted with," Arthur said. "But in my honest opinion, you're not half bad."

"You don't want to meet the worst ones," she shook her head. "I was shown that some humans are not ruthless like those of the fathers that took our land to build this Kingdom upon. Others refuse to believe there is any good with your kind." Her jaw clenched. "I do not wish to lose my daughter to prejudiced elders who will shun not only me but the family I have gotten myself involved with. Erin and Samqueel have done everything for me. I trust them. And now, I'll have to trust you."

Sariel's eyes widened in shock. She clearly wasn't expecting her mother to let her go.

"I swear on my life, I will protect your daughter," Arthur said. "Even if it means putting my own life on the line. Samqueel did a lot for me, and now it's time I returned the favour."

"I expect big things from you, Pendragon," Laruen said. "Do not allow yourself to let yourself down. I may not care for politics, but I see you can be better than the brat on the throne currently."

"Yes, ma'am," Arthur nodded at her. "You have my word."

Sariel stood up from the ground, standing in front of her mother. Laruen looked down at her and threaded her fingers through her hair gently. Arthur looked down at Sariel with a slight grin, placing his hand on her shoulder gently.

"You'll be fine in Reigate," he said warmly.

She looked at him for a moment and turned to Laruen, burying her face into her leg and wrapping her arms around her. Laruen smiled slightly at her and tapped her back. "Go on, child. You will be okay."

"I'll miss you," Sariel whimpered, letting her mother go.

"You will see me again when the moon and the nightmares set and the sun and the warmth rise high over the horizon," she smiled. "Let the sun guide you, my girl."

Arthur smiled at the two, watching the exchange between the both of them. Laruen petted her hair softly and rumbled - no, *purred* - at her, looking at Arthur.

"Where will you go?" Arthur asked curiously.

"Home," she answered. "Where I belong." She turned Sariel towards Arthur gently and prodded her on. "Go. Before the carriage leaves."

Arthur reached his hand out to her with a warming smile, nodding over to the carriage. Sariel glanced back at

her mother a moment and took Arthur's hand, her small
chest heaving great breaths. The both of them walked over
to the carriage, Arthur rubbing her back gently.

"You'll be safe with us," he reassured her. "I won't let
anything happen to you."

Lucy poked her head out of the carriage, looking at
them with slight confusion. "Laruen?" she asked, looking
behind them.

"Laruen isn't coming," Arthur said, lifting Sariel onto
the back of the carriage. "I'll do one final look before I
jump on."

Lucy bent down to Sariel's eye level, compassion on
her face at the anxious child. "Aw, you'll be okay," she said
to her. "We'll take care of you." She wiped away the tears
that spilled over, Sariel looking back over Arthur's shoulder
to find nothing standing there anymore.

"Tell Hannah to wait for five," Arthur said, walking
away from the carriage.

"Will do," Lucy nodded. "Be careful."

"I'm always careful," Arthur reassured, tapping the side
of the carriage before moving back away from the door,
Lucy pulling it halfway shut. The Rebels remaining in the
street were already packed in their carriages, the street bare
of people other than packing up vendors. *It must be three
o'clock.* Generally, at that time, the vendors traded their
morning spots over to the afternoon vendors who sold
different products that catered more for the nightlife than
the average morning market.

Arthur followed the alleyway down further, peering
down alleyways with his hood up. Everything was quiet,
surprisingly. *Escaping this time around will be easier than I
initially guessed.*

He turned down an alleyway corner to check a tunnel
trapdoor, fixing up a plank that moved out of place. But
what he didn't do was look up as something barreled down
on his shoulders, a great force shoving him into the wall

with a crack. Arthur cried out as something blacked out his vision, the air becoming stuffy as it surrounded his head. Strong hands gripped him against the wall, the planks beneath his feet scattering as he kicked at his attackers, the wood clattering down the alleyway loudly.

*What in the name of the Gods?!* He cried out and flailed, a hand clamping the potato sack against his mouth, silencing him as pain shot through his stomach at a harsh blow, doubling him over with a whoosh of air before something smacked into the side of his head, the world going numb and dark as he fell.

"Where the Hell is Pendragon?" Owen asked with impatience.

Lucy rolled her eyes at her brother's insistence. "Gone to shop for onions," she said sarcastically. "Where do you think, genius? He's doing rounds." Lucy didn't think it was an excellent idea for him to do so, but what could it hurt?

"He better hurry up," Owen growled.

"Or you'll do what, cupcake?" one of the Rebels jousted. "Cry?"

"I'll beat his ass for, one, leaving us *again* and, two, wasting our time," Owen said with a scowl.

"Let me stop you right there, sunshine," the Rebel said with a raised hand. "If you hurt Arthur, I'm afraid we will have to report it back to the authorities, and the authorities consist of a man that's well versed in kicking ass that will most certainly kick your ass for kicking royal ass, which will also get *our* asses kicked. We don't want that. Two, sure, he can be a smart mouth who can waste time, but I'd rather listen to him than you."

"And who are you?" Owen asked.

"Eylan Muyta," he said. "And you?"

"Owen Lucan."

"What's so special about you for Arthur to smuggle you in here?"

Lucy snorted. "Certainly not his ability to think or lead," she said.

"I lead these refugees to safety," Owen argued. "And I am a strong asset to the group."

"Don't listen to a word he says," Erin shook her head. "He just likes the sound of his voice."

"He'll fit in with Kyan," Eylan huffed, and a few of the Rebels laughed softly.

"Where is this guy?" Owen scowled, looking around for Arthur.

Lucy sighed, exasperated, and turned to her brother, raising her hands. {Can you shut up before someone here gets the urge to stab you?}

Owen scowled at her. [Fine]

"What was that?" Eylan mused.

Lucy turned to him. "Telling my brother to shut up," she shrugged.   {Should I go and check?}

[Make it quick]

{Don't let them go without me, please}

"That's a lot of hand movements to say shut up," Eylan smirked.

Lucy looked at him for a moment before she slipped out through the half-open door, closing it behind her softly. The muffled protests in the carriage became quickly distant as she jogged around the alleyways, peering around them.

*No sign of Arthur anywhere.* Worry coursed through her as she kept searching around, finding no trace of the prince.

*What was that name Hannah called him?* "Benjamin?" Lucy called out. "Are you around here?"

Nothing but the echo of her voice called back. "Oh Gods, where are you?" she mumbled to herself, walking further. "Benjamin!"

She paused to listen, the tap of marching boots on cobblestone making her heart jump as Barons rounded the corner, and she quickly turned around to flee back down the alleyway. *Arthur, where in the Gods' names did you go?*

She ran back to the carriage, the call of the Barons' voices sending her faster. Boots echoed after her, and she yelped, sprinting to the carriage. She flung open the door and jumped in, pulling it shut behind her with a speed she didn't know she had. "Go," she said.

"Go? What about-" Eylan frowned.

"Go! There's Barons coming!" Lucy barked, and Hannah deftly flicked the reins, the carriage wheeling down the street away from the Barons.

"So where's Arthur?" a small voice asked from beside a crate, Sariel staring up at Lucy. The whole carriage was staring at Lucy expectantly, her anxiety rising at their stares. *What are they going to think? They're going to blame me for leaving him behind, and it'll be my fault-*

Owen looked over at her, leaning forward in his seat. "What happened out there, Lucy?"

Lucy sat against the door, puffing too fast to be catching her breath. Her hands flew to her face, brushing back the hair strands behind her ears nervously. *They're going to hate me; they already hate me-*

"Lucy," Owen asked, looking at her in worry, seeing the stress clear as day on her face. "Where is Arthur?"

"I don't know!" she blurted, looking at her brother with wide eyes. "He wasn't out there, I-I couldn't find him, he wasn't there," she stammered, covering her face.

"The Barons got him," Owen sighed, shaking his head.

"I know it's my fault; I let him go; I should've said something. I thought he would be fine, but now he's gone-"

"Lucy, it's not on you," Owen said, placing a hand on her shoulder. "Arthur made his choice, and now we need to report it back to the higher-ups." He threw Eylan a look.

Eylan sighed. "We're going to die," he muttered.

Lucy felt tears prick her eyes, ducking her head into her knees. *Gods damn it, Lucinda, you messed up again.* She could feel the daggers being thrown her way from the glares of the Rebels, her skin on fire from their stares. *Can never get anything right.*

Something shifted on the floorboards, and Lucy turned her head to look, her vision blurred. Owen shuffled closer towards Lucy and wrapped his arm around her. "It's not your fault," he said quietly.

"It feels like it is," she muttered, turning her head back to rest on her leg.

"We're going to get him back," Eylan said to them. "We'll report to Gawain when we get back."

Anxiety spiked through her, her hands balling into fists. Gawain would kill her for this. He was ruthless enough to the trainees to make a statement not to mess around with him; Lucy could only imagine what his reaction would be when he found out she was the last person to see Arthur. She didn't like imagining it.

"Hannah," Eylan called out to her. "Let's move on."

"Working on it," she called from the front, the carriage bumping along the path at a high speed.

Owen held Lucy to him, rubbing her shoulder in comfort. It was rare for her brother to be so caring, and it usually didn't last long. Lucy leaned against him, sniffling with her head on his shoulder.

"Hold on to your hats!" Hannah called from the front, and the carriage jolted violently as the wheels hit something large. The Rebels exclaimed in fright as the crates started shifting down and around, one spilling over to land on top of Eylan's leg. He barked in pain as it landed and shoved it off, cursing. "What the Hell was that?" he called to the front.

"I dunno, probably a Baron," Hannah laughed, a dark shadow flitting overhead as they passed through the Southern Gate.

A small flash of light brightened the cabin a moment before Sariel ran to Lucy, the kitten clawing up onto her lap in fright. Lucy grabbed her and sat her properly, petting her fur. "You'll be okay."

*I don't know about me, though.*

The gravel under the carriage crumbled below the wheels, scattering away from the pathway. The cabin swayed at the sudden change of stability of the Earth, Lucy looking up tiredly from her resting place on her brother's shoulder. *I fell asleep?*

Owen stared out the front, trying to see exactly where the carriage was heading. Lucy rubbed her eyes before following his gaze; dim afternoon light from the sun made the winter trees turn red, the forest around them thinning out the further they went on the gravel road.

Lucy sat up, wary of the kitten still on her stomach. She peered out the window to her right and saw an entrance to a massive cave, decorative sandstone slabs paving the gravel path to the gaping mouth like a civilised establishment. It was naturally beautiful, with a courtyard out the front filled with people, fresh grass and cut shrubs and flowers around the edges.

"Is this..?" Owen asked, looking over to Eylan.

"Welcome to the Reigate Caves," Eylan nodded, looking out towards the entrance.

Lucy looked at the people and felt off. They didn't look happy to see the carriages. In fact, their weapons were at the ready in their hands as if expecting an attack. At the entrance, a band of men stood watching the carriages, their bodies tense. Lucy looked at Owen.

{This doesn't feel right}

Owen glanced over to Eylan with a glare. "Is this your way of welcoming people?" he asked.

"Not usually," Eylan mumbled, looking out the window in confusion. He moved towards the front of the carriage, slipping through the gap between the driver's seat and the roof, jumping off the carriage and walking beside it with a shake of his sore leg.

"Where is he going?" The boy, Tyler, asked from the corner confusedly, moving to watch outside the window.

Owen watched Eylan carefully, glaring up at the men and their weapons. The carriage pulled to an eventual stop at the mouth of the cave, the door unlocking and sliding open. Lucy stood up and faced the door, a Rebel holding it open for them to flow through. She glanced at Owen for a moment before jumping out, her feet crunching the gravel beneath them loudly. More followed after her, refugees and Rebels alike standing on the courtyard grass, watching each other curiously. Lucy looked towards the men gathered at the cave and watched one approach the carriage.

"Good to see you're in one piece," Geraint said to Hannah, walking up to the carriage.

"I wouldn't say that," Hannah mumbled, smiling faintly at him and shifting to sit on the edge.

"Touchè," Geraint nodded at her.

"We've got a bigger problem than what you're thinking of," Hannah said quietly to him.

"We had the Barons raid the caves while you were gone," Geraint said, leading the carriage over to the loading bay. "A whole group of them. They threatened to kill Baeydn if Galahad didn't tell them where Arthur was."

Hannah looked at him speechless, her eyes wide. "W-what?" she stuttered, going pale.

"What was your problem?" Geraint asked curiously.

Gawain's hulking figure stormed out from inside the cave, making a beeline for the carriage. Lucy's stomach sank; *this won't go down well.*

"Where is he?" Gawain asked, looking around at the gathered Rebels for the familiar blonde head. "Tell me no one lost his royal ass."

Hannah shrunk back a bit, avoiding his gaze. Eylan stood beside the carriage, looking up at Gawain with a nervous glint in his eye. "You see, we *had* him," he started.

Gawain turned to him, his glare like a brand of death. "What do you mean, *had*?" he barked. "So you *did* lose him?"

The gathered Rebels all averted their eyes, a few turning pale at his outrage. Lucy wanted to shrink into a tiny ball and roll away.

"They're back," Lancelot called from behind them, walking up beside Gawain.

Gawain spun around to face him, the rage on his face like fire. "What did I say? They damn well *lost* him, Rodney," he growled.

"Lost who?" Lancelot asked, looking at the others around them. The refugees stared at the Knights in fear and awe.

"Who else would I be talking about other than Arthur? Do you see him standing around anywhere?" Gawain snapped, waving his hand to the group.

Lancelot flicked his eyes over to Eylan. "What happened?"

"He went to check something, apparently, and didn't come back," he said with fake confidence, glancing at Lucy.

Lancelot glanced at Gawain, folding his arms. "The Barons got him."

"Yeah, and guess who has to go and get him now," Gawain growled in frustration. "First, the Barons mess up the caves, and now they get what they want. The stupid lad shouldn't have left. I told the both of you, but neither of you would listen! Stupid young tool!"

"You shouldn't be mad at Arthur, Jonathan. He wouldn't have meant to get caught," Lancelot narrowed his eyes on him. "And you watch who you're speaking about. That is your King you're calling a stupid tool."

"He's not the King yet," he snapped. "And he might never be now that Ergott's got him. He's not safe as long as he's at that bastardly castle. *What* did he think he was *doing*?"

From behind Lancelot, the other Knights walked over, overhearing the conversation. Lancelot glanced at them for a moment before turning back to Gawain. "Have you given up on the boy?"

"I've given up on his common sense," Gawain growled, pinching the bridge of his nose.

"Then you've broken Benjamin's promise, haven't you?" Lancelot said quietly to him.

Gawain turned furious eyes on him. "If somebody had said to the fool he was too in over his head to be doing a stunt like that, he wouldn't be stuck in Baron land, now would he?" he sniped.

"He would've gotten taken by Jackseye if he was here anyway, Jonathan," Lancelot protested.

Gawain growled and turned to look at the Rebels angrily. "Who did it?" he barked at them. "Who let him go?"

The Rebels looked at him frozen, some flicking their eyes amongst themselves. Lucy crumbled on the inside, the blood draining from her face.

"Why does it matter who?" Bedivere muttered, rubbing at a sore spot on his face.

"They did their best, Gawain," Percival groaned, rubbing his left shoulder.

"Well?" Gawain growled, ignoring them. Eylan flicked his eyes to Lucy again, and she finally felt the tether inside her snap, her legs giving out beneath her as the weight of her guilt crushed her to the gravel. Hot tears fell over her cheeks in waves, and she covered her mouth to keep from sobbing aloud.

Lancelot glanced over to her, his eyes widening in shock. "Miss, are you alright?"

"I'm sorry, I'm sorry, I'm sorry," she sobbed, her body trembling.

"What are you sorry for?" Lancelot asked, kneeling beside her and rubbing her back gently.

"I let Arthur go," she admitted. "I let him check around for Barons. I thought he would be fine and that he wouldn't be long, but I couldn't find him when I went out to look for him-"

"Just slow down, take deep breaths," Lancelot said warmly. "Did you see the Barons take him?"

Lucy took a shaky breath and looked at him, pushing her hair back. "I didn't see him at all. I got chased back to the carriage by a patrol and told Hannah to go," she sobbed. "I'm so sorry."

Lancelot looked back up at Gawain. "Arthur is in trouble."

"You don't say," Gawain said sarcastically, looking at Lucy.

"How about some compassion and sympathy for once, Jonathan?" Lancelot growled at him. "One of the reasons why Arthur wanted to go is because you weren't even giving him what he needed. You were just a commanding figure that bossed him around because you were entitled to."

"He didn't *need* the skills at that point in time. He *wanted* the skills," Gawain growled. "He doesn't need to be coddled like a toddler. That's not my job. I'm not his daddy, and I'm not here to treat him like he's made out of glass."

"Benjamin told you to watch out for Arthur and protect him, yet here you are telling me that he's a failure and a fool for wanting to take back what is rightfully his."

"I tried to protect him. I warned you not to send him, and now look what's happened," he snapped.

"The boy had every right to see what was happening in *his* Kingdom," Lancelot argued.

"That argument is the same reason the other half of the Roundtable *died*," he roared, glaring at Lancelot. "Pelleas knew it too and still went with your plan, and look where it sat him - three feet under ashes with nothing but bones left!"

"Do *not* bring them into this!" Lancelot snapped at him.

"Too late," Gawain spat. "Their burnt corpses speak for themselves of how good your leadership is."

"Enough!" Galahad shouted at the both of them, walking up to them. "You both are wasting your time arguing instead of doing something about it."

Gawain turned his gaze on him. "And I suppose *you* have a plan?" he spat. "You spill the beans to save a life and now you're the mastermind?"

Galahad folded his arms and nodded lightly. "I have somewhat of a plan if you're willing to hear it. And for the record, if you had a son, you would've done the same thing."

"Families are a tool to use against people. You saw that in there yourself. Everyone in there did. Jackseye is a bastard for knowing how to do that."

"Gawain, just shut your Gods damned mouth for once and listen," Percival scowled at him, rolling his eyes.

"Keep your shit together long enough to figure out a way to kick Baron ass, and *then* you can figure out a way to tell Arthur not to do that again," Kay said, standing beside Geraint. "You've got enough of that attitude to fight; you can use it against them instead of us. We've had enough."

"Kay has a good point," Gaheris nodded. "Your anger should be used upon the Barons, not your allies."

"We need to get Arthur back," Geraint said, looking around each of the Knights. "It's what we would do for Ben."

Gawain looked around at each of them, his jaw clenched as he heaved a great sigh. He placed a hand on his head and leaned into it, the frustration roiling off him in waves. "I don't know why nobody listens to me in the first instance," he muttered.

"Because you're too strict," Percival said, smirking at him lightly.

Gawain looked up at him flatly. "It is my job to be strict. You may not *like* it, but that's how it is. It got you all this far, and it's worked for everyone else. You lot just piss me off more."

"But you still love us," Percival grinned.

"'Love' is a high overstatement. 'Tolerate' would be a better word. You're all tools."

"So what are we going to do?" Bedivere asked. "Are we saving the fool from the castle?"

"No, we're just going to leave him there to rot, Ryan," Kay snorted.

"Wasn't talking to you, drunkard," Bedivere sniped at him.

"Shut your gob before I flatten it."

"Make me," Bedivere said, turning to him. "I'd like to see you try."

Kay's hand balled in a fist, and Lancelot frowned. "You both are children," he sighed.

"This child can punch," Kay growled.

"Have a few more drinks before you fight. That'll get your endurance up," Bedivere smirked at him. Kay glared daggers at him, and Lucy watched as the muscles in his arm bunched, his fist lashing out at him in a blur. Bedivere barked at the impact on his arm, moving back away from him and holding his shoulder with a glower.

"Alright, since that's out of your system, get inside," Gawain said, frowning.

Percival glanced over at the both of them. "You two have issues."

"Don't pretend like you're innocent, Aaron," Kay said, walking towards the cave.

"Don't call me Aaron," Percival frowned, following him.

"What's that, Aaron?" Kay called back to him. "Go eat all the soup? Sure thing."

"I hate you," Percival sighed.

"Whatever."

Gawain looked at Lancelot for a moment, calmer than before. "We're figuring out a plan, but it's not just going to be *your* plan. I've been in Camelot the longest. Londinium is different from all those years ago. I want a say."

Lancelot looked over at Galahad. Galahad nodded at him. "I'm listening."

## *Chapter 24: Lesser Evil*

The stone floor was hard and cold underneath Arthur. A shiver slid along his body as he stirred awake, his head screaming at him. *Where am I?*

Arthur groaned as he got up slowly, his eyes opening and closing as he cleared his tired head, looking around his surroundings. His body felt like a carriage had run over it. A wind draft crept in from somewhere, sending goosebumps along his arms.

Everything was cast in a deep shadow, the only light coming from a vent high on the wall through the bars on the other side of the room. A pile of hay sat in the corner with a bucket, and that seemed about it. Arthur frowned. *The castle dungeons.*

"I must say," a familiar voice said coldly, "your efforts were impressive, besides getting yourself caught in the end."

Arthur glared to the right side of the bars, a silhouette sitting down on a wooden crate. Metal gleamed on the figure's head in the torchlight, the orange gems catching the fire spectacularly.

"I hope it was worth the risk," he said. "Helping those refugees out of Londinium to end up exactly where you don't want to be."

"You've ruined this place," Arthur growled. "How could you do this?"

"Everything you've seen is the result of collateral damage," Ergott dismissed. "They got in the way, they didn't obey, they suffered for it. They are slowly starting to learn."

"Why did you destroy this Kingdom?" Arthur asked, sitting himself up against the stone wall. "You spent so long pining for it just to let it crumble."

Ergott leaned forward onto his forearms, his eyes glowing that stark orange Arthur had seen so many times before in his dreams. "What's one Kingdom's destruction for the control of an entire realm? What does it matter if you ruin one thing when you've got everything?" he smirked. "Control of the people by force, starting with one Kingdom, will spread like a plague. It will overtake them all until there's no one left to oppose it."

"You have no idea what you're doing," Arthur growled. "Being a King doesn't involve terrorism."

"In order for people to respect you, you must make them fear you. If there is no fear, there is no obedience. The people do not matter as long as they obey. What matters is gaining the power to rule over everything in Braynor."

"Do you hear yourself?" Arthur asked, glaring at him. "Ruling with fear is just a way for you to gain more hatred from the people you rule over."

"The people are learning that obedience keeps them alive. As long as they don't stand in my way, they get to live their lives just fine. You, on the other hand," Ergott clenched his jaw, "are standing in my way. Your death would set my will for power free with no barriers."

"How could you? How could you dump me to die and blame me for your murders?" Arthur sniped, standing up from the ground. "I knew you were a manipulator, but I never thought you'd have the grit to betray your own family."

Ergott smirked at him, watching him rise. "Wouldn't you want to get rid of the problem that stopped you from getting what you wanted?" he asked. "Like how you fought to train with that sword, but they wouldn't let you? You disobeyed them to make your own rules. You decided your ideals were more important than theirs, didn't you?"

Arthur leaned his arms on the bars, placing his head on his forearms. "How do you know about that?" Arthur asked with creased brows.

Ergott chuckled darkly, his voice skittering off the walls. "The things you don't notice when you're not paying attention until it's right in front of your face," he laughed. "Did you ever wonder about that wolf in the woods? About whether you imagined that it stopped to grin at you? Whether your friend was attacked on purpose or not?"

Arthur stepped back from the bars in shock. *Did he order Tristan's attack?* Arthur's head spun with the impossibility of how the wolves connected with Ergott. *Could he shift?*

Ergott's eyes flared brighter as he grinned, his teeth sharp. "Family ties are one hell of a bond," he growled wryly.

"You're a bastard, Ergott," Arthur barked at him. "You're nothing but a false King, an usurper to Camelot."

"That may be true," Ergott shrugged, standing up from the wooden box. He stalked over to the bars, standing in front of them with his hands folded behind his back. "But look where we are right now, Arthur. You're in a cage, and I'm on a throne. You can bark all you want, but I've got you trapped beneath my claws, boy. And when you're finally disposed of this cursed land, there will be *nothing* left to stop me."

Arthur snarled at him. "You're wrong about that."

"Really? Take a look around. Your closest companions are the fleas in the hay in the corner. I have Barons guarding the castle at all hours and throughout Londinium at my beck and call."

"I have Knights," Arthur smirked at him. "Knights of the Roundtable."

"As I've heard," Ergott spat through the bars at his feet. "The Knights were supposed to die with your father, but it seems they've made a name for themselves more than what they did before."

"What do you mean, *supposed*?" Arthur glared at him.

Ergott's teeth bared in a grin. "Did you believe it was an accident that the forest on the edge of the Darklands was destroyed by fire like the rest of the hive minds?" he drawled. Arthur frowned at him, his jaw clenching tighter the longer he looked at his uncle.

Ergott moved closer to the bars, his eyes lit in delighted mischief. "The fires weren't just any match-lit wildfire, boy," he smirked, his hot breath washing over Arthur's face.

"How did you know this?" Arthur growled at him, moving up to the bars again.

"You're truly dumber than you seem," Ergott sniffed, looking to the side of the dungeon. "Normal fire doesn't burn an entire forest as savagely as black-"

A sudden hand gripped Ergott's shirt and tugged him forward sharply, Arthur bashing him against the iron bars as hard as he could. Heat flared like a brand along Arthur's hand, Ergott's body igniting with black flame. Arthur yelled in pain, flailing his hand around in the air like a madman. Arthur's arm was blotchy with already formed blisters, the skin a bright red. His arm hairs were singed off, replaced with waves of pain as air touched the sensitive skin.

Heat radiated off Ergott like a second sun, the flames disappearing with an audible whoosh of air. Ergott's skin cracked and glowed like burning coals, the light from the red-hot iron bars matching his eyes. "Never, *ever*, touch me again," Ergott roared. "The next time you do, I'll burn your whole Gods damned corpse to nothing but cinders!"

"Go to Hell," Arthur snarled at him. *His magic must be extraordinary. Where is he gaining it from?*

"You're already in it, Arthur," Ergott huffed, moving back away from the bars, his face swelling red. "Welcome to the rest of your pitiful life."

Arthur bashed his hand against the metal bar with a roar, the heat sizzling against his hand, too angered at Ergott to care about the sensation of his burning flesh.

Ergott smirked at Arthur, turning around and walking out of the dungeon hallway, shutting the door behind him. Arthur sighed and slid down against the bars, leaning his head back against them, ignoring the stark warmth biting his skin. He looked down at his hand, the red flesh on his forearm blistering quickly. If Ergott was right about him being here for a while, then it was going to get infected in a matter of days. *Just great.*

Never had Arthur wished for Ms Enid to come bail him out and help him or Aunt Guinevere to convince Ergott to let him be. He looked down. *Whatever even became of the old Maiden?*

Ergott marched up into the castle hallway from the dungeon staircase, passing by a few Black Cloaks guarding the passage to the dungeons. They regarded him with a nod, standing up straight from leaning against the walls.

*That fool doesn't know what will become of him.* His plan was falling perfectly into place now that that boy was in his claws. He smirked at his thought as he walked, reaching the main foyer near the High Gates. A few Maidens clean around the hall with Enid, the older woman cleaning the dust from the engravings on the pillars.

"That dust won't clean itself, Maiden," Ergott said, looming over her shoulder.

She jumped in fright, looking at him with wide eyes and a hand over her heart. "Sire, you frightened me half to death," she breathed, a few of the Maidens turning to look.

"Perhaps it would've been a favour to you," Ergott said coldly.

"Pardon?" she frowned.

"I'm sure you're not deaf," Ergott narrowed his eyes.

"With all due respect, Your Highness," she started. "If I were not here living in this castle, you and your guards would have empty stomachs and no clean laundry. I think it would disadvantage you greatly if I-"

"Speaking of empty stomachs," Ergott interrupted her. "Our new guest in the dungeons would be hungry. It wouldn't be a bad idea to feed them now, would it?"

The old Maiden lowered her cloth and sighed dismally. "Right away, sire," she muttered.

"You're a lucky woman, Enid," Ergott said coldly to her. "If you weren't doing anything for this castle, you wouldn't be living here. Consider yourself privileged."

Ms Enid frowned up at him and tucked the cloth into the front of her apron. "It's just your luck that I have nowhere else to go and that you're the King," she mumbled. "If anybody else acted this way towards me, I would've clipped their ears."

Ergott smirked at her lightly, then walked off to the Round Hall, his boots echoing through the foyer. Behind the door sat a hollow room, the once grand table of legend no longer seated on the dais in the centre of the room.

The Barons had done their job to rid the castle of any traces of the Roundtable, the entirety of their history and presence wiped from existence within the walls. The only thing left behind was their memory and the abandoned cabins in the Eastern Wing.

Ergott smiled at the sight and walked up the stairs, heading to his grand room. The blood had long been cleaned up from the floors, and the bodies of dead Barons were disposed of only the Gods knew where.

Ergott walked into his room, smiling at the sight of Vivien sitting on the edge of the bed. "Hello, my Queen."

The dark-haired woman turned her head to look at him, her yellow eyes aglow with delight. "A fine evening to you, my King," she purred. She wore a devilishly short dress, the material hugging her shoulders up to her neck before stretching to reveal the gap over her chest and extending down her arms with long sleeves, the black material sheerer than water. The split along the leg showed an edge of sin, an unconventional garb for a Queen of any Kingdom to be adorned in.

Ergott walked over to her, sitting down on the bed next to her. "Arthur has had his talk," he smirked.

She turned her body to face him, crossing a leg over the other and leaning on her elbow. "Has he been a good lad while he was down there?" she asked, inspecting the swelling on his cheekbone.

Ergott looked at her, frowning. "He's stronger than I thought."

"The Knight trainer knew what he was doing," she purred, resting a hand on his leg. "They wasted no time, it seems."

Ergott moved his hand over hers, nodding at her words. "They were preparing to make him fit for his destiny."

"He almost reached it, too," she said. "But now you've stopped it, put a cork in it. But how long will it last, I wonder?" she mused with a smirk.

"The Knights will want to take him back. I can sense it."

"They will enter their territory easily," she agreed, her eyes glinting. "The legend has not yet been extinguished. The future is still written in stone."

"We must make it so it *will* be extinguished," Ergott said coldly. "Even if it means sacrifices."

"You know what to do," she said, her hand trailing up to his chest, "to keep your future the way you want it." A pulse wave flowed through him at her touch, his mind numbing over as his vision turned yellow for a moment.

Ergott smirked at her. "I won't let you down, my Queen," he promised, bringing her hand up to his mouth.

Vivien leaned against him, tilting her head up to look at him. "I'm counting on you," she whispered.

Ergott leaned down to her and kissed her lightly, a zap of electricity jolting him slightly. "You have my word," he whispered back.

Horses' hooves crunched gravel loudly in the bunched group, the sound harsh to Edward's ears. Nightfall was beginning to follow the dusk, the forest turning a deep shade of green and gray. The breeze was beginning to turn warmer; the Winter was starting to end.

Beside him, his father rode emotionless, his eyes set on the path forward. They hadn't spoken a word since they left the cave; Edward knew it had to do with his interference in the cave. Publicly outing his father or any other *Muharí*, was highly taboo. The repercussions would come eventually. Edward wasn't so much a fool to believe he'd escape them.

Barons rode behind them, silent as the wind that blew over them. Their hoods and masks were still fixed in place despite the darkness that cloaked them all around. *The masks are insufferable. I have no idea how you tools handle them for longer than you need to.* Come to think of it, he wasn't sure if he'd ever seen another Baron without their mask off outside of Ariendal while they were on duty.

Jackseye's horse began to slow down on the path, his hand patting its mane softly. "Take a break," he grumbled, dismounting his horse. "We'll head out in fifteen," he told the group behind him.

The Barons slowed their horses, a few of them dismounting instantly and leaving them on the path; the horses were trained well enough to know not to flee from the group. They didn't bother to secure them because of that reason. Edward rode his horse closer to the treeline, dismounting his horse beside a tree. He ruffled its mane between its ears gently, petting along its forehead.

"Edward," Jackseye said with a growl in his voice. He flicked his eyes to look at his father over his shoulder. *Judgement Day already.*

"You're aware of what I'm about to tell you, aren't you?" Jackseye asked, standing behind his son.

*You should know.* "Read me the riot act," he muttered, looking back at his horse.

"You are not a Baron," Jackseye growled. "Neither you nor your brothers were."

"Oh?" Edward said flatly, turning back around slowly with low brows. "Should I bother asking exactly what we were then, or should I make the assumption you're drawing out your words for your dramatic flare?"

"A disappointment."

"Yeah, 'cause that's new." *Get on with it.*

"You're not fit to be a Baron," Jackseye huffed. "Nor will you ever be. You're relieved from your duty, son."

Edward chuckled softly to himself. "You know what's funny, *Father*?" he asked, looking back at his horse and threading his fingers through its tack, loosening the buckles. "The fact that *you*, the self-proclaimed great Baron *Muharí*, was never a true Baron. No, you came from a position where everybody in this league hated you. The Legion General for King Benjamin. Or was it just Commander? You were the number one enemy once. But now look at you," he smirked, "the one who throws away everything opposing him just because titles empower you to do so. Interesting how you can just dispose of me because I decided it was pure mutiny to murder a child for information, to lead you to a royal you're tasked to kill. Which, ironically, is illegal. But the laws don't apply to you, do they? You enforce them, yet don't follow them."

"Silence!" Jackseye interrupted him, glaring at his son.

"I'm not finished," Edward growled, gripping the horse's bridle tighter. "And the worst part is, you and the others lie and cheat for the sake of that Gods damned usurper-"

"I don't care," Jackseye interrupted once again. "Give me your *Harí* cloak, Edward."

*Come and take it.* "Maybe I should take yours instead since you can't use it right. Is this what happens when someone says enough? Did Jase try and say something, too?"

Jackseye huffed in amusement, stepping closer to him. "You've asked me before about how your brothers *truly* died," he whispered into his ear.

*Yeah, and you still refuse to say anything.* Anger flooded his chest as he turned around to face his father. *Screw the Rites to Hell, he deserves what he gets.* "Why don't you just own up to the truth that we've all figured out? Just say it now while-"

A sudden pain shot through Edward's side, the feel of his skin parting like fire ripping up his body. Edward hissed and looked at his side, his hand shooting towards the pain. Jackseye's dagger was buried in past his leather armour, blood gushing out in painful bouts.

"The same way you're about to," Jackseye said coldly, launching his boot into Edward's knee with a crack and ripping the dagger out of his side and up across his chest. The horse behind Edward reared with a loud neigh, bucking backwards away from the scent of blood. Edward roared through his teeth, his side barking in pain and throbbing.

He gripped the wound as much as he could, stuffing the material of his cloak against it.

"You backstabbing traitor," he spat, glaring up at his father. *No, this man is not my father.*

"For what this is worth," Jackseye crept over him. "I am sorry."

"No, you're not," Edward scoffed in scorn, inspecting his face. "I can see it on your face and in everything you've ever done that you never intended to keep your bonds. You're a sadistic bastard; I hate you!"

Jackseye looked down at his son, a slight hint of silver glimmering at the bottom of his eyes. He turned away, then stopped. "I'm not the villain of this story," he looked back over his shoulder.

"Don't you dare walk away," Edward seethed. "You coward! Face the sight of watching your son die!"

"My King is expecting me," Jackseye said. "And I've watched too many of my sons die before."

"And whose fault is that?" he spat. *You are a disgrace.* The hatred flowed pure with every drop of blood that left Edward's side. His teeth clenched against the ache of the wound in the wind. "You murdered your sons. If I die and I see you murder my family, I will *haunt you.* I will find a way to kill you." His hands started to tremble, his skin turning paler. He would do it. He would find a way to protect Lana from this prick. He would break the Otherworld to break him.

Jackseye turned around to his son, a rare sighting of a tear falling down his face. It was like watching a war unfold before him, the stone-cold face giving way to grief just to flicker back. It made Edward's head swim. *Or is that from the blood loss?*

"I didn't want to kill you. I didn't. But as a father, I couldn't make the same mistakes as I once did," Jackseye said softly. "I'm sorry, my son."

Edward laid his head back on the mud, panting through his teeth. "Jase deserved better than a rigid father's murder. Arlo was not ready to die. Was Marley the hardest to fight? Your favourite son?" he huffed.

"No," Jackseye shook his head. "This was the hardest one…"

Edward laughed breathlessly. "You never were a good father, you know?" The pain was numbing him, the ground cold underneath him. "You left us to suffer so many times."

"I know."

"Was it worth it?" The world was spinning around him faster than a flicked coin. *Was all of this pain and suffering really worth the Hell you've put my mother through?*

"I wish it were," Jackseye murmured to himself. "But it wasn't."

"Bastard," he snarled. His vision was going dark at the edges like a burned piece of paper. Breathing became harder; it felt as though he was being crushed beneath his horse.

Jackseye groaned, holding his temple as if in pain. Edward blinked slowly, trying to clear his vision enough to look at Jackseye. Rohin Jackseye shook his head sharply, his face confused. He looked down at Edward and gasped in surprise, kneeling beside him.

"My son! Edward!" Jackseye breathed, his skin paling as he touched Edward's face. "What have I done?"

All sense left Edward as he stared at his father with bewilderment. *What the Hell?* His eye wasn't the usual amber hue anymore; the old stormy blue-gray that stirred up memories of his childhood replaced it, and both eyes were flooded with tears of shock. *Shock? He's the shocked one?*

Jackseye looked down at his son in agony, tears falling down his rugged and unclean face as he tried to stop the bleeding across his chest. It was as if he'd been released from a trance.

Jackseye's expression turned to anger, glaring towards the castle just over the hill. "That evil witch," he spat, his hands clenching on Edward's cloak.

*Witch*... Edward's sight flickered between darkness and doubling, pain blinding him as he tried to move his hand to touch Rohin's arm.

"You lot! Saddle up!" Jackseye's voice commanded the group, the pressure on Edward's chest lightening.

He grunted as his father's touch left, his hand falling to twitch at his side. Longing for answers pinged through his mind, his breath matching the rapid thundering of his heart that began to slow.

The scuffle of boots turned to the shifting of horses on the ground as the Barons got ready to continue, waiting for Jackseye. Edward watched as Rohin looked back at his son and stood up from the ground, walking around to mount his horse. His eye had returned to its amber hue, all traces of grief dashed from his face and tear trails burned away.

Jackseye mounted his horse and rode away, the *Shueba* following after him without a second glance. Edward watched as they left, the rush of blood in his ears turning to a high-pitched whine. Air huffed onto his face gently, the silhouette of his horse's head coming into his vision as he leaned his head back.

He huffed in slight amusement. "At least you're here, *Rafiq*," he murmured to the beast, his vision finally winking out.

The caves sat adorned to the dusk falling overhead, a few of the Rebels lighting fires in the courtyard's dugout pits. The smell of cooking meat wafted through the air, overpowering the scent of the flowers around the sandstone slabs.

It was enough to draw Tristan out of the cave, following his nose to the source. He hadn't left the infirmary since the Barons came through and dragged him out, and everything was itchy and sore. But this… he would do whatever it took to get that steak.

"He's walking again," a familiar voice called, Peter walking over to him. "Glad to see you on your feet."

Tristan paused for a moment, looking at Peter with a slight frown. "You're okay after the attack?" he asked. "I saw you were bound."

"I wouldn't say *okay*," Peter murmured, lifting his shirt to reveal a massive bruise on his ribcage. "One of the bastards landed a kick."

Tristan cringed a bit, wincing. "That would be sore," he murmured. He should know. He was peppered with them.

"I guess it's time to take those bandages off," Peter said, looking at the bandages along his body.

Tristan quirked his mouth. "I don't know," he muttered. "Galahad didn't say to take them off yet."

"He is the healer of the Knights. What he says goes," Simon said from behind Tristan.

Tristan jumped a mile in the air, spinning around to face Simon. He immediately regretted it as his body barked at him, letting out a small groan. "Gods, why did I do that?"

"I scared you?" Simon asked, looking at Tristan in worry.

"No, he's just easily frightened," Peter shrugged. "It's always been that way."

Tristan sighed, trying to move his limbs without a dull throb of pain shooting through him. "I know, I'm a scaredy cat," he muttered.

"Lucy! Where did you put the onions?" a voice shouted across from him.

Tristan froze. *Lucy?!* He swivelled his head back around behind him, scanning over the courtyard. "Do we have a Rebel named Lucy, or am I hallucinating?" he asked quickly.

"You're not hallucinating," Peter assured.

"They're next to the fire, you tool," a very familiar voice called back.

Tristan's heart leapt. *It was her!* He quickly made his way out of the tunnel entrance, heading towards the sound of her voice.

"Lucy?" he called, looking around in the dark.

A woman turned to look at him from beside a fire pit, her eyes widening. "Tristan!" she gasped, running towards him.

"Is he your boyfriend?" Owen asked with a scowl.

Tristan didn't hear him as she barreled into him, his wounds barking in pain as she squeezed his sides. He didn't care; he wrapped his arms around her, too. "I never thought I'd see you again," he said breathlessly to her. "How did you get here?"

He flicked his eyes to Owen, looking at his scowl with a lifted brow. "Hi?"

"Hi, who are you?" Owen asked.

"I'm Tristan Garrison," Tristan said. "Who are you?" He looked around with more attention, finding more unfamiliar faces. *What is going on?*

"Owen Lucan. Lucy's older brother," Owen said.

Tristan's brows raised, and Lucy pulled back from him, grinning before she spied the bandages on him. "You're hurt?" she blinked, looking up at him. Her eyes widened. "Your eyes! They're blue!"

"I know, it took me a while too," he agreed.

"What happened to you?" she asked, looking at him with worry.

"I'm okay," he assured. "Just a few scratches."

"Tristan?" an old voice said from beside him. His eyes widened, and he looked toward- *Erin Torona!*

"Erin?!" he said astoundedly. "Holy mother of Gods and the Holy Otherworld, you're here too?"

Erin grinned, moving over to hug him tightly. "It's been a long time."

"I'd say," Tristan grinned. "Around six months now. Are you doing okay?"

Her face dropped slightly. "I still miss him," she said quieter.

He smiled sadly. "I know, I do too." He let her pull back and looked down at the older woman. Samqueel was definitely her son; the same quicksilver gray eyes and straight nose, and her attitude could undoubtedly match the fiery temper Samqueel was known for on the fields when she was particularly fussed about something, too. Although it was a rare sight. "He was a legend."

"I'm sure you'll become one, too, by the looks of your wraps and those eyes," she said, looking at him closely. "What happened to earn those scratches you were talking about?"

"Tristan here was brave. He fought off a pack of wolves," Peter said, walking up to the two.

"Fought? More like threw." Kyan walked over to them, holding a mug of tea. "Fought with his arms and sides, no less."

"Ignore Kyan," Peter shrugged him off. "Tristan was incredibly brave."

"You fought *wolves*?" Lucy asked, astounded.

*Uh...* "Kind of, I suppose," Tristan said slowly, looking sideways at Peter. *He thought I was brave?*

Peter looked towards Tristan, winking at him. A small smile crept on Tristan's lips, his chest warming.

"How long have you worn those bandages?" Kyan asked, nodding to his arms. "Surely you'd be right by now since you were magically healed."

Tristan hadn't thought of that. But at the same time, he'd thought of what his arms would possibly look like underneath. The images of stretched, mutilated skin didn't really increase his confidence in wanting to take them off. He wasn't sure what to expect, and it scared him. "I mean, I'm still a little sore," he muttered.

"Nonsense," he dismissed. "Go ahead, Pete, just roll them off. Get it over and done with so he doesn't smell like old linen anymore."

Tristan frowned and folded his arms against his chest. "Why does it matter?"

"I want to see the scars," Kyan shrugged. "It makes people look tough, and chicks dig scars, right?" He looked at Lucy, who frowned.

"Go on," Owen nodded. "Let's see if your story is real."

"It *is* real," Tristan frowned at him. "How would you know if it wasn't?"

"If it wasn't real, then why would he lie? And why would his eyes change colour for no reason?" Erin frowned at him.

"What happened? Exact details, please," Owen said, crossing his arms.

Insecurity flashed in Tristan's chest, looking away from him. "The dogs sprang on me in the woods. What else is there to know?" he protested.

"And for the record, I've never met you before, so I don't know what colour eyes you *had* before you were attacked," Owen pointed out.

"He had brown eyes," Lucy said to him.

"Wasn't asking you," Owen spat at Lucy.

Tristan's jaw clenched. "Watch your attitude," he warned.

"Or what?" Owen huffed.

"Or you'll learn to watch it better than what you're doing now."

Owen chuckled at him, shaking his head. "You don't scare me."

"I'm not supposed to be scary," Tristan said. "I'm not the violent type. But I would like it better if you showed some respect to your sister."

"Let's get one thing straight," Owen said, walking up close to Tristan. "She's my younger sister, and I'm responsible for her. If you have a problem with that, say it to my face."

"Okay, I have a problem with the way you think you're responsible for your twenty-year-old sister," Tristan growled. *Who does he think he is?* He saw Erin shift back away a reasonable distance. Probably a good idea.

"Listen to me very clearly," Owen growled. "I've been looking after her since I was eight years old. Both our parents died, and no one was there to look after us until we found our fosters," Owen bared his teeth at him.

"You lived in a broken-down house on the edge of town with the river a mile away before that," Tristan said, watching him flatly. "You were repeatedly chased by Knights for stealing your food source to feed Lucy, and you slept on the floor huddled together for warmth with a stray dog. I know your story because it's hers, too. I understand, Owen. But none of that corresponds with why you treat her the way you do."

"How about you keep your opinions to yourself?" Owen suggested. "Just because you're allowed to speak your mind, it doesn't mean you're smart."

Tristan's arm lashed out before he realised what he was doing, Owen's hands grabbing for his fist too late. The force of his punch shoved Owen's hands back into his face, the lad staggering back with the force as his grip on Tristan tightened. Lucy gasped and moved back as Tristan was flipped over Owen's shoulder, landing on the ground with a huff. Owen twisted his arm and pinned him down on his back. Tristan growled and launched his boots up into

Owen's stomach, pushing him back with a whoosh of air. His boots tripped over a wood log, and Owen fell to land inches away from the campfire to his left.

He got back up and glared at Tristan, stalking over to him. Kyan swore under his breath, the Rebels watching the fight murmuring in surprise. Tristan stood back on his feet a moment later, raising his fists, ready to fight. He paused for a moment and looked at Owen's hand, something dangling in his fist. *What is that?*

"Enough!" A commanding voice echoes through the air. Tristan pivoted to the voice, keeping one eye on Owen.

Lancelot walked over to the two, his hands folded behind his back. "What is the meaning of all this?"

Tristan lowered his arms, the fight dimming in him. "He started it," he frowned. "He couldn't keep his gob shut."

"Not good enough, Tristan," Lancelot shook his head. "And you, don't you be a rude loudmouth to my trainees."

"He's like this all the Gods damned time," Lucy sighed frustratedly, turning to Owen. "And Tristan's right; I don't need to be looked after. I'm old enough to be left alone now."

Owen scoffed at her and walked away, dusting himself off and throwing whatever he'd held into the fire to burn. Lancelot shook his head at him, looking back at Tristan.

"How are you feeling?" he asked.

Tristan didn't hear him. He was too busy staring at his arm. *Owen was holding the bandage...* "What the Hell?"

His arm wasn't all twisted and scarred; it was *splotchy*. His skin was smooth but patterned with light patches across where there should've been scars, contrasting with his darker skin like marbled chocolate. He twisted his arm around in wonder.

"He's got vitiligo?" Erin asked softly.

Lancelot nodded. "Unfortunately."

Tristan grabbed the other bandage off his arm, unwrapping it quickly to find the same thing: white skin where scars should've been. "Is this another side effect?" *This is so strange.*

"Your eyes changed colour," a familiar voice sounded from beside the group. Tristan turned around to face Galahad, lowering his hands. "When I heal people, my magic has a few side effects, but they're different for each person. The closest reason I can come up with as to why you've got vitiligo is because of how much magic it took to knit your skin back together. It must have destroyed the melanin in your skin."

"If you wish to hide it, we have gloves for you to wear," Lancelot suggested.

"No," Tristan said. "I don't understand it completely. I'm not sure if I ever will, but… this is better than what I thought." He looked up at the gathered people. "I expected worse. It's fascinating, to say the least. I'm spotty."

"If I'm honest," Lancelot started, "It gives you a unique outlook, and it looks… quite fancy. I should know about fancy things."

"Geraint is the flamboyant one," Percival chimed in, patting Lancelot's shoulder as he walked past.

"It looks like you dipped your arms in milk," Kyan said with a lifted brow.

"Well, I think it looks cool," Tristan pouted at him. It was odd as heck, but something about it was almost hypnotic.

"If Arthur was here, he'd agree with that," Lancelot smiled.

Tristan looked at him blankly. "He's not back?" he asked confusedly.

The group fell silent, Lancelot and Galahad sharing the same wide-eyed expressions. Tristan swallowed the nervous lump in his throat. "He came back from the search in Camelot, right? With the rest of you guys?"

Lancelot glanced at Lucy, his mouth quirked. "Do you want to tell him?"

She shrunk in place, and Tristan looked at her, seeing the guilt on her face. "Huh? You know where he is?" he raised a brow in confusion. "What's all the secrecy?"

She shook her head, looking elsewhere. *Something has happened, and Arthur is gone. Did the Barons do something?* "Did it happen when we were stormed? Is he lost in the forest or something? We can find him, right?"

"Arthur went to Camelot with the Rebels, and the Rebels returned with Lucy and a few refugees. Arthur didn't," Lancelot said softly. "He wanted to know what the Barons were up to in the Kingdom, and he saved the refugees from suffering more. But unfortunately, they got him as they left."

"Why didn't he take me with him? I would've gone," Tristan brushed his hair back from his face. "The silly tool, he never leaves without me."

"Arthur didn't want you to worry or end up more wounded than you currently are," Galahad said.

Tristan turned to him with a confused face. "But you healed me," he reasoned. "I was healed, but I was angry and upset…" he groaned in frustration. "Gods be merciful. Why did I shove him away?"

"He was trying to protect you," Lancelot said. "He cares too much for you, Tristan."

His mind raced over everything they'd told him. "Barons caught him, took him away, he's in the castle- he's in the castle!" He looked at them with wide eyes. "We gotta get him out! Ergott will kill him over whatever happened to the Roundtable. We gotta go!"

"The Rebels are not invading Camelot," a familiar deep voice said. "It's too risky for our alliance to be revealed."

"Gawain, this is *Arthur* you're arguing about with me," Tristan said. "No matter what anybody says, I'm going to get him; I don't care if I die. I'm getting him."

"Tristan-"

"Don't 'Tristan' me! I know what I need to do, and this time, you lot with your opinions of me not being able to fight will be shocked when I actually manage to bring him home. I either have you guys with me to go and get him or-"

"You didn't let me finish, Tristan," Gawain frowned.

Tristan paused, his bravado crumbling. "Sorry," he muttered.

"I said the Rebels, not us," Gawain said.

"Gawain and I will be leading the rescue. Kay will be staying here and watching over the caves," Lancelot said, a warm smile going across his face.

"Even though this is a risky and stupid plan, Arthur needs to be rescued, and I can't break a promise I made," Gawain grumbled, a small smile forming.

Tristan looked at the lot of them, Lucy's face interested in the conversation, Erin watching him with a small, proud smile. Behind Gawain and Lancelot, the other Knights stood proudly. Peter and Kyan stood by his side, Simon and Maria watching on from beside the fire pit.

"I thought you didn't like Arthur?" Percival asked Kyan.

"Let's be honest here," he started. "Would you prefer to be led by a bastard King that had black-clad posers in the castle walls or someone the people liked?"

"He's got a point," Gaheris nudged Percival. "Let's get our King back!"

Tristan tried his hardest, really, to absorb everything going on around himself, but… "Huh?" he blurted.

Everyone looked at him, the group falling silent. The sound of crickets chirping replaced the crackle of fire.

"Were you listening to anything spoken for the past two minutes?" Bedivere asked.

"I mean, yes, but actually… no," he said, his face drooping slightly.

"Tell me what's happening then," Gawain folded his arms.

Tristan raised his hand and counted on his fingers, "Uhh, Kay is staying here," he listed slowly.

"Not to my amusement or willingness, I'm not," Kay muttered.

"Get over it, stumpy," Percival teased.

"Stumpy? I'm taller than you."

"Not when you're going to be six feet underground in the next two or so years," Bedivere chuckled, the other Knights joining him.

"Shut your gob, Ryan," he growled.

"...Gawain and Lancelot are leading," Tristan said, ticking off another finger. He then frowned. "Am I gonna lead?"

"No," Gawain sighed. "You're coming with us, and you're going to be with Percival, Maria, Peter and Kyan to get Arthur out of the castle while the rest of us fight off the Barons and save more refugees."

Tristan paused for a moment before counting another finger. "You broke something," he said to Gawain. He turned to Gaheris. "You're scary." He pivoted to Kay. "You're short?"

"No," Kay scowled, looking down at him.

Tristan turned to Kyan. "And you like Arthur."

Kyan frowned and went to open his mouth, then stalled. Tristan raised his brows. "Well, you can't say you don't 'cause you've stuck around this long," he teased.

Kyan frowned and crossed his arms. "No comment."

Tristan's eyes lit up as he looked at Peter. "And you think I'm brave," he grinned.

"You're getting off-topic," Peter said, his eyes lit in amusement.

*Oh.* Tristan looked at Lucy, her brown eyes looking up at him in humour. He smiled down at her softly and brushed a stray hair back from her face. "And now I know you're safe here, or as much as you can be."

She smiled at him and flushed slightly. He winked at her and looked up at them. "And the Rebels are staying here. That's all I got."

"We're going to get Arthur, Tristan," Maria said behind him.

His eyes lit up. "We're going to get Arthur!" he grinned. The Knights laughed and took up a cheer.

"Finally, he gets it," Percival chuckled. "So, when are we going?"

"Tomorrow at dusk," Gawain said, looking at the Knights. "You'll be needing a different style of clothing, and you lot too," he looked over at the others.

"What type?" Peter asked.

"Armour," Lancelot grinned.

"I almost feel sorry for the Barons," Geraint chimed in. Percival nudged him with his elbow, Geraint rubbing his arm with a frown. "What? I said *almost*."

Armour. Oh, how Tristan despised armour. And he'd only worn chainmail. *I hope it isn't chainmail…*

"Get some rest," Gawain said to the group. "We've got training in the morning."

Simon looked at Maria. "Are we going?"

"Apparently so," she shrugged. "You might be with the escape party, though, since your leg is busted." It was a wonder Gawain thought to put her in the search party, if she was honest. She would've thought he'd make her stay.

"I'm not much of a fighter, anyway," Simon shrugged. "I don't find joy in violence."

"You don't have to fight," she said. "You can just help out with getting the refugees away."

"I'm guessing you're Arthur's girlfriend?" Owen asked, walking up to the two.

Maria looked over at Owen, a frown on her face. "Here comes trouble again," she muttered. "Have you come back to pick another fight with the rest of us?"

"I'm here to ask questions," Owen said, folding his arms. "You look a bit like the lad, I must say."

She raised a brow at him. "Is that because of the hair? Because I don't think so," she said. *Arthur's hair looks mud-stained compared to mine.*

"You have the same coloured eyes," Owen examined.

"So does Kyan, but we're not related." Owen made her feel on edge like he was a thief with a hidden dagger just waiting to spring.

"So you're his lover?"

"No, we're just friends," she frowned, shifting uncomfortably. "What's it to you anyways, sticky beak?"

"Just common curiosity," Owen shrugged. "I'd be surprised if Arthur was taken."

Defence stirred through her, and she straightened her back. "Why? Would you be jealous if someone was happier than you?" she sniped. *Why am I being so standoffish?*

"Who in all of Camelot would date a royal?" Owen asked her. "Queen Guinevere learnt that the hard way."

"Owen!" Lancelot shouted, walking over with a frown.

Owen turned and raised a brow, Maria watching on. "Yes?"

"What did you just say?" Lancelot scowled at him.

"That Guinevere took the hard way out of life, chose the tool in the castle like a blind mad-woman," he shrugged. "What's it to you?"

Lancelot glared at him. "You do not talk about anyone in that way. While you're here at Reigate, you are to show respect to everyone, especially Arthur and the Knights. If you cannot follow those instructions, then you will be forced to leave."

Wicked delight entered Owen's eyes, and Maria clenched her jaw. *The bastard can't handle shit for brains.* "Is Rosaline a touchy subject for you, good Sir Knight? My apologies, really. I wasn't aware the Queen had friends outside the castle."

"You better watch your mouth," Lancelot frowned at him. "You will learn some respect, or I will show you some."

"Good luck, people have already told me I'm too far gone," Owen chirped.

*No kidding.* Maria didn't like this tool at all.

"Some even tell me my attitude makes me likeable," he grinned, winking at Maria.

Maria scoffed, cringing back away from him slightly. "Creep," she muttered. She felt Simon's hand steady her on the small of her back in comfort.

"If you want to teach me respect, you'll have to do it for ten or so years before I start to show it to you," Owen grinned.

"Is that right, boy?" Gawain walked forwards to him, stopping beside the fire.

Owen turned around to him. "For certain, Sir Knight."

"Would it be helpful to let you know I can knock ten years' worth of sense into you at any given time? The people around you have certainly learned that lesson," he said calmly.

"I'm sure you can," Owen scoffed.

"Test me," Gawain shrugged. Maria smirked. *The challenge appears.*

"Prove that you can knock sense into me; go on," Owen challenged, facing Gawain.

"Would you like to learn it the nicer way first?" Gawain unfurled his arms to his sides.

"No," Owen grinned.

Gawain raised his brows in feigned shock. "Oh? The hard way?" he asked in surprise.

"The hard way, old man."

Gawain shrugged nonchalantly and walked towards him, his bulk towering over Owen's slim frame. "Okay, but don't forget, you insisted," he said. Owen crossed his arms and nodded.

The trainees and Knights around him started backing up a great deal away, Maria and Simon smirking to themselves as they sat on a sandstone slab. *He needs to learn.*

Gawain shook his arms slightly, looking around the courtyard. "Have you ever moved at record speed before?" he asked Owen.

Owen looked at him, a confused expression forming on his face. "What record speed?"

Suddenly, Gawain barreled into Owen, driving him across the courtyard pinned onto his shoulder, the breath whooshing from him at the impact. The world disappeared from beneath him as Gawain flung him across the courtyard, landing on the grass and rolling over and over like a loose log down a mountain.

Owen finally came to a stop and groaned on the ground, surprise overflowing his expression. He'd been launched the entire way across the courtyard!

"New record, Gawain," Maria laughed, the Rebels around her laughing at the bedraggled Owen.

"What the Hell?!" Owen growled at him, his teeth bared.

Gawain grinned at him widely, amusement on his face. "Come on then," he goaded. "Get back up and fight if you want. You'll end up back in the same spot."

Owen roared and sprinted towards Gawain, curling his hand into a fist and swinging it towards him in a fit of rage. Gawain simply stepped to the side and spun around to boot his behind, sending him stumbling down once more with the momentum. The Rebels continued to laugh, cheering and whooping.

"See, now you're not learning," Gawain said to him. "You're channelling your anger into your movements and not your smarts."

Owen snarled, standing back up and glaring at him.

"You're trying to fight a man with years of prior experience, son. Is that really a smart move on your behalf?" Gawain raised his brows.

"You never gave me a chance," Owen said.

Gawain spread his arms wide. "Alright, here's your chance," he said. "I won't move from this spot."

Owen smirked and swung his fist towards Gawain's jaw, his wrist barking in pain as Gawain's hand squeezed it and pulled his arm to the side, spinning him around and shoving him back.

"Are you trying, Owen?"

"Bastard!" Owen snarled at him.

Gawain beckoned him back and shifted his feet. "One more shot," he growled.

Owen turned back to him, panting heavily. He swung his arm again, this time towards Gawain's side, and was grabbed again. He rocketed his shoulder towards him and barged his chest, the old Knight staggering backwards. Owen's eyes lit in victory, and he spun to launch his elbow into his jaw; he forgot about the arm Gawain held.

Gawain dodged backwards and twisted his arm, Owen barking as he manoeuvred himself to try and stop the pain. His legs were swept out from beneath him, and he went crashing face-first into the dirt, Gawain pinning him at the wrist and back of the neck.

Owen struggled to move against his strength, growling at the mouthful of grass. Gawain leaned down to his ear.

"You will learn quickly here that you are not above us," he whispered. "You aren't worth the space you take up here."

"I'm above Arthur," Owen growled at him.

The pressure on his neck tightened, and he snarled in pain. "You, Owen, are *not above anybody*," Gawain hissed. "You aren't worth the waste of food that we hunt for. You don't deserve the life you've gotten right now. Arthur saved your miserable ass from that shithole of a Kingdom, the least you can do is show him some Gods damn gratitude!"

"He left us to suffer!" Owen protested. "He left us to die and be controlled by a man who killed our protectors!"

"He left the Kingdom to prosper," Gawain snapped. "He left so he could come back to save you flea-ridden assholes. He went to train to become the King. He left to protect the city. You just can't see past the selfish self-pitied bullshit you've convinced yourself to believe. Stop thinking of yourself and think of the long run. Do you want the Kingdom to get better? You need the time to wait for it to do so.

"Arthur isn't a miracle worker; he is human, just like your sulky ass. Be grateful that he'd give you the time of day 'cause the rest of us wouldn't."

Gawain shoved him into the dirt before letting him go, standing back up and watching him. Owen sat up slowly and stared at Gawain. The Rebels fell silent around them, watching them with interest.

Maria watched Owen's face change, processing Gawain's words. *Hopefully, the prick learned not to be like that around him now. If he hasn't, then he's a goner.*

Owen sighed and nodded at Gawain slightly. "You make a good point," he said, standing up from the ground and rubbing his neck.

Gawain watched him flatly. "Nobody wanted these circumstances, nobody wanted to go live in a cave for eighteen years, nobody wanted to hide away from the radar or leave their Kingdom they were destined to rule," he said. "But things happen whether we like it or not. We didn't want to abandon our people," he swept his arm around to his companions behind him. "We didn't get a choice. Just like you. Just like Arthur. You should learn to accept that life just doesn't work the way you want it to. It's easier to live that way. Do you understand?"

Owen nodded at him. "I understand."

Gawain nodded and clapped his shoulder. "Good. Now, let's eat."

# Chapter 25: Unbroken Destiny

The heated metal of the dungeon bars didn't hold their bite on Arthur's skin anymore. His back had gone numb hours ago, so long that he had forgotten how long he'd been leaning against them. He sighed quietly to himself and leaned his head back on the bars, closing his eyes in frustration. *How am I going to get out of here?*

He'd already tested the bars; they were too thick to bend and too slim to squeeze through. The door lock was warded with some kind of magic Arthur didn't have a clue about, and the hinges were rusted on. The vent wasn't any help either since he couldn't even reach it.

He didn't hold much hope for the Knights to come get him. Reigate was hours away from here, and even if they did come for him, there were too many Barons to deal with. They would be recognised as soon as they passed the Gates. Arthur turned his head around to see through the bars; the dungeons were unclean, to say the least. All the cells hadn't been used in what felt like ages. He was just the lucky one to be thrown into one of them. *And I'll probably be left here to rot.* At least he'd suit the aesthetic.

Light footsteps echoed from the dungeon stairs, an old grumbling voice cursing quietly. Arthur's eyes widened, and he looked over to the far end of the dungeon hallway, seeing a silhouette of a small lady walking down the hallway. She held a tray in her hands, the scent of warm food wafting to him past the stench of mold.

She paused for a moment, looking around at each of the cells. "Hello? I've brought food. Which cell are we in?" she asked in the open air.

Arthur stuck his arm in between the bars, waving to her. "Down here."

The voice gasped and moved quickly towards his cell. "Arthur? What are you doing in the cells? Where have you been?"

Arthur couldn't believe it; Ms Enid was still here! "Far away from here," he said, standing up from the ground. "What are you still doing here?"

She stood in front of his cell, inspecting him quickly with the worried look of a fussed mother. "I've been waiting for you to come back," she said. "I've been set to ridiculous duties and far-out tasks for these people. I've hoped you'd come back every day."

"Here I am," he smiled faintly. "I've been at the Reigate Caves training with the old Knights of the Roundtable-"

"Shh," she hushed, wide-eyed. "If anybody overhears what you've been doing, you could get your mates in trouble." She lifted the bowl off the tray and handed it to him through the bars: warm, chunky beef stew with chopped vegetables. His stomach rumbled at the smell.

"Smells freshly made," Arthur said.

"Everything I make is fresh," she replied. "It was a wonder anything was left. Those Barons just don't stop eating. They're worse than Karsol."

"More of them have arrived?" Arthur asked, taking the bowl from the tray. Arthur examined the food in his hands and immediately brought the bowl up to his mouth, sipping the stew.

"They've been flooding the Kingdom in waves," she said. "I don't know if any of them are actually new because they never take their masks off. It feels like there's way more than what we started with, like they're growing."

"Thankfully, we got Lucy and a few refugees out when we did," Arthur said. "I went to see if any Barons were around, then they snatched me up and took me to this cell."

Ms Enid sighed through her nose, watching him through the bars. "How are we getting you out of this pickle?" she muttered.

"You shouldn't risk your life for me," Arthur said, leaning his head on his forearms against the bars, the bowl of stew placed on the ground beside him. "It's my mess, and I need to find a way out or pay the consequences."

She looked at him worriedly. "Arthur, you understand what is going to happen next, don't you?" she asked quietly.

Arthur nodded slightly. "Execution trial."

"I'm not going to sit aside and watch him murder you for something you never did," she said firmly. "You weren't born to be killed off by an undermining uncle. I won't stand for it. I didn't put that crate under your bed just for you to get cut off."

"Ms Enid," Arthur said quietly. "I know what I need to do."

"And what's that?"

"Face the consequences. All of this has been because of me. And it's only right if I finish it, even if it's the solution no one wanted." Arthur reached his arm out in between the bars and rubbed her shoulder gently, looking at her with a faint smile.

Ms Enid watched him with a sad, determined look. "This isn't the solution you will use," she replied. "I know you will find a better way to solve this. Dying won't help your people, Arthur. It'll only help your uncle win." She touched his hand on her shoulder gently.

"And win I will do," Ergott's voice echoed through the dungeon.

Arthur flicked his eyes over to the entranceway, seeing his uncle, along with two other Barons, standing behind Enid. She turned around to face Ergott with startlement, her body shrinking away from him. The King wore a regal gold-trimmed black jacket, his knee-high boots polished and armoured. A simple sword hung at his side in a black leather scabbard, his hand resting on the rounded pommel.

Ergott looked down at her, scowling at the old Maiden. "Ms Enid, I'm sure you're needed elsewhere within the castle?"

Ms Enid glanced at Arthur with a pleading look and tucked the food tray beneath her arm, keeping her head down as she moved past Ergott.

"Goodbye, Ms Enid," Arthur said quietly, his expression turning sad. *Maybe this is the end...*

"I think we both know what happens next," Ergott growled.

"Sorry, I didn't hear you. Step right in front of the bars again," Arthur scowled up at him.

Ergott stayed right where he was. "Your beloved people have already heard the news of how their famed 'Born King' has been captured by me. They've stopped their rallies against my men. They've already become more obedient. The majority of them are outside the High Gates waiting to catch a glimpse of your trial."

"You know that won't last after you kill me," Arthur said, standing upright from the bars. "They'll cause riots, protests. If you think you're going to win by getting rid of me, you're poorly mistaken. You've just ruined your reputation."

Ergott smirked slowly, the wry grin stretching his face gruesomely. "You're kidding yourself, Arthur," he laughed. "You truly believe that the people will rebel? They haven't got an ounce of fight left in them from when we abolished them at the funeral. I have successfully captured their last hope, and I will use you to show them that I will not be overshadowed by myths and legends that don't exist. And once your head rolls down the castle steps, your friends will be quick to join you in the Otherworld."

Arthur interrupted the King with a loud bash on the metal bars, his eyes glowing in anger and frustration. "I'd like to see you go through the shit I have and see if you still call yourself a hero," he spat. "You exiled me from the castle and took away my right to the throne. You aren't anything to these people. I have just one question for you, uncle. Why?"

Ergott leaned forward slightly, his orange eyes flaring. "If you were in my position, then wouldn't you want to rule the world?" he asked quietly. "Wouldn't you want to have the people who spat at your feet, who called you second best to a destined brother, who called you a waste of resources the moment you were born, to be bowing at your feet as you sat on the throne of the world? *You* ruined *me* first, boy."

"No," Arthur said simply. "You brought that upon yourself, uncle."

"If you were never born, I would've been first in line to the throne!" Ergott barked. "This was *my* destiny first! Your father took that away from me the moment you were screaming from your mother's womb."

"Cause he knew what type of King you would turn out to be!" Arthur spat. "A horrible, selfish man with no respect for anyone but himself!"

"Nobody respected me before you came along, and nobody respected me when you were born," Ergott growled. "You do not respect the people who hated you in the first instance. Those people made their choice to tie their loyalties to Benjamin's life only. Anything else that wasn't in his limelight was a waste of space and time. You should know how it feels to be invisible beneath others who don't pay attention to you."

"I do," Arthur nodded, stepping back slowly. "You made me feel that way."

"Face it, Arthur. The people in this world are cruel, bigoted idiots. They choose the people they want based on

what they think is best, not on what they know is best. You
were a *child*, Arthur. You were seven years old. A Kingdom
does not have Kings who cannot rule. I stepped up after
Benjamin died because I knew I was the one who could
lead that was still in the bloodline. I was old enough to do
this. The people were foolish to want a child to lead them."

"Even when I was of age, you never gave me a chance
to step up and *try*. You never encouraged me to do anything
of use, never allowed me to do anything independently,"
Arthur argued. "And you had every opportunity to do so,
but you were, and still are, trapped in your own fantasy.
You pushed me away, you forgot about me, all because I
was born. You're a coward of a man."

"Why fix something if it isn't broken? I was leading the
Kingdom just fine," Ergott shrugged. The door of the cell
clicked as the magic on the lock moved, the Barons moving
to the door. "And then that damned prophecy resurfaced.
You are at fault for the destruction that has been caused. I
am protecting my people from themselves with their foolish
beliefs of a wizard's drunken words scrawled on a piece of
parchment. And so I will shut this down for good."

"I hope it's worth it," Arthur snorted. "You're a
disgraceful King and a worse uncle."

"It runs in the family," Ergott smirked. The Barons filed
through the door, unslinging chained metal cuffs from their
belts. "Don't struggle, or it'll hurt more."

Arthur watched them gain closer, backing away slowly.
The closer Baron grabbed his arm tightly, the other looping
one cuff over the held arm's wrist. Arthur shrugged around
in his grip, looking at his uncle with a death stare.

They pinned him roughly against the cell wall and
cuffed his other wrist, the other Baron holding a more
complex cuff; it was bigger, with a clip on the end of it that
they looped through the chain links of his wrist cuff. The
Baron holding him pinned his head back, and he tensed as

they cuffed the metal around his neck, the locks sliding into place.

Arthur remained silent, his expression bland and empty. They gripped his arms and the length of the chain, pulling him out of the cell. The metal cuff around his throat bit at his skin where the hinges shifted, keeping his head forward. Ergott watched him with a sideways glance of victory as they walked him up the stairs, trailing after them with footsteps that echoed around the chamber.

*This is it, huh? This is the end of my supposed destiny?* The past three months were all just a waste of time. Everything he did has met him to this point. The best he'd done was get those refugees out, and he didn't even know if they'd made it out of the Gates.

All that effort was just in vain. All those dreams he had meant nothing anymore. The words that were written on the walls in murals were nothing but graffiti now. As they dragged Arthur down the castle hallway, he let himself slump. He let them carry him out. *Fighting is useless now. Nobody will be here to stop them.*

Maidens pivoted to watch with shock from where they cleaned, Barons lined against the walls every ten paces keeping them back. Each held a spear as they stood along the length of the torn-up red carpet that sat on the bloodstained marble. Everything was a mess.

*And it was all because of me.*

The willowing breeze blew at their backs as the horses trotted towards the Gates on the deserted cobblestone streets, the Barons setting their eyes on the castle courtyard. Jackseye led them up the slope, glancing around the empty alleyways. Something had definitely happened here while he was gone. He stopped his horse at the base of the castle

steps and dismounted, the rest following suit. The Barons
on the ground led their horses to the stables, Jackseye
looking up at the castle. A murmur of loud voices came
down the steps from inside the wall of the High Gates; the
citizens were inside the castle boundaries. A knowing
smirk stretched across his face.

The Barons guarding the Gates stood straight, saluting
Jackseye with no emotion. He nodded briskly to them as he
ascended the steps, his body sore from the extensive horse
ride.

*Ergott must have heard.* Their plan had worked
flawlessly; the King's powers were extensive beyond
anything Jackseye knew. Learning that the King could see
miles away from the eyes of another subject and hear from
the same visions was a game changer. So much so that
relaying back to him that Arthur was in the city had proved
the method effective. Satisfaction coursed through him.

The guards lowered their arms as he vanished from
their vicinity, the Black Cloaks remaining silent and
focused on their job. He passed through the arch of the
Gates and entered the courtyard, the space packed full of
citizens of every variation. Nervous, disbelieving murmurs
were rife through it all, and it only fueled Jackseye's smirk
more.

He walked through the castle doors, ignoring the
glances from the citizens outside. King Ergott was nowhere
to be seen within the area, only patrolling Barons standing
off to the side. They shifted back as he walked through,
following the ripped red carpet towards the throne room.

The pews were void of people both on the higher and
lower levels, Barons shadowing the walls. The dais at the
front of the room no longer had the two wooden thrones
that had sat there for centuries; instead, one finely crafted
metal throne sat against the back of the dais, both currently
empty. Ebony thorns and branches of ivy wound through
the metal structure, meeting at the points topping the seat

like castle spires, the obsidian-like stone glistening like the night sky.

Jackseye hummed to himself and turned away to ascend up the staircase to his left, weaving through the multiple levels and dodging rushed servants and Maidens. At the top level of the castle was Ergott's quarters, a massively oversized space composed of a separate entertainment area, living area, and, of course, his room.

A walk-through wardrobe sat with its door open as if expectant of him. He approached it and peered through, knocking three times on the door. "Sire," he said gruffly.

"I suppose the search went well," Ergott said, putting on a newer jacket than before. Brown fleece lined the green velvet coat, black buckled straps pulling the jacket shut all the way up to his neck, the collar standing up to his jawline. "Arthur was here as you left, but now we know of the Reigate Caves."

"He left the morning we got there," Jackseye said. "We must have missed the carriages on the way through."

"No matter," Ergott dismissed. "We got what we needed. Arthur is being trialled for execution, and the citizens get to suffer by watching their last hope crumble before them."

The small voice inside him protested against that, but he shut it off, clamping down against it. He would not allow it to break through again. "I assume he's being prepared for his trial," he mused.

"Indeed," Ergott smirked, turning to where his crown sat on a plush cushion on top of a small pillar. "I suppose you'll be attending the trial?"

He nodded. "I'll be making sure the Barons do as they're told. If the people revolt, they'll have a great force to deal with."

"And your son?"

The voice in him screamed again, fighting to get through again. His face remained impassive.

"Unfortunately, he will not be joining us at the castle any longer."

Ergott's jaw shifted in amusement, and he raised his hands to place his crown on his head. "I see you've done the witches bidding."

"Albeit not willingly." His eyes flashed. *Why did I say that?*

"Not willingly?" Ergott asked, raising a brow at him.

*That damned voice is breaking through again...* "I meant to say 'swimmingly', sire," he cleared his throat. "He put up a struggle."

"As to be expected," Ergott mused. "And the Rebels' location?"

"The cave is several hours south of here, hidden within a discreet part of the forest. They've been there a while, by the looks of things. The caves were outfitted accordingly."

"No wonder why it took days to find them," Ergott huffed, walking up to him.

"It would've taken more time to find them without the aid of your ally," Jackseye said, standing tall. "She was very helpful indeed in tracking Arthur down."

"She's quite useful when it comes to priorities," Ergott grinned faintly, his orange eyes flaring lightly.

"Her powers work well when it comes to animals," Jackseye smirked. Indeed, the girl's power to communicate with the beasts was extraordinary.

"Her abilities are quite substantial to consider natural," Ergott said. "But, she is a perfect eye to watch over Arthur's moves."

*And the best part was that the boy had no idea.* "Has she returned to the Kingdom yet?"

"No," Ergott said simply. "But her arrival is to be expected soon enough."

"When she does return, let her know of the Barons' gratitude."

"For certain," Ergott smirked.

It was a pity, really. If Edward were still alive, the two would've been a powerful force to fight for them. But, Jackseye supposed, the weeds had to be pulled. "What time will this trial commence? The people are jam-packed in the courtyard."

"Give it time, my notorious friend," Ergott said, placing a hand on Jackseye's shoulder. "The Executioner needs to prepare his target."

Jackseye's brows flicked up. "Are we succumbing him to torture first?"

"It wouldn't be an execution without it."

*Brutal. And to his own nephew, nonetheless.* "Surprising decisions," he mumbled.

"But necessary ones," Ergott mused.

"Has anyone reported back to you about the remaining League's positioning? I requested them to guard the gateways before I left."

"As far as I've heard, they had troubles in the South with a band of three rogue wagons. The rest have doubled security. That's all I understood from the jumbled words Wilhelm babbled on about," Ergott waved.

Jackseye's brows lowered slightly. *Come to think of it...* "Where is the General, anyway? He wasn't at the Gates as per normal."

"He has been relieved from duty."

That made Jackseye pause. His breath slowed as he thought over Ergott's words. "I see." Jackseye had known Wilhelm for many years before he'd joined the Barons. He was one of the only men left behind that Jackseye would've counted as a friend. His jaw tensed a little.

"I understand he was your friend. But what was done had to be done," Ergott said coldly.

Jackseye sighed quietly through his nose and stood back up straight. "Whatever the reason, I'm sure it was valid," he said, the lie crumbling to ash on his tongue.

Ergott nodded and turned to the door. "The execution shall begin soon," he said. "It would be beneficial to prepare ourselves."

Jackseye turned to face him, nodding in agreement. He needed to change from his riding clothes, anyway. One month on the road didn't do much for his overall appearance. "I will see you at the courtyard."

The citizens were all clustered up towards the top of the castle steps; something had got their attention. Tristan watched from underneath a brown hood, pulling the shawl around his shoulders close against the wind.

Though it didn't matter. The furnace-like heat underneath all of this cloth stuff was thanks to the armour Gawain made him wear. And it was *heavy. This is way worse than the chain mail...* He was almost out of breath, his feet dragging on the cobblestones with all the weight.

Something nudged him forward semi-roughly, a mutter sounding from behind him. Tristan looked over his shoulder, frowning. "I bet you didn't like the weight of your first armour set either, Bedivere," he frowned.

"At least I didn't drag like a sorry cat," Bedivere said, frowning at him under a large hat.

"You dragged multiple times," Percival nudged him from the side, sporting a green cloak torn at the edges. "You complained about it every day."

"With reason," Bedivere sniffed. "Unlike yourself."

"I had plenty of reasons," Percival protested. "Do you know how heavy that armour was?"

"I wore the same armour as you, you chip idiot," Bedivere rolled his eyes.

"That's a nasty word," Tristan muttered.

"Isn't nasty when it's true," Bedivere shrugged.

"Yes," Percival said. "It makes it more nasty when it's true, and it's called antagonising."

"Did you just confirm you're a chip idiot?" Kyan raised an amused brow. His hair was pulled up underneath his cap, a cloak covering over his back.

"No one was talking to you," Percival and Bedivere snapped in sync. Kyan scowled at them.

"Can we focus on doing what we're here for instead of bickering like children?" Gawain growled under his breath at them. He glowered at them from beneath his own dark hood, the cloth around his body loose; easier to conceal weapons that way.

"Bedivere started it," Percival said.

"And Gawain is finishing it," Lancelot muttered from behind him. He wore the same kind of clothes as Gawain, the same loose-fitting cloak and scuffed boots. His white hair was smudged with charcoal to blend in underneath the hood.

Tristan watched as a group of citizens huddled together on their way towards the staircase. "The castle is letting them in," he mused. "That isn't usual."

"We're here to watch the execution," an elderly man said to Tristan, his grizzled face dirtied and smudged with charcoal.

Tristan frowned. "Execution? Is Ergott going to get his head lopped off?" he asked confusedly.

The elderly man shook his head. "The Born King has his trial."

Tristan's eyes widened, and he took a breath. A hand clapped over his mouth before he could say anything, Peter standing beside him. "They caught the lad?" Peter asked him in character. His face was altered, kohl lining his eyes and his beard shaved in strange swirls. Tristan took a double look at the beard swirls in confusion.

"Indeed they did," the man chuckled. "He was rescuing refugees from the training grounds, then he was snatched up."

"When is this trial?"

"Now."

Tristan tried to move his mouth and wretched at the smell of Peter's hands. *What was the last thing he* touched*?*

The Knights shared a brief look before following after the groups of people, Peter moving his hand away from Tristan's mouth. He grimaced and wiped his mouth with his sleeve. "Did you touch Kyan before you did that?"

Peter gave him a look before facing forward, following the group of citizens. Tristan sighed and looked up, watching the silhouette of an eagle circling high above. *I don't know how you'll pull this one off, Maria, but if we do, I just hope we can get out on time.*

At the top of the staircase, the crowd of people got more restless. It looked like the entirety of the Kingdom was here! *How do you fit so many people in such a space?* Not an inch of grass was spared in front of the courtyard altar. The citizens were packed shoulder to shoulder like cans of sardines.

The Barons beside the moving citizens scoured over them, their masks emotionless and their eyes following each individual carefully. Gawain nodded to a Baron, and the Knights peeled off to separate areas, disappearing among the crowd. Tristan watched as Peter went a different route, his brows knitting together as they left on their own accord, Kyan remaining.

"Come on, Garrison," Kyan muttered, making his way towards the crowd. Tristan followed begrudgingly and glanced up at the castle.

Above the gathered citizens stood an overlooking balcony, and King Ergott, along with Vivien and Jackseye, looked over each gap in the railing. Ergott walked forward and placed his hands on the edge, smirking over the people coldly.

Tristan looked forward again to find Kyan gone, his eyes widening. *Uh oh.* He swivelled his head around, trying to not look like he was lost but ultimately failing. He made his way cautiously forward, pressing through the crowd and keeping an eye out. *Damn it, Kyan, where are you?*

A hand shot out and grabbed him from his left, and he flinched and spun to see Kyan frowning at him. "Come on, you tool," he growled. "Keep up."

Tristan clenched his jaw and followed him better this time.

Arthur gritted his teeth at the flash of pain lancing his eye, growling and spitting blood to the floor. His whole body ached and screamed with agony; he'd been stuck here with the Executioner for almost an hour.

"That could've been a lot worse," a voice growled at him.

"If that statement is true, then why wasn't it?" Arthur panted through his teeth, his voice defiant.

"I still want you to be conscious when I take your head off," the Executioner replied, circling around him.

Arthur turned his head to watch him fighting against the chains that held him. The brace on his neck felt like a noose more than a collar. "When is the big show anyway? Are you delaying to keep the interest of the crowd?" Arthur huffed.

The Executioner lashed his hand out to Arthur's head and tugged him back by the hair, Arthur hissing in pain. "It will be on when I am ready for it to be."

Arthur bared his teeth at him in defiance, fighting the tears of pain that threatened to flood his eyes.

"Sylvester!" A voice called from the doorway, the Executioner turning to it. "It's time."

"Under whose orders?" the Executioner growled.

"Ergott's. Now move it."

"Come on then, Sylvester," Arthur grinned wolfishly. "Let's end this little game."

The Executioner snarled at Arthur and turned to the Barons standing on either side of the room. "Drag him out and make it hurt."

*Fantastic. More pain is* just *what I need.* Arthur ground his teeth as the Executioner let his hair go with a shove, watching as the Barons neared him and pulled him from the seat. The Barons walked him roughly outside the torture room and shoved him down the hallway, his body barking in pain.

Arthur growled at the Barons and walked in front of them slowly, his eyes adjusting to the bright sunlight as opposed to the darkness of the torture room. His chains jangled as he walked along the torn red carpet, the marble beneath stained with red. But the pillars were spotless.

Arthur looked around to observe the walkway; the engravings in the walls, the glass alcoves, and the paintings were all spotless. *Odd...* Although the paintings of his father and Aunt Guinevere had been removed from their spots. *Obviously, Ergott is expecting more fighting to not fix the flooring.*

It puzzled him as to why he'd remove Rosaline's portrait. Even if he did murder her, he still loved the Queen, or so Arthur thought. Arthur sighed and continued on, trying to ignore the sharp stings of pain that shot through his side every step he took.

Something was more off than normal; the air felt different. Arthur wasn't sure how, but he just had a feeling.

They approached the High Gates, a cool breeze blowing through the opened doors. As Arthur stepped out onto the staircase, the Barons immediately turned him to the left, taking him to the courtyard. The Executioner grinned at him over his shoulder and led Arthur to where he was sentenced to death.

He could hear the buzz of multiple voices gathered around the corner, more Barons standing along a path leading to the altar at the front of the crowd pressed against the Gate wall.

He watched as they all turned towards him, the crowd falling silent in waves. His heart pounded at the lost hope and shock on their faces, guilt stilling him a moment before the Barons shoved him forward. He scoured his eyes over the heads that stood tall above the rest; not one familiar face stood out. His heart sank at the realisation that nobody was here to save him. *I really am going to die.*

The Barons gripped his chains as they led him up the altar stairs, his view towering over the crowd. A clerk stood at the far corner of the altar, his head held high above his adorned orange and black jacket. The Executioner stood beside a large stone block, his axe embedded in a stump beside it. He wore a black hood over his head, a Baron's mask covering his face. If that wasn't a statement, Arthur didn't know what was. The Barons stood him in front of the stone block, forcing him to look out over the crowd and up at the castle balcony overlooking the courtyard.

Ergott nodded over to the clerk beside the altar, the clerk nodding back and clearing his throat. He stepped forwards to the front of the altar, unfurling a roll of paper. Ergott smirked coldly to himself and watched the clerk prepare to read out the crimes, amused by the slight fear on Arthur's face.

"The Kingdom of Camelot in the land of Braynor has summoned her citizens to witness the trial of Arthur Loholt Uther Pendragon, the firstborn son of Deadking Benjamin Uther Constantine Pendragon, Crown Prince of Camelot," the clerk announced. He smirked and looked sideways at

Arthur for a moment. "And the people's supposed Born King."

The Barons pulled his chains down, and he grunted as his jaw hit the stone roughly, sending his head spinning. His arms strained against the chains as they looped the links underneath hooks bolted into the stone, his neck pinned on the rock as the cuff bit at his skin.

"The charges read as follows," the clerk continued, raising the paper higher. "One account of the murder of the late Queen Rosaline Guinevere, the beloved wife to His Majesty King Ergott Pendragon; twelve accounts of organised murder against King Ergott's Knights of the Roundtable, the names including Knight Commander of the first rank, Sir Samqueel Torona."

Arthur thrashed in the chains, growling in protest. The hooks wouldn't budge. "I didn't kill anyone!" he barked.

"Knight Commander of the second rank, Sir Reuben Solas, Knights of first ranking as follows: Sir Taryn Dawn, Sir Henry Brannagh, Sir Caleb Lorsaw…"

"You have the wrong person!" Arthur protested, glaring up at Ergott. "*He* killed them!"

Ergott frowned at him and nodded at the clerk to continue.

"Sir Craig Karsol, Sir Liam Carsen…"

As the clerk listed on and on the names of the Roundtable, the crowd began to grow restless, shouts of protest splitting the air at random spouts. Arthur gritted his teeth and looked out over the crowd, seeing their disbelieving faces and outrage.

"Theft on the streets of the grand city of Londinium," the clerk smirked. More people protested against that statement, shop owners in particular raising their voices.

"I didn't steal anything!" Arthur bared his teeth.

"The aggravated attacks against lawful citizens of Londinium, including brawling against shopkeepers, Baron patrols, innocent bystanders and Knight trainees, conspiring in the act of thievery against the Kingdom of Camelot and her people, the alleged association amongst rebel forces and the conspiring of overthrowing His Majesty King Ergott from the throne of Camelot," the clerk cleared his throat once more, smirking over the riled crowd gathered in front of him. Barons fought to keep them in line, pushing them back from the stage with batons and pointed spears. "And finally, one account of attempted murder against His Majesty King Ergott, a highly illegal act that will not go unpunished by law. All claims against the accused have labelled him guilty of each crime listed."

Arthur continued to stare at his uncle, outrage and anger coursing through his veins. *This man is a liar!* The crowd were protesting against the charges fiercely, a few fighting against the Barons at the front of the line.

The clerk raised his voice against the chaos of the crowd, a wicked grin spoiling his face. "And so by the name of His Majesty King Ergott, and under the Lawful Act of Braynor and her people across her land, I sentence thee, Crown Prince Arthur Loholt Uther Pendragon of Camelot, to death by execution."

Arthur shook his head, sighing through his nose. It was no use. They weren't going to be convinced otherwise, no matter how hard he tried. Arthur sat his chin down on the block, and the Barons unfastened his neck cuff, letting it hang down to the altar floor.

The world went muffled in his ears, the shouting of the crowd distant. His heartbeat began to rise, the thump echoing in his mind. Arthur looked up at the balcony and saw his uncle grinning in amusement and victory down at him. A woman stood beside him that Arthur hadn't seen before, and she wore Rosaline's crown. His eyebrows knitted together. *Who is the new Queen?*

The Baron to his right shoved his head back down on the block roughly, his jaw banging into the stone with a clang. He growled and looked out to the crowd. The struggle grew intense, Barons pushing them back under command. *They're wasting their efforts. There's no stopping this.*

He watched as they fought, and a flicker of a brown hood caught his eye to the left. The Executioner pulled his axe free from the stump, the razor-sharp blade catching the midday sun. Arthur squinted at the hooded figure, and the figure lifted the hood slightly. Dark skin showed beneath the shadow, the glow of white teeth grinning at him a bright contrast. Blue eyes winked at him, and Arthur froze, staring. *Tristan?!*

The lad disappeared back amongst the crowd, and Arthur strained to see where he went, the Barons pinning him to the spot. The Executioner lifted his axe in the air and-

The whizz of an arrow through the air sounded over Arthur's head, the thump of it hitting its target followed by a strangled cry from the Executioner. The axe dropped to the altar with a clang, and the crowd exclaimed, some cheering while others started to run.

"Arrow!" one of the Barons warned, the two looking around to locate where it came from.

Suddenly, another arrow hit the Baron in the neck, followed by more shots coming from high above. They fell to the ground limply, and Arthur looked to his right. Up on the High Gates, Peter crouched on a small guard platform, his bow raised and ready.

"Get Arthur out of here!" he shouted, continuing to fire more arrows.

"Now!" a voice shouted from the crowd, and the crowd scattered as a group of men brandished swords against the Barons. Arthur's eyes widened; not just any men, that voice was Lancelot! And there was Gawain fighting off the Barons at the Gates with Percival and Gaheris, and Geraint by the castle doors, and Bedivere and Galahad in the middle of the crowd!

Heavy, quick footsteps rushed up the wooden staircase on the side, and Arthur pivoted to look, his arms still stuck in the cuffs locked in the hooks. Tristan and Kyan rushed to him, moving over the Barons with ease.

"I was beginning to think you wouldn't make it to the grand occasion," Arthur said, shifting around in his cuffs.

"You really think I'd want to miss this special day?" Tristan grinned. "Once in a lifetime opportunity, you know?"

"I'd like to keep it as a one-time thing," Arthur grinned back.

Kyan rummaged over the Barons' belts and grabbed a keychain, moving over to Arthur. "Good on you for keeping your head on," Kyan snorted, shifting through the keys and trying each of them.

"Lovely to see you too, Kyan," Arthur huffed.

"He's been sulky since you left. I've had to put up with it," Kyan smirked and turned the key. The cuffs fell to the floor, freeing Arthur's wrist. "Finally!"

Arthur stood up from the block and rubbed his bruised wrists. He glanced at Kyan and nodded at him. "Not bad."

"To your left!" Peter shouted from above and fired an arrow down towards them.

Arthur turned to his left, the three of them ducking as the arrow flew overhead into the chest of a Baron, the corpse collapsing to the ground at the foot of the altar.

Arthur looked back up to the balcony and saw Ergott and the woman fleeing with Jackseye on their tail, his eyes narrowed at them. Peter saw it too; he knocked an arrow and let one fly towards Ergott's back, the mark true.

Ergott spun around and flung out his hand, catching the shaft to a sudden stop. He looked at the arrowhead inches away from his chest, then to the source, his orange eyes flaring at Peter. Peter's eyes widened, and he moved, disappearing back around the side of the pillar. Kyan and

Tristan surrounded him on both sides, shoving back any Barons that threatened to reach the altar.

The woman on the balcony stopped and started to back away from the door, Ergott turning back around to do the same. Arthur narrowed his eyes and heard the growling of multiple dogs coming from the balcony. "What the Hell is going on up there?"

"Maria's plan," Tristan said over his shoulder. "I don't know what it is exactly, but it sounds like it's working."

Ergott backed away from the doorway, Vivien doing the same beside him. The pack of royal wolfhounds had somehow escaped the kennels and stood snarling in front of them, teeth bared. Their eyes glowed golden with anger, snapping their teeth in warning at them. Jackseye and the Barons stood in front of the royals, their weapons pointed at the feral hounds.

"What's gotten into them?" Ergott mused. First, Benjamin's old Knights returned to fight for Arthur's freedom, and now the court hounds had gone wild. *What other surprises await me?*

"Stand back, sire," Jackseye said, his sword pointed directly at the leading hound. It snapped its jaws at him in hostility, and the dogs pounced, snarling and barking as they leapt onto the Barons. One of the hounds jumped towards Jackseye, and he flung his arm out, grabbing the hound by the neck. It fought against him, snarling and digging its claws against his armour.

Jackseye glared at the wolfhound, slamming the dog into the wall with a loud thud. It yelped and got back up, barking savagely at him. Jackseye grabbed his sword and embedded the blade into its stomach as it leapt at him, twisting the sword and swinging it around to fall over the balcony ledge.

The Barons yelled as the dogs began to overpower them, the sheer size of the hounds too much to pick off easily. "*Muharí*, there's too many!" a Baron yelled, screaming as a dog jumped and pinned him by his throat to the ground.

Jackseye glared at the number of hounds, watching another making a beeline for him. He raised his sword to slash towards the dog, ready for it to leap. The dog paused, shaking itself out and looking up at Jackseye in surprise, its tail tucked beneath its legs.

Ergott watched as the rest of the dogs began to do the same, the hounds backing off of the Barons one by one as if released from a spell. Ergott knew only one person who could control animals to do her bidding like so. He narrowed his eyes. *If she is behind this...*

"What is going on?" one of the Barons breathed, watching the closest dog lay on its stomach in front of him.

Vivien smirked absently to herself, watching everything happen quietly. Ergott looked at her sideways. The Witch was able to see events before they happened. *She knew this would unfold.*

Irritation flew through him, and he turned to face Jackseye. The castle was as good as gone; the people had rebelled on the hopes given by the return of the old Roundtable and were still following the prophecy that had given him such a headache from the very first uttering of the Born King.

Besides, he could think of better places to reside in the meantime while he gained more power.

"Prepare your leagues. We leave immediately," he commanded. "Let them have their pitiful Kingdom."

*Arthur will win for now.*

*But this is not the end of my reign.*

Jackseye nodded to him and moved past the whimpering mutts. "Gather your things," he commanded. "We move to Dolorous Gard."

## Chapter 26: Rise of the King

"They just don't stop coming," Tristan breathed, fighting off another Baron trying to climb the altar. Arthur turned to his side, one of the Barons charging towards him. As he swung his sword, Arthur bent down, and the Baron rolled over his back right into the path of a waiting Kyan, who punched him back off the altar.

"Incoming!" Tristan warned, looking up and moving to the side.

Arthur followed Tristan's gaze; a large lumpy object was falling right where Arthur stood and falling fast. He dodged out of the way right as it landed, the dog's bones cracking with a loud yelp of pain. Tristan froze, staring at the dog.

Arthur glanced at Tristan, the lad awfully pale. "Tristan," he said quietly. "We have to go."

The dog whined as it bled out on the altar, and Tristan couldn't take his eyes off it. "It's a dog," he murmured. "It's not a wolf, it's a dog, it won't hurt you - it's dying, oh my Gods, it's dying…"

Arthur looked over to Kyan, then back at Tristan, moving him along. Tristan peeled his attention away from the dying dog, trying not to flip out while Arthur moved him.

From the bottom of the altar stairs, Percival and Gaheris fought attacking Barons, their skill too great for the Black Cloaks to handle.

"We need to get you out of here," Percival said.

"Where did Ergott go?" Arthur asked, looking up at the balcony.

"He disappeared back inside," Peter panted, running towards them. "The whole lot of them. Something went wrong with the dogs."

"Tristan, go with Peter," Arthur said. "Mind if I borrow that sword?" he pointed to Peter's scabbard.

Peter pulled his shortsword free of the scabbard and handed the blade to him pommel first. "Be my guest, don't lose it," he said.

"Get the citizens to safety," Arthur said to them. "Make sure they get indoors."

"Where, exactly, is *safety*?" Kyan asked.

"Anywhere the Barons aren't," Arthur looked at him.

"And where exactly are *you* going?" Percival asked him.

"Hunting," Arthur grinned and ran towards the castle.

Percival watched as Arthur ran off and sighed through his nose. "Gawain is going to kill me."

"You know you could just *not* let him go, right?" Kyan frowned at him.

"Easy for you to say," Bedivere called to him. "You haven't tried stopping the bastard."

"And where is he going?" Galahad asked, running up to the gathered group.

"Somewhere he shouldn't," Gaheris muttered.

"Let's get these citizens to safety!" Lancelot called to them, shoving a Baron off him.

They ran towards the Gates, Kyan lagging behind with a scowl. "So we're just going to let him get his ass kicked?" he asked incredulously.

"You go and get him if you think you're capable of turning him around," Bedivere snapped at him. Kyan glowered and followed after them with a sigh.

Leading the group, Percival ran through the courtyard as more Barons began to join in on the fray. *The silly bastards don't know when to stop.* A whole litter of their mates were thrown around the courtyard dead; Percival didn't know how they could keep coming when the evidence that they wouldn't win was right in front of their smooth black masks. He raised his sword, ready.

A Baron swung his sword towards Percival's chest; he deflected the attack with a parry and shoved the Baron back onto the ground, knocking him out with a swift kick to the temple. The others quickly disarmed and knocked out the rest of the Barons surrounding them and headed down the stairs, spotting the tail end of the fleeing citizens heading Northbound.

"They're heading towards the training hall," Gawain barked from behind them, fighting off the Barons that followed behind. "Oliver, you genius! Help him herd them towards it; it'll hold them all!"

"It'll hold a whole city?" Bedivere raised a brow.

"You'd be surprised."

"No time for questions, Bedivere," Lancelot said from beside him. "Let's get moving."

"What about Arthur?" Tristan questioned. "He's in the castle."

Gawain snapped to him. "He's *what*?" he roared.

"Back in the castle," Percival repeated. "Dealing with Ergott."

Gawain growled in frustration. "If I have to save this lad's ass one more time this century, then I swear to the Gods, I'm going to lock him in a room and leave him there," he cursed, turning back to charge up the stairs.

"Gawain! Not the time!" Galahad interrupted him. Gawain ignored him as he ran back up towards the castle, shoving Barons down the staircase as he went.

"I guess it's the time," Lancelot rolled his eyes. "Geraint needs our help."

A small figure ran towards them from the bottom of the stairs, their arms waving above their head. "Hey! Hey guys!"

Percival immediately frowned at the boy, coming to a stop as they neared him. "Tyler? What in the Gods' names are you doing here?!"

Tyler paused a few steps down, panting fast, holding his side. "Oh my Gods, that was a run," he puffed. "Why is this city so big?"

"What are you doing here, Tyler?" Galahad asked firmly.

"I came to help," he panted. "I saw Geraint herding them towards the North. I stayed back to-"

"Tyler," Lancelot stepped forward. "You were told to stay back at the caves. This is too dangerous for you."

Tyler shrunk a bit. "Well, yeah, you did say that, but I thought I'd come along to help and look!" He pointed towards the alleyway he came from. "No tailenders! I told them where they all went and made sure they caught up, but Gods, the run here was unbearable."

"Tyler Agravian," Gaheris snapped at him, his voice deep as thunder. Tyler flinched and looked at him in fear. "You were given specific orders by the commanding Knights of the Roundtable to stay at the caves, and you disobeyed their orders."

"You could've gotten yourself hurt," Percival said. "Or worse, killed."

Tyler seemed to shrink in on himself, the small lad wide-eyed. "I'm sorry," he said quietly. "I just thought I'd do something outside of my comfort zone."

Lancelot gave him a warm smile and placed a hand on his shoulder. "Your bravery is considerable, young Knight, but you need to listen once we give out orders, especially if they're from me, Gawain, Galahad, and soon Arthur."

Tyler nodded, then paused. "Wait," he said. "Young Knight? I'm not a Knight."

"That could change," Lancelot smiled. "But right now, I need your help to gather the citizens."

Tyler's eyes widened, and he nodded fast. "Okay, okay, uh," he stammered, looking around the alleyways.

Percival rolled his eyes in amusement. *This kid has no idea.*

"Oh! They went this way!" Tyler said and ran down the alleyway at an incredible speed.

Percival's eyes widened, and he looked at the others. "Did anyone else see how fast he just ran?"

"He's a kid," Galahad mused. "They're fast."

"I'm pretty sure no normal kid reaches a building three hundred metres away in five seconds flat," Bedivere said, astonished.

"You're just jealous he's faster than you," Percival smirked at Bedivere.

Bedivere raised a brow. "Want to race?" he challenged.

"You know I'm faster than you," Percival dismissed.

"Just follow the citizens, will you?" Gaheris sighed, jogging after Tyler.

Bedivere took off at a sprint before Percival could move. "Are you now?" he teased.

"Not fair!" Percival called after him, sprinting behind him.

"Those two keep trying to one-up each other," Galahad sighed, jogging after the group.

"Seems natural," Peter said, keeping pace. "Everyone I've seen in training tries it too."

"Targeted much," Kyan frowned.

"He's not wrong," Tristan shrugged.

"Shut up."

Adrenaline surged through Arthur as he ran up the castle staircase, his breathing heavy but his focus clear. No Barons were to be found around the hallways peeling away from the stairs; they must all be outside or with Ergott. Wherever they were, Arthur was going to find his uncle. Arthur ran through the castle, searching every corridor.

A strangled cry sounded from a distant hallway, the sounds of struggle echoing towards him. Arthur paused; he looked towards the sound and walked over to it slowly.

"You girls have had it too easy for long enough," a muffled voice snarled from around the corner. A choked sound protested against the voice, whimpers following it. Arthur turned the corner, the shortsword gripped firmly in his palm.

One of the younger castle Maidens was pinned up against the wall by the throat, a Baron holding her there. Two more of the girls were crouched against the wall in fear, another Baron holding them at swordpoint.

"It's time now that we get what we want," the Baron snarled, tightening his grip. The Maiden bucked beneath his hand, straining to get free.

"Oi," Arthur said firmly. The Barons turned to him sharply, the Maiden looking at him with wide eyes. "Aren't you meant to be following your King?"

"Aren't you meant to be dead?" the Baron sneered. The other Black Cloak moved away from the girls against the wall, standing beside his comrade, weapon raised.

Arthur grinned and twirled the sword in his hand. "Some people manage to avoid death," he shrugged.

"Clearly," the Baron snorted, dropping the girl who fell to her knees coughing. The other Maidens moved to her, pulling her away from the Barons.

Arthur shuffled his feet in place and eyed both of the Barons. *Two daggers on the left one. The right one has a shortsword.*

"Let's see what the supposed Born King is capable of," the left Baron growled and launched forward, drawing both daggers.

Arthur moved towards the Baron, narrowing his eyes at the Black Cloak as he met the daggers with the shortsword. The Baron spun his arm and sliced towards his side, Arthur jumping out of the way and grabbing his forearm, twisting it. He yelped and shot his leg out, hitting Arthur's shin with a mild crack. Arthur grunted in pain, glaring at him and snapping his arm with his knee.

The Baron yelled and reefed out of his grip, rolling away from him and clutching his arm, his daggers scattered across the floor.

Arthur turned to the other Baron, quickly ducking beneath the arc of their blade and driving his shoulder into his stomach, the Baron stumbling back with a whoosh of air. A fist launched up towards Arthur's jaw, clipping him with a shock like lightning. His eyes went fuzzy as he stabilised himself, and his breath rushed out of him as the Baron kicked his stomach, sending him into the wall with his head rocketing back against it.

Arthur slid down the wall, his head pounding at the force of impact. The Baron moved again, and Arthur rolled, the clash of metal against stone echoing down the corridor. He swung the shortsword in a wide arc towards the Baron and felt the crunch of bone against the blade as it buried itself in the Black Cloak's thigh.

The Baron hissed in pain and collapsed to the floor beside his mate, blood spilling as the blade pulled free. Arthur got back up and caught his breath, picking up one of

the scattered daggers and thrusting it through the fallen
Baron's forearm, the both of them crying out in pain behind
their masks.

He turned to the young Maidens, panting heavily. "You
lot alright?"

The Maidens watched with pale faces and wide eyes,
the girl that was pinned holding her bruised throat gently.
Arthur walked towards her and crouched down in front of
the scared girl. "Are you alright?" he repeated softly.

She looked at him with big blue eyes and nodded,
trying to clear her throat. "Thank you, Arthur," she croaked.

"Do you know where the training hall is?" Arthur
asked, glancing at the other two in the corner.

"I do," one of them says. "My brother was a Knight. He
showed me once."

Arthur handed her the dagger hilt first. "Take this and
as many Maidens as you can find," he said. "The Knights
of the Roundtable are there waiting for you all there."

The girl's eyes lit up in hope as she took the dagger.
"They returned? They're not dead?" she gasped.

"The Old Roundtable," he smiled warmly at her.

A little bit of the light died from her eyes, her face
falling. "Oh," she murmured. "Silly me, I thought you
meant Ergott's."

"It doesn't matter," he said. "Right now, I need you to
do me a favour. What's your name?"

"Elain Dawn."

Arthur's eyes widened. *Taryn had a sister?* "Your
brother will be missed by us all," he said softly.

Elain smiled slightly. Arthur could see it now: the same
shiny black hair and sharp features, the same ocean-blue
eyes. *She's definitely a Dawn.* "I'm sure he's having the
time of his life up there, picking on Lorsaw probably," she
huffed.

"I'm sure they're all picking on Lorsaw," Arthur smiled.

"I wouldn't doubt it," she laughed. "Or maybe Lorsaw finally clapped one over his ears. Taryn would have deserved it."

"He would be proud of you," Arthur said. "'Cause right now, you're going to do something important for me."

She looked back up at him. "Whatever it takes," she said, determination on her face.

"Don't stop running, Elain," Arthur said. "All of you," he glanced at the others. "Stay together, and go straight to the training hall. Don't stop until you get through those doors. Do you understand?"

"Yes, my liege," she said, and the other two nodded.

"Go," he said, a small smile forming on his face.

The Maidens got to their feet and ran off down the hallway, heading towards the servant stairwell. The servants' quarters were full of hidden routes and guaranteed to be harbouring scared Maidens and servants alike; one tunnel was destined to get them out of the castle without them being followed. *Smart girl.*

Arthur stood up and ran further down the hallway, ignoring the groaning Barons as he turned down the corridor. A few fleeing servants rushed past him as he neared the balcony, the door left wide open with no one in sight around it.

He turned to look out the door and stopped, the strange woman from before still standing on the balcony. Her black hair floated around her head like it was being held aloft, her elaborate black dress shifting as she turned to face him. Glowing golden eyes watched him with interest, red lips turned in a smirk. "So you made it through into the castle?" she purred, her voice like sour honey.

"Is that a common eye thing?" Arthur huffed, his sword pointed at her.

"It seems like it, doesn't it?" she hummed and lifted a hand. A bright yellow orb formed quickly in her hand and began to spin fast, glowing brighter and brighter. "I suggest you duck."

"I don't take suggestions from a witch," Arthur sneered at her.

She raised a brow and huffed. "Your choice," she dismissed and launched the orb high into the air, a great gust of wind whooshing around the balcony with the explosive sound of a sonic boom.

Arthur yelled as he rocketed back inside the castle to roll down the hallway, his ears ringing as his head cracked against the marble. Splintered pieces of the wooden balcony door scattered around him in shards, the door completely destroyed.

The orb pulsed a bright yellow light from the doorway, flooding the castle as it dimmed and brightened. Arthur tried to shake his head clear, his vision swimming. The witch walked back inside the castle and looked at him, his blurry vision flickering her appearance from a young woman to an old wrinkled hag, her face contorted as she laughed. The sound echoed in his ears as he tried to clear his head, rubbing his eyes.

He looked back up as his hearing somewhat cleared and saw nothing but the castle hallway covered in debris. She was gone, along with the light from the orb. Arthur's head still throbbed as he stood up, using the wall to help him. Arthur looked around, disoriented and stumbling. All he could feel was the dust harassing his nose and making him cough uncontrollably.

A muffled bark sounded behind him with the thud of footsteps coming towards him from the hallway. Arthur turned around slowly, squinting his eyes through the thick cloud of dust and debris.

Gawain emerged through the haze, grabbing his shoulders and staring at him with an angry face. "Arthur! What… the castle?" he questioned, his voice cutting in and out of his hearing.

"The witch," Arthur coughed. "She got away with E...Ergott."

"Witch? That's not..." his hearing faded again, and Arthur shook his head, stumbling forward slightly. He could see Gawain's lips moving, but nothing was coming out. "... gotten into you? You look... got a concussion..."

"Gawain..."

"Come on boy... are waiting for you... training hall." Gawain's hand moved to the top of Arthur's head, and he looked at his eyes. Arthur's vision doubled, his head shaking around to try and clear it.

The next thing he knew, the world was tilting around him, and he felt the hard bone of Gawain's shoulder on his stomach as the world turned upside down and moved all around in thuds, his legs held by a strong bond. *Gawain is carrying me?*

Indeed, the old Knight had lifted Arthur over his shoulder as if he were a small child or a heavy sack of potatoes. "Don't throw up on me," Gawain warned, Arthur's hearing clearing especially to hear that. Arthur huffed in amusement. *Typical.*

But what was the witch doing on the balcony? And why did she let off that orb? *Perhaps it was some kind of signal?* His head swam too much thinking about it. Or was that from being upside down? He tried not to think too much about anything else other than keeping his food in his stomach at the repetitive lurch of motion.

The boy had gotten a lot heavier since he first came to training, and it started to show. Gawain panted as he walked down the North alleyway, sweeping his vision to keep an eye out for anybody.

Not even the glint of a Black Cloak showed up. *Has Ergott and his kind finally retreated?* The explosion from the orb at the castle *had* to be a signal of sorts. Witches don't just waste mana for the sake of it.

Gawain climbed up the stairway of the training hall, tucking Arthur in close to avoid hitting his head on the doorway. The hallways were still coated with debris, all the alcoves where the historical armour was kept were ruined, the armour gone. It hurt his chest to think about priceless history and its stories, artefacts from the people's ancestors, gone to whatever Hell Pit the Barons had cast them to.

*I didn't kill enough of them.*

The chatter of voices echoed quietly around the training hall, the seats down in the training pit standing once more and packed with thousands of citizens, the doors to each separate room wide open and filled to the maximum amount. The kitchens wafted all sorts of scents, the citizens all harbouring at least one cup of water and a makeshift plate. None of them noticed their King being carried over Gawain's shoulder down the tighter hallway.

"Do you think Arthur survived?" a familiar voice echoed from the medical ward.

"I don't know at this point," another voice said. "Gawain hasn't returned, and neither have Simon and Maria. It'll be a miracle if any made it out after that explosion."

"Well, hallelujah," Gawain announced as he walked through the door.

Inside the medical ward, the Knights were gathered around a few injured citizens, a few of them standing up to face him.

"Gawain, where have you been?" Bedivere questioned, looking at Arthur draped over his shoulder.

Gawain shifted Arthur to a standing position, holding him steady. "Fetching this dizzy tool," he replied. Arthur looked as if he had been hit by a horse's hoof in the head; it worried him somewhat. Head knocks were never good.

"Where's Tristan and Maria?" Arthur asked, rubbing his eyes.

"I think you better worry about yourself first before worrying about them," Galahad said, taking the woozy Arthur and sitting him on a spare chair.

"I have to admit," Percival started, "you're a brave soul, Arthur."

"He's either very brave or very stupid," Gawain said, sitting himself down against the wall and panting. "All the way here, he was muttering about a witch. Ergott's new Queen isn't what she seems to be."

"A witch?" Lancelot asked. "They originate in the Willow Keep in the Darklands. What is a witch doing in Camelot?"

Gawain flicked his eyes to Lancelot. "My best guess is that Ergott is using her to gain his powers." *And if he truly believes that it is a good idea, then he deserves to find out his true fate.*

"Only a tool like him would do that," Geraint huffed. "And why would he get her to be Queen?"

"The Witches of the Darklands are very manipulative creatures," Gawain said. "Their magic is enticing to their targets, so much so that anyone who falls into their trap fails to see the benefits the witches are milking from them."

"So she's also using him for her own benefit," Lancelot said. "Intriguing."

"Do we know where they're heading next?" Percival asked, his arms folded.

"My guess is Dolorous Gard," Gawain growled. "If the rumours from the letters are anything to be believed." The infamous Kingdom of Dolorous Gard was fraught with Drow Elves and guarded better than any prison, seated right on the edge of the Darklands itself. The legends of the

Kingdom were enough to scare any great warrior away and enough to attract any fool wanting to prove himself.

"Great," Bedivere sighed. "I'm guessing Arthur would want to go there, too?"

"Arthur isn't that stupid to head to Dolorous Gard on his own," Lancelot said. "Especially since you must traverse the Darklands in order to reach it."

"Legend says that only a few people have made it to Dolorous Gard," Gaheris said. "And Benjamin was one, himself."

*And he was lucky to come back alive.* "The Barons and Ergott have teamed up with this witch, who I suspect was the catalyst to this whole thing unfolding," Gawain muttered.

"I wouldn't doubt that," Geraint nodded. "Witches are always catalysts for events like this."

"And they'll stop at nothing to get what they want," Percival chimed in.

"They are infamous for using bargains with hidden repercussions," Gawain agreed, looking at Lancelot. "She may have convinced Ergott to do things to gain more power, like murdering the Knights. Although her motive is not easily as predictable, it seems."

"Witches only have their own goals for success," Lancelot said. "She's using him for something, and I would like to know what."

"Wouldn't we all," Bedivere muttered.

"What of Camelot?" Percival asked. "Who will rule it now?"

"According to a little bird that tweeted in my ear, King George will be taking over," Gawain said.

Percival raised a brow. "From Rheged?" Rheged was a little-known Kingdom on the Western shores of Braynor; it specialised in harvesting seafood and maintaining the river flows from the ocean. As you would imagine, the rulership of a local peasant wasn't well received among the royal ranks in the rest of Braynor.

"Since when did a fisherman rule Kingdoms?" Gaheris chuckled.

"Why would Ergott choose a tool like him?" Percival asked.

"King George, despite his flaws, is a good leader," Lancelot said softly. "He knows how to handle situations when under a lot of pressure, and he is a respectable man."

Bedivere snorted. "The most amount of pressure that looney has been through is deciding what he wants for dinner," he huffed. "He's nowhere even close to being of royal blood either. My left pinky toe is more royal than him."

"Being a King is no easy task, Bedivere," Lancelot said. "I'm sure you would struggle to rule an over-exhausted Kingdom like Camelot."

"Hey guys," Tristan panted from the doorway, holding onto the skirting. "We have an issue. Several, actually."

The Knights turned to him, their brows flicking up at the same time. "What is it?" Gawain said.

"One, we're out of apple buns," he puffed.

"Not relevant, but alas," Percival said.

"Two, there's a whole lot of food missing."

"Again, not relevant," Geraint frowned.

"Well, how are we going to feed the entire city then?" Tristan frowned.

"Find more food," Gaheris said simply. "The market stalls are only a few blocks away.

"*You* go find more food," Tristan pouted at him. Gaheris gave him a look that shot fear through Tristan, the lad grinning nervously. "Three, Simon and Maria just showed up. She's not in a good way."

Arthur's eyes flew open, and he sat up. "Maria?"

"Where are they, Tristan?" Gawain asked, moving to stand back up with a groan. He wouldn't admit it, but everything was starting to wear him down. His old bones were creaking more and more as the day went by. *And* he'd copped a bad blow to the side.

Arthur got up from the seat and limped over to Tristan. "Where are they?"

"Arthur, sit back down," Galahad said, reaching for him. "You've got a concussion."

"I need to see her," Arthur protested, moving away from Galahad.

Tristan looked at Arthur with worried eyes. "You look like something the cat dragged in," he muttered.

"Take me to them," Arthur said, his head spinning.

"Arthur," Galahad warned. Arthur looked back at him, going pale. "Sit."

Arthur shook his head. "No."

"She'll be coming in here. Just wait for her," Gawain said to him and moved outside of the door.

Arthur nodded and collapsed to the floor in front of Tristan, the lad cursing and reaching for him. Gawain turned back around and cursed along with him, the other Knights moving quickly to Arthur's aid.

"Get him on a bed," Gawain commanded. "And keep him there, for the Gods' sake."

Gaheris stood from the chair and walked over to Arthur, picking him up from the floor. Tristan helped him to shift Arthur onto a bed, Arthur hanging limply between them. Gawain turned back around and continued down the hallway, Tristan following after him quickly to take the lead.

"Where has she been?" Gawain asked from behind him.

"According to Simon, they got found in their hiding spot," Tristan shrugged. "Whoever found them was pretty rough, by the looks of things."

"What are the damages?"

"See for yourself," he said, turning the corner down the long hallway.

Gawain followed him around the corner and saw Maria and Simon seated on the foyer floor beside the doorway. He frowned lightly as he walked towards them, examining her wounds from afar; a black eye darkened the left side of her face, and she clutched her right shoulder, her skin peppered with light bruises and cuts, a particularly nasty one dashing across the left side of her neck.

Gawain crouched in front of her, lifting her chin up with his finger. "What happened?"

Her green eyes widened as she took him in. "I had the dogs there, I had the control over them, and then I felt something interfere with the connection," she stuttered. "It was like another force was overtaking them, then I lost the hold over them, and by the time I figured out that I couldn't tap back into their minds, they were right behind us…"

"Maria, calm your breath," Gawain said, patting her shoulder gently. "Who controlled the dogs?"

Her breathing started to slow a bit, and Tristan sat beside her, looking over to Simon and helping him out. "I don't know," she murmured. "But whoever it was, they had a lot more control of their power than I did."

Gawain furrowed his eyebrows and looked over to Simon. "Did you see anyone else near the border wall?"

Simon nodded. "I tried to ward them off while Maria got out of trance; three Barons and a strange woman."

"A strange woman?" Gawain echoed.

"She was the one who gave Maria a black eye. We fought them off the best we could, then a loud bang happened, and they disappeared."

"What did the girl look like?"

Simon waved his hand in the air in uncertainty. "Hood covered the face, but the eyes were glowing gold."

"Another witch," Gawain scoffed. As if that's what this Kingdom needed. Ergott had set himself in a position that he would learn to regret later on. "Did you see which direction she went?"

"No, they quite literally vanished," he said. "One moment they were there, next minute they were gone."

"Witches have the tendency of vanishing," Gawain frowned.

"Where is Arthur?" Maria asked, shifting to sit up and wincing. Gawain turned back to her and gently sat her back down.

"He's fine," he said. "Just recovering."

Maria nodded slightly and held in a groan, moving her hand to the cut on her neck. "I need some water."

Gawain looked at the wound on her neck and frowned at it as blood leaked through her fingers. "We'll take you to the medical ward."

Simon shifted against the wall and used it to stand up, his braced leg making him grunt. He offered a hand down to Maria, and she took it. Tristan grabbed her other hand, and the both of them pulled her to her feet.

"Easy now," Gawain said, helping her ease herself. She gritted her teeth and started walking down the hallway with Simon, her hand still pressed on her neck.

Gawain led the group down the hallway, a few citizens passing by them glancing at Maria while continuing their path. Tristan quickly ducked back into the kitchen and reemerged with a cup of water, following after them through the crowd.

They turned the corner and reentered the medical ward, Arthur lying unconscious on the bed, Galahad sitting beside him. His hands pulsed a dim yellow light as they waved over him, his eyes closed. Galahad's magic wasn't much of a secret amongst the Rebels and the Roundtable. Still, to anyone outside of the bubble, it came as a shock, even though the legends told of his abilities. Gawain supposed that even though the legends were true, it was hard for some people to believe.

*Like that ratbag back at Reigate. Gods, Owen gets on my nerves.*

Galahad looked up from Arthur, his eyes fading from the bright yellow back to blue. "He's stable, he's just got the-" he flicked his eyes to Maria. "Oh, Gods! Don't you look like you've been chewed up and spat out?"

"Feels like it too, don't worry," she winced and sat in a vacant chair.

"Any room for a second patient?" Gawain asked Galahad.

"There isn't," he admitted, standing up and walking to Maria's seat. "There are too many casualties from the street rallies with the Barons, and not a single bed is available. There's just too many people." Gawain sighed and shook his head, looking down.

"And here you were saying it could fit the city," Bedivere muttered, fiddling with a coin.

Gawain looked over at him. "It can," he said firmly.

"And it *is*," Tristan said, handing Maria the water cup. "Just not very well."

"King George will arrive soon with his men," Lancelot said. "But until then, we need to be here for these people."

"I'm with Lance," Percival said.

"How do we know if King George is even coming?" Geraint asked.

"We don't," Gawain muttered.

"Oh, we'll know," Bedivere snorted. "You'll smell the brine on the wind before you see him."

"Percival," Lancelot said. Percival flicked his eyes over to him. "Take Bedivere and Gaheris to gather more food; the citizens will need more than what we've provided. Take a few marketers with you."

"Done," Percival smirked, looking at Bedivere. "Come on."

"Look at you, all leader-like," Bedivere mocked, standing up. "Rodney gives you one task, and your chest is more puffed up than a bellow on a winter's night."

"Better than you," Gaheris chimed in, nudging Bedivere's shoulder roughly.

"I still won that race," Bedivere goaded, stumbling slightly and glaring up at Gaheris. "Do you know how much you hurt people?"

"I'm fully aware," Gaheris chuckled.

Percival nudged Bedivere on the way out of the door. "Don't be a wuss."

"Says the one who can't stand being called by his first name," Bedivere scoffed, following after him and shoving him from behind.

Gawain shook his head at them. "Those two just don't stop butting heads."

"It gets worse when they've had drinks," Geraint mused.

Galahad threw him an incredulous look. "You can't say anything about 'getting worse when drunk', little miss dancing-on-a-bar-chair," he teased.

"That was one time, and I never did it again."

"You learned real quick after cracking your melon open, didn't ya?" Galahad grinned.

"It was worth it," Geraint grinned at him.

"Did you end up impressing anyone? Or do you just have a flair for embarrassing yourself now?"

"Both."

Galahad raised a brow, and Simon chuckled to himself. "Who's the lucky lass? Or lad, even?"

"Hannah," Geraint said, leaning back in his chair. "She's got herself a good personality."

"So *that's* where that came in," Galahad smirked. "She fell head over heels for a man that quite literally fell head over heels." The Knights left in the room laughed, a few of the conscious citizens listening in quietly chuckling with them. Geraint joined them and shook his head.

Gawain smirked at them and turned back to face Arthur, watching his face twitch in his sleep. The boy was a tool, for sure. He couldn't keep his temper cool for the life of him, he couldn't follow orders for the life of the good Gods, and he always came up with the most reckless, stupid plans Gawain had ever seen in all his years of existence on this Gods forsaken continent.

But the boy was most definitely his father's son. He had more than Benjamin's blood in him; Arthur had his courage. Deep down, Gawain could see that prophecy in him. The steel will of a King steered him true. Even if it often led him in the wrong direction.

He sighed through his nose and turned around to face the door. None of what he normally would teach trainees worked on Arthur besides bringing his anger out of him. *A new approach would be highly considerable with this lad. It'll come with time.*

But right now, he was in safe hands; he'd gotten his Kingdom back from his bastardly uncle. Gawain smiled softly towards the hallway. *He's got the first step under wraps, at least.*

"Gawain," Lancelot called back to him.

Gawain turned back around to look at him, dropping his smile.

"You've made him proud," Lancelot smiled warmly.

*Benjamin...* Gawain smiled again at Lancelot. "I better have," he said. "It was an awful lot of effort for nothing if I hadn't."

"Arthur has learned he can count on you," Lancelot said, walking over to him. "It's time you be his trainer *and* his mentor. Become his biggest supporter."

Gawain's mouth quirked. "You can keep the father figure part," he joked.

"All Ben wants from you is to watch over the boy, care for him, nurture him," Lancelot assured. "You can leave the father business to me. I'm not going to expect that of you."

And that's just the way Gawain liked it. "Deal."

## Chapter 27: The Epilogue

The morning sky clouded over Londinium, the birds overhead chirping in delight, mixed with the chatter of the lively citizens down below the castle staircase. People from all around the city made their way up to Camelot, the new castle guards allowing them inside the castle and leading them to the throne room. The pews on both the lower and upper levels were packed with citizens, all eager to see the rare event of a new King taking over the Kingdom.

Arthur stood in the front line along with the Knights, awaiting the arrival of King George to sit on the throne that adorned the dais at the front of the throne room. He'd made sure the servants had found the removed paintings of his aunt and father and got them to put them back in their rightful place on the hallway wall with the rest of the royal portraits before he got himself ready. He didn't want them to miss this.

The Knight Guards from Rheged were more sophisticated than Arthur would've thought, considering they were actually knighted and trained to use the weapon on their side. Even Gawain was surprised to see the way they carried themselves through the process of getting rid of the traces of the Barons. They now lined the hallway at each individual post, standing at attention so still Arthur would have thought them mannequins.

From the right side of the throne, three Knights marched together, the front one wearing the typical

Commander's armour, the gold inlaid Braynor Cross shining brightly on his shoulder pad.

"It is with great honour that I announce the arrival of His Grace, King George Derva II of the Eastern Kingdom of Rheged," his voice boomed from beneath his helmet. "Second born son of King Frederick Derva, and now, temporary King over the land of Camelot and her people through arrangement by the Pendragon royal family. All rise for the entrance of His Grace."

Everyone in the pews stood where they were, Arthur straightening himself as he fiddled with his hands. Tristan leaned over to whisper in his ear, "Do you think his brain is rattling around in his head from the amount of shouting he just did inside of a helmet?"

"Why don't you ask him yourself?" Arthur gave him a look and nodded to the throne.

"I may be dumb, but I'm not stupid," he smirked.

The Commander turned to face them and raised his brows. "What was that?" he asked them quietly.

Tristan straightened quickly, his eyes wide slightly. His shoulders shook as he held in a laugh, his lips pressed together tighter than a vice. Arthur chuckled as he shook his head.

"Cut it out, Tristan," Lancelot whispered to him.

"It doesn't matter what I say, Lancelot. He can't bloody hear me," Tristan snorted in quiet laughter.

"Maybe if you shouted at him he'll hear better," Percival said from behind him.

"I'm sure it'll echo around in that tin can just fine," Bedivere said, holding back laughter. It was true; the helmets did look a lot like fashioned buckets, the visors on the helmet held on to the tin by screws and wing nuts.

"Still think he can hear the waves from Rheged?" Percival smirked.

"He probably thinks the Castaral is a boating channel," Geraint snorted, standing beside Percival.

"I think I can hear a whale from here," Arthur said, holding in a laugh. The Knights pursed their lips as they tried not to laugh, keeping their eyes forward as the Commander looked at them in suspicion.

"Quiet," Gawain murmured down the line. "George is coming through." The pews pivoted to look down the castle hallway, a tall, dark-skinned man making his way towards the dais. His fine clothing was adorned with red and gold accents, with rings on his fingers and a woollen cape drooping behind him. His face was sharp, and his jaw was strong, with a small goatee on his chin. He carried himself about as gracefully as a fish out of water, his posture slouched as he walked up the dais steps.

King George sat in the chair and moved his arm down, all the people in the pews sitting back down, Arthur and the Knights still standing in front of him.

"So when is the real King getting here?" Tristan murmured to Arthur.

Arthur looked over at him. "*That's* King George."

Tristan looked at him with brows flicked up. "*That's* him? He looks like how they describe him, alright," he quirked his mouth in uncertainty.

A sudden force hit the back of Tristan's head, making him flinch and turn around, touching the back of his head. Gaheris glared at him and put his finger to his mouth. Tristan pouted and turned back around, rubbing his head gingerly.

Arthur stepped forward from the line and bowed to King George. "My liege, it's an honour."

"Prince Arthur," George nodded to him. His voice was light, almost nonchalant with his regard. "I'm glad to finally be here."

"The people of Camelot can say the same," Arthur straightened himself.

"Once I heard the call from Ergott, I knew it was time to come and pick up his mess," George said somewhat bitterly and slouched slightly on the throne.

"Your sacrifice is well appreciated," Arthur nodded at him. The citizens in the pews looked at one another, murmuring quietly.

"I just hope my reign over Camelot is as short as I'm sure we all wish it to be," he said. "For the people are wanting their legend. I can see it among the ones gathered here now. They expected you to be crowned today, isn't that right?" he asked the room, the people falling silent. He smiled slightly, his eyes flicking around the pews.

"My time will come eventually," Arthur said. "But for now, it's crucial you rule this Kingdom until I'm ready."

"Nobody is ever really ready to become a King," he shrugged, turning back to Arthur. "The way you become ready is to be thrown right into the thick of it. But I understand these are different circumstances. You were not raised with the essentials of becoming a King by your father or uncle, correct?"

Arthur nodded at him, his face flat with slight annoyance. "Yes, my liege."

"And I can tell this Kingdom is in dire need of a rebuild. Ergott is terrible at maintaining something for a long time," he sighed. "It's typical. Alas, the brute has disappeared to whatever hole he's gone to and left me with this, so I'm rolling with the punches."

He sat up higher on the throne, clearing his throat. "Whilst I'd much prefer to be back home in Rheged by the sea, I will agree to rule over this Kingdom until the day you decide you are ready to take over the reins. Your destiny requires you to become a Knight, yes?" he questioned.

"It does," Arthur said. "Though I need more training."

"Good, you're committed," he smiled and stood up from the throne. "On your knees, son."

The pews collectively murmured, and Arthur looked back at the Knights, Gawain nodding to him. "Go on," he muttered to him.

Arthur smiled at him faintly and turned back to George, lowering himself onto one knee. King George stood in front of him and turned to the Commander, holding his hand out to grab the sword he handed him.

King George lifted the sword and tapped the blade onto Arthur's right shoulder. "I, King George Derva II, grant thee Prince Arthur Pendragon an honorary knighthood," he said, touching his left shoulder. "By my power as King, and under the watch of the Holy Gods of the Overworld, it shall be so. You may rise."

Arthur stood up from the ground and smiled warmly to himself. "Thank you, my King," he said to George.

"Serve your destiny well, son," George smiled, and the pews erupted with cheering and applause. Arthur looked back at the Knights with a grin, the lads applauding him the loudest.

Percival looked at Kay beside him and nudged him slightly. "Clap faster, you're not a sloth," he grinned.

Kay looked at him sideways flatly. "I'll clap your ears," he muttered.

"Gawain, Kay is being rude again," Geraint laughed.

"I'll clap yours, too," Kay growled.

"Why so violent?" Percival asked.

"Why so picky?"

"Be happy for the lad," Percival said, turning back to Arthur. "He deserves it."

"Have you ever seen me applaud for anybody else?" Kay scowled, lowering his hands. "He should count himself lucky I'm even here."

"You poor thing," Galahad muttered. "How dare you attend an important event such as this one here."

"I'd put up with it better if it didn't start at nine in the morning," he growled, folding his arms.

"You wake up at seven every day," Geraint raised a brow.

"I had to watch the entirety of the caves for a week on my own," he argued. "You think I got any sleep?"

"Do we care?" Bedivere smirked at him. "It's the same answer for both questions."

Kay glowered at him darkly and sat back down, rubbing his eyes with a hand. Gawain rolled his eyes and looked back forward again, focused on Arthur. Arthur smiled widely and glanced over to Maria and the others seated in the corner pew, her bruised face smiling at him warmly.

Arthur walked over to them and glanced at Kyan beside her. Kyan nodded to him faintly, a small smile on his lips. Arthur nodded back and stood in front of Maria.

"I wouldn't be here if you didn't convince me to go to the training hall," he said. "Things would've turned out a lot different."

Maria huffed in amusement. "I'm surprised you let me drag you there in the first place," she said.

"Me too," Arthur smiled warmly. "But I'm glad you did." He took her hand and lifted it to his mouth, her eyes blinking in shock as he brushed his lips against her knuckle. Her face flared bright red as he let her hand go, and he held in his laugh, moving back to look around the pews.

The people grinned at him, their eyes alight with renewed hope. Their Born King was beginning to rise, the prophecy unfolding before them.

*I'm doing it, Father. I'm becoming what you asked, what you wanted.* Arthur grinned back at his people and felt that hope stir inside of him, too.

The light of dawn turned the night sky a deep shade of blue on the horizon to the East, the stretch of pine forest silent aside from the quiet footsteps of the horses and the occasional scrape of armour plate. The rows of Knights behind Samqueel might be a large batch of newcomers, but they were certainly as well versed in combat silence as the veterans.

*Gawain must be solid on the boys nowadays. It seems to be working a lot more effectively than what Mordred or Jackseye taught.*

Reuben rode beside him on his usual spot to the left, his attention turned forward. All of the Roundtable kept their gazes straight ahead; it was better to focus on the battle in front of them rather than distract themselves with the little things.

The night had gone more smoothly after the werewolves had left; the post guards hadn't reported any more activity from the woods, and no sign of anything to do with the Giant's footprint the young lads had found outside the camp. Perhaps it was just passing through, or they had just missed it. Either way, Sam was grateful it wasn't around to cause more problems.

The trees began to thin out, the edge of the forest coming into view. Sam broke through the line of trees onto the bare meadow, his horse snorting as the shadows fell away to the slowly rising sun. He pulled the reins to a stop, the legion behind him pausing their pursuit.

It had been eighteen years since the fall of Catarina. Eighteen years, and the Kingdom still had not been rebuilt. Catarina had been a dear ally to Camelot once, a sister Kingdom, if you will. Sam was old enough to remember the news of the Kingdom falling and to remember the day King Benjamin fell. To see a Kingdom on the horizon reduced to nothing but rubble and debris unsettled him.

Reuben paused beside him, looking at the ruin of granite and sandstone. His face was as solemn as Sam's. "To think that a whole civilisation that had no quarrels with the Kingdom that killed them could fall as easily as they did makes me feel insignificant," Reuben said quietly.

"An entire city of people, a royal bloodline exclusive to that Kingdom, wiped out in a matter of days," Samqueel muttered. "It makes you wonder what the motivation was."

"Power," Reuben answered. "Control, more land to bicker over. None of it is worth it, and they refuse to see that. They lose good men for the sole purpose of gaining the upper hand they never needed."

Ariendal was like that; always at war with some sort of Kingdom, always fighting their enemies that they made themselves. It was sickening to think that they raised their sons for the sole purpose of fighting to die in a battle that nobody asked for.

"This is what we're here for," Sam said, looking at him. "To stop them from making that mistake again. Hopefully permanently."

"The stories that are told of the strength of their numbers and forces are well known by most people," Reuben mused. "They won't be easy to beat. Do you have a plan in mind?"

*No.* Samqueel never thought he'd ever go up against the might of Ariendal. Only a fool would plan an attack on a side that you had no hope of winning against. Ergott had thrown him a curveball he didn't know how to hit.

He took a deep breath through his nose, watching the smoke plumes rise from the campfires dotting the ruins. "The best chance we have to defeat them is to find their weakest link," he murmured. "If we can kill the heart of the operation, we can shut down the whole thing. We just need to find out what, exactly, it is."

"And how hard is that going to be?" Reuben asked him, looking at him with a thoughtful glint in his eye.

"About as hard as it gets." It didn't help that Ariendal's method of attack wasn't well known. Sam hadn't found one single history book detailing any movements or hints as to how Ariendal moved, and it frustrated him. Now, he was expected to figure out how to win over an enemy he knew nothing about other than where they resided.

"Lead on, Commander," Reuben said, his horse stomping impatient hooves into the tough ground.

*Lead on into the unknown.* Samqueel straightened his back and lifted his head. After all, how many battles had he won where he hadn't known about the enemy until he got there to observe?

Sam picked up the reins and kicked gently, his horse shifting forwards towards the ruins of Catarina. The swish of armour and clank of metal weapons filled the air, the familiar feeling of the focus of war washing over him.

*I will find a way. I always do.*

# Knights of the Roundtable

## THE RISE OF REBELLION

### BOOK TWO

# COMING SOON